REMEMBER ME

ALSO BY
Christopher Pike

THIRST NO. 1
THIRST NO. 2

REMEMBER ME

Christopher Pike

INCLUDES *REMEMBER ME*, *THE RETURN*, AND *THE LAST STORY*

Simon Pulse
New York   London   Toronto   Sydney

SIMON PULSE

An imprint of Simon & Schuster Children's Publishing Division
1230 Avenue of the Americas, New York, NY 10020
This Simon Pulse paperback edition July 2010
Remember Me copyright © 1989 by Christopher Pike
The Return copyright © 1994 by Christopher Pike
The Last Story copyright © 1995 by Christopher Pike
All rights reserved, including the right of reproduction in whole
or in part in any form.
SIMON PULSE and colophon are registered trademarks of
Simon & Schuster, Inc.
For information about special discounts for bulk purchases, please contact
Simon & Schuster Special Sales at 1-866-506-1949 or
business@simonandschuster.com.
The Simon & Schuster Speakers Bureau can bring authors to your live event.
For more information or to book an event contact the
Simon & Schuster Speakers Bureau at 1-866-248-3049 or
visit our website at www.simonspeakers.com.
Designed by Paul Weil
The text of this book was set in Adobe Garamond.
Manufactured in the United States of America
4 6 8 10 9 7 5 3
Library of Congress Control Number 2009938063
ISBN 978-1-4424-0596-7
These titles were originally published individually.

Contents

REMEMBER ME   1

THE RETURN   309

THE LAST STORY   537

REMEMBER ME

For Pat

CHAPTER I

MOST PEOPLE WOULD probably call me a ghost. I am, after all, dead. But I don't think of myself that way. It wasn't so long ago that I was alive, you see. I was only eighteen. I had my whole life in front of me. Now I suppose you could say I have all of eternity before me. I'm not sure exactly what that means yet. I'm told everything's going to be fine. But I have to wonder what I would have done with my life, who I might have been. That's what saddens me most about dying—that I'll never know.

My name is Shari. They don't go in much for last names over here. I used to be Shari Cooper. I'd tell you what I look like, but since the living can see right through me now, it would be a waste of time. I'm the color of wind. I can dance on moonbeams and sometimes cause a star to twinkle. But when I was alive, I looked all right. Maybe better than all right.

I suppose there's no harm in telling what I *used* to look like.

I had dark blond hair, which I wore to my shoulders in layered waves. I also had bangs, which my mom said I wore too long because they were always getting in my eyes. My clear green eyes. My brother always said they were only brown, but they were green, definitely green. I can see them now. I can brush my bangs from my eyes and feel my immaterial hair slide between my invisible fingers. I can even laugh at myself and remember the smile that won "Best Smile" my junior year in high school. Teenage girls are always complaining about the way they look, but now that no one is looking at me, I see something else—I should never have complained.

It is a wonderful thing to be alive.

I hadn't planned on dying.

But that is the story I have to tell: how it happened, why it happened, why it shouldn't have happened, and why it was meant to be. I won't start at the beginning, however. That would take too long, even for someone like me who isn't getting any older. I'll start near the end, the night of the party. The night I died. I'll start with a dream.

It wasn't my dream. My brother Jimmy had it. I was the only one who called him Jimmy. I wonder if I would have called him Jim like everyone else if he would have said I had green eyes like everyone else. It doesn't matter. I loved Jimmy more than the sun. He was my big brother, nineteen going on twenty, almost two years older than me and ten times nicer. I used to fight with him all the time, but the funny thing is, he never fought with me. He was an angel, and I know what I'm talking about.

It was a warm, humid evening. I remember what day I was born, naturally, but I don't recall the date I died, not exactly. It was a Friday near the end of May. Summer was coming. Graduation and lying in the sand at the beach with my boyfriend were all I had on my mind. Let me make one point clear at the start—I was pretty superficial. Not that other people thought so. My friends and teachers all thought I was a sophisticated young lady. But I say it now, and I've discovered that once you're dead, the only opinion that matters is your own.

Anyway, Jimmy had this dream, and whenever Jimmy dreamed, he went for a walk. He was always sleepwalking, usually to the bathroom. He had diabetes. He had to take insulin shots, and he peed all the time. But he wasn't sickly looking or anything like that. In fact, I was the one who used to catch all the colds. Jimmy never got sick—ever. But, boy, did he have to watch what he ate. Once when I baked a batch of Christmas cookies, he gave in to temptation, and we spent Christmas Day at the hospital waiting for him to wake up. Sugar just killed him.

The evening I died, I was in my bedroom in front of my mirror, and Jimmy was in his room next door snoring peacefully on top of his bed. Suddenly the handle of my brush snapped off. I was forever breaking brushes. You'd think I had steel wool for hair rather than fine California surfer-girl silk. I used to take a lot of my frustrations out on my hair.

I was mildly stressed that evening as I was getting ready for Beth Palmone's birthday party. Beth was sort of a friend of mine, sort of an accidental associate, and the latest in a seemingly endless string of bitches who were trying to steal my boyfriend away. But she was the kind of girl I hated to hate because she was so nice. She was always smiling and complimenting me. I never really trusted people like that, but they could still make me feel guilty. Her nickname was Big Beth. My best friend, Joanne Foulton, had given it to her. Beth had big breasts.

The instant my brush broke, I cursed. My parents were extremely well-off, but it was the only brush I had, and my layered waves of dark blond hair were lumpy knots of dirty wool from the shower I'd just taken. I didn't want to disturb Jimmy, but I figured I could get in and borrow his brush without waking him. It was still early—about eight o'clock—but I knew he was zonked out from working all day. To my parent's dismay, Jimmy had decided to get a real job rather than go to college after graduating from high school. Although he enjoyed fiddling with computers, he'd never been academically inclined. He loved to work outdoors. He had gotten a job with the telephone company taking telephone poles *out* of the ground. He once told me that taking down a nice old telephone pole was almost as distressing as chopping down an old tree. He was kind of sensitive that way, but he liked the work.

After I left my room, I heard someone come in the front

door. I knew who it was without looking: Mrs. Mary Parish
and her daughter Amanda. My parents had gone out for the
night, but earlier that evening they had thrown a cocktail party
for a big-wig real estate developer from back east who was
thinking of joining forces with my dad to exploit Southern
California's few remaining square feet of beachfront property. Mrs. Parish worked as a part-time housekeeper for my
mom. She had called before I'd gone in for my shower to ask
if everyone had left so she could get started cleaning up. She
had also asked if Amanda could ride with me to Beth's party.
I had answered yes to both these questions and told her I'd be
upstairs getting dressed when they arrived and to just come in.
Mrs. Parish had a key to the house.

I called to them from the upstairs hall—which overlooks a
large portion of the downstairs—before stealing into Jimmy's
room.

"I'll be down in a minute! Just make yourself at home—
and get to work!"

I heard Mrs. Parish chuckle and caught a faint glimpse of
her gray head as she entered the living room carrying a yellow
bucket filled with cleaning supplies. I loved Mrs. Parish. She
always seemed so happy, in spite of the hard life she'd had.
Her husband had suddenly left her years earlier broke and
unskilled.

I didn't see Amanda at first, nor did I hear her. I guess I
thought she'd changed her mind and decided not to go to the

party. I'm not sure I would have entered Jimmy's room and then let him slip past me in a semiconscious state if I'd known that his girlfriend was in the house.

Girlfriend and *boyfriend*—I use the words loosely.

Jimmy had been going with Amanda Parish for three months when I died. I was the one who introduced them to each other, at my eighteenth birthday party. They hadn't met before, largely because Jimmy had gone to a different high school. Amanda was another one of those friends who wasn't a real friend—just someone I sort of knew because of her mother. But I liked Amanda a lot better than I liked Beth. She was some kind of beauty. My best friend, Jo, once remarked—in a poetic mood—that Amanda had eyes as gray as a frosty overcast day and a smile as warm as early spring. That fit Amanda. She had a mystery about her, but it was always right there in front of you—in her grave but wonderful face. She also had this incredibly long dark hair. I think it was a fantasy of my brother's to bury his face in that hair and let everyone else in the world disappear except him and Amanda.

I have to admit that I was a bit jealous of her.

Amanda's presence at my birthday party had had me slightly off balance. Her birthday had been only the day before mine, and the whole evening I remember feeling as if I had to give her one of my presents or something. What I ended up giving her was my brother, I brought Jimmy over to meet her, and that was the last I saw of him that night. It was love at first sight. And that evening, and for the next few weeks, I thought Amanda loved him, too. They were inseparable. But then, for no obvious reason, Amanda started to put up a wall, and Jimmy started to get an ulcer. I've never been a big believer in moderation, but I honestly believe that the intensity of his feelings for her was unhealthy. He was obsessed.

But I'm digressing. After calling out to Mrs. Parish, I crept into Jimmy's room. Except for the green glow from his computer screen, which he was in the habit of leaving on, it was dark. Jimmy's got a weird physiology. When I started for his desk and his brush, he was lying dead to the world with a sheet twisted around his muscular torso. But only seconds later, as I picked up the brush, he was up and heading for the door. I knew he wasn't awake, or even half-awake. Sleepwalkers walk differently—kind of like zombies in horror films, only maybe a little faster. All he had on were his boxers, and they were kind of hanging. I smiled to myself seeing him go. We were upstairs, and there was a balcony he could theoretically flip over, but I wasn't worried about him hurting himself. I had discovered from years of observation that God watches over sleepwalkers better than he does drunks. Or upset teenage girls . . .

I shouldn't have said that. I didn't mean it.

Then I thought of Amanda, possibly downstairs with her mom, and how awful Jimmy would feel if he suddenly woke up scratching himself in the hall in plain sight of her. Taking the brush, I ran after him.

It was good that I did. He was fumbling with the knob on the bathroom door when I caught him. At first I wasn't absolutely sure there was anyone in the bathroom, but the light was on and it hadn't been a few minutes earlier. Jimmy turned and stared at me with a pleasant but vaguely confused expression. He looked like a puppy who had just scarfed down a bowl of marijuana-laced dog food.

"Jimmy," I whispered, afraid to raise my voice. I could hear Mrs. Parish whistling downstairs and was becoming more convinced with each passing second that Amanda was indeed inside the bathroom. Jimmy smiled at me serenely.

"Blow," he said.

"Shh," I said, taking hold of his hand and leading him away from the door. He followed obediently, and after hitching up his boxer shorts an inch or two, I steered him in the direction of my parents' bedroom and said, "Use that bathroom. This one's no good."

I didn't wake him for a couple of reasons. First, he's real hard to wake up when he's sleepwalking, which is strange because otherwise he's a very light sleeper. But you practically have to slap him when he's out for a stroll. Second, I was afraid he might have a heart attack if he suddenly came to and realized how close he'd come to making a fool of himself in front of his princess.

After he disappeared inside my parents' room, I returned to the bathroom in the hall and knocked lightly on the door. "Amanda, is that you?" I called softly.

There was a pause. "Yeah. I'll be right out—I'm getting some kitchen cleanser."

Since she wasn't going to the bathroom, I thought it would be OK to try the knob. Amanda looked up in surprise when I peeked in. She was by the sink, in front of the medicine cabinet and a small wall refrigerator, and she had one of Jimmy's syringes and a vial of insulin in her hand. Jimmy's insulin had to be kept cool, and he'd installed the tiny icebox himself so he wouldn't have to keep his medication in the kitchen fridge downstairs where everybody could see it. He wasn't proud of his illness. Amanda knew Jimmy was a diabetic, but she didn't know he needed daily shots of medication. Jimmy didn't want Amanda to know. Well, the cat was out of the bag now. The best I could do, I thought, was to make a joke of the matter.

"Amanda," I said in a shocked tone. "How could you do this to your mother and me?"

She glanced down at the stuff, blood in her cheeks. "Mom told me to look for some Ajax, and I—"

"Ajax," I said in disbelief. "I wasn't born yesterday. Those are drugs you're holding. Drugs!" I put my hand to my mouth. *"Oh, God."*

I was a hell of an actress. Amanda just didn't know where I was coming from. She quickly put down the needle. "I didn't mean to—" she began.

I laughed and stepped into the bathroom. "I know you weren't snooping, Amanda. Don't worry. So you found the family stash. What the hell, we'll cut you in for a piece of the action if you keep your mouth shut. What do you say? Deal?"

Amanda peered at me with her wide gray eyes, and for a moment I thought of Jimmy's expression a moment earlier— the innocence in both. "Shari?"

I took the syringe and vial of insulin from her hand and spoke seriously. "You know how Jimmy's always watching his diet? Well, this is just another part of his condition he doesn't like to talk about, that's all." I opened the medicine cabinet and fridge and put the stuff away. "It's no big deal, is what I'm saying."

Amanda stared at me a moment; I wasn't looking directly at her, but I could see her reflection in the medicine cabinet mirror. What is it about a mirror that makes the beautiful more beautiful and the pretty but not exceptional less exceptional? I don't understand it—a camera can do the same thing. Amanda looked so beautiful at that moment that I could imagine all the pain she would cause my poor brother if her wall got any higher. And I think I resented her for it a tiny bit. She brushed her dark hair back from her pink cheek.

"I won't say anything to him," she said.

"It's no big deal," I said.

"You're right." She nodded to the cupboard under the sink, "I suppose I should have been looking down there."

We both bent over at the same instant and almost bumped heads. Then I remembered that Jimmy was still wandering around. Excusing myself, I left Amanda to find the Ajax and went searching for him. When I ran into him, coming out of my parents' bedroom, he was wide awake.

"Have I been sleepwalking?" he asked.

"No. Don't you remember? You went to sleep standing here." I pushed him back into my parents' bedroom and closed the door. "Amanda's here."

He immediately tensed. "Downstairs?"

"No, down the hall, in the bathroom. You almost peed on her."

Sometimes my sense of humor could be cruel. Jimmy sucked in a breath, and his blue eyes got real big. My brother's pretty cute, if I do say so myself. It runs in the family. He's the solid type, with a hint of refinement. One could imagine him herding cattle all day from the saddle, playing a little ball in the evening with the boys, taking his lady to an elegant French restaurant at night where he would select the proper wine to go with dinner. Except he would mispronounce the name of the wine. That was Jimmy. He was totally cool, but he wasn't perfect.

"Did she see me?" he asked.

"No. I saved you. You were about to walk in on her when I steered you this way."

"You're sure she didn't see me?"

"I'm sure."

He relaxed. Jimmy always believed everything I told him,

even though he knew what an excellent liar I was. I guess he figured if I ever did lie to him, it would be for his own good. He thought I was a lot smarter than he was, which I thought was stupid of him.

"What's she doing here?" he asked with a note of hope in his voice. I couldn't very well lie and tell him Amanda had come over to see him. When I had been in the bathroom with her, she hadn't even asked if he was home.

"Her mom brought her over. She's downstairs cleaning up the mess from the cocktail party. Amanda wants to ride to Beth's party with me."

"Why's she going? Is she a friend of Beth's?"

"Not really. I don't know why she wants to go." I had to wonder if Amanda had had time to buy a present, if she even had the money to buy one. She and her mom didn't exactly enjoy material prosperity.

"Is she still in the bathroom?" he asked.

"I don't know. You're not going to talk to her, are you?"

"Why not?"

"You're not dressed."

He smiled. "I'll put my pants on first." He started to open the door. "I think she's gone back downstairs."

"Wait. Jimmy?" I grabbed his arm. He stopped and looked at me. "When was the last time you called her?"

"Monday." He added, "Four days ago."

"That was the last time you talked to her. You called her

yesterday. You called her the day before that, too. Maybe you should give it a rest."

"Why? I just want to say hi, that's all. I'm not being fanatical or anything."

"Of course you're not," I lied. "But sometimes it's better, you know, to play a little hard to get. It makes you more desirable."

He waved his hand. "I'm not into all those games." He tried to step by. I stopped him again.

"I told her you were asleep," I said.

"She asked about me?"

"Yeah, sure." I wasn't even sure why I was so uptight about his not talking to her. I guess I couldn't stand to see Jimmy placed in a potentially humiliating situation. But perhaps I was just jealous. "We have to leave for the party in a couple of minutes," I added.

He began to reconsider. "Well, I guess I shouldn't bother her." He shook his head. "I wish her mom would tell her when I've called."

"Jimmy—"

"No," he said quickly. "Amanda really doesn't get the messages. She told me so herself."

I couldn't imagine that being true, but I kept my mouth shut. "I'll drop sly hints to Amanda tonight that she should call you tomorrow."

He nodded at the brush in my hand. "Isn't that mine?"

"Yeah, mine broke."

"You have a dozen brushes."

"They're all broken." I gestured to our mom's makeup table behind us. She never went out of the house without fixing herself up for an hour. Some might have called her a snob. I had called her that myself a few times, but never when my father was around. We didn't have a lot in common. "And mom wouldn't let me use one of hers."

"What did Amanda ask about me?"

"If you were getting enough rest." I patted him on the shoulder. "Go to bed."

I tucked Jimmy back in bed so that he could be fresh when his alarm went off at three in the morning and finished getting ready. When I went back downstairs, I found Amanda and her mom in the kitchen discussing whether a half-eaten chocolate cake should be divided into pieces before squeezing it into the jammed refrigerator.

"Why don't we just throw it in the garbage?" I suggested.

Mrs. Parish looked unhappy about the idea, which was interesting only because she usually looked so happy. Maybe I should clarify that. She wasn't one of those annoying people who go around with perpetual smiles on their faces. Her joy was quiet, an internal matter. But if I may be so bold, it often seemed that it shone a bit brighter whenever the two of us were alone together. I could talk to her for hours, about everything—even boys. And she'd just listen, without giving me advice, and she always made me feel better.

Jo, "Little Jo," had given her a nickname, too—"Mother Mary." I called Mrs. Parish that all the time. She was a devout Catholic. She went to mass several times a week and never retired for the night without saying her rosary. That was the one area where we didn't connect. I was never religious. Oh, I always liked Jesus, and I even went to church now and then. But I used to have more important things to think about than God. Like whether I should try to have sex with my boyfriend before I graduated from high school or whether I should wait until the Fourth of July and the fireworks. I wanted it to be a special moment. I wanted my whole life to be special. But I just hardly ever thought about God.

I'm repeating myself. I must be getting emotional. I'll try to watch that. Not everything I have to tell is very pleasant.

Back to that blasted cake. Mrs. Parish felt it would be a waste to throw it out. "Shari, don't you think that your mom might want some tomorrow?" she asked.

"If it's here, she'll eat it," I said. "And then she'll just complain about ruining her diet." I ran my finger around the edge and tasted the icing. I had already tasted about half a pound of it earlier in the day. "Oh, wow. Try this, Amanda. It's disgusting."

Amanda looked doubtful. "I'm not a big cake person."

Mrs. Parish suddenly changed her mind about saving it. "Maybe we should throw it out."

"You don't like cake?" I asked Amanda. "That's impossible—

everybody likes cake. You can't come to Beth's party with me unless you eat cake. Here, just try it. This little piece."

I could be so pushy. Amanda had a little piece, along with her mother, and I had a slightly larger little piece. Then I decided that maybe there was room for it in the refrigerator after all. I didn't care if my mother got fat or not.

Mrs. Parish sent Amanda to check to see if our vacuum cleaner needed a new bag. For a moment the two of us were alone, which was nice. I sat at the table and told her about the party we were going to, while she stacked dishes in the dishwasher.

"It's for Big Beth," I began. "I've already told you how she's been flirting with Dan at school. It really pisses me off. I'll see the two of them together on the other side of the courtyard, and then when I walk over to them, she greets me like she's really glad to see me, like nothing's been going on between them."

"How do you know something *is* going on?" Mrs. Parish asked.

"Because Dan looks so uncomfortable. Yeah, I know, why get mad at her and not at him?" I chuckled. "It's simple—he might leave me and run off with her!"

I was forever making jokes about things that really mattered to me. I doubted that even Mrs. Parish understood that about me. I may not have been obsessed with Daniel the way Jimmy was with Amanda, but I couldn't stand the thought of losing him. Actually, I honestly believed he cared for me. But I continued to worry. I was never really cool, not inside, not about love.

"Is Dan taking you and Amanda to the party?" Mrs. Parish asked, carefully bending over and filling the dishwasher with detergent. She had an arthritic spine. Often, if we were alone in the house, she would let me help her sweep the floor or scrub the bathrooms. But never if anyone else was present. I'd noticed she particularly disliked Amanda knowing she needed help.

"Yeah. We're picking Jo up, too. He should be here in a sec." I paused. "Mary, what do you think of Dan?"

She brightened. "He's very dashing."

I had to smile. *Dashing.* Great word. "He is cute, yeah." I took another forkful of cake, although I needed it about as much as I needed another two pounds on my hips. "What I mean, though, is do you like him? As a person?"

She wiped her hands on her apron and scratched her gray head. Unlike her daughter's, her hair was not one of her finer features. It was terribly thin. Her scalp showed a little, particularly on the top, whenever she bent over, and she was only fifty. To be quite frank, she wasn't what anyone would have called a handsome lady. She did, however, have a gentle, lovely smile.

"He seems nice enough," she said hesitantly.

"Go on?"

"How does he treat you?"

"Fine. But—"

"Yes?"

"You were going to say something first?"

"It was nothing."

"Tell me."

She hesitated again. "He's always talking about things."

"Things?" I asked, even though I knew what she meant. Daniel liked *things*: hot cars, social events, pretty people—the usual. Since the universe was composed primarily of things, I had never seen it as a fault. Yet Daniel could be hard to talk to because he seldom showed any deep feelings or concern for anything but "things."

Mrs. Parish shrugged, squeezing a couple more glasses into the dishwasher. "Does he ever discuss the two of you?"

"Yeah, sure," I lied.

"You communicate well when you're alone together then. That's good. That was the only thing I was concerned about." She closed the door on the washer and turned it on. The water churned. So did my stomach. I pushed away the cake. I'd heard a car pulling up outside. It must be Daniel, I thought. I excused myself and hurried to the front door.

I found him outside opening our garage. Graduation was a couple of weeks off, but my parents had already bought me my present. I can't say what it was without giving the impression I was spoiled rotten.

It cost a fortune. It was fast. It was foreign.

It was a Ferrari.

Oh, my car. I loved it. I loved how red it was. I loved everything about it. Daniel loved it, too, apparently. He hardly noticed my shining presence when I came out to greet him. He fell in love with my car at first sight.

He had taken longer to fall in love with me.

I had officially met Daniel after a high school play in which he played the lead. I have an incredible memory for facts, but I cannot remember what the play was about. That says a lot. He blew me away, and he wasn't even that great. He had forgotten several lines, and he'd been totally miscast. None of that mattered, though. He just had to strut around up there under the lights, and I felt I just *had* to go backstage afterward and commend him on his artistry. Of course, Jo had to drag me kicking and screaming to his dressing room. I was sort of shy, sometimes.

Since we went to the same school and were in the same grade, I naturally knew *of* him before we met after the play. I would like to record for posterity that the reverse was also true, that he had noted with approval my existence the four years we had spent together at Hazzard High. But the first thing he asked when Jo introduced us was if I was new to the area. What a liar. He didn't want me to think I was too cute.

But he asked me out, and that was the bottom line. He asked me out right there in front of his dressing room with Jo standing two feet away with her mouth uncharacteristically closed. Later, it seemed so amazing to me that I wondered if Jo hadn't set it all up beforehand. But she swore to the day I died that it wasn't so. . . .

I must talk about his dashing body. It was smooth and hard. It had great lines, like a great race car. Except Daniel wasn't red. He was tan. He hugged the road when he moved. He had legs, he had hips. He had independent rear suspension. We used to make out all the time in his bedroom with the music on real loud. And then, one warm and lustful evening, two weeks before Beth's birthday party, we took off our clothes and *almost* had sex.

I loved to think about sex. I could fantasize six hours a day and not get tired, even if I was repeating the same fantasy with only slight variations. I was a master of slight variations. But one can think too much. When we got naked together in bed, things did not go well. Daniel couldn't . . . Oh, this will sound crude if I say it, so I'll say instead that I shouldn't have overdone it comparing him to my Ferrari. Yet, in a sense, he was as *fast* as the car. I left the room a virgin.

He was *so* embarrassed. I didn't understand why. I was going to give him another fifty chances. I wasn't going to tell anyone. I didn't tell anyone, not really. Maybe Jo, sort of. But she couldn't have told anyone else and had enough details to sound like she knew what she was talking about. Unless she had added details of her own.

Daniel and I had other things in common, other *things*

we liked to do together. We both enjoyed going to movies, to the beach, out to eat. That may not sound like a lot, but when you're in high school, it often seems like that's all there is.

Anyway, when I went outside to welcome Daniel, he was in ecstasy. He had turned on the light in the garage and was pacing around the car and kicking the tires like guys are fond of doing when they see a hot set of wheels. I didn't mind. He had on white pants and a rust-colored leather coat that went perfectly with his head of thick brown hair.

"Did you have it on the freeway today, Shar?" he asked.

"Yeah, but I didn't push it. They told me to break it in slowly over the first thousand miles."

"This baby could go up to one forty before it would begin to sweat." He popped open the driver's door and studied the speedometer. "Do you know how many grand this set your dad back?"

"He wouldn't tell me. Do you know how many?"

Daniel shook his head. "Let's just say he could have bought you a house in the neighborhood for the same money." He went to climb inside. "Are you ready to go? Can I drive?"

"We can't take it. Amanda Parish is here, and she's riding with us. And we have to pick up Jo."

Although Joanne had introduced the two of us, Daniel didn't like her. It would be hard to pinpoint specifically what she did that bothered him, other than that he was a boy and she had a tendency to make the male species as a whole feel inferior.

I had no idea what he thought of Amanda.

He showed a trace of annoyance. "You didn't tell me."

"I didn't know until a little while ago." The Ferrari had no backseat. "We can go for a drive in it tomorrow."

He shut the door, sort of hard, and I jumped slightly. To be entirely truthful, I never felt entirely comfortable around Daniel. He strode toward me and gave me a hug. His embraces were always unexpected.

"Hi," he said.

"Hi."

He kissed me. He wasn't an expert at lovemaking, but he had a warm mouth. He also had strong arms. As they went around me, I could feel myself relaxing and tensing at the same time. I didn't know if other girls felt the same way when their boyfriends embraced them. But when his kisses grew hard and deep, I didn't mind.

"Oh, sorry," we heard behind us a minute or so later. Daniel let go, and I whirled. There was Amanda, as pretty and as unprepared as when I walked in on her in the upstairs bathroom. Her big eyes looking down, she turned to leave.

"No, it's OK," I said, taking a step toward her, only mildly embarrassed. "We should be leaving. Stay here. I'll go say goodbye to Jimmy and Mother Mary. Be back in a moment."

Amanda stopped. "What did you say?"

I suddenly realized I'd brought up Jimmy. "If Jimmy's

awake," I said quickly, the remark sounding thin in my own ears. "He was asleep a few minutes ago."

Amanda stared at me a moment. Then she muttered, "Say hello for me."

"Sure."

Jimmy was awake when I peeked in his door. He motioned me to come and sit on his bed. His computer screen was still on, and, as always, I found the faint green light hard on my eyes.

"Why don't you just turn it off?" I asked, gesturing to the CRT.

He smiled faintly, his muscular arms folded across his smooth chest, his eyes staring off into space. He was in a different mood now—more contemplative. "I might wake in the night inspired."

"The way you get around in your sleep, you wouldn't have to wake up."

"I was dreaming about you before I bumped into you in the hall."

"Oh? Tell me about it?"

He had just opened the window above his bed, and a cool breeze touched us both. Later, I thought it might have been the breath of the Grim Reaper. It was a warm night. Jimmy closed his eyes and spoke softly.

"We were in a strange place. It was like a world inside a flower. I know that sounds weird, but I don't know how else to describe it. Everything was glowing. We were in a wide-open space, like a field. And you were dressed exactly as you are now, in those jeans and that shirt. You had a balloon in your hand that you were trying to blow up. No, you *had* blown it up partway, and you wanted me to blow it up the rest of the way. You tried to give it to me. You had tied a string to it. But I didn't catch the string right or something, and it got away. We watched it float way up in the sky. Then you began to cry."

Far away, toward the front of the house, I heard Daniel start his car. He wasn't a good one to keep waiting. But suddenly, I didn't feel like going to Beth's party. I just wanted to sit and talk with my brother until he fell asleep. I pulled his sheet up over his chest. The breeze through the open window was getting chilly now.

"Why was I crying?" I asked.

"Because the balloon got away."

"What color was it?"

"I don't know. Brown, I think."

"Everything's brown to you! What was so special about the balloon?"

He opened his eyes and smiled at me. For a moment I thought he was going to ask me about Amanda again. I felt grateful when he didn't. "I don't know." He paused. "Will you be out late?"

"Not too late."

"Good."

"What's the matter?"

He thought a moment. "Nothing. I'm just tired." He squeezed my hand. "Have fun."

I leaned over and kissed him on the forehead. "Sweet dreams, brother."

He closed his eyes, and it seemed to me he was trying to picture my balloon a little more clearly so maybe he could answer my question about it a little better. But all he said was, "Take care, sister."

People. When you say goodbye to them for the last time, you'd expect it to be special, never mind that there's never any way to know for sure you're never going to see them again. In that respect, I would have to say I am thankful, at least, that my brother and I got to talk one last time before I left for the party. But when I got downstairs, Daniel was blowing his horn, and Mrs. Parish was vacuuming the dining room. I barely had a chance to poke my head in on her as I flew out the door.

"We're going," I called.

Mrs. Parish leaned over as if she was in pain and turned off the vacuum. "Did you bring a sweater?" she asked, taking a breath.

"Nah! I've got my boyfriend to keep me warm!"

She laughed at my nerve. "Take care, Shari."

"I will," I promised.

But I lied. And those little white lies, they catch up with you eventually. Or maybe they just get away from you, like a balloon in the wind.

CHAPTER II

I LET AMANDA sit in the front seat with Daniel. His Audi didn't have much of a backseat, and since I'm a lot shorter than Amanda, I figured it was only fair. I'd always been kind of sensitive about my height. I won't tell you exactly how tall I was—suffice it to say that I was only an inch taller than Little Jo and that she hadn't gotten her nickname by accident. A lot of people thought Jo and I were sisters.

Amanda perked up once we got on the road. Or at least she began to do more than nod her head and smile faintly. Amanda was awfully shy. Maybe it was the sugar in the cake that got her talking a bit. For a girl who didn't like desserts, she had gone to enough trouble to sneak back into the kitchen and grab another piece of the chocolate monster. As Daniel raced toward Jo's house at warp eight, Amanda fought to balance the cake between a napkin and her mouth. She must have known how paranoid Daniel was about getting crumbs on his upholstery.

"Thanks for inviting me to the party," Amanda said between bitefuls. "I've been cooped up in the house all day painting."

"I'm glad you're coming," I replied. In reality, I had not invited Amanda. She had invited herself through her mother.

"You're an artist?" Daniel asked. "What were you painting?"

Amanda hesitated. "Our bathroom."

"Really?" Daniel said. Amanda could have told him she'd been cleaning toilets; he was amazed. He had obviously never painted a wall in his life. His parents were almost as well-off as my own, as were the parents of most of the kids we went to school with. Amanda was our token pauper. I sometimes kidded her about it.

"What color?" I asked.

"White," Amanda said.

"White's so boring," I said. "Why white?"

"It's all the same to me," Amanda said.

"You must be color-blind," I said. "You're as bad as Jimmy. He keeps telling me I have brown eyes."

"What color *are* your eyes?" Amanda asked.

"Look at them," I said, slightly exasperated. "Can't you tell?"

Amanda glanced over her shoulder. "It's too dark. Are they green?"

"Good girl," I said. "We'll let you live." Daniel took a corner at the same speed he was taking the straightaways. "Hey, Dan, slow down. It's only a party we're going to."

"I just don't want to be late," he said. "Jo had better be ready."

"She'll be ready," I said. "Jo is always ready."

Jo wasn't ready. I told Daniel and Amanda to wait while I ran in to get her. Jo's mother answered the door. I didn't mention this earlier, but Jo's mother and Amanda's mother were sisters, which meant, of course, that Jo and Amanda were cousins. The reason I didn't mention it before was because Jo and Amanda were so different I forgot they were related. Their mothers were even less compatible. The only thing they had in common was that they both were divorcées. Mrs. Parish would have given me her right arm had I needed it, but Mrs. Foulton wouldn't have twisted her left wrist to let me see her watch had I asked the time. The lady wasn't hostile toward me, just *busy*. That was her excuse for everything— she had *so* much to do. She was head nurse at a hospital with a million hospital beds, and Jo had grown up practically an orphan. That was Jo's excuse for being so weird.

But Mrs. Foulton *was* hostile toward her sister. She loathed Mrs. Parish. Jo said it was because her mother blamed Mrs. Parish for the collapse of her marriage. Years ago Mrs. Parish was supposed to have had an affair with Mr. Foulton. When Jo told me the story, I didn't believe a word of it. But that was one of the things with people older than your parents—it was impossible to imagine they had ever had sex.

"Oh, Shar, Jo's in her room," Mrs. Foulton said when she saw who it was, quickly pushing open the screen door before turning back to the kitchen, a cup of coffee in her hand, a cigarette in her mouth. It always cracked me up to see someone in a starched white medical uniform with a cigarette in her mouth.

"Thanks," I said, stepping into the house over a pile of newspapers and magazines. Mrs. Foulton had *so* much to do, how could she possibly have time to clean up? Yet it was a beautiful house, a big house. Mrs. Foulton didn't have to kill herself going to work every day. Her husband had left her with enough bucks to give her the leisure to follow all the afternoon soap operas. It was Jo's opinion that her mother was obsessed with helping people because she felt guilty about not really liking them.

"Off to work?" I asked.

"I *am* at work," the lady replied, throwing her coffee into the kitchen sink and stubbing her cigarette out on the top of an open beer can. "This is my 'lunch break.'" She picked up her car keys. "Tell Jo I don't want her bringing her Ouija board to Beth's party."

"I don't think it's going to be that kind of party, Mrs. Foulton."

She stopped at the door, digging in her bag for her lipstick.

When she wasn't in a hurry, she could be attractive.

She had a great Roman nose, very authoritative. I couldn't imagine Mr. Foulton having left her years ago for a roll in the hay with Mrs. Parish. Then again, I couldn't remember when Mrs. Foulton had not been in a hurry, nor had I ever seen Mrs. Parish anything but patient. I often wondered what Mr. Foulton must have been like. Jo wouldn't talk about him.

"How do I look?" she asked, touching up her lips.

"Like a nurse," I said.

She flashed me a dangerous smile. "You're worse than Jo. Who's that out in the car? Dan?"

"And Amanda, yeah."

Mrs. Foulton brightened, which was the equivalent of smog forming a rainbow. Amanda was the one person Mrs. Foulton felt—besides those dying in hospital beds—was worthy of her time. She threw her lipstick back in her bag. "I'm going to say hi to her. 'Bye."

"Goodbye, Mrs. Foulton, and you take special care of yourself, 'cause we love you so much."

"Shove it, Shar."

I found Jo in her room carefully combing her hair. She had only recently begun to worry about her appearance, the way most girls did at age nine. She had fallen in love. His name was Jeff Nichols, and he was Big Beth's boyfriend. I knew it was going to be a hell of a party.

Jo was fascinated with the occult. She was into the usual

New Age fads such as astrology and crystals. Yet she leaned toward the darker edge of the esoteric circle. Nothing excited her more than a method to tap into a supernormal power. Her latest craze was a magnetic pendulum that she said could be used to *broadcast* or send substances into a person's body from any distance. When I was sick with a cold the week before Beth's party, she had called and told me she had broadcast vitamin C into my throat. It was ethereal vitamin C, of course, but she said it worked as well as the real thing. I can't say I felt a thing.

Did she believe in all that stuff? I don't know. When I was alive, I never gave it much thought, and now that I'm dead, I consider myself too close to the subject to voice an objective opinion. But Jo was no one's fool, that I can say.

"Dan's got the car running," I said as I stepped into her room. Friends at school who knew of Jo's interest in the supernatural were often disappointed when they visited her house and discovered that her bedroom was perfectly normal. In fact, it was usually the cleanest place in the house. The only things in her room that suggested her hobby were a box of incense and an incense holder on top of her chest of drawers.

Her appearance was also fairly normal. Although we resembled each other, her hair was dark enough that I made fun of her every time she described herself as a blonde. We had the same petite builds, the same kind of mouths that laughed at the same kind of jokes. But whereas I did have *striking* green eyes, hers were at best hazel. She did have great taste in clothes, however. I was forever borrowing outfits from her. The yellow shirt and jeans I wore to Beth's party actually belonged to Jo.

"Tell him I'm going to be a minute," Jo said, finishing her hair and hurrying to the closet.

"It'll take me more than a minute to walk down to the car," I said, sitting on her rock-hard bed. Jo also practiced yoga and would never stand for a mattress that would let her spine sag. "You look fine. Let's just go. I don't think Dan's in the best of moods."

Jo glanced up from digging in her closet and grinned. "Does Spam feel uncomfortable around you now that you two have engaged in bestial activities together?"

"I didn't say we had sex." Jo always called Dan "Spam." I had long ago ceased trying to free her of the habit. It is interesting that I was one of the few people Jo never gave a nickname to, and I was her best friend.

"Yes, you did," Jo said, finding what she was looking for, which appeared to be a lump of metal. "You said he undressed you, you undressed him, and then the two of you let things take their natural course."

"Stop," I pleaded. "We have to drive to the party in the same car in a few minutes, for Christ's sake." I paused. "What's that? Another magnet?"

"Yeah."

"What happened to the last one?" I asked as I picked up a small pile of typed papers lying on her bed.

"I still have it. But this one's stronger. It's used for a different purpose." She squeezed it into the pocket of her black pants. Like any good witch, Jo loved to wear black. "We can talk to the universe with this one. We'll play with it at the party." She gestured to the papers in my hand. "You know what that is?"

"What?"

"A short story by Peter Nichols—Jeff's brother."

A couple of years back, when I was a sophomore and he was a senior, I had shared a biology class with Peter. He was great—he could crack me up like no one could. He would tell me these totally ridiculous stories about all the weird things that kept happening to him. For example, once he told me how he picked up an old man with a white beard hitchhiking, and how the old guy started telling Peter his whole past history, beginning with when Peter was in second grade right up until Peter helped the Hazzard High baseball team win the city championship. Peter had an amazing arm—his coaches said he had pro potential. He also had an incredible way with words. I could picture the old man and his story perfectly. Before the old man got out of Peter's car, he also told Peter what his future would be. I remember how Peter smiled and shook his head when I asked what the guy had said.

I must emphasize that Peter was not—at least to the best of my knowledge—interested in the occult. I don't know why he told me that story. Usually his stories were about crooked cops and crazy people he constantly ran into while simply walking down the block.

Peter died not long after that—some kind of car accident. I missed him terribly. He had been the best part of my day, and I always felt I'd know him all my life.

I instinctively dropped the papers when Jo said his name. "Oh, God," I whispered. "Peter. How did you get this?"

"Jeff gave it to me," Jo said, picking up the sheets and sorting them into a neat stack. "He gave me a whole bunch of Peter's stories. He wanted to see if I could help get some of them published."

"Peter wasn't a writer. He was always playing baseball. When did he have the time to write? He never showed me any of his stuff."

"He never showed anybody. Jeff only found the stories a couple of months ago at the back of Peter's closet. You should read this one."

I don't know why the news disturbed me so. I brushed off Jo's attempts to hand the story to me. "Why are you reading them? Are you trying to get on Jeff's good side?"

Jo didn't flinch at my remark. It took a lot for her to show she was hurt. "I'm doing this because I want to," she said in a normal tone of voice. "He was a pretty good writer, and he had great ideas. But he seldom finished anything. That's one of the things Jeff asked if I could do for him—put some endings on Peter's stuff."

I continued to feel uneasy about the whole thing but couldn't pinpoint the reason why. Could it have been that the mention of his name had triggered a wave of painful memories? I asked myself.

Jo wrote for the school paper and was acknowledged to be Hazzard High's sole master of grammar. She tried to hand me his story again. "You should read it," she said.

I finally took it and glanced at the title: *Ann's Answer*. "What is it?" I asked reluctantly.

"It's about a girl our age who buys a VCR and then discovers it can tape tomorrow's TV programs today. She starts out taping the local news, spotting all the tragedies that are about to happen, and then she goes out to try to prevent them."

"How does it end?"

"He never finished it."

"But what was the last thing that happened to this girl?"

So my middle name was Ann, I told myself. He hadn't written the story about me. Yet the icy breeze that had blown through my brother's window earlier that night felt as if it had taken a detour into Jo's bedroom. And her windows were all closed. A cold sweat broke out on my forehead. *Omen* might be the word for what Jo said next, and for the balloon Jimmy watched float away. I suppose it was all a question of interpretation. A part of me must have seen the black ax rising slowly into the air above my head.

Maybe Peter had seen the same ax.

But of course he'd seen it. Far more clearly than I.

"She taped a program of a news story that was about herself," Jo said.

I swallowed. "Had she died?"

"The tape was jammed in the machine. She didn't get to see the entire piece, only the beginning where her name was mentioned and her picture was shown. Then Peter stopped."

"He stopped?"

"In midsentence. But read it. It's fun."

I handed the papers back to Jo. "I'll wait until you write the ending."

CHAPTER III

I HAD FORGOTTEN to tell Jo that Amanda was in the car. The fact didn't seem to faze Jo. She may have had little in common with her cousin, but there was no known hostility between them. Jo climbed into the backseat with me, however, a seating arrangement that may have been unwise. Dan had once complained to me that whenever Jo and I got together, we drowned out the rest of the world. Remembering the remark, I endeavored to be quiet. Jo immediately took it upon herself to make up for my silence.

"Spam," Jo said to Dan as he pulled out of her driveway. "What did you get Big Beth for her birthday?"

Dan frowned. I could tell he was frowning even though I was looking at the back of his head. He frowned whenever Jo spoke to him. "Why don't you call people by their real names for once?" he asked.

"All right, Daniel," she said. "What did you get Elizabeth for her birthday?"

"Earrings," he said, flooring the accelerator and racing up the street as if he were late to his own wedding.

"What?" I asked, amazed. "I got her a present from both of us. You didn't have to get her something."

"What did you get her?" Jo asked me.

"An old Beatles album," I said.

"Beth has a CD player," Daniel said.

"Elizabeth hates the Beatles," Jo said.

"Oh," I said. I had been aware of both facts, but there had been a sale on Beatles albums at the store.

"What did you get her, Bliss?" Jo asked Amanda. Jo had once explained the choice of nicknames to me. Apparently, in India, the Sanskrit word for "bliss" is *ananda*, which Jo obviously thought was close enough. Her reasoning might have had an element of sarcasm in it. Amanda seldom smiled.

"I didn't have a chance to stop at the store," Amanda said softly. If I hadn't been so overwhelmed with disgust at Daniel's having gone to the trouble to buy Beth a separate gift, I probably would have told Amanda she could put her name beside mine on the album.

"Isn't anyone going to ask what I got her?" Jo asked, fiddling with the pink tissue paper on the package in her hands. A moment of silence followed. "Specimen jars," Jo said finally. "My mom got them from the hospital for free."

"You can't give Beth that," Daniel said, irritated.

"Sure I can," Jo said. "She'll think they're crystal."

"She's not that stupid," Daniel said.

"She's pretty stupid," I said.

"And we'll tell her they're crystal," Jo said. "Hey, slow down, Spam. The party won't start until I get there. What's the hurry?"

"I always drive this fast," Daniel said.

"Is he always this fast?" Jo asked me.

"Always," I said without thinking. The question, and answer, might have been innocent enough, to start with. Except Jo suddenly burst into hysterical laughter.

"Always?" she asked, gagging.

I gave her a hard poke in the side—too late. I didn't have to see Daniel's face. I could feel the vibes. They were *bad*. He knew that Jo knew he had not performed up to expectations when we had gone to bed.

"What's so funny?" Amanda asked.

"Nothing," I said.

We drove the rest of the way in silence.

Big Beth met us at the door. Her parents' condominium was on the top floor of a four-story building that overlooked the ocean. It had a view, of course, and it had been built with lots of money. My father had been involved in the construction. The sound proofing in the walls between the condos was excellent.

Beth had music up loud and pumping, and there wasn't one complaint. I handed Beth my gift as we went through the door. A fool could have told what it was. Beth glanced at it after saying hello and smiled.

"It's not a painting, is it?" she asked hopefully.

"It'll never wear out on you," I said, remembering her CD player. My eyes flickered to Daniel. Whenever someone is madder at me than I am at them, it is hard for me to stay mad. Guilt, I suppose. Daniel handed Beth his tiny box, and you would have thought he had given her an engagement ring. She planted a kiss on his cheek, gushing.

"You shouldn't have," she said.

"No problem," he said, by no means pushing her away.

"It's your birthday, for God's sake, he had to get you something," Jo said, quickly scanning the room for Jeff Nichols. He was standing alone in the corner of the room, a beer in his hand. He didn't even glance over at us. Why a shy, intelligent fellow like Jeff Nichols was going out with someone like Beth was beyond me. Jo's eyes lingered on him a moment before she turned back to Beth and handed her the specimen jars.

"Whatever you do, don't shake the box," Jo said seriously.

Beth nodded and pressed her ear to the package. Don't ask me to explain it.

Yet I'm giving the wrong impression of the girl. Beth was not totally stupid, nor was she a complete knockout. She did as well as I did in school—A's and B's—and her SAT score was

high. It's my belief that she had cultured her air-head qualities to pacify her subconscious anxieties about her looks. Guys
often say there's nothing sexier than a girl with brains, but just
watch them drool over *Playboy*'s Miss September, whose turn-
ons are sincere guys and windy nights and whose turn-offs are
rude people and dogs that bite. I mean, it's no wonder that
a girl like Beth with breasts out to the moon would develop
the idea, while growing up in a society as superficial as ours,
that if she just smiled a lot and didn't demand regular cerebral
stimulation, guys would be more likely to ask her out. That's
my theory, at least, but then again, what the hell do I know?

Beth had more to her body than a chest. She had a bumpy
nose, two ordinary brown eyes—devoid of even a hint of gorgeous green—and a head of brown hair which, although long
and straight, didn't shine in any light. All the guys at school
thought she was sex incarnate, and she wasn't even that pretty.
And as I said, I think she knew it. Studying her as she stood
next to cool, soft Amanda, I thought Beth looked like nothing
to worry about.

"I'm sorry," Amanda said to Beth. "I didn't have a chance
to get you a present."

"That's OK," Beth exclaimed, hugging Amanda, whom
she scarcely knew. "I'm just glad you're here!"

"You're shaking the box," Jo warned Beth, silently muttering *Christ* under her breath. For his part, Daniel kept silent.

And so the party began, and at first it was a fairly ordinary affair. I won't go into every blessed detail. Beth's parents were gone for the night. We ate a little. We danced a little. We ate some more. We gossiped; lots of people came and went, so there was plenty to gossip about. And all the time I kept my eyes on Daniel and Beth, and Jo kept her eyes on Jeff and Beth, and the world went right on turning. Nothing out of the ordinary happened.

There are, however, a few things I should mention before I get into Jo's idea of entertainment. Beth opened her presents close to eleven o'clock, and even though it was early, the party had begun to thin out. There couldn't have been more than a dozen people left when Beth sat in the middle of the floor in her pink summer dress and proceeded to break every one of her nails. She really did—each time she dug into a fresh package, she ripped another manicured nail. It was excruciating to watch.

"I should have bought you a bottle of calcium supplement instead," Jo remarked, busting up the group. Beth laughed at the joke, but I could tell she hadn't appreciated it. Yet all was forgiven a moment later when she opened Jo's present. To be fair, the specimen jars at Mrs. Foulton's hospital were a bit larger and more elaborate than the usual. But in no way did they look like expensive crystal. When Beth unwrapped them and held them up for the room to see—a hint of utter confusion in her eyes—Jo broke in with smooth sincerity.

"I know they're not the usual crystal," she said. "But I

thought you would like something different for your collection." Jo added humbly, "They're from China."

Beth beamed and hugged Jo. I almost died. The rest of the room nodded and tuned out. Only Jeff gave any sign that he knew Beth was being suckered, and it was a faint sign at that; he finished his beer and silently crumpled the can between his palms. Amanda sat quietly in the corner, casting me furtive glances, probably wondering if I was going to lose it, or maybe still embarrassed that she had nothing for Beth to open.

Daniel's earrings had diamonds in them. Diamonds! They sparkled as he helped Beth put them on her earlobes. Again, I almost died. I almost cried. I almost said something. But what could I say? Daniel hadn't said much to me all night. I knew he was still pissed at me for speaking to Jo about his excitable bedsheet manners. I was afraid that if I spoke then—or even later—I would ask why and he would say 'bye.

I began to think it was a stupid party.

Beth finally finished with her presents. ("Oh, Shari, the Beatles! My favorite!") Several more people left. Then Beth brought up the idea of swimming. The condominium complex had one huge heated pool and two steaming Jacuzzis. But how could we go swimming, I wondered, without bathing suits? That was no problem for those who had been told in advance to bring their suits, I soon learned. Daniel was one of those people. And strangely enough, Amanda was also one. Apparently, after asking her mom to ask me for a ride to the party, she must have called Beth directly to see if she really could come and had received the word on the suits. Daniel and Beth had theirs on under their clothes.

"We could go skinny-dipping," Jo said as we watched everyone except Jeff parade out the front door. Jeff was standing alone on the balcony drinking another beer when Jo made her suggestion. He had been putting them away all night, one after another, but he did not seem drunk.

"No," I said. "I always feel naked without my clothes on." I nodded toward the dark balcony, which lay—relative to our cozy spot on the living room couch—beyond an intervening kitchen. We could see Jeff's silhouette against the night sky, the shadow of his beer can resting on the supposedly strong and secure wooden rail. "Besides, this is your chance. Go give him a bite."

"I think he wants to be alone," Jo said.

"He wouldn't have come to a party if he wanted to be alone."

"He had to come to the party. It's his girlfriend's birthday."

"His girlfriend's not here. She's gone swimming with my boyfriend."

"You're not upset?"

"I'm not?" I asked.

"They were the gaudiest earrings."

"Gaudy costs money. You should have given her used specimen jars."

"Who says I didn't? Are you really upset?"

"I don't know. Are you really afraid to talk to Jeff?"

"I don't know," Jo said and sighed. "Yeah."

"Do you want me to talk to him?"

"I don't care. Just don't tell him I love him."

"Do you love him?" I asked, surprised. I hadn't realized he meant that much to her. Coming to the party was probably hard for her.

Jo began to make a flip remark, at which the two of us were masters. Then she paused and lowered her eyes. "Yeah, maybe. I don't know. Do you love Spam?"

I stood. "I always hated it when I was a little kid."

Before going out onto the balcony, I made a quick stop in Beth's bathroom. But it wasn't because I'd been drinking beer. I was never into depressants like alcohol and health food. I liked good old blood-rushing caffeine: coffee, Cokes. Pepsis. I'd had all three that night.

The design of the condo was common for the beach area, although it would have been unusual a few miles inland. It had two master bedrooms, which meant, of course, that the condo's two bathrooms were located in the bedrooms. Beth's room had the better view, with a wide sliding glass door that led directly onto the west-end balcony that overlooked the ocean. But it was smaller than her parents' room and, being next to the kitchen, was also less private.

When I finished in the bathroom, I joined Jeff outside on the balcony without having to backtrack to the living room.

He was lighting up a cigarette when I first stepped into the night. That is my last impression of Jeff Nichols—the side of his rugged face in the orange flare of a wooden match. He wasn't particularly handsome. He had none of the warmth and humor in his face that his older brother had had. His bone structure was not well defined, and he didn't have to narrow his eyes for you to feel he might be angry. Still, you had to look at him. He had magnetism, buried deep, perhaps, and probably rusty, but pulling hard. He was unlike most of my friends—he didn't give a damn what anyone thought of him.

We'd only talked a few times at school, although we shared a couple of classes. Sometimes it seemed to me that he purposely avoided me.

"I hope I'm not disturbing you?" I asked.

He glanced over, waved out his match, and took a drag on his cigarette. "No."

I went and stood with my hands resting on the smooth-sanded railing, six feet from Jeff. The view of the ocean at night was nothing—all flat, black, and depressing. It depressed me then, that's for sure. Or maybe it was the faint sounds of splashing and giggling I could hear coming from the far side of the complex.

Jeff seemed kind of down, too. I wondered if he was remembering Peter. He wasn't saying anything, and I felt I had to speak.

"It's a nice night," I remarked. It was essentially warm,

with layers of cool, damp air drifting up to the balcony—not unusual for that close to the sea.

"It's all right."

"Am I bothering you?"

He shrugged. "I'll probably be going home soon."

"Before Beth gets back?"

"Maybe."

"Jeff?"

"What?"

"Nothing. I just wanted to, you know . . . say something." That was clever. What I wanted to say was that he shouldn't be with a girl who would put specimen jars in with her crystal collection and that I missed his brother, too. Jeff had idolized Peter, the way Peter could stand on the mound and make another team's hitters jittery just by the way he chewed his bubble gum. Peter had been funny but cool, without having to act it.

"I wish I'd brought my suit," I said. When he didn't respond, I added, "I wish Dan had told me we'd be swimming."

"Maybe he forgot."

I may have imagined it, but his reply seemed to contain a note of sarcasm. "You two don't know each other very well, do you?" I asked.

"No."

"That's too bad."

He peered over at me. Neither the lights in the kitchen nor those in Beth's bedroom were on. I couldn't see his eyes;

nevertheless, I shifted uneasily. "For whom?" he asked.

"For the two of you. I mean—What do you mean?"

Jeff looked back toward the ocean, took another drag off his cigarette. "Never mind, Shari."

I moved a step closer to him. "You don't like Dan, do you?"

"Why ask?"

"Come on, Jeff."

"Dan, he's OK." He shrugged again. "If you like assholes."

I did not appreciate the remark. Yet I think it disturbed me mainly because it reflected on me as Daniel's girlfriend.

"You're the asshole," I said, deciding that any sympathy I might have felt for him had been misdirected.

"I suppose."

"What's your problem?"

"I don't have any problems."

"You've got an asshole for a girlfriend."

It was not a particularly nice thing for a sweet little girl like me to say, I admit. I half expected him to throw down his cigarette and walk away. Yet his upper lip curled into a slow smile beneath the glow of his cigarette. "She's not that bad. She's too good for him."

"For who?"

He shook his head, and now he turned to leave. "Nothing."

I hate it when people start to tell me something that I will hate and stop right in the middle. That's my only excuse for saying what I did next. It *was* cruel.

"You know, Jeff, you're such a shallow jerk compared to your brother."

He stopped suddenly, and I wished I could have reached out and retrieved my words. Like in the car with Dan on the way to the party, I only had to look at the back of his neck to feel the bad vibes. He turned slowly, though, casually raising his cigarette to his mouth and sticking it in the corner in such a way that I thought it would fall out any second. It was too dark for me to read his expression clearly, and I was glad.

"He used to tell me stuff about you," Jeff said. "He thought you were all right. But I always thought you didn't know what was going on. I just had to look at the way you strolled along with your head up your ass." He pulled out his cigarette and dropped it, crushing it beneath his black boot. Then he cleared his throat. "Yeah, and he died, Shari, and you haven't changed. Not in my book."

He went inside but didn't leave. Jo met him in the kitchen, and I saw the two of them sit down on the living room sofa together and talk. Maybe they talked about me. I never did know.

Neither did I know that I had less than two hours to live.

I turned back to the ocean. It was black. Then I looked straight down. A concrete sidewalk ran just below, alongside a plot of green grass lit by a hard white globe on top of a shrunken lamppost. It was a long way down.

CHAPTER IV

I COULD TELL YOU how I died. How my skull cracked open and the blood gushed out. All the gory details. But gore is for the living. Fading mortals don't always close their eyes when becoming naked spirits, but they seldom watch. At least, I didn't.

Jo played a strange part before the fun started—and ended. But before even that, Bliss told me all about Big Beth and Spam. I think I understand now why Jo was always giving people nicknames. The living really have only one point of view—their own. Oh, there are wise men here and there on earth who can see things as others do, but they are rare. Most people can't see other people as quite as real as themselves. It is forgivable when you realize they have to see everyone from inside a body that can be in only one place at one time. When I was alive, some people at school seemed to me like little more than mannequins in a store window. They were simply there for my greater shopping enjoyment.

Jo must have had the same problem. For her, Daniel was easier to relate to as Spam because Spam was a *thing*, and she could always return a thing to the store if she didn't like it. And Big Beth was like a cartoon character; Jo could change the channel on the set and watch another cartoon if she was no longer amused. Or she could pull the plug, and they would all be gone. All of them.

I believe her nicknaming people gave Jo the feeling that she had control over her environment.

But I'm digressing. While Jo and Jeff sat in the living room, I went back into Beth's bedroom and lay down on her bed. I figured if she could swim with my boyfriend, I could wrinkle her sheets. I didn't go straight from the balcony to the bedroom. I discovered that the sliding glass door I had used a few minutes earlier automatically locked when I closed it. I had to reenter the condo through the kitchen and return to the bedroom. Jeff and Jo didn't even look up as I went by. God knows what they were talking about.

I had a headache. I was tired. When I lay down, I had no intention of sleeping, but I must have. I didn't dream, however. My omens were over for the night. Except for one last big one. Before my headache blossomed into a skull-shattering mess, the gang rehearsed my funeral.

Amanda awakened me. She was sitting on the bed by my side when I opened my eyes. Her black hair looked so long and lovely to me right then, I remember thinking how awful it would be if she were to go prematurely gray. I knew from a picture album Mrs. Parish had shown me that her mother had. Amanda must have blow-dried it after swimming.

"What time is it?" I muttered. My headache was worse than when I had lain down.

"After twelve."

I sat up. "Is the swimming over?" Amanda had changed back into her clothes. She stared at me for a moment with her gray eyes before answering.

"Most of the kids have left," she said.

The condo did seem unusually quiet. "Where's Dan? Is he back?"

"No."

"Where is he?"

She looked down, and even in the gloom I could see the lines form on her forehead. "I don't know how to tell you this, Shari."

"What?"

"Dan and Beth are still out."

"So?"

Amanda took a breath, her hair hanging over the side of her face. "I was walking back when I remembered I'd left my watch by the diving board. I went back to get it. Dan and Beth must have gotten out of the pool. They weren't there. But I . . ."

"What?" I demanded as she paused. She glanced up.

"They were in the Jacuzzi."

"So?"

"They were naked."

"No. How could you tell?"

"I could tell."

I swallowed, and my throat wasn't merely dry, it was parched and bleeding, like my soul. I have a confession to make. Daniel was a lot better than I've described him. He wasn't just a pretty face. He had style. He was funny. He had done a lot of nice things for me. He had taken me to the prom in a gold-plated Rolls after pinning the biggest corsage of the night on my long white dress. I liked him, I really did like him. And all those doubts I had about him and Beth—deep down inside I knew I was just being paranoid.

I hated Amanda right then for telling me I had been right all along.

"What were they doing?" I asked.

She shook her head. "Nothing."

"What?" I insisted.

"They were kissing."

"And she had her top off?"

"Yes."

"How could you be sure?"

"I could see, Shari. There was enough light." Amanda shook her head again. "I shouldn't have told you." She started to get up. I grabbed her arm.

"What else were they doing? Was he fondling her?"

Amanda broke free of my hold and retreated to the end of the bed, where she stood and looked down on me. "I'm sorry," she said.

I laughed out loud for a second. "What are you sorry about? She wasn't kissing Jimmy—if you would even care. You know he was home when you came over? You could have said hi. I know how much you love him. Anyway, I don't care. Dan can do what he wants. You can do what you want. I ain't going to stop you, sister. The whole world can go to hell for all I care."

Amanda left. And I cried, alone and to myself.

The party should have ended when Dan and Beth returned. I should have openly accused them, ignored their pleas of denial and forgiveness, and then stormed off into the night with Jo chasing after me to make sure I was OK. The problem was that when Dan and Beth finally did come through the door together, I was too heartsick to speak, and Jo was still busy entertaining Jeff on the couch. It struck me then that my best friend might actually find reason to celebrate the news of Dan and Beth's passionate public make-out.

The party *would* have ended if Jo hadn't insisted we talk to the universe after everyone finished dressing. She pulled out her magnet.

"I read about this technique in a book on Taoism," Jo said, holding up the magnet so that we could all see that it had a brass cap over one end. "It was originally used thousands of years ago to diagnose health problems. It allows you to question the body directly about what's wrong with it."

"Is it like a Ouija board?" Beth asked wearily. Even I could sympathize with her. Beth was afraid that Jo was going to get out her Ouija board, as she had done at so many parties before. This is not to say that Jo insisted others share her fascination with the occult or that she couldn't sometimes liven up a dead party by invoking a few dead people. It simply meant that Jo never knew when it was getting late.

"It's similar but different," Jo said.

"Oh," I said.

Jo cast me a look that said she knew I wanted to leave but that she also thought we should let the magnet decide when to call it a night. "Why don't I demonstrate it rather than talk about it?" she said.

"What do you need?" Jeff asked, seemingly interested. He had put away his cigarettes and didn't look nearly so fierce in the light as he had in the dark. There were six of us in the room right then—Amanda, Dan, Beth, Jo, Jeff, and myself—all arranged in a rough circle in the cluttered living room. Sad six, one short of lucky seven.

Jo smiled at Jeff. "A body."

"I have one," Beth volunteered, raising her hand, showing more enthusiasm now that her official boyfriend had made the whole matter respectable with his question. Daniel looked at her and smiled, the bastard.

"We know," I said, sitting on the floor against a wall.

They ignored me. They wanted to talk to the universe. Only Amanda appeared uninterested. Or else afraid. She continued to hang back in her corner chair. She might have been afraid of what I was going to say. Or else what the universe might know. I suppose we all have our secrets.

But Dan and Beth weren't afraid of anything. They gathered around as Jo slid onto the floor. "What's the heel like on those shoes you're wearing?" Jo asked Beth.

"They're all right," Beth said, not having the foggiest idea what Jo was asking. Jo leaned over and gave Beth's sneakers a brief inspection.

"They'll work," Jo said. "Lie down flat on your back."

"What are you going to do?" Beth asked, now a tad nervous.

"I'm going to put this magnet on the floor at the back of your head," Jo said, doing precisely that as she spoke. "And then I'm going to take your ankles in my hands and ask your body questions. When your body wants to answer yes, one of your legs will get longer than the other."

"Why don't you use her nose?" I asked, thinking of Pinocchio and telling lies and that sort of thing. No one seemed to care. They continued to ignore me.

"Are you serious?" Dan asked.

"You'll see," Jo said. "One leg will actually get longer than the other."

"How does that happen?" Jeff asked.

"Her hip must rotate," Jo said, cradling Beth's shoes in her palms. Beth had closed her eyes and appeared to be concentrating hard on something unknown to the rest of us.

"No, how does her body know to respond?" Jeff said.

"No one knows," Jo said. "Somehow the magnet triggers an answering reflex in the body."

"Why did you cap one pole of the magnet?" Jeff asked.

"The book said to do it," Jo said. "It doesn't work otherwise." She turned her attention to Beth. "How do you feel?"

"Different," Beth whispered.

"Should she feel different?" Daniel asked.

"No," Jo said, looking down and pressing Beth's heels together. "Your body must be in good alignment. Your legs are exactly the same length."

"Thank you," Beth said.

"She probably has her hips worked on regularly," I said.

One person in the room didn't ignore me this time. Daniel caught my eye and stared. I stared back in such a manner that I made it clear I knew what had happened in the Jacuzzi. And somehow I knew he was thinking of the comment Jo had made in the car on the way to the party, about how fast he always was—thinking about what an untrustworthy bitch I was. There was something unhealthy in the way we looked at each other right then.

"Is today Beth's birthday?" Jo asked aloud, simultaneously raising Beth's heels off the floor. Jo then nodded for Jeff to check Beth's leg lengths.

"They haven't changed," Jeff said.

"It's not working?" Beth asked, obviously worried that her body might not be connected to the universe. Jo was unconcerned.

"Think for a moment," she said. "It is after twelve. Today is the day after your birthday."

"Ask an affirmative question," Jeff said.

"Is Beth a girl?" Jo asked, again raising Beth's feet up. I was too far away to tell, but apparently there was a shift in the length of one of her legs. Jeff leaned forward from his place on the edge of the couch and nodded his head.

"There is a slight difference, yeah," he said.

"It's not that slight," Jo said, continuing to keep Beth's heels tightly pressed together. "The right leg is now an inch longer than the left."

"And this is her body's way of saying yes?" Jeff asked.

"Yes," Jo said.

"You can only ask yes-or-no questions?" Jeff said.

"You'd be surprised how much information you *can* get," Jo said. "Now, I know what you're going to say, but go ahead and say it anyway."

Jeff shrugged. "Beth heard you ask the question. She knows she's a girl. Her body's response could have been subconscious."

Jo smiled. "What if I told you it doesn't matter if I say the question aloud or if I just *think* it?"

"You want me to think about being a girl?" Beth asked, frowning, her eyes still closed.

"The legs will still shift?" Jeff asked.

Jo let go of Beth's ankles, climbing to her knees and scooting toward Jeff. "I'll whisper three questions in your ear that we already know the answers to," she said. "Then we'll see if her body responds correctly each time."

They had a brief huddle, and then Jo got back to Beth's ankles. Since the rest of us didn't know the questions, the demonstration was not exactly overwhelming. When it was done, however, and Jeff had finished comparing Beth's leg lengths, he nodded his approval.

"You did them in the same order you told me?" he asked Jo.

"Yes," Jo said.

"What did you ask?" Daniel asked.

"First I asked if Beth was pregnant," Jo said. "And the answer was no. Her heels didn't shift."

"Thank God," Beth said, smiling. It struck me then how cool Beth was playing it for someone who had only a few minutes earlier been sinning in a hot tub with a guy who didn't belong to her.

"Then I asked if Beth was alive," Jo continued. "And as I raised her feet off the floor, her right leg got an inch longer. Right, Jeff?"

"It did, yeah," he said thoughtfully. I suspected that if he knew about Beth's unfaithfulness, he would have cared less.

But he did seem to be totally absorbed in what Jo was doing. And she knew it. Her cheeks were flushed with pleasure.

"My third question was if it was Saturday morning," Jo said. "And once again, Beth's legs moved." Jo glanced down at Beth. "Are you comfortable? Can we keep using you to ask our questions?"

Beth squinted her eyes without opening them. "Yeah, but turn off that lamp. The light's bothering me."

Jo gestured to Daniel to turn the light off, although it was clear Jo still did not understand why Beth should feel any different. The rest of us pulled in a little closer, including Amanda, who finally came and sat on the floor beside me. The door to the balcony in the kitchen lay wide open. I could feel the night air on my bare feet; it seemed to hug the carpet like a cool sheet. I wanted to go home. My headache refused to go away.

"What should we ask?" Daniel asked.

"Anything," Jo said, a glint in her eyes. She again took hold of Beth's sneakers. "Anything at all."

"Ask if there's going to be another war," Daniel said.

Jo asked the question out loud, raising Beth's heels a foot or so off the floor and then checking for a shift in leg length. Now that I was close enough to see, I realized the shift was genuine. It was clear-cut.

"Yes," Jo said.

"Oh, no," Daniel said, distressed. The poor baby, I thought.

The bombs would probably catch him in bed with his neighbor's wife. God, how I wanted to grab that magnet and glue it to the back of his head so that every time he lied his left leg would get shorter and he would trip and fall on his face.

"Of course there's going to be another war," I said. "There are small wars going on all the time all over the world. Ask if there is going to be another world war in the next twenty years."

I noticed that Beth's heels returned to an even keel the moment Jo set Beth's feet back on the floor. At the back of my mind, I wondered if Jo was tugging on Beth's ankle whenever she wanted a yes answer.

Jo asked about another world war. Beth's legs shifted a tiny bit.

"What does that mean?" Jeff asked.

"That there might be," Jo said, obviously taken off guard.

"Did it say in the book you read that a slight movement means maybe?" Jeff asked, obviously not trusting Jo a hundred percent on this point.

"Yes," Jo said quickly.

"Ask if I'm going to be rich," Daniel said.

Jo asked. Beth's right leg didn't budge.

Jo laughed. "You're going to be a poor can of Spam, Dan."

Daniel frowned. "Ask if I'm going to live to an old age."

"Yes," Jo said a moment later.

Daniel perked up. "Am I going to be happy?"

"No," Jo said. Beth's heels had not moved. Daniel sat back, discouraged.

"I don't know how a magnet can know my future," he said.

"It's not the magnet," Jo said. "It's only the trigger. It's Beth's body that's answering our questions."

"Her body might have some effect on your future," I muttered.

That time my comment did not go unnoticed. The room became filled with tension. Yet no one said anything. What was there to say when we had God to talk to? Jo wasn't going to let my bad mood spoil the festivities. She nodded to Amanda.

"Anything you want to know, Bliss?" she asked.

Amanda got up slowly and crawled over beside Jo. "Can I do it myself?" she asked.

Jo smiled. "It takes a little practice. Why don't you just let me ask for you?"

Amanda gestured to Beth's feet. "But you just ask the questions and lift her heels up. I can do that."

"But why not let me ask?" Jo asked.

"She wants to ask something private," Jeff said.

Amanda nodded. "Please?"

"All right," Jo said reluctantly, moving away. "But be sure to have your question clearly in mind, or it won't work."

The magnet did work for Amanda. Sometimes Beth's right leg would get longer when Amanda thought her question and raised Beth's feet, and sometimes Beth's legs would stay the same. It was eerie watching Amanda go through the routine silently. Amanda asked many questions. Or else she asked one question a number of times. I didn't know why I got that impression—that she was hung up on one point. When she was done, she stared off into empty space for a few seconds.

"Are you satisfied?" Jo asked.

"One question," Amanda said. "Is this thing always right?"

"I've found it to be," Jo said carefully.

Amanda looked at her. "But I just asked it if it was always right, and do you know what it said?"

"What?" Jo asked.

"Maybe," Amanda said.

Jo motioned for Amanda to scoot aside and took hold of Beth's feet. "Does the leg-length reflex in Beth's body always respond correctly to our questions?" Jo asked.

Beth's right leg got more than an inch longer.

"Yes," Jo said.

"That's not the answer I got," Amanda said. Because she was so often solemn, it was difficult to tell if the magnet had upset her. But she certainly didn't appear to be bursting with joy.

"You must have done it wrong," Jo said.

Amanda thought a moment. "Maybe."

Jo let Jeff ask his questions next. He questioned her out loud, not worried about what we thought. He let Jo handle Beth's feet.

"Is everything in our lives predestined?" he asked.

Jo frowned down at Beth's shoes. "Her heel budged slightly."

"Is there a yes-or-no answer to my previous question?" Jeff asked.

"No," Jo said.

Jeff was getting awfully heavy awfully fast. "But are certain things in our lives destined?" he asked.

"Yes," Jo said. "It's very clear this time."

"Is the force that we understand as God *directly* answering these questions?" Jeff asked.

"No," Jo said, and she seemed disappointed.

"Is there a God?" Jeff asked.

"Yes," Jo said.

"Is he as we imagine him?" Jeff asked.

"No," Jo said.

"Is there life after death?" Jeff asked.

Jo paused. "Of course there must be life after death if there's a God, Jeff."

"Ask," he insisted.

Jo asked. "Yes," she said. "I told you."

Then he asked the question that on the surface started me on my long fall to my death. He definitely must have had Peter on his mind. "Is someone who was once alive but is now dead using this leg reflex to try to communicate with us?" he asked.

"Yes," Jo said.

"Did we know this person when he was alive?" Jeff asked, sitting forward.

"Yes," Jo said.

"Is this person anxious to talk to us?" Jeff asked.

"Yes," Jo said, letting go of Beth's feet and looking at him. It was then I noticed that Beth had fallen asleep. She wasn't snoring or anything, but I could tell by the way she was breathing that she was out of it. Jeff had lowered his head and was thinking. Amanda was doing much the same, her expression lost behind a curtain of hair. Daniel shifted uneasily.

"This is creepy," he said.

Actually, that was an astute observation. The atmosphere in the room had definitely changed. It was no longer simply tense. It was distorted, as if the room we were in had somehow been overlapped with another room, a place almost the same but not quite. The room felt *heavy*.

"Beth's gone to sleep," I said. "Let's call it a night."

"No," Jo said suddenly, firmly. She shook Beth's feet. Beth opened her eyes.

"I'm floating," she whispered.

"We have to find out who we're talking to," Jo said. "Right, Jeff?"

Was Jo trying to win Jeff's favor by giving him a last chat with his brother? The idea struck me as so perverse I almost screamed. But screaming's not supposed to be cool. There are times, though, when it can save your reputation. Oh, yes, indeed.

Jeff touched Jo on the shoulder. I could practically see the thrill go through Jo's body. It has been said that nothing is as powerful an aphrodisiac as a brush with the supernatural. Well, maybe I'm the one who said it. But Jo was primed. She wasn't going to deny Jeff anything. Beth had closed her eyes again.

"Did you bring your Ouija board?" he asked.

"No," Jo said.

"I need more than these yes-or-no answers," Jeff said, his hand still on her shoulder. "I want whole words."

Spirits were fine, but this was real male flesh that had a hold of Jo. She nodded quickly. "We can do it without a board."

"How?" he asked.

She swallowed. "One of us can channel this entity."

"Not me," Daniel said and giggled foolishly.

"How?" Jeff asked.

"I can put one of us in a hypnotic trance," Jo said.

"Who?" Jeff asked.

"Shari," Jo said.

"No way," I said.

"Why Shari?" Jeff asked.

"It has to be someone I've known all my life."

Now, Jo was Amanda's first cousin and had known Amanda all her life, but I didn't bring that up. I imagined Amanda would be too shy to invite an entity into her body. Also, I suddenly had a change of heart. I decided I wouldn't mind channeling. My reasoning was simple: it would put me in a perfect position to stop all the nonsense. Once Jo *thought* she had me hypnotized, I was going to say all us entities were exhausted and wanted to go home to sleep.

"All right," I said. "What do I do?"

Before we could proceed, we had to wake Beth up once more—no small feat. We got her eyes open, but before she could climb into a vertical position, she passed out again.

It was almost as if having the magnet resting at the back of her head had drained her. When she finally was sitting up, I noticed that her eyes looked glazed.

Jo made me lie on my back on the floor in the spot Beth had just vacated. Surprisingly, the spot was not warm. Jo told Daniel to bring a blanket from the bedroom, and he covered me to my chin. Then Jo turned off all the lights and lit a red Christmas candle, which she set on the glass coffee table, off to my right. It was pretty dark, but I could still see everyone clearly enough to identify them. Jo positioned herself just behind my head and had the others kneel around me. Amanda was on my right near the candle, Daniel and Jeff were to my left, and Beth was hanging out near my feet. I thought the whole setup typically New Age.

The candle flame caught my eye. I had always been fond of fires—those of the safe and sane variety—and I found the steadiness of the burning orange wick oddly comforting. I wished, though, without knowing why, that the candle had been any color but red.

"We're going to start the same way as we did when we played that 'dead girl' game at Tricia's party," Jo said. "Does everyone remember? We'll pretend that Shari is lying here about to be buried. We'll talk about her as if she's dead. Just as important, we'll try to *feel* as if she's dead. We should get sad. But unlike the other game, we won't start to talk about how light she's getting. We won't try to lift her into the air with our fingertips. When we have her in a deep trance, we'll start to ask her questions, just as we asked the magnet. Only Shari should be able to answer us out loud. All right?" Everyone nodded. "Close your eyes, Shari, and just listen to my suggestions. *You* don't have to worry about anything. *We'll* take care of everything."

I closed my eyes and thought back to the last time we had played the "dead girl" game. I hadn't been one of the subjects, but the two girls we used, Tricia Summers and Leona Woods, did get amazingly light after we went through the whole burial ritual. In fact, it had taken only one finger each from Jo and myself to lift Tricia all the way to the ceiling. She had seemed as light as a feather. Amazing, I had thought at the time, yet I was glad they weren't going to be floating me into the air. I was afraid of heights.

"Take a deep breath, Shari," Jo said, her voice soft but firm. "And let it out slowly. Feel the air leaving your lungs. Feel the life leaving your body. That's good, that's fine. Now, take another breath, and again let it out very slowly. And this time, feel your heart slowing down, becoming faint. Listen to me, Shari, and don't be afraid. You're going to be all right. It is only your body you're leaving behind, not your soul."

It may have been because I was tired, but the suggestions had a profound effect on me. I started to relax immediately. The tension in my shoulders and neck began to dissolve, and I could feel the pulse of my headache diminishing. It was almost like Jo had said—my actual heartbeat was slowing down. The muscles of my back eased deeper into the carpet. I began to feel as Beth said she had, as if I were floating.

Jo continued her suggestions for a while—I'm not sure exactly how long—and then there seemed to be a long period of silence. I was still conscious of my body, of where I was, and yet at the same time, I felt removed from the situation. I didn't even feel like thinking. I just wanted to drift, like a balloon on the wind. But even though I was relaxed, I didn't feel content. The wind was pulling me along, but I wasn't sure if I liked the direction it was taking me. I was afraid, however, to try to move, to stop what was about to happen.

That was it right there. I *was* a tiny bit afraid. Despite what Jo had said about my being safe, I felt as if I were about to lose something precious to me, that I had, in fact, already lost it. The idea of Daniel kissing Beth in the Jacuzzi flashed across my brain, and with it came a stab of pain. Then it was my brother's face that I saw swim by and fade away, drowning in the darkness inside. Daniel's voice came to me from far off.

"She was a good friend of mine. We had a lot of good times together, and I'm going to miss her."

That was all I heard him say. Two lines about his poor dead girlfriend and not one word about how much he had loved her. My sorrow deepened and, with it, the darkness. It was suddenly so dark inside that it seemed as if I were about to be devoured, soul and all.

I was no longer floating. I was sinking, and fast. I don't believe I could have opened my eyes if I had tried. It was Jeff Nichols's turn to remember Shari Cooper.

"I really didn't know her that well, not as well as my brother did. I suppose if I had known her better, I would have liked her more. We never talked that much. It's too bad she's dead, though. It's a real shame."

None of them sounded sad. It was almost as if they were remembering someone they had murdered. Amanda spoke next.

"I didn't know her very well, either. I knew her brother better. But she loved her brother—Jim. She was crazy about him."

She sounded like a record that had already been played. Beth went to speak next. She was a broken record. I remembered that was what I had gotten her for her birthday, a Beatles album from the discount bin. I could remember the party. I knew I was still at it; I hadn't disappeared into the ozone. I knew everything that was happening and that it was only a game. Yet a portion of me, a huge portion, continued to fall, deeper and deeper, down through the earth to where it hid its most terrible secrets. They could have already lowered me into my grave and covered me over with dirt.

Beth couldn't speak. Some kind of entity must have crawled inside her and bit her tongue while she lay on the cold floor. Jo spoke instead. *She* sounded sad.

"She was my best friend. She was more important to me than anything. I used to tell her everything, and now she's gone. I can't believe it."

Jo had to pause to collect herself. Yet she, too, seemed far away. I felt that if I were to reach out to touch her, I would snatch only thin air.

"But she's still alive to me, because I won't forget her," Jo continued, her voice gaining strength. "None of those who have died is really gone. They're always near, speaking to us in whispers we don't ordinarily hear. But occasionally we can hear them, *if* they find someone to speak through."

Jo paused again. She might have cleared her throat. Or I might have cleared my own. I couldn't tell what was happening. I had stopped falling finally, but I doubted if I would be coming up for air soon. Something strange was happening, stranger than all that had previously transpired. Maybe it was a delayed reaction to discovering I was now an *ex*-girlfriend. Perhaps it had something to do with Jo's suggestions.

Then again, it could have been one final omen.

When Jo spoke next, a weight of sorrow heavy enough to

crush the world descended on me from nowhere and every-where at once. I felt it on top of my chest, crunching my ribs, my heart.

"Who are you?" Jo asked.

My voice sounded. But it was not mine. It was not me.

"Most people would probably call me a ghost," the voice said. "I am, after all, dead. But I don't think of myself that way. It wasn't so long ago that I was alive, you see. I was only eighteen. I had my whole life in front of me. . . ."

Someone gasped. Someone else cried out a name—*Peter*. More cries followed. Everyone was talking at once. The candle had been knocked over. There was a danger of fire.

I snapped out of my trance. At last my body was my own again. For a moment. I threw off my blanket and jumped up. At first, I couldn't see a thing. I wasn't even sure if I had my eyes open. The room was pitch black. Then Jeff turned on the lamp near the sofa, and the glare hit me like a hot flare. Jeff was mad at me. They all were.

"Why did you stop?" he demanded.

"You shouldn't have jumped up," Jo said.

"You were faking that," Daniel said.

I wasn't a fake, I wanted to shout at them. But I couldn't get out a word. I was too choked up. When I looked around at their faces, I couldn't find a trace of a thing I had assumed had been with me all the days of my life to one degree or another. There was no love. Daniel just wanted to be back in the tub with Beth. Jo just wanted to be alone with Jeff. I hung my head low, smelling smoke. Amanda was on the floor at my knees, turning the toppled candle upright. The red wax on the carpet was blood red and still hot. But my body was cold; I was shivering. I felt so overcome with loneliness right then that I thought I would be consumed and die of it.

"What is it?" Amanda asked, her clear, cold gray eyes holding mine.

"Nothing," I whispered. "It's nothing."

I ran from the room then, through the kitchen and out onto the balcony and into the night. I remember standing by the rail, feeling the smooth wood beneath my shaking fingers. I remember seeing the flat black ocean and thinking how nice it would be if I could only exercise my magical powers and fly over to it and disappear beneath its surface for ages to come. I remember time passing.

Then things went bad.

I felt a sensation. It was not one of being pushed; it was, rather, a feeling of rising up. Then of spinning, of being disoriented. I saw the edge of the condominium roof, the stars. There were only a few of the latter, and they weren't very bright. Not compared to the lamppost standing beside the cement walkway, which suddenly began to rush toward me at incredible speed. It was only in the last instant that I realized I had gone over the edge of the balcony. That I was falling head-first toward the ground.

I didn't feel the blow of the impact. But I do remember rolling over and looking up. Now there were millions of stars in the sky. Orange ones and green ones and blue ones. There were also red ones. Big fat red ones, whose number rapidly grew as I watched, blotting out all the others in the heavens, until soon they were all that remained, part of a colossal wave of smothering hot wax. I blacked out. I died.

CHAPTER V

WHEN I CAME TO, I was home in bed, lying on top of the sheets in the dark. At first I didn't question what I was doing there. Many times throughout my life I would wake up in bed and not know what the hell was going on. I was a deep sleeper; in fact, it was normal for me to take several minutes after sleeping to figure out what planet I was on.

On the other hand, I did feel *strange*. I was mildly surprised when I sat up that I wasn't dizzy. For some reason I expected to be dizzy. Yet when I paused to ask myself why, I had no answer. I remembered being at the party, but I didn't remember the end of the party. Certainly, I had no recollection of falling to my death.

I climbed to my feet and walked to the open door and peeked out. As I have already mentioned, my bedroom was off a hall that overlooked a large portion of the downstairs.

Because most of the downstairs lights were off, it was natural that I wasn't able to see well. Except I couldn't see for what appeared to be the wrong reasons. It was less dark than it should have been; the walls and furniture were not glowing or anything, but they weren't exactly not glowing, either. They were brighter than they should have been with nothing shining on them.

Then there was the *stuff* in the air. It was the stuff, I decided, that was blurring my vision. It was everywhere, translucent, vaguely gaseous, and flowing, very slightly, around the entire room, up the curtains and over the bookcase. In fact, the vapors actually seemed to be flowing *through* the walls. I blinked my eyes, but it did not go away. And yet I had to wonder if I was really seeing it all. It was very fine, almost invisible.

I walked down the hall to Jimmy's room and stuck my head through his partially opened door. He was asleep, lying on his back, his sheets thrown off, his right arm resting behind his head. If I hadn't known that he had to get up early, I would have tried to wake him up. The feeling of dislocation refused to leave me, and I wanted to talk to him about it. But I left him alone. His computer was still on, of course.

I went downstairs. My parents were in the kitchen; I heard them talking before I actually saw them, and even before I went inside and joined them at the table, I thought they sounded different. My mother had one of those high-society voices that could be the embodiment of charm when she was in a good mood and nothing short of bitchy when she wasn't. My dad had a deep, authoritative voice that never changed no matter what his state of mind. It certainly never sounded muffled, as it did now. Their words seemed to be coming to me through a layer of invisible insulation. Yet I mustn't overemphasize the effect. I could understand what they were saying. They were talking about money.

"Hi, Mom. Hi, Dad," I said as I stepped into the kitchen and grabbed ahold of one of the chairs to pull out so I could sit down. But it was weird—it felt stuck to the floor. I couldn't get it to budge. I couldn't be bothered hassling with it, so I slumped down in a chair near the stove instead, a few feet away from the table, off to my parents' right. They didn't even look over at me, which I thought was rude of them.

"Did you hear what Mrs. Meyer had to say about that loan you and Bill got from Mr. Hoyomoto's firm?" my mother asked my father, taking a bit of the chocolate cake Amanda and Mrs. Parish and I had talked about at length.

"No," my father replied, lighting up a cigar and leaning back in his chair. "But I imagine she said something about us helping the Japanese buy the world out from under us."

He looked tired, as did my mother, but they both looked good. They were dressed to the hilt, and they were a handsome couple. My father was of medium height, solid, with shoulders that could ram down a door. He radiated strength and masculinity. He didn't smile often, but he wasn't a cold man. He was just too busy to smile. There was too much building to be done. He had closely clipped rust-colored hair, a tan, and small, sharp blue eyes.

My mother bore him scant resemblance, except that she also was attractive. She was tall and sleek, quick and loose. Her wide, thick-lipped mouth and her immaculately conceived black hair were her prizes. At present she had on a long black dress slit up the side to reveal one of her smooth white legs. It was odd she was eating cake that late. She usually took such good care of herself. In fact, taking care of herself took up so much of her time that she couldn't take quite as good care of us. But she loved my father, and she also loved her children. It was just a shame that she loved us all in a way she had learned from her therapist.

"She didn't say it in those words," my mother replied, her voice cracking slightly as if it were being electrically interfered with. "But you'd think you were selling secrets to the Russians from the tone she took. Really, she's nothing but a pain in the ass."

"Her husband's not a bad fellow, though," my father said, blowing a cloud of smoke toward the ceiling. It was a strange cloud. It had that *stuff in* it, that mysterious haze that could have been a super-refined blend of smoke and gas and water all rolled into one.

"Oh, Ted," my mother said, putting down her cake fork and waving her hand. "He's adorable, absolutely wonderful. I can't imagine how he's stayed with that shrew so long."

"I almost threw out that cake," I said.

"He's a good man," my father said.

"He's too good for her," my mother said. "But you know, I heard from Wendy that Colleen Meyer's got six wells down in Texas."

"Ted told me only three of them are pumping," my father said.

"Three pumping wells can make up for a lot of character flaws," my mother said.

"Hello," I said. "It's me. I'm here, waiting patiently to have my presence acknowledged."

They continued to ignore me. I couldn't understand it.

Then the phone rang. My mother stood up and walked over and picked it up, carrying her cake with her. But just before she answered it, she said something really weird.

"That's probably Shari," she said.

"Huh?" I said.

My mother lifted the handset to her ear. She was smiling. She was tired, but her life was in order. She had a big house, a rich, hard-working husband, great clothes, cool jewelry, one wonderful son, and one OK daughter.

"Hello," she said. "Yes, this is she. Who is this, please?"

My mother listened for several seconds, and as she did so, her hand holding the cake plate began to shake. But her smile didn't vanish immediately. It underwent a metamorphosis instead, slowly tightening at the edges, bit by bit, until soon it could not be confused for a smile at all. She dropped the plate holding the cake. It shattered on the tiles. Her mouth twisted into a horrible grimace. My father and I both jumped up.

"What is it?" my father asked.

"It's Shari," she whispered, slowly putting down the phone and sagging back against the counter. My father grabbed her at the waist, steadying her.

"What's happened?" he demanded, anxious now.

"Yeah, what's going on?" I asked, coming over to them.

"Shari," my mother whispered, closing her eyes and shaking her head.

"What?" I asked. "What's wrong?"

Still holding on to my mother, my father snapped up the phone. "This is Mr. Cooper," he said. "Who is this?"

His face paled as he listened. "Will she be all right?" he asked after a minute. "What do you mean?" He paused, listened some more, biting his lower lip all the while, something I had never seen him do before in my life. "You don't know?" he asked finally. "Why don't you know? I see, I see. Yes, I know where that is. Yes, we'll be there shortly."

My father didn't thank whoever had called. He just hung up the phone and hugged my mother, who was close to collapsing in his arms.

"Hey," I said, beginning to get emotional. "Would someone please tell me what the hell is going on?"

They ignored me. Yet that was not it. They didn't hear me. Something terrible must have happened, I thought, that they could get into such a state that they blocked me out altogether. I reached out for my father's arm.

"Dad, please," I said. "I need to know, too."

I might as well have not been in the room. My father helped my mother over to the table, sat her in the chair, and took her hands in his. "We don't know yet, Christine," he said.

My mother kept shaking her head, her eyes closed. "It's no good," she whispered. "It was too far. Oh, God. Shari."

"I have to go get Jim," he said, letting go of her.

"Yeah, go get Jimmy," I said, nodding vigorously. But my mother suddenly opened her eyes and grabbed my father's arm.

"No, we can't tell him," she said. "Leave him alone."

My father shook his head. "I have to get him." He leaned over and kissed her on the top of the head as she squeezed her eyes shut again. "The three of us should be together."

"Aren't there four of us?" I asked. Obviously, something dreadful had happened, but there was a note of bitterness in my question. Jimmy had always been their favorite. I had never been jealous of him, but I had never felt that parents should have favorites, especially my own.

My father left. My mother cradled her head in her arms on the table. She wasn't crying, but she was having a hard time breathing. I sat beside her and put my hand on top of her head, my resentment of a moment ago disappearing.

"It'll be all right, Mom," I said.

She sat up suddenly and stared right at me, her mouth hanging open slightly, and I was mildly relieved that I had at last made some impression on her. But when she kept staring at me and didn't speak, my relief quickly changed to something quite different. A splinter of fear began to form deep inside me—a faint fear, true, but a cold one.

Something was not right, I told myself. Not right by a million miles. I prayed Jimmy would come quick and make it all right.

My brother appeared a minute later. He was suffering, however, from the same problem as my parents. He was so shook up that he had totally blotted me out of his awareness. He was not as pale as my father, nor was he trembling as my mother was. His symptoms were more subtle, worse in a way. His eyes—those warm, friendly blue eyes—were vacant. Even as he crossed the kitchen and hugged my mother, they remained blank.

"Jimmy!" I cried. But he didn't hear me. I thought he couldn't even see me.

They were all going to a hospital of some kind. I had gotten that much from my father's remarks. They were hardly dressed for it. My father had on a wrinkled black tux, my mother a tired evening gown. Jimmy had pulled on a pair of blue jeans and a white sweatshirt, but he had forgotten his shoes and socks. As I followed him out to the car, I said something about it being chilly. I could have been talking to myself.

So far the night had abounded with extraordinary events. Yet nothing had prepared me for what happened when I reached the front door. In keeping with recent developments, Jimmy ignored the fact that I was behind him and opened and closed the door without giving me a chance to get outside. Naturally, I tried to open the door myself.

But I couldn't.

The doorknob wouldn't turn. I twisted it as hard as I could, clockwise and counterclockwise, but still it wouldn't budge. It seemed to be not only stuck but somehow *different*. As I shifted my hold to try again, the difference hit me like a bucket of ice water.

The doorknob and my hand were not connecting. I was touching it, I knew, but it was as if an extremely fine barrier was preventing me from having any effect on it. Oh, was I confused. To touch something and not to have it respond to your touch. I stepped back and waited for my father to open the door for me. There seemed nothing else to do. He came by a few seconds later, leading my mother by the shoulder, and I managed to slip outside in front of them.

Jimmy was already in his car. He sat hunched over the steering wheel, with the engine running, staring straight ahead. He didn't have a red Ferrari like me. He had a white Ford station wagon, and he was paying for it with the money he earned working for the telephone company. My father helped my mother into the front seat of the Ford, fastening her seat belt for her. She was holding a handkerchief to her face now, and I believe she was weeping quietly. I hopped in the backseat when my father opened the rear door on the passenger side. I wasn't about to wrestle with another door. It was amazing, I thought as I settled in the seat behind Jimmy, that I had not bumped my father as I squeezed past him.

But I wasn't in the mood to be amazed. I was suffering from the worst kind of fear—fear of unknown origin. No one in the car was speaking, and I chose to remain silent. I sat by the window and stared up at the sky, at the stars. Never before had I found them so numerous, so bright and varied in color. But it was the red ones that drew my attention. There was something about them that filled me with dread. I kept expecting them to suddenly swell and drown out the others. They were dark red, like dripping candles seen through blood-smeared glass.

I recognized the hospital—Newport Memorial. It was located on a low hill only a couple of blocks from the beach, a fifteen-story cube. I had taken Jo to the emergency ward there the summer before when she had slipped on the rocks on the Newport jetty and cut her knee open. The nurses and doctor had been nice. As Jimmy parked near the emergency entrance, I wondered who we could possibly be going to see. My grandfather—my mother's father—had a bad heart. My father's brother had also been having serious stomach ulcers.

Climbing out of the car with the others, I prayed it wasn't family.

We went inside, and I was surprised when my nose didn't react to the hospital's medicinal smell; ordinarily, the odor of alcohol and drugs made me cringe. But I smelled nothing, although I continued to see things I knew I shouldn't be seeing. The stuff in the air had not gone away, and now, walking with my family toward the front desk, I noticed threads of shadow weaving through the film, growing and fading in front of me, almost as though the shadows were alive and seeking me. I didn't want them to touch me; I was afraid they'd hurt me.

My mother and father went to talk to the nurse on duty while Jimmy stopped at a drinking fountain in the hallway leading to the examination rooms. I went with him. He didn't appear to be thirsty. He just ran the water up high for a few seconds, without leaning over for a sip, and then thrust his hands in his pockets and stared at the floor.

"Jimmy," I said. "Why won't you talk to me? Why won't you even look at me?"

He ignored me, and in desperation I reached out to grab his arm, to scream his name so loudly that they would hear it on the top floors of the building. But I choked on the word.

For an instant, my fingers appeared to go through the material of his sweatshirt. To go right *into* his arm. I recoiled in horror.

Jimmy rejoined my parents. The woman at the desk picked

up a phone and requested a doctor somebody. The young white-coated gentleman appeared within seconds; it seemed he had been waiting for us. I would have tried to say hello to him had I not still been in shock over my hands' newfound powers of penetration. He spoke quietly to my dad for a few seconds, and then we were off.

I expected the doctor to lead us to one of the examination rooms, or perhaps to the critical care ward. But he immediately whisked us into an elevator and pushed the bottom button. The doors rifled shut. My father turned to the guy in confusion.

"Why are we going down?" he asked.

"I told you, I'm just an intern," the young man said. "Dr. Leeds is in charge of the case." He added, almost ashamed, "I'd rather you saved your questions for him."

"But what's in the basement?" my father asked. And then, more reluctantly: "Is she all right?"

The intern spoke to the elevator wall. "Ask Dr. Leeds."

Downstairs, we walked along a short, narrow hall that dead-ended in twin green metal doors. They opened from the inside just before we reached them. A white-haired man appeared and clasped my father's hand. He looked like a kindly old country doctor. I could imagine the twinkle in his eyes as he handed a little girl patient a lollipop and told her that if she took her medicine like a big girl, she would be outside and playing with her friends in no time. But now the doctor was not smiling.

The intern nodded and left.

The white and black letters on the doors said: MORGUE.

"Mr. and Mrs. Cooper," the elderly gentleman said. "I'm Dr. Leeds. I'm afraid I have bad news for you."

"How is she?" my father asked. "Is she going to be all right?"

"No, she's not." Dr. Leeds let go of my father's hand and looked him straight in the eye. "She's dead."

"Who's dead?" I asked.

It must have been a stupid question. The rest of my family knew the individual's name. My father paled again, much worse than he had in the kitchen when he had picked up the phone. My mother literally doubled over in grief. Jimmy had to grab her to keep her from passing out. I couldn't bear it. I had to turn away. When I looked back a few seconds later, my mother had somehow managed to straighten herself up, although she was crying openly now.

"I want to see her," she said.

Dr. Leeds looked concerned. "Later would be better."

"No," my mother said, wiping her damp cheek. "Now."

"Honey, please," my father said, reaching out to take her from Jimmy. My mother would have none of it.

"I'm seeing her!" she cried, brushing off both Jimmy and my father. "I *have* to see her." Then she suddenly stopped, clenching her eyes shut, her whole being shaking. "My baby."

Her baby? I said to myself. My mother didn't have a baby. She didn't even like babies.

"Would it be possible to see her?" my father asked.

"She fell four stories, headfirst, onto a cement sidewalk," Dr. Leeds said reluctantly.

"You just can't take her," my mother pleaded pitifully, her head bowed. "Jim, don't let him take your sister."

Your sister? I thought miserably.

"But *I'm* his sister," I whispered.

My father and Dr. Leeds exchanged uneasy glances. Jimmy stepped forward. His eyes were still vacant, but there was a trace of life around his mouth, a flicker of strength.

"It'll be hard for us to see what happened,' he said quietly. "We know that. But I think it could be harder for us to have to think what happened, without seeing her. If you know what I mean?"

Dr. Leeds considered a moment. "All right," he said finally, turning toward the green metal doors. "Give me a few minutes."

While waiting with my family in the bleak hallway, I started to get a funny feeling. I was already scared and confused, but this new feeling was worse. My cold splinter of fear had grown long and sharp in the last half-hour. Now it was like an icy blade that was threatening to cut my sanity in half and leave me floundering in darkness for eternity. Yes, eternity— that was the element that hit me then. Something terrible had happened, I realized, and whatever it was, it was forever.

The deduction wasn't that clever.

"Morgue," I whispered aloud to myself, to no one.

Dr. Leeds reappeared approximately five minutes later and led my family through the double green doors. Apparently everyone had gone home for the night; there were only the five of us in the morgue. And maybe, I thought with growing understanding, there were fewer.

Off to the right was an open square room stacked with rows of lockers. Only they weren't lockers. I'd seen enough police shows. They were the cubicles in which they stashed the stiffs.

Off to the left was a white-tiled wall. In the middle were three tables. The center one was occupied. There was a person there, a short dead person, lying under a thin white sheet. Dr. Leeds stepped to the head of the table. The rest of us followed. We had asked for it, and now we had to take it.

Dr. Leeds slowly pulled down the sheet. He appeared to be starting at the head. The first thing we saw, however, was not a head; it was a green towel, and it was stained dark and wet. The doctor had obviously just wrapped the towel around the girl's hair. I could tell it was a girl. The conversation on the other side of the green doors had made that clear enough, and a lock of her dark blond hair had peeped out from beneath the towel. There was no blood on the hair, on those particular strands, but it didn't require a great deal of imagination to see that the rest of her hair must be a disaster.

It was, of course, silly of me to wonder what kind of shampoo it would take to clean that hair when it was clear that the entire top of the girl's skull had been crushed to a pulp.

Even before Dr. Leeds folded down the sheet farther and revealed the girl's face—washed clean of blood—I knew what we would see. I knew that hair. I had fought with it all my life, and now it would rest in peace forever, along with that face.

A moment later Dr. Leeds folded down the sheet, tucking it under her chin as if it were a blanket that could keep her warm. He stepped back. Her eyes were closed, thankfully, and although a ghastly black and blue patch had colored her forehead and sent bruised streaks down the sides of her cheeks almost to her mouth, death had not stolen her beauty. You see, that's how I felt then, in the presence of a person who could have lit many lives with her beauty had she just been given the chance.

My father didn't move. My mother couldn't move. But Jimmy reached out and touched the girl's lips with the tip of his finger. It was fortunate his fingers strayed no higher. I remembered the long fall toward the sidewalk then, the fat red stars, the wave of hot wax covering the sky, my blood flowing over my open eyes. Maybe it had been Dr. Leeds who had closed them. It was good. Better she remain a sleeping beauty, I thought. I knew if Jimmy were to open them, they would no longer be the sparkling green she had told him they were, nor even the warm brown he had thought they must be. They wouldn't be beautiful. They would only be flat and colorless.

It was me lying there. Just me.

CHAPTER VI

I HAVE READ articles describing how hard it is to accept the death of a loved one. How people often go through phases where they actually deny the person is really gone. I can imagine how difficult it must be. Yet I must say it is harder to accept one's own death.

As long as I stood in the morgue with my body, I could intellectually understand that the fall off Beth's balcony had killed me. But when my family left the room a few minutes later and I followed them out the green doors and back down the hall, I began to have doubts. I began to get upset, angry. I couldn't be dead, I told myself. I was too young. I had too much to do. I hadn't done anything wrong. Besides, how could I be talking with myself if there was no one left to talk to? It simply made no sense that I was dead. It was illogical.

I decided I must be dreaming.

This decision didn't last long. The death state can vary in the extreme, yet it is usually much closer to the waking state than dreaming. I didn't try pinching myself or anything silly like that. I simply paused for a moment and examined my thinking process and realized I could not be unconscious.

On the other hand, that didn't mean I couldn't help believing that someone somewhere had made a terrible mistake. I tried telling my family just that after the doctor bid them a sympathetic farewell and they climbed into the elevator.

"Hey," I said as the doors closed and we started up. "I know you can't hear me too well for some reason or other, but you've got to listen to me. That girl in there was not me. She couldn't be me. I'm me, and I'm right here. Mom, look at me. I'm all right. Dad, that doctor's a nice guy and all that, but I swear, he's messed me up with someone else. Jimmy, you know I can't be dead. I wouldn't die on you." I reached out and hugged my brother. My hands did not go through his flesh this time, but they did not touch him, either. I could have been trying to hug a reflection in the mirror. "Jimmy?" I cried, pleading.

It was no use. They exited the elevator without a glance over their shoulders to make sure I had gotten off safely. But I continued to follow them. What else could I do? There was a handsome blond policeman waiting by the emergency front desk. He wanted to have a word with them. I chose not to listen. I went and sat on one of the chairs in the waiting room. A young couple were there with their three-year-old son, who had split his upper lip open. It didn't look serious. The child was coloring in a coloring book, and the mother and father were talking about how much fun they were going to have in Hawaii on their vacation.

A few minutes later the policeman and my family started for the exit together. I had to pull myself out of my chair to go after them. I didn't have a headache or a stomachache or any other specific physical complaint. I just didn't feel well.

Outside, I realized dissension had entered the group. Apparently Jimmy wanted to go somewhere that the others— particularly the policeman—didn't want him to go. It took a moment for me to understand that he intended to go to Beth's place.

I got all excited at the idea. If we went to Beth's condo together, I thought, we would be able to figure out exactly what had happened. Then we could prove that I was really all right, and people would start seeing me again!

Jimmy finally got his way. The policeman agreed to take my parents home. My brother embraced my mother and father as he said goodbye. It was hard to look at my mother, even though I could see her much clearer than I had any right to in the dark parking lot. She just kept shaking, and I kept thinking that if she didn't stop soon, her heart would begin to skip beats, and she'd have a heart attack. I felt guilty as I ran away from my parents, chasing Jimmy as he jogged toward his car. But I had no difficulty climbing over the driver's seat into the passenger's seat when Jimmy opened his door. I was already getting good at it.

We were almost to Beth's house, coasting along the coast highway at a high speed, the ocean off to our left, when the worst possible thing happened. It was worse than seeing a pretty young girl lying on a cold morgue slab and realizing it was me. Jimmy suddenly pulled over to the side of the road and laid his head on the steering wheel and began to cry.

I had seen my brother upset before, but I had never seen him cry. I would not have thought it possible. Oh, he wasn't so tough that I couldn't imagine him breaking down. It was just that I couldn't imagine him doing it where I could see him. That was what made it all so horrible; I was here, and he was there, and there was hardly anything separating us—nothing at all, really.

Only the entire span of an uncaring universe.

"No, Shari," he whispered as he closed his eyes and sobbed in his clenched fingers. I tried to unclench them, to soothe him, but I could not. I couldn't because his sister was dead, and I was his sister, and it was only right that we should both grieve. It was then, finally and forever, that I accepted the fact that my life was over.

"Yes, Jimmy," I said and wept with him.

When we reached Beth's place, I made the mistake of letting Jimmy climb out of the car in front of me, and then, of course,

I couldn't get the car door open. Fortunately, he had left the window down, and I was able to squeeze through the space. It took me a couple of minutes, however, and by then Jimmy had already entered the complex, leaving me trapped at the front gate, unable to turn the knob or ring the bell. I realized I was a ghost. I considered trying to walk through the gate. But I had a horrible fear that I'd get stuck. I just couldn't bring myself to make the attempt.

There were a couple of police cars sitting in the visitors' parking lot. As I paced the gate area waiting for someone to appear and let me in, a blue truck pulled up and parked beside them. But the driver didn't get out, and I started to become frustrated. I headed over to his truck to try to hurry him along.

He was a man on his way down in life. In his mid-forties, he had on a frumpy green sports coat and a wrinkled white shirt with a loosely knotted purple tie caught beneath his over-size belt. He needed a good meal. His thin brown hair was going gray, and his red wizened face had seen either too much sun or too much life. He looked burned out. He was lifting a pint of whiskey to his lips when I tapped on his window.

"Hey, mister," I said. "They're talking about me in there, and I want to hear what they're saying. Let's get a move on."

In response, he took a deep swallow and coughed. I probably would have left him right then if I hadn't noticed that he had a CB radio in his truck. It cracked to life, and he set down his bottle and flipped it off. He withdrew a handful of breath mints from his coat pocket and began to chew them down, one after another. When he was done, he picked up his pint and took another huge hit. It amazed me that such a wasted individual could afford such a nice truck.

After finally capping his bottle and stowing it under the seat, he climbed out and grabbed another handful of mints from his jacket. I followed him to the front gate. I couldn't smell his breath—I couldn't smell anything—but I doubted that he was drunk; his step was firm and direct. He pressed the button to Beth's condo—number 413.

"This is Garrett," he said, clearing his throat.

"Do you know Beth's family?" I asked, for all the good it did. The gate buzzed open, and I followed Garrett inside. I trailed him all the way up to the fourth floor. He was headed the same place I was. He walked into Beth's place without knocking.

All those who had been at the party—Daniel, Beth, Jeff, Jo, and Amanda—were sitting in the living room. They looked shocked, but no one was crying. Daniel was on the loveseat with Beth. Jo and Jeff were seated in individual chairs. Amanda was alone on the couch. Standing with Jimmy in the dining room were a couple of police officers. One strode over to greet Garrett, holding out his hand.

"Hello, Lieutenant, I'm Officer Fort," he said. "This is my partner, Officer Dreiden. And this is the deceased's older brother, James Cooper. Have you been assigned to this case?"

"Yeah," Garrett said, shaking his hand briefly.

This was the lieutenant who had been assigned to my case? I asked myself, horrified. I didn't even know what my case was, but I certainly didn't want a boozer put in charge of it.

"Just you?" Officer Fort asked.

"Yeah." Garrett turned to Jimmy. "Why don't you have a seat, son." Jimmy did as he suggested, sitting on the couch beside solemn Amanda, who took his hand and held it in her lap. Garrett spoke to Officer Fort. "What are we looking at here?"

Fort was cut in the same mold as the cop at the hospital: young, blond, handsome. He had, however, a high, annoying voice. He began to annoy me the moment he opened his mouth.

"It looks pretty clear-cut," he said. "The kids were trying to have a seance when the deceased, Shari Cooper, got upset over a couple of remarks the kids made and ran to the balcony and jumped off."

"*What?*" I shouted, standing in the center of the floor. "I jumped off the balcony? I didn't jump off the balcony. I *fell* off it. I—"

I stopped. How could I have fallen? The blasted rails reached practically to my neck. I looked toward the balcony. The rails were still in place, standing straight and firm. It was funny, but it wasn't until then that I began to question how I happened to be dead.

"Shari would never have done that," Jimmy broke in, bitter.

"Were you here when this happened?" Garrett asked.

"No," Jimmy said. "I was home in bed, sleeping."

"Were the rest of these young people here?" Garrett asked Officer Fort.

"These were the only ones present."

Garrett addressed the group. "Does everyone agree that Shari jumped?" he asked.

"She must have," Beth said.

"Yeah," Daniel agreed.

"No!" I screamed.

Garrett looked at Jeff. "Well?"

Jeff shrugged, trying to light a cigarette. He appeared as cool as usual, except he couldn't get his match to light. "I don't know what happened."

"You didn't see her jump?" Garrett asked.

"No."

"I didn't, either," Jo said. She didn't appear unusually upset, which upset me a great deal. But Jo, I had to remind myself, seldom showed anything when she was hurt or hurting.

"Did anyone see her jump?" Garrett asked. No one responded, although Amanda moved closer to Jimmy. Sighing under his breath, Garrett turned to Officer Fort. "I want to have a talk with these kids," he said.

"Now?"

"Yeah. Alone."

Officer Fort didn't like the idea. "The couple who lives here has been notified about what happened. They should be here any second."

"So?" Garrett said. "You and your partner go downstairs and welcome them. Tell them the place is off-limits for tonight."

"The whole night?"

"Yeah."

Fort glanced at his partner. "Dreiden and I have already questioned the kids at length. Don't you want to hear our report?"

"I can't imagine there could be anything you could add to the report you've already made," Garrett said dryly.

"Are you sure you don't want our help?"

I could not be certain, but the way Fort held Garrett's eye as he spoke made me feel that Fort believed Garrett incapable of handling the situation, that Fort might in fact be aware of Garrett's drinking problem. But since Fort had already classified me as a suicide, I wasn't inclined to favor him over Garrett.

"Yeah," Garrett said, obviously growing tired of the sameness of the questions. He made a gesture of dismissal toward the door. The two uniformed policemen left reluctantly.

"Can I stay?" Jimmy asked.

"That'll be fine," Garrett said. Then he spoke to the group. "I know all of you have had a bad night. Try to relax for a few minutes while I take a quick look around."

Garrett disappeared into the hall. Nobody spoke for a long while. Finally, Daniel asked nervously, "What's he looking for?"

"Evidence that Shari didn't jump," Jo said.

"She didn't jump," Jimmy said softly.

That killed the conversation right there. Amanda stroked Jimmy's hand. I had to look away. I had tried to do the same thing in the car on the ride over.

When Garrett reappeared, he took a chair from the dining table and placed it at the end of the living room, sitting down and pulling a pen and notepad from his coat. I was just glad he didn't pull out a bottle. Yet I was having to revise my initial impression of him. His blue eyes were bloodshot, true, but they were also sharp. As he scanned the group, I didn't believe he missed much. Except me, of course, and I could have told him a thing or two.

"We have a simple floor plan here," he began. "We have a living room, with attached dining area, a kitchen, and a balcony. We have two master bedrooms. The one at the end of the hall has its own separate balcony, which faces south, down the coast. The other bedroom leads directly onto the west-facing balcony and faces the ocean. Tell me, when Shari ran from here, did she go through the kitchen or the first bedroom?"

"The kitchen," Jo said.

Garrett apparently wanted to get that point out of the way before anything else. He leaned back in his chair, crossing his legs and resting the tip of his unpolished black right shoe a fraction of an inch from the edge of Beth's beautiful glass coffee table and a foot above the red wax stain on the floor. They had put the candle away.

"Tell me what happened," he said to Jo.

"Me?" Jo asked.

"Yes, you," Garrett said. "Please."

Jo didn't hesitate. "We were trying to talk to the spirits. We were using Shari as a subject. She was lying on the floor here near the table. We were trying to put her in a trance by talking about her as if she had crossed over."

"Come again?" Garrett said.

"We were pretending she was dead," Jo said. "It's a common method of putting people in a state where they can channel. We had her pretty deep, I thought, when she suddenly jumped up and ran out onto the balcony."

"You say *we*," Garrett said, obviously wondering if this was a normal teenage activity. "Wasn't one of you leading this thing?"

"Yes, I was," Jo said.

"While you were putting her into her *trance*," Garrett said, "what kind of suggestions did you make?"

"Like I said," Jo replied, "we were acting like she was dead, saying how much we were going to miss her and stuff like that."

"You didn't by any chance make any suggestion as to *how* she had died?" Garrett asked.

"No," Jo said, surprised at the question.

"Did she say anything while she was in her trance?"

"Not really," Jo said.

"She did say something," Daniel broke in.

"What?" Garrett asked.

Daniel glanced at Beth. "I don't remember," he said.

"She said she was a ghost," Jeff said.

"That's right," Jo said, nodding.

"Anything else?" Garrett asked.

"No." Jo glanced around the room. "I don't think so."

"Why did she suddenly leap up?" Garrett asked.

"I'm not sure," Jo said. "I think she got scared."

"Did she say anything when she jumped up?" Garrett asked. "Was anything said to her?"

"Yes," Jo said. "Jeff asked her—that's Jeff there—asked her why she had stopped. Then I told her she shouldn't have jumped up. Like I said, she looked scared. Amanda asked her what was the matter. Shari said it was nothing. Then she ran out to the balcony."

"And jumped?" Garrett asked. "She jumped right away?"

"Oh, no," Jo said.

"How long was she on the balcony before she jumped?"

"A few minutes," Jo said.

Garrett frowned. "Did anyone leave the living room during this time?"

Now Jo hesitated. "We all did."

Garrett sat up and clicked down the point of his ballpoint pen. "Who was the first one to leave the living room after Shari?"

"I was," Amanda said quietly, speaking for the first time. Garrett glanced over at her and stopped. I don't know why.

Maybe it was her beauty. Maybe it was her sorrowful eyes. Then again, Garrett could not have known that Amanda was often grave.

"What's your name?" he asked.

"Amanda Parish."

"How long after Shari left did you leave?"

"A couple of minutes."

Garrett jotted down a note in his pad. "Where did you go?"

"I went into Beth's bedroom."

"The bedroom at this end of the hall? The one that leads to the west balcony?"

"Yes," Amanda said. "I had to go to the bathroom."

"Did you see Shari on the balcony before you went into the bathroom?"

"No."

"Do you recall if the sliding glass door that leads onto the balcony was open or closed?"

"No."

"How long were you in the bathroom?"

"A few minutes."

"What did you do when you left the bathroom?"

"I returned to the living room."

"Who was there?"

"No one. At first. Then Jeff came in from the hall."

Garrett paused and then scanned the room again. I waved to him, but he didn't wave back. "Who left the living room after Amanda?" he asked.

"I did," Jeff said, a lit cigarette in his hand.

"What's your last name, Jeff?"

"Nichols."

"How long after Amanda left the living room did you leave?"

"A minute or so."

Garrett made another note in his pad. "Tell me about it."

"I had to go to the bathroom," Jeff said. "I went into Beth's bedroom, but there was already someone in there. So I went into the bedroom at the end of the hall and used that bathroom instead."

"Did you see Shari on the balcony when you went into Beth's bedroom?"

"Yeah."

"You're sure it was her and not Amanda?"

"Yeah, it was Shari."

"What was she doing?"

"Standing by the rail, looking out at the ocean."

"Anything else?"

"No."

"Was the sliding glass door open or closed?"

"It was closed."

"Was it locked?"

"I don't know. I didn't try opening it."

"Could there have been anyone else on the balcony besides Shari?"

"I doubt it."

"How close did you get to the door?"

Jeff took a puff of his cigarette. "Maybe ten feet."

"Did you have a clear view of the entire balcony?"

Jeff hesitated. "No."

"What portion of the balcony couldn't you see?"

Jeff considered a moment. "The area behind the wall between the kitchen and the bedroom."

"How did you know there was someone in the bathroom?"

Jeff shrugged. "The door was closed; the light was on."

"It was you who was in there, right?" Garrett asked Amanda.

"Yes," she said, her hand on Jimmy's knee.

Garrett turned his attention back to Jeff. "How long were you in the bathroom in the master bedroom?"

"A couple of minutes. Then I came back into the living room."

"Who was in the living room at that point?"

"Amanda."

"What was she doing?"

"Sitting on the couch, looking at a magazine."

"Who left the living room after Jeff?" Garrett asked the group.

"Beth did," Daniel said. He glanced over at his big-breasted object of desire. He had to shake her. "Beth?"

"Yes, we were good friends," Beth said suddenly, blinking. Garrett uncrossed his legs and leaned toward her.

"You were a good friend of Shari's?" he asked.

"Yes," she said. Studying her closer, I realized she must have been crying before Garrett and I had arrived. Good girl, I thought. But she was still a slut.

"What is your full name, Beth?"

"Elizabeth Palmone."

"How long after Jeff left the living room did you leave?"

"Not long."

"How long?" Garrett asked.

"Less than a minute."

"Where did you go?"

"Into my bedroom."

"Did you see Jeff or Amanda in there?"

"No."

"Did you see Jeff leaving your room?"

"No."

"Did you notice Amanda in the bathroom?"

"No. I mean, I noticed there was someone in the bathroom. But I didn't know who it was."

"What did you do in the bedroom?"

"Nothing."

"Did you see Shari on the balcony?"

"No."

"You're sure?"

"Yes." Her eyes strayed to Daniel. "I went out on the balcony. I didn't see her. She wasn't there. Right, Jo?"

"Right," Jo said.

"Wait a second, Beth," Garrett said. "Jo was on the balcony when you stepped outside?"

"Yes," Beth said. "I think."

"Was she or wasn't she?"

"It was dark." Beth was confused. "I think she was."

"How long were you in your bedroom before you went outside?"

"A little while."

Garrett leaned forward even more. His next question was to be the important one, I knew. "Was the door to the balcony open or closed when you went outside?" he asked.

"It was closed."

"Was it locked?"

"Yes," Beth said. "It locks when you close it."

"And when it's locked, you can't get back in from the outside, right?"

"No. Unless you come in through the kitchen."

"Does that door also lock when you close it?"

"Yes."

Garrett nodded to himself and made a note in his pad. "Who left the living room after Beth?"

"I did," Jo said.

"What's your full name, Jo?"

"Joanne Foulton." She added, "I was Shari's best friend."

"How long after Beth left the living room did you leave?"

"A few seconds. I went through the kitchen to the balcony. I wanted to see about Shari, make sure she was all right."

"Why did you take so long to go after her?"

"I wanted to give her a few minutes to settle down."

"Did you by any chance tell the others to leave her alone for a few minutes?"

Jo paused. "Yes."

"What did you all do after Shari ran off and before you started to leave the living room?"

"Nothing really," Jo answered. "Amanda picked up the candle and then went to the bathroom. Jeff went after her. Dan helped me turn on the lights and straighten the furniture. I flipped on the stereo."

"You turned on the music? How loud?"

"Medium volume."

"When you started for the balcony, did you leave Dan in the living room?" Garrett asked.

"We left the living room at the same time."

"Did you see Shari on the balcony?"

"No. I only saw Beth."

"Beth was there before you?"

"Yes."

"You're absolutely sure?"

"Yes."

"Was Dan?"

"No. But he walked out a few seconds after I did. He came out of the bedroom and put his arm around Beth."

"Did he have to slide the door open? Was it shut?"

"I think so, but I couldn't swear on it."

"Who was the first one to see Shari lying below?"

"I was," Daniel said, uneasy.

"What is your full name, Dan?"

"Daniel Heard. I didn't kill her."

Garrett smiled. It was not a particularly handsome smile. He looked as if he was out of practice. "Why do you say that?"

"Because I didn't."

"What was your relationship with Shari?"

"She was a friend of mine."

"Oh, Christ," I muttered, disgusted.

"She was your girlfriend," Jo said sharply. I was surprised Jimmy hadn't said it. But Jimmy was sinking, I realized, down deep inside. He hadn't spoken in a while. I was glad, in a way, that Amanda was there for him to hold on to.

"I didn't know I was investigating a murder here," Garrett said slowly, watching Daniel carefully. "If I believed that, I should have first advised you of your rights." He leaned back in his chair. "Have I made a mistake, Dan?"

"I don't know. No. I think Shari jumped."

"You think she was suicidal?" Garrett asked.

"Well, no. I wouldn't say that."

"But you're saying she killed herself?"

Daniel shifted uncomfortably. "I'm not the only one."

"*Were* you her boyfriend?"

"Yeah, sort of. We were about to break up, though."

"Why?"

"No particular reason. I wanted to date other girls."

"Did she know this?"

"No," Jo broke in.

"She did," Daniel said. "I had told her." He looked down at his sweaty palms. "But I still liked her. She was a good kid."

"I was too hot a babe for you," I grumbled. "You liar."

"What did you do when you left the living room?" Garrett asked.

"I went into Beth's bedroom," Daniel said.

"Was Amanda still in the bathroom?"

"Yes."

"Could you hear her in there?"

"I could hear the water running."

"Was the door leading onto the balcony open or closed?"

"It was closed."

"Was Beth on the balcony?"

"Yes."

"What was she doing?"

"Nothing."

"Nothing?"

"She was just standing there, looking out."

"She wasn't by any chance looking down?"

"I don't think so."

"When did you notice Jo on the balcony?"

"The second I stepped outside."

"Was Jo looking down?"

"No"

"Why did you look down?"

"I just did."

"How long were you out there before you did so?"

"Not long."

"What did you see?"

Daniel bit his lower lip. "Shari."

"You knew right away it was her?"

"Yeah."

"What did you do? When you saw her?"

"I told Beth and Jo. Then Jo went and got Jeff and Amanda. Then we called for the paramedics."

"Before you called the paramedics, before you saw Shari, did you notice Amanda leaving the bathroom?"

"Yes."

"You're absolutely sure?"

"I noticed her in the bedroom behind me, yeah."

"Jo," Garrett said. "Were Amanda and Jeff both in the living room when you went to get them?"

"Yes. They were sitting on the couch together."

"Listening to the music?"

"No," Jo said. "The music was off."

"Who turned it off?" Garrett asked.

"I did," Amanda said. "It was giving me a headache."

Garrett stopped his barrage of questions for a full minute to study his notes. The gang watched and waited without making a peep.

"Let me sum this up," he said finally. "And if I've made a mistake anywhere, let me know." He straightened himself up in his chair. "Shari jumped up from the floor and ran to the balcony. A couple of minutes later Amanda went into Beth's bedroom. She didn't see Shari on the balcony. She didn't know if the door leading to the balcony was open or closed. She went into the bathroom. A minute later Jeff came into the bedroom. He noticed Shari on the balcony. He also noticed that the bathroom light was on and the bathroom door was closed. He definitely saw that the door to the balcony was shut, although he wasn't sure if it was locked from the inside. He left Beth's bedroom for the master bedroom, where he stayed in the bathroom for a couple of minutes. Less than a minute after Jeff left the living room, Beth entered her bedroom. She stayed there for a little while doing nothing.

"She noticed that there was someone in the bathroom and that the door to the balcony was locked. She didn't see Shari on the balcony, however. Not even when she unlocked the sliding glass door and stepped out onto the balcony. But she did see Jo on the balcony, even though she wasn't sure if Jo had been there before she was or not. And it's feasible that Jo did reach the balcony before Beth. It, in fact, appears likely, because Jo left the living room only seconds after Beth did. But whereas Beth dawdled in her bedroom before stepping onto the balcony, Jo went straight from the living room to the balcony."

"Beth was out there before me," Jo interrupted.

Garrett nodded thoughtfully. "We have a bit of a problem here. If Jo and Dan left the living room only a few seconds after Beth, and Beth hung out in her bedroom for a little while before going out on the balcony, then Dan should have caught up with Beth while she was still in her bedroom." Garrett turned to Daniel and Beth. "Well?"

"Jo and I didn't leave that soon after Beth," Daniel said. "It was more like a minute."

"Maybe half a minute," Jo said.

"Did I see you in the bedroom?" Beth asked Daniel.

"No." Daniel shook his head. "No."

"Why did you put your arm around Beth when you did catch up with her on the balcony?" Garrett asked Daniel.

"We're friends," Daniel said quickly.

"Are you good friends?" Garrett asked.

"Pretty good."

"Tell him about the Jacuzzi, Amanda," I shouted.

But Amanda was not telling.

"Do you two date?" Garrett asked.

"No," Daniel and Beth said simultaneously.

Garrett found the coherence mildly amusing. But he frowned as he rechecked his notepad. "It seems to me that Shari must have jumped after Jeff entered the bedroom but before Beth did. Do the rest of you agree?"

Everyone, with the exception of Jimmy and Amanda, nodded. Jimmy didn't look like he was doing much of anything except trying to breathe and stop thinking. But Amanda spoke up.

"Do you think that one of us pushed Shari from the balcony?" she asked.

"Why do you ask?" Garrett said, and he might have been toying with her a bit, not knowing he had picked the wrong person.

"Because you keep asking us so many questions."

Garrett shrugged. "It's my job."

"I see," Amanda said evenly.

Garrett held her eyes a moment. He might have been admiring their cool beauty. I don't know. He certainly couldn't have suspected her of foul play. Unless he also suspected her of the ability to be in two places at once. He addressed the group.

"I have only one more question, and then I'll let you all go." He paused. "Did any of you hear Shari scream?"

No one did, and I couldn't remember if I had. Like I said, screaming wasn't supposed to be cool. I probably hadn't made a sound. I hadn't had a chance. Four stories is not that long a fall, and whoever had pushed me had taken me by surprise.

Whoever had pushed me?

Getting my head burst open must have slowed me down a step. It wasn't until that moment that I realized I had been murdered. It really pissed me off. Especially because I didn't know who had done it. Oh, I can't tell you how mad I got. I was seeing things.

Actually, I *was* seeing things. There was the stuff in the air, of course, and now it had traces of color throbbing on and off, in complex crystalline patterns, deep within its depths. Yet it was so faint, I could not be absolutely sure I wasn't imagining it. But even that concern made me crack a bitter smile. A ghost worried that she was imagining things. It was funny in a sick sort of way.

Everybody got up to leave. Garrett called downstairs and learned that Beth's parents had arrived. He told them, and Beth, that he was placing the condo off-limits for the night while he evaluated the situation. Officer Fort came on the line and expressed the belief that Garrett was putting Beth's family through unnecessary hardship. Garrett didn't seem to care. In some ways he appeared a hard man.

He must have had a soft side, though. Jimmy and Amanda were the last two to leave, and when my brother stopped to speak to the lieutenant near the door, Garrett didn't brush him off.

"My sister didn't kill herself," Jimmy said.

"You two were close?" Garrett asked.

"Yes. She wouldn't have killed herself. It's not possible."

Garrett was listening. "Did she have any enemies among those present tonight?"

Jimmy glanced at Amanda, pained. "I don't think so."

"There was no reason anyone here would have wanted to kill Shari," Amanda said.

"Was there enough reason for her to kill herself?" Garrett asked Amanda.

"Excellent question," I observed.

Amanda took Jimmy's arm. "No," she said.

Garrett nodded and put his hand on Jimmy's shoulder. "Try to get some rest, son. The truth has a habit of emerging in time. I'll do what I can from my side."

Amanda and Jimmy left. I hoped she was driving him home. I didn't consider following them. I wanted to see exactly what Garrett had cooking on his side.

The first thing Garrett did when he was alone was take down a bottle of scotch from the liquor cabinet.

"Come on, Garrett!" I shouted at him as he plopped down on his chair in the living room and poured a stiff one into a dirty glass he'd swiped from the coffee table. "Gimme a break. You're on duty."

Garrett didn't give a damn. He finished his drink in three burning swallows and poured another. This one he nursed. I doubt he would have enjoyed it nearly so much had he been able to see me pacing back and forth across the floor in front of him. Actually, he probably wouldn't have seen me had he been able to see me. His eyes had settled on the red wax stain on the floor. At least, that was what I thought he was staring at. But then he suddenly set his glass and bottle aside and got down on his hands and knees near the couch. I knelt beside him.

"What is it?" I asked.

There was a dust of fine orange chalk on the carpet. Garrett touched the stuff and then held it up to his eyes, rubbing it between his fingers, feeling its consistency. I thought maybe he was on to something and started to get excited, but then he rubbed the chalk off on his pants leg and reached for his glass again.

He didn't get back in gear for another half-hour. By then the bottle was half-empty, and he had definitely slowed down. He began to stroll around the condo, wandering from one room to the next, seemingly in a random fashion. He ended up on the balcony, hanging over the rail. He had to be drunk by now, I figured, and I was concerned he was going to fall and kill himself. Then again, if he did, I could have told him to his face what I thought of his investigative preparations.

He did look around a bit while he was out there, and then he stumbled back inside and plopped down on the floor beside his bottle. Now he'd finish it, I thought to myself. But he didn't touch the scotch. He pulled out his notepad instead and began to draw a diagram. I stood behind him as he worked. He could have been an architect; he was good at proportions. Yet when he was done, I failed to see the point of it all. He had not put down everybody's position at the moment I had supposedly jumped. He had just marked my place. And I didn't understand the dotted lines that he had sketched in, crisscrossing behind me on the balcony.

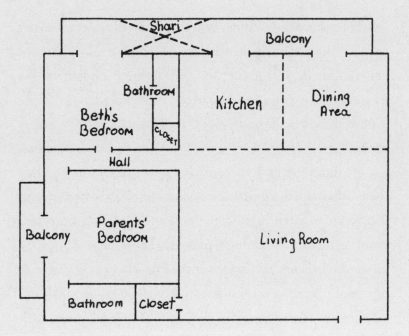

Garrett decided to call it a night. The clock in the living room read four in the morning. I followed him out and into the elevator down to the ground floor. He looked pretty fried; I was worried about him driving home in his truck. My concern was not purely altruistic. I figured if he was all I had, then he'd better stay alive.

He did not, however, head straight to his truck once we were outside. He strolled instead over to the cement walkway that ran beneath Beth's balcony. I followed with great reluctance. The police had roped off the spot and had wiped up most of the blood. But I could still see the wide, dark, lopsided memento my plunge had left on the ground. I began to feel sick.

"Hey, Garrett, let's go," I said. "This was just a place to land. It's not important."

He didn't share my opinion. He stared for a long time up at the balcony, and it seemed to me he was trying to picture my fall. Then he did something very strange; he actually sat on the ground beside the stain on the concrete. He pulled out his wallet. There was a picture of a girl my age inside. She had dark hair, sharp features—we didn't look alike. She was probably a shade more beautiful than me. Sitting alone, with me by his side, the picture in his hand, Garrett's face visibly sagged.

I figured whoever she was, she must also be dead.

I didn't know what to do. I felt too shaky to try to console him. And I knew it would be a waste of time. I sat down across from him on the other side of the stain.

"It wouldn't be so bad for us," I whispered, "if only you knew we were still here."

I didn't know how bad it could get.

Garrett sat there awhile, but eventually he put his picture

away and stood up and walked away. I didn't chase after him. He was probably going home to bed. Also, although I had approached the spot with many reservations, I was finding it had a peculiar allure for me now. Twice I tried to stand and leave, but I couldn't. I felt my hand reach out and touch my lost blood. But unlike the doorknob at home or Jimmy's arm at the hospital, I did touch it. When I pulled my fingers away, they were dark and dripping. I could see it, the warm red life running out of my hand.

My surroundings began to whirl, and I had to lie down. It seemed only appropriate that I should lie on my back with my head in the center of the mess. I was where I belonged, I thought miserably. Where it had all ended. There was the annoying lamppost off to my left, and far above I could see the balcony. But I didn't have to picture my fall as Garrett had done. I could remember it, especially the hot wave that had come upon me at the end and washed me away.

Only now, unlike then, I began to feel pain in my head, a throbbing, skull-cracking pain. My hand instinctively tried to reach up to the top of my head. It tried, but it didn't succeed. Something kept pushing it down.

No. Some*one*.

Suddenly I was not where I had been. I was back in the hospital, in the morgue. Dr. Leeds was standing above me, a glaring white light at his back. He was trying to put me in a green bag. But my right arm kept popping out. He had taken away my towel. It had been gross and disgusting, but I wished with all my heart that he had left it alone. My brains literally felt as if they were spilling out of my head.

Stuffing my arm back under the plastic, Dr. Leeds pulled the fat zipper toward my face.

"No!" I shrieked in horror. I fought to pull my arms up, to kick the bag off with my feet. But I was paralyzed. The zipper kept coming, past my sewn lips, over my glued eyelids. The doctor, looking down at me, sadly shook his head one last time. Then there was darkness, and he was lifting me up and shoving me into a locker. I heard the door slam shut. I felt the cold go deep within my black heart. Oh.

Lord, yes, it was black then. It was the abyss I had glimpsed as I had lain on the floor at the party.

But darkness inside, outside—it is not so different as the living might believe. In the next instant I was back on the messy walkway, the balcony above me. Only now there was something standing up there.

It was my first glimpse of the Shadow.

It bore no resemblance to a human being, and yet, from the start, it reminded me of a person. There was no reason it should have. Its shape and color were difficult to comprehend. It seemed a dark cloud caught in a state of flux between a solid and a vapor. It also appeared to be a part of the surroundings, a dam of some sort on the plasma that continued to flow through my new world. Or perhaps, I thought, it was a scar on the world. It was painful to behold.

It was watching me.

I got up very slowly and began to back away from it. It shifted as I moved, following me. I couldn't see its eyes, but I could feel them on me—cruel and penetrating. The thing didn't like me. I didn't like it. When the concrete walkway came to an end and the asphalt parking lot began, I ran.

It ran after me.

Someone had left the gate open. I dashed out of the complex, down a short road, and onto the deserted coast highway. I could see no one—no cars, no lights, no signs of life anywhere. I had a monster on my tail and no one around to help. Many times, when I was a child, I'd had a nightmare in which I tried to flee from a hungry creature with scales, claws, and dripping teeth. I had awakened in a cold sweat, crying for my mother. Sometimes she would come to my bed and comfort me. But other times she wouldn't hear me, and there'd be no comfort, and no sleep, until the sun came up.

I knew it was hopeless, but as I raced across the highway and onto the sand toward the vast ocean, I called for her once more.

"Mother!"

It was a hundred feet behind me, and in the next moment it was on top of me. I had run out of room. I'd run straight to the water's edge, boxing myself in. I turned to face it, to plead for mercy, but I couldn't bear to look at it. Without looking, I knew there could be nothing more horrible than what it had planned for me.

It stopped several feet from me. For several seconds it appeared to study me, and I could feel wave upon wave of loathing radiate from it like dark swells in a poison ocean. And what made it so utterly terrible was that it *knew* me. It had reason to hate me. It reached out a distorted hand to touch me.

"No!" I shrieked, turning and fleeing into the water.

I was no saint. I couldn't walk on water. I began to go down, but still it pursued me. "Mother!" I cried. "Save me!"

"Shari."

I heard my name. I opened my eyes. It was dark. I was home, in bed with my mother. She lay with her back to me, and I was holding on to her, trying to. I couldn't see her face, but I could hear her crying. I could feel her heart breaking. I tried to squeeze her tightly.

"I'm here, Mom. I'm here. Please don't cry."

There was a pause, and then, when she said my name next, it was as if she had heard me. "Shari?"

"Yes!" I cried. "It's me! I'm here! I'm here! I never left!"

She didn't respond, not directly. But she did stop crying, and soon she was asleep. And so I also slept, holding on to her as best I could, and swearing to myself that I would never, ever let go.

CHAPTER VII

I AWOKE TO a sunny day. My mother was gone. So was her bedroom. I had moved again. I was at Amanda's house. I jumped up from the bed on which I was lying. I still had on the jeans and yellow blouse I had worn to Beth's party. They were wrinkled, as if I had in fact slept in them, and I felt greatly relieved. It was not as though I had forgotten what had happened the previous night, but I had a sudden rush of confidence that it couldn't have *really* happened. People died all the time, I realized, but it was simply too ridiculous to think I could have been so unfortunate.

My confidence lasted long enough for me to walk into the living room. Mrs. Parish, dressed in mourning black, was sitting on the couch holding a rosary.

"Hello, Mrs. Parish," I said, flipping a spunky wave at her. Nothing. Not even a puzzled glance in my direction. I plopped down in the chair across from her. "Damn," I said. Apparently, dying was one condition a good night's sleep couldn't remedy.

"You better finish your breakfast," Mrs. Parish said to Amanda. "They'll be here any minute."

Amanda, wearing a long gray dress that matched her wide gray eyes, was seated at the dining room table, a bowl of oatmeal in front of her. The table, in fact the whole place, was fairly undistinguished. There wasn't a piece of furniture one couldn't have found at the Goodwill.

"I'm not very hungry," Amanda said.

"You'll need your strength," Mrs. Parish said, although it was clear from her shaking hands that it was she who needed the strength. "Please eat."

"All right," Amanda said, spooning down another soggy bite. "Where's the service going to be?"

"At the chapel at the cemetery," Mrs. Parish said.

"Now hold on a second," I said. "I just died. I'm not ready for any funeral. I'm not ready to—"

Why say it? Who was ever ready to be put in the ground?

But there was still a scheduling problem here. No one was buried the day after they died. The only logical explanation was that I had slept away several days. My, I thought, how time flies when one splits open one's skull.

"Will it be a Catholic service?" Amanda asked.

"I don't know. I don't think so."

"You might not want to bring your rosary. They only use those at Catholic masses."

Mrs. Parish looked down at her string of tiny black beads. "I can pray quietly," she whispered, squeezing her eyes shut.

"What?"

Mrs. Parish looked up. "Nothing, honey. Are you almost done? They should be here soon."

"I'm almost done," Amanda said, nodding patiently.

"How are you feeling?"

"Fine."

"You're remembering to take care of yourself?"

"I'm fine, Mother."

"Good," Mrs. Parish said weakly. "That's good."

Jo and her mother, Mrs. Foulton, arrived shortly afterward. I felt honored that they were all going to my funeral in the same car since they seldom did anything together. Mrs. Foulton had on a black dress—somehow it still looked like a nurse's uniform—but Jo was wearing orange pants and an orange blouse. It was incredible. Who would wear orange to a best friend's funeral?

"This isn't Halloween, for God's sake," I told her, insulted.

Amanda set her bowl of half-finished oatmeal in the sink and headed to her room for her bag. Jo went with her. Mrs. Foulton sat beside Mrs. Parish on the couch. Neither looked as if she had been getting much sleep lately. But Mrs. Foulton clearly had no intention of showing any weakness.

"You've got to get a handle on yourself," she said to her sister, pulling out a cigarette and a Bic lighter. "This is going to be hard enough on the girls."

Mrs. Parish nodded, bunching up her rosary in her hand. "I know," she said.

"How's Amanda taking it?"

"I thought I heard her crying last night." Mrs. Parish took a breath. "How's Jo?"

"She doesn't say a word."

"Have you tried to talk to her about it?"

Mrs. Foulton lit her cigarette and exhaled a large cloud of smoke. "I don't want to talk about it. She's gone. It's done."

Mrs. Parish looked at her. "How can you say that?"

"It's true."

Mrs. Parish held her eye. "You're not going to forget her."

Mrs. Foulton went to snap at her sister but then thought better of it. She ground out her cigarette, lowering her eyes and voice. "No, I don't suppose I ever will forget."

The girls reappeared. We went outside and climbed into Mrs. Foulton's Nissan. I sat in the back between Jo and Amanda. The sky was a sparkling blue, and the sun was cloaked in a dazzling aura of purple. That was another thing—I could stare right at the sun and not hurt my eyes. Mrs. Foulton lit another cigarette and started the car.

Cruising down the road, the breeze through the open windows didn't mess my hair one tiny bit.

The cemetery was not very close to my house. My parents had lived in another neighborhood earlier. I suppose they had purchased a couple of local plots back when things were cheaper. In other words, I was being stuck in a plot they had one day planned on using for themselves. That was fine with me. I didn't plan on spending a lot of time underground.

But I felt a morbid curiosity as we drove through the flower-lined cemetery gates and started up the grassy hill along the narrow winding black road that led to the chapel. I leaned over Amanda and stared out the window. I was looking for other ghosts, but I couldn't find any, not even a little white Casper to go for a walk with. I began to feel lonely.

Part of the reason I had never been much of a churchgoer when I was alive was the minister of our church—the Reverend Theodore Smith. He wasn't an old-school fire-and-brimstone preacher; he was just straight, so straight you could line up your wallpaper next to him. He was one of those rare men you just knew had never been to bed with a woman. He was about thirty-five and by no means bad looking, but the only suits he wore were the ones his father had left him in his will. He was always talking about Jesus. You would have thought they were old friends. He could have bored any empty pew. But I wasn't surprised that he was there to host my funeral. I bet he figured this was one service I couldn't walk out on.

I was in for a big disappointment when I walked into the chapel with Jo and Amanda and their moms. Besides seeing

Reverend Smith up front, I discovered that few kids from school had bothered to come. At first I figured we must be early, but the service started almost immediately, and there were no latecomers. I couldn't understand it. I had gone to Hazzard High for four years. I hadn't been on the cheerleader squad or anything, but I had gotten around. I had been invited to every damn party there was, and, all told, there couldn't have been more than a dozen kids present.

Then it hit me. Everyone thought I had committed suicide. It angered me for a minute that that should make any difference, and then I started to feel a bit better. If they'd known I'd been murdered, I told myself, they would have had to turn people away at the gate. I probably would have got my picture on the front page of the paper.

My casket rested at the altar on a wooden table. Black and shiny, with gold trim and smart angles, I supposed it would do. As long as they kept it closed. I was relieved to see I wasn't on display.

My family was sitting up front. I didn't want to sit near them; I didn't think I could handle it. Amanda and Jo and Mrs. Foulton, however, headed straight for them. Fortunately, Mrs. Parish decided to stay in the back where she could say her rosaries in peace. I sat beside her. Beth and Daniel were three rows up from us. If they hadn't come together, they would probably be leaving together. It was only fair, I supposed. A girl wasn't much good to a guy without a body. Of course, he mustn't have been that crazy about me when I had a body. He must have been wondering how he could get rid of me without hurting my feelings,

I wondered if he had killed me. I didn't see Jeff Nichols anywhere, and I wondered about a lot of things.

Reverend Smith stepped to the podium.

"I would like to welcome everyone to this service on behalf of Mr. and Mrs. Cooper, and their son, James Cooper," he said in his smooth, sympathetic voice. "We are gathered here today to pay our final respects to a wonderful young lady—Shari Cooper. It warms my heart to see how many of her friends have taken the time to remember her. She was, in all truth, a very special person. I knew her well. . . ."

"You didn't even know what color eyes I had," I muttered, already tuning him out. My gaze wandered to the pew across from me. There was a guy about my age sitting there who looked familiar, but I couldn't place him. His clothes made me laugh. He was wearing baggy white shorts and a red T-shirt. To *my* funeral? At least he'd come, I thought. He must be someone from school who had loved me from afar. I wished I knew who he was.

Mrs. Parish had tuned the reverend out as well. She was praying: ten Hail Marys preceded by an Our Father and followed by a Glory Be to the Father. I knew the prayers. I had even said a few of them during my days on earth. But I doubt I had ever said them as Mrs. Parish was now—with feeling.

She was whispering softly, but I found, as I turned my attention her way, that I could hear her clearly, better even than the reverend, who had a loud voice, not to mention a microphone.

There was something about her praying that began to charm me in a special way. I didn't understand it. Mrs. Parish was crushed. Her fingers trembled as she slipped from one bead to the next. Yet, as I listened, I began to feel lighter. I would go so far as to say I felt a thrill of joy. The weird plasma in the air began to shimmer with a cool silver light. It was faint, true, but it was there, beyond question. I wondered if it was coming out of Mrs. Parish. I wanted the light to keep coming. I began to become quite engrossed in it. I closed my eyes, but still I could see it—better, in fact. My mind began to drift with the words without actually listening to them. The meaning was unimportant, I began to realize. All that mattered was that they were being said with love. The light increased and seemed to encompass me. As the brilliance intensified, so did my peace. It was the first peace I had felt in a long time.

And then it stopped, and it was like a mountain crushing down on my soul. I opened my eyes. The light was gone. The service was over. I couldn't believe it. We had just got there! It should have taken at least an hour to remember how wonderful I had been. What about my favorite song—"Stairway to Heaven"? Jo could have played it on her acoustic guitar. What about my closest friends getting up and saying a few words about how much they were going to miss me? I wanted to be remembered!

People began to file out. I had no choice but to follow. A hearse was brought around front for the coffin. I stood on the chapel steps and wondered what had gone wrong with time. Every time I closed my eyes, the hands on the clock would spin forward.

I rode to the gravesite in the hearse. It seemed the thing to do. But I sat in the front with the driver, not in the back with the black box. That was how I had begun to think of it now, a prison they would lock my body in beneath the ground while my spirit wandered alone and forsaken on the surface. I had begun to feel sad again and lonely, terribly lonely.

We lost a few people on the short trip out to the lawns, about half, actually. I couldn't blame them. They had things to do. And what the hell, Shari had been a nice girl, but she hadn't been that nice. Oh, it was awful. It was true. I had done nothing in my life that was worth remembering. Why should they remember me? I watched them unload the coffin and set it on the ground next to a pile of brown dirt and a black hole.

They had another short service. Reverend Smith read a few verses from the Bible. They were nice, but they were nothing; he just read them because he was supposed to read them. Daniel stood next to Beth and held her hand. Mrs. Parish and Mrs. Foulton stood next to each other and behind their daughters. Out of the group, only Mrs. Parish was weeping.

My mom and dad were also there, of course, and Jimmy. They looked as if time had been moving slowly for them, as if they had no more tears to shed. They held individual white roses. I liked roses; orange ones for parties and red ones for love. White ones were OK, too, I guessed. They set them on the top of the coffin at the reverend's bidding. Then the minister closed his Bible. There was a note of finality in the way he did it. People began to walk away.

The last person to leave was Jimmy. He knelt for a moment by the coffin and placed his hands palms down on the shiny black surface as if he were trying to touch me one last time. But I was standing behind him, beyond reach.

Finally, he left, and it was only minutes later that the grave diggers appeared. They seemed to be in a hurry to get me in the ground. They came in a truck with concrete liners and ropes and pulleys. They also brought shovels. They sealed my coffin up so it would be safe from robbers and perverts, but not so safe, I thought, that it would be beyond the reach of the slimy creatures that lived deep in the soil. After they had lowered me into the ground, they began to throw shovel after shovel of dark moist earth on top of me.

"No!" I pleaded irrationally, panicking, trying to grab their arms, to stop them. "You can't do this to me! I was just getting started! I was going to do all kinds of neat stuff! Please don't cover me up! People will forget that I'm here!"

They buried me quickly. Eighteen years to become the person I had become and thirty minutes to disappear forever. They threw their equipment in the back of their truck and drove away, leaving me alone and crying on top of a pile of unsettled earth that probably wouldn't give up my bones until the day the world came to an end.

"Oh, God, help me," I wept. "Please help me."

I don't know how long I sat there before I noticed the pair of sandaled feet in front of me. I glanced up. It was the boy from the chapel with the baggy white shorts and the red T-shirt. I had been happy to see him before, but now I resented the fact that he hadn't even brought a flower to lay on my grave.

"Go to hell," I told him, looking back down.

"We're already there, wouldn't you say, Shari?"

My head snapped up. I didn't understand how I could have failed to recognize him before. "Peter," I whispered.

CHAPTER VIII

My RELIEF IN that moment was wondrous. It was as glorious as my sorrow had been horrible. I don't remember jumping up and stretching out my arms, but I do remember how sweet it felt to hug him, to *feel* him and know that he could feel me. I think I held him for quite a long while before I let go. I was afraid he'd disappear.

"Peter," I said again, shaking my head in amazement as I finally stepped back. He looked great, and I don't mean that he looked great for someone who had been dead a couple of years. He was as I remembered him from biology class: thin and wiry, his blond hair thick and curly, his broad smile wide and wild. That was one thing I had missed so much about Peter when he died; the mischievous way his mouth would twist up whenever he told me something that he swore was the absolute truth and which in most cases was a complete fabrication. He had eyes as blue as my brother's but even more clear; they shone in the bright sun, although his head cast no shadow.

"You remember," he said, pleased.

"Of course I remember! God, this is incredible. I never thought I'd see you again. How are you?"

"All right. How are you?"

"Great," I said. Then I made a face and giggled. "Well, I'm OK, considering that I'm dead."

He nodded and spoke softly. "I know." Then he smiled again, but it, too, was soft. "It's good to see you, Shari."

"Yeah? Thanks. It's great to see you." I laughed, gesturing to the pile of dirt at our feet. "So here we are. At my funeral!"

"Yeah."

"Some place to get together, huh? How was yours? Did you go?"

"Yeah. It was pretty good."

"That's good." I hadn't gone to his funeral. I had stayed home and cried. In fact, I had never gone to a funeral before, and had Peter not shown up, I would have regretted attending my own. I surveyed the cemetery. We were alone now, just us and the tombstones. It seemed much more peaceful than before. "So there is life after death, after all," I said. "It's hard to believe."

"For some people."

"Is that true?"

He shrugged, and the gesture reminded me of his brother. "It can be."

"No. I mean, did I screw up by not believing, or what?"

He shook his head. "Not at all."

"That's a relief," I said, and I meant it. "So what's the deal? Is there really a God?"

"Sure."

I brightened. "That's neat! Where is he? Can I see him?"

"He?"

"You mean he's a *she*?" I said. "Oh, wow, that's cool. What's she like?"

"God isn't what we used to think he was like when we were alive, Shari. He isn't a he or a she."

"Is he an *it*?" I asked.

Peter laughed. "These are deep questions, and I don't have a lot of deep answers for you. From what I've been able to tell, everything's much simpler than we used to think. It's so simple you can't even talk about it. God just is. He exists. He is everything. He is us. We are him." Peter turned away and looked over the green lawn. I could not remember where he had been buried, but I doubted it had been in the same cemetery. He added, "And that's all I know."

I thought a moment. "Why are you here?"

"To help you." A note of seriousness entered his voice. "As long as you want my help."

"Oh, I do," I said.

"Good."

The dirt at our feet caught my eye. I hadn't forgotten what lay beneath it. "What I mean is, why are you here *now*?"

"And not before?"

I nodded reluctantly. "Yeah."

His expression softened, and he reached out and rubbed my shoulder. "It was hard for you, wasn't it?"

I didn't feel the tears coming. They were just there, falling silent and invisible to the ground. I wanted to fall, too, into his arms again. But I hadn't known him *that* well. We had never kissed. We had never gone out. I wiped at my cheek, unsure if it was damp or not.

"It was hard," I said.

Peter hastily took back his hand, almost as if he were ashamed. "I'm sorry, Shari. I couldn't come earlier."

"I understand. Well, actually, I don't understand. Why couldn't you come?"

"You hadn't asked for help," he said.

"You mean, since I've been dead, all I've had to do was ask for help and I would have gotten it?"

"Yes."

"But I didn't know that. Why didn't someone tell me?"

"You didn't ask," he said.

"But—"

"It says in the Bible, Shari, if you knock, the door shall be opened."

"Since when did you start reading the Bible?" I asked.

"I haven't actually been reading it. But your minister read that line during your service."

I had been crying a second ago, and now I burst out laughing. "That's the most ridiculous thing I ever heard!"

"It's the absolute truth," he said.

"What a crazy system," I said, not sure if I believed him. Then I remembered how I had cried to my mother for help when the monster had tried to eat me, and how I had been immediately transported to the safety of her bed. I peered at him curiously. "Why is it you were sent to help me?"

"I told you."

"Why you in particular?"

He hesitated. "I was available."

"*Who* sent you?"

The question amused him. He tugged at his red T-shirt. "I don't suppose I look like a messenger of God."

"Damn right, you don't. Why are you dressed that way?"

"This is what I was wearing when I died."

"You died riding your motorcycle," I said.

"It was a warm night."

"We don't get a change of clothing?"

"Soon you'll be able to wear whatever you want." He stepped past me then, walking to the edge of the hill where I had been buried, looking up at the sun and its glorious purple halo. At least, I thought he was looking at the sun. When I came up at his side, I realized he had closed his eyes and that the light playing over his face had nothing to do with sunlight. There was a faint silvery luster to his skin, and it seemed to brighten as he stood there—listening, perhaps, to some internal voice.

"Peter?"

"You can't stay here," he said.

"Where should we go?"

He opened his eyes, stared at me. "You know where to go."

"Where?" I asked.

"Where you started to go when you were in the chapel."

I was confused. "Where was that?"

"When Mrs. Parish was praying," he said.

"But I didn't go anywhere then." I paused. "Do you mean the light? I have to go into that light?"

"Exactly."

"How do you know? Did God tell you just now?"

"No," he said. "I read about it in the *Enquirer*."

I socked him. "Peter!"

He grabbed my hand, stopping me, trying to be serious in spite of his laughter. "I mean it, Shari. You mustn't stay here."

"But what am I supposed to do? I didn't have a rosary with me when I died. And I hardly remember those prayers."

"The rosary and prayers are not as important as where you put your attention. Put your attention on the light, and the light will come."

"How do I do that?"

"You just have to want to do it, that's all." He began to sit down, gesturing for me to do likewise. "It's very simple."

I sat so close to him that our knees touched. And I suddenly began to feel uneasy and was at a loss to explain why. I remembered the serenity of the light in the chapel. If Peter was going to lead me into it, I reasoned, I should be happy.

Then I thought of Jo and the party. The trance.

"You're not going to give me suggestions, are you?" I asked.

"No. The desire to be with the light must be from your side."

"But do I have to close my eyes?"

"You may close your eyes, if you wish," he said. "But it isn't necessary."

"Are you coming with me?" I asked.

"This is between you and the light. I'm just here to point you in the right direction." He smiled and reached over and patted me on the back. "Don't worry, Shari. Soon you're going to be happier than you can imagine."

"Will I know who killed me?"

He hesitated. "Does that matter?"

"Yes! I want to know who did it."

"Why?" he asked.

"What do you mean, why? If someone killed you, wouldn't you want to know who had done it?"

"Not really," he said.

"That's only because you've been dead for a while. Believe me, if you had just been snuffed out, you'd want to know who the murderer was. Now, tell me the truth—will I know who killed me?"

"I don't know."

"What do you mean, you don't know?"

"I don't," he said.

"Is there someone who does?"

Peter looked uncomfortable. "Shari, you're dead. You had a nice go of it on earth, but now it's time to move on."

"Exactly where am I moving on to? Heaven?"

"Heaven is a word the living use to describe a place. Over here, places do not exist, not as they existed for you when you were alive. Have you noticed since you've been dead that sometimes you'll be in one spot, and then suddenly you'll be in another?"

"Yeah."

He nodded. "Again, it's a question of where your attention is. Put your mind on your house, and you'll be back home. Put it on the light, and the light will be with you."

"But what about my family? They think I'm dead."

"You are dead," he said.

"Yes, I know. But they don't know what death means."

"That's not unusual."

"But it is unusual to have your family think you killed yourself when you didn't." I paused. "They all must think I was crazy."

"They don't," he said.

"They do. Did you see how many kids from school came to my funeral?" I sighed. "I bet you had ten times as many."

"Neither of us is running for student office."

"If I go into the light, can I still come back here and snoop around?"

"I don't think you'll want to do that."

"But could I?" I insisted.

"Didn't the police assign someone to investigate you your death?"

"Yeah, but the guy's a drunk!"

"He's not that bad."

I stopped. "You know Garrett?"

Peter hesitated. "I've seen him around."

"Were you there when he was interrogating the group?"

He looked down. "Yes."

"What were you doing there?"

"Hanging out."

"Were you at the party?"

Peter obviously wished he had not made the slip about the lieutenant. "Some of the time," he replied carefully.

"Why were you at the party?"

"I like parties."

The cool air of coincidence touched me. "Were you there because you knew I was going to die?" I asked.

He glanced up, not at me but toward the north end of the

cemetery, where a residential street ran alongside the sloping green lawns. Two little girls were riding their bikes on the sidewalk, laughing together. They looked like sisters.

"That's an interesting question," he said.

"Yeah, it is," I said, thoughtful. I'm not sure why, but I took his response to mean yes. I remembered Jeff's question at the party concerning destiny. "Was I meant to die that night?"

He nodded. "Nothing happens by accident. We are born with so many breaths. When they're used up, we die. Nothing can stop it."

"Nothing?"

"Nothing."

I tried to digest the concept. I couldn't say it made it any easier for me to accept what had happened. In fact, I think it depressed me further. "Are you sure about that?" I asked.

My doubt made him smile. "The girl falls off a balcony and she turns into a philosopher."

"Come on."

"I would rather talk about baseball," he said.

"I hate baseball."

"Did you know that running head-on into that truck at sixty miles an hour didn't slow my fastball one bit?"

"Peter, please."

He saw how serious I was. "I've already told you, Shari, I can't answer these kinds of questions, not to your satisfaction. I say you were destined to die that night, and from everything

I've seen since I've got over here, I know that to be true. But I also know you have free will. You are totally in charge of your destiny. You did not have to go to the party last Friday."

"But if I hadn't gone, I'd still be alive. You're contradicting yourself."

"That is the trouble with these discussions. Let me try an analogy. Say you took out a bank loan. Being a person of your word, from that point on, it's predetermined you will pay it back. But how fast you pay it back is up to you. You can take eighty years, or eighteen. So you have both: destiny and free will. Life is like that. And death."

"But this stupid bank foreclosed on my house!"

He smiled. "You must have exceeded your credit limit. Don't worry, this is just an analogy. You're in debt to no one. Words explain so little. You have a chance to go into the light. That will mean much more to you than anything I can say." He touched me again on the shoulder. He had beautiful hands, large and strong, perfect for a big-league pitcher. I had only been kidding him. I had loved baseball, especially watching him play. "Do you have any other questions before we say goodbye?" he asked.

I sat upright. "You're not coming with me?"

"I can't."

"Why can't you?" I asked, and I almost choked on the words. I don't think I could have told Peter how much it had meant to me to see him again.

He looked back toward the children on the bicycles. For mortals, they would have already been out of sight, but with us, they were still crystal clear.

"I have a responsibility," he said. "There are others like you who, when they die, wander around lost and confused, unaware that they are dead."

"And you help them?"

"I try."

"Do you need another helper?"

My offer startled him. He shook his head. "You cannot stay here, Shari. You must go on."

"But why? What's the hurry?" It might be kind of fun, I thought, helping out other novice ghosts like myself. I would definitely advise them to stay away from morgues. "I'm not getting any older," I said.

"That makes no difference. You are *supposed* to go on."

"Who says? Don't I have free will?"

"Yes, but . . ."

"Then I decided to stay. And my decision must be destined."

"How so?" he asked.

"Because I just made it. Look, I want to find out who killed me. I want to clear my name."

"You can't clear your name. Even if you did figure out who killed you, you wouldn't be able to communicate the information to the living."

I had forgotten about that. "Is there no way to get through to them?"

"No," he said.

"Are you sure?"

He shook his head again. "Shari, you've got to leave it to the police. They're better equipped to deal with the situation."

"I told you, Garrett's a drunk."

"Yes, but he has an advantage over you. He's alive."

"I would think dead people would make better spies," I said, remembering how my mother had twice seemed to hear me, in the kitchen immediately after the hospital had called and, even more distinctly, in her bedroom when I had tried to comfort her. There must be a thread that connects us to the living, I thought. There had to be a way to talk to them. "Why are you so anxious to get rid of me?" I asked.

"I'm not anxious to get rid of you."

"Do you have a girlfriend over here? Some big-bosomed wench from the Middle Ages, maybe? I bet she doesn't know about women's liberation. I'd like to meet her."

He wasn't laughing. "It's dangerous for you to stay."

I stopped my teasing. "Why?"

He was watching me. "You know why."

Sitting on the grass in the bright sun with a friend by my side, it might have been possible to forget the creature on the balcony. But I was never going to forget, I knew. "What was it?"

"The Shadow," he said.

"The what?"

He closed his eyes and lowered his head. The thing scared him. "It's the most awful thing."

"Is it like a devil?"

"It can't be. . . ." He opened his eyes, staring down at the grass. I had never seen him this way before. He was as pale as a ghost, and that was no joke. "Yes, it's like that. It's evil."

"If it's evil, why did God make it?"

"I don't know."

"Is there just one of them?"

He turned toward me. "Listen, Shari, you mustn't give it the chance to catch up with you. You must leave here."

"What would it do to me?"

"Imprison you."

"How?" I asked.

"I can't explain. That's just what it does."

"Can't you protect me from it?"

"No," he said.

"How do you protect yourself from it?"

"I avoid it. And that's not easy."

"But wouldn't the two of us be safer together?"

He went to argue with me some more when he suddenly stopped. I didn't know what was happening. He closed his eyes as he had done before. It was almost as if he were meditating. Only this time his face didn't brighten. I let him be. When he finally did open his eyes, he looked down at his open left hand.

He had been a southpaw; he had pitched left-handed. He had been so good.

"I didn't know," he said.

"You didn't know what?"

"That you were going to die that night."

"You didn't see who did it?"

"No. I left the party a few minutes before it happened.

"Oh," I said.

"You won't go on?"

The Shadow had scared me more than death itself, but there was Jimmy still grieving alone and a murderer walking free. Plus there was Peter. He continued to study his open palm. I thought to put my hand in it and tell him that I wanted his company as much as I wanted my name cleared. But I didn't. It was not to be, I guessed. A lot of things aren't.

"No," I said.

He closed his hand into a fist and gently pounded the grass beside his knee, bending back not a single blade of grass. "You're making a mistake," he said.

"We'll see."

He raised his head, and I was relieved to see him smile. He was giving up, at least for now. He offered me his hand. "I guess we're partners again," he said, referring to the days when we were lab partners in biology.

"There is no wench from the Middle Ages?"

"No such luck."

CHAPTER IX

WE DIDN'T LEAVE the cemetery right away. We had to decide how we were going to conduct our investigation. I started out by asking Peter if he could read people's minds. He thought it was a weird question.

"Of course not," he said. "I'm not psychic."

"I was just asking. I figured it would make our work a lot easier if you could."

"I can't."

"All right," I said. "So what should we do now?"

"Who at the party do you feel was capable of murder?"

"No one."

"We're off to a great start," he said.

"But if I had to choose someone, it would be Amanda.'

"Why? She seems like a nice, soft-spoken girl."

"She's too soft-spoken. I haven't trusted her from the day she started going out with my brother."

He chuckled. "Do I detect a hint of jealousy here?"

"No. Well, maybe. But I think that girl's hiding something."

"When did you start thinking that?" he asked.

"I've always thought that."

"But if she is the one, then she only just killed you a few days ago. What could she have been hiding before?"

"I don't know," I said.

"We should review where Garrett had everybody when you went over the balcony."

"All right." Something struck me. "How come I didn't see you in the condo when he was doing his questioning?"

"You're easy to hide from," he said.

"I am?"

"You've always been that way." He thought a moment. "Wasn't Amanda supposed to be in the bathroom when you died?"

"Yeah," I agreed reluctantly. "When your brother came into Beth's bedroom, I was still on the balcony. Wait! What if she came out of the bathroom after Jeff left, shoved me off the balcony, and then reentered the bathroom before Beth came into the bedroom?"

"She would have had to have moved extremely quickly."

"But it's possible," I said.

"It's unlikely. Beth said she left the living room less than a minute after Jeff. Besides, you haven't given me a single reason why Amanda would have wanted you dead."

"Let's look at Dan, then. Amanda said he was fooling around with Beth in the Jacuzzi. He had a motive to knock me off."

"A slim one," Peter said. "Dan only had to break up with you if he wanted to date Beth. He didn't have to kill you."

"But I had humiliated Dan."

"What did you do?"

I hesitated. "It's a long story." A disturbing idea occurred to me. "Peter?"

"What?"

"Since you've been dead, how much have you been hanging out with us guys, you know, who were still alive?"

He smiled. "Are you asking if I ever spied on you while you were taking a shower?"

I would have blushed had I real blood in my veins. "No."

"I did once."

"*What?* You didn't!"

"Just once," he said, giggling.

"When? Was it last summer? Did I have a tan?"

"I don't remember."

"You don't remember! How did I look?"

"Fine."

"*Fine?* What does that mean?"

He continued to laugh. "You looked great."

I hit him. "You're disgusting."

"I was curious."

"Why did you choose me? Or did you go around peeking through curtains all over the city? I bet you did. I bet you still do. And here you were trying to give me the impression you're a guardian angel."

"You were the first one I checked out," he said.

"And I suppose I should be flattered?"

"Yeah."

I thought a minute and decided I *was* flattered. Of course, I thought, I couldn't let him know that. "I hope you weren't disappointed," I said.

"I found the entire experience spiritually exhilarating." He stood and began to pace in front of me at the edge of the grassy bluff, returning to business. "Dan may be the last person we can pin your murder on. He was one of the last people to leave the living room, and he didn't come out onto the balcony until after Jo and Beth were already there."

"He could have been on the balcony before Jo got there and then gone inside before coming back outside."

"But he left the living room at the same time as Jo," Peter said. "He wouldn't have had time to kill you before Jo got to the balcony. Also, Beth would have had to have been in cahoots with him."

"Then what about Beth herself? Jo said Beth was on the balcony before her."

Peter nodded. "From the point of view of timing, Beth has to be considered the number one suspect. But what about a motive? So she had the hots for your boyfriend. That's not a good enough reason to kill you."

"But Beth was acting weird that night. After Jo used the magnet on her, she looked spaced out. Peter, when exactly did you leave the party?"

"I told you. A few minutes before you died."

"What was the last thing you saw? Did you see the seance?"

He stopped his pacing. "What seance?"

"When Jo was hypnotizing me," I said.

"I caught some of that."

"Why did you suddenly leave?"

"It was getting late," he said.

"But you don't have to sleep. Do you?"

"Not exactly. But I do rest sometimes."

"Why did you leave?"

He shrugged. "I just did."

"Well, I don't know what was wrong with Beth. Do you?"

"How would I know?"

"I don't know." Something was bothering him. I think I knew what it was. There was no sense avoiding the matter. "Peter? What about Jeff?"

"He didn't kill you."

"He says he saw me on the balcony. But when Beth came into the bedroom, she said I was gone."

"It wasn't my brother. He couldn't harm a fly."

"He didn't like me," I said.

"Why do you say that?"

"I could tell."

"He wouldn't have had time to kill you before Beth appeared."

"It doesn't take a whole lot of time to shove someone in the back." Peter didn't say anything. "Why didn't your brother like me?" I asked.

"Shari, as far as I know, when I was alive, Jeff had nothing against you."

"All right. I believe you."

"What about Jo?" he asked.

I had to laugh. "Jo's my best friend."

"Did you trust her?"

"What kind of question is that? Of course I trusted her. Anyway, she didn't get to the balcony until after Beth."

"Beth thought Jo was there before her," Peter said.

"Beth didn't know what she was talking about."

"You shouldn't automatically eliminate Jo."

"You shouldn't automatically eliminate Jeff," I snapped. Dying obviously hadn't improved my disposition. I felt ashamed. "I'm sorry," I muttered.

He nodded. "So am I. It's no fun dissecting your friends."

"And your family," I said.

"Yeah."

"Are we making any progress?" I asked.

"Who knows?"

"God must. Can't you give him a call?"

Peter smiled. "Did you notice how Garrett drew those crisscrossing lines behind your position on the balcony?"

"You saw those too?" I asked.

"I was peering over your shoulder when you were peering over his. Do you know what those lines meant?"

"No."

"Garrett's considering the possibility that someone was standing at your back on the balcony in the one spot that wouldn't have been visible from the center of Beth's bedroom."

"Amanda," I whispered.

"It would seem that she could have been behind you even when Jeff was in Beth's bedroom."

"It must have been her!"

Peter shook his head. "It would seem so on the surface; but let's look at it a little closer. Jeff said the sliding glass door to the balcony was closed when he went into the bedroom. Garrett made it clear that when you close that door, you lock it. Amanda would have had no way to push you off the balcony and then get back inside, unless she went through the kitchen, where Beth and Jo and Dan would have seen her. Amanda *must* have been in the bathroom. Dan noticed her at his back when he was on the balcony, and when Jeff came back into the living room, Amanda was there."

"So we've determined it couldn't have been Dan or Amanda?"

"Maybe." Peter glanced up at the kaleidoscope sun. "What if it wasn't someone at the party?"

"You mean someone from the outside might have murdered me?"

"No. We may be too caught up on the idea of some-*one*. What if two people were involved? Or three? And they arranged their stories for Garrett so that the facts we're taking for granted might be completely false."

My jaw dropped. "What if it was *all* of them?"

"Then we're really in trouble."

We decided the best course of action would be for us to try to pick up clues by following my friends around for a few days. A ghost can't do much else, really—or so Peter said. Yet I was secretly determined to explore any imaginable way to make contact with the living.

We were leaving the cemetery when Peter remarked that it was time for my first lesson in spirit transportation.

"We don't use cars on this side of the fence," he said.

"What do you use?"

He tapped his head. "Our minds. But let's go over to the park before I show you what to do."

He didn't say it, but he meant he wanted to get me away from my burial plot. The whole time we had talked, my eyes had strayed to the mound of fresh brown dirt. Like the spot where I had died, it held a perverse allure for me. I couldn't help thinking how my body would decompose beneath the earth. I wished I had been cremated and my ashes thrown into the ocean.

The park was across the street from the cemetery. The two girls we had seen earlier had set aside their bikes and were playing on the swings. Peter steered me toward a bench beneath a shady tree.

"We're going to perform a little experiment," he said when we were comfortably seated. "First, close your eyes." I did so. "Now, picture to yourself the courtyard at Hazzard High. Think of how the benches surround the snackbar area. Think of the buildings and the trees, the people we know who go to school there. Then say to yourself—"

"There's no place like home," I muttered, giggling and thinking of Dorothy in *The Wizard of Oz*.

He laughed with me, but only for a moment. "Keep your eyes closed, Shari. Think to yourself: I want to be there. I want to be at school. You mustn't try to concentrate on the desire. You simply want to have it, quietly, innocently. Now go ahead. Do it for a minute or so."

I did as he requested. At the end of the minute, I opened my eyes and asked, "How am I doing?"

"You're still here."

"This is supposed to teleport me to school?"

"It's the way I get around," Peter said. "You've done it yourself, remember? Close your eyes, try again. But don't try too hard. Just picture the school and imagine yourself there. We have plenty of time."

"Indeed we do."

I worked at it for half an hour, and I would have to say that was one of my problems; I couldn't help trying. Finally, I opened my eyes. "I can't see this working," I said.

"That's why it isn't."

"Thank you, Yoda. Feel the force, Luke."

He smiled. "*Star Wars.* Good. Do you remember Peter Pan?"

I began to shake my head. "I'm not flying. No way."

He bounced up. "Anybody can fly, even the living. There are yogis in India who float from one mountaintop to another. I've seen them. But it's easier when you don't have a physical body. Watch this."

Taking an extraordinary leap upward, Peter crossed his legs lotus-style in midair and hovered a half-dozen feet above my head. "Christ," I whispered.

"Just Saint Peter, please. See how easy it is? Come on up."

"I can't. I can't get into a full lotus."

"How your legs are crossed is unimportant. All that matters is that you understand you can do it and that you have no fear of hurting yourself. Let's fly, Shari Poppins."

"*Can* I hurt myself?" I asked.

"That's impossible at this point. Now jump up."

I jumped. I didn't go very high, and I landed quickly. I tried it again, trying to pretend I was light as a feather. It didn't work. "Can't I hold on to you like Lois Lane did in *Superman*?" I asked.

"No. Your lead-foot mentality would make me sink."

"Why do I have to *learn* to do this?"

"You are not learning to do it. You're unlearning the belief that you *can't* do it. Try again, without trying."

It's hard not to try when you're trying not to. I couldn't get off the ground, not even far enough to break Hazzard High's high-jump record. Peter finally floated down to my side.

"It'll come in time," he said.

"I feel that if I had a broom I could pretend better."

"I could get you one if you think it would help."

"Really? Where?" I asked.

"I could make you one."

"How?"

He gestured to the stuff in the air, which I had begun to forget about. "When you were alive," he said, "you were in a realm of matter. There's matter here, too, but it is of a finer nature and more easily manipulated. All I have to do is put my attention on a broom and the ether around us will generate one."

"Could you make me some new clothes?"

"Sure."

"Could you change the color of my eyes?" I asked.

"Yeah."

"My body?"

"What's wrong with your body?"

"I didn't think anything was wrong with it until someone told me it was just *fine*."

He laughed. "Would you like bigger breasts?"

"No, I'd like—What color are my eyes?"

"Green. Why?"

"You are a saint." I hugged him. "Never mind, I'm satisfied with the way I look. And forget about the broom. I was never into witches like Jo."

"You'll have to walk," he warned, sounding like the good witch in *The Wizard of Oz*.

"Can't I hitch rides?"

"If you get through the car doors." He pointed to the tree. "Walk through that trunk."

"No way. There're bugs beneath the bark. Hey, that's something I wanted to ask you about. How come I touch things, but don't really touch them?"

"Because you're dead."

"Yes, we've already covered that. What I mean is, my feet are touching the ground right now. The ground is supporting me. How come I don't just sink into it?"

"Because you *expect* the ground to support you," Peter said. "It's all in your mind." He paused. "Since you died, has a part of your body passed through anything physical?"

"Yeah. When I tried to grab Jimmy at the hospital, my hand went right through his arm."

Peter nodded. "You were probably desperate at the time and dropped your psychological inhibitions. The point is you've already seen that it can be done." He gestured to the bench. "Walk through that."

"All right." I had finally decided it was time to stop messing around. I strode toward the bench as if it wasn't there. I was furious when I cracked my shin on the wood. "Ouch!" I cried, bending over in pain.

"It only hurts because you think it hurts."

"Would you shut up! It hurts! I don't care why it hurts!"

"Imagine that it doesn't," he said.

"I'd rather have an aspirin and a glass of water."

Because I was bent over and rubbing my poor leg, I didn't see any flash and glitter. Maybe there wasn't any. The next thing I knew, he was handing me an aspirin and a glass of water.

"Swallow it, and let's get out of here," he said.

CHAPTER X

WE TOOK THE BUS. The doors opened automatically. We didn't have to worry about correct change. I was thankful for small favors. We had to catch a couple of connections to get to my neighborhood. The last bus we got on was jammed. I stood with several people while Peter sat on a cute blonde's lap.

"Pervert," I said.

"You think sex is dirty. You have a dirty mind."

"I think sex is fine between two consenting *living* adults."

"What about between two dead adolescents?" he asked.

I just laughed. I didn't believe he was serious.

Daniel's house was closer to the bus stop than my own. I told Peter I wanted to check on my old beau. A window around the side was open. Peter had to help me up. He didn't need any help. As I turned around inside, he was already heading from the kitchen into the living room. There were voices. Big Beth and Spam.

They were making out on the couch. Daniel had his hand under her blouse. She was undoing his belt. They were both groaning. Peter stood above them shaking his head.

"And you're not even cold in your grave," he said.

"Peter," I moaned, deeply hurt. He was by my side instantly.

"I'm sorry. That was tactless." He put his arm around my waist. "Are you OK?"

"I think I'm going to be sick."

"No, you're definitely not going to do that. Let's go in the kitchen."

"I want to leave!"

"Not yet. This might get interesting. I mean, as far as your case is concerned. Come on."

We sat at the kitchen table. I could still hear them in the next room. I stared at the apples in the fruit bowl and wished I could stuff one down each of their throats. "I thought he cared about me," I whispered.

"You get used to it," Peter said.

"No."

"Forget him. He was trash."

I chuckled sadly. "Your brother said he was an asshole."

"He's a smart guy."

"Yeah. If he was so smart, what was he doing with Beth?"

"Well," Peter said, peeking around the corner of the kitchen into the living room. "I suppose he had a couple of good reasons."

Someone knocked at the front door. We jumped up, but not nearly so fast as Daniel and Beth. They were busy pulling themselves together when we reentered the living room.

"Just a minute!" Beth called.

"Shh! This is my house," Daniel said. "Just a minute!"

Peter peeked out the window. "We're in luck, Shari. It's Garrett. He's caught them red-handed."

"He's a couple of minutes early," I growled.

The kids finally got themselves presentable and answered the door. Garrett was not wearing his frumpy green sports coat, but his unironed black shirt was a questionable improvement. He looked as if he had spent the night with his head bent over a toilet. He needed a shave in the worst way.

"May I come in?" he asked Daniel.

"I don't know." Daniel glanced at Beth. "This is sort of a bad time."

"I bet," Garrett said, stepping inside anyway. "Are your folks home?"

"No," Daniel said.

"Good." He took out the notepad he had brought to Beth's condo. "I'd like to ask you two a couple of questions." He gestured to the couch. "Have a seat."

Daniel and Beth sat down. Garrett pulled up a footstool. "Did you go to the funeral?" he asked.

"Yes," Daniel said.

"It was sad," Beth said.

"They usually are." Garrett coughed as he clicked open his ballpoint pen. "Did either of you push Shari off the balcony?"

Daniel gave a ridiculous smile. "What?"

"Did you kill your girlfriend?"

"She jumped," Beth said.

"Did you see her jump?" Garrett asked.

"No," Beth said.

"I didn't push her," Daniel said. "Jo can tell you that."

"She wouldn't tell me if she stood by and let you push her," Garrett said.

Daniel stopped smiling. "I don't believe, sir, that we have to answer your questions."

"You do have the right to remain silent," Garrett agreed.

Daniel nodded self-righteously. "I know my rights."

"But that's only if you've been arrested. I'll have to arrest you if you want to remain silent."

"I love this cop," Peter said.

"Shh," I said.

Daniel and Beth exchanged uneasy glances. "We didn't kill her," Beth said. "What else can we tell you?"

"Was Jo on the balcony before you?" Garrett asked her.

"She says she got there after me," Beth said.

"What do you say?"

"I don't know. I told you, it was dark."

"It wasn't that dark. The balcony's not that big. What was the matter with you that night, Beth? Were you drunk?"

"She doesn't drink," Daniel said.

"I'm asking her," Garrett said.

Beth put her hands to her mouth and grimaced. "I don't know what was wrong with me."

Garrett leaned forward. "Were you mad at Shari?"

"No."

"Why not?"

"Because . . . s-she was my friend," Beth stammered.

"How could she be your friend when she was going out with your boyfriend?" Garrett asked.

"Dan wasn't my boyfriend."

"Is he your boyfriend now?"

"No," Daniel interrupted.

"No," Beth echoed weakly.

Garrett turned to Daniel. "When you were on the balcony, did you see Amanda come out of the bathroom? Please try to remember as best you can, or I might have to arrest you."

"I saw her."

"Are you positive?"

"Yes."

Garrett closed his notepad and stood. "That's all for now."

Daniel's fear turned to anger. "Why are you hassling us like this? You have no right."

Garrett stared down at him for a moment—way down; he

appeared to be studying Daniel's feet. Then his eyes flickered upward, and he reached over and plucked something from Daniel's shirt pocket before Daniel could stop him.

It was an unopened condom.

"What's this for?" he asked.

"It's none of your goddamn business," Daniel snapped.

Garrett tossed the condom into Daniel's lap. "You may think you're practicing safe sex, son." He smiled and put his notepad away. "But you're not even close."

Garrett left. Peter wanted to go after him.

"He's probably going to question the others," Peter told me. "We can ride in the back of his truck and not have to worry about the buses. Come on."

"No. I want to see what these two have to say."

"They're just going to have sex." Peter paused. "I suppose we could stay."

They did not have sex. The instant Garrett was out the door, Beth burst out crying. Daniel tried to comfort her.

"He was just bluffing," Daniel said. "He's not going to arrest us." He put his hands on the back of her neck as she wept into the couch cushion. "Hey, babe. I'm here. It's all right."

She sat up suddenly, throwing off his hands. "I shouldn't be here! We shouldn't be together!"

"Why not? You said you liked me."

Beth gave him an incredulous look. "Dan, Shari's dead. We just buried her." She glanced around, obviously confused about how she had come to be where she was. She stood. "I've got to get out of here."

Daniel tried to stop her. "I'm upset, too. You know, she was *my* girlfriend."

"If she was your girlfriend, why are you trying to make like you hardly knew her?"

"That's not true."

"Let me go. It is." She went to shove him away and then stopped. Looking at his face, her own changed. The ding-dong expression vanished. "It is true," she said, a note of regret in her voice.

Beth left. Daniel let her.

"Shari," Peter said. "We have to get into Garrett's truck."

"Just a second," I said. Daniel just stood there staring at the closed door before finally trudging upstairs to his bedroom. I went with him. Peter remained behind. Plopping down on his bed, Daniel opened a drawer in his nightstand and took out a picture of me in my white prom dress. My corsage was huge, as big as my smile. He had pinned it on me only a couple of hours before the picture had been taken. He had told me how beautiful I was, and that night he had been beautiful.

Now he looked old.

"Shari," he said, biting his lower lip. I had to move closer. I couldn't believe what I was seeing. They were tears.

I might have taken pleasure in them or even wept with him. But he didn't give me the chance. A second later he hurled my picture against the far wall, breaking the glass. Then he buried his face in his pillow, and all I could hear was his heavy breathing.

"Catch you later," I said.

Downstairs, Peter hurried me out the window. We hopped into the back of Garrett's truck as he pulled away, heading in the opposite direction from Beth. Garrett did not fail to note Beth's hasty departure.

"I heard something break?" Peter asked.

"It was nothing," I said.

Garrett went to Jeff Nichols's place next, Peter's old house. I could tell that's where we were headed a couple of blocks before we got there. I had an eye on Peter, but he appeared undisturbed by our destination.

"I never asked you," I said. "What was it like when you died?"

"What do you mean?"

"Did you know you were dead?"

"Oh, yeah," Peter said. "I didn't black out like you did. I was on my motorbike one moment with the wind in my face, and the next thing I knew, I was standing on the road beside my body and a huge semi." He shrugged. "There was a lot of blood. I knew it was over."

"It was the truck driver's fault, wasn't it?"

"No."

"That's what I read in the papers."

"It was my fault."

"Really? What happened?" I asked.

"I was careless."

"Did someone meet you on this side and help you along?"

"I was worse than you," he said.

"What do you mean?"

He smiled faintly but refused to elaborate.

Jeff was out front, working on his motorcycle. The love of fast machines obviously ran in the family. Jeff had grease on his hands, a cigarette in his mouth, and a half-finished six-pack sitting beside a ratchet set. He hardly glanced up as Garrett climbed out of his truck and walked toward him.

"Busy?" Garrett asked.

"I suppose."

"Can I have a beer?"

Now Jeff looked at Garrett. He set down his tools and handed Garrett a can. "It's not cold," he warned.

"That's all right, I'm on duty," Garrett said, popping the beer and taking a deep drink. "Thanks. I wanted to ask you a couple of questions."

"I have nothing to add to what I said the other night."

"You like beer, Jeff?"

"Yeah. Do you?"

"I like whiskey." Garrett finished his can and set it beside Jeff's pile on the cement driveway. The Nicholses were fairly well-off. Their house was roughly the size of my own. Jeff appeared to be the only one home. Garrett pulled out his note-pad. "Were you drinking the night of the party?" he asked.

"Yeah."

"How much did you have to drink?"

"I wasn't drunk," Jeff said.

"How much?"

"Two or three cans."

"Following the seance, why did you try to go to the bath-room in Beth's bedroom when you had just seen Amanda go in there?"

"Beats me."

"You can do better than that," Garrett said.

"I had to take a leak. I just went in there. I didn't give it a lot of thought. Want another beer?"

"No. When you were in Beth's bedroom, did you hear any-thing that would indicate Amanda was actually in there?"

"I don't know. Maybe," Jeff said.

"Could you be more specific?"

"I thought I heard water running."

"What was your relationship with Shari?"

"I didn't have one," Jeff said.

"Weren't you friends?" Garrett asked.

"No."

"Did you dislike her?"

"Not really."

"Would you say she was suicidal?"

"I told you, I hardly knew her."

"What is your relationship with Beth?"

"I used to go out with her," Jeff said.

"When did you stop going out with her?"

"The night of the party."

"Why?" Garrett asked.

"It started to get old."

"What is your relationship with Joanne Foulton?"

"We're friends."

"Have you ever dated?"

"No," Jeff said.

"Might you in the future?"

"I doubt it."

"What's your sign, Jeff?"

"Huh?"

"Your astrological sign. What is it?"

"I'm a Scorpio."

"You don't strike me as the type who'd be into astrology."

"I'm not," Jeff said.

"How did you know what sign you were? Did Joanne tell you?"

Jeff hesitated. "That's right," he said flatly.

The phone inside the garage rang. Jeff went to get it. I tagged along and pressed my ear to the receiver as he answered it. Garrett stayed in the driveway.

"Hi, Jeff, this is Jo. Am I calling at a bad time?"

"Sort of," Jeff said.

"I won't keep you. I just wanted to tell you that I'd like you to come over to my house tonight at ten o'clock."

"What for?"

"You'll see when you get here, but it's important."

"I can't make it," Jeff said.

"It has to do with Shari. The group's going to be here.

Jeff glanced at Garrett. "Can't make it."

"Come on, Jeff. Please? It really is important."

"I'll think about it."

Jo paused. "All right. I hope you come."

Jeff set down the phone and returned to Garrett and his bike. He picked up his ratchet. "Finished with your questions?" he asked.

"Just about," Garrett said. "Who was that?"

"Some girl."

Garrett gestured to Jeff's greasy white sneakers. "Are those the shoes you wore to the party?"

"Maybe."

"Are you sure you didn't have on black shoes?"

"I don't remember."

Garrett put away his notepad. "Those sneakers are a mess. I doubt Beth would have let you into her place with them on." He turned to leave. "Take it easy, son."

"You, too, Lieutenant."

Peter and I climbed into the back of Garrett's truck again. Garrett started the engine, and we were on our way. It had to be close to seven; the sun was nearing the horizon. I couldn't get over how the breeze was not messing up my hair.

"Who was on the phone?" Peter asked.

"Jo. She wanted Jeff to go over there tonight. She said the gang would be there. It's supposed to be about me."

"We'll have to stop by," Peter said.

"You bet. What did you think of Jeff?"

"He didn't do it, Shari."

"But he was so evasive."

"That's just the way he is."

"Why do you think Garrett asked Jeff about his shoes?"

"I was wondering that myself," Peter said.

I soon regretted hitching a ride on the truck. Garrett left our neighborhood and got on the freeway. He headed west, toward downtown L.A. Peter told me I could jump off any time I wanted, but my shin still hurt from the park bench.

We got off the freeway in a crummy part of town. It was dark by then. Garrett stopped at the first liquor store we came to. He bought himself a pint of whiskey and drank half of it before he left the parking lot.

"I think we should get off now," I said as Garrett restarted the truck.

"I wouldn't worry about him crashing," Peter said.

"I am worried. I don't want to be late to Jo's get-together."

"I won't be late. I can always just pop over."

"Lucky you. What do you think Garrett's doing in this sleazy part of town?"

"He's probably going to buy drugs," Peter said.

For a while I thought maybe Peter *was* psychic. Garrett rode several blocks north to Sunset Boulevard, to the bad end of Hollywood, where the porn shops and hookers carved out their existence. Garrett could have been searching for a pusher. He parked on a side street a hundred yards off the big boulevard and reached for a pair of binoculars. I noticed again the telescopic vision I'd had at the cemetery; I was able to follow Garrett's magnified gaze without effort. He was studying a tall, pasty white dude leaning against a streetlight. The guy looked like a threat to young girls everywhere. He had on tight black leather pants and an orange Day-Glo shirt. A thin gold chain circled his shaved head.

"He wasn't at the party, was he, Shari?" Peter asked.

"Hardly. What's Garrett doing?"

"Let's wait and see."

A half hour later, I began to fret. I could see Garrett's watch through the rear window. It was just past eight-thirty. "We have to go," I complained.

"Not yet," Peter said, gesturing to the dude on the corner as Garrett simultaneously leaned forward inside the truck. Someone was approaching. "Look at her. Wow."

The girl had long straight black hair and a cute heart-shaped mouth. Her face was bony, her dark eyes set deep and wide. She needed a decent meal; she was thin as a rail. Yet her dress was conservative: a longish gray skirt and a freshly pressed white blouse. I understood Peter's wow—she was beautiful.

"I know her," I said.

"She was at the party?" Peter asked.

"Would you shut up." She was several years older, but it was definitely the girl in the picture Garrett carried in his wallet. I cringed as she embraced the slime on the corner. "What could she be doing with him?" I asked. "Is he her pimp?"

"I doubt it," Peter said. "She doesn't have the hooker look. But she could be an addict. The guy could be her connection. How do you know her?"

"I've seen her before."

"I hope Garrett invites her for a ride in his truck."

Garrett, however, did not make his presence known. He continued to follow the couple until the slimeball kissed the girl on the neck and slipped a plastic Baggie holding white powder into her hand. Then Garrett lowered his binoculars and leaned his head back on the seat, reaching for what was left of his bottle.

"It's his daughter," I said, understanding at last. The couple parted company, heading in opposite directions along the boulevard.

"Are you serious?" Peter asked. "A cop with an addict for a daughter? Sounds like TV. Hey, where are you going?"

"I want to follow her," I said, leaping out of the truck.

"If you insist," Peter said, catching up with me in the blink of an eye.

The girl did not go far before she turned into a discount motel half a block off Sunset. The place was not only run-down, the stuff that clung to its walls was choked with the threads of shadows I had first seen in the hospital. Only these threads were thicker and twisted at sharp angles like a form of astral barbed wire.

"What is that?" I asked, pointing.

"Pain," Peter said.

"Is that what people mean by bad vibes?"

"Most definitely."

"Can it hurt us?" I asked.

"If we let it."

We followed the girl into the lobby. The guy at the desk nodded to her as she strode by. Her room was on the second floor. She opened it with a silver key she took from her black boot. Surprisingly, inside it was fairly neat. The sheets on the bed were clean, and the paint on the walls was a fresh blue. But the threads of darkness were now rope thick. I kept thinking they would cut me if I bumped against them.

I don't know what I hoped to discover. She was in the room less than a minute when she got out the Baggie of pow-der, a syringe, a spoon, and a rubber tourniquet on the stand beside her bed. It was sickening to watch. She set a portion of the powder into the spoon and mixed it with water. Then she pulled out a lighter and ran the flame beneath the solution. I had to turn away a minute later when she steered the needle toward her vein.

"Why don't we leave?" Peter asked.

I nodded weakly. "All right." But the girl had closed the door as she came in. I had to go out the window. As I peered into the night with Peter and tried to estimate what the fall to the pavement would do to my supposedly invincible legs, I noticed the girl staring at me with wide, dilated pupils.

"Hi," I said.

"Hi," she whispered.

I jumped so high I almost hit my head on the ceiling. "Peter, she can see me!"

He was not impressed. "Sometimes, when the living are in an altered state of consciousness, they can glimpse the realm we're in."

"Are you serious? Why should a drug give someone special powers?" The girl continued to stare at me with her weird, unblinking blue eyes.

"It is hardly a power," Peter said. "At best, drugs can give a peek at where we are. They never give people an insight into the higher realms you would now be enjoying had you followed my advice this morning. They often do the opposite, opening the mind to dark levels, to madness."

"I want to talk to her," I said.

"Why? She's stoned. You'll be late to Jo's meeting."

"Just a sec." I strode to the bed, where the girl now lay stretched out. Her head followed me as I moved.

"Hi," she said again.

"Listen," I said, sitting beside her. "You're blowing it. You're a great-looking girl. This is no life for you. You're messing up your dad's life as well. He's drinking himself into the grave because of you. He's so screwed up he can't find the person who murdered me."

"Murder," she mumbled.

"Careful," Peter said. "Don't give her any ideas."

I stood. "We're going to have another talk, you and me," I told her. "As soon as I figure out what you need to hear."

The jump to the pavement didn't slow me down a beat. We rode a fire truck back to the freeway, where we caught an ice-cream truck heading east. We didn't exactly get invited into the front seat. The freeway rushed beneath us, and Peter laughed at me for hugging the brightly lit cherry snowcone on top.

CHAPTER XI

JIMMY AND AMANDA were sitting in Jimmy's station wagon at the end of Jo's driveway when we arrived. I told Peter to go on ahead while I eavesdropped on their conversation. I did it without feeling a twinge of guilt. That's one good thing about being a ghost. When all you can do is watch and listen, you feel you should be allowed to watch and listen to everything.

Amanda had her arm around Jimmy's shoulder, and that annoyed me. Here she wouldn't even return his calls, I thought, and I die and now she's in love. It was sort of a ridiculous thought. Actually, I was happy she was taking good care of him. He looked pretty messed up. He had his window down, and I stood by his side as they talked.

"I don't know," Jimmy was saying. "Maybe I should have stayed home. I wasn't invited."

"Jo won't mind you coming," Amanda said.

"I guess not."

"Are you worried about your mom?"

"I probably shouldn't have left her alone," Jimmy said.

"We can always go back."

"We're here. We may as well see what Jo wants." He glanced toward the house, shaking his head. "Someone in there—"

"What?"

"Nothing."

Amanda knew what he meant. Jimmy thought my murderer must be in the house. She let it pass. "Are your parents still thinking of going away tomorrow?" she asked.

"Yeah. My dad wants to get my mom out of the house."

"Are you going to go?" Amanda asked.

"I haven't decided."

She kissed him on the cheek. "If you don't, I'll come over to see you."

He looked at her. "I'll be lousy company."

She smiled. "I don't mind."

They got out of his car and walked toward the house. They almost bumped into Mrs. Foulton coming out the front door. She had on her nurse's uniform and was in her usual hurry.

"I didn't know everyone was coming over," she said, and I immediately understood why Jo had set the meeting for ten o'clock and not earlier—she had thought her mother would already be at work. "What's up?" she asked.

"Jo just said to come," Amanda replied. "She said it was important."

"Yeah, well, she thinks everything she does is important," Mrs. Foulton said, turning to Jimmy. "How are your parents?"

"Not good," Jimmy said.

Mrs. Foulton nodded sympathetically. "I thought that service was never going to end. That minister read practically the whole Bible. I wish that—that he hadn't done that." She had been on the verge of saying something else. Jimmy was making her nervous. She fussed over Amanda's hair, brushing it away from her eyes. Amanda was her favorite niece. "Your mother just called," she said. "She was looking for you."

Amanda took Jimmy's arm. "Really?"

Mrs. Foulton's uneasiness increased, for no apparent reason. "She wanted to know when you would be home."

"I'll call her," Amanda said.

"I'm really sorry about Shari," she said to Jimmy, leaving in a hurry.

I followed Jimmy and Amanda into the house. I had never seen the place so clean. Everyone was in the living room. I was surprised to see Jeff—he was lounging on the couch with Jo. Beth and Daniel were not close to each other; they were sitting stiffly in chairs and avoiding each other's eyes.

"What's Jo want?" I asked Peter, who was planted cross-legged on top of the TV.

"She's been waiting for everyone to get here," Peter said.

"But as soon as her mother stepped outside the door, she went for her Ouija board."

"Oh my," I said, interested. "Do those things really work?"

"What do you mean?"

"Can we talk to them through it?"

He shrugged. "They can work. Sometimes."

"I guess you're all wondering why I invited you here," Jo said as Jimmy and Amanda took a seat on the floor. Jo had finally put on her black dress—better late than never, I supposed. The Ouija board rested on the coffee table at her knees. Jeff gestured to it and snorted.

"You want to use that thing again," he said, annoyed. "You should have told us. We wouldn't have come."

If the remark hurt her, Jo showed no sign of it. "I know this may seem like the wrong time," she said. "God knows this has been an awful day. But think back to the party just before Shari jumped up and ran to the balcony. Something remarkable happened. I think we contacted Peter."

Jeff took a deep drag on his cigarette and ground it out. I wouldn't have been surprised to see him leave. Yet he said nothing, nor did he move to get up. I turned to Peter.

"Is that true?" I asked.

He spoke reluctantly. "Yes."

I grabbed him. "You used *my* body to talk to them?"

"Yes."

"But that's—that's obscene!"

"You volunteered to act as a channel."

"But I didn't know it was real!"

Peter was embarrassed. "I know, Shari, and I'm sorry. I just wanted the chance to talk to my brother."

I refused to accept his apology. I was furious with him, and I wasn't even sure why. But I was a hypocrite. I was wondering if it could be done again.

"It was just Shari talking," Daniel said.

"It was more than that," Jo said. "I can't be the only one who thinks this way. What do you say, Amanda?"

"I hardly knew Peter," she said.

"How about you, Beth?" Jo asked, sounding less sure of herself.

Beth didn't answer immediately. I remembered that Peter used to talk to her frequently—probably out of respect for her big breasts.

"There was something in Shari's voice," Beth said finally, confused. "It gave me gooseflesh."

"Why?" Jeff asked sharply, sitting up.

"It sounded like him," Beth said. "I mean, it sounded like Shari, but also like Peter, using Shari's voice."

"She's smarter than she looks," I said, scowling at Peter.

"You knew Peter best of all," Jo said to Jeff. "*Did* it sound like him?"

He began to snap at her. He was mad. But he was also confused. He pulled out another cigarette. "If you want to use the board, then let's do it and get it over with," he growled.

"Excuse me," Jimmy said, breaking in. "I'm missing something here. Why do you want to do this now? Tonight?"

"I want to talk to Shari," Jo said. She raised her hand when the group started to protest. "What happened at the party makes me feel it's possible. I don't think she's left yet. I've read a lot on this subject. It's normal for someone who has recently passed over to hang around for several days. We must try to contact her before she leaves."

"That's my girl," I said.

"Don't get carried away," Peter warned.

"But Jo knows what she's talking about," I said.

Peter was unconvinced. "She has some knowledge. But a little knowledge is often dangerous."

"But can we talk to them?" I insisted.

"Let's see," Peter said.

"But Peter has been dead two years," Daniel said. "How did we get ahold of him?"

"Sometimes people have reasons to stay," Jo said.

"Showers they have to attend," I agreed.

"I don't believe any of this," Daniel said.

There followed an uncomfortable silence. Except for Jo, I doubted any of them honestly believed they could communicate with either Peter or me. Yet I also realized even before they took their vote that most of them probably felt that if there was one chance in a thousand it wouldn't hurt to try. It both excited and depressed me to see from Jimmy's expression that he was willing to give it a try. He had never been into such nonsense, and it didn't matter now that it might not be non-sense; it just hurt to see how desperate he had become.

Jo called for a vote. Daniel was the only one who was opposed. The others went along. They moved to the kitchen table. Jo lit a candle and turned down the lights, handing Jimmy a paper and pencil to keep notes. That surprised me, since he had obviously been closer to me than anybody. Per-haps Jo felt he was too upset to act as a medium, I thought. Jimmy did not appear to mind his role. The Ouija board was placed in the center of the table, and Jo instructed everyone to lightly rest the fingertips of one hand on the planchette. Daniel continued to be stubborn.

"I'd rather watch," he said.

"And I'd rather you joined us," Jo said. "I want the same group mind we had at the party."

"The same what?" Beth asked.

"It won't hurt you," Jo told Daniel.

He finally gave in. I strode back to Peter, who was still on top of the TV. "I am getting tired of your vagueness," I said.

"Why don't we see what they come up with on their own before we interfere," he said.

"They won't come up with anything. How do we interfere?"

Peter stood. "You have to put your hands inside their hands."

"*Inside?* I can't do that."

"You could if you really wanted to," Peter said.

"Come in here," I said, taking him by the arm. The session was already under way. The planchette was coasting wildly over the board beneath their fingers. Jo was the only one who had two hands on the plastic indicator. Jeff still had a cigarette dangling from his mouth.

"Who's there?" Jo asked.

"Peter and Shari," I said loudly.

The planchette continued to roll in meaningless circles. "Who's doing this?" Daniel asked.

"I'm not," Amanda said.

"You're making it move," Daniel accused Jo.

"Shh," Beth said.

"Give it a few minutes," Jo said. She asked again. "Who's there?"

The indicator looped over the letters for a minute more before beginning to swing in an arc between YES and NO. It was amazing how fast it moved.

"Is anybody there?" Jo asked. "Shari?"

"They'll quit soon if we don't answer," I said to Peter, beginning to panic. "Do something!"

"You can do it, if you must," Peter said. "Blend your hands in with theirs. If they don't resist, you should be able to steer the indicator where you want."

"I can't," I said. "You saw what happened when I tried to

walk through the bench. If I put my flesh inside theirs . . ." I shuddered at the thought. "I might start bleeding."

"You don't have any blood," Peter said.

"This is stupid," Daniel remarked.

"Why aren't you helping me?" I pleaded.

Peter looked me straight in the face. "It's what I've been trying to tell you all along. The dead shouldn't mingle with the living. It only leads to problems."

"But you mingled," I said in a cold voice. "More than once. Why did Beth feel so weird when Jo used the magnet on her? Was it because you merged your legs with hers? Was it because you were *inside* her?"

Peter hesitated, then nodded. "You're very perceptive. I used to think that even when we were both alive."

"Please answer if you can, Shari," Jo said as the planchette swung back and forth like a dead man at the end of a short rope.

"Then it's true," I said.

"Yes," Peter said.

It made little sense, but it was only then, when I no longer trusted him, and when I ached because of it, that I realized how much he meant to me. "Did what you do have anything to do with how I died?" I asked, so softly that even a ghost might not have heard.

"I don't think so, Shari." He lowered his head. "I don't know for sure, but I really don't think so."

"I'm getting a headache," Beth said.

"We should stop," Daniel said.

"Do it," I ordered Peter, pointing to the board. "I think you owe me."

Peter sighed and moved to the table, standing between Jo and Jeff. As he plunged his hands into the others, I felt my guts heave, even though I probably didn't have any of those, either. Yet it was fascinating to watch. Faint blue sparks flickered in the places where his fingers moved in and out of the group's. He directed the planchette toward the happy-face sun in the corner of the board.

It followed his direction.

"Something's happening," Jo said, excited.

"Who's doing this?" Daniel asked.

"Shut up," Jeff said, taking his cigarette from his mouth and grinding it out in the glass tray that held the candle. It was a green candle this time, but on my side of the mirror the flame looked more silvery than orange, more like ice than fire. The indicator stopped above the sun. I stepped to Peter's side.

"Who's there?" Jo asked.

"Spell my name," I told him.

"I'll try," he said.

"It's coming," Jo said. "S—H—E—R—"

"No!" I shouted. "Goddamnit, Peter! It's Shari with an *a*."

"How should I know?"

"It was on my tombstone, for Christ's sake," I said.

"Your tombstone isn't up yet," Peter said.

"In biology, the whole stupid year we were partners, it was written in big block letters on my lab notebook!"

"What's wrong?" Jimmy asked, clenching his pencil tightly.

"It's stopped," Jo said.

"Start over," I said. "No, finish it. Then spell out your name."

"We have to concentrate harder," Jo said.

"Oh, no," Peter said.

"What?" I asked.

"When they strain, they block me out," Peter said, shifting his hands so that they overlapped as many living fingers as possible. The faint blue sparks brightened and took on a purple tinge. The planchette began to move again. "Something's wrong," he muttered.

"Are you being blocked?" I asked.

"I don't—" Peter began.

"P—E—T—E—R," Jo spelled out loud.

"It's working," I said.

Peter frowned, started to speak, then stopped.

"Peter," Jo said. "Is that you?"

The planchette swung to YES.

"Is Shari there?" Jo asked.

The planchette circled the YES.

Jo smiled. "I told you guys."

"We could be making this happen," Jeff said, doubtful.

"Tell them hello for me," I said, excited. "Tell them I'm all right and that I didn't kill myself."

"This is real," Jo said.

"I don't know," Peter said, still frowning.

"You do it!" I said.

"Ask how Shari is," Jimmy said, his eyes big.

"Shari," Jo said. "Are you all right?"

The planchette went to NO.

"Peter!" I cried.

"It's not me," he said.

"What's wrong with her?" Jimmy asked.

"We have to be careful how we phrase our questions," Jo said. "Naturally, as far as we're concerned, she's not all right. She's dead."

"Ask if Shari and Peter are together," Jimmy said.

"We've already asked that," Daniel said, and there could have been a twinge of jealousy in his voice. "It said yeah."

"Ask again," Jeff said.

"Shari," Jo said. "Is Peter there with you?"

The planchette glided to YES.

"Good," I said.

"No," Peter said.

"What is it?" I said. "Don't stop."

Peter took his hands out of the others, put them back in, trying, so it seemed, to get a better grip on the situation. "There is another force at work here," he said.

"Where are you?" Jeff asked directly, bypassing Jo.

"T—O—G—E—T—H—E—R," Jo spelled out.

"Good," I said. "Tell them we're happy."

"Where are you together?" Jeff asked. "Is it a place?"

The planchette went to NO.

"Where?" Jeff insisted.

"B—U—R—N—I—N—G," Jo said and winced. "What?"

"Burning," Jimmy said softly, staring at the candle.

"No!" I yelled at Peter. "Stop it!"

Peter did not respond. He was struggling with the planchette. Tiny sparks cracked at the tips of his fingers—I could hear them as well as see them. But the indicator kept moving.

"H—E—L—L," Jo said slowly.

"Hell," Beth whispered. "Burning in hell."

I should not have exploded at Peter right then. I could see he was having trouble directing the planchette. I knew he would not have willfully tried to hurt either me or Jimmy. I suppose his admission of having used my body was still bothering me. Also, when I saw Jimmy, his face pinched and withdrawn, suddenly stand and run from the room, I lost all control.

"You bastard!" I yelled. "Look what you've done!"

"I didn't write that," he protested, removing his hands from the planchette. As if it had become too hot to touch, the others did likewise. Amanda pushed away from the table and went after my brother.

"Don't suicides always go to hell?" Daniel asked.

"My brother didn't kill himself," Jeff said to Jo, disgusted, knocking the board off the table, almost knocking the burning candle onto the floor.

"I'm sorry," Jo said miserably.

"You did it on purpose!" I screamed at Peter.

"No," he said.

Jimmy was already out of the house. Amanda had her hand on the front door as I turned after her. She slammed the door shut behind her. Fortunately, it bounced open, and I was able to get outside. I followed her down the driveway. Jimmy wasn't in his car. Amanda searched up and down the dark street but couldn't find him. She didn't have my magical eyes. I could see him running fast beneath the shadows of the oak branches that hung like tired arms over the deserted sidewalk. I knew how foolish he could be when he was upset, and I feared for his safety. I went after him.

But I never reached him.

The faster I chased my brother, the slower I appeared to move, and the greater my anxiety became. I was trapped in the nightmare again where I was fleeing from the monster with the scales, claws, and dripping teeth. Only now the monster was in front of me.

It came out of my brother. One instant my eyes were focused on the clear outline of Jimmy's back, and the next the outline blurred into a whirling vortex of dust and pain. A pair of gaping green holes in place of eyes peered at me from deep inside it.

It was the Shadow.

I stopped dead on the street. Yes, I was dead in this arena, it seemed to say to me, while it was very much alive. It was still strong and powerful while I was only a shadow of my former self. It was hungry, and I was easy pickings.

I turned to flee but tripped over a mound of unsettled earth that shouldn't have been there. I landed in a terrible place. The sidewalk was gone. I was back in the cemetery, my hands buried in the mud that covered my dead body. I raised my head and glanced over my shoulder to see if my assailant had followed me in my leap through space. But the cemetery was empty. I saw only a rectangular tombstone standing tall at the foot of my grave: SHARI ANN COOPER.

My name was carved on the top in red block letters. The stone shone a faint purple, and as I watched, it began to clear, like a mirror as the dust is wiped away. I stood, brushing off the dirt that I imagined would have stained my pants if I'd fallen wearing real pants. I knew my tombstone couldn't be up yet, not the night after my funeral, but more than anything else I had encountered since I had gone over the balcony, the stone looked real to me.

It continued to clear, to brighten with the purple light, and my name began to dissolve. It *was* a mirror. I could see myself in it. I couldn't look away. I looked as I had the hour before the party when I had stood half dressed before the mirror in my bedroom with my broken brush in my right hand. And I had thought I had problems then.

Then I began to change. I started to get younger. I looked as I had when I entered high school, my hair long and straight, braces on my crooked teeth. The image held for only a moment; the march back through time continued. Suddenly, I was twelve years old, skinny, and tan as a deer from a summer of swimming in the Gulf of Mexico at my uncle's house in Mississippi. Then I was only five years old and had a joyful gleam in my eyes that I would lose the following year when I entered school.

The years rocketed quickly backward until I was a healthy pink baby sleeping in a white crib. Here the picture froze, inviting my inspection. I leaned closer. A hand was entering the scene from the side. It was a big hand, with red nails as long and sharp as claws. It grabbed my infant form. I screamed.

It was a trap. The light of the mirror died. The tombstone vanished. The Shadow stood in its place. It had a hand out to grab me. I screamed and turned and fled.

"It's awful. It's the most awful thing."

I remembered Peter's warning as I ran down the hill from where I had been buried, and my fear was a knife in my heart. Leaping over a tombstone, I tripped on the steep hill and went sprawling, striking my nose hard on the ground. A bolt of pain exploded in my head. The sound of the Shadow's slobbering breath filled my ears. I scampered to my feet, my lungs burning on the ethereal night air. It was getting closer.

"Peter!" I cried. "Help me!"

He did not appear. I knew I had to get out of the cemetery. If the Shadow caught me in this wasteland of memories and grief, I knew it would drag me under the earth and imprison me in my coffin, where I would be forced to watch the rot of my body for the next hundred years. It knew what frightened me most.

I didn't pause to ask myself how we understood each other's minds so well.

I got as far as the fence that surrounded the cemetery. The black poles and bars that made up the barrier were tall and slippery, crowned at the top with a row of spikes that would have made the most adventurous young lad decide on another place to play. I leaped up and caught hold of a narrow bar a few feet above my head. For several seconds I struggled to pull myself up, my feet thrashing uselessly against the smooth metal. Then I lost my grip and fell into a rose bush ripe with petals of red and thorns of pain. They only cut me because my mind let them, Peter would have said, but they cut me nevertheless.

"Shari."

The word came out like the hiss of a snake as the Shadow halted approximately ten yards from the fence and held out its hand to me. It wasn't an ordinary hand with fingers and a thumb. It didn't even have claws. The hand was more a force that the Shadow wielded to draw me toward it. It was not actually something I saw—more something I sensed. I should have been repulsed—and I was—but I was also drawn to it. Slowly I pulled myself out of the thorns and took a tentative step in the direction of the dark being. Another appendage appeared out of its other side, and the Shadow's pull on me grew stronger. Then I looked up into those eyes again, those pale, bottomless green pits into madness, and I retreated, horrified, pressing my back against the metal poles. I told myself that I was a spirit, that I could slip through the fence and vanish on the wind. It didn't work. The poles remained firm against my flesh. The Shadow took another step toward me.

"Hello," a voice said above me. My head shot up. Peter was relaxing on the top of the spikes.

"Help me up, it's coming!" I shouted.

"What?"

I gestured to the Shadow, which was now less than fifteen feet away. Peter stared at it for several seconds without making a move. I wondered if he had frozen in fright, then dismissed the idea. His expression was relaxed, although slightly puzzled. It was almost as if he couldn't see it.

"Hurry!" I cried, holding up my arm.

"Of course," he said, suddenly reaching down and gripping my hand. He pulled me up without effort. I didn't wait to be lowered gently onto the other side. I jumped and then ran, not looking back.

Peter caught up with me in the park across the street where

he had tried to teach me to fly. I was a trembling wreck by then, but I was still running.

"Shari," he said, trying to stop me.

"We've got to keep going," I said, shaking him off.

"It's gone."

"We've got to get out of here!"

"Shari!" He grabbed me. "It's gone."

I glanced back toward the cemetery. There was nothing, not as far as I could see. "Are you sure?"

"Yes. It's all right," he said. "You're safe."

"Oh, Peter," I moaned, collapsing against his chest.

He led me to the same bench we had sat on before. I don't know how long we sat there with me shivering in his arms. I couldn't get a grip on my fear, and I think it was because I didn't know what was causing it. There was the Shadow, of course, but what was the Shadow? Peter had called it a devil, but only because I had suggested the word. Why had he chosen the name he had? I wanted to ask but was afraid of the answer I would get. It seemed to know my thoughts, I remembered, and vice versa.

A shadow—that no sun had ever cast.

I didn't want to know whose shadow it was.

Peter was talking about escaping into the light again.

"When you least expect it, Shari, it will come after you. You've got to give up trying to find your murderer. You've got to go on. You don't know what you're risking. It's more than your life now."

I raised my head and looked around the park. There wasn't a soul around, not a sound in the air. I wished I could say I felt at peace. "You saw Jimmy's face as he ran out of the room," I said.

"I didn't tell them that we were burning in—"

"I know," I interrupted quietly. "I shouldn't have said what I did. Can you forgive me?"

"Sure." He was so cool.

"But Peter, what happened? What went wrong?"

He shook his head. "I don't know. It started out all right, but then the indicator just went out of control."

"You mentioned that there seemed to be another force at work. Could there have been another spirit in the room that we were unaware of?"

"I doubt it."

"But is it possible?" I asked.

"Yes."

"Is it also possible that a member of the group was purposely manipulating the indicator?"

He had thought of that, of course. He was no dummy. But he didn't want to encourage any line of reasoning that would make me continue my investigation. "If someone was writing what he or she wanted," he said, "that does not necessarily mean that he or she was the one who killed you."

"But to spell what they did—that person would have to hate me." I nodded to myself. "It was one of them."

"So what? Everyone's fingers were on the indicator, and you haven't eliminated a single suspect." He leaned close. "Shari, please, listen to me. You could close your eyes right now and in a minute be in bliss."

I got emotional. "How can I be in bliss when my murderer is walking free? How can I leave my brother thinking I'm in hell? Why can't you see that I can't leave?"

"Because Jimmy can't see you. He can't hear you. He can't feel you. As far as he's concerned, you're already gone."

I shook my head. "There must be some way to get through to them."

"There isn't."

"But what if we found a psychic? Could we communicate with one of them?"

"No."

"They can't all be phonies. Are they?"

He sighed. "There are people who can tap into our realm—without the aid of drugs. There are even some alive on the earth today whose minds can reach to the infinite. But these people are rare. They are not found at your local psychic fairs reading palms. As a rule, they never display their powers."

"But if these people are so enlightened, wouldn't they want to help me?"

"They would help you by instructing you to listen to me and leave the problems of the living to the living. Jimmy is alive, Shari, and your death—terrible as it was—is simply something that he has to go through in his life." Peter paused, his eyes raised to the sky, to the many-colored stars and pulsating nebula that the living would never see. "Jeff had to go through the same thing."

"It must have been terrible for him," I said, thinking how terrible it had been for me when Peter had died. Indeed, with his next question, I could have told him exactly how difficult it had been. I don't know why I didn't.

"Did anyone close to you ever die?" he asked.

"My aunt Clara. She was my father's sister. She helped raise me." I smiled at the memory. "When I was a kid, I saw more of her than I did my mom. She was crazy but such a sweetheart. She used to feed me a diet of soda and cookies. She figured if that's what kids liked best, then it must be good for them." I stopped smiling. "I was fourteen when she died. She got cancer. One day she was fine, and the next . . ." I gestured helplessly. "It went right through her body like poison."

"You must have missed her an awful lot."

Was he trying to tell me I could see her if I would go into the light? I might have asked if the "Big Idea" hadn't hit me a few seconds later.

"That's strange you should say that," I began. "I didn't, not really. I don't know why. It might have been because of these dreams I started to have of her not long after she died, where she would talk to me and tell me that she was—" My voice didn't just trail off. It got caught in my throat. Then it exploded. "Peter!"

I startled him. "What's wrong?"

"That's it!"

"What's it?"

"My aunt used to talk to me in my dreams! I can talk to Jimmy in his!" I jumped up. "Let's get back to my place."

"How?"

"I don't care how. We'll take another fire engine if we have to."

"No. How are you going to get inside his dreams?"

I sat back down. "I don't suppose there's a book lying around here that I could read on the subject?"

"If there is, I haven't seen it," he said.

I studied him. "Have you done it?"

"Done what?"

"Don't play dumb. And please tell me the truth. Please?"

He took a breath, which had to be an act of desperation for a dead person. "Yes."

"Did it work?"

"Sort of," he said.

"Come on. Were you able to get through when you did it?"

"Did Jeff strike you as someone I had gotten through to?"

"No," I said, disappointed. "Why didn't it work?"

"Because people have to be asleep for you to get into their dreams. And when they're asleep, they're—asleep. They don't know what's going on. Worse, they forget almost everything you tell them the instant they wake up."

"*Almost* everything?" I asked, grasping at straws.

He nodded reluctantly. "You saw with your aunt that you can sometimes remember certain things."

"You think she was really talking to me? That's amazing."

"Someone in your position shouldn't be amazed by anything."

"How do you get into a dream?" I asked.

He stood. "It's not hard. You'll figure it out, if you must." He checked his watch. I hadn't noticed before that he was wearing one. It blew my mind that it worked. I mean, where did he buy his batteries? "I have to go," he said.

I scurried to my feet. "Where to? Aren't you going to come with me?"

"I can't."

"Why not?" I demanded.

"Finding out who killed you is one thing, but I'm not supposed to help you try to communicate with the living. It's against the rules."

"Whose rules? God's?"

"Mine," he said.

"You helped me at the seance."

"And see where that got the two of us." He began to walk away. "Catch you later. Don't get lost in anybody's nightmare."

"Peter!"

I don't remember blinking. I don't think ghosts do blink. Just the same, he was gone.

CHAPTER XII

I HAD A HARD TIME getting back to my neighborhood. It was late, and there weren't many trucks on the road that I could catch a ride with. At least not many going my way. I waited at a couple of big intersections and did manage to get aboard a flatbed, but it ended up turning away from the coast, and I had to wait till it stopped at a light to hop off. If anything, my paranoia about hurting myself was increasing. Finally, though, I found a truck that took me practically to my doorstep. It was a dump truck. I had to sit in the back with the garbage. It was fortunate my nose was no longer working on the terrestrial plane.

I had no difficulty entering my house. The front door was wide open. My father was loading a couple of suitcases into his white Cadillac, which was parked in the driveway. My bright red Ferrari must still be in the garage, I thought sadly.

I remembered Jimmy's remark to Amanda about my parents going away for a few days. I followed my dad back into the house, getting out of the way before he could close the door on me. I didn't need my nose to tell he had been drinking. His face had that puffy red look that took a solid bout with the bottle to develop. The uncapped quart of expensive scotch sitting on the kitchen table did more than reinforce my suspicion.

My mother was holding a tiny blue pill as my dad sat down at the table beside her. A prescription bottle stood beside the toaster. My mom had on a baggy nightgown she might have worn eighteen years ago when she was pregnant with me. The whole situation could not have been more depressing.

"We can leave first thing in the morning," my dad said, refilling a shot glass. "I figure we'll head north."

"Why north?" my mom asked wearily, her jawbone visible as she swallowed her pill with the aid of a glass of water. I would not have believed anyone could lose so much weight in so few days. I doubted that she'd eaten a thing since her last bite of the chocolate cake I had wanted to throw out.

"Do you want to head south?" my dad asked. "That's fine with me. We could drive all the way to Acapulco if you'd like."

My mother smiled faintly. "Remember when we went there a couple of summers ago and Shari made us stay three extra days because she had a crush on that lifeguard?"

I hadn't realized my parents knew about my infatuation with the handsome twenty-five-year-old Mexican who had watched over our hotel swimming pool. I should have been embarrassed, but I wasn't. I was glad they'd had some knowledge of my personal life. My father nodded and tilted his shot glass to his lips.

"She had a lot of love in her," he said.

"I wonder if that young man is still working there?"

"Probably not."

My mother put a hand to her head, massaging her temple, losing whatever smile she had. "Maybe we should go north."

My father swallowed his whiskey. "All right," he said.

I couldn't stand it. I had to get out of the kitchen. I went searching for Jimmy. I was surprised to find him at the top of the stairs kissing Amanda good night outside my bedroom door. She was sleeping over. She was going to sleep in my bed!

"Try to get some rest," she said as they parted. She had on a plain white bathrobe. Had it been one of mine, I think I would have freaked out altogether. "We'll have a good day tomorrow together," she said.

Jimmy wore blue jeans, no shirt. He was developing a slouch. He looked like he could have used a shot of scotch. "What should we do?" he asked.

Amanda smiled and ruffled his hair. "It doesn't matter."

Jimmy looked past his girlfriend, into my room. "We shouldn't have gone to that meeting."

She hugged him. "It was stupid. Forget about it. Someone there probably made it say those things."

He jumped slightly at the suggestion. He held her at arm's length. "Do you honestly think one of them killed her, Amanda?"

She lowered her eyes. "Please don't ask me that, Jimmy."

Jimmy, I thought. Only I called him that.

I went back downstairs. I had to wait for Jimmy to fall asleep. The door to the garage lay slightly ajar. The light was on. Sucking in my breath, I squeezed through. Someone had rolled down the window on the driver's side of my Ferrari. I climbed inside and rested my hands on the steering wheel. My birthday present. Some people would have given their right arms for a car like this. Well, I thought, I had certainly paid my fair share.

I must have dozed. It was a bad habit that I had probably carried with me to the grave; I had always loved to nap. When I came to, it was dark. I had a moment of panic when I thought I had been locked in the garage for the weekend. But the door to the house, I quickly saw, was open farther than before. I climbed out of the Ferrari and went inside. The clock in the kitchen said almost two-fifteen.

Upstairs, Jimmy's door was the only one not closed all the way. I counted my blessings. If it had been shut, I would have been out of business for the night. With the rest of forever ahead of me, I shouldn't have been concerned about wasting one night. Yet I was, and it wasn't just because I was worried that the Shadow would get to me before I could communicate with my brother. I just had this feeling that I had to hurry.

Dreams were not my expertise. I knew that people's eyelids fluttered when they had them and that they supposedly aided in the release of stress. That was it. I certainly didn't know how to climb into one. Jimmy was sleeping on his back, the sheet tangled around his waist, his chest bare. Sitting on the bed by his side, I silently cursed Peter for deserting me in my hour of need. I had no idea what to do next. Yet Peter had said I should be able to figure it out. I decided to experiment. I reached out and touched Jimmy's hands.

The brush of mental dullness caught me by surprise. It was not strong, and it stopped the instant I let go of Jimmy, but it gave me a rush of hope. I assumed it must have been caused by a partial merger with Jimmy's unconscious mind. I couldn't think of another explanation. I sat back to wait for his eyelids to begin to flutter. I figured he should be in the midst of a full-fledged dream before I made a determined effort to say hello.

A half-hour must have gone by before his long black lashes began to twitch. I immediately reached for his hands. The wave of dullness returned, but this time it was mixed with a sinking sensation. The feeling was far from pleasant. Internally, I could sense Jimmy's presence, although he seemed light-years away. I was caught between two universes, split in two, and the desire to be whole again wrenched at my heart. His world was so painful!

But I refused to let go. I wanted to get closer to him. I wanted to pull him up. Instinctively, I moved my hands up his arms toward his face, and the light-years changed to miles, and then to mere feet. Spreading my fingers over the crown of his head, I glimpsed him wandering lost along an endless corridor of shadows, and I felt the same weight on top of my chest that I had on the floor of Beth's condo when my so-called friends had tried to bury me before my time. The bedroom vanished. The new background was thick with smoke and dust, devoid of color or definition. He was dressed in black. His eyes were open. He was looking at me. No, he was looking for me. And he couldn't find me. Tears ran over his sunken cheeks, and then fell, mingling with the pale clouds that dogged his weary feet.

"Jimmy," I called to him. "I'm here, Jimmy. Over here."

He didn't look up. There was a veil between us made impenetrable by his sorrow. I didn't want to let go, but I had to. I simply could not bear it! I felt for my invisible hands and yanked them upward.

I landed facedown across his chest as he turned uneasily in his bed.

"Oh, Jimmy," I whispered, brushing his cheek and kissing him goodbye. Maybe we were still partially connected. I could feel the dampness of his skin, and it was no dream.

There was a window downstairs in the laundry room that had been left open. I used it to climb outside. It was almost a relief, I thought, that my parents had closed their door. I doubted that I could stand to be that close again to grief caused by me.

But I was frustrated by what little I had accomplished. I did not leave the vicinity of my house right away. Crossing the backyard, I noticed another window open. It was on the second story, and it led to my bedroom. A peek behind Amanda's cool gray eyes, I thought, might be educational.

I needed a ladder. I really needed to get my ghostly wings flapping. I had to settle on a network of ivy and the frail wooden framework it entwined to help me up the side of the wall. Being the psychologically inhibited ghost that I was, I expected my support to break beneath my feet with each upward step I took. It was with a sigh of relief that I climbed through the window and plopped down on the floor.

Amanda was sleeping snug and secure beneath the quilt Mrs. Parish had knitted for me on my fifteenth birthday. She looked so beautiful with her long black hair spread over my pillow that I couldn't help but feel disgusted.

I waited for a half-hour for her eyelids to flutter, as I had with Jimmy, but the best her gorgeous lashes would do was bat every now and then. I finally decided to grab her head and just go for it.

My awareness began to alter. It was different this time. There was no crushing grief, no sudden change of location. Slowly, almost imperceptibly, the room around me was overlaid with the faint image of a flat gray landscape riddled with thousands of narrow poles that reached high into the sky. As I held tight to Amanda's forehead, the image grew in clarity and depth, and I began to realize that the poles were actually tall steel needles. They glittered bright and hot beneath the light of an unseen sun. There was no feeling associated with the scene. It was simply there, although Amanda was not. I understood I was seeing the landscape through her eyes, despite the fact that I was still aware of the dimensions of my bedroom.

One by one, gigantic bubbles of air began to form at the tips of the needles, breaking off and drifting into a hard white sky toward a long translucent pipe, which floated miles above the ground, stretching out of sight in both directions. Flowing with a dark pulsating liquid, the pipe appeared to draw the bubbles toward it. But even though the bubbles bounced harmlessly off the side of the pipe, I sensed they were anxious to get inside it and flow with the liquid.

I wondered if there was a particular significance for Amanda in the scene, and why, no matter where I looked, there wasn't a trace of color.

The image started to fade a few minutes later, and a wave of drowsiness began to overcome me. I let go of Amanda's forehead. The night was getting on, I thought. I had other dreams to walk. I stood and turned toward the window. I did not kiss her goodbye.

My next stop was Daniel's house. A Hell's Angel unknowingly gave me a ride most of the way there on the back of his

Harley-Davidson. The dude was most gracious. He knew Jimi Hendrix's songs word for word and sang several for my personal entertainment. He had a pretty good voice.

The open kitchen window I had used that afternoon to walk in on Daniel and Beth's sexual sinning was still available. I hoisted myself inside without difficulty and headed upstairs. Daniel had his door shut, however. I was about to leave when his mom got up for a drink of water and stopped to have a peek in at him. I'm sure she would have been shocked to know she had just let her offspring's supposed love into his bed. But I did not enter the room without first checking that there was an open window I could jump out of in the event she closed the door on me—which she ended up doing.

Daniel lay in the center of his bed with his arms and legs wrapped around a big stuffed teddy bear. I laughed, thinking the poor boy must be in desperate need of affection. As I made my way toward his bed, his eyelids were twitching. I didn't wait. I grabbed his head and dived in.

I probably should have gone slower. His bedroom instantly vanished and was replaced by his dream bedroom. This one had a naked blonde with Beth's chest and my face lounging on a circular waterbed. A silver tray stocked with caviar and champagne sat beside it. Hundreds of lights were on, and the ceiling was all mirrored. Better to see you with, my dear, I thought. Or was it Daniel saying it in response to the girl's question? He stood to the side of the bed with his mouth hanging open and his eyes wide. He had on a full black wet suit and flippers.

If only I'd brought Freud along for the ride.

"I love you, Danny Boy," the girl on the bed crooned, shifting provocatively on top of the satin sheets. It pissed me off that she sounded just like Beth. I mean, if he was going to steal my mouth, why didn't he take my voice as well? The guy was disloyal to the core—as well as being a pervert. He flapped his flippers on the red velvet floor like a fish in heat.

"I love you, Marsha," he said, excited.

"Who the hell is Marsha?" I asked.

He heard me. He looked over and almost fainted. "Shari," he said. "What are you doing here?"

I strode toward him. "What am I doing here? I'm your girlfriend!" I pointed to the bed. "What's she doing here?"

"Who?"

"Her!"

He put his hands to his mouth and began to bite his nails, his teeth chattering as if he were a cartoon character. "I don't know," he mumbled.

"Get rid of her," I ordered. "And take off that stupid suit. You look like a senile penguin."

He turned to Marsha. "Could you come back later?"

"Later?" I yelled. "You cheating bastard! Here, I'll tell her myself. Miss, get your tight ass out of this room and never come back."

She took the hint. She gathered up her clothes—they were all over the floor; he had probably torn them off her—and hurried from the room. Daniel sat down on the edge of the bed and began to pull off his flippers.

"Gee, Shari," he said. "I didn't know you were coming over."

"Who's Marsha?" I demanded, sitting beside him. He had really fixed the place up since he had been awake. Besides the velvet carpet and the mirrors, there was a plush lavender loveseat near the closet and a swirling blue Jacuzzi in the corner. There was, in fact, color everywhere, like in an ordinary dream.

"She's a cousin of mine visiting from Florida," he said.

"Did you have sex with her?"

He looked guilty. "We took a shower together once."

"You took a shower with your cousin! Were you going out with me at the time?"

He hesitated. "No."

"Liar!"

"I wasn't."

"Then what are you doing with her now?"

He appeared confused. He couldn't get his stupid flipper off. It looked like it had melted on his toes. He finally gave up on it and put his foot back down. "Shari, you're supposed to be dead."

Here was my big chance. "How did I die?" I asked.

He scratched his head like a cartoon character, his nails on his scalp sounding like files rubbing against wood, it was getting to be too much. "I don't remember," he said.

Just my luck, his subconscious was as dumb as his conscious state. Yet he had told me something. If he'd murdered me, he wouldn't have forgotten. "Somebody killed me," I said.

He suddenly snapped his fingers. I couldn't believe it when I actually *saw* an exclamation point zoom off the top of his hand. "I know what happened!" he said. "You jumped off the balcony!"

"No, I didn't!"

"Yes, you did!"

"I did not!"

"I saw you!"

I froze. "You saw me jump?" I asked softly.

His face fell. "You were lying in a puddle of blood."

"But before that, what did you see?"

He lowered his head between his knees. He was having trouble breathing. He began to cry. "Oh, Shari. Your head. Oh, God."

"Dan! Tell me, what happened?"

"Crushed. Splattered. Oh, Jesus."

"What did I do!?" I screamed, reaching out and grabbing his hands. And as I did so, his eyes swung toward me, and a look of pure horror filled his face. For an instant I saw everything from his perspective. I saw the girl I had found lying on the table in the morgue, minus the green towel that had hidden the worst of the damage. Had I a meal in my stomach and a stomach in my body, I would have vomited.

Then I was back in his bedroom, his *real* bedroom, sitting by his side in the dark as he stirred restlessly in a nightmare I knew intimately. I had accidentally removed my hands from his head. Perhaps it was just as well. I touched my own head gingerly, drawing small comfort from the fact that it appeared to be all in one piece. Shaken, I stood and ran to the window. I had to get out of that room.

Jo's was my next stop. I walked the whole way there, hoping the exercise would calm me down, quiet my fears. It didn't help a bit.

Jo's mom, Mrs. Foulton, was sitting on the front porch in the dark smoking a cigarette. She had probably just gotten off work; she had on her uniform. I estimated the time at about four-thirty. The sun would be coming up soon.

A newspaper lay across Mrs. Foulton's lap. I could read it without a light, even though she couldn't. The paper was a couple of days old. She had it open to page three. There was a picture of me in the upper right-hand corner beneath the headline, "HIGH SCHOOL SENIOR JUMPS TO HER DEATH." They'd plucked the photo right out of my junior year annual. I looked all right.

I sat in a chair beside Mrs. Foulton and noticed she was using her cigarette for more than just smoking. Between puffs, she would hold it close to the picture. Either she wanted to burn out my eyes, or else she was trying to get a better look at me. Remembering back to the indifferent tone she had taken with Mrs. Parish before my funeral, I wondered why she would bother one way or the other.

Her hands were trembling slightly, yet her face betrayed no emotion. After a while she ground out her cigarette and went inside, leaving the paper on the porch chair. Naturally, I followed her.

Mrs. Foulton went straight to bed. She didn't even bother to remove her uniform; she just lay on top of the sheets and closed her eyes. I reasoned that she had to return to the hospital in a few hours. Because she hadn't been at the party and couldn't possibly have pushed me from the balcony—if I had, in fact, been pushed—I didn't try to probe her dreams.

Jo's door was wide open, which struck me as unusual. Jo normally guarded her privacy vigorously. Entering the room, I found her sleeping with her blanket thrown off, her head buried under her pillow. I had to wait for several minutes until she turned to get even a glimpse of her head. But as I let my fingertips brush close to her hair, I almost passed out. Yet Jo had to be dreaming, I thought; her eyelids were twitching violently. Moving cautiously, I gently touched the top of her head with my right hand.

I was not cautious enough.

I fainted and began to dream myself. . . .

~   ~   ~

The parlor was dimly lit. Dull buff-colored curtains had taken the place of the walls, and if I'd looked up I knew I wouldn't have cared to see the ceiling. The furniture was Victorian, old and splintered, and the forlorn statues that haunted the four corners were dismembered remnants from forgotten places. At the far end of the room, propped up in an overstuffed rocking chair in front of a large crystal ball, sat the witch.

It was Jo, clothed in a stained and ragged black gown, an ancient Jo of many wrinkles and aching bones, who had seen the best years of her life wither away with the burden of the knowledge that she had lost everything of value in her youth. Her expression was a mask of deep secrets, but I recognized it for the lie it was and was not afraid. She knew nothing of significance. She didn't even remember my name, although I remembered her clearly. She raised a bony finger and bid me approach. I was there to have my fortune read.

"Have a seat, child," she said in a tired voice, making an effort at a smile but coming up short. I sat before her on a low brown stool. Two squat red candles stood on either side of her crystal ball, their smoky flames watching each other through a prism of polished glass. The woman regarded me with flat hazel eyes. "What concerns you?" she asked.

I had the question prepared and already knew its answer— it was part of a play. "I want to know if I will live a long and happy life," I said.

She thought it was a silly question for one as young as myself. She leaned toward me, and now she smiled. "Yes."

"You're sure?"

"Yes, child, you have no need to worry." She held out her left hand. "Ten dollars, please."

"Look in your crystal ball," I said.

"It is not necessary. I can see your destiny in your face."

"But I *want* you to."

She cocked her head to the side. "What is your name?"

"My name is not important," I said, doing my best not to sound rude. I gestured to her ball, feeling my confidence grow. "I've heard your magic is very powerful."

She withdrew her money-seeking hand and nodded. "You have heard correctly."

"Friends of mine said you told them exactly what was going to happen to them. And it happened."

"Who are these people?" she asked.

"Just friends. They had great respect for you. You told one of them he would live to an old age and be miserable all his life. And he did."

She started to get suspicious. "But you are young. How is it that you have old friends?"

I shrugged. "I get around. I've met many interesting people. I once knew this extraordinary girl. She was in a state of pure joy all the time." I added, "Pure bliss. She came to you for a reading."

The old lady sat back uneasily. "I remember no such person."

"I can understand how you might have forgotten. Actually, she wasn't that happy. She was as miserable as my other friend. I think you were a little off on her reading. Are you sure you don't remember seeing her?"

"No."

"You gave her a nickname," I said.

"What nickname?"

"It was—oh, I've forgotten. It doesn't matter." I pointed to the glass ball again. "Please, tell me my fortune."

"I've already told you."

"But you haven't looked in the crystal. Come on, I'll pay you double. Twenty dollars."

She was undecided. Twenty dollars was obviously a lot of money to her. "Why did all your friends come to see me?"

"They didn't. You came to them."

"Tell me some of their names," she said.

"What for? They're all dead now."

"How did they die?" she asked.

"You know. You told them how they would die. They were old like you are. They died of old age."

She clasped her hands together to keep them from shaking and glanced down at the dry and cracked flesh of her fingers. She was beginning to remember. "Who are you?" she whispered.

I smiled. "A friend."

She closed her eyes. "I've never met you before."

"Look in the crystal." I put my hand over hers and squeezed gently. "I'll pay you triple."

"What do you want to know?" There was fear in her voice.

"How I'm going to die." I squeezed harder. "Open your eyes, old woman. Look in the crystal."

She looked. She had to. I moved my grip on her frail hands to the top of her brittle skull and forced her to look. I was through playing with her. I lowered my gaze and peered through the other side, seeing her lifeless hazel eyes, poor imitations of my clear green eyes, and her tired parched mouth, pressed to the surface of the ball so tightly that I wondered if she was able to breathe, if I wasn't in fact smothering her. I wanted to kill her right then, but I also realized that it would be a mistake to do so before I learned what I had come for. I loosened my grip on her head slightly, expecting her to pull her lips off the glass and catch her breath.

It didn't happen that way.

Things started to get confused. Suddenly, I couldn't tell what I was holding on to. I worried that I had shifted my hands too far forward. The rough scalp of sparse hair had disappeared beneath my fingers. Now I was touching glass.

I was holding on to the crystal ball.

The old woman was inside it.

She was dead. I had killed her. A long time ago. She was dead and now decayed beyond recognition. Staring into the glass, I saw a white skull that a swarm of insects could have picked clean. But the top of the skull was badly cracked, and somehow that didn't fit. Jo had never been shoved off a balcony. It was I who had died that way.

All of a sudden, I was very afraid and in terrible pain. I couldn't get my hands off the damn ball. Somehow, the candles had become attached to the side of the glass, heating the crystal to an intolerable level, and the flesh of my fingers was melting and sticking, and no matter how hard I pulled, I couldn't get them off.

I began to scream.

I still didn't know how bad it could get.

What happened next—It wasn't good. I began to lurch about the parlor, trying to knock the crystal ball with the old woman's skull inside it out of my dissolving hands. It was almost, but not quite, like burning in hell. To be there, I thought, I would have had to be *inside* the ball.

I should never have considered the possibility.

It happened next. I don't know who put me inside. I guess it was myself. Events were unfolding with perverse irony. People had always said that Jo and I looked like sisters. And when I had peered through the crystal ball and seen the old face on the other side, it had been like looking into another mirror. I had seen myself as I would have appeared if I'd lived to an old age.

I hadn't lived, though, and my dream wasn't an ordinary dream a mortal girl could have survived with her sanity intact. I found myself careening wildly around the parlor, surrounded by flames, with my hands locked on top of my cracked skull. The dance went on forever and a moment. I heard devils applauding.

Then I heard Jo cry out to her mother.

I came to on the floor beside Jo's bed. A bundle of typed sheets lay scattered around my knees, the pages of Peter's story about the girl who could videotape the future. They had been sitting in a neat pile on Jo's nightstand when I entered the room. Jo must have knocked them down. It couldn't have been me; I was no poltergeist, and besides, my hands were clamped to the top of my head. I practically had to pry them loose. I thanked God I was awake.

Jo was sitting up in bed crying. Her mother was by her side, holding on to her. Jo was close to hysterics.

"Shari says I killed her!" she raved. "She blames me for pushing her off the balcony! But I didn't, Mom. I swear I didn't!"

"Jo."

"She thinks I murdered her!"

"Shh, honey, no." Mrs. Foulton hugged her daughter to her chest. "Shari was your friend. She couldn't blame you."

"She does! She came back to tell me she does! She grabbed my head and tried to stick me in a crystal ball! It was horrible! There was a skull grinning at me, and I was burning!"

"Jo, it was only a bad dream."

"No, it was real! She was really here! I kept telling her, I didn't kill you! I didn't kill you! I told her a thousand times! Why wouldn't she listen to me?" Her head collapsed on her mother's shoulder, and she moaned softly. "I wouldn't have hurt her for anything. I loved her."

Mrs. Foulton held her at arm's length, staring into her face. Jo was not calming down. Her nightgown was soaked with sweat. I kept waiting for Mrs. Foulton to say something, to reassure Jo some more. But in the end, all she did was hug her daughter again and say, "You were the lucky one. She knew how you felt."

My guilt was a miserable thing. I understood more clearly why Peter had insisted I leave the living alone. I was becoming a nightmare for all of them. I don't know how I could have suspected Jo.

But if she hadn't killed me, if none of them had killed me, then that must mean that I had . . .

I couldn't say it; I couldn't even think it.

I was standing to leave, to jump out the open window headfirst if that would have helped to get away from it all, when I heard the desperate cry. It came to me through my mind, not my ears. It was still loud and clear.

"Shari! Help me! It's after me!"

It was Peter.

CHAPTER XIII

I FOUND HIM not four blocks away, cowering at the end of an alley behind a trash can. His call had led me to him like a cosmic homing beacon. I had run the whole way. But when he saw me, he waved frantically for me to stand back.

"Don't move," he cried.

I froze, knowing he must be talking about the Shadow. Yet I saw nothing. Even more important, I sensed nothing. Always before, the Shadow had announced its arrival by filling me with dread. "Where is it?" I whispered.

He nodded in the direction of a green garbage bin that stood between us against a grimy brick wall, his eyes wide with fright. I could actually hear his rapid breathing.

But there was nothing there.

"Peter?" I said.

He put his finger to his lips to silence me and began to creep toward the wall that blocked the rear of the alley. He obviously was going to try to make a run for it, and this was a guy who could beam himself to the top of the Himalayas at a moment's notice.

He was halfway up the wall when I grabbed his foot. That was a mistake. Letting out a yelp, he kicked me in the face and scampered over the wall out of sight. I went after him, clearing the wall with far more ease than he had.

"Peter!" I cried.

It took me less than a block to catch up with him. It amazed me; in real life he could have easily outrun me. And as an experienced dead person, he had far more powers to draw on than I had. It was as if he was suddenly handicapped.

"Would you stop!" I said, grabbing hold of him in much the same way he had grabbed me after my flight from the cemetery. He fought me off.

"It's coming."

"No," I said.

"We've got to keep going!"

I had said the very same words. Leaping onto his back, I tried to slow him down. "There's nothing there!" I yelled.

He threw me off, and I landed on my butt on top of a manhole cover. But a glance over his shoulder made him pause. "Where is it?"

"God knows," I replied. He continued to search the street for a full minute. Finally, though, he drew in a deep breath and relaxed.

"It's gone," he said.

"It was never there," I said.

He looked down at me. "How would you know?"

"I knew before. What gives?"

He turned away. "Never mind."

I jumped up. "No, tell me. Why is it I couldn't see it just now? And why couldn't you see it in the cemetery?"

He stopped. "You don't want to know."

"Why do you call it the Shadow? Is there a different one for each of us?"

He closed his eyes briefly at my question, and I believed it scared him almost as much as the thing he imagined had been chasing him. "Yes," he said finally.

I let go of his arm and sat down on the curb. We were near the corner of Baker and Third. A memory of the place tugged at a corner of my mind, but I forced it back. I had more pressing concerns. "What is it?" I asked.

He sat beside me. He wouldn't look at me, only up at the sky. It was as if he wished he could get up there and far from all earthly concerns. Although the sun couldn't have been far away, the stars were very bright, the colors pretty.

"It is the worst thing we could ever have to face," he said. "It is ourselves."

"I don't understand."

He smiled at the remark, a weary smile; he could have been running from it since the day he died. "I would give you a long, involved explanation if I knew one, Shari. Maybe it would cover up what I don't understand, or how I lied to you about it in the first place."

"Peter?"

He kept his focus upward. "There is a different Shadow for each of us. While we live in the world, it is with us all the time. It colors our thoughts, how we feel, how we see others, and even how others see us. But it is not different from us. It is a part of us. It is with us from birth. We simply add to it as we grow. It is the product of our experience on earth. It is the sum of our thoughts and feelings."

"Then why is it so horrible?" I asked.

"It is not horrible in and of itself. It is only horrible to the person it belongs to. When you come face to face with it, you see yourself as you really are."

"But I wasn't that rotten a person while I was alive." I thought of what Daniel had started to tell me before the memory of my cracked head had made him sick. "Was I?"

"No, you were fine. But like most people, you refused to accept yourself as fine. In the presence of the Shadow, any judgment you hold against yourself is magnified a millionfold."

"Is that why I felt such hatred from it when it was near?"

"Yes," he said.

"But you've said that if I go into the light, I will escape from it. How can I escape from myself?"

"You've asked a question that has many answers. Even

though the Shadow is you, it is not all of you. It is not what you would call the soul. The true soul is never tainted by what you think or do. When you enter the light, you leave the Shadow behind. Imagine—how could you possibly enjoy the joy of heaven carrying such a burden with you?"

"I just leave it behind? Where does it go?"

"Nowhere," he said.

"What does it do?"

"It waits for you to return for it."

"You mean, I pick it up again when I'm reborn?" I asked. "Like reincarnation?"

"We need not bring religion into this. Reincarnation is a model mortals use to explain the unexplainable. Heaven is another model. Who is to say which is more accurate? As I told you before, reality is so simple there is nothing that can be said about it. But if you wish, you can imagine that the Shadow does wait for your return and that it does remember everything that has gone before and that it doesn't let you accept yourself as perfect until *you* let it. There is truth in that. This is why a child usually cries as soon as it's born. With its first breath, the Shadow returns."

"But knowing all this, why does it still terrify you?"

He lowered his eyes from the sky toward the ground. "You saw for yourself, Shari, in the cemetery. The fear it brings is not something you can reason away. It is just there, and you have to run from it."

"Has it ever caught you?"

He looked at me. "No."

"Then how can you know what would happen if it did?"

"I don't."

"So it might not imprison me? It might do nothing to me?"

He shook his head. "It would do something."

"Why do you stay here, on earth, where it can keep chasing you?"

"I can't—it's my job."

"What job is that?" I asked. "I haven't seen you rush off to smooth anybody's crossing since you've been with me. Tell me the truth, Peter, are you here because of me?"

He stared at me oddly for a moment. Then he rested his head in his hands. "No."

"Why, then?"

"I can't tell you why."

He sounded so sad; I didn't have the heart to press him. I switched to a more cheerful subject. "What about suicide?"

His head shot up. "What?"

"Suicide, you know, when you kill yourself. I've been in a few of my friends' heads since I saw you last." My voice began to crack. "I don't think any of them killed me. Maybe everybody's right. Maybe I jumped, Peter."

"Shari, that's ridiculous."

I had been holding back the tears since I had run from Daniel's bedroom. Now they burst from my eyes like cold rain. "It's not. You said yourself you weren't there when I died. You don't know what I did. I don't know what I did! I was upset. I ran to the balcony. All I remember is thinking how good it would be if I could fly over the ocean and disappear forever." I nodded to myself. "I must have jumped."

"That's not possible."

I hung my head low. A spider was walking toward my foot. I moved my shoe to kill him. Then I decided to let him live. For all it mattered. I couldn't have hurt it had I jumped up and down on it a hundred times. I had no say in anything anymore. "It is more than possible," I muttered. "It is likely."

"Garrett doesn't think so."

I got up. "Garrett's just doing his job. I was wrong about him. He's a good detective. And if he hasn't been able to find my murderer by now, then it's because there isn't one."

"You didn't jump, Shari."

"You keep saying that. How do you know?"

He looked at me again in that odd way he had a few seconds ago. But this time a faint smile played across his lips. I couldn't understand the reason for it, or for his next remark. "I was glad when I got you for my lab partner in biology."

"You wouldn't have been so glad had you known your partner was a loony." I turned away. "I've got to go."

He stood quickly. "Where are you going?"

"To see what it can tell me about myself."

"Your Shadow?" He grabbed my shoulders from behind. "No, Shari. You don't know what will happen."

I didn't fight him. I just let myself fall back against his chest.
I took him by surprise, but then he wrapped his arms around
me, and I was able to hold his hands in mine close to my heart.
I could feel it beating still, and I was happy for that. For a few
moments we stood together in the middle of the silent street, and
I remembered back to the week before the prom my sophomore
year, when I had purposely bumped into Peter in the hallways at
every opportunity. I had been trying to suggest to him that if he
needed a date for the dance, I was available. But he hadn't asked
me. He hadn't asked anybody. I had stayed home that night and
read a book. He had probably gone for a ride on his motorcycle.

I realized what had been bothering me about our location.

"You died right here, didn't you?" I asked.

" Yes." He tightened his hold on me and rested his chin on
the back of my head. "It was my fault."

I released his hands and let his arms fall by my side. "I've
got to know if it was *my* fault."

"It wasn't," he said, a soft plea in his voice.

"We'll see." I turned and faced him. I was scared, but I
joked for his benefit. "I hope it doesn't have my bad breath."

"You never had bad breath, Shari."

"How would you know?" I kissed him quickly on the lips.
"You never got a chance to know." I stepped back. "Goodbye,
Peter. Don't try to follow me."

I walked briskly up the road toward Beth's place. He let me
go. I felt as if I was hurrying to my death.

CHAPTER XIV

THE GATE TO the condominium complex, was closed. I didn't bother waiting for someone to come along and open it for me. A tree hung over the brick wall that circled the estates. I was becoming quite adept at climbing and was inside fast as a cat.

The stain of blood from my head had been scrubbed off the walkway that ran under Beth's balcony. At least a mortal might have thought so. But I could still detect signs of my demise. Kneeling, I touched a finger to the dried particles of blood that had fallen between the tiny imperfections in the cement. And unlike anything else in my realm, I could *really* touch them and feel the life that had once sparked within and which had now grown cold.

I looked up. I half expected to find the Shadow standing on the balcony four stories above. It was on that spot, after all, that it had first shown itself. But it wasn't there now, and

I was more relieved than disappointed. But I vowed not to leave until it came to me. An idea popped into my mind that I believed might hasten its arrival. It was sort of a sick idea; it might have sprung from the same desire that drove criminals to return to the scenes of their worst crimes.

What if I got up on the balcony?

I stood and ran my hand through my hair.

I felt drawn.

The entrance was locked tight, and I didn't have the proper identification card to buzz my way inside. But Beth's place, I reminded myself, had the best view in the complex; the top floor and the roof were not that far apart, and there was a flight of emergency stairs on the south side of the building. Jogging around the side of the condos, I ran up those steps as far as I could and then went a little farther; a rain drain helped me onto the roof. Except for the part about the nine lives, Catgirl was doing well.

Adobe tile covered the roof, sun-baked Spanish clay. As I walked above the sleeping city, I noted the hint of color in the eastern sky off to my right. Just then something about the flaking orange dust that coated the tiles troubled me. But I could not pinpoint the source of my disquiet.

The slant of the roof was mild; I was in no danger of falling as I knelt at the edge of the tiles above the accursed balcony. The Shadow had yet to put in an appearance, and this time I sent a prayer of thanks heavenward. It struck me as insane that

I was going to such lengths to embrace something that I was hoping with all my heart to avoid.

It surprised me how easily I was able to lower myself over the side and swing onto the wooden rail that guarded the edge of the balcony. The upraised ends of the tiles made excellent handholds—a child could have held on to them.

The sliding glass doors to the kitchen and Beth's bedroom were both locked. I didn't know what to do with myself. I had reached my destination, and I had nowhere to go. I paced the balcony back and forth. The eastern glow took on a yellow tint.

It was half an hour later, and I was on the verge of leaving in spite of my vow, when I suddenly saw my nemesis kneeling beside the stain on the walkway three stories below. What was left of my dried blood looked more alive and darker with the Shadow beside it. Now the gook was literally boiling up from the concrete. As I watched in horror, the Shadow leaned over and put its head into the cauldron. I didn't want to believe it was licking the blood up. Yet when it raised its head and looked up at me, the walkway was clear.

"Oh, God," I whispered.

Dawn was near, and the eastern light was playing havoc with the Shadow's form. It was no longer an insubstantial cloud of revolving darkness. Yet, if anything, it had moved farther away from a human semblance. Strange colors sparked and cracked from its depths like electrical shorts on a logic circuit gone mad with emotion. It was deep, this thing that was supposed to be me. But not with wisdom or love. Only with life, crazy and fearful as that always was. It had drunk of my blood because it craved my life. It raised a hand and beckoned for me to come to it.

"Shari."

My name—it might have known a thousand things to call me by, although I would have remembered none of them. I understood what it wanted, however. It was quite clear.

It wanted me to jump.

It was promising to catch me.

The night of the party, the doors had been unlocked behind me but only in a physical sense. I had closed another door forever when I had run frightened and upset from the others. My death might have been destined, but not so the reputation of failure I had left behind with my supposed suicide. At least, that was what I imagined the Shadow was trying to say with its challenge. I could hear it clearly in my mind. Now that I thought about it, it was, and always had been, a part of my thoughts.

Suddenly, I felt no fear.

I climbed up onto the rail and jumped.

I didn't fall. Not right away. That was for the end, I was told. The sun was coming up. The only place to start was at the beginning.

The world vanished, and a baby cried.

My skin cringed at the dreadful cold. My eyes winced under the harsh white light. I was being taken from my warm, wet home, and I didn't like it. Big grubby hands pulled me through the air. Rough material scraped my face clean. No wonder I was crying.

But then I was set beside a soft face. A gentle mat of hair touched me. Sweet words sounded in my ears. This was my home, I realized, talking to me. I decided maybe I could stay for a while. This was my mother.

I went to sleep happy.

Later, I awoke, and my mother was gone. But it was OK. I opened my eyes and looked around. Everything was a white blur, but it was still neat to have eyes and be able to see through them. I sniffed the air. I had a nose, too, and that was good.

I wondered when I would get to be with my mother again.

I went back to sleep.

I awoke moving through the air in the hands of a huge white person. My nose did not like this huge person. This huge person's smell made breathing difficult. Nor did my ankle like the way in which the huge person was tugging at a plastic band snapped around it. When the band slid off, I was glad.

The huge person set me down in a warm white box similar to the one I had just been in. But I knew it was not the same box; it smelled different, and besides, there was another baby in it. I knew it was a baby because it looked like me, and I was a baby.

The baby was crying. The huge person was pulling on the poor thing's ankle band, too. I began to cry in sympathy. And then I cried in pain as the huge person began to put the other baby's ankle tape around my leg. It didn't quite fit; I must have had fatter ankles. Even when the huge person finally got it on and carried the other crying baby away, the band continued to cut into my poor leg. I cried myself to sleep.

When I awoke, another huge white person was carrying me through the air to see my mother. The band had stopped hurting. This huge person smelled nice. I knew where I was going because the huge person was telling me. I understood telling and talking. I did a little of it myself as we flew down the hall, but I did not think the huge person understood me or even heard me. These huge people were going to take some getting used to.

Then something very scary happened. The huge person gave me to another huge person who was not dressed in white and told me that she was my mother. But this huge person did not smell like my mother. She didn't have her soft hair. She didn't even look like her! What was wrong with that huge person in white? She had made a mistake. Where was my mother?

I began to cry. I cried and cried, and the huge person who was not my mother didn't know how to stop me from crying.

I never did find my mother. Not for a long, long time.

But I grew older. I saw it all. I did more than see. I lived it all, quickly, at light speed, but also completely. Down to the last tiny detail, I went through everything Shari Cooper did. I grew to know the people she called mother and father but who I knew were not her parents. Through Shari Cooper, inside her, I met the boy named Jimmy and loved him, clung to him. And he loved me back, and even though he was not my brother, he was just as good, if not better, than any brother. He was so good I didn't want to share him with anybody. It made me uneasy when I had to. It sometimes made me angry.

Or it did that to Shari. I just watched and listened. I was the silent witness. Occasionally, though, I tried to raise my voice and speak in silence. I tried the day Shari Cooper met her real mother and Jimmy's real sister, but by then she was too old and couldn't hear what I was saying. Too confused to listen to me, who was inside her, but also apart from her. Who was more than the Shadow that had taken hold of her as she had come from the womb. Who loved her more than life itself and who would stay with her even when her life was over.

It was I who watched her as she stood on the dark balcony and stared out over the wide ocean in those last moments.

But even I did not see who lifted her up and pushed her forward. I saw only through her eyes and knew only what she knew. But I knew it better. I knew she would never have willingly given up her life, not without a fight or for anything less than a great purpose. Shari Cooper—I knew her greatness.

CHAPTER XV

THE SUN WAS touching the western horizon when I came to. It was going down. The day had passed me by, as fast as my life. I sat up and rubbed the top of my head. I was lying in the spot where I had died. My bloodstain was now gone for good. I had not lived through my first fall, but I had survived my second.

I was confused.

I remembered most of what the Shadow had shown me. I knew I had not committed suicide. There were, however, several crucial incidents that would not come into focus. Worse, I could not review what I had seen from the perspective of the person who had watched the review. Yet *I* had been that person, only I wasn't who I thought I was. I was the somebody else, I realized, who always watched me.

The realization didn't help much. I decided to ignore the heavy stuff for the time being and just deal with the facts.

I was somebody else's child.

No wonder I had never gotten along with my mother.

But who did I belong to?

Peter was coming up the walkway toward me, wearing his usual baggy white shorts, red T-shirt, and sandals. I jumped to my feet.

"Peter! The most amazing thing just happened to me!"

"What?" he asked anxiously.

His tone surprised me. "What's wrong?" I asked.

"What's wrong? I followed you here to this complex and saw you jump off a balcony and fall three stories headfirst onto a concrete sidewalk and not wake up for twelve hours, and you ask me what's wrong?"

"But I'm a ghost. You've been telling me since we met that I can't hurt myself."

His face darkened. "I couldn't get to you. I tried to, but something kept pushing me back." He lowered his voice. "Did you see it?"

"Yeah. We had an intimate get-together."

"What?"

I glanced at the setting sun. "Never mind. It's getting late. We've got to get out of here. We have to go see Mrs. Parish."

"Why?"

I could almost touch the answer, only I think I was reaching with the wrong hand. "I'm not sure," I said.

~   ~   ~

We rode on a variety of interesting vehicles to the Parishes': van tops, car hoods, the backs of skateboards, anything going our way. We made good time. There was still light left in the sky when we reached the lower-middle-class neighborhood where Amanda and her mom lived. Peeking through the curtains, we could see Mrs. Parish sitting inside and sewing. Unfortunately, she had the place locked up tight. There wasn't even a window cracked that I could slip through.

"What if we go down the chimney?" I asked Peter.

"Like Santa Claus?"

"Yeah." The idea appealed to me. Until I studied the roof. "Wait, she doesn't have a chimney."

"Why don't you close your eyes and imagine yourself inside?" Peter asked.

"That's not going to work."

"It won't with—" Peter began.

"With my attitude, yeah, yeah—heard you the first time. All right, I'll give it a shot. What do I do?"

"Just do as I said, and don't be afraid."

"Afraid of what? That I'll get stuck in a stucco wall? That I'll rematerialize with a vase on top of my neck instead of a head? What's there to be afraid of?"

Peter sighed. "Don't even bother."

I pointed up the street. "Look, Jo's mom's coming over to visit her sister. She'll let us in."

One might have thought the timing very lucky. That is,

until Mrs. Foulton parked a few houses down the block from Mrs. Parish's place and proceeded to smoke half a carton of cigarettes. Well, maybe not quite that many. But it was dark when she finally emerged from her car and walked toward her sister's front door. She looked stressed. She hadn't even had a window rolled down the whole time she had been in the car.

"There's one huge person I'm glad I can't smell," I said to Peter as we followed Mrs. Foulton up the steps.

"One *what*?" Peter asked.

"She—I'm not sure what. Let's get inside."

Mrs. Parish let her sister in, and the two of them sat at the kitchen table. Mrs. Foulton lit another cigarette. Mrs. Parish poured them both coffee.

"This is an unexpected surprise," Mrs. Parish said.

"Cut the crap," Mrs. Foulton replied. "Where's Amanda?"

"She's out for the evening."

"Where is she?"

Mrs. Parish set down her coffee cup, her face worn and tired but her eyes steady. "It sounds like you already know."

"As a matter of fact, I do. Amanda called me from the Coopers' house. She's spending the night. And I've heard Jimmy's parents have gone out of town. What do you think of that?"

"Amanda knows what's right and wrong."

"Christ, you are stupid." Mrs. Foulton leaned forward. "You may have raised her Catholic, but she doesn't have a drop of your bleeding religious fervor in her veins."

"Don't talk that way."

"I'll talk as I please. What penance do your priests prescribe for incest?"

"No!" I cried, understanding at last.

"What are they talking about?" Peter demanded.

I shook my head miserably. "This can't be."

Mrs. Parish also shook her head, not as shocked as me, perhaps, but every bit as sad. "You know she doesn't have any idea."

"I wonder," Mrs. Foulton said.

Mrs. Parish showed anger. "You have no right to come into my house and say such things."

Mrs. Foulton ground out the cigarette she had just lit. "Don't I? You had no right to ruin my marriage!"

Mrs. Parish started to speak, thought better of it, and took a sip of her coffee instead. "I've paid for what I did wrong," she said finally, softly, glancing out the window. "We've both paid."

Mrs. Foulton sat back in her chair and closed her eyes, trying to control her anger and her grief. A tear slipped by, however, and was halfway down her cheek before she wiped it away. Reopening her eyes, she stared down at her trembling hands as if the tear had tainted them. I noticed then the nicotine stains on her fingertips, and I remembered them, from so long ago. "Who was worse?" she asked. "You or me?"

"You," Mrs. Parish said without hesitation. "I made a

mistake in love. You made one out of hate." Mrs. Parish studied her sister. "Do you still hate me?"

"No."

Mrs. Parish raised a surprised eyebrow. "When did you stop?"

"Last week."

Mrs. Parish reached across the table and squeezed her sister's hand. "You do miss her, don't you?"

Mrs. Foulton nodded. "So does Jo. She woke up last night crying about Shari. I wanted to tell her who her best friend had been." She shrugged and reached for her lighter. "But it only would have made her feel worse."

"Maybe. Maybe not."

It was Mrs. Foulton's turn to study her sister. "When did you stop hating me?"

Mrs. Parish sighed. "A long time ago. But also a long time after you told me what you had done."

Mrs. Foulton struck her lighter. "Do Catholics really believe that people can go to hell?"

"Some do."

"Do you?" Mrs. Foulton asked.

"No," she answered simply.

"No matter what they've done?"

Mrs. Parish nodded. "No matter what."

Mrs. Foulton closed the cap on the flame and set the lighter on the table. "I never hear from him," she said.

"David?"

"Yeah. Do you?"

"No," Mrs. Parish said.

"Do you ever hear from Mark?"

"Never."

David had been Mr. Foulton. Mark had been Mr. Parish.

"Tell me what they're talking about," Peter said again.

"Amanda and me," I said. I had to sit down on the couch in the living room. Peter came and sat by my side. He took my hand.

"What does it mean, Shari?"

I wanted to cry. I had cried over lesser things in my life, and in my death. The calmness of my voice as I answered his question sounded forced. Yet I did feel a peculiar sense of satisfaction mixed with my sorrow, a sense of having finally arrived. They were discussing something a part of me had always known.

"Jo once told me the reason Mrs. Foulton didn't like Mrs. Parish was because Mrs. Parish had had an affair with Mr. Foulton," I said. "At the time, I thought Jo was kidding me. But she must have been serious. Mrs. Parish and Mr. Foulton must have wrecked both their marriages."

"What does that have to do with you?" Peter asked.

"Mrs. Parish is my mother."

"*What?*"

"Mr. Foulton is my father. Jo is my half-sister." I had to put a hand to my head. "Amanda is Jimmy's sister."

"That's insane," Peter said.

"No, it's logical," I said. "Mr. Foulton had an affair with Mrs. Parish, and she got pregnant with me. But Mrs. Foulton found out about it. Maybe they told her, I don't know. Mrs. Foulton was working as a nurse at the hospital where I was born. Imagine how she must have felt when she looked at her sister's child and knew it was her husband's child."

"But how can you know all this?" Peter asked.

"Because I was there! Trust me, the Shadow showed it all to me. When I was only a day old, Mrs. Foulton exchanged the identification tag on my ankle with Amanda's. Don't you see? Amanda's birthday is the day before mine. No! It's the day *after* mine. Mrs. Foulton switched us in our incubators."

Peter shook his head. "That's not logical. No one could swap babies like that and get away with it. You don't look anything like Amanda."

"I don't know. I did then. I had dark hair as a baby. We would both have the same blue eyes. We were both only a few hours old! You've been to a hospital. It's hard to tell one baby from another. Besides, for all we know, the only time our mothers saw us before the switch was made was while they were under the influence of pain medication."

"But Amanda is your brother's girlfriend."

"That's why they're talking about incest! That's why they're so worried!" I stopped my raving. I let go of Peter's hand. I didn't want to let go of the most important person in my life, but I had to say it. "He's not my brother."

"Hold on a sec," Peter said. "What exactly did you see when you were with your Shadow?"

My lower lip quivered. "We don't need what I saw. Think how much Amanda and Jimmy look alike. They both have the same beautiful black hair. They have similar eyes." I stopped, struck with a cold realization. "They're both color-blind!"

"I never knew Jimmy was color-blind."

"I didn't either," I said. "But he could never tell what color my eyes were. Amanda couldn't tell either. And when I was in their dreams, everything was black and white. It makes sense. Color-blindness is hereditary."

"Color-blindness is rare among females," Peter said.

"It doesn't matter. Some girls are color-blind. And there's one other thing. When I was running from the Shadow the first time, I called out to my mother for help."

"So?"

"I assumed I was teleported to my mother's bedroom. It was pitch-black in the room when I materialized beside her. I couldn't see clearly. But I could tell there was no one else in the room, which doesn't make sense. Where was my dad?"

"He might not have come to bed yet," Peter said.

"That's possible. But when I finally did wake up, three days later, I wasn't at home. I was here. In fact, I was lying on Mrs. Parish's bed. Peter, she's got to be my mother. I've always loved her as one."

Peter appeared doubtful and confused.

The front doorbell rang.

Mrs. Parish went to answer it. Peter stood and peered out the window. "It's Garrett," he said. "I wonder what he wants."

"Hello," he said when Mrs. Parish opened the front door. He held his badge out. "I don't believe we've met, but Amanda must have told you about me. I'm in charge of the investigation into Shari Cooper's death." He offered his hand. "The name's Garrett. May I come in for a few minutes?"

Mrs. Parish shook his hand and glanced uncertainly over her shoulder. "I do have company at the moment."

Garrett poked his head in the door. He had on the same clothes he'd worn when we'd met. "Ah, Mrs. Foulton," he said, slipping his badge back into his coat pocket. "Your sister. I wanted to have a talk with her, too. I would appreciate it greatly if I could speak with you both. I promise to be brief."

"Fine," Mrs. Parish said, coming to a decision, opening the door farther. "Jan, this is the police officer who spoke to our kids the night of the accident."

Mrs. Foulton gave him a cordial welcome, and the three of them sat at the table together with fresh cups of coffee. I expected Garrett to launch into a barrage of questions concerning Jo and Amanda. But once he learned Amanda was not present, he appeared happy enough to relax in his seat, talk about the weather, and enjoy the coffee. He drank three cups of the latter at a truly remarkable speed. One might have thought he was trying to sober up, but he didn't seem the least bit drunk.

"What's going on?" I asked. "He's not doing anything."

"He's here for a purpose," Peter said, watching him.

A minute later Garrett made an unusual comment. "You know, Mrs. Parish, I'm no stranger to this neighborhood. I used to live around the block on Willow."

"Really? Which house?"

"The one at the end of the block with the fence. I think I had the same floor plan as you do." He stood suddenly. "Do you have two bedrooms and one and a half bathrooms?"

Mrs. Parish got up. "We have two full bathrooms here."

"Do any of the bedrooms have a huge closet?" Garrett asked. "I had one of those at my place. Loved the design of that house."

"The master bedroom's closet is plenty big," Mrs. Parish said. "That's my daughter's room. I'd be happy to show it to you."

Garrett smiled, showing a trace of discomfort. "Maybe I should go myself. I'm afraid all that coffee I drank has gone straight to my bladder. If you ladies will excuse me for a minute."

"There's a bathroom in the hall," Mrs. Parish said.

Garrett waved aside her suggestion as he turned and started off. "I'd like to see if Amanda's room is the same room as mine."

"He wants in her bedroom," Peter said.

I nodded as Mrs. Parish sat back down. "And he wants to be alone," I said. "Let's follow him."

We barely got into the room before he closed the door. He didn't even bother with the bathroom. He flipped on the light and quickly scanned the gray carpet. Then he strode to the closet door and flung it open, getting down on his knees and examining the soles of the three pairs of shoes that sat beneath the hems of Amanda's clothes. He didn't appear to find what he was looking for. Staying on his knees, with his nose in the carpet, he turned and carefully made his way across the floor to the bed. There he pulled up the corner of the bedspread.

A pair of white Nike tennis shoes lay under the boxspring.

"He's studied everybody's shoes that he's talked to," Peter said, thoughtful.

Garrett picked up one shoe and turned it over, tracing the sole with the tip of his finger. A fine orange chalk caught at the edge of his nail. I recognized the color.

I had seen it on the roof of Beth's condo.

"Wait a second," Peter said. "Isn't that the chalk Garrett found on the carpet in Beth's living room?"

"That bitch," I swore. "She pushed me off the balcony and then went over the roof!"

Garrett didn't have to hear me. He knew what was what. He must have suspected such a scenario from the beginning; that was why he had drawn the crisscrossing lines on his diagram between the wall that separated the kitchen from the bedroom, a few feet behind where I had been on the balcony. He stood and carried one shoe into the bathroom. He wrapped it in wads of toilet paper.

"He's preserving the evidence," Peter said.

"That bitch," I said again, my fury knowing no bounds.

"But why would she kill you?" Peter asked.

When Garrett had the shoe completely covered, he took it to the window and threw it into a bush at the side of the house. Then he straightened the bed—leaving the other shoe where he had found it—and returned to the living room. He was an amazing actor. He looked as natural as ever. But he made no move to rejoin the ladies at the table for more coffee.

"That room could have been mine," he said. "I guess that's how it is with tract houses, and I mean that as a compliment." He smiled. "Go into a neighbor's around here, and you can always find the bathroom." He took a step toward the door. "I promised to be brief, and now I must go. Thanks for your time."

"Nice meeting you," Mrs. Foulton called out, a bit puzzled.

"Let me see you out," Mrs. Parish said, hurrying to the door.

"Do you know when Amanda will be back tonight?" he asked casually as he stepped onto the porch with Peter and me.

"She's spending the night at a friend's," Mrs. Parish said.

"With Joanne?" he asked.

Mrs. Parish hesitated. "No. She's at another friend's."

He glanced at his watch. "I'd like to talk to her tonight if possible. I have a couple of small questions I'm sure she could clear up for me. Would you know where I can reach her?"

He asked the question with an air of complete nonchalance, but Mrs. Parish was suddenly alert. He was inquiring about her daughter, she must have realized, and policemen did not normally spend a lot of time investigating suicides. Despite what she knew, she must have still thought of Amanda as her child. Mrs. Foulton had probably told her the truth too late, when Amanda was hers for good or bad.

"No, I'm afraid not," she said.

He caught her eye. "She wouldn't, by any chance, be at her boyfriend's house?"

She did not flinch. "No. They've gone out of town for the week."

"I see." He handed her his card. "Well, please have Amanda give me a call at this number when you see her. Thanks again for the coffee."

Mrs. Parish smiled tightly. "It was nice of you to stop by."

She had no sooner closed the door than Garrett dashed for the side of the house. He reappeared a moment later with the shoe in his hand and ran to his truck. Pulling open the door, he put a foot up on the floor near the clutch, took out his notepad, and grabbed his cell phone.

"He's dialing my number!" I exclaimed.

"Mrs. Parish didn't fool him," Peter said. He added a moment later, "He's getting a busy signal."

"We have call standby on our phone," I said, my anxiety growing in leaps and bounds, "You never get a busy signal unless the phone's off the hook."

Garrett threw down the phone and reached for his CB. "Ten-forty, this is Garrett," he said into the receiver.

"Ten-forty, over," a voice cracked with static.

"Code sixteen. Send the two nearest available units to three-four-two-nine Clemens. Cross streets Adams and James. Repeat, code sixteen. This is an emergency. Locate and restrain Amanda Parish. Over?"

"Ten-forty, copy. Two units to three-four-two-nine Clemens. Code sixteen. Restrain Amanda Parish. Over."

"Out," Garrett said, hanging up the receiver and climbing in.

"Quick, let's get in the back," Peter said.

"No!" I cried. "It's twenty minutes to my house from here. We've got to get there now!"

"Jim's in no danger," Peter said. "Amanda won't hurt him."

"She killed me! She's crazy! God knows what she could do!" Garrett started his truck.

"If you don't go with Garrett, you'll be stuck," Peter said.

I couldn't think. I had to go by my gut feelings. I knew Peter was wrong. Alone with that witch, Jimmy was in grave danger. It was almost as if God himself was telling me that my brother needed me. Garrett began to pull away.

"Oh no," I moaned.

Peter touched my arm. "If you're worried, Shari, I can beam myself there and return in a few minutes and tell you what's happening."

"No! I have to go with you!"

Garrett laid down rubber as he raced up the street. He was worried, too.

"Why?" Peter asked.

"I don't know why!" I shouted. "Look, I have a mental block against ending up as part of a piece of furniture, all right, but I think I can fly. I was never afraid to go up in planes. What do I do?"

"Did you ever see the Superman movies?"

"Yeah, all of them. I saw *Supergirl*, too."

"Good. Just recognize the fact that you are Supergirl. You can do anything, and nothing can be done to you. Your arms can propel you on the breeze faster than any set of wings. Close your eyes, Shari, and let yourself float into the air. Don't concentrate, don't strain. Simply desire the ability. It is easier to fly than it is to walk."

I closed my eyes and did as he suggested. Nothing appeared to happen. "It's not working," I complained a minute later.

"Open your eyes, Shari," he said.

I did so. I almost gagged. I was ten feet off the ground!

"You're safe," Peter said quickly, floating up by my side.

"You're not going to fall, and even if you do, you won't

get hurt. Trust me. Trust yourself. Look around you. See, you can fly."

"Do I have to flap my arms to get going?" I asked, shaking my hands in the air like a tar-soaked pelican.

"Does Supergirl?"

"No." I raised my arms over my head and held them firm. "Let's haul ass," I said. "Warp eight."

CHAPTER XVI

My ANXIETY RUINED my first experience of flying, and that was a pity. It should have been a glorious moment. We rose up rapidly to about a thousand feet and then turned toward my street and let rip. Direction and speed seemed to be purely a function of will, and my desire to get there was overpowering. We flew like mad witches on burning brooms. The houses and yards raced beneath us in a blur. I felt no wind in my face, only the fear in my heart.

One thing I did notice, however, was that the city looked much brighter from high up than it did on the ground. I was reminded of the time I had returned to Southern California on a night flight, how easy it had been to identify the cars moving in slow motion up and down the square map of roads, to spot the miniature people walking the paper-thin sidewalks and even tell what color clothes they wore. Yet now plasmatic auras of violet and red drenched the neighborhood, shifting lazily from one end of the rainbow to the other as the thoughts and feelings of those beneath us waxed and waned over the spectrum of love and hate.

Even from high above, I could feel Amanda's hate. Or perhaps it was another dimension of my Shadow, my own hate for her closing in on me. Despite all I had learned and seen, I wished to God someone would choke her to death so I could get a hold of her and choke her some more.

I saw the smoke pouring out of my chimney from far off. It made no sense. It was summertime.

My window was open. We swooped into my room like gods of vengeance. But we had sacrificed our thunderbolts for wings when we died. We were here, but so what? What could a thousand angry ghosts do against one insane mortal?

We found Jimmy downstairs in the living room with Amanda.

They had a regular blaze going in the fireplace. The lights were all off. It looked as if Amanda had had Jimmy carry in half my family's winter supply of logs from out back. They were lounging together on the cream carpet in front of the flames, with Amanda sitting up on her knees and Jimmy resting on his back on a bundle of brown pillows. They appeared tired but relaxed.

They had on white bathrobes, nothing else.

"He looks like he's doing all right," Peter said.

"No," I said, pointing to a partially eaten chocolate cake and a largely empty bottle of red wine resting on the nearby coffee table. "She's been feeding him that junk."

"So what?" Peter asked.

"He's diabetic. She knows that. I don't like this."

"Don't panic. Garrett will be here in a few minutes."

We didn't have to listen long to learn that a few minutes would be too long.

"Would you like some more cake, Jimmy?" Amanda asked, reaching for the big knife near the dessert tray.

"No, I better not," Jimmy said, his voice drowsy. "I'll get sick."

Amanda made a long face. "That's not saying much for my baking, is it?"

He smiled and reached up to touch her long hair. "You're so beautiful."

She continued to hold the knife in her hand. "But you can't eat me."

"Oh, I don't know," Jimmy said. "I could try."

"Are you sure you don't want another piece? It'll go to waste."

Jimmy let go of her hair and put his hand over his tummy and groaned. "I'm sure. How come you don't have some more? You hardly touched that piece you cut."

"I never eat cake. It has a bad effect on me. The last time I ate cake was the time Shari made me."

Jimmy blinked. "When was that?"

" The night of the party."

"But why does cake have a bad effect on you?" he asked.

Amanda slowly set down the knife and turned and faced the fire. "For the same reason it bothers you."

Jimmy stared at her profile, which must have been difficult for him; his eyelids were half-closed. "You know I'm diabetic?"

"Yes."

"How do you know?" Jimmy asked.

"Shari told me," Amanda said.

"She did?"

Amanda nodded. "But I knew anyway. I could read the signs."

"You're diabetic too?" Jimmy asked, confused.

"Yes." Amanda tugged softly on the ends of her hair, her face warm in the glow of the fire. "We have that in common."

"She never told me." He was dumbfounded. "Why did you tell her?"

"She caught me giving myself a shot of insulin," Amanda said. "She tried to pretend like she didn't know what I was doing, but she did. She knew all kinds of stuff." Amanda shrugged. "I went along with it. For as long as I could."

"But I didn't know," I cried. "Peter, she's wrong."

"Shh," Peter cautioned. He was getting worried.

"She never told me," Jimmy repeated.

"She would have," Amanda whispered.

"What?" Jimmy asked.

Amanda turned toward him. "She was a funny girl, Shari. She and Jo. They used to give people nicknames. Do you know what Shari used to call my mother?"

"Mother Mary. She didn't mean anything by it."

"Oh, I thought it was a perfect name. Mother was always saying the rosary. Did you know she would sometimes pray in the middle of the night? Mother would think I was asleep, but I could hear her right through the wall. Praising the Blessed Virgin and asking God to forgive her for her sins." Amanda chuckled softly. "Her sins and mine. I used to listen to her sometimes. I told you that I'm a virgin, didn't I, Jimmy?"

My brother shifted uneasily, sluggishly. Amanda had probably tricked him into drinking most of the wine. I hated to think what his blood sugar level must be. "The way I feel right now," he said, yawning, "I think you'll still be one tomorrow." Jimmy sat up with effort. "It's late. We should get to bed."

"It's only ten o'clock," Amanda said.

"I have to get up for work tomorrow."

Amanda put her hands on his chest and gently pushed him back down. "No you don't," she said sweetly. "You're not going anywhere."

"She's going to hurt him," I moaned.

There was evil in the room. A perceptive mortal might have sensed it, but I could *see* it. The astral barbed wire from the addict's den was growing in the ether, hanging from the rafters like red and black celebration threads strung for a party in hell.

"Garrett's coming," Peter said, dropping all pretense that the situation was not critical. He could see the blossoming decadent products of Amanda's mind as well as I could.

Jimmy smiled. "Is that so? Who's going to stop me?"

In response, Amanda kissed him long and deep on the lips, her bathrobe breaking open partway at the top. She was definitely naked underneath. "I am," she said when she finally pulled back. "I'm going to keep you awake as long as I like, and then I'm going to put you to sleep with a bang."

"Sounds dangerous," Jimmy said, getting interested but yawning again.

Amanda moved back on her knees. "You're tired because you didn't take your medicine this evening. You don't have to be embarrassed. I take insulin, too, remember?" She tossed her head as if she had just been struck with a brilliant idea. "Hey, let me give you your shot. And you can give me mine."

"Peter," I cried. "Do something."

Jimmy pushed himself up on his elbow. "Are you serious?"

"Sure. And then you'll have the strength to make love to me. Would you like to make love to me, Jimmy?"

He nodded as he sat up farther, even though he couldn't stop yawning. "Yeah, but I'm bushed. I don't want a shot. I need rest. I haven't been sleeping well the last few days."

Amanda became very still. "Have you been dreaming of her?"

"Shari? Yeah." It broke my heart to see him glance at the

flames at the mention of my name. "I dreamed about her last night."

"So did I," Amanda said. "I dreamed we were blowing bubbles. But she kept trying to burst mine. It made me mad."

"Shari wouldn't have done that."

"She was doing it."

Jimmy gave her a puzzled look. "Shari liked you, Amanda."

Amanda lowered her head. "No she didn't. She didn't like me seeing you. She tried to keep us apart. She thought our relationship was—wrong. She was going to tell you, I know she was. She was just waiting for the right time."

"She was the one who introduced us," Jimmy said.

"She didn't know we were going to fall in love."

Jimmy forgot about his poor dead sister for a moment. He brightened. "You never said that before."

Amanda smiled sadly. "That I love you? Couldn't you tell?"

Jimmy reached out and took her hand as it rested in her lap. "I wanted to think you did, but I wasn't sure. Especially when you stopped returning my calls."

"My mom didn't always give me your messages,"

"Was that all there was to it?" Jimmy asked gently.

Amanda bit her lower lip. "No. The main reason was because of what I heard my mother saying."

"When?"

"Late at night, when she was praying. I told you. I thought I had to stay away. And I tried, too, but I couldn't."

"What did she say?" Jimmy asked.

Amanda raised her head and stared him in the eye. "That we were related."

Jimmy chuckled. "Really?"

Amanda stared at him a moment longer and then slowly nodded. "I'm glad you don't care. I don't. I remember a line I once read in a poem. It said, 'Love knows no reason.' That's how I feel about you. That I would do anything for you. Anything to keep you for myself."

Jimmy was amazed. "Have you always felt this way?"

"Yes. I can't even imagine your being with anyone else." Amanda took his hand and kissed his knuckles. "Especially her."

Jimmy wasn't sure he had heard correctly. "Who?"

Amanda's eyes lingered on the portion of his arm not covered by his sleeve. "I can see your needle marks," she said, which was a lie. I couldn't see anything. "I wouldn't leave marks like those."

The smoke from the fire seemed to back up in the chimney and choke the room. Jimmy took hold of her chin and looked longingly into her cold, clear gray eyes, noticing, perhaps, the way her rosy lips trembled at his touch, but failing completely to see the spiked halo that spun like a sticky cobweb from the core of her black-widow heart.

"You know I love you," he said.

She smiled faintly. "More than anyone?"

"Yes."

"You trust me?"

"Yes," he said.

"Then let me do it," Amanda said.

"What?"

"Let me give you a shot. And then you can give me one."

"Do you need insulin?" Jimmy asked, obviously not keen on the idea. "Have you tested your sugar level?"

She leaned closer, enclosing him in her claws. "I need it. You need it. We can make love afterward. Then we can sleep."

"But why?" Jimmy began. Amanda put her finger to his lips.

"Because I want to do it," she said. "Please?"

Jimmy thought a moment and then shrugged. "All right."

"Where is Garrett?" I cried.

Peter checked his watch. It had a luminous dial. "He could be as long as another ten minutes."

Amanda kissed Jimmy quickly and stood up and walked from the room. Leaving Peter with Jimmy, I went after her. She headed upstairs to the hall bathroom, where I had unknowingly caught her sticking herself before the party. There she retrieved three syringes and one vial of insulin from Jimmy's refrigerated supplies. Going back down the stairs, I tried tripping her, but she didn't care.

"Bitch," I swore at her.

In the flickering shadows outside the door to the steaming living room and the cracking fire, Amanda poked a needle into the vial. Like most diabetics, Jimmy took two forms of insulin: regular and long-lasting. Regular acted far more quickly, and it was that kind Amanda held in her hand. It was the medication of choice to rid a diabetic of sugar blues.

But whereas Jimmy's normal dosage was ten units, Amanda filled the hundred-unit syringe to the hilt.

"What will that do to your brother if she gets it in his bloodstream?" Peter asked, rejoining me and watching Amanda's secret preparations.

"It could send him into insulin shock," I said, unable to stand the tension.

"But could he survive it?" Peter insisted.

"Yes. But even if it just puts him to sleep, that's no good. The girl's nuts!"

"How long till it takes effect?"

"It requires half an hour for its effect to peak," I said. "But he'll be out in less than fifteen minutes."

"Still, time is on his side," Peter said.

"Time is never on your side when you're alive," I said.

Amanda stuffed the loaded syringe into her bathrobe pocket and strode into the living room. The bad black vibes were alive and hungry and everywhere to be seen. Jimmy continued to lie on the pillows by the fire. He had his eyes closed and only half opened them as his true love knelt by his side.

"I'm thirsty," he muttered.

"Your pancreas is probably freaking out," Amanda said,

the two empty syringes and the half-filled vial clearly visible in her hands. "You need this."

"I don't know," he mumbled, yawning and rolling over. "I just want to sleep."

Amanda put her left hand on his right ankle, setting down the insulin and unused syringes and carefully slipping the full needle from her pocket. "Let me take care of you, and then you can rest," she said.

Jimmy suddenly sat up. Amanda deftly dropped the needle back into her pocket. He nodded to the unopened syringes lying on the rug near the fireplace bricks. "Maybe I should test myself first."

"We can estimate your dosage," Amanda said.

He was doubtful. "You use synthetic, right?"

"Yes. In the evenings, I usually take ten units of regular. How about you? The same?"

Jimmy yawned and nodded wearily. "All right. Let's do it."

"Turn over," she said.

"What?"

"I'll give it to you in your backside like a nurse." She smiled at his discomfort. "Don't be embarrassed, Jimmy."

"I usually just do it in my arm."

"Your arms are all sore." She picked up one of the unopened syringes and gestured for him to turn over. "It'll just take a sec, and then you can do me in the same spot."

Amanda was convincing. Jimmy lay down on his belly and

closed his eyes. Yet she made no move to pull up his robe. "If it will make you feel better," she said, undergoing an abrupt change in tone, "I can put it in your leg."

"That would be fine," Jimmy muttered.

"Or your foot," she said, setting down the empty needle and picking up his right foot. Once again, she removed the loaded syringe from her pocket.

"Won't that hurt?" he asked.

"You'll hardly feel it," Amanda promised.

"Be careful not to hit a vein," Jimmy said.

"Peter!" I cried. "She's going to put it in his vein!"

"What will that do?" Peter asked.

"The insulin will go straight into his bloodstream! He'll be out in minutes!"

I had guessed Amanda's plan well. Quickly and smoothly, she pinched the skin around the big vein closest to his ankle and slid the needle home. Jimmy's eyelids barely flickered. It took Amanda only a few seconds to empty the syringe. Then she gathered together all the needles, plus the insulin vial, and put them in her pocket. She patted him on the rump as she stood.

"Rest there a minute," Amanda said.

"What about you?" Jimmy asked.

"I have to go to the bathroom," she said.

"Watch him," I told Peter as I chased after her.

Amanda returned to the bathroom upstairs and put away

both the unused needles and the tiny bottle of insulin. Yet she left the opened needle in her pocket, even though it was now drained. I could not imagine what she wanted it for.

Amanda stopped to wash her face before she left the bathroom. I stood to her left and watched her in the mirror as I had done the previous Friday night when I had been admiring her beauty.

"Please don't do anything else to him," I pleaded.

Amanda dried her face and put out the light.

Jimmy was sitting up on the pillows when she reentered the living room. "I don't feel so good," he mumbled.

Amanda strode to the pile of wood to the left of the fireplace. "You'll feel better in a few minutes," she said.

Jimmy frowned in her direction. "What are you doing?"

Amanda picked up a log. "Keeping the fire going."

"Don't. I'm hot." His head swayed atop his shoulders, and he raised a hand to steady it. "What's happening?"

Amanda threw the log into the fire. The sparks cracked like cheap fireworks. She came and knelt by his side and placed what might have been a cool palm over his sweaty forehead. "You poor darling," she said. "Can I get you something to drink?"

"No." He bent over. "I feel like I'm going to be sick."

"That's the insulin," Amanda said. "I gave you a hundred units."

He sat up and winced. *"What?"*

Amanda sat back on her knees. She looked sad. "Mrs.

Foulton called me earlier. She's over at my mother's house right now. They're discussing us. They don't want me seeing you anymore."

"What are you talking about?"

"I thought it would stop with Shari. I thought they would leave us alone. But they're not going to."

Something darker than sickness touched Jimmy's face.

Too late, he was beginning to get the message. "Why do you bring up Shari?"

Amanda looked to the fire and appeared to go blank for a few seconds. When she spoke next, it was with a peculiar mixture of bitterness and confusion, a small girl mad at a world suddenly grown big and complex.

"When I decided to go to the party," she said, "I didn't know what I wanted. I thought maybe I would talk to Shari about us, bring it out in the open and get it over with. I didn't want to, though. Then she kept me from having my shot when I needed it. She forced me to eat cake. It made me feel weird—I shouldn't have had a second piece. I could hardly think. Then, at the party, there was this magnet that you could ask questions. I asked about us, and it said that our love was real. It said that I should protect it. The magnet told me I had to take control of my own destiny." Amanda lowered her head, her pale face disappearing behind the fall of her long hair. "But what I did, I did on the spur of the moment."

I glanced at Peter, silently asking if he knew what she was

talking about in regard to the magnet answers. He quickly shook his head.

"What did you do?" Jimmy whispered. He was having trouble breathing. Sweat no longer merely dampened his forehead; it poured off his brow and into his eyes. Amanda raised her head, and her arm, too, and gestured to the richly furnished living room.

"I grew up in a slum," she said, her tone harsh. "She grew up in a mansion. She was given everything she wanted: new cars, new clothes. I had to take the bus to school and wear hand-me-downs. She was spoiled rotten. Do you know my own mother had to make her bed for her? She should burn in hell!"

"The message on the Ouija board," Peter gasped.

Jimmy sagged forward and had to throw out an arm to keep from landing face-first in the carpet. "What did you do to my sister?"

Amanda was suddenly concerned. "Are you still sick?"

"What did you do?" he demanded.

Amanda smiled. "Nothing. Your sister's fine."

Jimmy swallowed thickly. "You killed Shari."

Amanda nodded. "I did push her off the balcony. She deserved it. She was standing there and thinking mean thoughts about me. I pushed her, and then I climbed onto the roof and went over to the fire escape and came back in Beth's front door. I thought I had blown it, that everyone would know. But I was lucky. When I came back into the bedroom, Dan saw me and thought I had just come out of the bathroom." Amanda's face softened, and she touched Jimmy on the shoulder as he huddled before her in the throes of his insulin fit. "I know you liked her, but she really was no good. She wasn't even your sister."

He fought it but was unable to stop from toppling over onto his side. He glared up at her with glazed eyes. "You're crazy."

She looked hurt. "No, I'm not. I had good reason to do it. And *I* am your sister." She leaned over to give him a kiss. "If I can't have you, no one's going to have you."

Then she jolted upright, blood on her face.

He had bit her on the lip.

"Go to hell," he gasped, his eyes falling shut.

Amanda stared at him for a long time after he had lapsed into unconsciousness, the blood trickling over her chin in a steady stream. "Yes," she said finally.

Still, I didn't know how bad it could get.

Amanda put more logs on the fire. Then she took out the empty syringe and drew back the plunger, filling it full of air.

"She's going to put a bubble in his vein!" I groaned.

"That will give him a heart attack," Peter said grimly. "Or a stroke. I'm surprised she didn't shoot him with the bubble with the first shot. But maybe she didn't want him to have to suffer."

I looked at Peter. "You have to stop her."

He sighed. "I can't."

"Go into her body. Make her put the bubble in her own vein."

Peter was shocked. "That would be murder."

I gestured to Jimmy sprawled before the sacrificial flames. "This is murder. What you do would be justice."

Amanda kissed Jimmy on the forehead and picked up his arm.

"She would resist me," Peter said.

"Resist her back," I said.

"I can't make her commit suicide!" Peter cried.

Amanda rolled up the sleeve of Jimmy's bathrobe.

"And you can't let Jimmy die!" I yelled.

His face filled with dread, Peter bowed his head. I was quite prepared for him to say again that he couldn't interfere. But then he suddenly stepped forward and went into Amanda.

Amanda paused. Had she been able to see what I could see, she would have got out of the room while the going was good. The phenomenon was similar to when Peter had overlapped his hands with the others during the seance, only a dozen times more intense. Most of Peter had vanished; I could catch only a faint glimpse of his face through the thousand miniature geysers that had erupted like psychedelic discharges over every square inch of Amanda's body. The girl knew something was wrong. She raised her arm and peered at the syringe in her hand.

The point of the needle bent toward her eyes.

Amanda jumped to her feet. She tried, but she couldn't drop the syringe. Peter, I supposed, did not have the control to aim for a tiny vein. I didn't mind, as long as he kept her occupied until Garrett arrived. Amanda twisted around the living room like an epileptic caught in a fit, the blood from her torn lip splattering the lapels of her white robe, screaming for help. It was a wonderful sight.

Then she stopped in midstride. Peter reappeared by her side, staring anxiously into the dark doorway at the north end of the living room.

"It's coming," he said.

"What?" I demanded.

"My Shadow."

Amanda shook herself, still holding on to the needle, and turned toward Jimmy. I jumped to Peter's side and grabbed hold of him. "You can't run," I said.

"It's coming," he said, panicking.

Amanda knelt by Jimmy's side. Pulling back the plunger, she refilled the syringe with deadly air.

"It's not as bad as you think," I said. "I faced it."

"It wouldn't be the same for me," Peter said, throwing off my hold.

"You can't leave till you kill her!" I yelled.

"I can't kill again!" he yelled back.

I stopped. Even Amanda paused in the middle of her evil

deed. She was wiping the blood from her mouth. She had everything ready; she just wanted to kiss Jimmy goodbye. "When did you kill someone?" I asked Peter.

He pressed his arm over his eyes and sucked in a deep breath as if he were about to shout. But all that came out was a shameful whimper. "I crossed the lane in front of that truck on purpose," he said. "I killed myself."

Amanda touched her bloody lips to Jimmy's sleeping mouth.

"That's not possible," I said, echoing his words to me about my own conviction of suicide.

He nodded miserably. "It's not something I'm likely to forget." He turned to go. "It's not something my Shadow will ever forgive."

Amanda reached for Jimmy's arm, searching for a vein.

"But we need you, Peter," I pleaded.

His gaze strayed again to the dark doorway, and he trembled. "I can't, it's too close," he said.

Amanda squeezed the flesh on the inside of Jimmy's elbow.

"All right," I said, my voice empty. "Leave, if you feel you must."

He looked at me with pain in his eyes. "I'm sorry."

I turned my back on him and stepped toward my brother. "So am I," I replied, and I heard the disgust in my tone, even though I did not want him to hear it.

There followed another pause, in both realities. Amanda

had found the desired vein and was pressing the tip of the needle to it. But she couldn't stop looking at Jimmy's face. Peter, it seemed, couldn't stop looking at me; I could feel his eyes on the back of my head.

"I love you," Amanda told Jimmy.

"Shari," Peter said. "I love—"

He didn't finish. It wasn't the time for confessions of the heart, he must have realized. He went by in a flash toward my brother. Unfortunately, he had waited too long. Before he could reenter Amanda's body, something came through the dark doorway at the north end of the living room. I couldn't see it as I could my own Shadow, but I could sense its movements. Peter only had time to throw a single terrified glance in its direction before it crossed the room and was upon him.

He crumpled to the floor precisely as Amanda stabbed Jimmy with the needle and began to depress the plunger.

I had previous information about the dangers of air in the bloodstream. A relative was a registered nurse and had once explained how careful RNs had to be when giving people injections to clear away any bubbles from the medicated solutions. She had added, however, that if the system could quickly break down a large bubble into a number of tiny ones, then the person would most likely survive.

It gave me an idea. And if I could fly, I thought, I should be able to do anything.

I dived *into* the air in the syringe.

I don't know how I did it. Once again, the power must have simply come to me because I wanted it badly enough.

I saw little before I was thrust into Jimmy's body: a blur of curving plastic walls, the vague shape of a gargantuan thumb, the distorted flames of the fireplace blazing before my microscopic vision like a sun gone nova. Then there was the motion of powerful winds, and I was riding a wild and pulsing current of liquid night.

Yet not everything was dark for me inside Jimmy's vein. Outside the window of the air bubble, I detected huge spheres of tumbling tissue chasing me along an endless tunnel of blood. Even more remarkable was the sound, a pounding thunder that grew so rapidly in volume and force that I feared it would drown out my mind. A fool could have recognized it—the beating of Jimmy's heart—and I was racing toward it with the speed of an angel.

A dark angel.

The thunder skipped as I plunged into a spacious chamber of churning blood. It skipped twice, three times, and then it halted altogether and everything was silent.

Dead silence. The bubble had caused Jimmy's heart to stop.

A golden light began to dawn in the strange night.

A realm of beauty and bliss unfolded.

It was Jimmy's dream. I remembered.

"We were in a strange place. It was like a world inside a flower. I know that sounds weird, but I don't know how else to describe

it. Everything was glowing. We were on a wide open space, like a field. And you were dressed exactly as you are now, in those jeans and that shirt. You had a balloon in your hand that you were trying to blow up. No, you had blown it up partway, and you wanted me to blow it up the rest of the way. You tried to give it to me. You had tied a string to it. But I didn't catch the string right or something, and it got away. We watched it float way up in the sky. Then you began to cry."

It was all true. It was a miracle. We were on a field that stretched almost to infinity, to the borders of an all-encompassing lotus that sent a thrill through every particle of my being at the sight of it. A brilliant white light shone in the sky, radiating a peace and joy beyond understanding. It was the light Peter had spoken of. It was all knowing. It knew our situation. Yet it was not there to interfere. It was merely there to observe. It was the silent witness of the movie of my life finally uncloaked. Jimmy turned to me and smiled.

"This is nice," he said.

I had on my jeans and yellow blouse. Jimmy was wearing his white bathrobe. The balloon I held in my right hand at the end of a thin string was not the brown Jimmy had told me after he had awakened from his dream, but red. And he had been wrong about me wanting to blow it up further. I wanted to pop the balloon. It was the bubble that had stopped his heart.

Still, it was impossible not to be happy. The field we stood on was like a living jewel.

"Yes," I said. "It's beautiful."

Jimmy took more notice of me. "Shari," he said, puzzled. "What's going on? You're supposed to be dead."

"I am dead," I said. "But being dead isn't like people think it is. Anyway, I can't go into that now or you'll die." I pulled down the balloon and tried to pop it in my hands. Unfortunately, it had a surface as firm as steel. "Oh no."

"What's wrong?" he asked.

"This is an air bubble that Amanda put into your bloodstream. It has to be broken up."

His eyes widened. "That's right. She was trying to kill me. Did she succeed?"

"Not yet, I don't think," I said, continuing to wrestle with the balloon. "Your heart's only been stopped a few seconds."

Jimmy gazed about the glass field, and his concern quickly receded. "But it's so peaceful here. And that light's so nice. I want to stay. I want to die."

"No," I said firmly. "You have to live."

"Why?"

"Because you're young and beautiful. You're wonderful. The world needs you. Mom and Dad need you. If you die, it'll break their hearts."

"But I want to talk to you," he said. "I miss you."

"I miss you, too. But you have to live a long life. And then, when you're done, you can be with me."

"Where is this place? Are we in heaven?"

"No, we're in . . ." I began, hesitating, wanting to say we were in his heart, before deciding we might be talking about the same thing. "Yes, this is heaven."

"I'm glad you made it here," he said.

"So am I." It occurred to me then that because the bubble was in his heart, it might be better if *he* tried to pop the balloon. But when I started to give it to him, it began to slide from my grasp. It was only the warning of his dream that enabled me to react quickly enough and pull it back in.

There was slippery gook on the palms of both my hands. It was like black chimney soot. Jimmy had a little on his hands, too, I saw a moment later, although not nearly as much as myself.

"What is this stuff?" he asked, brushing with his fingers. Neither of us could get it off. It was the only stain in our entire world of light. We had brought it with us, I realized. The light itself must have helped me with the realization. When I spoke next, I did so with the certainty that I spoke the truth.

"It's hate," I said. "We've got to get rid of it. We have to forgive Amanda in order to be able to burst the balloon."

"That bitch. She pushed you off the balcony."

"So she did. But what's done is done. I see that now, Jimmy. I really do. Don't you see?"

"But she murdered you," he protested.

"Amanda is sick. She needs your help." I added, "Besides, she told you the truth. She *is* your sister."

He raised an eyebrow. "You can't be serious."

I nodded. "I'm afraid I am."

"Oh no." He shook his head. "I knew I should have gone away with mom and dad."

I had to laugh at his discomfort. And it has been said there is nothing more forgiving than a hearty laugh. When I looked down, my hands were clean; so were his. Jimmy had never been one to hold a grudge for more than two minutes. I estimated that was how long his heart had been stopped. We were running out of time. I handed him the balloon, and he held on to it.

"Pop it," I said. "It's the bubble in your heart. It's killing you."

"Will I remember any of this?" he asked, worried.

"I don't know," I replied, my voice faltering as a tear ran down my cheek. "It doesn't matter. You will always remember me. And I will remember you. You were the best brother a girl could've had." I started to hug him goodbye and found I couldn't budge from my place. Neither of us could move, and it was getting late. "Pop it, Jimmy," I said. "Live. Be happy. Be happy for me."

"You know, Shari . . ." he began as he squeezed the balloon in his fingers. But he didn't get a chance to finish the sentence. I didn't get a chance to hear it. The golden lotus exploded with the flash of a thunderbolt. It was not, however, real thunder that I heard. It was the beating of his heart.

CHAPTER XVII

I REAPPEARED STANDING beside Jimmy. He was still lying on his back on the pillows. Only now he was coughing. He was alive!

For the time being. Amanda had scattered logs across the carpet and was transforming the living room into a furnace of flame and smoke. A funeral pyre for both of them. She really was off her nut. She had the needle in her hand and was going to put a big balloon in her own vein. Fine, go ahead, I thought, before I remembered my promise to forgive her. Ten seconds, and I was already forgetting.

Someone was hammering on the front door.

Amanda had the needle up to her skin. The someone at the door was going to be too late to save her.

I crossed the room in one leap and jumped inside her. It was weird. It was like having a physical body again, only one that didn't fit. I felt so *thick*. I decided not to worry about it.

I whipped my right arm upward and flexed my palm open. Amanda did the same and dropped her needle on the floor. She was bending over to search for it, coughing her blessed lungs out, when the front door burst open.

"What the hell," Garrett shouted, running into the room.

Amanda dashed behind her barrier of burning logs. I got out of her quick. "You can't have me!" she screamed.

"Honey," Garrett said, hurrying to Jimmy's side and grabbing him by his wrists. "I don't want you."

Garrett dragged Jimmy away. Amanda appeared to be set on going to an agonizing end until a spark landed on her bare foot. Letting out a silly cry, she ran after Garrett. I loved it.

Peter lay where he had fallen. Following Garrett's lead, I took hold of his arms and pulled him out into the night air. I was surprised at how light he felt, forgetting for a moment that he didn't weigh anything at all.

The house survived. Two black and white units arrived on Garrett's tail, and the policemen were quick to gather the front and backyard hoses and get water on the flames. A fire engine appeared shortly afterward. They had paramedics with them. Jimmy got plenty of attention. He sat propped up beside Garrett on the neighbor's front lawn while a medical man pressed an oxygen mask to his face. Leaving Peter still unconscious but out of the way of the stampede, I walked over to check on him.

"How's he doing, doc?" Garrett asked, concerned.

"I'm not a doctor," the man replied. "But he appears to be doing fine."

"I can breathe," Jimmy said, pushing away the face mask. The excess insulin in his blood was not affecting him as much as it should have. I could only believe the light had somehow detoxified him.

The paramedic put down the oxygen. "Then breathe," he said. "But you're still going to the hospital."

"No, I'm not," Jimmy said. "I feel fine."

"What did she do to you?" Garrett asked.

Jimmy's voice hardened. "She killed Shari. She pushed her off the balcony. She tried to kill me. She shot me up with too much insulin and knocked me out. Then she put an air bubble in my vein."

"If she knocked you out with insulin," the paramedic said, reaching for an instrument that resembled the tool Jimmy used to check his blood sugar, "how do you know what she put in your vein?"

I crossed my fingers *and* made the sign of the cross waiting for Jimmy's response. But I was in for a disappointment. "I don't know," he said after a moment's hesitation.

"We're going to keep him in the hospital overnight," the paramedic told Garrett.

"Oh, no," Jimmy muttered.

Garrett slapped Jimmy on the side. "Son, remind me some-day that I've got to introduce you to some nice girls."

Satisfied that Jimmy was in good hands, I returned to where I had deposited Peter. The flashing lights of police cars bathed the surrounding houses. The whole neighborhood had poured out to watch the spectacle. Her white robe gross with bloodstains, Amanda stood pale and bent in the custody of a police officer.

Peter had not moved an inch. Kneeling by his side, I shook him gently.

"Peter? Can you hear me? Wake up, it's Shari."

He stirred and opened his eyes. "Where am I?" he mumbled.

"It's not Newport Memorial, and I'm sad to say you didn't make it." I helped him up. "How do you feel?"

"Embarrassed," he said. "How's Jimmy?"

"Fine. Everything's fine. Why are you embarrassed? You stayed. That took guts. Believe me, I know."

He wouldn't look at me. "I lied to you."

I sat by his side and put an arm around his shoulder. "What happened?" I asked.

He was ashamed. "I committed suicide."

"I don't believe it."

"Believe it. I was out on my bike, driving like a maniac, when I saw this truck coming at me the other way. I jerked my bike into its path."

He was serious. "But *why*?" I asked.

He shrugged. "I'm not sure. It was a number of things. Everybody at school was ecstatic about how I'd pitched Hazzard to the city championship. But what they didn't know was that the coach pressured me into starting the last four playoff games. I let him pressure me. Anyway, I blew out my arm, tore my rotary cuff. I wasn't going to pitch again."

"*That's* why you ended your life?"

"No. There's more. It's complicated. I was depressed."

"Why?" I asked.

"I was lonely."

"But you had lots of friends. You had me."

He looked at me. "You heard what I said before the Shadow arrived?"

"Yes. You were going to say you loved me, right?"

Ordinarily, he would have snorted at my nerve. Now he just nodded. "I've always been crazy about you."

I laughed. "You are so dumb. I was crazy about you!"

He shook his head. "Don't, Shari."

"I'm telling you the truth! Why didn't you ask me out?"

"You wouldn't have gone out with me."

"I would have given my right arm to go out with you! God, I'm so angry at you! We could have had so much fun together!" I sighed. "And I wouldn't have had to suffer so when you died."

"You suffered?" he asked in disbelief.

"Of course I did. I never got over losing you."

"But you didn't even go to my funeral."

"Because I was too upset. I stayed home and cried for days."

He stared at me strangely. "Are you serious?"

"Yes! I loved you! I love you now! When you found me in the cemetery after they buried me, it was the happiest day of my life. I mean, it was great! You didn't have to kill yourself over me."

"I didn't do it just because of you."

"Oh. All right. What else was the matter?"

"I was curious," he said.

"You were *what*?"

"I was curious to see what it was like on the other side. Jo showed you some of my stories. I was obsessed with death. It was an unhealthy obsession."

"I should say."

"There was something else. This is hard to explain. Remember when we were in the park and trying to figure out who killed you? Remember how I kept insisting we needed a motive?"

"Yes," I said.

"I should have known better. Did you hear what Amanda said in the house? She had all these reasons for what she did, but when it came right down to it, she did it on the spur of the moment."

"Are you saying you pulled in front of the truck on the spur of the moment?"

"It sounds strange, but it's true."

"That's dumb," I repeated.

"I can't argue with you."

"Did this have anything to do with why Jeff dislikes me?"

"He knew I cared for you," Peter said. "But he thought you were a tease. I'm not sure, but from watching him the last couple of years, I sometimes got the impression he blames you for what happened that night."

"Does he think you hit the truck on purpose?"

"No. He thinks that I had reasons for living dangerously. But that's not quite the same thing."

"And that I was one of those reasons?"

"Yes," Peter said. "Does that bother you?"

"No. I understand."

"I'm glad. He's a great guy."

"I have another question for you," I said. "Why did you put me in your story?"

"That wasn't you," he said.

"You used my middle name—Ann."

"I didn't know that was your middle name."

"That's right," I said. "You don't even know how to spell my first name. OK, let's back up a sec. You were driving along, and you decided to add some excitement to your life by dying. What happened next?"

"I realized I had made a terrible mistake."

"Is there a penalty over here for committing suicide?"

"Yes. Remember I told you I knew you couldn't have killed yourself?"

"Yes," I said.

"The reason I knew was because you have the opportunity to go into the light." He paused. "I haven't had that opportunity."

I wrinkled up my face. "Why?"

"Until all the years my life *should* have lasted have gone by, I have to stay on earth. I am earthbound."

"Who bound you? Who told you this?"

"Those are the rules," he said.

"That's B.S. Peter, I've been in the light. I went into it when Jimmy's heart stopped. And I can tell you from personal experience that it wouldn't hand out penalties. It can't—it's too nice. It's completely nonjudgmental. The reason you're stuck here is because you're keeping yourself here. You're feeling guilty."

"Wouldn't you?" he asked. "I threw away my life. It was only by blind luck that I didn't kill the driver of the truck."

"Yes, I would feel guilty. But not for the rest of eternity. Who told you that you have to stay?"

"Other ghosts in my predicament," he said.

"Oh, swell, go to the man on death row for advice about your trial. They're obviously as screwed up as you are."

"I am not screwed up," he said indignantly.

"Yes you are. Here you give me all these boring lectures on how anything is possible, and you don't even know how to knock on the door to ask to be let in. And another thing, if you haven't been in the light, how can you know anything about it?"

"I didn't lie to you about everything. I really have helped many people that have just crossed over. Dozens of times I've seen what happens when the light comes over an individual, the joy they experience, the peace—even before they leave."

"But you've only watched, Peter. Tell me, have you ever tried to go on?"

That got him. "No," he said.

"See? Tell me another thing. What happened when your Shadow caught you?"

"My whole life passed before me."

"And?" I asked.

"And what?"

"Was it so horrible? Were you such a bad guy? The Peter I remember couldn't do enough for people."

"The Peter you remember wasn't the real Peter."

I stood and spoke to the sky. "Listen to this guy—Mr. Suffering Servant himself!" I kicked Peter in the shin, and I honestly believe he felt it—he winced. "Stay here, then. Go play with your other unhappy ghosts. Spend the rest of eternity peeking in at girls in the shower. I don't care. I have better things to do with my time."

He raised his head. "I didn't peek at you in the shower."

"You said you did."

"I was kidding," he said. "I left before you took off all your clothes."

"*All* my clothes? How much did I have off?"

"Ah, your top," he said.

"How did I look?"

"I told you, fine. Great."

"Why did you leave at all?" I asked. "I thought you were lusting after me."

"I didn't say that."

"Crazy about me, love me, lusting after me—it's all the same thing."

"I didn't peek at you in the shower."

"Why not?" I asked, feeling mildly insulted.

"That would have been unethical."

"Ah-ha!" I exclaimed, pointing a finger at his nose. "That's your problem. You think sex is dirty. You have a dirty mind. No wonder you can't get into the light."

He took hold of my finger. He surprised me when he pulled it down and gently kissed the back of my hand. "I can get in," he said quietly.

I took a step back at his change in tone. "Did I convince you that easily?" I asked, surprised.

Peter stood and put his hands in his pockets. We had almost forgotten the commotion going on around us. The fire was out, although smoke continued to pour from the from door and the side windows. My dad would probably have to replace the downstairs furniture and carpeting. I wasn't worried; he could afford it. Slowly, in twos and threes, the neighbors were returning to their homes, probably thinking those Coopers were crazy.

"You did the most for me when you made me stay and face the Shadow," Peter said. "I'm not afraid of it anymore. I don't have to keep running. It helps that I was able to talk about it right now. I guess I've finally accepted what I did. And what you said just now, yeah, it makes good sense. I can go on, I think, as long as I can go with you." He paused. "You were serious about liking me?"

"*Loving* you," I corrected, squeezing up against him. "But don't make me out to sound like a soul winner, all right? It's not what I want out of this relationship."

"What do you want, Shari?"

I thought a moment. "Kisses. Two years' worth."

He grinned. "For that, you'll have to take off your top."

Later, we rode to the hospital in the back of the ambulance with Jimmy. Garrett was also there, and that was good. I put my arm around the detective and gave him a big hug. Maybe he felt it, I don't know. He belched.

"I owe this man," I said.

"He saved your brother's life," Peter agreed.

"He also saved my reputation. There's got to be something I can do for him."

"Shari."

"I'm going to give it some thought," I insisted, calling over to my brother, who was sitting with a wary eye on the paramedic. "Hey, Jimmy, what do you say?"

Others might have disagreed, but I believe what happened next meant Jimmy remembered a portion of our talk in the golden lotus. At my remark, he turned to Garrett and finished the sentence the popping of the red balloon had interrupted.

"You know," he said, "Shari was the best sister a guy could've had,"

I burst out crying, I was so happy.

EPILOGUE

PETER AND I did not leave immediately. I wanted to see what happened after all the excitement died down. I also wanted to offer what help I could to smooth out what I believed was going to be a rough period for those I loved.

The truth about Amanda's biological parents came out. It was, I suppose, inevitable. Yet Mrs. Foulton's full involvement in the switch of infants was never brought to light. Mrs. Foulton and Mrs. Parish got together and led the authorities to believe that they had "felt" for many years that some "mistake" had been made long ago at the hospital. It was amazing how vague they were about what this mistake was, and even more amazing that the police didn't haul them both over the coals. It may have been because nobody was pressing any charges.

The police did, however, take a print of Amanda's feet and mine—lifted from inside one of my shoes—and compared them to the ones in the hospital's files. This verified that the mistake had indeed been very real. I was worried about how my parents would react when they learned that their pretend daughter had been murdered by their real daughter. My concerns proved to be groundless. They were both so elated to have a daughter again that they went out and hired the best lawyer in town to defend Amanda for killing me!

It is a strange universe.

Amanda got off light—she was sentenced to five years of state-supervised psychiatric care. I guess the judge figured she had been subjected to psychological pressures of a most unusual nature. I didn't mind; I felt no need for vengeance. Nor did Jimmy. He provided Amanda with moral support throughout the course of the trial. He never, however, let himself get caught alone with her again. He was a nice guy, but he wasn't stupid.

Two days after the red balloon and the big fire, I had my picture on the front page of Los Angeles's two biggest papers: "HIGH SCHOOL SENIOR'S SUICIDE TURNS OUT TO BE MURDER" and "SHARI COOPER DIDN'T JUMP." I liked the sound of the second one the best. The latter headline was also above a color picture of me—not a black and white—and everybody in town got a chance to enjoy my sparkling green eyes.

The gang—Jo, Jeff, Daniel, and Beth—got together at Beth's condo shortly after the articles came out to discuss how they knew all along that I wasn't the jumping kind. I just listened and laughed. Especially when Beth slapped Daniel across the face for trying to grab her breast after Jo and Jeff had left holding hands and cuddling.

But through all this, I fretted over Mrs. Parish the most. She had, in a sense, lost not one but two daughters. I would like to say her quiet strength allowed her to accept Amanda's crime with a sense of equanimity. Regrettably, besides being strange, the universe is often hard. Mrs. Parish suffered terribly with Amanda's trial. One consolation, however, was that my mother bore no malice toward Mrs. Parish for not having brought the mix-up to light sooner. Quite the contrary, she supported and encouraged Mrs. Parish at every opportunity. I was proud of my mother, finally proud to call her Mom, even though she no longer was.

In the end, Mrs. Parish did gain a measure of peace. I am happy to report that I had a hand in it. For many nights after Amanda was arrested, I would visit Mrs. Parish in her dreams and tell her that I was doing well and that I held no grudge against Amanda. For a while it seemed my interludes did no good and that she would remember nothing upon waking. But then one afternoon when she was sewing in her living room and I was sitting by her side and listening to the melody she was humming, she suddenly put down her needle and thread and stared off into empty space.

"Shari," she said. "If you're there, if you can hear me, I want to tell you something that I almost told you a thousand times while you were alive. Finding you again after losing you all those years was wonderful. It was the best thing that ever happened to me. It brought me so much joy, I thought I would never again ask God for anything, because he had given me everything. And I kept that promise, until right now. You see, I have to ask him one more thing, to tell you this, that I loved you as much as any mother loved a child. You were always my daughter."

Then she went completely still for a moment and smiled, and there was the same light on her face that I had seen in the church above her head when she had prayed for me. "Thank you," she whispered. "So it is done. I've heard you, too, Shari. Don't worry about me, I'll be fine."

And from then on, she was much better.

But I still had my debt to Garrett to repay and, more important, the desire to do something for him. I thought about the problem a long time, and finally a solution came to me.

Peter helped me implement it. He showed me how to alter my form at will and acted as my accomplice. Together we journeyed to the seedy motel room where Garrett's daughter spent her miserable nights.

I returned as a radiant angel of light. My hair was long and golden. I had eyes of emeralds and a beautiful silver robe. I spent a long time getting my translucent wings to shimmer with a celestial glow. A fine sight I made standing beside Peter.

He played a devil, and it was hard to look at him and not cringe. His mouth was a chopping maw of pointed green teeth, his hide a red and purple map of dragon scales. He had short, squat reptilian legs and took particular delight in drooling dark clots of blood and poking me with his huge black pitchfork.

We waited in the closet of the motel room for the girl to shoot up with her drugs. After my recent bad experiences with needles, it was difficult for me to watch. But Peter was encouraging. He made an excellent devil.

"This is going to be fun," he slobbered with glee as we trooped out of the closet. The girl lay sprawled in her underwear on the bed, deep in the spell of her narcotic, her pupils dilated. But she blinked at the sight of us. She knew we were there, though I'm sure she couldn't have guessed why.

We were going to fight over her soul.

"Let me eat her alive!" Peter cried, jumping toward the bed with his pitchfork held high. "Let me chew off her fingers— one through five!"

Garrett's daughter recoiled against the bedstand, her nails going to her mouth, her face turning white. I leaped in front of Peter and held my arms and wings out wide. "You cannot have her!" I cried. "Not while she lives!"

Peter halted and snorted like a fiend. "She will be dead soon! With all the drugs she takes, she will die in this very room!" He tried to squirm around me. "Then I will come for her! I will peel off her skin and wear it like fur!"

I barred his way. "She might not die! She might turn away from her evil ways!"

Peter laughed uproariously. "She will never change! She is already in my cage! Soon I will carve her dry! I will lick her bones and make her cry!"

"You cannot do this!" I said.

"Let me have her tonight!" He fought to get by me. "Let me have a bite!"

"Stop him," the girl pleaded, shaking like a leaf.

"I can't," I said, looking over my shoulder and through my wing, barely holding Peter at bay. "I cannot stop him without your help, child. If you die on drugs, he will come for you."

"A leg!" Peter chortled. "Give me her legs! They taste so good with sausage and eggs!"

"Please," the girl cried.

"Leave here," I told her in as clear and urgent a tone as I could muster. "Go to your father. Only your father can keep this devil away."

"I must have an eye!" Peter howled. "A soggy eye for my sandwich of ham and rye!"

The girl nodded frantically. "I will go."

"You must promise me," I said. "I can do nothing for you without your promise."

"An ear!" Peter yelped. "An ear to mix in my salty beer!"

The girl tried to grab my hand and kiss it. "I promise."

Peter stopped his struggling and took a step back, falling silent. I laid my hands atop her thick black hair. She was very pretty.

"You are stronger than you know," I said. "You will be able to keep your promise." I leaned over and kissed her on the forehead. "Close your eyes now, child, and be at peace. All is well. Tomorrow you will return to your father's house and start a new life."

The girl did as I requested and lay back on her bed. Peter and I hurried out the door. (I had no trouble walking through them nowadays.)

"We scared the hell out of her," Peter said. "It might work."

"What was the deal with the rhymes?" I asked.

"Devils always speak in rhymes."

"How do you know?" I asked. "Have you ever met any?"

"No. But I read about it in the *Enquirer*."

The girl did return home to Garrett. In fact, she called him the next morning, and he drove across town to pick her up. She tried to tell him about her vision. He nodded in understanding and told her to get into the truck. These days they're living together in a tidy house with a white picket fence and two-car garage. They're driving each other crazy. But at least she's no longer tripping, and he has stopped drinking. I'd say they're happy.

I'm happy. Peter and I are going to be leaving soon. The light is waiting. The sun is rising. It really is rising. Jimmy hasn't gotten over his bad habit of leaving his computer on, and he is still sleepwalking. He will probably be waking up soon, and I'm sure he's going to be tired. He has never spent an entire night typing at the speed of a supernatural being. He has never spent so long with a ghost sitting, not beside him, but *inside* him.

It was Jimmy who unknowingly wrote this story. I merely provided the inspiration.

I am going to miss my brother, but he is getting on with his life. The wonder he experienced when we stood together inside his heart has not left him, even if he does not consciously remember it. I watch him even now, through the images that flash behind his fluttering eyelids. And I know he dreams of me, of everything I have gone through since I last bid him farewell on my way to Beth's party. His touch lightens as he types this happy ending. Mrs. Parish is not the only one who knows I'm doing well.

If you who read this story are really there, then it means my brother did not accidentally erase this computer disk I store my words on. It means that my last wish has been granted.

In the beginning, I called myself a ghost and said this was because I was dead. But those were Peter's words that I borrowed when he tried to communicate with his brother using my body. Even though Peter is a fine writer, I think he could have put it better.

I am not dead. Death does not exist. I am alive! That is the purpose of this tale, to let everyone know that they do go on and that they don't need to be afraid, as I was afraid.

Yet I also have a selfish reason for wanting my story told.

I was young when I died. I didn't have a chance to make nay mark in the world. I didn't do anything unique, nothing that will change the course of history. But I wasn't a bad girl. I don't want to be forgotten.

I want people to remember me.

THE RETURN

For all the Wanderers of the world. May they one day remember where they came from.

CHAPTER I

JEAN RODRIGUES did not want to become her mother. A not quite forty-year-old woman with five kids, a dead husband lost to booze, working sixty hours a week at a coffee shop just to pay the rent on a rundown house in the wrong part of town and to put food in the mouths of children who could not have cared less about her. Most of the time Jean couldn't give a damn, not about school or work or even about herself. Yet sometimes she'd watch her mother as the woman got dressed for work, the lines of ruined dreams on her weary face, and Jean would feel sorry for her. She'd think, There must be something that would make my mother smile. There must be more to life than what I see waiting for me. Yet Jean could never see that "more," and so she seldom smiled herself.

Jean Rodrigues was eighteen years old and it was two weeks before her high school graduation. Her father had been

Mexican, pure Aztec—at least that's what she was told. Her memories of him were few; he had died of pneumonia and heart failure while she was still in first grade. Her mother—she wasn't positive what her mother was. Half Hispanic, a quarter Italian, two-thirds the rest of the world. The numbers and genes never added up. Jean supposed the same was true for her. But Jean knew she looked good, no matter what her gene pool or how broke she was. Her long dark hair was her glory. She wore it unadorned and straight down to her butt and washed it every night with an herbal shampoo—one of the few luxuries she allowed herself. Her face was strong; relatives said she took after her father. Her nose was big, but since her mouth was as well, the flaw only enhanced her beauty. She may have had her father's fearless expression, but she had her mother's body. They were both voluptuous. Her looks were one of the things Jean felt good about. There were so few things.

That evening was a warm Friday. If Jean had read the papers closely and had an excellent memory, she would have remembered it was exactly fifty-two Fridays after the death of another eighteen-year-old in another section of Los Angeles, a certain Shari Cooper. Like Shari of a year ago, Jean was in her bathroom preparing to spend Friday night at a birthday party for a friend. Her friend was Lenny Mandez. Jean had been dating Lenny for about three months and had a special surprise for him tonight. It was so special that she wondered if she should let him know about it on a night reserved for celebration. She was six weeks pregnant with his kid.

My mother got pregnant with me when she was eighteen. The same sad story, all over again. I don't want to become my mother.

Jean knew why she was pregnant, besides the obvious reason that she'd had sex. Six weeks earlier when Lenny and she had made love, their condom had broken. And there they were being so responsible, practicing safe sex and all. She'd been a fool to believe all that hype, she thought. The only hundred percent safe sex was between Barbie and Ken, and she'd heard rumors they weren't doing it anymore. What made it worse was that she wasn't sure if Lenny knew how badly things had misfired that night. She worried that he might think the kid belonged to someone else. But it wasn't a huge worry—Lenny was cool—not as huge as the kid growing inside her. She didn't know what to do. She didn't want to think about it, so she planned to get loaded that night.

Jean was brushing her hair when the car horn outside startled her, although she'd been waiting for it to sound. Her best friend, Carol Dazmin, was driving her to the party. Jean did not have a car. She did work after school and most weekends at a Subway Sandwich but only to supplement her mother's meager income and to buy clothes and pot. Not for a car. Jean smoked pot practically every day; it was the only thing that made the clocks on the walls at school fun to watch. Carol got loaded with her, too, but spent her days staring at the other girls. Carol was a lesbian, but she never hit on Jean or anything and it was OK. In fact, Carol was another of the few things in Jean's life that could be called positive. Carol was one of the kindest and funniest people Jean had ever met.

At the sound of the horn, Jean jerked her hand the wrong way and ended up breaking the handle off her brush with it right in her hair. Even if she'd possessed a perfect memory and had read every paper in town, Jean wouldn't have known that Shari Cooper had broken brushes regularly. Jean stared at the plastic handle in her hand before pulling the clump of bristles from her hair. She had never broken a brush before.

Jean left the bathroom and walked into the living room. It was getting dark, but her younger stepbrothers and -sisters were still outside playing, even four-year-old Teddy. The only one Jean really felt close to was Teddy; the world had yet to ruin him. As for the rest, she didn't care if they ever came inside. Her mother had crashed on the couch in front of an old "Star Trek" rerun on TV. Jean had no interest in science fiction or anything to do with space. She would just as soon the government spent the money on nuclear bombs.

"Hey, *Mamá*," Jean said softly, staring down at her mother. "I'm knocked up. Knocked up and dropped down."

Her mother stirred. Her hair was already gray; she couldn't be bothered dying it. She had on green coffee-stained pants, a white blouse she had worn the past two days. Her lipstick was a cheap color; it looked as if she'd put it on in front of a dusty windshield rather than a clean mirror. Most of all she looked tired. She had to be up at four to be at work on time. Jean felt that somehow she was standing before a mirror as she studied her.

Her mother yawned. "Did you say something, Jean?"

Jean hesitated. She'd have to tell her sometime. Or would she? Maybe Lenny would talk her into an abortion. Or perhaps he'd just take her out and shoot her. There were all kinds of possibilities, when she thought about it.

"No," Jean said. "I'm going out."

Her mother opened her eyes. "Where are you going?"

"Lenny's having a party. It's at his house."

"Will his parents be there?"

"His parents are dead, Mom. I told you that."

"Well, who will be there? Just you kids and a cloud of smoke?"

Jean acted bored. "Mom, nothing like that's going to happen."

Her mother snorted. "Yeah, like it doesn't happen every day. What do you take me for, *mija*? One of your teachers at school?"

"I don't know."

"What time are you coming home?"

"Midnight, maybe a little later."

"Don't you have work tomorrow?"

"Yeah. I'll be there. Do I ever miss?"

Her mother shook her head. "I don't know what you do

anymore, Jean. Except that you don't stay around here much. What's this Lenny like? Have I met him?"

"You met him last week."

She scratched her head. "He wasn't that black fella, was he?"

"Mom! He's the same color as you and me. He's a great guy. I like him. It's his birthday tonight."

Her mother nodded. She liked birthdays. They were next to All Saints days in her book. "What'd you get him?" her mother asked.

Jean had passed the two-minute-get-your-ass-in-gear mark. Carol honked again. Jean stepped toward the door, saying, "I got him something special. I'll tell you about it later. Don't worry if I'm a little late."

"If you don't come home, I'll worry," her mother called after her.

Jean opened the door and stepped outside the house, the same house she'd lived in all her life. She drew in a deep breath of smog. North and south, east and west, her neighborhood was in the throes of a holocaust. Had been since the word *ghetto* was first used.

"I wouldn't," Jean muttered under her breath.

Carol had made herself up, much more than Jean had. Carol had on a tight black leather skirt, a long-sleeved red blouse, fake silver and gold chains. Jean wore blue jeans and a yellow shirt. Carol was not butch; she liked to attract the girls as a girl.

Jean knew Carol's fantasy, Darlene Sanchez, would be at the party. Jean also knew Carol was wasting her time on Darlene, who needed guys the way a smoking car needs a quart of oil.

But Darlene was not in a romantic mood these days. Her boyfriend, Sporty Quinones, had been gunned down near the projects in a drive-by only two weeks ago. Lenny had been with him at the time, but hadn't been hurt. Sporty had taken three shots in the chest and bled to death in Lenny's hands. At the funeral Darlene had not been silent in her mourning; there was too much fire in her blood. Even as they lowered Sporty into the ground, she shouted for vengeance. That was the trouble with drive-by hits; they were just guns poked out of dark windows. The killers didn't leave cards. Darlene said she knew who did it. Lenny didn't know how; he said he didn't even see the car. The whole thing confused Jean. She didn't know what the hell the guys were doing so close to the projects in the middle of the night. That was like walking into a sewer pipe and asking not to get dirtied. She missed Sporty as well; he had been a good friend. If it hadn't been for Lenny, she might have gone out with him. They had fooled around a little at some boring party just before Lenny and she got together.

"Guess what?" Carol said as Jean climbed into the car. Carol had a ten-year-old red Camaro that had once been hit by a school bus. It sounded like a tank under enemy fire, but it always started, which was the important thing.

"What?" Jean said, closing the car door.

"You have to guess." Carol put the car in gear and they rolled forward.

"I don't want to guess."

"I got asked out today."

"Who asked you out?" Jean asked.

"You know the guy with the Russian accent at the McDonald's on Herald?"

"That guy? His face is scarred."

Carol giggled; she often did. Her lips were glossy, her eyelids neon. She was skinny as a wire plugged into a shorted socket. She had a lot of energy. She could eat two Big Macs with fries at lunch break and still do situps in P.E. an hour later. She was pure Hispanic but wore so much white powder that she looked as if she were auditioning for a circus clown.

"What do you think?" Carol asked.

"About his scars?"

"No! About him asking me out. He knows I'm a lesbian, and he still wants to go out with me. Doesn't that make him some kind of pervert?"

"No. I bet he thinks he can turn you on. Are you going out with him?"

"I don't know. I told him to come to the party tonight. Do you think he'll come?"

"Why do you keep asking me questions like that? I don't even know the guy."

Carol nodded excitedly. "I hope he comes. It might make Darlene jealous."

"I wouldn't count on it"

Carol lost her smile. "Don't you think she likes me—just a little? And don't say you can't answer because you don't know her."

"Yes. I think Darlene likes you. I just don't think she wants to sleep with you. God, Carol, the girl is a complete horn dog. She's slept with just about every guy at school."

"Yeah. But she's just suffered a major personal loss. That can sometimes shake up a person's sexuality. I heard that on 'Oprah.' There was a woman on there who didn't become a lesbian until her husband's head was cut off by a helicopter blade."

Jean groaned. "Oh, brother."

"What is it?"

"I need some *mota*. Do you have a joint?"

"At home, not with me. But there'll be plenty of stuff at the party. Can't you wait?"

"I suppose."

"What's bothering you, Jean? You look like you're worried about your sexuality."

I'm pregnant."

"*Qué?*"

"I'm pregnant."

Carol almost rammed the back of a bus. "Wow! That's big. Whose is it?"

Jean was disgusted. "What do you mean, whose is it? It's Lenny's. He's my boyfriend. What kind of question is that?"

"I was just asking. I just wanted to be sure. Wow. What are you going to do?"

"I don't know. What do you think I should do?"

"I don't know. Get rid of it."

Jean shook her head. "Just like that? I don't know if I can do that."

"Have you told him?"

"I was thinking of telling him tonight."

"That should liven up his party."

"Shut up. Maybe I'll tell him later. I haven't even told my mom yet."

"Don't tell your mom. She won't let you go out anymore."

"I'll think about it," Jean said.

"What did you get Lenny for his birthday? I got him a book."

"What kind of book?"

"I don't know. It had a scary cover on it. Does Lenny like scary stuff?"

"I don't think he's read a book in his life. I don't know if he can read."

Carol laughed. "I was thinking the same thing! I was thinking this is the stupidest present I could possibly buy him! That's why I bought it. What did you get him?"

"Nothing so far. Let's stop at the record store. Maybe I can buy him a CD."

Carol settled back down. She reached over and touched Jean on the leg. Her voice came out gentle. Jean knew Carol was not as insensitive as she liked to pretend.

"If you do keep the baby, then we could all play with it," she said. "It might not be so bad. It might even be fun."

Jean sighed. "Nothing's fun anymore."

CHAPTER II

LENNY MANDEZ had a hilltop home with a view. Unfortunately, the house rested on a weed-choked plot of land between a slum and a ghetto. The surrounding area was covered with aged oil wells that creaked so badly in the middle of the night it sounded as if the house were under attack from an army of arthritic robots. The latest earthquake had actually made some of his neighbors' homes stand up straighter. The whole area looked as if it had been thrown together for the express purpose of violating every code in the book. Lenny's home had two bedrooms for the cockroaches and a bathroom for the real nasty creatures. Still, it wasn't a bad place to have a party, Jean thought, as long as there was enough booze and dope. Fortunately, that was never a problem with Lenny. Intoxicants followed him the way ants beat a path to the food across his kitchen floor.

Lenny Mandez was twenty, but if his age was measured by mileage rather than years, he was ready for retirement. He had joined his first gang while walking home from kindergarten. He was in juvenile hall for stealing a car he didn't know how to drive when he was thirteen. But that two-year stint inside sobered him some, and Lenny returned to public school and graduated from high school last year. He had a full-time job now, working as a mechanic at a gas station owned by an uncle. He owed allegiance to no particular gang, but had friends in all the wrong places and made as much money dealing drugs as he did tuning engines. Jean knew he was trouble, she was no fool, but she took solace in the fact that he didn't like being a pusher, anymore than he liked the idea of returning to prison. He told her that he was trying to change, and she could see that he was. He took a couple of night classes at the city college—general ed stuff. He didn't know what he wanted to do with his life any more than she did. They had that in common, at least.

She had met him through the late Sporty Quinones, who, at the age of twenty, had still been trying to get a high school diploma. They had been introduced in the middle of the street, literally, and for a moment, when she'd looked into his dark eyes, she forgot about the oncoming cars. There was passion in his eyes, she sensed, as well as danger. She wondered if that's what it took to turn her on—the possibility of a bad end. He had a great body; she had seen a few in her day. He had heavy muscles, generous lips, and wore his straight black hair long onto his shoulders. He had taken a hip tone with her. "Hey, baby, I heard about you. Heard you were hot. What do you say we get together tonight?" Of course she had told him where to stick it, and he had laughed, reverting to a more subdued tone, which she was to learn was more normal for him. He had taken her to the movies that night, and they had made out so hard in the back row they had turned a PG Disney film into a hard R erotic mystery. That was what she liked most about Lenny— the mystery. Even after months of dating, she still had no idea what he was thinking. At Sporty's funeral, as his best friend was lowered into the ground, he hadn't changed the expression on his face. He could have been staring at the sky for all the emotion he showed.

Jean ended up getting Lenny a Los Lobos CD, which he slipped into the CD player as soon as she and Carol arrived at his house, and cranked up the volume. Jean assumed that meant he liked it even though she hadn't had a chance to wrap it. He gave her a quick kiss and handed her a beer and she sat on the couch in the living room with a bunch of people she hardly knew and the party moved forward as they always did. There was alcohol, pot, music, laughter, and cursing. She and Carol cornered a hookah loaded with Colombian Gold near the start of the festivities and each took four hits so deep into their lungs that they could feel their brain cells leaving on the sweet cloud of smoke as they exhaled. They both began to laugh and didn't stop until they remembered they had nothing to laugh about, which was an hour later. So the first part of the party passed painlessly.

Even though Jean got loaded regularly, marijuana often had an undesirable side effect on her psychology. The moment her high began to falter, her mood sometimes plunged, so rapidly that she felt as if she were sinking into a black well. In other words, the pot bummed her out as surely as it made her laugh, and this was one of those unfortunate times when, after an hour of giggling, she felt close to tears. But since she seldom cried, and never in front of other people, she just got real quiet and tried not to think. She didn't want to know she was in a place she didn't want to be with people she didn't care about and who didn't care about her. That her whole life was headed in the wrong direction and that it wasn't going to change because that was just the way the world was. That she was pregnant and didn't want a baby and didn't want to have an abortion and didn't want to end up like her mother. It was this last thought, spinning around in her head, that caused her the most grief. And the weird thing was, her mother was one of the few people in her life she actually respected.

Come midnight, though, when the party began to thin out, and the dope began to filter from her bloodstream, her depression lifted sufficiently so that she was able to talk again. At the time she happened to be sitting on the end of Lenny's bed watching as Darlene Sanchez used the cracked mirror precariously attached to the top of Lenny's chest of drawers to replait a few loose braids. Darlene was Hispanic, but wanted to be black; a formidable task, to be sure, since she was naturally whiter than Carol after makeup. Sporty Quinones had been Darlene's first non-African-American boyfriend, a fact that was somewhat at odds with her reputation of having slept with most of the juniors and seniors in the school. But who was counting, colors or numbers. Darlene was hot, no debating that.

"How are you feeling, girl?" Darlene asked, gazing at her in the mirror.

"I'm all right," Jean said.

"You looked like hell all night."

"Thanks a lot."

"No, I mean your mood." Darlene lifted a few strands of hair above her head and, in the blink of an eye, braided them. Her braids made her look pretty scary when she wore them just right. Her long painted fingernails were just as bad. They reminded Jean of razors dipped in blood. Darlene added, "You look like someone just died."

Jean realized she had a can of beer in her hand and took a sip. "Someone just did."

Darlene acted pissed. "Great! You had to bring that up. I'm here to have a good time, and you have to talk about Sporty."

"I wasn't talking about him." Jean shrugged. "In this town someone dies practically every hour."

"Yeah, right. God, what a downer you are."

Jean burped. "Sorry."

Darlene waved her hand. "It doesn't matter. I don't mind talking about him. We're going to talk about him later anyway. We're going to have a little meeting when the party's over, Lenny and I. You should stay for it."

"What kind of meeting?" Jean asked.

"You'll see."

"I came with Carol. Can she be there?"

Darlene seemed exasperated. She could change her expression quicker than most people inhaled. "That girl. She doesn't know what she is. Do you know what she said to me this evening?"

"I can guess."

"She said, 'You know, Darlene, there are two sides to everything. You don't know what belongs on front until you check the behind.' Can you believe she said that to me?"

"I don't even know what it means."

"It means, dope head, that she's still trying to get in my pants. Lenny tells me you're straight as an arrow. How can you have a dyke as a best friend?"

"It's easy. She's not a dyke to me. She's a great girl."

Darlene paused. "Have you two ever done it?"

"Done what?"

"Had sex, for godssakes! Have you?"

"No. Carol's not interested in me that way."

"What is she interested in then?"

"She's my friend. She needs friends as much as straight people. Maybe more. Maybe you should try being her friend rather than always badmouthing her."

"Maybe she should quit hitting on me first," Darlene said.

"She's not hitting on you. She's just flirting with you. You should be flattered."

"I'm not. She makes me nervous. She makes me feel like I might be a *joto* and not know it."

"Maybe you are a *joto*, Darlene." Jean allowed herself a rare smile. "Anybody who goes around with a head looking like a snake fest has got to have something wrong with her."

Darlene laughed. "Hell, you're probably right." She finished with her hair and turned around. "How do I look?"

"Am I the right person to ask? I just told you. You look great."

"Thanks. You want to go get something to eat?"

"You mean, leave the party?" Jean asked.

"Yeah, I mean leave the party. You can't eat any of the rot in Lenny's refrigerator. We can hit the Jack-in-the-Box down the street and be back in twenty minutes."

Jean shook her head. "You go ahead. I don't feel very hungry."

Darlene sat on the bed beside her friend, concerned. "Really, are you all right, Jean?"

Jean shrugged. "Yeah, I'm just tired."

"Are you and Lenny getting on all right?"

"Yeah." Jean paused. "I think so. Do you know something I don't?"

Darlene hesitated. "No." She stood quickly. "I'll be back soon. Remember that meeting. I want you there."

"I won't be there unless Carol's there. She's my ride home."

"Aren't you going to spend the night with Lenny? It is his birthday, after all."

"No," Jean said. "My mother would freak."

Darlene seemed to think for a moment, then nodded. "That's what mothers are for."

Darlene left. Jean continued to sit on the edge of the bed and sip her beer. She studied herself in the mirror. It was only then she remembered the dream she'd had that morning. It had been wonderful yet simple, painful to wake from. She dreamed she was floating above her house and that just a few blocks away she could see a colorful amusement park, the rainbow of shimmering lights illumining her insides as much as the neighborhood. The feelings of the dream had been more important than the actual events. She knew that if she would just fly over there, she could enter that place of constant fun and excitement. Where there were people who cared and things to do that meant something. And in the dream she was being given that choice, to leave her house, her life, and never return. Why had she awakened? She sure as hell hadn't said no to the offer. Now the memory of the dream made her sad. Made her sad that it was gone, forever.

After some time Lenny entered his bedroom. He had on his black leather jacket; he seldom took it off, even on nights as warm as this. His long black hair was pulled back in a ponytail. They had talked little all night. Conversation wasn't big with either of them. They were better just sitting and watching a movie together, or smoking a joint, or making love. She had assumed they'd have sex tonight since, as Darlene said, it was his birthday. But now she had to wonder if she could talk herself into the right mood. Lenny sat on the bed beside her and leaned over to give her a kiss. She kissed him back—sort of. He sensed her lack of enthusiasm and drew away.

"What's wrong?" he asked.

"Nothing." She touched his leg. "How are you doing?"

"Good. Great party, huh?"

"Yeah. That was great dope. Where did you get it?"

He shrugged. "The usual sources. Where did Darlene go?"

"To Jack-in-the-Box. She was hungry."

"We have pizza in the living room," Lenny said.

Jean forced a smile. "It's on the living room floor. I think Darlene worries about hygiene."

Lenny chuckled; it sounded forced as well. "Then I don't know what she was doing with Sporty. That guy had equipment that needed to be machined to get clean."

"Was he that bad?"

Lenny paused and stared at her. "I don't know. He just told me so many stories."

"About so many girls?"

Lenny nodded. "Yeah. You must have seen how he carried on at school?"

"Yeah, he got around some, I guess. When Darlene wasn't around."

"But they weren't going out that long," Lenny said.

"Really? I thought it was a few months."

Lenny continued to watch her. "Something's bothering you, Jean. What is it?"

She lowered her head. "Well, there is something I wanted to tell you. I should have told you earlier, but I was afraid. But I don't know if this is the right time, either."

Lenny sucked in a deep breath and became still. She sensed his rigidity more than saw it because she continued to keep her head low. Finally he let the breath out.

"Yes?" he said softly.

"I'm pregnant."

The two words seemed to float out of her mouth and into a vacuum. The room became a bowl sitting on some troll's table, and they were breakfast. She raised her head and saw that Lenny had closed his eyes. A vein pulsed on his forehead. It looked as if it might pop if the pressure wasn't released soon. She wanted to say something to make him feel better like I'll get rid of it or maybe the test kit was wrong. But she doubted he would have heard her at that moment. His mind seemed to have fled to a place where there were no words. Finally, though, he opened his eyes and looked at her. His expression was strangely blank.

"Are you sure?" he asked softly.

"Yes." She paused. "I'm sorry. Lousy birthday present, huh?"

"I've had better. What do you want to do?"

"I don't know. What do you want to do?"

"It's up to you."

"No, it's up to both of us." She felt a painful lump in her throat. She had taken her hand off his leg, and she wanted to put it back, to hug him, maybe kiss him again. But they were like two strangers sitting in a cheap motel room. At least that was how the two people in the cracked mirror looked. Jean regretted having started the conversation in front of their reflections. It made her feel more lost. How did she really feel about Lenny? She had told him she loved him; he had told her the same. But those were just words. She didn't believe she could love him because she didn't know what love was. She didn't even know if there was such a thing, if it wasn't all hype. She added, "We can keep it or we can get rid of it. I'm not going to force it on you."

"How much does an abortion cost?" he asked.

"Three hundred dollars. About."

He smiled thinly and shook his head. "That's *mucha lana*. You were raised Catholic. Could you go through with an abortion?"

She sighed. "I don't know." His next question caught her off guard.

"What do you think he'd look like?" he asked.

She hesitated. "*Bueno.* Like the two of us. But it might be a she, you know."

"Have you ever seen pictures of me when I was a baby?"

"No. You haven't shown me any." She paused. "I'd like to see some."

"No, you wouldn't. I looked awful. But maybe he would look—better." He stood and eyed the door. "Let's talk about this later when no one's around. Right now I have to enjoy my twentieth birthday party. It's the only one I'm ever going to have."

"*Lo siento*, I'm sorry," she said again.

"Don't be sorry," he said as he left the room.

Ninety minutes later Jean was sitting in the living room with Lenny, Carol, and Darlene. After Lenny had left her, Jean had fallen back on the bed and passed out for an hour. She hadn't dreamed, only entered a black void where there was no sound or feeling and slept the sleep of the dead. She didn't even know who she was when she awakened in the dark. The disorientation had lingered. Who had turned off the bedroom light? She didn't know and it didn't matter.

The four of them were the only ones left at the party. Jean sat on the couch with Lenny. Carol was on the floor, acting bored. Her Russian boyfriend had never shown. Darlene, as usual, paced. Darlene wanted revenge, she wanted blood. Her little meeting was about planning a hit on Sporty's murderers, specifically on Juan Chiato. Juan was the biggest drug dealer at their high school, although he hadn't been to class in ten years. He was twenty-one years old, high up in the Red Blades, one of the most vicious of the inner city gangs. Jean knew Juan by sight; she had met him twice at Lenny's house. He'd been leaving as she went in. Out of necessity, Lenny said he occasionally had to deal with Juan, although Lenny clearly did not like to be in the same room as Juan, who was known for his violent temper. But Juan had direct contact with Colombian drug lords and practically set the price of cocaine in their neighborhood. His face was badly scarred from knife fights. Jean thought he looked like one of Satan's first lieutenants. She hadn't known Sporty was connected to Juan, but she supposed she'd been mistaken.

"Let me tell you why I know it was Juan," Darlene said as she strode back and forth in front of them, a cigarette in her hand. "The week before Sporty died, he told me about a deal he had going with Juan. You didn't know about it, Lenny. Sporty told me Juan had sworn him to secrecy. Anyway, Sporty told me about it because he could never keep his mouth shut when he was drunk. It had nothing to do with drugs. Juan had stolen a truckload of Levi's jeans. He had slipped onto a freight company's lot with a gun and put the barrel to the security guard's head and driven away with the trailer. He wanted to use Sporty to sell the jeans to certain stores. Sporty was game. The commission looked good, and he thought dealing with store owners would be a lot more pleasant than the jerks that hung around Juan. But what he didn't know was that Juan was just using him. The stores he sent Sporty to paid protection to the Bald Caps. You know them?"

Lenny nodded. "*Cierto.* They're a small gang, but they control much of downtown, especially around the convention center and the skyscrapers. Why did Juan want to piss them off?"

"I asked Sporty that," Darlene said. "He thought maybe Juan was trying to set something up between the Red Blades and the Bald Caps. Juan was trying to move up in the Blades, and he was impatient. He wanted some action that he could lead, show the others how strong he was. He wanted a fight. He sent Sporty out, not to sell jeans, but to start a war with the Bald Caps. Right away Sporty ran into trouble. The Caps cornered him and threatened to cut out his heart for daring to enter their territory. They stole his van full of jeans. Sporty went running back to Juan and told him what had happened, but Juan didn't want to hear about it. He gave Sporty an ultimatum—either he got the jeans back or *he* was going to cut out his heart. Sporty yelled at him, said he had just been set up. Then Sporty made a big mistake. He told Juan he was thinking of going to the police to tell them the whole story."

337

"No," Lenny said, shaking his head. "He wouldn't have been that *estúpido*."

Darlene paused in her pacing. "Sporty was pretty stupid sometimes, I can say that because I loved him. I asked him how Juan reacted, and he said Juan didn't say anything, which we all know is not the best response to get from a bloodthirsty sonofabitch like Juan Chiato. I tell you, Sporty was scared. He had a right to be scared." Darlene nodded, her eyes burning. "That all happened four weeks ago, and now look what's happened. Sporty's dead. Juan killed him, there's no doubt about it. We have to kill the bastard."

The room was silent for a full minute. Jean didn't know what to say. It did sound like Juan was probably the culprit, but who in his right mind would take revenge against someone who had a whole gang at his back? The Red Blades would re-earn their name hunting down and slaughtering whoever touched Juan. And if they just happened to murder a few who were only guilty by indirect association, then so much the better. Jean regretted having asked if Carol could stay for the meeting. Sitting on the floor against the wall, Carol looked full of regrets. Darlene must have been loaded to be talking about such things so openly. Yet she appeared in full command of her senses. It was Lenny who spoke first, and Jean was surprised when he didn't dismiss Darlene's proposal outright.

"I can't understand why Sporty didn't tell me he was having trouble with Juan," he said. "He should have come to me right away, before he tried to sell any jeans. I would have told him to stay as far away as he could from the guy."

"He wanted to make his own mark," Darlene said. "He wanted to make his own money. Sporty got tired of living in your shadow and wanted to do something about it."

Lenny shifted uncomfortably. "He picked a bad way to go about it."

"We've already established that he wasn't the most intelligent guy on the planet," Carol said.

"Shut up," Darlene said. "I can say those things, but you can't. You didn't love him."

Carol made a face. "I hardly knew him."

"Let's say, for the sake of argument, that it was Juan," Lenny said. "If we want him dead, we have to do it ourselves. Anyone else will talk to someone else. And if we do kill him, it's got to look like someone else did it. Because the second Juan's Blade buddies find his body, they're going to guess it was either Darlene or me who was behind it because we were Sporty's best friends."

"I hope you're not suggesting that it has to look like an accident," Carol said.

Lenny shook his head impatiently. "If Juan has a dozen bullets in him, it can't look like an accident."

"We could run him over," Darlene suggested.

"It might be better to blow him up," Lenny said. "The less left, the better."

Jean felt compelled to speak. "Wait a second. What are we talking about here? Sporty's dead and that's terrible. But we can't avenge his death, *especially* if it was Juan who killed him. His gang will know who did it no matter how you plan it. They'll kill us all."

"Why would they kill you?" Lenny asked, an odd note in his voice.

"Because I was Sporty's friend, too," Jean said, annoyed at the question. "Because I'm here with you guys talking about this foolish plan. You can't go up against someone that's high up in a gang. It's just not done. You know that, Lenny. Why are you even listening to Darlene?"

Lenny held her eye before answering, his face dark. He hadn't appreciated her remarks. "Because I was his friend. A real friend doesn't do nothing after his friend's gunned down. I was there. He died in my arms."

Jean returned his stare. When angered, few people intimidated her. "What were you two doing at the projects so late at night?" she asked. "So close to Juan's home ground?"

Lenny didn't blink. "I didn't know about Sporty's problems with Juan. I said that already."

"But that doesn't answer my question," Jean said. "At night that piece of turf is a death zone."

"No one's asking you to be involved, Jean," Darlene said bitterly. "I just thought since Sporty always told me what a great girl you were that you'd want to be in on the payback."

"What payback is that going to be?" Jean asked, her voice hot. "Kill Juan and live in fear every second until they come for us? And who's to say they'll simply shoot us? They might torture us first. You heard about what happened to that teenage bookie that the police found on Main? During the autopsy they found a pillowcase in his stomach. Do you know how scared someone has to be to swallow a pillowcase? Oh, and did I forget to mention that his throat had been cut from ear to ear? That was down on Main, Darlene—Red Blade territory, Juan's playing ground."

"Was it a *whole* pillow case?" Carol asked.

"Oh, would you shut up," Jean said this time.

Darlene glared at Jean. "I thought you were more than a chicken bitch. I guess I was wrong."

Jean turned to Lenny, her boyfriend, the father of her unborn child. He still hadn't answered her original question. Earlier she had been right to think of him as a stranger. Looking at his dark, cold, masklike face, she hardly recognized him. And to think, she had made love to him only two days before on this very couch. No, she had had sex with him—there was a difference.

"How can you let her talk to me that way?" she asked. "This is your house. Kick her out. You know she's talking crap. You know this whole meeting is insane."

Lenny took his time answering. Something on the floor between his legs had him fascinated. It must have been the dirt because that was all that was there. The heavy burdens on his attention—the filth and her request. Finally he spoke, his head still down.

"You just didn't care about him the way we did. You can't understand." He shrugged, adding, "We can't let Juan get away with it."

Jean jumped up from the sofa, feeling the blood suffuse her face. "I cared about him more than any of you know! I knew him before any of you knew him! But he's dead, and it's really sad, but why do we have to die with him? Why do we even have to talk about killing people?" Her throat choked with emotion; her voice came out cracked. "Why do we even have to live like this?"

Jean didn't wait for an answer to her painful questions. She ran from the living room, into the bedroom, and out onto Lenny's balcony. The platform was a haphazard affair, a collection of splintered planks thrown on top of a randomly spaced group of termite-zapped wooden stilts. Yet the drop to the ground was substantial: thirty feet straight down. Jean heard the boards of the railing creak as she leaned against them. The view was pretty at least, if you liked smelly oil wells and rundown houses that doubled as fear-infested fortresses. The downtown skyscrapers were visible, far in the distance; dark towers with dots of light in a bleary haze of pollutants. Really, Jean thought, it was all the same no matter which direction she turned. It wasn't a city, it was a dying monster. She wanted it to die. She wanted the big bombs to fall, the red mushroom clouds to form. She didn't know why she had argued so passionately for life when she felt so little life in her heart. It was ironic that ever since the seed of a new human being had started growing in her body she had felt more and more like ending it all. Not suicide, no, but something close to it. Something like a contract that could be entered into without serious penalties. Not a devil's contract certainly, more like a person-to-person handshake and a pat on the back and an understanding that it was OK. That it would be all right.

I did the best I could, God, but it wasn't good enough. But I don't hate you and I don't hate myself. I just don't know what the hell I'm doing. Help, please, help me.

Standing on the creaky balcony, time passed for Jean Rodrigues.

How much time, she didn't know.

But somewhere in the sand at the bottom of Jean Rodrigues's fallen hourglass, the colors of the nighttime city altered. The dull yellows turned to blues and the sober reds to fresh greens. The intensity of the light grew as well, as one after another tiny candles were lit in dark corners above homes that had never been built and atop skyscrapers that would never fall. The shift was subtle at first, and she didn't know it was even happening to her until she suddenly found herself staring out upon a landscape bathed in pulsing light. It was only then that she realized she was back in her dream, being given the chance again to lift up her arms and fly, over the wall and into the land where the wishes and the wisher were one. It was a chance she was not going to pass up twice. There, she thought eagerly, there, make me immortal.

Happy at last, still leaning against the railing, she lifted her arms.

But Jean did not fly; the human body could not. The floor of the balcony abruptly vanished from beneath her feet and she fell instead. Headfirst toward a ground that took forever to reach. Yet the plunge was not terrifying, as Shari Cooper's fall from a balcony one year earlier had been. The contract was signed and sealed. It wasn't suicide but an accident. Or at the very least someone else's fault. There would be no penalty for Jean Rodrigues. There would be no more pain.

CHAPTER III

FLOATING DOWNSTREAM in a boat on a river, you can see only a little way in front of you, a little way behind, the nearby shore, and if you're lucky and the river isn't lined with trees, maybe a far-off field or house. But if you go up in a plane and look down at the river, you can see the entire course of the waterway. You can see where it began, and you know where it will end. In a sense, the aerial view is like being given a vision of the future, at least as far as the life of the river is concerned.

Death is a vision that never dies. I am supposed to be dead, but I experience the entirety of my life as if it were all happening at once. I float above the river of personality that was once Shari Ann Cooper. I know her, I am her, but I am something else now as well, something blissful. Even as I poke into the dark corners of my life, my joy does not leave me. It is separate from personalities and events. My joy is what I am and has no name.

I did many things in my eighteen years on planet Earth. I was born. I learned to walk, to talk, to laugh, and to sing. I learned to cry as well, and I chased boys. I even got laid once. I was popular. My junior year, mine was voted the best smile in the whole high school. But few of the things that I considered important on Earth interest me now. As I view the whole of my life, a seemingly insignificant event holds my attention. I was sixteen years old. There was a girl in my biology class who was deaf, not a crime in itself, but she was homely as well. Those were two big strikes against her with my friends, and two strikes were completely unforgivable in those days. No one ever talked to her—I didn't either—or even thought about her, except occasionally to wonder why she wasn't in a special school. It never occurred to me that she might be a brave soul trying to live a normal life despite her handicap.

There was one day, though, as I was leaving biology class after the bell had rung, that I noticed the girl was having trouble finding her glasses. On top of everything else she couldn't see well and I knew that she would sometimes remove her glasses while the teacher talked and just sit with her eyes closed, trying, so it seemed to me, to absorb the lesson by osmosis. I didn't know at the time that someone had swiped her glasses, but I did know she was going to have a hard time making it to her next class without them. I walked over and gently tapped her on the shoulder. I scared her, made her jump, and immediately felt bad about it. But she smiled quickly at me after she'd recovered and squinted. I wasn't sure how much of me she could see.

"Hi," I said. "Can I help you?"

She leaned forward, closer to my mouth, and gestured for me to repeat myself. I realized she was reading my lips. I put my face right in front of hers and asked my question again. This time she nodded vigorously. She gestured that she couldn't find her glasses and if I would help her look for them. I didn't have to look long to realize someone must have taken them. I mean, it wasn't like there were a lot of hiding places on a school desk. I placed my face in front of hers again.

"Lost," I said. "Gone. Stolen. I will help you."

The news seemed to take her aback, but only for a moment. She nodded, collected her books, and stood up. She offered me her arm; clearly I would have to touch her to help lead her to her next class. I didn't mind, although at that time—that week I think it was—it was something of a taboo to touch anyone of the same sex. In fact, I was happy to help her. Very happy I had finally stopped to speak to her.

Her name was Candice, but she said to call her Candy in her uninflected, flat speech. I helped her around for the next two days while she waited for new glasses to arrive. We never did find out what happened to the original pair. During that time I learned to sign quite a few words. We became friends, and I learned something else as well—that life was good even when it was hard. That hidden beauty was much greater than physical beauty. Candy could not hear our teachers, she could hardly see them. But she taught me more than any of them had. I was sad the day I heard she would be coming to school no more. She had ended up returning to a special school for deaf kids, after all. I missed her.

But what I didn't know at the time was that from the moment the thought occurred to me to help Candy, and all the time I was with her, tidal waves of light and energy rolled from me and spread out over the entire universe, to the farthest planet circling the loneliest star in the most distant galaxy. I touched that much. But I could only see these waves as I reviewed my life when my life was over. My good grades, my good looks—none of that had mattered. None of it had affected the creation, but my simple act of service and kindness had been like a miracle. And the strange thing was that I had helped Candy only because I wanted to. Because, for once, I had stopped thinking of myself and thought only of someone else. As I watched the beginning and the middle and the end of the river of Shari Cooper, I could see then the answer to one of our age-old riddles. Does love survive? Yes, I thought, somewhere in some place it is saved and made sacred. I had not known how much love Candy had given to me, and how much I had given to her.

I had known nothing.

"Good," a voice said.

I opened my eyes and found myself sitting on a grassy bank on a sunny day beside a gently flowing stream. The still air was warm, fragrant, radiant with light and good feelings. In the distance were trees, snow-capped mountains, but no houses, no roads. I was in paradise but I wasn't alone. Beside me sat an extraordinary man.

He appeared to be thirty years old. He had an austere face, hollow cheeks, deepset blue eyes, a soft smile. It was difficult to specify his race. His skin was a deep coppery color; he could have been an ancient Egyptian priest come to life before me. Perhaps he was, I thought. He wore a blue silk robe. I had on the same clothes I had died in: jeans and a yellow shirt. I was going to have to change one of these days, I thought. My surroundings were pervaded by peace, but the man's aura was even more tranquil. I had no memory of seeing him before, yet I felt as if I had known him a long time. His smile widened at my thought.

"Very good, Shari," he said. Like his smile, his voice was soft, yet it carried great authority behind it. He was not someone with whom I would have argued.

I smiled. "Can you read my mind?"

"Yes. Do you want me to stop?"

"It doesn't matter. You were with me as I reviewed my life. I felt you."

"Yes. How do you feel about how you did?"

"Like a fool."

"That's a good way to feel. Only a fool can get into heaven."

"Is that where we are? Did I make it?"

"I joke with you. All this you see is just a thought. You created this place because you still feel the need to occupy a certain space and time. People usually carry that habit with them when they cross over. It is to be expected; it is fine. But you don't need to talk to me with a body. When you feel comfortable, you may drop it."

I rubbed my legs with my open palms. They felt the same as they had on Earth. "I'm still sort of used to this body." I paused, troubled. "But I suppose it's really back on Earth rotting in a grave somewhere."

"Is that real, Shari? After all you have experienced, would you say that any part of you could rot?"

I frowned. "I'm not sure I understand. I do know I have a soul and that it survived death. I learned that the hard way. But my body died. It's still on Earth. I saw them bury it. I went to my own funeral."

"I was there."

"Really? You should have introduced yourself. What is your name? Do you have one?"

"You may call me by a name." He considered. "Call me the Rishi. Rishi means 'seer.' When I was in a physical body, people often called me that."

"So you've been on Earth?"

"Yes. We're on Earth now, Shari."

I was amazed. I looked around. "Are we in Switzerland?"

He laughed softly. "We are in another dimension of Earth.

But these concepts—distance, space, time—they have no meaning for you now, unless you give them meaning. You're free of those limitations. You can be on any world in the universe just by wishing it."

His words made me smile. "How is Peter? Where is he?"

"Not far. You'll see him soon."

"Good. I mean, don't get me wrong, I like being here with you, but I want to know why you're here with me. What our relationship is." I stopped. "Am I asking too many questions?"

"I'm here to take your questions. When people first cross over, they often go through a question-and-answer period like this. But understand that not all your questions can be answered with words. Our relationship is a beautiful thing. We are, ultimately, the same person, the same being. But if that is too abstract a concept for you, then think of a huge oversoul made up of many souls. Throughout many lives on many worlds, these different souls learn and grow. Each life is like a day in class, and as you know, some people do better in class than others, but all will graduate if they keep going." He paused. "We are a part of the same oversoul, Shari."

"But you've already graduated?" I asked.

"Yes."

"To where? To what?"

He gestured around him. "To all that is. To God if you like. I see your surprise, but it is so. Yes, I am with God now as I speak to you. I see you as my Goddess." He reached over and touched my hand, his fingers warm, soothing. "You are very dear to me, Shari."

I felt so loved then I began to cry. He was like my big brother Jimmy. Or my father even, my real father, whom I had never known. I realized then that even when I had been alive he had been with me, just out of sight, helping me, guiding me. It meant so much to me to be able to see him again with my eyes. I felt as if finally I had come home. I clasped his hand in mine.

"Will you stay with me?" I asked.

"Yes. Always I am with you."

I laughed, I felt so foolish for weeping. "Wow. Who would have thought it would be like this?"

"That you would die and end up in Switzerland with an ancient Egyptian priest?" he asked with a twinkle in his eye. "I was in Egypt a long time ago as people *on* Earth measure time. I am there now. I teach beside the pyramids. People call me Master."

I was fascinated that he could be in many places at the same time, even as he lived outside of time. "What do you teach?" I asked.

"Hmm. Big question. I will give a short answer." He considered for a moment. "The teachings of a Master appear different in different times. The needs of the time and the place vary. When you were alive few would have said the words of Buddha matched those of Krishna or Jesus. But in essence they all said the same thing—that there is one God and that we are all part of him. That it is important to realize this great truth while we are on Earth. But over time the message becomes distorted. People take God out of man and put him up in an imaginary heaven, where he is of no use to anyone. Or else they found a religion based on the worship of a particular Master. Yet Buddha never founded Buddhism. Christ never founded Christianity. Krishna hardly spoke about religion at all. He was too busy dancing and playing his flute. He was too ecstatic to be dogmatic. I am very happy now as I speak to my followers in ancient Egypt. But I know a short time after I vanish from their view they will begin to squabble over what I really said and what I really meant. Even now they quarrel amongst themselves. I have to laugh—it is natural that a Master should speak from his level of consciousness but that his followers should hear the words at their level. A long time ago, as mortals are fond of saying, the Rishi was also worshiped as the only son of God. But we all deserve that title, don't you think?"

I nodded. "How about saying 'the daughter of God'?"

"Very good. You understand, I am not saying religion is bad. Where it turns men and women inward and helps them realize that they are as great as the creator who created them, that there is an ocean of love and silence deep within the heart, then it is useful. But where it divides people against one another, where one person is led to believe he is saved and another is damned, or where it leads a person to think that true happiness will be found only in an afterlife, then it is harmful. Each life on Earth is very precious. I called each one a day in class, but if you are wise, if you go deep inside, you can go all the way to the goal in just one life." He paused. "It's a wonderful thing to be alive."

I sat up with a start. "That's a line from the story that I wrote before I left."

"I know."

"Did you help me write that story?"

"Yes. And it has not been lost. Your brother saved it. He read it and believes it to be true. It means much to him. He keeps it safe."

There were tears in my eyes again. "That was my last wish before I left. To be remembered. How is Jimmy?"

"He's fine. He thinks about you often."

I dabbed at my eyes. "What I wouldn't give to see him again, to tell him I'm all right." I stopped and shook my head. "Here I am in paradise with you and I'm still complaining. I guess I'll never learn. I can't see him until he dies and I don't want him to die until he's an old man. I guess I'll have to wait."

The Rishi took his hand back. He stared at me with his beautiful eyes—the color of limitless sky. I sensed the joy behind them, but also the power of eternity. I knew I was safe in his company, yet something in his expression made me shiver. He was as gentle as an angel, but I sensed he could also be as firm as a king. I was still in class, I realized. He was the teacher. It was wise to listen to him.

"You don't have to wait," he said.

"What do you mean? I thought you said Jimmy was fine?"

"He is. But you can go back."

"To Earth? To a physical body? So soon? Will I be born as a baby?"

"No. You can, if you want, become what we call a Wanderer. You can enter the body of an eighteen-year-old girl."

I had never heard of such an idea. "Is that legal? I mean, what will happen to the girl? Won't she go running to the nearest priest for an exorcist to get me out of her?"

"She will leave the body altogether. She'll be fine. She's already made this choice. At night, when she sleeps, her soul converses with me. She feels she is going nowhere in her life. She wants to give you another chance. Her leaving is purely her choice. It is always that way." He paused. "She'll be with me."

"Who is this girl?" I asked.

"Her name is Jean Rodrigues. If you wish, that will soon be your name."

CHAPTER IV

THE FIRST SENSATION Jean Rodrigues felt was of pressure, as if she were under a thousand feet of water. Every square inch of her skin was being smothered. She wanted to cry out, to shove the water away, but was unable to make a sound or move. For a while she struggled in a black place, then she felt a prick of something cold and sharp, and her struggling ceased, at least for a little while.

Time went by, jumbled moments of consciousness and unconsciousness. Next, she heard voices. They seemed to come from far off, and she listened to them for what could have been hours before realizing that they belonged to her mother and Carol. She could make no sense of the words except to realize that they both sounded worried. She was about to doze off again, when someone shook her roughly. She moved to push the person away; she really didn't want to wake up yet. But she couldn't find her hand so she opened her eyes instead. Her mother was standing over her with bloodshot eyes. It looked as if her mother hadn't slept in a long time. Jean wondered where the hell she was.

"Mamá," she said softly.

Her mother glanced at someone to the side. *"Gracias a Dios*, she's awake," she said.

That someone came into view. It was Carol. She also looked exhausted. "How do you feel, Jean?" Carol asked, concerned.

"Tired." She coughed weakly. "Thirsty. Where am I?"

Her mother thrust her hand out and then held a glass of water to Jean's lips. "Sip this. You'll feel better."

Jean did as she was told. She realized her lips were badly parched, bleeding even. The water went down cool and delicious. Her heart pounded at the back of her skull. Her head did not hurt so much as it felt as if it were being steadily squeezed by a clamp. She swallowed and gestured for her mother to take away the glass. Her vision went beyond them, to the hallway beyond the open door. She saw nurses walking back and forth. She was in a hospital, she thought.

"What happened?" she asked.

Her mother and Carol looked at each other as if deciding how much to tell her. "There was an accident," her mother finally said.

"Lenny's bedroom balcony collapsed," Carol added.

"You fell down the hill and hit your head and broke a few ribs," her mother continued. "But now that you're awake, you're going to be all right. But I have to say you gave us quite a scare for a couple of days there."

"A couple of days?" Jean whispered. "What day is it?"

"It's Monday morning," her mother said. "You've been unconscious this whole time." Her eyes dampened as she leaned over and hugged her daughter gently. Jean had to stifle a groan. Her right side was extraordinarily sensitive. She wondered if the *few* broken ribs really meant her whole side was caved in. Clearly, to be unconscious as long as she had been, she must have suffered a serious concussion. Her mother added, "My poor girl."

Jean patted her mother's head. "Don't worry, *Mamá*, I feel better than I probably look. I'll be out of here in no time. How're my brothers and sisters doing?"

Her mother sat up and smiled. "Why, that's sweet of you to ask, since you're the one who needs special attention right now. They're fine. I'll call them and tell them you're awake." She stood. "In fact, I'll go tell the doctor. I think he'll want to examine you."

Jean smiled. "Is he cute? Did he examine me while I was asleep?"

Carol and her mother chuckled; they seemed so relieved. "He couldn't keep his hands off you," Carol said.

Her mother stepped toward the door. "I'll be back in a few minutes. Try sipping a little more water, Jean. Carol, maybe you can help her."

"*Cierto*, Mrs. Rodrigues," Carol said.

"*Mamá,*" Jean said. "Has Lenny been by to see me?"

Her mother hesitated at the door. Again she and Carol exchanged looks. "Yes," her mother said. "He's been by."

"Could you call him as well?" Jean said "Tell him I'd like some flowers and chocolates and an immediate visit."

Her mother lowered her head and nodded. "I will." She went to leave.

"*Mamá,*" Jean said.

Her mother paused once more. "Yes?"

"*Te amo,*" Jean said.

Her mother had to take a breath. The words had caught her by surprise. Again her eyes dampened—no, this time they spilled over and tears ran down her cheeks. "My," she said, touching her heart. "I haven't heard that in a long time. I love you, too, Jean. I'll be back as soon as I can."

When she was gone, Jean gestured for Carol to help her sit up. Carol picked a remote control off the nightstand. "This will make the top half of the bed move up," Carol said. "That way you won't have to bend so much. Ready?"

"Yes," Jean said. Carol pushed the button and the top of the bed moved her into a sitting position. The shift in the blood supply in her body brought a wave of new aches and pains. It felt as if her right knee was pretty screwed up as well; there was, in fact, a thick bandage wrapped around her right leg from the top of her calf to halfway up her thigh. An IV ran into the back of her left hand. But she didn't feel any bandages on her ribs beneath her wrinkled green hospital gown. She wondered what had become of her clothes. Carol carefully sat on the bed beside her. Jean offered her her right hand and Carol took it.

"You really had us scared," Carol said.

"Have you been here a lot?" Jean asked.

"Most of the time. To tell you the truth, the doctor didn't know if you were going to wake up or not. Not until early this morning."

"He could tell then?"

"*Sí.* Don't ask me how. It was only this morning they moved you out of intensive care. You should have seen yourself yesterday and the day before. You had a ton of tubes and wires hooked up to your body."

"Sounds kinky." Jean considered. "What's the deal with Lenny?"

"What are you talking about?"

"What you and my mother are afraid to talk about. I saw the looks you gave each other when I asked about him. What's going on? Why isn't he here?"

Carol sighed; she was trapped. "Jean, what do you remember about last Friday night?"

Jean frowned. "Everything, I think, up until I fell. I remember we had that stupid fight about whether to waste Juan or not. Then I ran out onto the balcony. I remember staring out over the city." She paused. "And the fireworks."

"What fireworks?"

"There weren't any fireworks?"

Carol laughed. "You must have seen those after you fell."

"No. I remember—just before I fell—the whole city was lit up with colored lights. And I felt so happy." She stopped and shook her head. "But you're right, they couldn't have been fireworks. Who would be setting them off in the middle of the night?" She studied Carol. Her friend had yet to answer her question. "You tell me what happened last Friday. Where were you when I fell?"

"I was in my car, on my way home."

"What? You left Lenny's house without me?"

Carol shrugged. "Lenny told me to go. Jean, don't look at me that way. You were out on that balcony for so long. It didn't look like you were ever coming back in."

"How long is *so long*?"

"More than half an hour."

"I wasn't out there that long. No way."

"Yes, you were. I came up behind you and called your name and you ignored me. You were out there at least thirty minutes when I left the house."

"Was Darlene still there when you left?"

"Yes." Carol thought for a moment. "It might have been Darlene who said I should go, instead of Lenny. Yeah, I think it was her."

"And you just did what she said without talking to me first?"

"I told you, I tried to get your attention but you weren't answering. I figured you wanted to be alone. Or at least alone with Lenny."

"This is too weird. What does Lenny say happened?"

Carol hesitated. "I don't know. I haven't talked to him."

"Why not?"

Carol averted her eyes. "I don't know how to tell you this. Lenny was on the balcony when you fell. He fell with you. He's in this hospital right now, but he's in worse shape than you."

Jean could feel her heart pound. "How worse?"

Carol's eyes filled. "He broke his back in the fall. It looks like he's paralyzed from the waist down."

"Oh, God," Jean whispered. She thought of Lenny's beautiful body, his powerful legs—now as good as dead. How could this have happened? Why did the balcony suddenly collapse? Carol was shaking her head.

"I'm sorry," she said. "I wasn't trying to keep the truth from you. It's just that your mother didn't think we should tell you when you woke up. She wanted to wait until you were stronger."

"I understand," Jean said softly, staring at the far wall, seeing only wheelchairs and impassable stairways, boredom and despair for Lenny. He was so active—how would he be able to live? She added, "Is there anything else you want to tell me? That you were afraid to tell me?"

Carol raised her head and nodded. "There is one other

thing. The fall was rough on you. While you were unconscious, you began to bleed, you know, down there. You lost the *bebé*, Jean."

Jean blinked. "What baby?"

"*Your* baby. You were pregnant, remember?"

Jean couldn't keep up with the barrage of information. It was true she could remember buying and taking the E.P.T., and failing it. She could also remember telling Carol about it. Yet, at the same time, she had trouble accepting the fact that she had indeed been pregnant. Like it was something that could not possibly have happened to her, not under ordinary circumstances. But there was no arguing with the facts. Strangely, she felt neither relief nor a sense of loss that the baby was gone. She simply felt nothing, as if the whole matter had been someone else's problem.

"Does my mother know I was pregnant?" Jean asked.

"Yes. The doctor told her, after your miscarriage. She took it well. She didn't freak out or anything."

"*Bueno.* Anything else?"

Carol smiled sadly. "No. Except that I'm glad you're awake and feeling better."

Jean patted Carol's hand. "You're a good friend. Thank you for staying with me while I was out. I won't forget that."

Carol did a double take. "I've never heard you talk that way before."

"Talk what way?"

"I don't know, just the way you're talking. You sound nicer than usual."

Jean nodded. "Maybe the fall did me some good."

Her mother returned with Dr. Snapple, who must have changed his name to his favorite drink because there was no disguising the fact that he had been born in the Middle East. Dr. Snapple had a thick accent and a face so dark he could have been conceived staring into the sun. He was a big man with fingers as thick as Cuban cigars. Jean didn't find him attractive but competent, preferable for a physician. Dr. Snapple asked her a few questions about how she felt and did a number of tests involving her vision. The results seemed to satisfy him, but when he touched her right side and the back of her head she groaned. Not mentioning her miscarriage, he explained that her concussion and broken ribs would take time to heal, that there was no magic procedure to speed her recovery. At the same time, he said she was to stay in the hospital for at least two more days, possibly three or four. Jean fretted over the cost. She had no insurance.

"Why can't I go home now?" she asked. "If you can't do anything for me?"

"Because you have been unconscious for over two days," he said. "Who's to say you might not slip back into a coma? We have to keep you for observation."

"But I won't go back into a coma," Jean said. "It's not possible."

Dr. Snapple was amused. "Since when did you develop the ability to see inside your own brain?"

Jean was annoyed. She knew her mother was too proud to accept help from the state. "I don't need to see inside my head to know how I feel. *Mamá*, I shouldn't stay here, you know. How are we going to pay for it?"

Her mother was staring at her. "You're worried about that? You're not worried about yourself?"

"Of course I'm worried about the money," Jean said. "We don't have any."

Her mother smiled faintly. "Don't worry, Jean, we'll find a way." She glanced at Dr. Snapple. "Thank you, Doctor. I'll make sure she stays here, and in bed."

Dr. Snapple left and a few minutes later Carol excused herself. For a moment Jean was alone with her mother. It was obvious to Jean that her mother had suffered terribly while she had been unconscious, and that the poor woman didn't know what to say or do now that the worst was over. Jean didn't know if anything had to be said. She just held her mother's hand and smiled at her, and after a while her mother seemed to feel better. Her mother kissed her goodbye and promised to come that evening, after work. She also warned Jean about staying in bed.

The moment she was gone, Jean got up. She lasted all of five seconds before a wave of dizziness made her sit down quickly. All right, she thought, her brain had to get used to gravity again. Taking several deep breaths, she got up slowly, then sat back down before she could fall over. She did this a few times and eventually was able to stand without feeling as if she were strapped to a Ferris wheel. Her side hurt awfully, as did her right knee. She wondered what she had looked like when they found her. She hadn't heard Lenny come up behind her on the balcony. Not that she could remember, anyway.

Jean knew she wouldn't rest until she saw him.

She limped across the room and found her clothes in the closet. The hospital dry cleaning service hadn't been by since Friday. She saw instantly how much she had bled. Her jeans and top were both stained dark red. She didn't know what to do. The green hospital gown she wore was drafty; she didn't want to go strolling down the halls with her ass hanging out, although she thought she had a very nice ass. Indeed, glancing over her shoulder at her bare behind, she was pleased to see she was still curvaceous even after her special coma diet.

Jean searched the closet for a robe but didn't find one. She was about to give up and return to bed when she noticed a door in the corner opposite the closet, one that didn't appear to lead into the hallway. Cracking it open a couple of inches she discovered—big surprise—that it led into an adjoining room. Her neighbor was a seventy-year-old white woman with a snore like Fred Flintstone's and a wardrobe the equal of Elizabeth Taylor's. The woman had so many clothes jammed in her closet it was as if she planned to attend numerous costume balls on the other side in case she failed to check out of the hospital. Jean took one glance at the woman stretched out on the bed and figured the woman would never know if she was missing a dress or not.

And so, not many minutes later, wearing a long print gown that she wouldn't have been caught dead in under other circumstances, Jean went searching for Lenny. She sneaked out of her wing without difficulty, but by the time she reached the hospital lobby she had to sit down to rest. She couldn't decide which hurt worse, her head, her leg, or her side. All together, though, it was one nasty ache. Yet the strange thing was that the pain bothered her only as far as her body was concerned. It didn't depress her *inside* that she was injured. She accepted it so well she actually surprised herself.

When she was sufficiently recovered, Jean strolled up to a woman at the reception area. She did her best to appear of sound body and mind but the huge bandage around her head was not something she could make vanish with witty conversation. To make matters worse, the bandage was even stained with blood. But the elderly woman behind the counter didn't seem to notice. She looked up as Jean approached.

"Can I help you, miss?" she asked.

"Yes," Jean said. "My brother, Lenny Mandez, is staying in this hospital. He broke his back last Friday. Could you please tell me his floor and room number?"

The woman put a hand to her mouth. "The poor dear. Is he going to be all right?"

Jean had to swallow before answering. She wondered what it would be like to see him. She reminded herself that she mustn't break down. "I hope so."

The woman turned to her computer. "How do you spell that last name?"

Jean gave her the name letter by letter. She thought it wiser to act like Lenny's sister rather than his girlfriend because surely he was still in intensive care and there might be restrictions as far as visitors were concerned. Indeed, a moment later the woman confirmed her suspicion that he was not in a normal room.

"He's on the eighth floor, Room Nine," the woman said. "That's a restricted area. You might have to show I.D. to get in."

"No problem," Jean said. "Thanks for your help."

"You look like you've been in an accident yourself," the woman observed.

"Yeah, I fell off a balcony."

"You were lucky you weren't killed."

Jean felt a cold wave, goose bumps all over. Had someone just walked over her grave? Felt like it. "Yeah," she muttered.

Room Nine turned out to be many small adjoining cubicles hooked up by wires and computers to a central nurses' station. One thing they didn't worry about in intensive care was people's privacy, Jean thought. The area was thick with the smell of alcohol and pain. The moment Jean walked in, she had to sit down. Her head throbbed. A young nurse who looked like a nun came over to check on her. Jean assured the nurse she was fine and explained how she was there to see her brother. The woman recognized Lenny's name. She didn't ask for I.D. Jean was helped into the last cubicle on the left and left alone with her boyfriend.

He was not a pretty sight, and it broke her heart because he had been such a pretty boy. Surprisingly, he was not in a body cast but held rigidly in place by a combination of plastic rods and screws and clamps. His bed, it was clear, was capable of rotating so that his body could be turned. Jean suspected it was necessary to circulate his blood and keep him from getting bed sores. He had no marks on his face, no wounds to any part of the front of his body, although she could see the edge of the large bandage on his back. Still, he looked like death itself. His skin was pasty white, as if a vampire on a binge got hold of him. His eyes were closed; he appeared to be asleep.

"Lenny," she whispered, her voice shaky.

He opened his eyes, but didn't look over at her, staring at the ceiling instead. "Jean," he said softly.

She moved to his side, went to take his hand, then thought better of it. The simple fear of touching him hurt her as much as anything had so far. It must have hurt him as well; he looked at her with such wounded eyes it was all she could do to not burst out crying. She remembered a dog she had had as a child.

He had looked at her the same way right after being struck by a car, right before he died.

"'*Ola,*" she said.

"'*Ola,*" he said. "How are you?"

"Fine." She touched her bandage. "Just bumped my head is all."

"Yesterday they told me you were in a coma."

"That was yesterday." She paused. "How's your back?"

He smiled bitterly. "I don't know. I can't feel it."

"What can you feel?"

He closed his eyes. "I can use my hands and arms. I don't know what else works."

She reached over and gently touched his big toe. He had on underwear, nothing else, but there was a vaporizer steaming in the corner and the cubicle was warm and humid.

"Can you feel that?" she asked.

"Feel what?" His eyes remained closed.

She took her hand away, the weight on her chest heavier than the one on her head. "Nothing. Lenny. Look at me, please, I need to talk to you."

He opened his eyes. "What do you want to talk about?"

She fretted with her hands and had to make herself stop. "You're going to get better."

His voice was flat. "No, I'm not. The doctor says my spinal cord's been severed. It won't heal, they never do. I'm crippled for life. I'm screwed, that's a simple fact. So don't stand there with that little bump on your head and tell me I'm going to get better."

Her throat choked with grief. "I'm sorry."

He turned his head the other way. "I don't want your sympathy."

"What do you want?"

"To be left alone. Get out of here and don't come back."

Finally her tears came; she couldn't stop them. "You don't mean that."

He turned his head back in her direction. His eyes were red, with anger as well as pain. "But I do, Jean. I can't stand to see you walking around while I'm stuck here in this bed."

"Damn you!" she yelled. "That's not fair! Just because I'm not paralyzed I can't be your girlfriend anymore?"

"My *girlfriend*?" he said sarcastically. "How can I have a girlfriend? I can't even control when I have to go to the bathroom anymore, never mind have sex. I'm no good to you. I'm no good to anybody."

"I don't care what you can and can't do. All that matters is that you're alive." She dared to touch his hand. "I mean it, I'm not going to leave you. We can work on you getting better together. And if you're unable to make a full recovery, then we'll work on that as well."

He looked down where she touched him. His eyes seemed to soften. "I can feel that," he whispered.

She nodded eagerly. *"Bueno."*

Unfortunately, the softness only went so deep. He shut his eyes and turned away again. "I have to sleep, Jean. I'm very tired."

She leaned over and kissed his hand. "I'll be back," she said.

He did not respond. He needed time, she told herself as she left the cubicle. Time and love. She couldn't remember having ever loved him so much.

CHAPTER V

THE RISHI WALKED WITH ME beside the stream. I still found it hard to understand how I had created the paradise we were enjoying when I had never imagined a scene so beautiful. The flowers that bloomed beside the water were like none found on Earth—or at least the Earth I knew—so many different colors and shapes. The joy of existence, of walking with this great being, was like a constant stream of gladness inside my chest, as clear and sweet as the water at our feet. I questioned him about Wanderers.

"Were there any on Earth that I knew personally?" I asked.

"You met many as Shari Cooper. But you weren't close to any."

"How about in history? Were any famous people Wanderers?"

"That is a perceptive question. The answer is yes, many well-known people were Wanderers. To be a Wanderer is a great honor as well as a great sacrifice. A soul has to be highly evolved in order to bypass the birth process. Because a Wanderer enters into a developed physical body, he—or she, sex is, of course, not an issue here—carries more of the knowledge of the spiritual plane with him to Earth. Always, he returns to the physical plane with a particular mission, and because he radiates so much soul energy, he often succeeds. By nature, Wanderers are charismatic, intelligent, loving. People are attracted to them. They want to be with them."

"Have you ever been a Wanderer?"

The Rishi smiled. "I wander all over the place."

"Will you ever return to Earth again?"

"I am on Earth now."

"I mean, somewhere in the time frame that I understand to be modern society?"

"Perhaps. It is up to God."

"Does he talk to you? I mean, like I am talking to you now?"

"God is an unbounded ocean of light and consciousness. I float in that ocean on whatever current or wave arises. I go with that, it is my joy to do so. I talk to God when I talk to you. I see God when I see the trees. I feel God when I touch my head. Who is there to talk to but myself?" The Rishi chuckled. "I'm sorry, I don't know how to answer your question."

I smiled. "It doesn't matter. Your answer was beautiful. Tell me some of the famous people on Earth who were Wanderers?"

"They're often hard to spot, but they do have one quality that makes them stand out from others. At one point in their lives they all undergo a huge change of heart and awareness. That, of course, is when the new soul enters the body. Einstein was an example. From a young age he was intelligent, but not the genius he became when the Wanderer who brought the theory of relativity to Earth arrived. That was his mission, to bring that knowledge."

"But wasn't the atomic bomb developed as a result of his theories?"

"Yes. His knowledge was insightful. But it is up to mankind to decide what to do with such knowledge. The theories themselves were neither good nor bad."

"Who was another example of a Wanderer?"

"Martin Luther King. I think his purpose must be obvious to you. But this will surprise you—Malcolm X was also a Wanderer."

"Him? But wasn't he a bigot?"

"He was many things while on Earth. Can any man or woman be defined by one word? But the Malcolm X whom history will remember entered while he was in jail. Immediately there was a huge change in his outlook. He became interested in religious matters. Many Wanderers go through this phase because in your society, religion is seen as the main source of spirituality, although, in reality, that is a great misunderstanding. But as I said, religion has its purpose and Malcolm X became deeply religious. He was extremely charismatic. He drew people by the thousands."

"But wasn't he a Black Muslim? Didn't he hate white people?"

"You just came from a predominantly Judeo-Christian society. Both Judaism and Christianity are fine religions, as are Islam, Buddhism, and Hinduism. One is not better than the other, no matter what the priests and ministers and rabbis would have you believe. Where religion awakens divine love, it is useful. Where it narrows the mind with dogma, it is harmful. And it is true that Malcolm X spent much of his adult life trying to separate Caucasians from African-Americans. But we must come back to what his mission as a Wanderer was. He came to give pride to people of color. At the time many African-Americans, particularly young males, felt a certain helplessness as far as dealing with society. Malcolm X showed them how to be proud and strong."

"But doesn't pride divide people?"

"It can. But it was a necessary step for that segment of population *at that time*. You cannot let go of pride until you've first had it. Malcolm X stirred things up—that was his purpose. You cannot judge people such as him. You cannot judge anybody."

"But if he was a Wanderer, why was he assassinated? Why didn't he have divine protection?"

"He had divine protection. But when a Wanderer is finished with his mission, he often leaves suddenly. Either in a blaze of bullets or quietly."

"Was Malcolm X happy when he got over here?"

"He did not accomplish everything he set out to accomplish. He was used by others, and his mission was distorted. But that happens. He had no regrets. Regret is the most useless of all emotions."

"I'm confused. You speak as if when he entered the body he didn't know he was a Wanderer?"

"That is correct. Few Wanderers realize what they are while in a physical body, at least consciously. But deep inside they know they are on Earth for a reason. They usually move toward their particular mission spontaneously."

"Will I realize that I'm a Wanderer?"

"It's possible. It's up to you. You have free will."

"What will my mission be?"

"I speak of missions because it gives you some understanding of why you would want to return. But in reality there is only one mission—to realize divine love. To awaken that divine love in others. But different people do that in different ways, and they don't have to be Wanderers to inspire others. Every man and woman born into a physical body On Earth has a mission. Your particular one will be to inspire the often forgotten segment of the poor Hispanic community. Jean Rodrigues is Hispanic and poor. As her, you will write stories that millions of people will read. They will not necessarily be spiritual stories. They can be about space ships or aliens or dragons or ordinary people. The topic does not matter. But the spirituality will be in your stories because it's inside you. It will flow into your words. People will read your stories and without understanding why, yearn for something greater. And because you are a young Hispanic woman, you will also serve as a role model for other young people like Jean Rodrigues."

I smiled. "I always wanted to be a writer. But where will I get my ideas? Will I have a muse?"

The Rishi smiled. "You will be inspired, don't worry. But perhaps you can write a story about where you get your ideas. I imagine it would be very popular."

"This is great. I couldn't ask for a better job. I loved writing that story about what happened to me when I died. Do you think I'll be able to find my brother and get my story published?"

He regarded me fondly. "It's possible."

"What does that look mean? You know something I don't. Will I find Jimmy?"

"Yes."

I clapped my hands together. "Great! Will I recognize him as my brother?"

"That is up to you."

I stopped walking. "But I have to know him. Can't you help me out here?"

The Rishi was amused. "I am always helping you, Shari."

"I know that. I appreciate that. But what can I do after I get in Jean's physical body to make it more likely that I will remember that I'm a Wanderer?"

"You can learn to enjoy silence."

"Come again? Do I have to learn to shut up?"

He laughed. "No. That would not be possible, or natural, for you. You can talk all you want But sometime during your busy life you will want to sit in meditation."

"But I don't know how to meditate. Can you teach me now before I return?"

"I will teach you. But you must be taught again while you're in the physical body. You must be taught by a Master. That is very important. There is a new consciousness entering your society, new ideas. Many people call this New Age information. Much of it is useful. Much of it is confusing. The New Age movement speaks of many of the same things I speak of, but there are major differences between what I tell you and what you will find in most New Age books. I will go over these differences with you. Even if you don't remember them consciously while you're in the body, you will have a sense for what is true and that sense will guide you on your path. You will even write about the things I tell you now."

"I can't imagine that a story about a dragon could bring out any profound truths."

"It all depends on the dragon, Shari. Listen attentively to these points. Meditation is never an act of mood making. Pure silence, pure consciousness, the eternal side of your nature—it is beyond thought. You cannot talk yourself into it. It comes by grace and by grace alone. But what is grace? How do you make it come? That is where a Master is important. Many in the New Age movement are too anxious to throw off all authority. They say that no one can teach anything, that it is all inside the student. And that is true to a certain extent. On the other hand, to uncover what is inside you must bow at the feet of someone who has already discovered that great treasure. I use the word *bow* carefully. Because until a person is ready to humble himself and admit that he doesn't know, then he can learn nothing of value. It takes great humility to even approach a Master. These are things the New Age movement sometimes forgets."

"The whole eighteen years I was on Earth, I never saw a Master."

"This time you will. They will begin to appear in the world at this time. They teach techniques: meditation, certain kinds of breathing, physical exercises. But a technique only points toward the goal. It is not the goal itself. It is like a branch on a tree at nighttime. You can say to a friend, 'Follow the way that branch points and you will see the most wonderful star.' The branch gives direction, but it is not the same as the star. The branch is made of wood, the star is pure energy. Or say you want to eat a bowl of cereal. To do that you need the technique of using a spoon: how to hold it, which end to put in the bowl, how it goes up and into your mouth. The spoon is crucial, but it is the cereal you want. The cereal is the grace. Grace flows from a Master. It has to flow because he embodies that divine love."

"I wish I had been on Earth with you in Egypt," I said.

"You were. You are. You are with me there as much as you are with me now."

I shook my head. "Let's stick to one time frame, please, or I just end up confused.'

"If you wish. But sometimes a Master is purposely confusing. He destroys preconceived ideas and beliefs. Always, though, he gives an aspirant a spiritual practice. That is very necessary to do even though many on the physical plane don't think so. They say, 'The time is changing and all will be taken care of.' They don't want to do any practice. And they are right, to a certain extent. The time is changing. That is why so many Wanderers are beginning to appear on Earth—to help prepare for this change. Mankind is entering a new age where spirituality will dominate. But many fear this change. They have heard about the disasters that are to come. Many so-called prophets say the majority of the world will be wiped out. That is not true. The world has an insurance policy. It has the Masters. There will be disasters, however, to shake things up a little. It can take a needle to remove a thorn. It can take a shaking of the Earth for people not to totally depend on the Earth, to make them look inside. You will write stories about the disasters as well.

People will read them and understand that when things appear the darkest, it is a sign that dawn is near. You will write stories of enlightened dragons and aliens, and people will want to learn to meditate. Even though the coming dawn is inevitable, it is good to be awake to enjoy it. Meditation helps with that."

"I am never going to remember all this," I said. "I can't remember half of what you just said."

"It doesn't matter. I see your mind has begun to wander. That is all right—you are a Wanderer, after all." He paused. "You want to see Peter."

I nodded. I knew I could hide nothing from the Rishi. "I miss him."

"Where would you like to see him?"

"What do you mean?"

The Rishi knelt for a moment and picked a red flower that resembled a rose. He gestured to the serene landscape. "I told you, this is all a dream. What would you like to dream with Peter? It can be anything. It can even be that you don't know that it is a dream. Really, that is all human life is. Just a dream people choose to enter into so that they can learn something. But people take it so seriously and become afraid of their own creation. They even fear to wake up. That is the one lesson humanity most needs to learn in the coming days. That there is no reason to be afraid. That things will work out for the best. That God knows what she's doing."

"She?"

He tapped me on the head with his flower. "When I am with you, Shari, you are my God. What universe do you wish to create for you and Peter?"

I considered. Boy did I consider. "It can be anything?"

"Anything."

I blushed; I could feel the blood in my cheeks even though I was a ghost. "Can it be an R-rated creation?"

"Yes."

"I don't want you to watch."

"I won't watch."

I laughed. "You promise?"

"I promise." He chuckled. "I swear it, Shari."

I rubbed my hands together in anticipation. "Awesome. Let the creation begin. Let there be light. Let there be boys!"

I never knew I had such a dirty mind.

Well, I may have suspected.

CHAPTER VI

JEAN RODRIGUES couldn't remember when she had last tied her little brother's shoes. Teddy sat above her on the kitchen table as she knelt at his feet and stared at her as if trying to remember the same thing. He was a cute four-year-old, with hair as long as a girl's and dimples. He touched the top of her head as she finished with his laces. She no longer wore her bandage, although she still suffered from a dull headache. But she couldn't complain; her ribs and knee were healed. She had been released from the hospital nine days earlier. She had just made it to her high school graduation the night before, and had been happy to be there. It was before nine on Saturday morning, two weeks after her fall.

"Is your head sore?" he asked.

She smiled and clasped his outstretched hand. "Now that you've touched it, Teddy, it's all better. Did you know you have magic hands?"

He blinked at her pronouncement and pulled his hands back to study them. His eyes went wide. "What can they do?" he asked.

"They can give love. That is their special magic. Go give Mom a hug and then you go play. Here, I'll help you down."

Jean lifted Teddy from the table and he hurried over to the sofa where their mother lounged in front of the TV. Today was their mother's only day off. Teddy gave her the briefest of hugs before dashing out the door yelling something about showing the other kids his hands. They both laughed at him. Her mother shook her head.

"You'll have that boy trying to heal all the kids on the block, Jean," she said.

Jean sat beside her on the sofa. "Maybe he can," she said thoughtfully.

Her mother continued to smile. "I don't think anyone's sick around here at the moment."

"There's sick and there's sick," Jean muttered.

"What do you mean?"

Jean smiled quickly. "Nothing, just mumbling. Are you still worried about me being a candy striper? I won't go if it really upsets you."

"I think you're still too weak to be volunteering for a job that pays nothing."

"But if it did pay well, I would be strong enough?"

Her mother slapped her playfully on the arm with a magazine. "That's not what I mean and you know it. You should rest while you have the chance. Why did you tell the nurses you were coming in anyway? Is it so that you can see Lenny? You can see him without working."

"I do want to be close to Lenny, that's true. But I volunteered because when I was in the hospital I saw a lot of patients who weren't getting any attention because the nurses are too overworked." Jean shrugged. "I don't want to sound like a saint. I just want to help out."

Her mother stared at her. "But you do sound different."

Jean started to deny it, but only nodded. "Carol said the same thing. But I don't feel any different since the accident, except for my constant headache."

Her mother continued to watch her. "I don't believe that. You seem freer in a way. You don't walk around like you have the weight of the world on your shoulders."

"I never used to do that."

"Yes, you did. You were always *triste*."

Jean shrugged again. "Well, maybe I had my reasons."

Her mother nodded. "Do you want to talk about it?"

"About what?"

"You know. Your pregnancy."

Jean acted shocked. "Was I pregnant? God, those comas are amazing things. Here I slept through an immaculate conception and a miscarriage all in the same two days."

"I was pregnant with you when I was your age," her mother said.

Jean quieted. "I know. I thought about that a lot."

"Before or after you had sex with Lenny?"

Jean looked over sharply. "Only after I failed the E.P.T."

"You took one of those? Where did you get one of those?"

"At the same drugstore where I bought the condoms that didn't work." Jean shook her head. 'They're not hard to use. All you have to do is be able to pee in a tube." Jean paused. "Why are you asking me these questions, Mom? You must know Lenny doesn't stand a chance in hell of knocking me up again."

"I'm sorry what happened to him. You know I mean that. I'm sure he was a fine young man."

"He still is, *Mamá*. Being crippled hasn't changed that. Not in my book."

Her mother touched her arm. "I'm going to say something harsh now, and you're not going to want to hear it. But I just want you to listen to me a second and think about it. I know Lenny is hurt and needs your help. You should go see him and help him in any way you can. But I think it would be a mistake for you not to see the facts for what they are. Lenny's going to be crippled for the rest of his life. At best he will be able to get around in a wheelchair. You can't let yourself get any more attached to him than you already are."

Jean spoke calmly. "Why not?"

"I just told you why. Because he's crippled for life. You can't be with a man tike that. You'll spend all your time taking care of him."

A tear sprang into Jean's eye, but she managed to keep her expression flat. "I like taking care of people."

"No, you don't. You've never liked it before. You can't be with half a man."

Jean drew in a painful breath. "First you're worried that I was pregnant. Now you're worried I want to be with someone who can't get me pregnant. What's the deal, Mom?"

Her mother sighed. "Maybe this is not the time to talk about this. You go see him. Do what you can for him. We'll talk later."

Jean stood and looked down at her. "I'll feel the same later. I love him. I didn't know that before, even when I slept with him, but I know now. Maybe my love can't heal him. Maybe I just lied to Teddy and there isn't any magic in this world. But at least my love makes him whole in my eyes. Lenny is not half a man." She turned away. "Now, if you'll excuse me, I think I'll wait outside for Carol. She's supposed to pick me up in a few minutes."

Her mother sounded sad. "I don't want to fight with you, Jean. I just want to protect you."

Jean paused at the door. "I know that. We're not fighting. We're just—arguing." She opened the door. "Have a nice day, *Mamá*. I don't know when I'll be home."

While waiting for Carol, Jean reflected on why those close to her were saying she had changed. There was truth in their comments. Despite Lenny's serious injury and her own wounds, she did feel lighter. Each morning she woke up anxious to start the day. Why, even the sun was brighter, the sky bluer. It was as if she had refound a childhood innocence she couldn't remember ever having enjoyed. Plus her head was filled with strange ideas she had never had before. She kept thinking of the stars and planets, dreaming of ancient civilizations, imagining vast supernatural dramas. She had begun to jot down her thoughts in a notebook, although she had no idea what she would do with them.

"What did happen that night?" she wondered aloud.

Carol arrived a few minutes later. She was on her way to a date with the Russian guy who worked at McDonald's, the guy with the scarred face. Seemed the guy didn't have a car. Carol was dressed to kill and excitedly smoking a joint. She offered Jean a hit the moment Jean got in the car. Jean took the joint and threw it in the garbage can at the end of their driveway.

"Hey!" Carol protested. "I just rolled that."

"I don't want any."

"Well, excuse me. I want it. You could have just said no and handed it back." Carol started to get out of the car. "I'm getting it."

Jean grabbed her arm and smiled. "I don't even want to have to smell it. Leave it in the can, *por favor*."

Carol looked at her as if she were an alien creature. "You don't want to get loaded anymore? What's gotten into you?"

Jean let go of Carol and gestured to the block. "You see

this street? There's graffiti on every wall. There's garbage on every lawn. Paint is peeling from the houses. Dogs and children are running wild. This is my street, but your street is just as bad."

"So? We live on the crappy side of town. When you get rich and famous, you can move to Malibu."

"I don't want to move to Malibu. I want to stay in this neighborhood because this is where I grew up. I want to clean up this place. I have given it a lot of thought. But I can't clean this place up by myself and, besides, it will just get dirty again because the minds of too many people around here are dirty. I know we get screwed in school. We have the worst teachers and the ugliest buildings. I know we get screwed at work because we're not white. But I think we're screwing ourselves with all the drugs we're taking. Look, you and I have been stoned since we were twelve. Haven't you gotten sick of it yet?"

Carol stared at her dumbfounded. "I don't know. I guess."

"I'm sick of it. I'm not getting loaded again, ever."

"But you'll still smoke pot now and then, won't you?"

"Carol. I'm not taking anything. And I don't want you to, either."

Carol was annoyed. "Right, great. If I don't want to be Miss Purity, I can't be your friend anymore. You know, Jean, you might be nicer nowadays, but you're also turning into a royal pain in the ass."

"I didn't say you couldn't be my friend anymore. It's just

that every time you light up a joint around me, I'm going to throw it away. And you won't be able to stop me 'cause I can kick your ass any day." Jean smiled sweetly. "But I still love you, Carol."

Carol put the car in gear. "Thank God for that"

They headed for the hospital. The day was hot and Carol's air-conditioning hadn't worked since the last ice age. Jean rolled down her window and looked at the houses she had seen every day of her life. Somehow, it was as if she were seeing them for the first time. It was true, most of them were in poor shape, but Jean could see the potential there. Everywhere she looked, she saw all kinds of possibilities.

"How long are you working at the hospital?" Carol asked.

"Three hours. That's all they'll let me with my injuries, and I had to push for those."

"Why are you doing it?"

"So I can steal hospital drugs."

"But you just said you don't want to get loaded anymore?"

Jean laughed. "*Menso!* See what all that *mota* has done to your brain? I'm not going to steal drugs. I volunteered to work at the hospital because they need help. That's the only reason."

Carol was impressed. "That's neat. Maybe you'll get to give some way-cool girl or guy a shot in the ass."

Jean couldn't stop laughing. "They don't let candy stripers give shots. Certainly not to way-cool girls and guys."

"Well, I don't know what they do."

"Tell me what's happening with you? Why are you going out with a guy?"

"He's not exactly normal, you know."

"I understand that. But he is a he. That makes him different from a girl."

Carol giggled. "That's true."

"Look, are you still a lesbian or not? I just want to know for future reference. If you're not, then I can quit defending you."

"Does it bother you to defend me?" Carol asked.

"No. It turns me on. But answer my question."

"I don't know the answer. I just know I like this guy. But I still like girls. Maybe I'm bisexual." Carol paused. "Does that gross you out?"

"No," Jean said honestly. "It makes you complex. I like that in a boy or a girl."

Carol nodded. "I like to think it gives me color."

"Just remember that a guy can get you pregnant where a girl can't."

"I have you to remind me of that." Carol paused. "Will you get to help Lenny today?"

Jean sighed. "I don't know if I can help Lenny. I've seen him every day since I woke up, but he hardly talks to me. I keep thinking he'll feel better when the bones in his back have healed enough so he can start physical therapy. Lying in bed all day would depress anybody."

"When will he be able to get into a wheelchair?"

"Not for a while. Another couple of months."

"That long?"

"At least. Where his back broke, they had to fuse the spine together. That takes time to heal."

"Will he ever walk again?" Carol asked.

Jean hesitated. "The traditional medical answer is no. That's the answer he's supposed to learn to accept. But I don't believe it. I can't help but think his condition is only tempo-rary." She shook her head. "Maybe I'm just fooling myself."

"I hope he gets better. Hey, have you seen Darlene lately?"

"No. She never talks to me. She never came to visit me at the hospital. What's with her?"

"I think she still plans to go after Juan," Carol said.

"After all that's happened? You can't be serious."

Jean was thoughtful. "I'd like to talk to her more about what happened that night Lenny and I got hurt. You know, weird as this may sound, I don't even know if she was still there when we fell."

"I think she was," Carol said. "I think she's the one who called the ambulance."

"But you're not sure?"

"No. What does Lenny say?"

"That he can't remember."

"Do you believe him?" Carol asked.

Jean shrugged. "I don't know why he'd lie to me." She

added, "We can't let Darlene go after Juan. It would be a death sentence for her."

Carol looked worried. "Maybe for all of us."

Carol dropped Jean off at the hospital twenty minutes later. She was going to spend the day with Scarface, and Jean assured her she could take the bus home. Actually, Jean liked riding the bus, especially since her accident. It was a good place to meet people.

Her candy-striper duties were simple: she delivered meals to patients. But even this job turned out to be complex with the elderly patients. Not one but two old women thought she was their granddaughter. At first Jean denied the relationship, but when she saw how much it meant to the women to have a visit from a granddaughter, Jean decided to play along, reminiscing about events she had no memory of and adding details the women had no minds to doubt. On the whole she had the most fun with the senior citizens and children. Really, helping people got her high, and somehow she had known it would happen.

The patient who affected her the most, though, was a teenage girl named Debra Zimmerer. She was eighteen, the same as Jean, and dying. Just before Jean delivered her food, the nurses told her that Debra had leukemia, and they felt she wasn't going to make it. When Jean brought in her tray, she found Debra lying in bed and reading J. R. R. Tolkien's *The Lord of the Rings*, which Jean had read in the hospital. Debra was worn-out pretty, with faded brown eyes as weary as those of a sick model in an old oil painting. She was five feet five and weighed maybe eighty pounds. Jean took one look at her and felt a painful stab in her gut, but somehow she managed to smile as she set down the tray.

"Awesome book, huh?" Jean asked.

Debra set the fat book aside. "I guess. I'm just near the beginning."

"Keep going. It keeps getting better and better. In fact, I think it's the best story I ever read." Jean lifted the lid off her plate. "Would you like something to eat? I brought you chicken, but if you don't like it they have some kind of fish."

Debra sat up weakly. "I'm not that hungry."

"How about something to drink? I have apple juice or orange juice or ginger ale."

Debra nodded. "I could drink some ginger ale."

Jean opened the can and poured Debra a glass. Debra's voice was dry, which Jean understood to be a side effect of the morphine she took to control the pain. Debra lifted it to her lips and took a sip. The act seemed to exhaust her, and she put down the glass quickly. Jean sat on the bed beside her.

"Is there anything else I can get you?" Jean asked.

Debra coughed. "No."

Jean patted her on the back. "Are you OK?"

Debra nodded and wiped at her colorless lips. "Yes."

Jean shook her head. "That was a stupid question. I'm

sorry, of course you're not OK." She paused. "I heard you have leukemia."

Debra watched her. "Yes. It's a drag. What's your name?"

"Jean. You're Debra, right?"

"Yes." Debra glanced at the book. "Could you tell me how the story ends?"

Jean forced a smile. "I don't want to do that. It'll spoil it for you." Then she stopped, hearing what Debra was really asking her. It was a long story, really three books in one. Debra was not going to live long enough to finish it and she knew it. "But if you want me to, I can. I can do it today after I finish delivering these trays."

Debra stared at the far wall for a moment. "How about tomorrow? That would be a good day for me."

Jean nodded. "I can come tomorrow evening and tell you the whole story." She added, without even thinking about what she was going to say, "Maybe I can tell you one of my stories as well." Debra was interested. "Do you write stories?" Jean shrugged. "I'm only working on one so far. It's about this famous writer and her muse. Only her muse is a troll who appears out of her bedroom closet one day and demands half her royalties. I'll tell you what I have of it so far and you can tell me whether you think I should bother finishing it."

"OK." Debra lowered her head. "It'll be nice to have a visitor."

"Doesn't anyone come to see you?"

"Just my father. But I can't talk to him because he's too scared about me being sick." Debra hesitated. "He's afraid I'm going to die."

Jean spoke gently. "Are you afraid?"

Debra raised her head and wiped her nose. "Yeah. I know it's going to happen, but I'm still scared. My doctor told me." Again she stared at the far wall. "I have no idea what it's going to be like." She shrugged. "Maybe it won't be like anything. Maybe I'll just be dead and that will be it."

"No," Jean said firmly. "Your body will die but you'll go on."

Debra smiled sadly. "I wish I had your faith."

It was Jean's turn to hesitate because she really didn't know what she wanted to say to the poor girl. But at the same time she felt compelled to speak, and she believed that what she would say would be the truth.

"It's not that I have faith. I just *know* that your time of death is no more important than when you change your clothes. Don't ask me how I know. I can't explain it. The main thing is, when death comes, you don't need to be afraid. That's important. Fear is the only thing that can hold you back."

Debra listened. "Hold you back from what?"

"From going on to more joy. It's a lot harder to be born than to die. You'll see, and when you do, you'll say to yourself, 'That foolish girl in the hospital was right.'"

"Are you a fool?"

"Sure. But you know, only fools get into heaven." Debra grinned. "Who told you that?" Jean stood up quickly from the bed. Debra's question had a profound effect on her. For a moment Jean felt as if there were two of her standing in the room, one visible, the other a reflection. She felt as if she should be able to glance over her shoulder and see her other half to answer Debra's question. She felt inexplicable joy even with a dying girl watching her.

"Someone wise," Jean said softly, turning away. "I'll see you tomorrow."

"I hope so," Debra said with feeling.

It was inevitable that when she finished her shift Jean would go and stand at the end of Lenny's bed and try to think of something inspiring to say. Lenny had been moved to a normal room with the motorized bed that allowed him to be rotated without the assistance of four nurses. At present, thankfully, he was lying faceup and she was able to address him rather than his scarred back. Unfortunately, no words of wisdom came to her and he had yet to open his eyes despite her saying his name several times. She heard her mother's words in her mind and had to convince herself they weren't true.

"I can leave if you want me to," Jean said finally. "But you're going to have to tell me to leave. Otherwise I'll just stand here feeling awful. But maybe that's what you want, Lenny, I don't know."

He opened his eyes. "You should know by now what I want."

Jean stepped closer, touching his bare arm. This room, like his previous one, was warmer than normal. Probably because they kept him scantily dressed to make it easier to care for him.

"What do you want?" she asked reluctantly.

"To die," he said flatly.

There was anguish in her voice. "No."

"Yes." Finally he looked at her face. "I can't live like this. You say you love me, Jean. If you do, then help me end this."

She clasped his right hand. "You just have to hold on for a little while longer. Soon you'll be in a wheelchair and able to get out. I'll take you to the beach. I'll take you to the movies. You can't imagine how many great films have come out since you've been in here. I can show you—"

"*You* can take me," he interrupted. "*You* can show me. That's true because I can't do any of those things without you. But how long will you be there? You say forever but we both know that's B.S. One day you'll get tired of pushing a cripple around and you'll meet some other guy and then you'll say, 'I'm sorry Lenny but you know it's a tough world.' Then you'll leave, and what'll I do? I'll tell you. I'll kill myself. But why should I have to wait for the day we both know is going to come? I don't want to go through the pain. I want to do it now. I want you to help me."

Jean wept. "I won't leave you, I swear to you."

Lenny strained to move his head as close to hers as he could. "You can get what you want if you keep your eyes open and move fast. A bottle of sleeping pills, a dozen packaged shots of Demerol—either of these would be enough to kill me. Are you listening to me, Jean? If you don't help me you just make it harder for me. I'll have to slit my wrists. No, that will be too slow. I'll have to cut my throat. The blood will be all over the place. You'll walk in here one day and the walls will be sprayed with red and—"

"*Cállate!*" she cried.

Lenny let his head fall back. "I'm going to do it. You know I'm going to do it."

She sighed, her tears sprinkling his arm. "You must have some reason to live."

"None."

"Don't say that."

"I want to die today."

"Lenny."

"Right now."

"Damn you! You have to give yourself time. If you can't think of a reason to live, then you have to find one. Think, Lenny, of everything and everyone in the world. Think of something you want to do. Hold on to that, at least until you get out of here." She squeezed his hand, a desperate note in her voice. "Can't you think of anything?"

He started to answer but then stopped, only staring at her

for several seconds. His expression became strangely blank. "Maybe," he muttered.

She nodded. "Good. That's a start. Hold on to that. It can make you strong."

"Don't you want to know what it is?" he asked.

She shook her head. "No. It doesn't matter. As long as it keeps you alive."

Lenny sucked in a weary breath and closed his eyes.

"But the day it stops doing that, then what? Will you help me end it?"

Her head throbbed. "Do I have to?"

"Yes. You must promise me."

She let go of his hand, let his arm drop. "I promise," she whispered.

CHAPTER VII

JEAN DID NOT take the bus home after she left the hospital, but rather, to the beach, Huntingdon Beach, located in Orange County. It was a long ride for her, and on the way she kept asking herself why she was going there when Santa Monica Beach or Venice Beach was closer and just as nice. Indeed, she couldn't even remember when she had last entered Orange County. Yet a wave of nostalgia spread over her as the bus headed for the Huntingdon pier. Staring at the brightly colored shops, she felt strangely at home, at peace even. She was glad she had hours of free time. The dull ache of her perpetual headache had eased somewhat.

Jean had forty dollars on her. The first thing she did after getting off the bus was buy herself a bathing suit, a navy blue single piece affair that showed her breasts and bottom to good advantage. She wanted to look sexy but she also wanted something comfortable to swim in. She also bought herself a beach bag and towel and headed for the sand with the suit on. The area immediately around the pier looked like the happening place; she found a spot in the shade of the first lifeguard station. The people around her seemed so different from those in her neighborhood, she thought, with their rich summer attire and perfect hair. Most of the kids looked like they were riding their daddy's credit card limits. Yet, at the same time they were young and confused like everyone else she knew. She couldn't take her eyes off them. Since her accident she was always observing and watching, like a spectator at a play she had no part in.

Jean did not spend long lying on the sand. Soon she was in the water, and the motion of the waves was more than enough to wash away the stress of the last two weeks. She had always been an excellent swimmer. Her worries about Lenny and Debra fell off as she swam out three hundred yards past the first break and let herself bob up and down on the huge south swells. The air was hot, the water cool, and there wasn't a cloud in the sky. It was almost as if she swam in paradise.

Wherever I am is paradise because I am there. I am joy itself.

Where had she heard that? From a book? A teacher at school? She couldn't remember and it didn't matter because it was true, she was that joy, and that was all that mattered. She swam farther out and felt the ocean welcome her. The blue horizon seemed to stretch to infinity and she felt as if she could keep going. She felt completely free.

Then she began to feel tired. The fatigue came on her all at once, and when she turned and saw that the beach was a half mile back, she felt a stab of anxiety. The water felt cold now. She wasn't out of the hospital that long. Her supposedly healed ribs suddenly didn't feel as if they were all knitted together. What if she cramped up? She might die. Yet it wasn't the thought of death that frightened her. It was the idea that she'd leave without completing an important task. For the first time in her life Jean felt she was on Earth for a purpose.

She slowly began to make her way back in, conserving her strength as best she could. She was halfway to the beach and experiencing exhaustion when the lifeguard boat happened by. The twenty-five-year-old-bronze god behind the wheel waved and asked if she'd like a ride to the shore. She humbled herself and gasped that she would. Once aboard, the lifeguard complimented her on her stamina and her bathing suit. But he didn't hit on her or anything. He probably rescued way-cool babes all day, she thought. His name was Ken, as in Barbie and Ken. He kind of looked like Ken.

The warm sand was a delicious treat for her weary goosebump-covered limbs. She lay back on her towel and was out in ten seconds. She slept for an hour, and dreamt of the sun and the heavens. She flew above mankind's burning star on the back of an angel, while all worlds spun below her. Worlds of light, worlds of pain—it was all there for her to choose, the angel said. If she wished to go back.

"Go back," Jean whispered as she awakened with a start. She sat up and looked around, feeling as if she had to start back. But not to the other side of town, to her side of town. But to another place, she thought.

She stood and collected her towel and clothes. Without knowing why, almost as if in a dream, she walked north.

Two miles from the pier, on a stretch of sand where Huntington Beach ended and Bolsa Chica Beach began, a row of expensive and multistoried condominiums had been erected to provide a view of Catalina on every clear day Southern California had to offer. Jean paused to stare at them. It was not their decor that drew her—if anything she thought they were something of an eyesore, with their oversize balconies protruding from their back sides like lines drawn on a blueprint by an architect on acid. She realized she had a prejudice against places she knew she'd never be able to afford. Still, the condos drew her attention, even though she didn't like them, even though they frightened her. How curious, she thought, to fear buildings she had never seen before. Yet it was as if the condos were bathed in black and red light, in memories of horror that someone had desperately tried to blot out.

"But I've never been here before," Jean muttered to herself.

Horror can attract as well as repel. She felt herself walking toward the buildings, pulled by invisible strings that could have stretched from the ground as well as from the sky. She continued to move as if in a dream, her angel long gone, replaced by a being from a lower region who whispered silently. Maybe it was a demon, she thought. Maybe it was just someone's past that had somehow passed by without touching her.

The condo on the right, in particular, drew her. It was three stories high, like the others, but somehow it appeared taller. The roof was covered with orange clay adobe-style tiles. A metal fence surrounded the building, but the gate was open. Without asking permission, without ringing a bell, she went inside.

She went straight to the spot.

What spot? She didn't know what to call it. A stain on the ground.

Going down on her knees, she touched the dark stain on the smooth concrete and wondered what had made it? Why did it fill her with such dread? Who had died here?

Yes. That's the real question. It's a bloodstain, I can see that. Only blood permanently turns concrete dark. Only blood refuses to fade. Only blood never forgets.

Jean felt her hair slip forward over her shoulders and fall on to the stain. It was almost as if the strands of hair strained to soak up the blood that had once flowed at her knees. Soak it back into her head, deep into her brain cells, suffuse them with the life and death of that night. Whatever had happened here, she knew, had happened in the dark. It had been an act of surprise, an act of vengeance. Jean could feel all those things as she knelt there. But most of all she felt sorrow. Whoever had died here, she knew, had come to a bitter end.

Jean didn't know how long she remained by the stain. But eventually she became aware of a shadow stretching over her from above. She raised her eyes into the glare of the sun and saw a tall elderly lady in a lovely white dress. She carried a smart gray handbag in her right hand and it was obvious she had just had her hair done. Although she was as old as some of the patients Jean fed in the hospital, she was nowhere near retirement. She stood erect and her blue eyes were clear and alert.

"Can I help you, miss?" she asked in a pleasant voice.

Jean stood reluctantly. The stain repulsed her, while at the same time she was afraid to leave it. Somehow, it connected her to a part of herself she felt she should know. She wiped her palms over her knees—the heat of the concrete had slightly burned her flesh. She still had her suit on.

"No," Jean said, realizing how foolish she'd sound if she spoke of how the stain preyed on her mind. She stooped to collect her bag. "I was just resting. I'll be on my way."

"The way you were kneeling there," the woman said. "The expression on your face—I thought you knew her."

Jean stopped. "Knew who?"

The woman nodded to the stain. "The girl who died here."

Jean felt dizzy. She had to stick out her arm and hold on to a fence to support herself. "Oh, God," she whispered.

The woman put her hand on her arm to steady her. "Are you all right, dear?"

Jean nodded weakly. "Yes, I'm fine. It's just—the heat." She

straightened up as well as she could, although the world continued to wobble as if the Huntingdon Beach fault had just decided
to try for the top of the Richter scale. She added, "I really should
be going," and turned in the direction of the gate but didn't move.

"If you'd like a glass of lemonade before you go, I'd be
happy to get you one." The woman stuck out her hand. "My
name's Rita Wilde. I manage several of the condos on this
block. Most are owner occupied but quite a few are rentals."

Jean shook her hand. Her eyes kept straying back to the
mark on the ground. "You were the manager here when the
girl died?" Jean asked.

"Yes. It happened a year ago. She was about your age." Rita
cocked her head upward. "She fell off that balcony right above
us." Rita frowned. "She might have lived if she hadn't landed
directly on her head."

"How did she fall?"

A shadow crossed Rita's face. "A bunch of teenagers were
having a party. The parents weren't home. The girl didn't die
until near the end of the party. At first everyone thought she
jumped. But then the police figured out she had been shoved.
It was all over the papers. You must have read about it."

"I didn't. Not that I remember at least." Jean nodded to the
stain. "This is from where she hit the ground?"

"Yes. I've tried a dozen times to scrub it away but it refuses
to go. The poor child. She was only eighteen."

"I'm eighteen," Jean said quickly.

Rita smiled. "Are you? That's a wonderful age. What I wouldn't give to be eighteen again. Can I get you that glass of lemonade now?"

"No, that's OK. I'm feeling a bit better." Jean hesitated. "Do you remember the girl's name?"

Rita stopped to scratch her head. "It was something Cooper. I can't remember her first name. But I do know her parents lived near Adams. The father came by a couple of days after she died. I talked to him and he told me a little about himself." Rita shrugged. "I guess he just wanted to see the spot where his daughter had died. Maybe I'd do the same, I don't know." Rita paused and studied her. "Are you sure you weren't friends with that girl?"

Cooper. Adams. Cooper. The father. Cooper.

The words chilled Jean to the bone.

"No," Jean said. "I didn't know her. Why do you ask?"

It was Rita's turn to look at the stain. "I don't know. It's just a thought I had."

Jean began to back away. "Thank you for your time, Rita. Have a nice day."

"You, too, child. Enjoy yourself."

Jean searched for a telephone booth the moment she left the complex. She found one outside on a liquor store wall a block over. There was a telephone book; she hastily scanned the white pages and found sixteen Coopers. She flipped to the map at the front of the book and located Adams, studied the streets around it, then returned to the list of sixteen. Only one man, Stewart Cooper on Delaware, lived anywhere near Adams. She memorized his number and again consulted the map. From where she stood it was approximately three miles to the man's house, but she figured she would probably have to walk half that distance just to catch the bus home. She decided to pay Mr. Cooper a visit.

But what are you going to say to him? I didn't know your daughter but I'm sorry she's dead. And, oh, by the way, her bloodstain really freaked me out. When my hair fell on it, I felt as if I were the one who had died. Imagine that?

Jean decided to cross that bridge when she came to it. She entered the liquor store and bought herself a tall Coke. Her walk already had her dehydrated. Taking a couple of slugs from the bottle, she set out for Adams, this time heading south, back toward the pier. She figured it would take her close to an hour to reach the Cooper residence. Plenty of time for her to figure out what the hell she was doing.

As it turned out, her estimate was overly optimistic. Between her long swim and her still healing body, she couldn't do twenty-minute miles. She was about to call a cab by the time she stumbled onto Delaware, *ninety* minutes later. Fortunately the Cooper house wasn't far up from the beach. In fact, it's just over there, she thought. The house with the white picket fence and the maple in front . . .

Wait a second! I have to check the address to know which house it is. I don't know anything about picket fences and maple trees. Hell, I couldn't tell a maple tree from an olive tree, even if it was growing maples.

That was true, she thought. But what was also true was that she recognized the house the instant she saw it. She didn't have to confirm her feeling by checking the number she'd obtained from the phone book. The Cooper house was the third house on the right. Still, as she drew closer, she did check the number against the numbers on the curb. The perfect match brought another wave of dizziness to her already overwhelmed brain. As did the sight of the young man in the driveway loading his pickup. He was tall and handsome with dark hair and a nice build and that was cool and everything. But what was not so cool, at least not at the moment, was that he looked so familiar.

He, in fact, looked like someone she had known all her life.

Yet she had never seen him before.

"He's the dead girl's brother," she whispered to herself.

Jean walked up to him, probably looking like the over-heated radiator that she felt like. His truck was loaded with a disassembled bed and a chest of drawers, plus a generous helping of wrinkled clothes and what appeared to be a PC. It didn't take a genius to realize he was moving out. He had a gold-colored lamp in his hand when he glanced over at her. His eyes were warm and blue and yet they sent a shiver down to her toes.

"Can I help you?" he asked.

"Yes," she mumbled. "Which way is the beach?"

He pointed toward the large blue body of water at her

back, the one with the waves and the salt in it, and the sandy beach beside it. "It's over there," he said.

She glanced over her shoulder. "Oh, yeah. I have a terrible sense of direction."

"You're not from around here?" he asked. The way he spoke, she knew he knew the answer to his own question—which he should have, because of her inner-city bad-girl accent. Yet, even though she liked him, she didn't like being categorized. She straightened up and cleared her throat.

"How can you tell?" she asked.

He shrugged and set down his lamp. "Your voice. Your bathing suit."

"What's wrong with my bathing suit? I just bought it. I bought it down here."

He paused and studied her up and down, perhaps wondering what he was getting himself into, and if it was worth it. "There's nothing wrong with it," he said carefully. "It just doesn't look like the kind of suit girls around here wear."

"Because my ass doesn't stick out?"

He smiled. "If you like. Where are you from?"

Jean took a step closer to him. "Guess."

"South Central."

"Close enough. Does that scare you?"

"Well, since it doesn't look as if you're carrying a switchblade or a gun beneath that suit, I'd have to say no."

"I might have one in my bag. You never know."

He gestured to his jammed truck. "If you are going to rob me, these are all the worldly possessions I have. Take what you want, I don't care."

Jean smiled. "I'm not as dangerous as I look. Are you moving out or is that a stupid question?"

He nodded. "Yeah, it's finally time to leave the nest. I found a studio apartment up on Baker. It's on the third floor. There's a pool, but the place is kind of small. But then I don't have a lot of stuff."

"Did you move that chest of drawers by yourself?"

"Yeah."

"I'm not impressed. That's a good way to wreck your back. Isn't any of your family home to help you?"

"There's just my mom and dad, and I want to move while they're out." He shook his head thoughtfully. "My mother isn't exactly crazy about me leaving."

"Is it because you're their only child?"

He hesitated. "Yeah. There are just the three of us."

Jean offered her hand. "My name's Jean Rodrigues. What's yours?"

"James Cooper." He shook her hand. "Pleased to meet you."

It was weird to touch him. It was like touching a mirror, while an old friend stood behind her. "I bet people call you Jimmy," she said.

Her remark made him stiffen. "Not usually. Most people just call me Jim."

"Then that's what I'll call you." She nodded to the truck. "It looks like you're about ready to take this load over. I'll give you a hand if you like."

Her offer took him aback. But then he smiled. "That's nice of you. But you're dressed for the beach. You should just go and enjoy yourself."

"I have an ulterior motive in wanting to help you, Jim. I took the bus over here and it'll take me two hours to get home. If I help you move your stuff, then I was thinking maybe you could give me a ride home." She added, "You're going to need some help if your place is on the third floor."

He raised his eyebrows at her offer. She could see he was shy, a sweet guy. By the faint lines around his eyes, she could also see that he had suffered in his life. It had to do with his sister, she knew. Yet she didn't feel this was the time to ask about her.

"Can you work in a bathing suit?" he asked finally.

"Are you afraid my breasts might pop out?"

He blushed. "I wasn't worried about that exactly."

"I have clothes in my bag here, along with my forty-four Magnum." She paused. "I would like to help you."

He watched her. "Why, Jean?"

She smiled. "Because I'm grateful to you. You showed me where the ocean is."

CHAPTER VIII

I LIVED IN THE REALITY of my own creation. I had put on my memory cap, however, and didn't know that I was both my own God and devil. I was Shari Cooper and I was alive on planet Earth and back in high school. It was my sophomore year and at the moment nothing was more important than Peter Nichols asking me to the prom. I could see him approaching in the crowded hallway. My heart pounded like a piston in my chest when he smiled at me. "Shari," he said. "How are you doing?" My hands were filled with school books and I worried they would be ruined with the sweat pouring off my palms. Peter looked so good then, his curly blond hair hanging in his blue eyes. Standing so cool in the hustle and bustle of the break between first and second period. Like he had just pitched nine innings of no-hit ball in the World Series and was about to be handed the MVP award. "Great," I said. "How are you?"

"Cool. Going to the prom tomorrow night?"

"Maybe."

"Why maybe?"

I shrugged like it was no big deal. "Haven't got a date yet."

"Do you want to go with me?" he asked.

I managed to hold on to my books. "Sure."

"What time should I pick you up?"

"How about six?"

"Six is good." He patted me on the back and stepped past me. "See you then."

Wow, I thought. Peter Jacobs. What a guy. Shari and Peter. What a couple.

Then it was Friday night, just like that, and I was upstairs finishing my hair and the doorbell rang. The noise startled me; my brush handle broke off in my hand, the bristles in my hair. But I just laughed; I was high as a kite. I ran down the stairs to find my mother and father opening the door for Peter. My father pumped his hand and my mother gave him a quick hug. They liked Peter, of course. He was a winner. He was my fastball. I was hoping for some fast times tonight as I hurried toward him. His tux was the color of sand on an ocean floor. He smiled at me and handed me a corsage as large and as white as the moon.

"You look great, Shari," he said.

"Thank you." I accepted the corsage. "You don't look so bad yourself."

My parents stood nearby and beamed happily.

We drove to the prom in a silver limo that Peter had rented. The dinner and dance were in the same expensive hotel. There was steak and lobster, music and candles. We danced long and slow and Peter put his arms around me and told me how much he cared for me. I whispered the same. A vote was taken on fancy folded cards and not long after Peter and I were crowned "Coolest Couple." The band played us a special song—"Stairway to Heaven." I felt as if I had died and gone to heaven. And the night was still young. Peter kissed my ear and told me he had rented a room upstairs. Did I want to see it? Sure, I said. If that's what he wanted. He nodded and took my hand and we strode toward the elevator, while all my girlfriends watched in envy.

The suite was plush. There were flowers, a bottle of champagne on ice, soft music on the stereo. We drank a toast to ourselves. Then Peter kissed me and led me into the bedroom. The light was down low. He began to undress me.

"Do you want to make love?" he asked softly.

"Yes. Yes. Do you?"

"Yes," he said. "Help me get out of these clothes."

"I love you, Peter," I said as I unbuttoned his shirt.

"I love you, Shari."

I opened his shirt and rubbed my palm over his hard muscles.

A metallic-colored monster burst out of the center of his chest.

"Eehhh!" I screamed and leapt back. In horror, I watched as Peter toppled to the floor, his blood and guts splattering the carpet. The monster climbed out of his ruined cavity and stood upright. Its head was enormous. As it peered at me, its mouth opened and a band of razor-sharp teeth protruded and snapped at the air. In the space of seconds it grew to eight feet tall. Too numb to shout for help, I backed into the corner and tried to be invisible. But the monster was hungry and wanted prime California girl flesh. Slowly it moved toward me, acid slime dripping from its mouth and burning the carpet. It would use the acid to digest me, I knew. I had maybe three seconds left alive. At last I found my throat and let out a bloodcurdling scream.

The monster stopped and peered at me curiously. It spoke in Peter's voice.

"Did I scare you?" he asked.

I was about to faint. "What?" I gasped.

"It's me, Peter," the alien said.

I frowned. "Is that a costume?" I pointed to his dead body. "What the hell is going on here?"

"We're at the prom," he said. "This is supposed to be the night of our lives."

I was having trouble taking it all in. "But are you inside that monster, Peter? It looks so real."

"Oh, it's real enough." It turned its huge head back toward Peter's body. "You want to see it eat what's left of me?"

"No!" I cried. "Get out of that suit now. You're making me

sick to my stomach." I was suddenly angry. "I didn't like being scared like that. You almost gave me a heart attack."

"I couldn't have done that to you."

"No, I'm serious. I almost had a heart attack."

The monster sat down on the floor. "You can't have a heart attack, Shari. Don't you remember? You're dead."

It all came back to me in an instant. Then I was really pissed. I strode over and whacked the monster on the head. "We both agreed to block our memories. We were supposed to go to the prom like it was real. Since when have you known this was all make-believe?"

"Since it started."

"That's not fair! Here I'm swooning under your attention and you're sitting in your fat head and chuckling at me. That's it, that's the last romantic fantasy I'm acting out with you. I'm going to find some other ghost. Maybe an Englishman from the last century. Those guys were supposed to have manners. I'm really angry at you, Peter."

The alien shrugged. "Sorry. I didn't mean to hold on to my memory. It just happened. Then as the night dragged on I started to get bored. I just wanted to liven things up."

"Oh, thank you! I feel much better now! You get to go to the prom with me and screw me afterward and you're bored. Thanks a lot Mr. MVP."

"We didn't exactly screw afterward."

"We were about to. Why did you choose that moment to

have an alien burst out of your chest? Do you know what that does for my self-esteem?"

"You're not supposed to have self-esteem problems."

"Why not?"

"You don't have a body for one thing."

"So? I'm still a person. I'm still walking around in the image of the body I had on Earth."

"Why?"

I stopped. "Why what?"

"Why don't you switch to another body?"

"What's wrong with this one? Is that why you got bored tonight? I wasn't cute enough for you? God, I'm happy I didn't date you when I was alive. I would have ended up killing myself. And would you get out of that stupid alien form? You really are making me sick. Not that the sight of your old self probably won't do the same thing."

The monster vanished, as did Peter's dead body. He stood before me just as I had met him at my funeral. "I just wanted to experiment is all," he said. "You don't have to get all bent out of shape."

I sighed. "I suppose not. It's just that I never got to go to the prom with you. I dreamed about it so much and this seemed like a good chance to have a dream come true. You can understand that, can't you?"

Peter put an arm around me, and in that moment it felt pretty real to me, and wonderful, his touch, like the touch of my oldest and best friend. I was still having trouble with all this consciousness business but I supposed the Rishi would explain it to me more if I asked. Once again I was glad he had promised not to observe my fantasy life. He was so wise—I didn't want to act the fool in front of him.

"We can do it again, Shari," Peter said. "We can start from when I asked you out. This time, I promise, I'll have my memory blocked. We can even have sex if you want."

I looked at him. "If *I* want? Don't you want?"

He shrugged. "Sure."

"What does that mean? Has being dead affected you more than you've let on?"

He took a step back. "Are you asking me if I'm impotent?"

"It's nothing to be ashamed of if you are. We can talk about it."

Peter was bored. "Shari, think for a second. How can I be impotent when I can sprout a dozen tentacles and talons in two seconds and eat you alive if I want to?"

I paused. "I see your point. Never mind."

"Do you want to start the date over?"

I paced the hotel room. "No. I want to do something more meaningful Let's go exploring. The Rishi said we could go anywhere we wanted in the universe just by wishing it. I've always wanted to see the solar system. Interested?"

Peter smiled. Such a lovely boy and smile. "Always," he said.

~ ~ ~

We hung suspended above planet Earth, seeing it as astronauts, and more. For our eyes were sensitive to colors and feelings ordinary humans failed to perceive. I saw that the Earth had both a physical and spiritual dimension. Much of the Middle East, for example, was clean desert covered with dark astral clouds. Intuitively I understood the darkness was from the constant strife there, and that the area could not go on the way it had been and survive. While other parts of the Earth shone with soft white radiance. The Himalayas in India, in particular, were beautiful to behold, and the West Coast of America also had some points of brilliance, as did a few other spots on the globe. But it saddened me to see that the lights were few compared to the darkness.

"Too bad *Time* magazine never had a picture of the Earth like this on their front cover," I said to Peter, who floated beside me.

"It is strange to see that hate is something you *can* see," he agreed. He pointed to the Middle East. "I do hope they get their act together there. It looks ready to explode."

"I feel that way, too. It's almost as if it would take an explosion to break the tension there."

"Or a huge wave of light," Peter said.

I nodded thoughtfully. "That would be preferable."

"Well, there's nothing we can do about it right now. Where would you like to go next?"

I turned around, seeing an old friend behind me. "Let's go to the Moon!"

There was no obvious sensation of speed as we soared toward Earth's natural satellite: no wind in our hair, no roar of a rocket engine. Yet the flight was exhilarating. Having the Moon rush steadily toward me, I never felt so free, so possessed by the certainty that all this was indeed my creation, as much as everybody else's, a playground made for all of us by God to learn in and enjoy. With a simple thought, I slowed as we neared the silver globe. But Peter was having too much fun and rammed headfirst into the Moon. We danced about on a crater-marked field, and then were off again, heading for the fourth planet from the sun, the red planet. Mysterious Mars.

Here I discovered both wonder and fear. On a purely physical level Mars appeared uninhabited, but studying it with the spiritual eye I was learning to use, I was treated to two interlocking visions. On what I can only describe as a low vibration, I saw a race of demonic reptilian beings. A cruel civilization that fought and warred with itself and every other living being in its dimension. Here there was no light, no love, and as a result, only pain. I could only tune into it for a few seconds before being forced to shut it out.

"Do you see it?" I asked Peter.

He nodded gravely. "It's like hell. Yet it's there with the other as well. How can that be? Two races on one world and our scientists on Earth can see neither."

"I think there's a lot that science has yet to learn." I focused on the other race. I say focused only in a manner of speaking. Actually, I found I could perceive more by "letting go" inside. Several octaves above the reptilians were enchanted cities of beings who looked similar to people on Earth. Immediately I was reminded of the haunting civilization the author Ray Bradbury had described in his book *The Martian Chronicles*. For these were a beautiful people with long shiny gowns, wine-colored faces, and sleek bodies. Canals filled with luminous dark liquids crisscrossed their globe and they floated from town to town along these watery highways on delicate boats that could have been made of glass. Music filled their towns, sad and serious, yet uplifting and beautiful as well, echoing softly over the stark red deserts as well as into deep space. If these people—I preferred to think of them as the real Martians—were aware of the hellish dimension around them, they gave no sign of it. Peter seemed to read my mind.

"I wonder if writers on Earth somehow tuned into these two races and wrote about them," he said. "Mars is often described in literature as both evil and magical."

"It's possible," I replied, thinking that when I returned to Earth as a Wanderer I wanted to write about Mars, preferably about the beautiful race.

We took off for Venus next, and even approaching the second planet from the Sun, we were thrilled by the light and joy that emanated from that white globe. We had to stop far off in space to observe it, the vibrations were so high our ghost bodies couldn't stand it. Through the radiance I glimpsed—and it was only a glimpse—a race of beings much farther along the path of evolution than either humanity or the lovely Martians. It was as if Venus were inhabited by angels, and I understood why on Earth it was usually referred to as the planet of love.

"I don't think we can get any closer," I said.

"We're probably too gross for them," Peter agreed. "I wonder why they are so much ahead of us?"

"I don't know if it's so much a thing of being ahead or behind," I said, once more feeling for the truth inside, something I had begun to do out of habit since talking to the Rishi. I wondered if he had rekindled the ability in me, and if it would follow me back to Earth as a Wanderer. "I think they started before us. They are as we will be in the future."

Peter laughed. "In ten millions years?"

"Maybe it won't take so long," I said, once more feeling I had spoken the truth. The Rishi mentioned a transitional time on Earth, in the next few decades. I wondered if we might not join our cousins on Venus sooner, ghosts included.

Without consciously deciding on our next destination, we began to drift away from Venus and the Sun. Soon we were out among the globular clusters and nebula. Never in my wildest imagination as a mortal had I imagined such colors, such beauty and vastness of scale. It was as if all my life I had lived in a great palace, but kept my head in the closet. On Earth all I had cared about was who was looking at me and talking about me, while I lived in a universe of mystery and adventure. I made another vow to myself, to study astronomy when I returned as a Wanderer. I did not merely float through the star fields, I merged with them.

"We're all stars," I told Peter.

"Yes. I was thinking how when my father died when I was ten years old I used to search for him in the sky."

A wave of sorrow swept over me, but it was sweet as well, bittersweet like sour candy. "When you died I looked for you in the sky." I reached out, across the light-years, and took his hand. My love for him then was like the light of the stars that shone all around us, and I knew it would burn for ages. "And now I have found you."

He squeezed my hand. He didn't have to say anything.

We floated for ages, seeing more wonders than any starship log could ever record. Eventually we found ourselves at the center of the galaxy. Here the stars were older, as were the myriad races, and the peace and bliss they radiated were like that from a million Venuses combined. Inside, I understood that these people had learned all that this universe had to offer, and that they were merely waiting for the "rest of us" to catch up so that they could go on, where, I didn't know, another dimension perhaps, another creation surely, where God was as real as the sky, and as easy to touch as water in the sea. In the center of this floated what I believe our astronomers would call a galactic black hole. The light that streamed from both the stars and the worlds swirled around the object in a cosmic whirlpool, disappearing down a shaft that seemed to have no bottom. Fascinated, I moved toward it but Peter stopped me.

"We don't know where it goes," he said, and for the first time since he had told me about the Shadow in the days after my death, there was fear in his voice.

"Nothing can harm us," I said. "I want to go inside."

"If you go inside, you might not get out."

I studied him. Throughout our starry journey he had been as enthralled as I was. But now I sensed not only his fear but the reason for it; something had happened to him while we were still on Earth. Yet I couldn't pinpoint the cause, and what it had to do with the portal to infinity that yawned before us. The black hole drew me like a magnet, and I realized we had not stumbled upon it by chance. I had to go in it before I could return to Earth and accomplish my mission.

"I am going," I said. "You can follow me if you wish."

He hesitated. "I'll wait for you, Shari. Take care."

"I am taken care of," I said.

I moved toward the portal.

As stars vanished behind me, so did the *I* that was Shari Cooper.

Words fail me here. How to describe the knowledge of anything without the presence of a knower? In the interior of the black hole the knowledge and the knower were one. I ceased to be aware of things. I was awareness itself.

Still, here, outside of all places, I sensed my true place and finally understood the Rishi's words.

"Our relationship is a beautiful thing. We are, ultimately, the same person, the same being. But if that is too abstract a concept for you, then think of a huge oversoul made up of many souls. Throughout many lives on many worlds, these different souls learn and grow . . ."

I was not singular. Many people were I, and yet we were one as well. All that they had experienced, I had experienced. The different lives the Rishi had spoken of, I had lived them all. I was the Master in Egypt instructing the young student outside in the pyramid. The student was also me. I was enlightened and ignorant at the same time, and I saw it was not possible to have one without the other. No light without darkness. No day without night. No compassion without suffering. No good without evil. Everything worked together, ultimately—a weave of different-colored threads forming an unfathomably rich tapestry. How foolish we were to try to explain the mystery of life, I thought. The mystery could be lived but never explained. Any more than the mind of God could be explained. I felt so close to God right then I imagined myself a perfect fool. And I was happy.

I sensed something else as well. Peter was part of me, as much as the Rishi. It was right that he should be with me enjoying this glimpse of our higher selves. But he was not with me because he was still supposed to be on Earth. He had committed suicide, I remembered that now, and I could see the effect that act had set in motion throughout our oversoul, like a ripple set out across a mountain lake that was finally settling down to freeze for the winter. He had feared to follow me because his fear still followed him. Even this far into eternity. It was this realization that jerked me back into normal space time. Normal as far as ghosts were concerned. I materialized outside the black hole beside Peter.

"What happened?" he asked.

"How long have I been gone?"

"Just an instant."

"It felt like ages." Looking at him I remembered his comment about how the situation on Earth was no longer our concern. I had not discussed what the Rishi told me about my going back as a Wanderer. Now I realized it was because his destiny was separate from mine. I could have fun with him for now, but the fun would have to end.

"What's the matter?" he asked.

"Nothing."

"What happened to you in there?" There was an edge to his voice.

"It's difficult to explain." I reached over and took his hand again. "We have to go back. I have to speak to the Rishi."

"Why?"

Would I miss him on Earth? I asked myself. I missed him now and I hadn't even left him. And he was a part of me. It was such a paradox. How could I succeed as a Wanderer without the love of Peter beside me?

"Because I need his help," I said.

CHAPTER IX

JEAN RODRIGUES drove with Carol Dazmin toward the cemetery where Debra Zimmerer was buried. It was late August; over two months had elapsed since Jean's fall off Lenny Mandez's balcony. The summer had been warm even by Los Angeles standards. Jean had spent the weeks working at her Subway Sandwich job as well as doing volunteer work at the hospital. She had also tried to raise her basic skills in math and science to enter junior college. She was to be tested the next week to see if she could avoid being placed in idiot classes. While she was in high school she had never considered going to college, but now it seemed inevitable that she should go. She was presently trying to talk Carol into joining her.

"I'm not saying a college degree guarantees happiness," Jean said. "But not having one guarantees that you'll be working grunge jobs the rest of your life."

"I don't know," Carol said. "I could become a hairdresser. They make pretty *mucha lana*."

"You can't spend the rest of your life cutting hair. You'd go mad from boredom."

"But how can I go to college? I'm too stupid. I was hardly able to graduate from high school."

"You're not stupid. You're just lazy. You need to focus. If you could be anything you wanted, what would you choose?"

Carol thought a moment as she steered them down the freeway off-ramp. Debra had been buried across the town from them, at Rose Hills in uptown Whittier. "I'd like to be a rock 'n' roll star."

"You can't go to college to study to be a rock 'n' roll star. Pick something else."

"But that's what I want to do."

"But you can't sing. You can't play an instrument. You can't even dance."

"That's what I'm saying. That's why I should be a hairdresser."

Jean sighed. "You don't have just two choices in life. You have a million. Why don't you study to be a nurse? I think you'd make a great one."

"Would I have to give people shots? Sporty once asked me to shoot him up with heroin and I couldn't do it. I told him to find his own goddamn vein."

"Giving someone a shot that's good for him is a lot different from shooting someone up with heroin. Which reminds me. I heard through the grapevine that Darlene was looking to buy a piece."

Carol nodded. "I heard she's shopping."

"If you heard, then everybody's heard. Surely she can't be planning to go after Juan after all this time."

"I don't know. The timing makes sense to me."

"What do you mean?" Jean asked, although she knew the answer.

Carol shrugged. "Lenny just got out of rehab. He's in a chair. He's mobile. Maybe she's buying the piece for him. Maybe he still wants Juan." Carol added gently, "Maybe he figures he doesn't have much to lose trying for him."

"Damn you! You have to give yourself time. If you can't think of a reason to live, then you have to find one. Think, Lenny, of everything and everyone in the world. Think of something you want to do. Hold on to that, at least until you get out of here."

Jean had not seen Lenny since they had transferred him from the hospital to the rehab clinic in the valley. He had not wanted to see her, which killed her. But she heard from friends that he was looking a lot better, and that gave her some comfort. It was her hope that now that he could get around, he'd call her. She waited for that call.

"He has everything to lose," Jean whispered.

Carol glanced over, concerned. "You're not going to want to hear this, but I'm going to say it anyway. You should start dating other guys."

"You sound like my *mamá*."

"You should listen to your mother. You love the guy, sure, I love him, too. But his body's wrecked. His life's wrecked. You can't fix it pining away for him."

"His life is not wrecked! He can do everything any other guy can do except walk. That's it. Who needs to walk nowadays? We have cars."

"Can he have sex?"

"I don't know if he can have sex. Many crippled people can. Many crippled people can't. It just depends. And who cares? Despite what all these stupid magazines say, sex isn't everything." Jean was suddenly close to crying. "I can't walk away from him. He needs me. And I need him. You're my best friend. Can't you understand that?"

Carol spoke carefully. "But he doesn't even call you, Jean."

Jean nodded. "He will. When he's feeling better, he'll call. I know it."

Carol stopped at a light and stared at her. "You're still so different from when we were growing up. Before your fall, you would have been out with another guy while Lenny was still in surgery."

Jean forced a smile. "I wasn't that bad."

"You were no saint." Carol sighed. "I'm sorry I said what I did. If you want to go on loving Lenny, more power to you. Look at me, I can't even make up my mind whether I want to sleep with guys or girls."

"Are you still seeing Scarface?"

"No. But I go out with his sister every now and then." She nodded at the manila envelope Jean carried. "Is that your story for Debra?"

"Yes. It was the first story I ever thought up. I told her the beginning, but I only figured out how it should end last week. I hope she likes it." Jean laughed at her own foolishness, and also got a little teary. "I know she's not there in that hole in the ground where they put her body. But I want to read it to her at her grave because I think maybe she'll know I'm there somehow. Does that make sense?"

"It does to me." Carol paused. "Maybe I should become a mortician."

"Just keep driving."

"Can I read the story after you've read it to Debra?"

"*Seguro.*"

"Are you going to try to get it published?"

"I hadn't really thought about that. But the main character is a successful author. I wonder if I subconsciously patterned her after myself." Jean added, wiping at her eyes, "I see myself being like her some day."

"Have you been working on other stories?"

"Yes. Late at night. I write in a spiral notebook with a Flair pen."

Carol cast her another look. "You never did that before your fall."

Jean nodded thoughtfully. "I know."

She never got headaches before her fall, either. They had become less frequent, but had never left completely. Sometimes she wondered if she had hurt herself worse than the doctors knew. She tried not to think about it.

Rose Hills was lovely. Many acres of well-tended lawns weaving in and around the Whittier Hills. Jean had attended Debra's funeral and still kept in loose contact with her father. Jean directed Carol toward a shaded meadow. Carol offered to stay in the car without being asked, and for that Jean was grateful. Jean had brought Debra a handful of flowers as well as her story. Jean laid the daisies beside the simple metal marker that was all that was left to say Debra had come and gone. Yet Jean felt her friend close as she lifted up the handful of pages to read aloud.

"Debra, I've reworked this three times and I don't know if I can make it any better," she said. "It's either completely brilliant or totally stupid. But it's my first story and I'm proud of it. If I ever do get it published, I'll be sure to dedicate it to you. Please forgive the crude spots ahead of time. What can I say? I have a dirty mind." She cleared her throat. "The story, as you might remember, is entitled, 'Where Do You Get Your Ideas?' If you get bored fly back to heaven. I won't hold it against you."

Debra Zimmerer was working on her latest novel when the creature came out of her bedroom closet. She almost fell off her chair when she saw the thing. She rubbed her eyes, hoping he'd go away, but he didn't. He was ugly, short, and dark as a dwarf from a deep cave, scaly and smelly as a troll from beneath an ancient bridge. Clearly, he was not human. As he walked toward her desk she couldn't help but notice his big yellow teeth and wide green eyes. He didn't smell especially pleasant, either. She had no idea what he'd been doing in her closet.

"Hi, Debbie," he said. "What's happening?"

Debra took an immediate dislike to him. She let no one call her Debbie. She was either Debra or Melissa Monroe, the pen name she wrote under, or else simply Ms. M & M. She had a few names because she was one of America's bestselling authors, and she felt it only fitting that someone as popular as she should be able to slip in and out of several identities. Just before the troll had come out of her closet, she had been typing hard on her new novel, *The Color of Pain*. She had a tight deadline, and as always was late. Indeed, she had been up most of the previous night working on the last chapters and was exhausted. She wondered if her fatigue had something to do with her seeing the troll. Her novel was in the horror genre, but otherwise it had nothing to do with the creature standing beside her desk.

"Who the hell are you?" she asked.

He smiled, and as he did so gray-colored slobber leaked out the sides of his wide toothy mouth. His nose was thick, the nostrils pointing almost straight out, choked with white hairs.

He wore a baggy pair of black shorts, snakeskin slippers, no shirt. The muscles on his hairy green chest were knotted and hard. Even though he was only three feet tall, he looked strong, perhaps stronger than she was, she didn't know.

"My name's Sam," he said. "I'm your muse."

Debra reached over and turned off her computer screen. "Come again?"

"I'm your muse. You know, the one who gives you your ideas. You get asked that question all the time—where do you get your ideas? Well, now you know. You're looking at him."

Debra shook her head. "That's ridiculous. Muses are supposed to be beautiful angels. You look like something the dog dug up."

He lost his smile. "Careful, Debbie. I don't like cracks about my looks. And if you think you have an angel for a muse, then you better think again. Look at the kind of stories you write. They're filled with ghouls and vampires and psychos. Somebody's always getting murdered in them. What do you think— an angel would give you those stories? Get a clue, sister. You want to write horror—you get a muse like me. It's that simple."

Debra frowned. "What is your name?"

"Sam. Sam O'Connor."

"Are you Irish?" He had a trace of the accent.

"On my mother's side. But I'm no leprechaun, if that's what you're thinking."

"What were you doing in my closet?"

"That's where I live. I have to stay close or you wouldn't be able to write nothing."

"You used a double negative. What you mean to say is, I wouldn't be able to write anything. That's pretty basic grammar. You should know that if you're really my muse."

Sam waved his hand. "I don't care about all that crap. Grammar is for editors and pansies. I'm the one who gives the blood and guts to your stories. If it wasn't for me, you would be writing about teen problems and teacher-student conflicts. You wouldn't be selling anything and you'd be living in a dump." He reached out to turn her monitor back on. "You sure as hell wouldn't be writing a book as clever as *The Color of Pain*. Let me see that last chapter. I think I can tell you how it should end."

She slapped his hand away. "Don't you dare look at my work. I don't let anyone see it till it's done."

Sam stared at his hand as if she had stabbed a knife in rather than knocked it aside. His face darkened; his teeth seemed to lengthen; the pupils of his eyes narrowed to hard green slits. He took a step back and glared up at her.

"Let's get one thing straight from the start," he said. "It's not *your* work, it's *our* work. And if you want our work to continue, you're going to have to learn to play by a few new rules. Understand, Debbie?"

"Don't call me that. No one calls me that."

"Liar. When you were in school all your friends called you that. But now that you think you're such a big shot, you go by Debra or that other stupid name you put on our books. But you're no big shot to me. You're nothing without me."

Debra gave a smug chuckle. "You keep saying that, but this house and everything in it belongs to me. I bought it with the money I made selling thirty million books. How many books have you sold? None, I bet. You look like a loser to me, Sam O'Connor. You look like a—something despicable."

Sam smiled grimly. "You were about to call me a colorful simile, but you couldn't think of one, could you? You can't think of anything clever without me. Go ahead, try, I dare you. I look like a what?"

Debra thought for a moment, but nothing special came to her. "You look like one ugly bastard," she said finally.

He laughed. "That's it? That's the best you can come up with? How many books are you going to sell describing your villains as 'one ugly bastard'? And what are you going to say about your heroes? Oh, they were so handsome? So pretty? You're going to be searching your thesaurus soon, Debbie, if you don't cooperate. And you'll find it can't help you with your plot." Again, he reached for her monitor button. "Let me see how you're wrecking my story."

She didn't stop him as he turned on the screen, but said, "How can you say it's your story when I thought it up, in my own head?"

Sam studied her last page. "All us muses are sort of tele-pathic. The story may have ended in your head, but only because I put it there in the first place." He grunted at the screen. "You can't kill Alisa here. You need her for the sequel."

"What sequel? There's no sequel to this book. Alisa's going to die and that's the end of it. Finished."

"You see what I mean? You don't even know that this first book is the beginning of a trilogy. The second and third books are going to be better than the first. You can't kill the girl. If you do you'll be out a million dollars in royalties."

Debra felt exasperated. Of course, when she thought about it, she remembered she had felt that way *before* Sam appeared. "How come I didn't know that?" she asked.

"Because I didn't tell you," Sam said. "I waited to tell you until after I came out of the closet. I knew it would make you more open to my proposition."

"What proposition is that?"

Sam's smile returned. He glanced around her well-furnished spacious bedroom, then out the window at the forest and the ocean. "You got it pretty good here, girl. You live in a mansion. You drive a hot car. You have a maid to clean up your messes and a secretary to take care of your bills and correspondence. You don't have to do anything except write."

"But writing's hard work. I deserve my success."

Sam snorted. "Writing's hard work when your muse goes on vacation. But how hard do you really work? You can sit down and knock out a novel in a month. That's because you got me working for you in the closet. I do all the heavy thinking. You're just a glorified typist. Sometimes I'm up till two or three in the morning trying to figure out a plot line, and then you get to wake up fresh in the morning and there it is all ready for you. I'm sick of this arrangement. I'm tired of the closet. I want to enjoy more of the fruits of my creativity. From now on, Debbie, you're going to give me a piece of the action."

Debra sat back and crossed her arms over her chest. "How big a piece?"

"For starters, fifty percent of everything you make."

Debra laughed. "Gimme a break. I make millions a year. You think I'm just going to hand over half of that to you? You get a clue, brother."

Sam lost his smile. "Fine. You want to play hard ball, let's see how hard your head is." He pointed to the screen. "Finish this book right now. Write the last page."

"I can't write with a slimy troll like you standing beside me."

Sam put his scaly hand on her knee. He pinched her leg, ever so slightly, and chewed on his tongue as if wishing it were one of her fingers. "I told you, no cracks about my appearance. If you spent as much time as I have in a closet, you wouldn't look any better. But as a favor to you, and to prove my point, I am willing to wait in the other room while you write the last page. You come get me when you're done. Or more likely, you come get me when you realize you have nothing in your brain to write about." He released his grip and patted her knee gently. He even smiled again, although his eyes remained cold. "You take as long as you want, Debbie."

Debra wiped the spot where he had touched her. "The name's Debra."

Sam walked toward the door, calling over his shoulder. "The *names* will be Sam O'Connor and Melissa Monroe. From now on, that's what'll appear on your books, in that order. That's another of my conditions."

Debra wanted to spit at him. "Never."

Sam laughed as he left. "Never say never."

He was gone two seconds when Debra turned back to her word processor and began to type furiously. His challenge was a piece of cake, she thought. What was one more page out of three hundred? She just had to have her heroine—well, all right, maybe she shouldn't kill her. Alisa was a great character and there were at least another two books in her. Debra could see that now. Sam was right. But she could finish with Alisa for now without his advice. She just had to have the girl—what? How could she save her? She had it all set up to kill her. Maybe she could—Maybe if she just—No, that wouldn't work. That would be stupid, and if she had a stupid ending, that's all people would remember. Three hundred pages of brilliant prose, and people would throw it against the wall and tell their friends not to buy it if the last page was flubbed. She always prided herself on her fantastic last pages. OK, she thought, stay cool and do what you do best. You know you're better than the rest, Ms. M & M, Ms. *New York Times* Bestselling Author. *Just write the goddamn page!*

Two hours later Debra went out to see Sam. He was sitting in her favorite chair with his ugly feet up on the coffee table eating the turkey sandwich she had planned to have for lunch. He had the TV turned to the sci-fi channel, some old black-and-white monster flick. He laughed uproariously as the alien monster ate a cute, well-proportioned brunette who bore a vague resemblance to her. He barely looked up as she entered.

"All right," she said bitterly. "How does the stupid book end?"

He glanced over and took another big bite out of her sandwich. "It ends in a cliff hanger," he said. "The reader doesn't know whether Alisa makes it or not."

"That's it? That's no ending."

"You're wrong. It's the perfect ending. But how you do it is important. I'll fix it up after my show." He paused and nodded to the nearby couch. "I want to go over a few more of my conditions. Just so we understand each other."

Feeling miserable, she sat down. He was right about the ending, she realized. He must have been helping her with her books since the days of *Slumber Weekend*, the first book she ever sold. Before then she had written plots like a—damn, she couldn't describe to herself how poorly she had plotted. Hell, and he knew it, too—he was snickering at her again.

"Besides wanting half your income and my name on every book," he began, "my picture is to appear on the back flap beside yours. We'll hire a professional photographer who can touch up my rough edges, give me a yuppie look. Also, we're firing your agent. He gets ten percent and he does nothing. From now on I'll negotiate all our contracts. I'll get us bigger advances, higher royalties. And I want to take over your fan mail. There are a lot of cute babes who write you. I want to get to know them, and let them get to know me. I want them to know just who turns them on in the middle of the night. And give me your car keys. I have a date tonight."

"But I just bought that car," she protested. "It's the only one I have."

Sam chuckled. "Then I guess you'll be staying home tonight. Maybe you can brush up on your grammar. It's all you're good for, Debbie." He took another bite from his sandwich and let out a loud belch. "You might as well face it—I'm the talent."

Debra had a horrible time firing her agent. He had been with her from the start. He pleaded with her to reconsider, begged her to tell him whom she had found to take his place. Finally, when she told him nothing, he threatened to sue her. She hung up. She had received a legal-looking letter from him a few days earlier but was afraid to open it. Sam told her not to worry. He said he knew a great lawyer. He seemed to know a lot of people for having spent so much time in her closet.

She had invited a photographer out to shoot Sam, but the guy had fled the moment he saw her muse, which put Sam in a bad mood. He continued to be sensitive about his appearance. She had ended up photographing him herself and had an expert rework the negatives. The expert kept asking her what the joke was. It didn't seem Sam would ever look like a yuppie.

Sam had taken over her bedroom. She now lived in one of the smaller rooms at the front of the house with no view. She had purchased another car, but Sam had put a ceiling on how much she could spend. She had ended up replacing her new Mercedes with a used Ford. Sam laughed at her every time she went out to start it.

He had *no* dates, however, even though he said he did. He went out often but returned fast, and usually in a lousy mood. He scoured her fan mail for eligible young women. She heard him flirting with them on the phone, setting up lunches and dinners. She could just imagine the women's reactions when they finally met the genius behind the books they loved. She had suggested he join a dating club, but he had told her to shut up.

They had started immediately on a new book, a horror story for teens. Debra had written Young Adult novels for several years before breaking into mainstream fiction, and still enjoyed the form. She'd wanted to take a break after completing her—*their*—adult novel, but Sam had insisted she keep writing. Yet his input from outside the closet was not as easy to take as it had been from inside. He paced ceaselessly behind her as she worked, muttering swear words and personal insults as often as he did fresh lines of dialogue.

"All right," he said when they got stuck in the middle of a particularly violent scene. "We can't pull any punches here. We've got to go for visceral impact. Write, 'Maria shot Tom directly in the belly. The blast went right through his guts and painted the wall behind him a lumpy red. Tom stared at Maria and tried to speak. A portion of his lower intestines and pieces of yesterday's lunch dripped out the side of his mouth. His breath stunk like an outhouse. Cursing Maria and her mother to eternal damnation, he slumped to the floor. A stunned silence choked the room.'" Sam paused and grunted in satisfaction. "Write that, Debbie, word for word."

"Wait a second," Debra said. "Are we forgetting something here? This is a Young Adult book. We don't have lower intestines and yesterday's lunch dripping out the side of people's mouths. Our editor won't stand for it. Neither will the teachers and librarians. We have to tone it down."

Sam was suddenly enraged. "I never tone down my words! What I have just told you is perfect. You write it that way or you stop writing altogether."

That was a typical retort from Sam. If she didn't do what he said, she could hang up her career. What he didn't seem to realize was how close she was to saying, "Fine. Take the money and the Mercedes. I can get another job. Just get out of my house and stop sleazing all over my fans." But she had books left on her contract to finish, this Young Adult novel being one of them. She feared getting stuck with half a dozen lawsuits and no income coming in. Plus she doubted there was anything else she could do, except maybe be a full-time secretary for some sexist male executive. She cautioned herself to speak carefully before responding.

"I have written dozens of Young Adult books," she said. "If what you say is true, I have written them with your help. Together we have pushed the limits of the genre. But there are certain limits it would be a mistake to go beyond. We can shoot Tom in the guts, and we can even talk about the blood that gushes out. But that's as graphic as we can get. There are even more rules when it comes to sex. None of our characters can have sex onstage."

"What do you mean onstage?" Sam growled. "None of our characters are in the school drama club. They can do it in their cars or at the park. Which reminds me. I have a great scene planned for the middle of the book. After Carol and Larry have been turned into aliens, and been killed by the police, we'll have them rise from the dead and make love in the morgue with formaldehyde dripping all over each other from their gory wounds. That will give us another half million in sales, I guarantee it."

Debra leaned over and turned off the computer. "If we write that scene we guarantee ourselves zero sales."

"No way!"

"Yes way! The publisher won't accept the book."

"Then we'll get another publisher. New York City is riddled with them! I don't know why you stay with that house you're at. Most of what they publish is written by failed actresses and politicians trying to lose weight."

"It's not that simple. The same rules will apply wherever we go."

"Rules?" Sam said indignantly. "I'm an artist. I don't have to follow rules. Do you think J.R.R. Tolkien was worried about rules when we wrote *The Lord of the Rings*?"

Debra paused. "Are you insinuating that you were Tolkien's muse?"

"Damn right I was. Where do you think he got the Ents and the Ores? I made those up, not him."

"Well, I can see you and the Ores," Debra mumbled.

Sam took a step closer. "I didn't quite catch that?"

Debra cleared her throat. "We're going to have to argue about this later. I have to meet my younger sister, Ann, for lunch."

Sam stopped and smiled. "Your sister, hey? I've seen Ann's picture in the other room. She's a babe. How about me coming to lunch with you two? You can introduce the two of us, tell her how creative I am." He grinned and winked. "In all kinds of ways."

Debra stood hastily. "You're not meeting my sister."

Sam stepped in front of her as she moved toward the door.

"Why not? You don't think I'm good enough for her? How many other guys can she meet that have my imagination?"

"None." Debra shook her head. "That's not my point."

"What is your point? You think she won't find me attractive?"

"You're not exactly her type."

"What is her type?"

"Well."

"Ah! You still think I'm ugly!"

"I didn't say that. It's just that, well, you are kind of short."

"I can wear my platform shoes. I bought some the other day."

"That would help. But it's not the main problem."

"What is the main problem? Is it my face? I can get these scales removed. I'm going to see a plastic surgeon on Thursday. I'll tell Ann I'm recovering from a fire."

"No! You won't tell Ann anything. You're not going to meet her."

Sam paused and nodded to himself. "So that's the way it is." He drew himself up on his hairy toes as he did when he was about to make a threat. "If you don't introduce me to Ann, I don't tell you how this new book ends. I'll let you work on it until the last chapter, and then when your editor's screaming for the manuscript, I'll leave you hanging."

Debra had had enough. She defiantly thrust her hands onto her hips. "Go ahead! Stop helping me! I've made enough money to live on for the rest of my life even if you take half. Go find another writer to play muse to. Get a nerdy teenage boy who looks up cheerleaders' skirts. I'm sure you'll get along fabulously."

Unfortunately, much to her surprise, Sam was not impressed by her retort to his threat. He let out a sly chuckle. "You'll live on half of what, Debbie? I copyrighted the plots of each of your books before you even wrote them. I have certified letters mailed to myself containing detailed outlines of every one of your stories. You walk out on me now, and I'll drag you into court and sue your ass off. The whole world will know that you're nothing but a scam. You'll owe me more money than you have. You'll have to sell that old Ford you're driving just to buy food."

Debra stared at him. "You're bluffing. You ruin me, you ruin yourself."

Sam grinned. "I can always make another you. But where are you going to find another me?"

Debra brushed him aside. "I'm going to lunch with my sister."

Sam let her pass. "That's fine," he called after her. "As long as you tell Ann I'll be calling her for dinner soon. At her place!"

Debra did not enjoy her afternoon meal, even though she ordered her favorite food at her favorite restaurant. She picked at her swordfish and stared out the window at the ocean. Her sister asked her what was bothering her, but she just shrugged and said she was under a lot of pressure because of a deadline. Finally lunch was over and she was able to kiss her sister good-bye and think seriously about what she was up against. Not for a moment did she consider telling Ann about Sam. It made her sick just to think of that smelly creature touching her sister.

She thought seriously but not creatively, and that was the core of her problem. Her enemy was her inspiration. She couldn't destroy him unless he helped her, which was not likely in the next fifty years. What to do? She had to go to someone else for her ideas. But who could she ask? Who would even believe her story?

Then it struck her.

She was a storyteller, still, at least in the eyes of the world, even if, apparently, she couldn't think up an opening line without her troll cackling in the background. But no one knew that yet, she reassured herself. Among other writers, she was seen as brilliant. Why couldn't she go to another writer, present her dilemma as a plot problem, and have him solve it? She knew just the man, Scott Alan. He was a local author of horror stories. He had yet to hit it big, but he had published a number of well-reviewed novels. She had considered him something of a beginner, but secretly she thought he was at least as, if not more so, creative than herself. He would probably be thrilled to help out the *New York Times* Bestselling Melissa Monroe.

She drove to Scott Alan's house after finding his address in the book.

His face shone excitedly when he answered the door. He invited her in. Wow, it was neat of her to stop by. Could he get her something to drink or eat? He'd loved her last book. How long had it stayed on the *Times* list? Four months? Amazing, he said. She was amazing.

"Thank you," Debra said as she took a seat on his couch. "I loved your last book as well."

He grinned. He was a handsome young man in his late thirties with sandy-colored hair and blue eyes and a nice round face that—damn! She couldn't think what his face was like. But it was attractive enough, she thought. Not that she wanted to have sex with him in a morgue or anything kinky like that. Where did Sam get such disgusting ideas?

"What did you like about it the most?" Scott asked.

Debra hesitated. Actually, she hadn't read his last book. "I liked how the main character changed as the novel progressed."

"Which main character was that?"

She smiled. "You know, Scott, the one who was on the most pages."

Scott was doubtful. "You mean Lucifer, the robot? I guess he did kind of change." Scott chuckled. "When he blew up."

"That's what I mean, yeah, exactly. You blew him up and his whole perspective changed." Debra paused. "Scott, I'm working on a short story for an anthology of major horror writers and I'm stuck." She batted her long brown lashes, knowing she could look pretty sexy to a struggling author. "I was wondering if you could help me get unstuck?"

He was interested. "What's the problem?"

"It's kind of unusual," she began. "My main character's a famous author and she has this troll for a muse. . . ."

It took Debra almost an hour to tell her story. She hesitated to leave out any detail for fear she might skip over the weak point in Sam's armor. Scott listened intently, as if she were telling him a real-life dilemma, which just happened to be the case. When she was done, he sat thoughtful for a moment.

"This story isn't like any of your others," he said finally.

"Tell me about it," she muttered.

"I'm not saying it's not clever. It's just that it's not as based in reality as most of your work."

"That may be why I'm having trouble resolving the main conflict. But you know what they say, if you don't take chances sometimes, you'll never know—you'll never know . . ."

"You'll never know what?"

Debra blushed. She had been about to make up a saying, but of course she couldn't think of what to say. "Never mind. Can you help me? How can my character get rid of her muse?"

"Does she still want to keep him as her muse? Or just put him back in the closet?"

Debra shook her head miserably. "At this point I think she'd be happy just to have him out of her life."

"How strong is this troll?"

"Pretty strong. Stronger than she is. Why do you ask?"

"For the obvious reason. Why can't she just buy a gun and kill him?"

"Believe me, she's thought of it"

"And?"

"She's not a killer—she's a writer, remember?" Debra added, "But if she were sure she could pull it off, and not get hurt, she might consider it."

"But the preferable ending would be to get the troll back in the closet and once more help your main character write her stories?"

"Yes."

"You mentioned that the troll said he was telepathic. Can he read the woman's mind?"

Debra had considered that point. For the most part, except when they were working together, Sam seemed unable to tune in to her thoughts. For example, the day before she had decided to cook them both vegetarian lasagna for dinner. But he had exploded when she served him the food. He needed meat, he yelled, didn't she know better?

"He's sensitive to the woman's thoughts," she said carefully. "But I don't know if he can read them, at least not all the time."

"But it would be better to distract him just before striking the decisive blow?"

"Yes. Definitely. But how is she supposed to distract a troll?"

Scott smiled. "I'm surprised it hasn't occurred to you, Debra. His weak spot is obvious. He's intelligent but insecure in his relationships with women. He worries he's unattractive. What we need your main character to do is pretend to seduce him, and then just when they're about to go to bed, she can ask him to get contraceptives from the closet. He'll be so excited he'll do anything she wants. The moment he steps inside, she can slam the door shut and lock him in."

Debra was appalled. "But she can't pretend to seduce him. Just being around him makes her nauseated."

"But she has to pretend. She has no choice."

"What makes you think he's interested in her?"

"Is she attractive?"

Debra brushed her hair with her hand. "Well, yes. She's pretty cute, I think."

"Then he'll be interested. It sounds like they have a love-hate relationship as it is."

Debra was shocked. "She can't stand to be in the same room with him. How can you say she loves him?"

Scott waved her objection away. "That's also obvious. The way they carry on together. There's got to be some attraction there, on both sides."

"No way."

"It doesn't matter. She just has to get him in the closet and lock the door. Now, if she wants to keep him as her muse, she has to give him some incentive while he's there. Perhaps she should have a phone installed in her closet. Then if he keeps helping her write, she can tell him, she'll keep slipping fresh fan letters under his door and pay for his AT&T bill."

Debra brightened. "That's interesting. He loves talking on the phone. It's practically his only pleasure in life, besides eating." She nodded. "You're pretty good."

"Thank you. You're not too bad yourself."

"Yeah." She glanced down the hall toward his bedroom, feeling a sudden chill from that direction. "Scott?"

"What?"

"Where do you get your ideas?"

He laughed. "You must get asked that question all the time. You know the answer as well as I do. I don't know. They just come to me." He paused. "What's the matter?"

She tried to hear if there was any other sound in the house. A pair of ugly feet scampering about in a closed space, for example. But there was no one about except the two of them.

"Nothing," she said softly. "I was just wondering."

At first Sam greeted her idea to go to a play with her that evening with suspicion. But when he saw she was serious, he did an about-face and got all excited, and even said a few kind words to her about her writing. It had been part of her plan to suggest he go out and buy himself a new outfit to wear on the date—so that she could have time to prepare the closet—but he beat her to the mark by bringing up the idea of new clothes.

He promised to be back by sunset and jumped in her Mercedes and was gone. She immediately got on the phone to a handy-man, telling him it was an emergency. He said he'd be right over.

Debra wanted two modifications made to the closet. Besides having a separate phone line installed, she instructed the man to add a sturdy dead bolt to the door. Once she had Sam inside, she swore to herself, she was not letting him out. The handyman worked quickly and was in and out in less than an hour.

She made a reservation for the play and dressed with care for their date. The trouble was, she didn't know what turned a troll on. She had to think back to what the naughty girls in her books wore to get a guy's attention and realized that probably with Sam, less was more. She put on a mini skirt from her high school days and let her thick brown hair hang down her back. Sam was true to his word and was back before sunset. He took one look at her, let out an obscene whistle and hurried off to one of the bathrooms with his col-lection of Nordstrom bags. She managed to keep him away from the master bedroom with the excuse that she needed to use it just this once because the lighting was better to fin-ish her makeup. He was in such a good mood he didn't argue with her.

She had said a play and not added dinner because she didn't want to be seen with him too much since she did have to live in the town. But Sam insisted they get a bite to eat before going to the theater. He took her to a French restaurant downtown. He had on a dark gray suit and a white shirt with a very chic green silk tie. She didn't know how he'd had them fit to his size. He wore oversize sunglasses to hide as much of his face as possible, and was somewhat successful with the maneuver. The maitre d' acted as if she was with a dwarf who'd just had skin grafts.

"To a long and successful partnership," Sam toasted when the wine arrived. He raised his glass and added with a wink that was visible even through his sunglasses, "To a deeply satisfying relationship. Cheers."

She smiled and raised her glass and tried not to vomit. "Cheers."

He took a sip of his wine and set his glass down and touched her right knee underneath the table. "You look lovely tonight, my dear. What is that perfume you're wearing?"

"Ecstasy."

Sam was in heaven. "My favorite. How did you know?"

"It's sensual. You're sensual." She blushed. "I just thought the two would go together."

He continued to stroke her leg, but he studied her as well. "What brought about the sudden interest, Deb—Debra?"

She shrugged. "I don't know. I guess it was spending time with you and seeing how brilliant you are. Nothing turns me on as much as intelligence." She paused, wanting to get a grip on just how much he could read her mind. "You should know that about me."

He grinned. "Opposites attract."

She nodded. "Ain't that the truth."

"*Ain't?* Isn't that poor grammar?"

She clasped his hand under the table and gave it a warm squeeze. "Tonight, for once, let's forget grammar. Let's use all the naughty words we want."

Sam licked his chops. "Jesus," he said.

Their meals came. Debra had halibut, Sam steak, a thick cut as rare as the health department allowed. Briefly she wondered how he had survived in her closet for so many years without food but assumed eating was a pleasure with him and not a necessity. She wouldn't be feeding him once she had him locked away.

The play turned out to be a nightmare. They sat in the back in the dark, and Sam couldn't keep his hands off her. Her pushing him away seemed to get him more aroused. She took in so little of the storyline that she couldn't have said what it was about. Her nerves were frayed. What if he escaped? What manner of revenge would he take? She thought of all the tortures the villains in her books had inflicted on her characters. All inspired by Sam. She could not fail, it was as simple as that.

He started to kiss her the moment they returned home. Or tried to—he was too short to do more than stick his face in her bosom and slobber on her blouse. He had brushed his teeth and gargled but his breath still stank. He dragged her toward the bedroom. With bile rising in her throat, she went with him.

He wanted her to undress in front of him with the lights on.

"Do it slowly," he said, his big yellow teeth chattering with excitement. "Not like they do it in teenage books. Like *you're* onstage."

She forced a smile. "Shouldn't we lower the lights? It's so much more romantic." She didn't want him getting too good a look at the closet when she steered him in that direction. He shook his head.

"I want to see you, Debra. See what you've got. I've waited a long time for this, you know."

She kicked off her shoes and began to unbutton her blouse. "Have you now? But *you* must know, Sam, that you can't tell what a girl's got until you've got your hands on her. And then it's so much better without all this artificial illumination." Sighing with pleasure, she removed her top and let it drop to the floor. Sam's big green eyes bugged out of his head. She crooned, "Something about the dark really turns me on."

"I'll get the lights," Sam panted. He tried turning off the lamp but his hands were shaking so badly he ended up having to yank the plug out of the wall to kill the light. The room was plunged into darkness. She could still see him, though, his phosphorescent eyes moving toward her. "Love me, baby," he whispered as his stubby arms went around her waist. He tried to press her down onto the bed. She stroked the top of his head and leaned over and spoke in his ear.

"You've got me so hot, Sam. I want to do it with you again and again. But I can't get pregnant. You understand. A baby would spoil everything we've got going here. You've got to wear something."

Sam's voice came out disappointed. "But I didn't buy anything."

She giggled mischievously. "Don't worry. I've got something in the closet, on the bottom shelf. You go get it and I'll help you put it on."

He let go of her and slapped her on her butt with pleasure. "That's my girl! Always thinking of the details. I'll get it and just pray it fits. Let me tell you, Debra, you haven't had a man until you've had your muse."

"Hurry," she whispered at him. Her eyes had adjusted to the dark somewhat, and she could see his short squat outline as he walked to the closet and poked his head inside. She took a step toward his back, but just then his glowing green eyes turned her way. She froze.

"I don't see them," he said. "Maybe I should turn the light back on."

"They're in the corner," she said quickly. "Keep looking. Please don't turn on the light. It will spoil the mood."

"Not for me." He snickered, turning back to the closet. "I'm always in the mood."

"So am I," Debra muttered. Suddenly she was sick of the charade, of having to constantly kiss his ass. She had planned to wait until she had talked him all the way into the closet before she struck, but now she couldn't wait a second longer. In two long strides she moved up behind him. He heard her approach; once more his green eyes turned in her direction as she raised her bare right foot and planted it firmly on his mid back. But even at that late a moment, he didn't realize his peril.

"Oh," he moaned with delight. "That feels good. Do it harder."

"My pleasure." She gave him one hard shove and he toppled forward into the closet. He might have hit his head on the far wall, she wasn't sure. She heard a loud bump followed by a soft thud. In a flash she grabbed hold of the door and slammed it shut, twisting the bolt counterclockwise as the handyman had instructed her. Hardly had she set the lock in place than he began to bang on the door.

"Debra!" he shouted. "Let me out!"

She laughed. "You didn't say please, Sam. If you had said please, I might have considered it. But now it's too late."

He threw his whole body against the door, but it was sturdy and didn't budge an inch. "If you don't let me out right now, it'll be the end of Melissa Monroe. There'll be no more warped teenagers. No more alien vampires. You'll be writing self-help and diet books for the rest of your life. You'll have to do talk shows to sell copies."

Debra couldn't stop laughing. "You say that now, Sam, but you're going to get pretty bored in there with nothing to do. Especially after your taste of freedom. I know you—you love your horror. Soon enough you'll be giving me stories again."

"Never!"

"Never say never."

He continued to pound on the door. "Let me out, you bitch!"

"What did you call me Sam? The *B* word? Golly, I don't know if that's allowed. I'll have to check with my editor and get back to you. We might have to cross that out."

"Debra!"

"That's my name. Be sure you don't forget it. Oh, by the way, I had a phone installed in the closet this afternoon. If you behave yourself and continue to help me on my stories, I might slip you a letter from a hot fan to call every now and then."

He stopped pounding. "Can I call long distance?" he asked.

"Only if our latest book makes the *New York Times* list."

Sam considered. "Can't I come out on weekends?"

"No way. I'll never get you back in the closet."

He sounded kind of sad. "Was all of tonight just a sham to lock me up?"

"I'm afraid so, Sam. You're just not my type."

He was curious. "Where did you get the idea to do this?"

Debra grinned in the dark. "I'll let you figure that one out."

A week later Debra stopped by Scott's house to thank him for help with *her story*. She was surprised when a short mole of a woman with a wide hat and thick sunglasses answered the door. Because the woman stood in the shadows, and it was bright and sunny outside, Debra couldn't get a good look at her. But she could have sworn the woman had *purple* hair.

"Can I help you?" the woman asked in a deep sober voice. She sounded like a cannibal might after a late-night dinner— the simile just popped into Debra's mind. Her thick red coat covered most of her squat figure. She wore black satin gloves and kept her right hand on the edge of the door.

"Yes," Debra said. "I'm here to see Scott. Is he at home?"

"Scott doesn't live here anymore." The woman started to shut the door. "Have a nice day."

Debra shot out her arm. "Wait a second. What do you mean he doesn't live here? I visited him here last week. Who are you?"

The woman stared up at her with her dark glasses. There was something wrong with her skin. It looked burnt, peeling, while at the same time it was ashen.

Debra couldn't help noticing how large her hands were, bigger than Sam's for that matter.

"A relative," the woman said.

"Where has Scott moved to? Do you have a forwarding address?"

"No."

"Do you know why he left so suddenly?"

"No."

Debra frowned. "If you see him would you tell him Melissa Monroe stopped by?"

"The writer?"

"Yes, that's me."

The woman seemed to grin. Yet the expression was hard to classify as a simple smile because there was gloating in it. As if the woman were still hungry after her late snack and wanted dessert. Her tone took on a false note of sweetness.

"I love writers," she said. "Would you like to come in, dear? Maybe for some tea? We could discuss books."

Debra swallowed and took a step back, feeling a strong sense of déjà vu. "No thank you. I have an appointment in half an hour. I really must run. But please, remember to give Scott my message."

The woman nodded. "It will be my pleasure."

"Thank you," Debra said. As she turned toward her car, just before the woman closed the front door, she thought she heard someone pounding on a wall somewhere deep in the house. She paused to listen closer, but just then the woman shut the door and she heard nothing more, not even the woman moving inside.

"Must have been my imagination," she muttered to herself.

Yet as Debra Zimmerer, *New York Times* Bestselling Author, started her car and pulled out of the driveway, she wondered if she wanted to stay in the writing business, even if Sam continued to help her. She had the feeling that being a horror author was a lot more dangerous than it was cracked up to be.

Jean laughed out loud as she finished reading her last line. "I like how Scott got put in the closet, too. It appeals to my ghoulish nature. But you know, Debra, it also makes me nervous about where I get *my* ideas." Jean paused to wipe away another tear. Her voice became softer. "But you might know that—wherever you are. If our ideas really do come from angels, then put in a good word for me with them. Have them send me down a story for a best seller. I can't make sandwiches at Subway the rest of my life." She paused and touched the marker. This date to that date, she thought. Eighteen years in between. It didn't seem right that an all-loving God could give a person so little time. She had only known Debra ten days, but she still missed her. Biting her lip, she traced Debra's name with her fingertips. "I will remember you," she whispered.

I want people to remember me.

Jean jerked back from the marker. Who had said that? The voice seemed to come out of the air. Of course, she thought, that was ridiculous. The voice had been in her mind. Just her own thoughts.

Yet the line felt as if it had been spoken by another.

The memory of that bloody stain on the condo concrete came back to her.

"I thought you knew her."

"Knew who?"

"The girl who died here."

Jean thought of James Cooper. After she had helped him move, he had taken her straight home and dropped her off. He had asked for her number, however, but he had not called hen She had been careful not to mention Lenny around him—not out of an urge to cheat on her boyfriend—more out of an innocent desire to get to know James better. Or was her desire so innocent? She did not lust after the guy. Nevertheless, she desperately wanted something from him, something she couldn't explain even to herself. Why hadn't he called her?

Because you spooked him as much as he spooked you.

Yet she had never asked him about his dead sister.

Something Cooper.

"I suppose we all want to be remembered," Jean said in a shaky voice to Debra Zimmerer's grave marker. Gathering her story together, leaving the flowers behind, she stood and walked slowly back to the car. Carol snored behind the wheel. Jean woke her and said, "Take me home,"

Yes, she thought, she wanted to go home. But first she had to find it.

~ ~ ~

Jean found James Cooper's phone number without difficulty. Information had it. But calling him proved to be more difficult. Alone in her bedroom, she dialed the number a half dozen times but quickly hung up before anyone could answer. She kept asking herself the same questions. Why had the spot where Sister Cooper died drawn her so? Why did the girl's incomplete name reverberate in her head like the echo of a lost cry off a high cliff? What was Ms. Cooper to her?

What could she be except a ghost?

Finally Jean let the number ring. He answered. She recognized his voice—she would never forget that voice.

"Hello?"

"Jim? This is Jean Rodrigues. Remember me? The girl who couldn't find the ocean?"

He hesitated. "Yes. How have you been?"

"Great. How are you?"

"Good. I finally have the place in order. You should see it. You wouldn't recognize it from the day I moved in."

"Can I see it today?" she blurted out.

He paused. "Is something wrong?"

"No. It's just, you know, I want to see you again. I had fun with you that day. I was disappointed when you didn't call." She lowered her voice, knowing she had no right to ask the question but wanting to do so anyway. "Why didn't you call?"

He took forever to answer. "The move was kind of rough for me, in a lot of ways I'd rather not go into. I didn't think I'd be very good company for anyone." He paused. "But if you want to get together that would be great."

"Would tonight be OK?"

He laughed—it sounded forced. "Sure. What time should I pick you up?"

"I'll come to your place."

"Are you sure? I don't mind driving over. I remember where you live."

"I'm sure. I think I can get my mother's car. I really do want to see your place. And that whole section of town is so much nicer than here." She added, "I feel more at home there."

CHAPTER X

JEAN WAS IN JIM'S PLACE five seconds—they had hardly said
hello—when she noticed Shari Cooper's picture. A four-by-
five color photograph in a gold-leaf frame, it stood on his
desk beside his computer. Jean had not seen it while helping
Jim move. Without asking permission, she crossed the single
large room of his studio apartment and picked it up. The
girl was attractive with layered blond hair and longish bangs.
Her face shone; her expression was intelligent. An eighteen-
year-old girl with plans for the future. Her big green eyes,
in particular, had depth. Yet, to Jean, the details of Shari
Cooper's appearance were unimportant. It was the person
behind the face that interested her. Holding the photograph, Jean's hand began to shake, and she realized that the
enchanted pool that granted the mysterious visions was not
only found in the deep woods. Sometimes a senior picture

in an unsigned yearbook pointed the way to profound mysteries.

She knew this girl!

Like she knew the reflection in her own mirror.

"Who is this?" she asked softly.

Jim came up at her back. "My sister, Shari."

Shari. Shari Cooper.

Jean nodded, swallowed. "She has such lovely green eyes."

"But they're brown, don't you think?"

"No. They're green, definitely green. What's the matter? Are you color-blind?"

"Yes."

She turned and looked at him. "I didn't know that."

He shrugged. "You hardly know me at all." Gently he took the picture from her and set it back down on the desk. The sight of it seemed to grieve him, but she did not wonder why he kept it so close. It seemed he couldn't turn away from it now. She watched him for a long moment as he stared at his dead sister.

"What happened to her?" she asked finally.

He shook himself as if from a trance. The feeling in the room was close to déjà vu, yet different. It was as if the sorrows of yesterday and the hopes of tomorrow had slipped from their respective time frames and crossed paths in this place as she had crossed his path, seemingly by accident, without reason, and also because it was meant to be. She realized then that she loved James Cooper more than she had ever loved anyone in her life. Not as an attractive young man with whom she wanted to have a relationship. But because he had been Shari Cooper's brother. He shook his head.

"It's a long story. I'd rather not talk about it."

Jean reached out and touched his arm. "I know she was murdered."

His eyes widened. "How?"

"I went to the spot where she died."

He frowned. "Did you know Shari?"

"No. I never met her."

"Then why did you go there?"

"I don't know. I went for a walk and found myself at the spot where she hit the ground. An elderly woman happened by and explained that she had been pushed from the fourth-floor balcony."

"Then you know what happened. You don't need to ask me."

"No. I don't know what happened. Why was she murdered?"

Jim turned away. "I don't know why you want me to talk about these things." He sat down on the sofa and put his hands to his head as if it hurt. He chuckled unexpectedly.

"What is it?" she asked, crossing to sit beside him.

"I was just thinking of what you said. How her eyes were green, definitely green. I would tell Shari they were only brown, and she would always say what you said back to me."

He looked at the floor. "For a second you reminded me of her."

Jean touched his knee. She couldn't stop herself from touching him. Deep in her chest, she craved for him to wrap his arms around her and tell her that everything was all right, finally, that the past was dead and buried and that they were both alive in a living universe. But she knew such a gesture on her part would disturb him. Yet she couldn't let it be, not without understanding what *it* was. The mystery of Shari Cooper's murder? No, she thought, it went much deeper than that.

"You remind me of someone as well," she said.

He looked up. "Who?"

"I don't know." She shook her head. "I am not trying to be purposely confusing. I am genuinely confused."

"About what?"

"You. And your sister. And why the stain of her blood on the ground—please forgive me—drew me like some kind of magnet." She pointed toward the picture. "Why does she have her bangs in her eyes?"

"Shari liked them that way."

"I knew that. I knew that before you said it."

"But you just asked me why she wore them that way?"

"I was being facetious. Or else I was mimicking your mother. I bet your mother didn't like the way Shari wore her bangs."

"She didn't. She always wanted her to cut them." Jim

stopped and drew back. "Why are we having this discussion? You said you never met Shari. Why should you care about how she wore her hair? Or for that matter, what else she did in her life?"

Jean fought to calm herself. "I'm sorry, Jim. I realize that by talking about these things I'm probably tormenting you. I assure you that is not my purpose. I'm not some weirdo who just happened to show up at your doorstep." She added sheepishly, "Even though I did just show up at your doorstep."

He eyed her cautiously. "Why did you come to my parents' house? Did the elderly woman you spoke to direct you there?"

"Not specifically. But she told me your last name. She had spoken to your father after Shari's death. I found the address in the phone book."

"So you *happened by* on purpose?"

"Yes."

"Why?"

"I told you, I don't know why. There's something about you and your sister that draws me. This morning I went to the grave of a friend. Her name was Debra Zimmerer. I do volunteer work in a hospital and she was a patient there. We didn't spend a long time together, but we were close, you know. Sometimes it doesn't take long to get to know someone. Anyway, I went to her grave to read her a story I wrote, and while I was there the thought 'I want people to remember me' popped into my mind. And then I thought of you and your sister and I felt I had to call you—and like I said, I really don't know why I am telling you all this." She paused to catch her breath. "I'll leave now if you want me to."

He was hardly listening. He was staring at the picture of his sister again. No, not at it but just to the right of it, at his computer. A great change had come over him. His face had become pale—he was ghostlike.

"Jimmy?" she said.

"She used to call me that," he whispered.

"Shari used to call you Jimmy?"

"Yes."

"I'd assume many people do."

"It's the way you say it. Just like her." He considered. "Besides being color-blind, I have a habit of walking in my sleep." He regarded her with something akin to awe. "Did you know that?"

"No. But that could be dangerous."

He nodded. "Shari always worried about me hurting myself while I was out for a nocturnal stroll." He continued to study Jean. Something she had said in her ramblings touched a nerve in him. She suspected she knew what it was. "You said you write stories?"

"Yes. A few. Why? Do you write?"

"No. I mean, I did write one story." He looked back at his computer. "While I was sleepwalking."

"Really? You were unconscious?"

"Yes."

"Wow. What was the story about?"

He drew in a breath. "My sister."

"That's nice that you'd write a story about her."

He shook his head. "No. I told you, I was asleep when I wrote it. And it wasn't exactly a story about her. It—it described what it was like for her when she died."

Jean sat stunned. "Are you serious?" Stupid question. Jim was near tears. He nodded weakly.

"I woke up one morning a few days after she died and found it in my computer. Apparently I had been up the whole night typing it in." His shoulders slumped. "That's the only explanation I have for its being there."

Jean felt cold then. Like a portion of the dark dirt of Mother Earth, a portion far beneath the surface that remained hidden as the years of man went by. A portion that was never supposed to be uncovered until the end of time. The cold was both terrifying and thrilling.

"Something I said reminded you of that story?" she said.

"Yes."

"She said in the story that she wanted to be remembered?"

"Yes. Those were her last words."

"But you wrote the story?"

Jim, Jimmy, wept then. He held his head in his hands as the tears trickled silently over his cheeks. "I don't know, Jean. I'm like you, I just don't know anything anymore."

Jean reached over and hugged him, and as she did so a wonderful glow radiated outward from her chest. The simple act of being able to comfort him meant so much to her. As if she had wanted to hold him in the past but had been unable to do so. She ran her fingers through his hair and pressed her face against his.

"I have to read that story," she whispered. "Please let me read it. If I don't I'll never know who I am."

He sniffed, embarrassed, his face damp. "But you're Jean Rodrigues."

She drew back, but continued to hold on to him. "Yes. But I don't know who *she* is. I feel like I've had two lives. At the beginning of the summer I also fell off a balcony. And since then I've been walking around in a dream. I have to wake up, Jimmy." She stared down at his hands, then let go of him and looked at her own. "I have to understand how I can now type stories I couldn't imagine before. I couldn't even write a one-page paper all the time I was in school."

"When did you fall off the balcony?"

"I don't know the exact date. It was a Friday night, two weeks before I was to graduate from high school."

"Shari died two weeks before she was supposed to graduate."

Jean looked over at the computer. It waited on his desktop like a modern Aladdin's lamp. She only had to rub the keyboard a little and the megabytes genie would appear and offer her any wish, except the wish for more wishes. But what could

Shari Cooper, sitting like an angel on her brother's shoulder as he labored unconsciously in the dark, have asked for in her story except for another chance to be alive?

I want people to remember me.

Sometimes memories just weren't enough.

"Let me see it," she pleaded.

Jimmy went over to the desk and sat down and booted the computer. A menu appeared on the monitor listing files. He moved his mouse around and the computer beeped. Then he stood and offered her his chair. "It's a long story," he said. "It'll take you several hours to read. I can leave you alone until you finish it."

She stood. "You don't have to leave."

He raised a hand. "I want to. I have never let anyone read it before. I think it will be hard for me, you know, to sit here while you go through it." He wiped at his face and forced a grim smile. "I might start crying again. Guys aren't supposed to cry."

Jean stepped toward him and gave him a hug. "I'm scared, Jimmy."

"What are you scared of?" he asked, holding her.

"What happened to her. Who she was. Is her story scary?"

He let go of her. "Much of it is, yes. But much of it is beautiful as well. You'll see. I think it ends happily."

Jean glanced past him at the computer. "I'm glad."

Jimmy nodded and left her. This strange girl he hardly

knew from the wrong side of town, all alone in his apartment with the most private aspect of his life. Jean wondered at his trust, but then realized he felt the same way about her that she felt about him. A love so old it must have been alive before they were born.

Jean sat down in front of the screen.

She moved the cursor. Words appeared.

Dark and disturbing and beautiful words.

> Most people would probably call me a ghost. I am, after all, dead. But I don't think of myself that way. It wasn't so long ago that I was alive, you see. I was only eighteen. I had my whole life in front of me. Now I suppose you could say I have all of eternity before me. I'm not sure exactly what that means yet. I'm told everything's going to be fine. But I have to wonder what I would have done with my life, who I might have been. That's what saddens me most about dying—that I'll never know. . . .

Jean read only a small portion of the book. She didn't have to read much. Before the party began, the birthday party that would stretch over a nightmare period of events and end days later in a dreary funeral, and finally days after that culminate in another murder attempt, she knew all the characters. All their names, their likes and dislikes, all their passions and hatreds.

All their secrets as well, and it was those especially that made it clear how it would end for Shari Cooper, and why it was that she did die so young. Jean, in fact, knew everything about the story. Because . . .

"I wrote it," she whispered aloud.

She remembered.

I remembered.

I, Shari Ann Cooper.

CHAPTER XI

I FOUND THE Rishi sitting cross-legged in meditation by the stream where I had left him. Peter was not with me; I told him I had to have a private talk with the Rishi, which hurt Peter's feelings a little. Peter had become worried on the flight back from the center of the galaxy. I wondered if he could sense my insight into what a problem his suicide was going to be. Quietly I sat down on my knees in front of the Rishi. He was still wearing his blue silk robe and looked as wise and wonderful as ever. After a minute or two he opened his eyes.

"More questions, Shari?" he asked softly.

"Yes. Is this a good time? I don't want to disturb you."

"No problem. What troubles you?"

"Several things. I was wondering when I would return to a physical body?"

"In a few minutes."

"*What?* Why so soon?"

"Because you are ready to return now. And I don't want you to postpone it. The more time you spend enjoying the freedom you have on this side, the harder it will be for you to go back. Besides, do you know how much time has passed on the Earth you knew since you died?"

"No."

"A year. I see your surprise. Time is not a constant throughout the creation. It is as much a product of consciousness as space. Here time is different. At the center of the galaxy it is even more different"

"But I thought I would have more time to goof off over here. I mean, there's still so much I need to learn before I go back."

"No. You know all you need to know. Also, I will continue to watch over you while you're on Earth. I will guide you, have no fear." He paused and briefly closed his eyes. "Besides, Jean Rodrigues is ready to take her fall. I see her now. She stands on a balcony overlooking the city much as you stood on a balcony before you left your body. Her mind turns to God. She prays for help." The Rishi opened his eyes and there was much love on his face. "We have to help her."

"But there are a few things that still confuse me. When we first talked, I assumed Peter was also talking to someone like you, a great teacher."

"Yes. He talked to me. But he saw me in a slightly different way and he called me Master."

"At the same time we talked?"

The Rishi smiled. "Time is time to me. It is all the same."

"What did you tell him?"

"Many of the same things I told you. I answered his questions. But we did not talk about Wanderers." He paused again and studied her in that gentle penetrating way he had. "I see what is in your heart, Shari. You want him to return with you."

I nodded. "Yes. Is it possible?"

"A better question would be, is it advisable?"

"You don't think it is?"

"Trust your intuition, Shari. What do you think? Or better yet, what do you feel in your heart would be best for him?"

I shrugged helplessly. "I don't know. But I sense the issue of his suicide is a problem, after all. More of a problem than I realized before we went into the light. Is that true?"

The Rishi nodded, and for once his expression was grave. "Human life is the greatest of God's gifts. Because it is only in a human nervous system that a man or woman can realize God. Even the angels in the highest heaven have to be born human to attain perfection, to become a Master. To purposely throw away such a gift is an unfortunate mistake. Don't misunderstand me—Peter is not damned because he killed himself, despite what certain religions might say. He will learn from his mistake and go forward like everyone else. It is simply that his suicide slows him down. He doesn't have all the opportunities open to him at present that you do. Naturally, though, these will be his in the future. God forgives all mistakes even before they are committed. It is important that we are able to forgive ourselves."

"But didn't Peter do that before he stepped into the light?"

"Yes. That is why he was able to follow you. You helped him in that way, as he helped you in other ways. But the consequence of his suicide will still be there when he returns to a physical body. There is a term for this—*karma*. His suicide created difficult karma for him."

"How will that karma take shape?"

"It can take a variety of shapes and forms."

"But you don't want to tell me?"

"Many of these things are up to Peter. As far as I know, he hasn't said anything about wanting to return to the physical right away."

"Because he doesn't know I have to go back. You said I am to return in a few minutes and I feel a lot of pressure. Can the three of us talk about it before I return?"

"There is no pressure, Shari. If you don't wish to go now, you may go later. It is simply that the time for the change is auspicious for you as well as Jean. But another auspicious time will arise. It always does. But certainly the three of us can sit and talk together before anything is decided. I can bring Peter here now."

"In a moment. I wanted to say that if you feel the time is ripe, then that's good enough for me. I'll go and quit whining.

I really am grateful that you set this all up for me. But I wanted to ask you—how long will I be on Earth? You said I'd write stories that millions will read. Does that mean I will live to a ripe old age?"

"No. It may be that you return for only a short time. I spoke of this period of transition that is fast approaching on the physical plane. Just as many Wanderers are incarnating on Earth to help with the transition, many with negative vibrations are also returning to stop it. They will not succeed, but they can upset the plans of many men and women of good will. In particular, they dislike Wanderers and attack them when they have the chance."

I shivered at the idea. "Can they spot a Wanderer?"

"Many of them can. Many of them are highly evolved, but in a negative way. I know that sounds like a contradiction, but it is not. One can evolve either positively or negatively. The interesting thing is whichever way you choose you end up merging into the divine. The divine is all there is. But the negative path takes much longer and is no fun. There is no love on that path. Those of negative vibration crave power and dominance. That is their trademark. You can spot them that way. They try to place themselves above others. They feel they are especially chosen by God for a *great* purpose. But God chooses everybody and all his purposes are great." He paused. "One of the negative beings might kill you. It's possible."

"But can't you protect me?"

"Protect you from what? Death? There is no death. I have nothing to protect you from."

I nodded. "If they do get me, then I'll be back here with you. That won't be so bad. But I would like to help humanity as much as I can while I'm on Earth. What else can I do besides write my stories?"

"Meditate. I will guide you to a genuine Master. Do service. Service performed without the expectation of reward brings a glow and richness to life. Study people who are always helping others. They are happy. You will have a happy life even if it doesn't last forever. That is my promise to you."

I bowed my head in gratitude. "Thank you." I sat back up. "And now I suppose the hour grows late. Please have Peter come."

CHAPTER XII

MY IDENTITY CRISIS was over, even though I didn't know I'd had one to begin with. Jean Rodrigues's memories were still there as clearly as was her body, and so was I. The fusion of her life with my soul brought me no confusion. Although I could not clearly recall everything the Rishi had told me, I remembered him well and trusted that he would not have put me in a body where I didn't belong. Before I did anything, even as I stood up from Jimmy's desk, I thanked him again, as well as said a prayer for the original Jean Rodrigues. But I knew she was well because she was with him. My Master.

I turned off the computer. I could read the rest of it later.

Stepping onto the balcony that adjoined the apartment, I saw my brother sitting three stories below beside the pool and staring at the water. I remembered how I had sat beside him in the car after I died, while he drove from the morgue to the condo where I had been killed. How he had pulled off to the side of the road and wept. How I had wanted to take him in my arms and tell him everything was all right. And now God had given me that chance, I thought, and here I was crying. The pool was practically right beneath me. My tears must have been landing on his head. He looked up in my direction.

"Have you changed your mind about reading it?" he called up to me.

I shook my head.

"Has it upset you?"

I shook my head.

"Do you want me to come back up?"

I nodded.

I was sitting at his desk when he came back in, studying the picture of my past incarnation. Honestly, I couldn't decide whether I looked better then or now. One thing for sure—Jean had bigger breasts. I was glad I hadn't gone out with Jimmy and let him touch them or anything. I would have just *died*.

Now what was I supposed to do? It took me two seconds to make a decision. I had to convince him who I was. If I didn't, I knew I would spend the rest of my life regretting that I hadn't at least tried. Also, I believed the time was ripe for revelations. I believed the Rishi had moved Jimmy to let me read the story. That was why Jimmy had gotten emotional around me, something I knew he seldom did. I believed the Rishi's grace was all around.

I couldn't get over how I had been dead and was now alive. I was so happy.

"What's wrong?" he asked quickly. "You look like you've been crying."

I set my picture down. "Yes. But that's all right. Please have a seat. I have something to tell you. You're not going to like what I say at first. You're going to get angry and order me to leave. But if you'll let me continue, then something wonderful will happen. Something beyond words."

He studied me quizzically. "What are you talking about?"

"I haven't read all of Shari's book. I don't need to. I know it from beginning to end. But I don't want to talk about particular incidents in the book. You could always say I happened to glance at a particular part and know what happened. Or else you could say I somehow got ahold of a copy and read it beforehand in order to confuse you."

He sat down on the couch. "You are confusing me. What are you talking about?"

"Jimmy, what do you think of me? I don't mean am I pretty or interesting or boring or crazy. I mean, is there something about me that you find familiar?"

He hesitated. "Yes."

"What is it?"

"I don't know."

"Do I remind you of anyone?"

He lowered his head. "No."

I understood that he was saying yes. But that it was not possible for him to say yes to his suspicion because what he suspected was not possible. Besides, the entire subject of Shari Cooper was so painful for him. I realized I'd have to punch a hole through that pain if I was to stand any chance of convincing him that I had come back from the grave. I took a deep breath. This was not going to be easy.

"I'm going to list a few events that happened between you and your sister. Only you two knew about them, no one else. None of them is discussed in her story. What I want you to do is just listen as I talk. Don't try to form any conclusions. Can you do that?"

"Yes. But you already said that you never met my sister. How can you know anything about us that isn't in the book? Have you talked to her friends? To Jo?"

"No. Even Jo wouldn't know the things I'm about to say. Please, just let me talk for a few minutes." I paused for effect. "On Shari's first day of high school she locked the number of the combination of her locker inside her locker. She was so embarrassed she didn't tell anyone what happened. But she came to you at lunchtime and asked if she could borrow some money to buy something to eat because her lunch was in the locker, too. She made you swear you wouldn't tell anyone what had happened and you kept your promise."

"No. I told my mother what had happened."

I jumped in my seat. "You told Mom? Why the hell did

you do that?" I stopped myself. Nothing was sacred, I thought. "Never mind. Let me take another example. On the night of your first date with Amanda, just before you went to pick her up, you entered Shari's bedroom and asked your sister how far you should try to go with Amanda. Like should you kiss her or just hold her hand—those kinds of questions. And Shari told you with a perfectly straight face that you should try to have sex with her before taking her to dinner. Do you remember?"

Jimmy sat up. "Yes. How do you know that?"

I raised my hand. "Be patient. When you were fifteen and Shari was thirteen, your parents took you for a trip to the desert. The two of you woke up early and decided to hike to a nearby rock formation. But what neither of you knew was that distances are deceptive in the desert and that the rock formation turned out to be five or six miles away. By the time you got to it you were both exhausted and thirsty. Then, on the hike back, while climbing through a dried ravine, you heard a rattlesnake in the nearby shrubs. Both of you panicked. You jumped out of the ravine and left your poor sister alone with the snake. She peed her pants. The rattlesnake looked at her and just crawled away. Afterward you both realized you had behaved like cowards, and you made a secret pact not to talk about what had happened." I paused. "You never told anyone about that incident, did you?"

"No." He was getting annoyed. "How do you know about it?"

"Let me tell you one more incident, and then I will try to explain myself. This happened after Shari died, but it is not recorded in her story. It did not happen between you and Shari but between you and Mrs. Parish. Listen closely here, it might sound a little confusing. After it became known that Amanda had killed Shari and that *she* was in fact your real sister, and not Shari, you went over to visit Mrs. Parish, Amanda's mother, who was in reality Shari's mother. While you were there you both talked about how great Shari had been. Toward the end of the conversation you made a touching comment. You said, "I think the things I loved most about Shari were all the things that made her different from me. In a way I'm grateful she wasn't my blood sister because then she wouldn't have been so different. She wouldn't have been who she was, which was the greatest sister in the world." After that you asked Mrs. Parish not to repeat the remark because you feared it would get back to your parents and they might be hurt by it."

There was a strange light in Jimmy's eyes. It was kind of scary, actually. But so is the fine line between fear and hope, pain and joy. It was as if I were being guided directly by the Rishi right then. I knew I had to take Jimmy to a place where he was about to explode before I hit him from just the right angle. I believed I was closing on that place fast.

"How do you know that?" he asked softly, his voice thick with feeling.

"Because I was there with the two of you when you spoke about Shari."

"That's impossible," he said flatly. "We were alone in her house. Amanda was under arrest at the time. How did you know about what happened in the desert?"

"Because I was there."

"I don't understand."

"In each of these incidents, I was there."

He spoke with exaggerated patience. "No, Jean. You weren't there. I would have known if you were there."

"Then how do I know these things? You explain it to me."

"I don't know. You must be lying. You must be a friend of Jo's. Shari must have told Jo these things and Jo told you."

"The phone is right there. Why don't you call Jo and ask her if she knows a Jean Rodrigues?"

His fear increased, as did his anger. "How do I even know your name is Jean Rodrigues? Why are you talking about these things? What are you doing here?"

"Do you want me to leave?"

"Yes." He stood. "As a matter of fact I do."

"Not thirty minutes ago you left me alone to read your most private computer entry. Now you're kicking me out. Sit down, Jimmy, I told you what I had to say would make you angry."

He sat back down. "I'm going to give you another three minutes."

"Good. That should be enough. If you were to call Jo, you would discover she knows no one who fits my description. If you were to call Mrs. Parish, you would learn she has never repeated your remark to anyone. Mrs. Parish is an extremely sensitive person. She would say nothing that might hurt your parents."

"So you know her at least? You're admitting that?"

I had to take another breath. "I know her in a manner of speaking. I know all of Shari's friends. I can tell you about them at length. But they do not know me. There isn't one of them who would recognize me." I paused. "Strange, isn't it?"

"Yes. If it's true, but I doubt it is."

"Why do you doubt it? Think about what I've just told you. Think about the things only you and Shari could have known."

"That's not true. Shari didn't know what I said to Mrs. Parish. She was dead at the time."

"No. That's what I'm trying to tell you. She wasn't dead. She was there in that house with the two of you!"

He stood again and pointed at the door. "I want you to leave. I don't know who you are or what you want. I just want you out. Now."

I stood and walked toward the door. But I stopped in front of him, I had to stop. He was my brother, after all, my big brother. My Jimmy. I stopped and rested my open palm on his chest and looked up into his eyes. He didn't brush me off.

He appeared to be transfixed by my touch, my eyes—there was a hint of green in them somewhere, I thought. Not that it mattered since he was color-blind. He had not been able to see the color even before I died. How could I hope that he would now? Still, I stared at him and I felt so much love for him that my own vision began to blur and he lost definition in my sight. Then I couldn't even tell what he looked like. It was then, however, that his face appeared to soften, and not just because of my tears, but perhaps because the old saying about the eyes being the windows of the soul was true. It was then he finally reached up to pull back the curtains a little. He reached up and squeezed my hand in that moment.

"Who are you?" he asked.

"It is me standing here. Just me."

"It was me lying there," he whispered, quoting from my story. "Just me." He brushed a tear off my cheek. He shook his head sadly. "It can't be you."

"I haven't forgotten you. How can you have forgotten me?"

He got choked up. "It can't be you."

I shook his hand. "Look at me! I'm here in front of you! What does it matter that my body has changed? It's still me."

He wanted to walk away, but I wouldn't let him. I held on to his hand as if it were a lifeline to safety. His head fell forward as if dragged down by weights. His eyes blinked at the floor. His anger was all gone now. There was just pain and a ray of hope.

"But you're dead," he said pitifully,

"Was I dead when I sat beside you that night and wrote my story? Jimmy, what was that story written for? To let everyone know that death does not exist! How can you have forgotten the main point of the stupid book?"

He shook uneasily, almost talking to himself. "But I didn't write it. I was asleep. I didn't know what I was doing. I just woke up in the morning and it was there."

"I wrote it!"

"It can't be. It can't be you."

"It is me! Look at me, Jimmy! Just look and you'll see. I've come back. I came back for you."

He looked up. I had the window at my back. Perhaps the light from it reflected on his face. Perhaps an angel brushed a wing over his forehead. I don't know. All I know is the scale finally tilted between the unequal balance of his longing and his grief. Just one more grain of sand had to be placed on our side, I saw. But he had to do it, not I. He had to say it.

Master! If you really are there now, please help us.

"Shari?" Jimmy said.

"Yes." I smiled. "You remember me."

CHAPTER XIII

TWO HOURS LATER we were both still talking our heads off and busting our guts laughing. And the funny thing was, it was as if I had never died. It was as if we were continuing a conversation we had started over a year ago. But the reverse was also true because it was the best talk we ever had. Sweeter than any I could remember. Neither of us would have come up for air if Jimmy hadn't suddenly begun to look tired. I commented on the fact and he shrugged.

"I've been working a lot of overtime lately," he said.

"For the telephone company? Still chopping down those telephone poles?"

He shook his head. "Is there nothing you don't know about me?"

"I'm sorry, but this Chicana babe remembers everything about her big brother." I reached over and felt his head. "I also remember you have diabetes. I think you need your insulin."

He nodded. "You're probably right. You know that was always one thing that amazed me about you. You knew when I needed a shot before I did."

"That's because I'm not color-blind, and I can see when you start to turn green."

"Do I look that bad?"

"No. I'm exaggerating. Are you still taking ten units in the afternoon?"

He stood and shook his head and stepped toward the bathroom. "I had to increase my dosage after you died. The doctor said stress has that effect on diabetics. I've never been able to bring it back down." He glanced back at me. He was obviously tired but hadn't lost his smile. "It just struck me how odd it sounds to talk to someone about her own death."

"I got used to it on the other side with Peter."

"That's right, good old Peter Nichols." Jimmy stepped into the bathroom and opened his medicine cabinet. "He didn't happen to wander back into a body, did he?"

I hesitated, feeling a lump in my throat. "No. He's still— gone."

Jimmy noticed my tone. "But you know he's fine where he is?"

I nodded. "But you can know one thing with your head and feel something quite different with your heart. I miss him."

Jimmy pulled out a short strip of paper he used to test the

blood sugar level of his urine. He closed the door only partway. The simple act meant a lot to me. He felt comfortable enough with me that he didn't have to close the door completely.

"You'll meet plenty of guys with those tits," he said casually.

I had to chuckle, although the topic made me a little sad. "To tell you the truth I already have a boyfriend. I inherited him from Jean. His name's Lenny Mandez."

"How do you feel about him?"

The question caught me off guard. So did my own answer; it just popped out of my mouth. "I love him," I said.

"Interesting," Jimmy remarked from the other side of the door.

"It is." I had to ask myself why I loved Lenny. He wasn't exactly Shari Cooper's type, not by about ten light-years. There was no question in my mind I had a distinct identity separate from the one Jean had formed over her eighteen years on Earth. Yet I had her memories; they were as much a part of me as they had been of her. When I sat quietly, it was easy to understand how someone like Malcolm X had not been able to pierce through the memory barrier. If not for meeting Jimmy and reading my own book, I doubted if I would have been able to do it. I realized so much of our identity was tied to our bodies, and wrongly, because we were much more than that. Still, the allure of the flesh was strong. I could close my eyes and feel exactly how Jean had felt on her first day of high school—she had been stoned, naturally—and what it had been like to make love to Lenny for the first time. The latter experience had been more satisfying than my one roll in the hay with Daniel. Lenny, at least, knew what it took to please a girl.

Or he used to know, I reminded myself.

I had to see him soon. I missed him.

"Damn," I heard Jimmy mutter.

"Did you pee on your hand?" I asked.

"That's a personal question if I ever heard one."

I giggled. "I'm glad you're testing your sugar level and not *estimating* like Amanda advised that night."

He popped his head out of the bathroom door. "You were there that night?"

"Of course I was there. You read that in the book. I saved your life, brother."

He shook his head again. "I have no doubt you're Shari, but it's still taking me time to absorb it all." He paused. "What did you see that night?"

"Are you asking if I saw the two of you screwing?"

"I never did it with Amanda."

"Gimme a break. When I got to our house that night the two of you were wearing bathrobes and nothing else."

"We didn't do anything."

"Yeah, right, sure. Why are you embarrassed to admit it? Is it because she turned out to be your sister?"

"Reread your own book, Shari. You will see we *definitely* did not have sex. Besides, what about you and Daniel?"

"I never did it with Daniel."

"Sure you did. It's in your book."

I was dumbfounded. "I put that in my book? God, you're right. You know I only wrote that because I was dead at the time. We've got to take that out."

"We've got to take out the part about Amanda and me. Even though we didn't do anything."

"No. We can't do that."

"Why not?"

"It's a major plot point. Daniel—he was just a minor character. The story doesn't revolve around whether I had sex with him or not."

Jimmy was worried. "You're not thinking of trying to get that story published?"

"I have to get it published. It's part of my mission on earth. To enlighten humanity about profound spiritual matters."

"But you can't publish that story."

"Don't worry, Jimmy. We can tone down things between you and Amanda."

"No. That story can't go out in that form. Mom and Dad will hear about it."

"Is that so bad? I want them to read it. I want to go see them next."

Jimmy came back into the room and sat on the couch

beside me. "You can't tell Mom and Dad who you are. They'll never believe you, no matter how many personal incidents you recount. You'll just end up hurting them."

"But my being dead hurts them."

"That's true. But it's been a year, Shari. They're getting over it. I know that must be hard to hear, but it's true. If you show up at their doorstep and say you're their daughter and a Wanderer— they'll freak. You know them. They'll never accept it."

"But you accepted it."

"Because we were very close. I can see beyond your body. Also, I have always been open to metaphysical ideas. Mom and Dad aren't. The only esoteric thing they do is read their horoscopes in the paper every now and then."

I sighed, knowing he was right. It was a painful realization. One of the first things I thought of when my memory had returned was to go see my parents and ease their grief. I had imagined all kinds of beautiful scenarios. Now I had to forget them.

"But can't I at least go over and see them?" I asked. "As a friend of yours?"

"Yes. But you'll have to be careful what you say."

"You never showed them my story?"

"No."

I nodded reluctantly. "Maybe that was wise. But I do want to try to get it published. I can always change the names and places."

"That's a good idea. We'll do that."

I hugged him. "You're so wise and yet I'm the one who's supposed to write the stories. Is it possible we could work together?"

"Only if I get half the royalties."

"No way! You're as bad as Sam."

"Who's Sam?"

"He's my muse. He's a troll and lives in my closet in South Central."

Jimmy's eyes widened. "Are you serious?"

I socked him. "You idiot! You still believe everything I tell you. Just because I came back from the dead doesn't mean there are trolls. Anyway, have you given yourself your insulin? I want to go out."

"Yes. Where do you want to go?"

"I want to see Jo and Mrs. Parish, my real mom. I want to see Detective Garrett, the guy who investigated my murder, as well. Boy, do I owe him. I hope he hasn't started drinking again. I'm telling Jo who I am. She'll believe me. She was practically born on the back side of a Ouija board."

Jimmy nodded. "We can see Jo. She lives on the other side of town. She's going to U.C.L.A."

"I was going to go to U.C.L.A."

"You can still go."

"My grades aren't good enough. Jean Rodrigues spent too much time in high school smoking dope. And I doubt U.C.L.A. will accept a transcript of Shari Cooper's grades on an entrance application. Besides, I don't have the money to go there. I live in the ghetto."

"We can change that. Tomorrow, you can move in here with me."

I stopped to think of the Rishi's words. My memory of my time with him was fragmented. I wondered if it was because we had spoken in a place outside of normal time. I knew he had told me to write and serve and meditate. But there were other things I sensed I had lost upon returning to the physical. He had given me some kind of warning—

"No," I said. "I have to stay with my new family. It's important that I work in that area of town to help improve things. Anyway, I never cared that much for material things." I paused again. "But I would like my Ferrari back."

"Who doesn't care about material things?"

"Well, it was mine. Where is it?"

"Dad sold it."

"*My* car? Who did he sell it to?"

"Your old boyfriend."

"Daniel is driving *my* car?"

Jimmy laughed. "It gets worse. He's still going out with Beth Palmones."

I waved my hand. "I don't care about that. He tried to make it with her an hour after my funeral. They deserve each other. But it pisses me off that he has *my* car. Could you buy it back from him?"

"That car cost a hundred grand. I don't have that kind of

money. Besides, you can't drive a Ferrari and live in the ghetto. It wouldn't last a night there."

"The ghetto is not as bad as rich white kids like you think. It has a lot of color. Take my best friend, Carol, for example. She's full of life. I have to introduce you to her. Maybe you two would hit it off." I paused. "Maybe not."

"Why do you say it like that?"

"Because she's a lesbian." I giggled. "But for a guy who's slept with his own sister, a lesbian might be a step in the right direction."

Jimmy was beet red. "Would you drop that? You know that's not true. Besides, I didn't know she was my sister. I thought you were my sister."

I quieted in a hurry. "You do still think of me as your sister, don't you? I still think of you as my brother. The fact that Amanda and I were switched at birth doesn't mean that much to you, does it?"

"Don't worry. You will always be my sister."

I was relieved. "Good."

"But there is something I think you should worry about. Should you see Mrs. Parish so soon after recovering your memory?"

"I'm not going to try to convince her who I am."

"I realize that. But she's a sensitive woman. She might sense something unusual about you and it might upset her. You might get upset around her."

I shook my head. "You forget, I have walked through the valley of the shadow of death. I am much stronger than when you last said goodbye to me. I don't mind getting upset. And Mrs. Parish is wise. If she does notice something about me, she'll be able to assimilate it in her own way. She doesn't have to understand that I'm Shari, but she can know that I am someone close."

"You want to see her now?"

"Yes. Please take me over. It means a lot to me."

He considered, then nodded. "That woman is an angel, as well as your mother. I suppose it's only right you should see her."

CHAPTER XIV

I HAD A PECULIAR EXPERIENCE as Jimmy drove me up to Mrs. Parish's place, a small apartment over someone's garage. She had moved since I'd last been on Earth. I thought of Mrs. Parish not in terms of how I remembered her, but how I had written about her in my story. My memory of my life as Shari Cooper, I realized, although distinct, also was blank in a few spots. I was Shari but someone else as well, and I wasn't just talking about Jean Rodrigues again. It was like I was a third person, a new and improved version of the other two girls. But the memories I had from after I died, the ones I could recall, didn't suffer from this veil, and perhaps that was the reason I thought of Mrs. Parish the way I did.

Mrs. Parish had an arthritic spine. Often, if we were alone in the house, she would let me help her sweep the floor or scrub the bathrooms. . . . Her hair was not one of her finer features. It was terribly thin. Her scalp showed a little, particularly on the top, whenever she bent over, and she was only fifty. To be quite frank, she wasn't what anyone would have called a handsome lady. She did, however, have a gentle, lovely smile.

Mrs. Parish smiled as she answered the door. Her right leg was encased in a walking cast. Her hands were covered with liver spots. She had lost considerable weight, and seemed more stooped, older than fifty-one. But her smile was lovely; it made my heart leap in my chest to see her.

"Jimmy," she said. "What a wonderful surprise. And you've brought a friend." She offered her hand. "Hello, I'm Mrs. Parish."

I shook her frail fingers. "I'm Jean Rodrigues."

Mrs. Parish stepped aside. "Please come in. I was just making myself coffee. Would you like some? I know Jimmy does. Black with cream, right? I have carrot cake as well, but I know Jimmy doesn't want any of that."

"The coffee would be great," Jimmy said. "Jean drinks it as well. How did you break your leg?"

"I was cleaning a friend of your mother's house," Mrs. Parish said as she limped into the tiny kitchen. There wasn't room to watch MTV in the apartment, but I supposed she didn't need much space now that Amanda was away in a state psychiatric hospital. Mrs. Parish opened the refrigerator and continued. "I was mopping the woman's floor when I just slipped and fell. I lay there for three hours before anyone came home. I couldn't even get to the phone. Have a seat, Jean, Jimmy, make yourselves at home."

"You poor dear," I said, sitting down.

Mrs. Parish chuckled. "It was my own fault. I'm getting clumsy. Anyway, I've been stuck in here for a couple of months. And the doctors say it will be another two months before I can go back to work." She finished putting on more coffee and came over and sat down near us. "Oh, well, at least I have a chance to catch up on my reading."

"I read a lot," I said. "I write stories as well."

Mrs. Parish was interested. "Do you now? That's wonderful, to be able to put your ideas down on paper. You must let me read your work. I'm sure I'll love it."

"I would be flattered to have you read it."

Mrs. Parish gestured to Jimmy. "So how did you two meet?" she asked.

"I knew his sister," I said quickly.

Mrs. Parish blinked. "Did you now? Shari?"

"Yes," I said, holding her eye, with Jimmy staring at me, fidgeting, no doubt wondering what I was up to. "I was one of her best friends. I only learned a short time ago that you were her actual mom. I told him I had to meet you."

Mrs. Parish had to take a breath. "I'm sorry, Jean, I never heard Shari talk about you. But it's always nice to meet someone who knew her. Did you two go to school together?"

"No. I live on the other side of town. But we often talked on the phone."

Mrs. Parish nodded pleasantly, but her face fell a little. "She was a lovely girl."

I leaned forward. "Another reason I wanted to meet you is because I wanted to share with you an experience I had a few days after Shari died. I thought that you would be the one person who could understand it. But if it's too upsetting to talk about her, I understand."

She straightened. "No. Please tell me. I want to hear."

I thought of what Mrs. Parish had said to the empty air as I sat beside her in the days after I died.

"Shari. If you're there, if you can hear me, I want to tell you something that I almost told you a thousand times while you were alive. Finding you again after losing you for all those years was wonderful. It was the best thing that ever happened to me. It brought me so much joy, I thought I would never ask God for anything else, because he had given me everything. And I kept that promise, until right now. You see, I have to ask him one more thing, to tell you this, that I loved you as much as any mother loved a child. You were always my daughter."

"I was sitting alone in my living room and thinking about Shari," I said. "There was no one at home, and somehow I dozed off in my chair. I had this dream that Shari was with a woman about your age and she was helping her sweep a floor. The woman had a sore back, and when Shari set her broom down, she rubbed the woman's spine to ease her pain. She said to her, 'Mom, finding you again was the most wonderful thing that ever happened to me. I know how much you loved me. Don't worry about me, I'm fine. I just wanted you to know how much I loved you. When I was alive, deep inside, a part of me always knew you were my mother.'" I paused. "Then something woke me up. A hand on my arm. But there was no one there, Mrs. Parish." I spoke gently. "Does my dream mean anything to you?"

A soft light shone on Mrs. Parish's face. In that moment, even with her wrinkles and her cast and her liver spots, she reminded me of the Rishi. They both had grace.

"Yes," she said quietly. "It means everything to me. Thank you, Jean, for sharing it with me." She touched her chest. "I know in my heart she's all right."

I stood and went over to hug her. I was crying again—for maybe the tenth time that day. A baby cried when it was born, and for me this was like my birthday. It felt so good to hug my mother again.

"I know she is, too," I said.

CHAPTER XV

WHEN WE GOT BACK to Jimmy's place, I asked if I could call my mother; Jimmy did a double take. "Jean Rodrigues's mother," I explained. "She'll be worried about me."

"You never used to ask if you could use my phone. Maybe you aren't really Shari. Maybe this is all just an elaborate hoax."

I picked up the phone. "I asked you once out of politeness, but I'm not going to ask you again."

"Oh, *that* sounds familiar. I guess you are Shari, after all."

I smiled at him. "Behave yourself. There are other secrets I can put in my book that will ruin your reputation." I punched out the number quickly. My mother, Mrs. Rodrigues, answered. I felt as close to her as I had the day before. That was the great thing about having two sets of memories. Overnight I had doubled my family. The only drawback was that I could think of twice as many people who annoyed me.

"Hello?"

"Hi, *Mamá*, it's me. I'm safe and sound. Haven't keeled over from any bad headaches. I'm with a friend in Orange County. I might be out late. Just wanted you to know. How are you doing?"

"I'm fine but Carol is upset. She's called three times. She wants you to call her immediately."

"Qué pasa?"

"I don't know. She wouldn't tell me. But whatever it is, I don't want you getting involved. You hear me?"

"Yes. Is she at home?"

"I think so. Who is this friend you're with?"

"He's an old pal. I'll tell you about him later. I want to go. I want to call Carol."

"Remember what I said," she warned.

I hung up the receiver and quickly dialed Carol. Jimmy watched me. "Do you still get headaches as a result of your fall?" he asked.

"Yes, and they're a real bitch. But don't worry, I'm not going to die on you again." Carol picked up. I turned my back on Jimmy and shielded the phone with my hand. "Hello, baby doll. What's the big emergency?"

Carol sounded agitated. "I got bad news. Darlene's got herself a piece. Freddy told me she bought it from a crack dealer on Hawthorne."

"That's no big surprise. We knew she was shopping."

"Yeah. But here's the scary part. Lenny checked out of rehab and went straight to Darlene's house. Freddy told me that, too. Maybe Darlene got the piece for Lenny. I hear he can drive. You hear what I'm saying?"

"That he might try a drive-by on Juan and take the heat?"

"Yeah. You better talk to him. Better talk to him now."

"I'm on my way. *Gracias*."

"Take care of yourself, Jean. I have a bad feeling about this."

"I'll call you as soon as I know something."

Jimmy was studying me when I set the phone down. I forced a smile.

"I have to go," I said. "A problem at home."

"You don't want me to get Jo? You were so excited about seeing her a minute ago."

"You can get her. I might be able to come over later." I edged toward the door. "I'll call you."

He stepped in front of me. "What was that remark you made about someone doing a drive-by and taking the heat?"

I laughed. "Oh, that's just tough girl talk. It's nothing."

He crossed his arms over his chest. "I'm not stupid, Shari."

I stopped laughing. "It's nothing to worry about, Jimmy, I promise. I'll be back in two hours. Go get Jo. Tell her what's happened. I bet you can convince her even without me there. I might be back here before you. Leave the door open for me."

"Can't I go with you?"

"No, and I can't explain why. The situation is complicated."

He stepped aside reluctantly. "Why do I feel like I did the last time we said goodbye?"

"Will you be out late?"

"Not too late."

"Good."

"What's the matter?"

"Nothing. I'm just tired. Have fun."

"Sweet dreams, brother."

"Take care, sister."

I went up on my tiptoes and kissed him on the forehead. "I will not be out late. I will come back. Trust me, I love you too much to leave you again."

"Love can't protect you from everything, Shari."

I opened his door. Outside, it was beginning to get dark.

"There's nothing I need to be protected from," I said.

Darlene Sanchez's house was a pile of old wood, plaster, and bad vibes. Her father had abused her when she was six. When she was ten he had taken two rounds in the chest from a double-barreled shotgun while trying to rob a liquor store. When she was sixteen her mother died from cirrhosis of the liver from having drunk half a liquor store. Darlene was tough, though, I knew from past life regressions. She could take a few setbacks and come out shooting. That was what worried me.

Darlene answered the door when I knocked.

"Jean," she said. "What are you doing here?"

"Is that how you say hello?"

"Hello already. What the hell are you doing here?"

"I want to see Lenny."

"He's not here."

"I don't believe you." I pushed at the screen door. "Let me in."

She pushed back; she was a strong devil. "No. I'm with a guy."

"You're with *my* guy. Open the goddamn door or I'll come in through the window."

Darlene was dark. "I wouldn't recommend that, Jean."

I laughed in her face. "What are you going to do, shoot me? Do you feel empowered because you bought yourself a piece today? Yeah, I heard about your gold credit card purchase. Do you think owning a gun makes you bad? You make me sick. You prance around like you're so hot to avenge your boyfriend's death, and then when it comes crunch time you drag a crippled guy into your stupid plot and tell him to do all the dirty work."

"I don't know what you're talking about."

"I'm sure you don't." I suddenly shoved hard on the door, catching her by surprise. I was inside before she could stop me. Lenny, in a wheelchair, sat beside the kitchen table. He glanced over as Darlene started to grab my hair.

"Let me talk to her alone," he said flatly.

Darlene stopped with her hand in the air. "Alone?" she asked, annoyed.

"Yeah," Lenny said. "Go for a walk."

"This is *mi casa*!"

"Go for a long walk," Lenny said.

Darlene went for a walk. I went over and sat at the table near Lenny. Physically, he looked better than when he had transferred from the hospital to the rehabilitation clinic, which was the last time I had seen him. He had some color and had put on weight. But his handsome face was still flat and cold. I felt as if I were about to talk to a perfect stranger. I'm sure the original Jean would have felt the same way. He offered me a cigarette, but I shook my head. The air was thick with smoke already. He took a puff on his own cigarette butt and ground it out in a filthy ashtray.

"You look good," I lied.

"For a cripple?"

"I'm sorry, I didn't know you would hear that when I said it. I'm glad to see you're up and around. What is it like handling the chair? I bet it takes some getting used to."

He snorted. "It's like riding a bicycle. The only difference is the ride never ends." He added softly, "Unless you decide to crash."

"You don't want to crash. You've come too far. Lenny, look at me. Talk to me. You're doing good. Ten weeks ago you were lying in a hospital bed. Now you're able to go places and see people. This is a fresh start for you. It can be a fresh start for us. I care about you—a great deal." I stopped and asked sadly, "Don't you care about me?"

He finally looked at me. "You look different."

I forced a smile. "Is that good?"

"I don't know." His eyes narrowed. "What have you been doing lately?"

"Waiting for you to call. But other than that I've been busy. I start school in a couple of weeks. I'm going to the JC. I've been working at the Subway and at the hospital." I added, "I've written a few stories. You can read them if you'd like."

He shrugged. "I never read. Why did you come here tonight?"

"I just told you. To see you. I'm worried about you."

He smiled thinly, as he had when Jean told him she was pregnant. "You don't have to worry," he muttered, leaning back in his chair and stretching. It seemed as if he had a cramp in his back.

"Are you all right?"

"Yeah. I just broke my back is all."

"Lenny!"

He shook his head. "I don't know why you're here."

I sat back, suddenly as tired as the whole sick house. "I heard Darlene bought a gun. I heard she wants you to kill Juan for what he did to Sporty. I'm here to talk you out of it."

He chuckled. "You know nothing."

I stood. The air in the house was too heavy. Reason could not prevail in such an atmosphere, I thought I had to get him somewhere else. "Let's go for a ride," I said.

"To where?"

"A friend's house."

"Who is this friend?"

"It's a guy I met. You'll like him. Let's go before the dragon lady gets back."

He surprised me. I thought I would have to drag him out the door.

"If you want," he said.

Jimmy's third-story apartment had an elevator as well as a stairway. The former had proved most useful when I had helped him move in, although the elevator had not been wide enough to accommodate his bed and chest of drawers. Fortunately, Lenny and his wheelchair fit in the elevator nicely, and soon we were rolling into Jimmy's apartment. The place was empty.

"Does he usually go out and leave his place unlocked?" Lenny asked.

"This is Orange County, not South Central," I said.

"They know what the word *crime* means over here. Do you have a key to this guy's place or what? How well do you know him?"

"I know him very well. But he's not my boyfriend or anything like that."

Lenny gave a bitter laugh. "Like I'm supposed to believe that. Like you're going to wait for me to get better when you know I won't. Drop the charade, Jean. You're screwing this guy. We both know it."

My temper flared. Maybe it was about time. Maybe it was the worst time. Time, I knew, was different in Orange County than it was in South Central. As it was different on Earth than at the center of the galaxy. What had I seen there? That we were all part of one another? If that was so, then Lenny had just become an aching head that I just wanted to rub softly or else pound furiously. I just wanted the madness to stop.

What I did not know was that he wanted the same thing.

"You drop the charade, you bastard," I said. "I am not screwing anybody and you know it."

I was very surprised when he pulled a black revolver, complete with silencer, from underneath his shirt and pointed it in my direction. His grin was the work of demons.

"Oh, I know a thing or two about you," he said. "I know you were screwing Sporty when you were supposedly going out with me. I know it was his baby you got pregnant with. And I know that you're going to die in the next two minutes."

I held out my hands defensively. I may have walked through the valley of the shadow of death and come back out again, but that didn't mean I was anxious to repeat the experience on a nice summer evening. His words had shocked me so much that I actually smiled instead of screamed. But it was an awkward smile, full of pain and fear. Yeah, it hurt me that he would even point a gun in my direction, my boyfriend. Of course, I knew it would hurt a lot more if he pulled the trigger.

"Hold on just a second," I said. "I never slept with Sporty. What gave you that idea? I was certainly never pregnant with his baby. You got it all wrong. Who have you been talking to?"

"I don't need to talk to no one. Last spring I drove by your house late one night and saw you kissing Sporty goodbye. It was kind of dark but what you gave him was no brotherly peck."

Frantically, I tried to remember that night, searching memories that not only didn't belong to me, but in more cases than not had been recorded with a stoned nervous system. There was one time, in mid-May, when I did recall that Sporty had been over late. He and Jean had been smoking pot and goofing off. She might have kissed him good night—he was an old friend of hers—but I had no recollection that it had been a hard kiss. The problem was, Jean might have been so high she momentarily thought she was making out with Lenny and went at it a bit. What a paradox, I thought. How could I defend myself for things she might have done? But one thing for sure, I knew Jean had never slept with Sporty.

"I might have kissed him, I can't remember," I said quickly. "We were high that night. But I didn't sleep with him. You have no proof of that."

He sneered. "No proof? You told me you were pregnant. You *were* pregnant. You lost the baby in the fall. You told me that as well."

"So? It was your baby."

"It couldn't have been my baby! What kind of fool do you take me for? I wore a condom every time we had sex."

I chuckled despite the situation. "You are a fool. The condom broke once. You didn't even notice, but I did. That's how I got pregnant with your kid."

"You expect me to believe that?"

"It's the truth. It happens all the time. Ask any doctor or pharmacist. They'll tell you the same thing."

My words seemed to shake him. The gun in his hand moved off to one side. But I didn't think to try to rush him and wrestle it away. Lenny was six feet away, and even with his injury I knew he had excellent reflexes. If I jumped him, I'd die, it was that simple. And I would have lied to my brother a second time.

"It can't be," he whispered, more to himself. His face went gray; his very soul seemed to tremble. "Sporty had to go."

"What did you say?"

He regained control of his aim. "You're a lying, cheating bitch. That's all there is to it. I'm going to kill you now. Move over onto that balcony."

"No! I heard what you just said. You were the one who arranged Sporty's death. You took him into Juan's territory that night. What did you do, tell him that you had arranged a truce for him with Juan?"

Lenny was enraged. "I didn't shoot him! I didn't pull the trigger!"

"But you set him up. I see it all. I should have seen it a long time ago. You told Juan where you'd be walking by and at what time. No wonder you didn't get hit. No one was aiming for you. And you call me a cheat. You grew up with Sporty, for chrissakes!"

"And he was screwing my woman! He deserved to die!" Tears sprung into his eyes as he glared at me with the dark hint of murderous guilt. It was then I understood, even before he said what he did next, that he felt he had to kill me to justify what he had done to his friend. To convince himself that he had not made a mistake. It was twisted logic, and unfortunately it was the kind practiced daily in the barrios every time some innocent person died.

"No one deserves to die so young," I said.

"I didn't want him to die! It was you who made him die! It was you and your goddamn slutty ways! Get out on that balcony. I tried to kill you once—knocking you off my balcony— and by God I'm going to do it this time. Get out there, you bitch!"

He was serious, there was no arguing with him. I stepped out onto the balcony, not taking my eyes off him. He followed me only partway. The wooden balcony was cramped, the sliding glass door that led to it even more narrow. He might be able to wheel his chair out, I thought, but it was obvious he didn't want to. The night air closed around me like a hand of doom. I couldn't comprehend that my time back on Earth was to be so short. Was my karma so bad? It didn't seem fair. The Rishi hadn't warned me.

Yet he had, I thought, in a way.

"What happened that night, Lenny? Did you set the balcony to collapse beneath me? At the critical moment, did your handiwork fail? Did you climb down beneath me to fix it and then—big surprise—me and the balcony fell on you? You know, you always were lousy at fixing things."

"*Cállate!*"

By his reaction I knew I had hit the bull's-eye. "Just tell me if Darlene was in on your little escapade."

"She wasn't."

"Great. That's a relief. Now what? This balcony isn't going to collapse beneath me, and I'm not going to jump off it. I've had enough of that stunt."

Lenny smiled grimly. "But you are going to jump. The pain is going to make you jump."

"What pain?"

Wrong question. Lenny took aim and fired.

The bullet burst from the muzzle in a silent flare of orange light. It tore through the right side of my right thigh with an agonizing red rupture. Even when I had hit the concrete with my head after falling three stories, I hadn't felt such overwhelming pain. Crying, I sagged to the side and instinctively covered the wound with my right hand. The blood poured warm and sticky into my palm. It soaked my pants and dripped onto the boards of the balcony. Lenny shifted the gun and aimed it at my left thigh. Where were Jimmy's neighbors? Watching cable TV? I had to scream, I knew, to get their attention. But I also knew if I did, he would just put a bullet through my heart. Oh, God, I thought. I should never have come back.

"You should jump now," he said. "I will take you apart piece by little piece. A few more bullets and the pain will become intolerable."

"You'll never get away with it," I gasped. "The police will come. They'll catch you. You'll go to jail forever."

My threat amused him. "Your new boyfriend will probably get here before the police. I'll do him like I'm doing you, slowly and painfully. I have plenty of ammunition. I'll save a bullet for myself. When the police get here, there will be no one to arrest." He put pressure on the trigger. "Would you like it in the crotch? You can cover the area with your hand if you like, but the bullet will go right through it and get you where it hurts most."

"Please." I wept, holding out my trembling arm, horrified at the thought of what it would be like to be shot there. "Give me a second. I'll get up on the railing. I'll do what you ask. I'll jump."

He was happy. He was sick. He was like some ancient beast dug up from a black tomb that the gods should have long ago covered with a sacred mountain. His eyes shone the color of blood, and I hardly recognized him.

"That's a good little slut." He cackled. "But do it fast, my finger is itchy. Dive headfirst if you don't want me to shoot at you while you're lying splattered on the concrete."

"I'm hurrying," I moaned, easing myself up onto the wooden railing. All I could think was that I couldn't let him put another bullet in me. From so many violent films and TV shows people have become anaesthetized to what it is like to be shot. It is a tragic thing. My lives were tragic. They kept bringing me to a precipice where there was no hope of escape. I eased my bloody leg over the railing. "Lenny," I pleaded, before I let go.

He was not there, not the guy I knew. But the gun was. It pointed through the railings at my crotch. "You have two seconds," he said. "One—"

I let go, partly. My hands slid down the wooden railings and I was left hanging on to the floor of the balcony. My legs dangled below me; it felt as if a river of blood dripped out of my torn thigh. The pain was already intolerable, and my plan was really no plan at all. My only hope was that now that I was below his line of vision, he wouldn't be able to shoot me, not without wheeling out onto the balcony, which I prayed was too narrow for his chair.

Unfortunately, my status as a Wanderer did not make it inevitable that God would take my prayers under consideration. Peeking up over the side of the balcony, I saw Lenny approach steadily, past the coffee table and through the sliding glass door. His big round black wheels coasted to the tips of my fingertips. It was there he aimed the gun, not at my head. He must have had some deep-seated perverse wish to see me fall. I swore if I did, I would let out a scream so loud everybody would come running. Before my brother could come running. A scream was the one thing I had failed to let out the last time I had died, and as a result most people thought I committed suicide. Of course, that would not be a problem this time with the bullet hole in my leg.

"One," Lenny repeated.

"Jesus, Lenny."

"Two."

He fired at my right hand. My fingers were sprayed; the bullet splintered the wood between them. Technically, he didn't hit me, but the shock of the striking bullet was enough to make me lose my grip with that hand. Careening wildly to the left side, I fought to bring my right hand back up onto the balcony. It was a loser's strategy. So what if I got it back up. He would just shoot my fingers off, and there would be that much less of me to bury.

Still, I fought.

Still, I could not comprehend that this was really happening to me.

Not again. Lenny's wild face loomed above me.

"Master!" I cried.

Lenny's face suddenly softened. "Shari," he said, as if surprised.

Time could have halted. I stared at him.

"What?" I said.

He reached down to save me. I reached up.

But he was too late. I lost my grip. I fell.

I saw the edge of the apartment roof, the stars. There were only a few of the latter, and they weren't very bright. Not compared to the lamppost that stood near the entrance of the apartment complex, which suddenly began to rush toward me at an incredible speed. I had been this route before. I knew how the stars would change when my head hit the ground and I rolled over and looked up. There would be millions of them in the sky then. Orange ones and green ones and blue ones. There would especially be red ones, which would multiply rapidly and blot out everything else in the heavens as a colossal wave of smothering hot wax—all the blood in my brain—ran out and covered my face.

I would black out. I would die.

CHAPTER XVI

WE SAT IN A TRIANGLE. Peter looked uneasy. I didn't feel so hot myself, not for being in heaven. The Rishi, however, had lost none of his equanimity. The clear stream trickled nearby. The air was still fresh with the fragrance of flowers. The sun shone; in this realm it seemed never to set. I wondered if Peter saw the Master as I did, but I supposed it didn't matter. I only hoped that Peter listened to him.

"What's going on?" Peter asked.

"I'm going back now," I said.

"To where?" Peter asked.

"Earth. A physical body. But I'm not going to be born as a baby. I'm going to enter the body of an eighteen-year-old girl named Jean Rodrigues. I'm going to be what is called a Wanderer."

Peter's face sagged. "You're going to leave? You can't leave.

We just got here." He appealed to the Rishi. "What's the big rush?"

"There are reasons," the Rishi said calmly.

Peter was distraught. "But I don't want her to leave. Shari, don't you have any say in this?"

"I do. It's all up to me. But I have to go. Not just for myself but for other people as well. I have something important to do on Earth."

"But won't you miss me?" he asked pitifully.

My eyes moistened. "Yes."

Peter turned to the Rishi. "Can I go with her? I have to go back if she's going."

The Rishi considered. "It is possible. But I wouldn't advise it. You have much to learn on this side, Peter, before you return. The last time you were in a physical body, you made some mistakes. If you return too quickly, you might repeat the same mistakes."

Peter was taken back. "Are you referring to my suicide?" he asked quietly.

"Yes," the Rishi said.

"But I won't do it again. Especially if I'm with Shari. I'll know how foolish an act it was."

"When we return this way," I said gently. "We don't necessarily remember the spiritual realm. The Rishi, the Master, has explained how easy it is to get caught up in matter again."

"The chance to become a Wanderer is a great gift," the Rishi agreed. "But it is also a huge responsibility. You would be more ready to accept that responsibility if you spent more time between lives."

Peter would not listen. "But I don't want to be here if she's not here. I—I love her. You told me when I arrived that the main thing in creation was love. Don't my feelings count for something in this decision?"

The Rishi smiled faintly. "They do. Divine love transcends all reason. It is the path to God. But is your love divine, Peter? Or do you wish to return simply because you will miss her?"

Peter was stubborn. "My love for Shari is as real as my love for God. I know that. You're so wise—you must know that."

The Rishi gestured innocently. "I know that I don't know. That is how I can feel the will of God." He briefly closed his eyes. "I feel many things right now. If you go back, it will be hard for you."

"I don't care," Peter said. "As long as I'm with Shari. Can you promise me that much at least?"

The Rishi regarded Peter gravely. "Yes. I can promise you that. But you threw away your last life. When you steered your motorcycle in front of the truck, you almost lived. Had you survived, you would have been crippled for life. If you return now, you will return as a cripple."

"No!" I cried. "That's too horrible. There must be another way."

"Those are the choices," the Rishi said. "It is up to Peter to chose."

"Don't do it," I said to Peter. "You know me, I live recklessly. I won't be gone so long. Stay here and learn what you have to learn. You don't want to be in a crippled body. You might not be able to have sex."

Peter smiled sadly. "But I would rather have love than sex. I would rather have you than have legs that work." He reached over and took my hand. "Even back in our bodies, you won't forget me and I won't forget you. It can work, I know it." He added, "If that's what you want, Shari?"

"I don't want you to spend years suffering."

"I won't suffer if you're with me."

I smiled through my tears. "What are you talking about? I'll drive you crazy."

"I enjoy being crazy about you," Peter said. He appealed once more to the Rishi. "Can I go? I accept that I will have to be crippled. I see the justice in it."

The Rishi nodded. "You may go."

I was still worried. "But is this the best course?"

The Rishi laughed easily. "I must confess this entire conversation has been something of a test for both of you. Everything I said about the reasons you should stay were true, Peter. But I love love more than anything in this creation. Don't worry, Shari. If someone makes a sacrifice in love, then only good can come from it in the long run. Good will come from Peter's decision, for both of you."

"Is there anything we can do on Earth to help us remember this time with you?" Peter asked.

"Shari has asked me this question several times," the Rishi said. "My answer to you is not the same. For you to remember, Peter, you will need a huge shock. You will have to return to that moment of despair that previously made you take your life. You will have to face it squarely. And this time you will have to decide to live." He paused. "What did you think of just before you died?"

Peter considered. "I thought of Shari."

The Rishi nodded and stood. "Then events will arrange themselves so that the lesson is repeated. I hope you pass the test. But if you don't, you will just have to take it again later." He offered both his hands, one for each of us. "Come children, it's time. Lenny and Jean are in the hospital, unconscious."

EPILOGUE

WHEN LENNY AND I had entered the apartment complex, we had, as I said, used the elevator because of his wheelchair. The lift was at the front of the complex. The pool was in the rear. Lenny, therefore—probably not until he wheeled himself out onto the balcony to try to shoot off my fingers—did not even know there was a fair-size body of water almost directly beneath the balcony. There was another important element in the scenario. Just before I lost my grip, as I fought to reach for Lenny's hand, I swung up with my right arm. The move was in one sense counterproductive and in another sense beneficial. It had the effect of making me lose my grip, but it also threw me away from the balcony and farther out over the central courtyard, just before I started on my long fall to my death. Yet I didn't die.

To make a long story short, I landed in the deep end of the swimming pool.

Boy, that was one bellyflop that stung.

I bobbled to the surface ready to scream. The water was already stained with my blood. Just then Jimmy and Jo came by. Jimmy took one look at me and appeared ready to faint. But Jo burst out laughing.

"Hey, Jimmy," she said. "You are right. That must be Shari. She's still jumping off balconies." Jo walked to the edge of the pool and offered me a helping hand. "If you are Shari, then I finally have a nickname for you."

I let Jo pull me out of the pool. My leg hurt something awful, but as long as it didn't have to be amputated, I didn't mind. I remembered that Jo often gave people nicknames. I noticed that she had bleached her hair blond. She always did want to have more fun.

"What's that?" I asked my old friend.

She giggled. "The *Fall Girl*."

"Shari!" someone called from three stories up. "Are you all right?"

"Yeah! Is that you, Peter?"

"This is turning out to be a weird day," Jimmy muttered.

"Yeah!" Peter shouted. "I remember! I remember you!"

I smiled. "That's what I wanted most!"

THE LAST STORY

For Marjorie

CHAPTER I

THE SILVER LINING of success often tarnishes before it can be enjoyed. For me, being rich and famous was both wonderful and awful. Wonderful because money and notoriety are necessary and useful in a world where almost everything can be purchased with them. Awful because that same wealth and fame caused me to forget that I can never truly own anything in this world. Like everyone else, I am here for only a short time and then, no matter how rich and important I have become, I will be gone. It's ironic that I, who have died and returned to life, should forget that. But forget it I did when I came face to face with my enemy.

Myself.

Shari Cooper. Jean Rodrigues. I have two names.

But perhaps I am being too hard on myself. After all, I was once a ghost who prayed only to be remembered. To have one more chance at life. And then, when that chance was miraculously granted, was it any wonder I should have run wild for a time? Yes, I can forgive myself, and hope those close to me can do the same. Because time is short.

Especially for me.

God, my head hurts. My heart aches.

Where to begin? Maybe at the beginning of the end. That would be a few days ago. My publisher had arranged a book signing for me at a large Barnes & Noble located in a California mall the size of Tokyo. The turnout was unexpected, even by my lofty standards. Two thousand young people showed up to have me scribble my name—my *real* name from my previous life, and now my pen name—on the inside cover of my latest bestseller. How young they seemed to me, although most were only a couple years short of my twenty-one years. Being famous does make you feel old and wise, like you know it all. Greeting each adoring fan with a quick smile and a flick of my pen, I felt like a queen.

"I'm your number-one fan," a cute redheaded girl said as she reached my table at the head of the line. She clutched a copy of *Remember Me*—my sixth book—to her chest, her eyes saucerlike and round. "I've read everything you've written."

"What's your name?" I asked, sticking out my hand for her copy of the book.

"Kattie. Is Shari Cooper a pen name, or is it your real name? I noticed you named the heroine of *Remember Me* Shari Cannon."

I glanced at Peter Nichols, in Lenny Mandez's body, sitting beside me, in his wheelchair. He smiled but didn't say anything. Peter enjoyed the signings more than I did. I didn't know why because all the attention was focused on me.

"It's real enough," I muttered. Taking the book, I opened it to the title page and scribbled: *For Kattie, Enjoy. Shari Cooper.* I don't use many different inscriptions inside my books. "Enjoy," "Best Wishes," "Be Good," and "Love and Kisses"—if the guy is cute that is. Actually, I didn't know what to say to people when they told me how great I was. Being a celebrity was fun but also confusing. Kattie lingered after I returned her book. The people behind her fidgeted. I had been signing for three hours straight and the line was still long. My right hand was numb. Kattie smiled shyly.

"I was just wondering," she asked, "where do you get your ideas?"

Had I been asked that question before? Once or twice, a million times. "I don't know," I said. "I really don't. They just come to me, at unexpected moments."

"But do you think you have a muse, like Sam O'Connor in that short story you wrote?"

I chuckled. Sam was a troll who lived in the closet. I said to Peter, "Do we have a troll in our closet?"

"There's only me," Peter said.

Kattie seemed confused. "Are you girlfriend and boyfriend?" she asked.

I hesitated, feeling Peter's eyes on me. "Yes. You look surprised, Kattie?"

She was not surprised, but embarrassed. "No. I just thought you were brother and sister." She shrugged. "I'm sorry."

"Don't be sorry," Peter said quickly. "We do look kind of alike."

Except for both of us being in Hispanic bodies, we looked nothing alike. My features were voluptuous, sensual. Since becoming a writing star, I had cut my hair short; my bangs brushed my eyes as they once did—in my earlier incarnation as Shari Cooper. Peter hadn't cut his straight black hair since he had wandered back in—he wore it long, down his back, in a ponytail I enjoyed tugging. Because he ate like a bird, he had become terribly thin, haggard even. Still, his dark eyes were bright and his smile seldom dimmed.

Like Peter, I understood Kattie's confusion. She saw me as a star, an idol, someone she dreamed of becoming. And here I was with a paraplegic. Knowing she'd never understand, I didn't try to explain. Plus anything I would have said would only hurt Peter's feelings.

"We've been through a lot together," I said to Kattie. "It's been great."

Kattie flashed me one last smile. "You're great." She held up *Remember Me*. "I've already read this new book three times. You wrote it like you lived it." She burst out laughing. "Or died it!"

I felt an unexpected wave of sorrow. But why? I asked myself. It was my decision to publish the book, even over my brother Jimmy's strong protests. He feared that one day our parents would find the story, read it, and see how similar the story was to that of the life of their dead daughter. Especially with the name Shari Cooper on the spine. But I felt the book was too important to be left in a desk drawer. Besides, I needed another bestseller. *Remember Me* had been out only a month, but already it had sold over a million copies.

My sorrow had nothing to do with publishing or the number of copies sold, however. The story was, after all, the story of my life and death. It felt weird to sit and sign *Remember Me* like any other book. But my expression was kind as I bid Kattie farewell.

"I'm glad you enjoyed it," I said.

Most of the people who appeared told me they were my number-one fans. Where do you get your ideas? Is Shari Cooper a pen name? Are any of your characters based on real people? How much money do you make? Are you going to write a sequel to *Remember Me*? Now *that* was a disturbing question, for more reasons than one. I continued to smile and speak, but deep inside my skull my blood vessels began to twist into demonic shapes and spread a thick band of pain across my forehead and around my temples. Since returning to Earth, I had experienced bad headaches off and on—as of late, more on than off. The damage was from the time Jean Rodrigues, the girl whose body I now inhabit, had taken an unintentional plunge off Lenny Mandez's balcony. I know from Jean's memories that she never had headaches until that night, over three years ago. But exactly what the damage was I didn't know, nor did I care to subject my brain to a CAT scan or MRI to find out the particulars. I suspected the news would not be good.

"Peter," I asked, "could you please get me a glass of water?"

He studied me. "Do you have a headache?"

"No," I lied. "I'm just thirsty. I'm sure they have something in back to drink. Could you check, please?"

He nodded and pivoted his wheelchair away from the table. "I'll be back in a minute."

The moment he was gone, I reached inside my purse and grabbed a prescription bottle of Tylenol-3, a potent combination of codeine and Tylenol. Without letting my fans see, I popped two pills into my mouth and swallowed, wishing I had water. I had sent Peter away largely because I didn't want him to know how much pain I was in. He worried about me, and I didn't want that. Being paralyzed from the waist down, he had so many health problems, and I hated to show any weakness. Peter returned with a full glass of water, and I drank it down in a single gulp. The drugs took twenty minutes to take effect and I bore the time patiently.

We ran out of books to sign, leaving five hundred fans empty-handed. It could happen, I knew—I was not upset with the bookstore. As I left the mall, I went down what remained of the line and scribbled my signature on pieces of paper, on kids' clothes, even. Most seemed grateful just to be close to me. The codeine was percolating between my synapses and I felt good again. At the end of the line I was surprised to find my brother, Jimmy, and my best friend, Jo.

According to Jimmy, he and Jo were not together, but were just occasionally hanging out. According to Jo, they were having incredible sex three or four times a week. Honestly, I didn't know whom to believe, and frankly I didn't care. They were both doing well. Jimmy was still working for the phone company, and Jo had graduated from college as a drama major, which, education-wise, was more than I could say for myself. I had dropped out of college the day I sold my first book—*First to Die*. It was this story I was about to make into a movie, with me as executive producer. I had gotten Jo a role as one of the victims, or, should I say, she had earned the role. She was quite the actress.

"How did the signing go?" Jimmy asked, studying the crowd. "Or do I need to ask?"

"She was a smash," Peter said. "They ran out of books again."

I massaged my wrist. "It's a good thing they did. I was getting a cramp. And everyone kept asking me about Sam O'Connor."

"Who's Sam?" Jo asked.

"Her muse," Peter explained. "They all want to know where she gets her ideas. I think it's a fair question."

Jo tugged on Peter's ponytail. "*We* know you're her sole source of inspiration."

Peter looked up at her and grinned. "And who inspires *me?*"

Jo and Peter often flirted, which didn't bother me, except much of it was overtly sexual, and Jo knew Peter was physically incapable of having sex. Yet I never spoke against it. I tried never to mention sex at all around Peter. It was a sore spot for him and—what the hell, for me, too. Since entering my new body, I had not made love once—the life of the rich and famous. Jo stroked the side of Peter's face. She was petite, as short as she had been in high school, although her hair was now blond, not brown, courtesy of a professional bleach job.

"I do, of course," she said.

I cleared my throat and grabbed the back of Peter's wheelchair. "I have a movie meeting in thirty minutes. Which reminds me, Jo, aren't you supposed to be at rehearsal?"

"I thought I'd ride with you," she said.

I considered. "You could do that, but we might not be on the same timetable."

"I'll wait," Jo said.

"This is a serious rehearsal. I might have to wait for you."

Jo snorted. "The big executive producer can't hang around for her best friend?"

"I don't want either of you to be late," Peter said. "Remember, we want to see that yogi tonight. He's only in Los Angeles for a few days."

Jimmy nodded. "Shari told me about him. I want to see him, too. What time's his talk?"

"Eight o'clock," Peter said. "It's in Santa Monica, at the Unity Church."

"I don't know if we'll be done by then," I said.

Peter acted pained. "You're the boss. You can be done when you want. I really want to see him. I think this guy is genuine."

I smiled. "You haven't even met him. How can you have an opinion about him?"

Peter was thoughtful. "I don't know. There was something about his picture." Peter paused. "He reminded me of you-know-who."

Peter was referring to the Rishi. I had seen the yogi's picture, and although he had had beautiful eyes, and lovely long hair and a beard, there had been nothing in his face that struck me as cosmic.

"I'll try to make it," I said unenthusiastically.

"He's supposed to teach meditation and certain kinds of breathing," Peter said. "You remember how often the Rishi spoke about such techniques."

"This yogi looks nothing like the Rishi," I said.

"You can't judge a book by its cover," Peter said.

"Not even a Shari Cooper thriller," I agreed.

Jimmy stared at me. "Shari, can I talk to you a minute before you run off?"

Jo pretended to be insulted, although she wasn't. "Private matters? Subjects Peter and I are unworthy of hearing?"

"We'll just be a minute," Jimmy said. He led me away from the others, into a toy store. Many of my fans continued to linger in the area, waving and smiling at me when I glanced their way. My brother and I stood near a stack of Ouija boards and I was reminded of the night I died. Not many people can say that.

"What's up?" I asked.

"It's nothing serious. It's just that I don't see you much these days."

"Is that why you came to the mall today?"

"I didn't come to buy one of your competitors' books."

I shrugged. "I'm not avoiding you on purpose. It's just that I've been busy. You know *First to Die* is going to start shooting in a couple of days, and we still don't know if Universal's going to let us use their large pond for the shark scenes."

"I didn't know that. I hope it works out for you guys. But why don't you just concentrate on your writing? Let your producer do all the worrying. That's why you hired him."

My defenses went up. I hate being told what to do, especially by my big brother. "I enjoy the movie business. I want to learn as much as I can about it while I have the chance." I paused. "I want to become a director."

"And quit writing? Is that why you're here?"

By *here* he meant on Earth. "No. I'll always write. I just want to broaden my horizons. What's wrong with that?"

"Nothing," Jimmy said.

"Are you upset that I was signing *Remember Me* today?"

"No. I'm just concerned about you."

"The book is sold as Young Adult. Mom will never even hear of it."

Jimmy's face darkened. "Mom has already seen the book. Yesterday she mentioned it to me on the phone."

I was stunned. "How did that happen?"

Jimmy shrugged. "It says Shari Cooper on the spine. It's on the bestseller lists. How can you be surprised? You wanted this to happen, and you know it."

"That's not true," I lied. Well, sort of. I didn't know what I wanted. Still, I longed to visit my parents and tell them I was back and alive. Yet I knew Jimmy was right when he said they'd never accept the truth, only be tormented by it. Jimmy had opposed my using my original name on my books. He said it violated the Rishi's desire to have me serve as a role model for the Hispanic community. Maybe he was right, but I liked being called Shari. I lowered my head and added, "Maybe I should have changed more of the names in the story."

"It's done. Anyway, you're right, she'll probably never read it."

I shook my head. "If she's talking about it, she'll read it. She might come looking for me."

"You're not that easy to find. Listen, I'm serious when I say I think you're taking on too much. You don't look good, Shari."

I chuckled. "You're full of compliments today."

He studied me closer. "You took pills this afternoon."

"No. I've been signing books all day."

"You may fool Peter, but you don't fool me. You speak differently with codeine in your system. How bad is your head?"

"Seen from the outside, it seems pretty bad."

"Shari. You have to see a neurologist."

I shook my head. "If there was anything seriously wrong with me, it would have become apparent in the last three years."

"That's not true. Injuries to the head often take time to manifest. I've done reading on the subject. You may have something wrong that can easily be fixed."

"Yeah, right, easily fixed with brain surgery. No thanks. I trust in the Rishi. If he put me in this body, it must be strong enough to last me."

"Having the Rishi's blessing doesn't mean you're exempt from using common sense." Jimmy glanced around and sighed. "The others are waiting. We can talk about this later."

"There's always later," I agreed.

Jo accompanied Peter and me back to our apartment in

Venice, which was close to the beach. I sat in the middle. We were in Peter's van, which had been especially outfitted to allow him to drive using only his hands. The van had cost a bundle. Not that I minded. Last year I made over three million dollars, but had promptly given half of it to the government. For me I'd bought a red Jaguar, which sent up a flag for every cop on the Coast Highway. In the last six months I got four speeding tickets and was in danger of losing my license.

The rear of the van was stuffed with track and baseball equipment. Peter coached a Special Olympics team and also did volunteer work with several handicapped baseball teams. He didn't get paid for his work, so the only money he brought in was from his business of finding rare books for people. He ran it out of our spare room. How he managed to locate the books for people, I didn't know. But he did well and had a growing list of clients. The trouble was that his commission on his finds was usually low—five or ten dollars. It was more of a hobby than a business, really, but he seemed to get a kick out of it. I just hoped my books never reached his list of hard-to-finds.

"Shari told me the pitcher on your baseball team is blind," Jo said to Peter as we cruised toward the beach. Our apartment was in a nice area of Venice and had a wonderful view of the ocean. Still, I was thinking of buying a house in Malibu, where my producer, Henry Weathers, lived, but was worried about tying myself down. For some reason I felt I would be traveling soon.

Peter nodded. "His name's Jacob and he's seventeen. He's been blind since birth."

Jo frowned. "I can understand that he can throw the ball as hard as anybody, but how can he throw strikes? In fact, how does it get anywhere near the batter?"

"He orients himself by the catcher's voice. As Jacob winds up, the catcher talks the whole time." Peter added, "The catcher's deaf."

"And the batters are all retarded," I quipped.

"Yeah," Jo said with a chuckle. "Doesn't Jacob hit the batters half the time?"

Peter shook his head. "He hasn't hit anyone in the last six games. His strikeout percentage rivals that of big league ball players. He's a phenomenon."

"He's probably just nearsighted," I said.

"He has no eyes," Peter said softly.

Boy, did I feel stupid. I touched Peter's leg. He could not feel the gesture but at least he saw it. "I'm sorry," I said. "I'd like to see him pitch sometime."

"You can come to any of our games," Peter said, quietly reminding me that I had never showed up yet. I enjoyed playing sports, but sitting and watching them somehow made me feel like a failed cheerleader. Visions of an old high school acquaintance, Candy, came to mind. She had been deaf and virtually blind. On the "other side," during my review of my previous life, I saw how important Candy had been to me. The few times I helped her at school had brought me better karma than the four years I studied to get good grades.

"The first chance I have," I said, "I will go see Jacob."

CHAPTER II

WHEN MY FIRST Young Adult novel came out and jumped on the *New York Times* bestseller list—the first YA book ever to do so—I was approached by numerous studios who wanted to buy the rights to film the book. They came to me with names of movie stars and forty-million-dollar budgets. I was wined and dined and finally settled on a large studio that swore the book would be on the screen within nine months, a year at the outside. Of course, nothing happened with *First to Die,* or the books that followed. They were optioned, I was paid a nominal fee, and then the stories sank into development hell. Such a slow-moving hell—nothing ever happened there. Hollywood's a strange place. All the clichés about it are true: executives like to make deals. They like to "do" lunch. They do not like to make movies. Movies might bomb. They might get fired. Better to just option stuff, pretend they're going to make it. I got tired of the scene.

I met my producer, Henry Weathers, by chance. I was buying popcorn at a movie theater in Westwood near UCLA. Peter and I went to two or three movies a week—at least we did before I became an executive producer. Anyway, Henry was standing behind me and he made a joke about how slow the line was, comparing it to how long it had taken to get the movie we were about to see on the screen. As it turned out a friend of Henry's had produced the movie, and even though it turned out to be a turkey, I liked Henry. We got to talking. I told him who I was and the experiences I'd had rewriting scripts for executives who needed readers to translate the labels on their afternoon bottle of mineral water. Henry was sympathetic, but otherwise didn't say a whole lot. We exchanged numbers and I thought that would be the last I saw of him. Yet a month later—after he had researched me and read all my books—he called to say he knew some people who had ten million dollars and wanted to get into the movie business. Was I interested in making *First to Die* into a picture? "When do we start?" I asked.

"Right away," he said. "We just have to sell them on the idea."

I liked that answer.

That had been three months ago. We had sold the idea to the investors, and things were moving fast. We had a director and cast, and the cameras were ready to roll. Well, almost. Our director, although highly talented, was insane. He had a pregnant wife who did astrological charts, and a gay lover who painted billboards with food coloring and a broom. Our director talked to the cameras when he thought no one was looking. Our leading man was addicted to cocaine. Our villain had just gotten out of jail for hot-wiring a car and driving it off the end of the Santa Monica pier. And we had no place to put our sharks. Yes, we had rented a pool full of sharks. We needed them to eat a few of our characters. You can rent anything in Los Angeles if you know where to look. Henry did; he was an old-time Hollywood producer. He could make a few million look like a hundred million on the screen, and, as he was fond of saying, he knew a hit the moment it collected two hundred million. Henry had had his ups and downs over the years. I was supposed to be his last great up. He thought he could build a dynasty from my work.

Before Henry and I gave our presentation to the investors, he had me prepare a scene-by-scene summary of *First to Die.* God forbid the businesspeople who wanted to give us millions should actually have to read a book. I would have read the blasted thing before spending seven bucks to *see* the movie. Maybe I'm cheap. Anyway, this summary turned out to be the outline from which I had prepared a shooting script because I had to cut large portions of the three-hundred-page novel to fit a hundred-minute film. While heading to Henry's for my meeting and Jo's rehearsal, I asked Jo to drive so I could reread my initial summary to see if there was anything I could do to improve the story at this late stage.

FIRST TO DIE
BY
SHARI COOPER

The story opens on a sailboat twenty miles off the coast of Florida. A group of seven high school students has been invited by Bob, the class nerd, to enjoy a weekend of sailing around the Florida Keys. What these seven do not know is that Bob has planned this weekend for many months. He plans to take revenge on these popular kids because he has hated them for years.

In the first scene our hero, quiet and shy Daniel, and our heroine, sweet and pretty Kathy, are talking inside a cabin when a scream brings them running up onto the deck. It is head cheerleader Susie who has cried out. Bob is holding a gun to her head and is demanding to have a meeting.

"This boat is rigged to sink in a few minutes," Bob says. "There are two lifeboats on board. Both are equipped with small outboard motors. Both are tiny; they will hold only two people, three at most. If you put more people in them, they will sink. In two minutes I am going to head back to shore in one of the lifeboats. I am going alone. That will leave the seven of you to decide who is to live and who is to die. The lifeboat

I'm leaving is equipped with a compass and enough gasoline to reach shore. With any luck, whoever departs in it will make it safely back. The hull of this boat is rigged to blow in two places. The seven of you can choose to stay and try to plug these holes. That way, working together, maybe all of you will survive. But the odds will not be in your favor. Because you cannot survive in these waters for even a few minutes. For the last two hours, while you've all been gossiping and eating, we have been trailing slabs of beef in the water. The blood has attracted a large school of sharks." Bob pauses to smile, to gesture to the surrounding fins. "The beef has only whetted their appetites."

Hearing the setup, football quarterback Todd swears at Bob and rushes him. Calmly, Bob lets go of Susie and shoots Todd in the head. Todd's blood soaks the deck as he dies. Bob shoves the body into the water. While the others look on in horror, the sharks begin to feed.

"Now you only have to decide among the six of you who is to die," Bob says.

From below deck come two sharp explosions. Water begins to pour into the sailboat. Taking his time, Bob climbs into one of the lifeboats. Smirking, he roars off toward the shore.

Now the tension escalates.

Susie wants to leave in the remaining lifeboat immediately. Because she is head cheerleader, and homecoming queen to boot, she feels she automatically deserves a place. The others do not agree with her, particularly class valedictorian Randy. It is his belief that the three guys—Carl is the third male—should go in the lifeboat. They are stronger and the girls—pleasant Mary is the final character—won't be able to stop them from taking it. Carl doesn't agree with this. He is captain of the basketball team and Susie is his girlfriend. While the water gushes in and the boat begins to wobble, Randy and Carl get in a fight. Good guy Daniel has to scream to shut them up.

"Let's at least try to plug up the holes," Daniel says. "A boat this size will take a few minutes to sink. Maybe if we work together we *can* stop the water."

They head below as a group, but they are not a cohesive group. They do not trust one another. They cannot concentrate on fixing the holes because they are concentrating solely on each other. It is only now they appreciate the cold cruelty of Bob's revenge upon them. In a sense, Bob is asking them to destroy one another.

As the water rises to the deck, the opportunity to fix the holes passes and Susie and Randy bolt for the raft. They are in it and ready to push off through the surrounding fins when Carl jumps in with them. Ironically, he accidentally knocks his girlfriend into the water. Susie's screams rend the air as the sharks tear her to pieces. Horrified, Carl blames Randy for her death, and the two get into a shoving match. In the end, of course, they both end up falling into the water and get eaten alive.

Now there are only three left: Daniel, Kathy, and Mary. They shove off in the lifeboat just as the mother sailboat goes under, but they do not head straight for shore. Something is bothering Daniel.

"Bob has planned this so carefully," he says, "that he must know if even one of us survives, he will go to jail for the rest of his life. There must be another level to his revenge. He emphasized how we have a compass, plenty of gasoline. But I'm certain if we head straight for shore we won't make it. He'll be waiting for us somewhere between here and there, and he has a gun."

Daniel convinces the others that Bob must be just out of sight, watching them through binoculars to see what they're going to do. Daniel advises them to head *away* from shore. The girls immediately consent because what Daniel says makes sense. But Daniel knows the change in course will not solve their problems. When Bob sees what they're doing, he'll come after them. For that reason, once they are clear of the school of sharks, Daniel has them cut speed while he hangs out of sight over the side of the lifeboat, in the water. Even though Bob must be watching them through binoculars, it will be hard for him to tell how many of them left the boat in the raft. It is Daniel's intention to swim under *both* rafts when Bob appears and attack him from behind. It is their only hope, he says.

Daniel has analyzed the situation well. The girls are hardly a mile from the sunken sailboat when Bob roars into sight. He has the more powerful motor; he catches up to them quickly. While he toys with their minds, pointing his gun at their heads and quizzing them about how the others died, Daniel swims under the rafts. At the last second Bob guesses Daniel's plan and spins around, catching Daniel in the sights of his gun. To save her new love, and her own life, Kathy dives across the space that separates the two rafts. A struggle ensues and Kathy is shot in the shoulder. She sags over the side of Bob's lifeboat and her blood drips into the water. Daniel does manage to climb back on board but is held at bay by Bob's gun. Daniel can only watch as Bob tries to shove the wounded Kathy into the water. But Bob makes the mistake of placing his own arm too close to Kathy's dripping blood, too close to the water. A shark rises from below and grabs hold of Bob's arm. Screaming, Bob begs Daniel to save him. Daniel, however, is not in the mood and he allows the shark to drag him under.

The evil villain reaps his just reward by becoming fish food.

The others head back to shore, Kathy recovering in boyfriend's arms.

"I like it," I said to Jo when I finished rereading the summary. "But I don't love it."

Jo waved away my comment. "You're too close to it. You've been over the story too many times. It's great."

"It seems too simple to me."

"Most successful thrillers are. That's why they work. There's motive. There's a crime. The hero catches the bad guy. Everybody is happy." Jo glanced over at me. "You're not thinking of writing out my part, are you?"

Jo was to play Susie, the pain-in-the-ass cheerleader. Jo could look as young as a high school kid. Most of the cast were about twenty-one. I sat back and frowned.

"I often think I should be making another of my books into a movie," I said. "One of the spiritual ones."

"You can do that next. After you make twenty million on this one."

After splitting up the shares with the investors and Henry and our crazy director, I still owned a third of the film. If the movie did modestly well, I *would* make twenty million, what with domestic and DVD and foreign rights. I had already considered what Jo was saying. Make what would sell before making what I wanted. *First to Die* was a huge bestseller. More people associated it with my name than any other book. Yet the reasoning didn't satisfy me. I wanted to work on what was important to me *now*. Actually, I wanted to make *Remember Me* into a movie. I suggested that to Jo. She almost drove off the road.

"You will never make that book into a movie," Jo said. "It's too esoteric. It has a sad ending. You die."

"I die at the beginning."

"Yeah. But you're still dead at the end. And you couldn't put in that part about how you came back. No one would believe it."

I laughed. "You believed it. You believe I'm here."

"Only because you are here," Jo said. "And because I'm crazy. Look, Shari, don't rock the boat on *First to Die*—no pun intended. Make the movie and make tons of money. Sell out—it's the American way. Then save the world. You'll have plenty of time—and cash—to do it."

"I guess you're right," I muttered.

"How are you and Peter getting along?" Jo asked.

"All right."

"Just all right? The two soulmates are not in constant ecstasy?"

"We're close. We're just not soulmates. Actually, I don't believe there are such things. The Rishi said it was a distorted concept. It comes from searching outside yourself for completeness." I paused. "How are you and Jimmy getting along?"

Jo smiled slyly. "Jim and I are fine."

"You never hold hands in public."

"We make up for it in private."

"Are you really screwing my brother?" I asked.

Jo acted shocked. "We are getting personal, aren't we?"

"You openly brag about the great sex you two have."

"Then you have no need to ask. Just believe."

"I don't believe you," I growled.

Jo saw it was time to change the subject. "How's Carol doing?"

Carol Dazmin, Jean Rodrigues's best friend—and now my

buddy as well—was not doing well. For the last two years she had fought heroin addiction. She would clean up her act, but then meet some crazy guy or girl and start shooting up again. Recently she had gotten off the junk only to end up in the hospital with hepatitis—the serious kind. Her liver was inflamed and she was the color of a spoiled lemon. The doctors thought she could live but would die for sure if she went back on drugs. Her addiction caused me a lot of pain. I had returned to Earth in Jean Rodrigues's body to try to help people, and I couldn't even help someone close to me. I told Jo what was happening and she was sympathetic.

"It's that neighborhood she lives in," Jo said. "It's crawling with drugs."

"It's not the neighborhood. It's Carol. Besides, I told her she could come live with me if she wanted. She doesn't want to. She'd rather get high." I sighed. "I have nothing genuine to offer people. Just stories."

"Your stories inspire people."

"Inspiration goes only so far."

Jo was concerned. "What's bothering you, Shari?"

My headache had returned.

"Something," I whispered thoughtfully. "I'll know it when it comes to me."

But I was wrong.

CHAPTER III

HENRY WEATHERS'S HOUSE was a castle built as a symbol of the good life. High on a hill above the sprawling town of Malibu, it commanded north and south views of the coast that stretched forever on clear days. There was a marble fountain out front, a pool in the back large enough to double as a small lake. Yet he had bought the place for a modest sum thirty years earlier from an actor who had gone from being number one at the box office to appearing as a host on game shows. Henry was good and frugal with money, a quality you want in a producer. We didn't plan to spend all ten million the investors had given us on *First to Die*, but decided to split it between two films. For that reason, how we used every penny counted.

Henry met Jo and me at the door. He was a short man with a six-course belly. Eating was one of his great pleasures in life—he loved hamburgers in particular, by the half dozen. Sixty-five years old, he softened his wrinkles with special effects makeup and dyed his hair the color of motor oil—then had the nerve to say it was his natural color. The thing that had struck me most about Henry when we first met was the twinkle in his eye, his goodness. He loved the movie business, even when it didn't always love him. He seemed to have a special affection for me. He had a daughter my age, Rico. She wanted to be in our movie, but her father said no, she was too plain for the part she wanted. Henry could be objective, when necessary, and that was another quality that I liked about him.

"Good news," he said as we went through the doorway. "We have a place to dump our sharks and tie our boat."

"Universal's going to let us use their pool?" I asked, relieved.

"Not unless we pay them a fortune." I started to freak out and he raised his hand to silence me. "It doesn't matter. I found a place out in the valley where we can dig our own pond."

"But that'll cost a fortune," I complained.

"It will cost us a quarter of a million when you include the backdrops and the support for the boat set. I know that's a lot of money but we'll have more freedom on our own set. We can shoot the hours we want."

"How long will it take to dig?"

"A day. It's just a huge hole in the ground. I have three bull-dozers heading out to the spot tomorrow. We'll dye the water green-blue—it'll look like the Caribbean. And the backdrops can be painted by Andy's boyfriend or be computer-generated."

Andy was our insane director. "This is a huge change of plan," I said. "It makes me nervous."

"Welcome to the movie business," Henry said. "Shari, trust me on this."

"All right, but I want to go out to the spot tomorrow."

"I'll go with you. Now we have something else to discuss." He glanced at Jo. She took the hint.

"I'll go wait by the pool," she said quickly.

When she was gone, Henry continued. "I think I've found a replacement for Darren."

Darren was our cocaine-snorting star. Personally I couldn't stand the guy but he was talented, and I didn't want to make such an important casting change so late. I told Henry as much.

"You're going to give me a heart attack," I said. "At least with Darren we know what we've got. Let's keep him."

Henry got up on his toes, which he did when his sense of dignity had been offended. "Darren knows we're going to start shooting in two days and he's using the situation to demand three times the salary we agreed on or he says he'll walk. Also, he wants half of it in advance—this evening. I told him that's just not done and he laughed in my face. He thinks he has us over a barrel. But no one talks to me like that—I don't care how talented he is."

"Who's the new guy?" I asked wearily, knowing Darren probably wanted the money for drugs. The five million we were spending on the film didn't belong to me, but I felt like it did, and I refused to squander any of my investors' funds.

Henry brightened. "His name's Roger Teller. An agent at CAA sent him over this morning after Darren issued me his ultimatum. This kid—I can't tell you how good he is. Andy loves him as well. He says he's better than Darren. Honestly, it was as if Roger was born to play Daniel. He's in the backyard. Do you want to hear him read?"

"Right now?"

"Yes. We have to decide in the next hour, one way or the other."

"OK, let me see him. How old is he?"

"Your age—twenty-one."

I made a face. "And he's a kid?"

Henry patted me on the shoulder. "You're all babes in the woods next to me. I'll bring him into my study. He can read for you there."

"Alone?"

"Yes. He won't bite you."

"OK."

Henry's study was piled full of screenplays rather than books. Henry had taught me a lot about the art of screenplay writing. It was easier than novel writing yet it made demands that were unique to the form. The main one was the limitation of space. Every word had to count, whereas in a novel I could go on about whatever happened to suit my fancy. Another thing about writing scripts I found maddening was that—with only dialogue to work with—I was unable to give my story a tone. *First to Die* was a straightforward thriller; however, in book form, I had managed to give it a haunted feeling, which was probably why it had become so popular. Now I had to rely on Andy to capture that same feeling. Andy, who was known to sleep with his film before he shot it—just to warm it up.

Roger Teller came into the study.

He was a babe. No question about it. Wow.

No problem. He can have the job.

I should never have been put in charge of casting.

"Are you Ms. Cooper?" he asked.

"Shari, please. Yes." I stood to shake his hand. "Come in. Have a seat."

"Thank you."

He plopped down opposite me on a wine-colored love seat. I sat cross-legged in an overstuffed chair. His face was perfection, molded in paradox. He appeared both strong and vulnerable. His eyes were large, dark; his intelligence shimmered behind them like reflections of the moon at night. He was broad shouldered but thin; his large hands reminded me of Peter's—before Peter died, the first time. When he was tall and blond. Roger didn't look like he would ever die. He had the handsomeness of eternal youth; the world would give him only good things, and take nothing away. In another age he would have been considered royalty. His expensive slacks were soft gray flannel, his dress shirt white. He wore a gold watch.

"Henry tells me you're a great actor," I said. When he didn't respond, I added, "What do you think?"

"I went to your signing this afternoon," he replied. "I watched as those teenagers told you what a great writer you were. I noticed you didn't know what to say to them."

"I didn't see you there."

He smiled faintly. "I hid in the shadows."

"Why did you come to the signing?"

"To see you. I read your books before auditioning for this part." He paused. "You're quite the writer."

"Thank you. What do you think of the Daniel part in *First to Die*?"

Roger shrugged. "He's a strong character. But I think I would play him slightly differently from how you wrote him."

A bold comment, from someone trying to get a part. "How so?"

"I would have him talk less."

"I'm curious how you'd do that. When there's a line in the script that belongs to him, what are you going to do? Remain silent?"

He shrugged. "I think more can be done with looks than words in some places. I may only be talking about four or five lines altogether."

His boldness continued to amaze me. Most actors pant

in front of someone who can give them a job. And here this guy was indirectly insulting my writing by telling me he could improve upon it.

"Hmm," I muttered.

My reaction amused him. "Of course, if you give me the role, I'll only be an employee. I can only make suggestions."

"I don't have final say on whether you get the role or not."

"Yes, you do, Shari. It's your movie."

Now he was calling me a liar, but subtly. He was subtle about everything—the way he was checking out my body, my face. I don't know why I liked him, besides his good looks, although they helped. Oh yes. And those deep, dark eyes.

"You have read *Remember Me?*" I said.

"Yes."

"What did you think of it?"

He met my gaze and held it. "It reads like a true story."

"Maybe it is a true story. Maybe a ghost told it to me."

"Are you thinking of making it into a movie?"

"Yes. But we need a larger budget than five million. It will require lots of special effects."

"For the death scenes?"

"Yes, and some of the other scenes as well."

"It sounds huge." He paused. "Do you want me to read for you for this movie?"

"Yes, please. Can I get you a copy of the script?"

"If you think it's necessary. I memorized the section where Daniel explains how Bob must be waiting somewhere between the sunken sailboat and the shore to kill them."

I nodded. "That's a crucial scene. Pretend I'm Kathy."

"It might help if you sat beside me. We can pretend we're alone in the lifeboat together."

I stood. "They're not alone. Mary is with them. Or is that one of those small changes you'd like to make? Eliminate Mary's character?"

"I would keep her. I would just kill her off."

I sat beside him. The love seat was old, cramped. Our legs touched. "How would you kill her?" I asked. "Feed her to the sharks?"

"No. Enough of them die that way. I'd have her die another way."

"Tell me?"

He shook his head. "I don't know. You're the writer. But there are a lot of ways to die—in the movies."

"Why kill her? Haven't enough people died by that point?"

"I think it's important that the hero and heroine are alone when they confront Bob at the end."

"Why?"

"It would heighten the tension."

"It won't work. You forget, Daniel is not even in the lifeboat. He is hanging on to the side. For his plan to have even a chance of working, there must be at least two of them in the lifeboat when Bob arrives. Otherwise, there is no explanation for why only one of them is in the lifeboat."

Roger seemed taken aback by my explanation, and I knew he couldn't argue with my logic. He acted impressed. "You understand structure very well."

"Thank you." I checked my watch. "I have to go to a lecture tonight. Let's do the scene now, please."

Roger suddenly sat up. And just like that, he slipped into Daniel's character. He required no transition period. He was like liquid mercury when it came to playing the silver star. He reached over and took my hand—Kathy's hand—in the lifeboat. The expression in his eyes changed from calm confidence to deadly seriousness.

"We cannot go back. If we do, he'll kill us. If we stay here, he'll kill us. All along he's intended for us to die. This whole scheme of who will be the first to die, and who will be left alive is just that—a scheme. Don't ask me why, but he hates us. Besides that he can't let any of us live and get away with what he's done."

"Then we're doomed," I said, mouthing Kathy's line from memory. His intensity was startling in its suddenness and effectiveness. I was mesmerized by his words, feeling as if I were indeed Kathy, trapped far out at sea with circling sharks and a madman in the area. Roger squeezed my hand.

"No," he said. "I have a plan. We have to head away from the coast. He'll come after us, I know he will. But we'll be ready for him. I'll hang outside the lifeboat. He won't see me. Then I'll swim under both boats and sneak up on him from behind."

I winced, or rather, Kathy did. "You'll die."

He smiled faintly. "I may die. But not today." He leaned over and—wow, the nerve—he kissed me on the lips! "Not with you here."

I sat back, stunned. "Jesus." The word was not in the script.

He laughed. "Does that mean I have the part?"

My blood was pounding. I had to assume he could make the blood in the veins of the girls in theaters do likewise. Yet his act had been presumptuous.

"I didn't give you permission to kiss me," I said firmly.

"I didn't kiss you. I kissed Kathy." He added, "It was in the script."

"Don't do it again."

He shrugged. "Not without your permission."

Discreetly wiping my mouth, I slowly nodded.

"All right, I forgive you." I hesitated for a moment. "You've got the part."

Henry and I enjoyed telling Darren to take a hike. At first the guy thought we were kidding, then he flew into a rage, saying we would be hearing from his agent and lawyer. He spat in the pool and stormed out of the backyard, where the others were rehearsing. Jo applauded his exit. She had been wanting to feed him to the sharks since she'd met him.

A few minutes later I wanted to do something painful to Bob, the actor who, ironically, was playing the nerdy villain Bob. The guy was much as I had written him: arrogant, overweight, rude. Actor Bob didn't have to stretch for the role—he'd been rehearsing for the part for twenty years. His face was pockmarked with acne, his greasy red hair a warning flag for dandruff. He was big—six-two, two hundred and fifty pounds easily. Had Henry found me a replacement for him, I would have fired him on the spot. But there were not too many Bobs in the world. To top it off, he wasn't chomping at the bit for the part. His parents were filthy rich. He had only taken up acting for the hell of it, and he could say "to hell with you" and split whenever he wished. Ironically, he was talented, more so perhaps than even he realized. His arrogance was all superficial, I believed. He struck me as being insecure inside.

We got into it beside the pool. Henry was barbecuing chicken and hamburgers to feed the hungry actors, and, as usual, Bob was stuffing his face. That didn't bother me—I can eat like a pig when I want. But he was drinking beer as well, belching loudly, and throwing the empties onto the lawn. Slobs piss me off; I don't know what it is.

"Hey," I said, pointing to the can he had just let fly onto the grass. "This isn't your house. Pick that up and put it in the garbage."

He gave me one of his dangerous looks. It would probably

work well on the screen, but not on me. "Are you the new director?" he asked.

I stood up. "You don't need a director. You need a nanny. What zoo did you grow up in anyway?"

"You're great with those one-liners, aren't you?" As he got up, I noticed he was a little drunk. "I don't need your abuse."

I tried to be patient. "I just want you to learn some manners. We're going to be working together every day for the next six weeks."

"You're going to be here all the time, huh? What for? To beautify the set?"

My patience ran out. "You idiot! Don't you realize you're getting the break of a lifetime being in my movie!"

Bob laughed. "Your movie! It isn't your movie. It's the director's movie. Besides, it's going to flop. The story sucks."

That really got me. I mean, I knew *First to Die* wasn't a masterpiece. I had told Jo as much on the way over. It was all right for me to criticize my story, but it wasn't OK for a guy who might get famous off my name to criticize it. If I'd wandered back to Earth in a male body, I would have smacked him right then. Instead, I did what I thought was the next best thing. I threw the Cherry Coke in my hand in his face. Bob's face turned cherry red, and I thought he was going to belt me. But *he* did the next best thing, from his perspective.

He shoved me, his executive producer, in the pool.

Actors.

I landed with a big splash. The slap of water hurt my already sensitive head and my right leg, which had once taken a bullet fired by a friend who couldn't remember who he was. Bursting to the surface, I heard the laughter of the others and stabbed my arm in Bob's direction.

"You're fired!" I yelled. "Get the hell out of here!"

Henry ran to the side of the pool. Even in his vast experience, I'm sure, he had never fired his two lead actors in the space of thirty minutes. He stretched out an arm to fish me out. Bob remained where he was, a smug look on his face.

"Shari," Henry said. "You should be an actor, not a producer."

"Get me out of here," I grumbled.

Henry pulled me onto the deck. Even standing soaking wet, I was still burning.

"I'm serious," I said. "I want him out of here." I pointed a finger at Bob. "Now!"

Bob was unimpressed. "Am I fired, Mr. Weathers?" he asked.

Henry hesitated. "No."

"Yes!" I screamed. "He pushed me in the pool. No one pushes me into a pool."

"I pushed you in the pool once," Jo remarked.

"Shut up!" I said. "I refuse to work with a pig who doesn't know an outhouse from a barn."

"Huh?" Jo said.

"Please," Henry said. "Let's talk this out. We start shooting in two days."

"Excuse me," Roger Teller said, stepping between us. "I think Shari's right. I think your callous act deserves retribution."

Bob was annoyed. "What are you talking about? Say it in English."

"All right," Roger said calmly. He turned and slugged Bob in the face. Roger was stronger than he looked. He just about took Bob's head off. Bob didn't fall in the pool but on the beer can that had started the whole mess. He flattened that piece of aluminum bad. He sat up dizzily, blood dripping from his nose, his eyes unfocused. Roger went and stood over him. "Apologize to Shari," he said.

Bob glanced up, and his eyes quickly came back into focus. Roger's expression was still calm but also strangely cold. Bob had to wonder, I knew, what Roger would do if he refused his order.

"I apologize, Shari," Bob said.

"That's all right," I muttered. Despite my momentary desire to hit Bob, the sight of blood sickened me. My books were occasionally violent, but I couldn't stand real violence. From experience, I knew too well how far it could go. I went over and helped Bob to his feet, brushing him off. "Do you still want to be in my movie?" I asked.

He wiped the blood off his face. "Your movie, huh?" he said.

I nodded. "I am your boss."

He cast Roger a wary glance. "Only if we get to change the ending," he mumbled.

Roger held his eye. "I like the ending as it is, Bob." He stepped past him and offered me his arm. I took it without thinking. "Let me take you home, Boss," he said.

He *was* awfully cute. "All right," I said.

CHAPTER IV

WE DIDN'T HAVE TO GO to my place. Henry's daughter, Rico, was about my size so I was able to change out of my wet clothes right at Henry's. Roger and I split after that, however, in his car. I left my Jaguar for Jo. It was only when we were on the road that I remembered the lecture I was supposed to go to with Peter and my brother. Sitting beside Roger in his luxurious black Corvette, the thought of a talk by a yogi from India sounded boring. The other reason I didn't want to go to my apartment was that Peter would be waiting for me there. How would I explain Roger?

He just hit someone for me. It turned me on.

Yeah, the violence made me sick, but I had to admit the guy did intrigue me.

Roger looked over at me and smiled. His teeth were white as ivory.

"What do you want to do?" he asked.

"Did you eat at Henry's?"

"No. Are you hungry?"

"Sort of."

"Do you like seafood?"

"Love it," I said.

We went to a place by the water in Pacific Palisades, at the end of Sunset Boulevard. The sun had recently set; the western sky was the color of candle flames. The candle on our table shone in Roger's eyes as he sat across from me and ordered a bottle of wine.

"Do you drink?" he asked.

"Seldom." I always felt the Rishi wanted me sober during my stay on Earth. "But I'll have one glass."

"Or two," he remarked. "I know this place. Let me order for you."

"OK."

We had lobster, burnt fiery red, and it was delicious. I ended up having three glasses of wine, toasting things I later couldn't remember. Then we went for a walk along the beach. The day had been warm but a chilly breeze came up as we listened to the sand crunch under our shoes. At some point Roger took my hand and I let him because it seemed so natural. I mean, it wasn't as if he tried to kiss me again. The wine had me feeling as if I were floating two feet above my body.

"Do you have a boyfriend?" he asked.

I hesitated. "I live with a dear friend." I added, "He's paralyzed."

Roger nodded. "I saw him at the signing."

"That's right, you were there." I paused. "I still don't understand why you came."

"I told you, to see you."

"Because you were auditioning for the part in the film?"

"Partly. But I've followed your career from afar."

"Really?" He seemed a little old to be reading Young Adult books. I reminded myself that as much as a quarter of my audience was adult.

"I've been reading you since *Magic Fire* came out," he said.

Magic Fire was one of my more esoteric works. It dealt with interdimensional travel. Realities constructed out of words on the paper. Demons who appeared as angels. Gods who were terribly flawed. Humans born without souls.

"What did you like about it?" I asked.

He thought for a moment. "It was not the kind of story I'd say I liked. But it stimulated me. I think that's more important than simply enjoying something. Do you know what I mean?"

"Yes." *Magic Fire* was a dark work. I hadn't enjoyed writing it, but felt compelled to do so. It was often that way with my books. "Do you think I should try to make it into a movie?"

"No. It wouldn't work."

I was curious. "Why not?"

"It's too abstract. People wouldn't understand it."

"You sound like Jo. She said that about *Remember Me*."

"Jo is your friend—the one who plays Susie?" he asked.

"Yes."

"How did you meet her?"

"We went to high school together," I said.

"Interesting. I would have thought you came from opposite sides of town."

His comment was perceptive. Especially since being in Jean's body the last three years, I had begun to talk the way I used to as Shari Cooper. For example, I almost never spoke Spanish anymore, except when I was around Jean's mom, whom, regrettably, I never saw often enough.

"Tell me about yourself," I said. "Where are you from?"

"Chicago. Have you heard of it?"

I chuckled. "Yeah. It's located somewhere between New York and L.A. Is that where you learned to fight like that?"

He was silent for a long moment. "No. I learned that somewhere else."

I had hit a sensitive spot. "What brought you out here?"

"I want to be a star."

"You didn't act like that during the audition. You criticized my writing."

"I noticed you didn't like that."

"Hey, I worked my butt off on that script. If you don't like it, too bad. You say what I wrote and that's that." I added, "Henry loves the script."

"He's a decent man. I like Bob as well."

"Are you serious? The guy's an animal."

"But he's true to what he is. I think we'll get along."

"If he doesn't try to drown you first," I said.

"I can handle him. Tell me more about your friend who's crippled."

"Peter?" I felt guilty talking about Peter. I hoped he didn't wait for me before going to the lecture. "He's an incredible person. He's my personal editor. I bounce all my story ideas off him. Without his help, I wouldn't be nearly as successful."

"Do you support him?"

"Ah—sort of."

"Where did you meet him? At school?"

"Yes."

"Do you love him?"

His question caught me off guard. "Of course I love him." I let go of Roger's hand and took a deep breath. "Why do you ask?"

Roger smiled at me in that cool calm manner he had. "Just checking."

We went to a movie. An action flick with plenty of blood and special effects, and a budget probably ten times ours. The story line was dreadful, as usual, but I had fun anyway. Then, even though I was tired, Roger dragged me to a club and we danced for two hours to music so loud I couldn't hear myself talk when we finally left. My headache was back, and although

I was longing for my pills I was afraid to take them because of the alcohol I'd drunk. While at the club, I'd had another couple of drinks.

It was two in the morning when Roger took me back to my apartment.

The light in my window was still on.

Peter was up. Waiting.

Roger followed my gaze as I checked out the scene.

"Are you in trouble?" he asked.

"No," I said. "I'm a big girl. I go where I want."

He ran his hands through his thick dark hair, looking very handsome in the dim light. The inside of his car smelled of leather, money. Despite having questioned him several times about his background, I still didn't know much about him. Like where he got his money. If he had a day job. Yet I found his secretive nature tantalizing. He didn't have to say a lot to communicate. Briefly I wondered if he was right, if he could play Daniel with fewer lines. Sometimes less was more. I wished I had more time to spend with him that night, and less guilt to hide. This close to Peter, I didn't feel so single.

"How paralyzed is he?" Roger asked as if reading my mind.

"He has complete use of his arms and hands. But from the waist down he has no feeling."

"Can he control his bowels?"

I swallowed. "Yes. But I think these questions are getting a bit personal. Don't you, Roger?"

He leaned closer and draped his arm on the top of my seat. "You don't want me to get personal?"

"Not about Peter. It's not appropriate."

"What about you?" he asked.

"What about me?"

"Isn't that the question of the night?"

Before I could respond, he kissed me again. Hard on the lips. He wasn't kissing Kathy this time, and there were no sharks in the vicinity. Yet, as I sunk unresisting into his embrace, I felt as if I could drown. It was not an unpleasant sensation. Actually, it was kind of euphoric. I had known from the moment I saw him that he would be a great kisser. Almost as if I knew him from somewhere else, another time and place. Yet, for my tastes, too much of the thrill of being intimate with him came because it was forbidden. When he reached out toward my left breast, I pulled back.

"No," I said, catching his eye.

His expression was eager. "What's wrong?"

I opened the car door. "I have to go. Goodnight, Roger."

"I'll see you tomorrow, Shari Cooper," he called after me.

There was no transition for me. One minute I was in Roger's arms and the next I was in the apartment with Peter. He was sitting on the couch in his underwear in the corner of our living room beneath a tall lamp, reading a book. He glanced up as I entered and didn't seem to be upset with me.

God. What if he'd been looking out the window?

"Long meeting?" he asked sympathetically.

"Yes." I was close to tears. "Give me a second, I have to go to the bathroom."

In the washroom I splashed cold water on my face and quickly brushed my teeth to get rid of the alcohol on my breath. The person in the mirror—I hardly recognized her. I no longer understood what she wanted. My head throbbed. I could see the pulse of a large vein on my right temple. Still, I did not reach for my pills, because I had too much alcohol in my blood. I didn't want to wake up dead. Not again.

"You didn't have to wait up for me," I said as I went back into the living room. Peter needed his sleep, nine or ten hours a night. He tired easily; often he had to take naps during the day. Yet at the moment he appeared radiant and I didn't understand why.

"I wanted to wait up," he said, excited. "I wanted to tell you about this man."

I pushed his wheelchair aside and plopped down on the sofa beside him. "The yogi? You went to his lecture?"

"Yes. Shari, you've got to see this guy. He's incredible. I think it's him."

"Who?"

"The Rishi."

I smiled. "Peter, the Rishi is not on Earth now. It can't be him."

"We don't know that for sure. Besides, it doesn't specifically have to be him to be him. You know what I mean. The Rishi is a Master. This man is a Master. They're both one with God. He gives off the same feeling as the Rishi. He's . . ." Peter paused, at a loss for words. "I've never met anyone so at peace with himself and the world."

"Did he teach you to meditate?"

"No. But he's going to. I'm going to take his course. It's this weekend."

"What does it cost?"

"Two hundred dollars."

I snorted. "If he's so spiritual, why does he charge?"

"His organization is nonprofit. They have to charge some fee in order to support their movement. I think two hundred dollars is reasonable."

"Where does the money go?"

"I don't know. I didn't ask. Shari, I'm talking about something important. Why are you talking about money?"

I rubbed my head. "I'm just tired. Did Jimmy go to the lecture?"

"Yes. He's taking the course with me. He's really excited."

I closed my eyes and slumped back. "That's nice."

Peter put his hand on my arm. "What's wrong with you?"

"Nothing."

"Where did you get these clothes?"

I yawned. "Bob pushed me in the pool. They're Henry's daughter's clothes."

"Why did Bob push you in the pool?"

"Because he's a bastard." I opened my eyes and patted Peter's arm. "I'm glad you liked the yogi. I'm sorry I couldn't be there to see him."

"You can see him tomorrow night. He's going to give another lecture."

"I'm busy tomorrow."

"That doesn't matter. You have to come. He won't be in L.A. long."

"We'll see," I muttered.

Peter shook his head. "Shari, he's what we've been looking for. He's why we came back."

I chuckled. "You can't say that. You just met him. He hasn't even taught you anything yet. You don't even know if his meditation techniques will work."

Peter was thoughtful. "It's not what he says that's important. It's the love he radiates. Already, I think, he's taught me a great deal."

I stood. "Let's talk about it in the morning. I have to go to bed now or I'm going to fall on the floor. Are you coming?"

Peter nodded, and quickly lifted himself into his wheelchair. "You'll understand when you meet him. Everything will make sense."

I shook my head doubtfully. "Not much makes sense these days."

CHAPTER V

I WOKE UP outside my body. Standing and looking down to where Peter and I slept. The room was dark but I could see. Not for a moment did I think I was dead, although my disorientation was similar to when I woke up back home in my bed after Amanda had shoved me off the balcony. There was *stuff* in the air now, the same stuff that I had wandered through for days when I was first on the other side of the grave. It was everywhere, translucent, vaguely gaseous, and flowing around the room, around the furniture, through the walls. It blurred my vision but not too badly. I could see my body breathing, hear myself snoring softly, Peter stirred as I stepped closer to the bed. He rolled over and wrapped his arm around me as I slept. Being crippled, he didn't usually move much during the night. He was nice and warm to sleep beside.

There was a reason I was outside my body, I realized.

I was to learn something. What, I didn't know.

I sat on the bed and reached out to touch Peter, to stroke his head. But soon after I touched him, I was gone. Touching a sleeping person while traveling out of body usually drags one into the sleeping person's dreams. I fell fast but not very far.

On the *inside*, a slight Indian man was sitting cross-legged on a sheet-draped chair. There were bunches of flowers around him and a candle flickered on his right side. He sat with his eyes closed and Peter sat at his feet, his eyes also shut. With his long black hair and beard, the man looked nothing like the Rishi, but Peter was right—there was an aura of peace around him so strong it was like being wrapped in an angel's embrace. As I moved closer, the man opened his eyes and gazed at me. A soft smile touched his lips, and he bid me sit beside him, also at his feet. A red rose lay on his lap, and he picked it up and gave it to me.

"Shari," he said. "You are here."

I accepted the flower, the fragrance strong in my nose. Never before had I smelled anything in a dream and I wondered if other people did. The feeling of love emanating from the man was almost overwhelming. Something in my chest loosened, and I found myself growing emotional.

"Where is here?" I asked.

"It's a place to meet. The place is not important. What is important is that you came to see me."

"But I didn't go to see you. I didn't go to the lecture."

"Why not?"

"I'm too caught up in what I have to do. And I want so many things."

"What do you want?"

"I don't know. Recognition. Love. Sex. I'm a young woman. I feel I should have everything that other women have." I lowered my head. "I feel so ashamed."

"Why?"

I glanced at Peter. "Can he hear us?"

"This is a private meeting."

I continued to stare at Peter. "I've betrayed him. And I'm going to betray him again. I know it."

"You don't betray him. If you know something is wrong, and you do it anyway, you betray yourself." The yogi paused. "Peter is doing fine. Don't worry for him."

"Who are you? Are you the Rishi?"

"Who are you? Are you Shari Cooper? Or are you Jean Rodrigues?"

I nodded. I wasn't these people, these personalities. I was the infinite soul, but I had forgotten that. He was saying he was the same soul as the Rishi, that we were all the same. Yet the realization brought me no peace. I lowered my head again.

"I can understand these things when I'm with you here. But I know I will forget them when I return to my body."

The yogi nodded. "It is true we have met here many times

lately. But each time you remember a little more. Don't worry—the time of decision comes soon."

I raised my head and took his hand. He did not seem to mind. His touch was gentle. "Will I decide wisely?" I asked.

He picked out another rose from a nearby vase and tapped me lightly on the head with the petals. Then he chuckled. "I hope so."

The comment did not reassure me. "Do I have a problem with my head? I feel sometimes like there's something inside me—" I couldn't continue.

"Are you afraid that it could kill you?"

I nodded, feeling a wet drop run down my cheek. Another first. Dream tears. "Is it true?" I asked.

He was thoughtful. "Come see me soon. We will see what can be done."

I kissed his hand. "Thank you. Please let me recognize you for who you are."

He touched his flower near my ear. "The rose is soft. The fragrance is gentle. You can only feel my presence, my being between my words. Remember, Shari, when we meet, to listen inside. Keep the voice of the other at a distance."

My head snapped up. "Who is the other?"

My question put an end to the audience. Suddenly I was flying over the city, high above it. The moon blazed, yet my ghostly form cast no shadow on the ground. The yogi's last remark had left me in doubt. I had no clear course. Yet I was lying to myself. He *had* told me what I had needed to know.

I just didn't want to listen. But if a Master couldn't help me, who could? I thought of my brother, my oldest guide, and in the blink of an eye I was with him.

He slept on his back in his bedroom, Jo wrapped in his arms. They were naked but covered with a sheet, and I had to smile as I looked down on them. Jimmy, I knew, was intensely private. Let him carry on his affair without my intruding. I felt no desire to touch him, to probe his dreams. As I turned to leave, Jo suddenly stirred and sat up.

"Hello," she whispered.

"Jo." I sat beside her. She didn't seem to feel me, but sitting still, she strained to hear—what? Me? I didn't know. Leaning over, I whispered in her ear, "I love you, old friend. I know I never tell you that but I do."

Maybe she heard me. A smile crossed her face. "Shari," she said softly.

I sat back and also smiled. "Yes."

Then, in another blink of an eye, I was sitting on the bed in my old room. To my surprise, my mother was sleeping in my bed, or trying to. Clutching a childhood doll of mine, she cried quietly. Close by, on my bedstand, I saw a copy of *Remember Me*. My hand flew to my mouth.

"Oh God," I muttered. What had I done?

Quickly I sat down beside my mother and stroked her hair. Her tears began to subside and not long after that her breathing relaxed and she fell asleep. I drew my hands far back. I did not want to probe her dreams, not after she had just finished the story of my death.

"What am I doing tonight?" I said aloud. "What am I looking for?"

I must have thought of him then, although I didn't do so on purpose. There was no movement through time and space. I was in my bedroom, then I was in Roger's bedroom. His place was opulent, more like an expensive hotel suite than personal quarters. He lay sleeping on his side, in his underwear. Cast in the rays of moonlight, his near-naked physique was exquisite. A young David cut from Michelangelo's marble. My hands were on him before I knew what I was doing. I gripped his head, his heart.

Was he dreaming of me?

Then I was inside his dreams, in the realm of make-believe where he wandered during the dark hours. The setting was vast—the third arm of a galaxy known as the Milky Way. A thousand billion stars burned cold in the endless firmament. Green and blue planets shone overhead. Meteor-scarred moons revolved nearby. And into all of this moved the spaceships, long, sleek purple ones closing in on white ships. Blue and red beams erupted from the purple ships, striking the white ones. Soundless explosions splashed the vast black canvas with light. Yet this was the light of death; for each of the white spheres was gigantic and filled with thousands of people.

The purple ships were not bent solely on destruction, however. Even as I watched, they maneuvered to corral in the white fleet, to capture its millions of occupants, ultimately to force them into submission. But for what purpose I didn't know, only that the invaders' ultimate goal was evil beyond words. Better to die, I thought, than surrender to *their* will. The will of the others.

CHAPTER VI

OPENING MY EYES, I stared at the black ceiling. For a moment I was surprised there were no stars embedded there. Yet I had no conscious remembrance of having dreamed. I sat up and looked out the window. The moon was a shade past full; its pitted surface, yellowed by the curve of the atmosphere, hung close to the sea. It was odd that I could see the marks of meteors on it without a telescope. Yet as I blinked and rubbed my eyes, my supernormal vision fled, and I was left with Peter's soft breathing, a normal-size moon out our window, and fragments of dreams I couldn't quite piece together. I remembered the yogi flying in a white spaceship beside me. No, I remembered my mother clutching a rose and crying as she asked me to sign a book for her. Shaking my head, I climbed out of bed and headed for the bathroom.

"It must have been the wine," I muttered.

After I peed, however, I didn't climb back into bed. My mind was alert. My headache was gone, as well as my fatigue. A subtle *power* swept over me, as often happened when I did my best writing. Not entirely sure what I was doing, I went into my office and sat down in front of my computer. The screen glowed eerie blue white as I booted my hard drive. For the first time in a long time, I found myself not working on a particular project. My efforts to get the movie going consumed all my energy. But I missed telling stories; there was nothing like it in the world. The strange thing about writing is that you never know when the magic will strike to let you tell the stories. In fact, you never know if the magic will ever come again.

I felt the magic then.

I opened a new file, thought for a moment, then began to type.

THE STARLIGHT CRYSTAL

Captain Sarteen smiled with satisfaction as her starship, the *Crystal*, materialized out of hyperspace far beyond the orbit of the tenth planet. The familiar yellow light of Sol glistened on the main screen, faint at this great distance but nonetheless welcome. Over a thousand years had elapsed since Sarteen had seen the sun of her birth. The travels of her starship had been vast, and the knowledge gained—invaluable. But now the journey was complete. Today was mankind's birthday. Today they would be welcomed into the Galactic Confederation, and no longer be bound by the laws of the physical realm. The contact with the elder races had come only recently, while Sarteen and her crew had been thousands of light-years away, searching for other intelligent races they feared they would never find. Now the doubt was past, the loneliness over. The call had gone out. All of mankind was returning home. Sarteen knew her starship was the last to reenter the solar system.

"Begin deceleration," Sarteen said from her command seat on the bridge of the starship. The vessel was vast, over a mile in diameter, and carried a crew in excess of a hundred thousand. It could jump in and out of hyperspace only at close to light speed; they would have to cancel out most of that great velocity before they reached the inner planets. In a split second, their last hyperspace jump had carried them over a hundred light-years. But now that they were in real space, the ship's great graviton engines would have to labor to keep them from flying past Earth. As she gave her order, she heard a faint hum as the engines were brought to full power.

"Deceleration initiated," First Officer Pareen said. "We should reach Earth inside ten hours."

Sarteen stood up from her chair and strode over to her first officer, noticing the excitement of her bridge crew as they stared at the sun and thought of the glorious destiny that awaited them. Sarteen could remember well her first and only brush with the collective consciousness of the Elders, as her people were now calling them. The feeling of coming home, of completeness, and of a love that transcended all their ideas of what love could be. It was impossible to think that soon it would be their natural state. Never again would they have to struggle, to be afraid. They would enjoy the limitless state of being of those other races that had gone before them and perfected themselves. Not only that, the Elders had assured them that their entry into the Confederation would greatly uplift them as well. Mankind was special, they said. Mankind held the keys to the knowledge of the universe. It was in their genes, they said. The twelve strands of their DNA. Mankind had been a glorious experiment and now the experiment was going to reach its conclusion.

Sarteen did not doubt the Elders for a moment. It would have been the same as doubting herself. When the Elders had linked with her mind, she realized that she was them, that she had come from them. And now she was going back to where she belonged.

Pareen gestured to the crew at her approach. "They're excited."

Sarteen nodded. "Aren't we all? It's not every day that the heavens open up. I still can't believe this is happening for us, after our long search."

"But the whole time we searched," Pareen said, "we knew we would find what we were looking for."

"You did, perhaps. You always had faith. But I had begun to think we were wasting our time."

"Did you?" Pareen asked. "You never said."

She smiled. "I'm the captain. I can never show weakness." She glanced at the screen. "At least I couldn't before."

Pareen shook his head. "I think your weaknesses are few. If it had not been for you, none of us would have survived to enjoy this day. How many times did your quick thinking save our mission from disaster?"

Sarteen was thoughtful. "But what was the usefulness of our mission? To find what we sought, we have come home. Don't you find that ironic?"

"No. I find it appropriate." He paused. "Something bothers you, Captain?"

She shrugged. "It's nothing. It's just that I feel somehow our journey was cut short. That we came to our goal too soon." She touched her chest as she stared at the sun. "I felt in my heart that it would be longer before we reached paradise."

Pareen chuckled. "A thousand years was not long enough for you?"

She had to smile. "I agree. It should be long enough for anybody."

The hours passed slowly, as time was wont to do when the present moment was not as enjoyable as the promised tomorrow. The sun grew in brightness, the outer planets became visible, the gas giants shimmering in the glow of a star that had given life to a race that supposedly could tap into universal truths. Over the long distance from the galactic core, where the Elders resided, had come a partial explanation for the purpose of humanity, and why they had been isolated from the Elders the last million years.

Mankind was the creation of the creator gods, who had been directed to this part of the universe by the Prime Creator itself, that glorious being that could only partially be comprehended even by the brilliant Elders. The creator gods had been directed to build a biological creation in the physical realm that would be capable of manipulating matter and energy over the entire spectrum of frequencies. From the pure inexhaustible white light of the Prime Creator all the way down to the most inert matter. The secret to mankind's role was in its twelve chakras, or centers, which resonated with its twelve strands of DNA. Each center in each human being was able to tap into a different frequency. When they were "plugged" back into their power source, the rest of the Confederation, these centers would vibrate with incredible energy. The whole of the galaxy would shine, and stand as a beacon for the remainder of the universe. In a sense, being contacted by the Elders was the same as being contacted by their more subtle half. At least that was what they said.

"They are me," Sarteen whispered to herself in her quarters. "But they are not me. I had forgotten them. They did not forget me."

THE LAST STORY

She was alone. Her room was dark, except for the glow of her viewing screen, which remained fixed on the distant sun, and the glimmer of her crystal column, which, by some strange alchemy, shone without an external power source. After linking with the Elders, she had been inspired to build a staff made up of different precious stones that she had collected from a dozen worlds. No one had told her to construct the thing and so far she had shown it to no one, not even her dear friend Pareen. The staff was roughly as tall as a human being. The first seven stones were set at equal distances along the top half of the gold rod; the remaining five were fixed in a silver wheel that crowned the pointed top. These last five were the unseen centers, Sarteen believed. The ones above and beyond the body. They were the cosmic centers that connected them directly to the Prime Creator.

Each of the jewels she had used had come to her as if by magic: one she had found in the cave of an asteroid that tumbled between the stars; another in the many-tentacled arms of a giant insect that had crawled out of a burrow in a tree as tall as a mountain; and still another had fallen from a sweet fruit she had bitten into on a planet where there was only one tiny island, the rest water. When the jewels began to glow, as she set them in place, she leaped back in surprise. And since then she had been unable to stop staring at the staff. It was almost as if looking at it were like staring into a mirror and seeing a goddess.

"How did I forget?" she asked the crystal staff.

The communicator on her desk beeped. "Yes?" she said.

"Pareen here. Something is terribly wrong."

"Specify?"

"Our fleet is under attack. A large fleet of alien vessels, with incredible speed and power, has appeared close to Malanak. The fifth planet is under heavy bombardment. What is your command?"

Sarteen stood. For some reason, the news did not surprise her.

"I will be on the bridge in a minute," she said. "For now, veer us away from Earth."

Pareen was shocked. "Turn away? But our people need our help."

"Do as I say. I am on my way."

How different the mood on the bridge was from when they had exited hyperspace. Rather than coming home to a wonderful party, they had returned to invasion.

Sarteen found it impossible to believe the Eiders had anything to do with the attack, yet the coincidence was disturbing. Why today, when all sorrow was supposed to end?

"Report?" she snapped as she stepped onto the bridge.

Pareen glanced up from his monitors. "Approximately three hundred alien vessels have materialized inside the orbit of Malanak. We are fighting back, but these ships, though small, are exceedingly powerful and maneuverable. Already, in this short time, ten percent of our fleet has been destroyed. The aliens have demanded our immediate and unconditional surrender. Our admiral is considering giving in to their demand."

"Have you been able to confirm the status of Malanak?" Sarteen asked.

"It has been destroyed," Pareen said.

Sarteen was shocked. "The entire planet? That's not possible."

"The destruction is confirmed. It is rubble."

Sarteen was confused. "How were these alien ships able to exit hyperspace so close to the sun?" Ordinarily they could come out of a hyperjump only far from the powerful gravitational pull of the sun, or any star, for that matter. Gravity greatly distorted travel through hyperspace, ripping ships to pieces.

"Their technology would appear to be far in advance of our own," Pareen said. "They are able to change speeds rapidly. Certainly their weapons are far superior to anything we have."

"Has our fleet been able to ascertain the nature of their weaponry?"

"No. It appears to be a new form of energy. Our shields can stand against it for only a short time."

"Has Earth been attacked?" Sarteen asked.

"Not yet. But many of the alien vessels are moving in that direction."

"Have we any communication with the alien fleet besides the ultimatum?"

"No, Captain."

"Have you altered our course to head away from Earth?"

"Yes. But to what purpose?" Pareen was angry. "Our place is with our people."

Sarteen ignored him for a moment. "Put the relative positions of our ship, the alien ships, and our fleet on the viewing screen."

"Captain?"

"Do it!"

Pareen manipulated the controls. A mass of purple and white lights appeared. Their own vessels outnumbered the aliens three to one, but as she watched several white dots blinked, and then vanished altogether. Surrender seemed the only course—for the others.

"We are still far from Earth," she said aloud, talking to herself. "We might be able to escape." She turned to Pareen. "Are any of the alien ships heading our way?"

Pareen consulted his instrument. "One seems to be breaking away from the main pack. It's accelerating sharply." He looked up, fear in his eyes. "It's coming in our direction."

"How long before it reaches us?" Sarteen asked.

"At its present rate of acceleration, four hours. We would not be able to return to near light speed and make a jump through hyperspace before then."

"How much time do we need to regain enough velocity?"

"Five hours."

Sarteen was thoughtful. "The ship that's chasing us might not be able to keep up its present rate of acceleration."

"I wouldn't count on it. I think we have to surrender."

"We will not surrender!" Sarteen shouted at him.

Pareen stepped toward her. "Then turn our ship around and let's fight. Let's at least have a noble end. Why do we run?"

"Because perhaps this is the end. The end of everything. But we can't let it finish, not like this. If humanity is so special, as the Elders say, we must survive."

Pareen sneered. "You believe anything they said after this?"

Sarteen was surprised that he automatically assumed the Elders were responsible for the attack. Yet as she glanced around the bridge, she saw the rest of her crew nodding agreement.

"We do not know who is in these alien ships," she said quietly.

Pareen burned with bitterness. "Of course we do. The Elders told us to recall all our ships so that they would all be in one place, easy to wipe out. Then this murderous fleet materializes. They must have intended to exterminate us from the beginning."

"But when we linked minds with them," Sarteen said, "their love was so great"

"They cast a spell over us. And we fell for it."

"No," Sarteen said. "I trust in that love. It was real."

"So is the ship that chases us. Love will not turn back its

energy beams. We either turn and fight or we surrender. There is nowhere to run."

"There is the whole universe." Sarteen considered. "If we could gain an extra hour, we would be able to jump into hyperspace. Then we would be safe."

"The mathematics of their speed versus our speed will not give us that hour," Pareen said. "It is a simple fact."

"We have to slow them down, catch them by surprise." Sarteen pointed to Pareen's monitors. "In three hours we will reenter the cometary cloud. Find me a gaseous cloud."

"This far out, comets have no tails or gas surrounding them. It is only when they approach the sun that they begin to boil and throw off material. You know that—it is elementary astronomy."

"Yes, I do know that Pareen. What I am asking of you is to find me a gaseous cloud of even *minute* size, which you should be able to locate up ahead of us. Not all comets are simple balls of ice out here. Some have faint coronas."

"May I ask the purpose of finding such a *minute* cloud? It will not stop the alien ship that chases us, I can tell you that now."

"But it will provide the camouflage we need to deposit thousands of nanoeggs in it."

Understanding crossed Pareen's face. The nanoeggs were the invention of the *Crystal*'s scientists, a weapon they had put together during the centuries they had explored far from home. A nanoegg was only as large as a chicken egg, but contained within it a million tons of compressed antimatter—

sealed inside a magnetic bottle. When matter and antimatter collided, the release of energy was phenomenal, complete. One nanoegg could wipe out an entire planet. The corona of a sleeping comet could disguise the presence of their eggs, and if the alien ship were to unexpectedly sweep through them, chasing in their wake, it should explode, shields or no shields. Pareen nodded as he considered her strategy.

"We must release the eggs with the alien ship practically on top of us," he said. "Otherwise the eggs—sharing our high velocity—will sweep out of the corona."

"True. But we can fire the eggs into our wake at high speed. There will be room for error."

Pareen shook his head. "Not much. If their weapons and engines are so superior, we must assume their sensors are likewise. The eggs must make contact with the alien vessel inside the corona or else they will be spotted and avoided."

"It is worth the risk. Especially when we don't have another option." She stepped toward the elevator. "Let me know when you have located a suitable cometary cloud. I will be in my quarters."

"Why are you leaving the bridge at a time like this?"

"I have to see to something important," Sarteen said.

I stopped writing. Tiredness had begun to creep back in. Besides, I didn't know what happened next. I didn't understand half of what I had written. *Twelve* strands of DNA that reverberated with twelve chakras? I knew that humans had *two* strands of DNA, spun in a double helix shape. I did not know what a chakra was; the word had just come to me as I wrote. I didn't even know if Sarteen was right, if the Elders were behind the attack or not.

Yet I loved the story, the feel of it, the mental pictures and feelings it evoked in me. Often I started a story simply with a single powerful image and waited to see where it went. Backing up what I had written onto the hard drive, and onto a jump drive, I turned off my computer and crawled back into bed beside Peter. Just as I began to doze off, another piece of my dream came back to me, or I thought it did. I had been talking to Roger and we had been discussing this very tale. The thought made me smile. I had only known Roger a few hours and already he had inspired a story.

CHAPTER VII

AT THE CONSTRUCTION SITE the next day, I came close to losing my mind. I could not see how this hole in the ground—even with the bulldozers plowing hard and Andy's gay lover painting wildly—was going to look like the Caribbean anytime in the next year. I told Henry as much, in a surprisingly hysterical voice.

"It will be perfect," he said. "You're a writer, not a director. You don't understand the magic of camera angles and film splicing. Remember, the sailboat set piece is complete. We just have to tow it over here from the studio."

I stepped to the edge of the wide pit. "When we fill this with water," I said. "Won't the water just soak into the ground?"

"Some will. We'll just put in more."

"And you're going to color the water? Will the sharks like that?"

"The sharks don't have a contract. They have to like it."

I chuckled. "What if someone falls into the water?"

Henry lost his easy manner. "We don't joke about that. No one gets near the sharks while they're feeding."

"Do we have to feed them?" It was a stupid question, I knew.

"We have to *film* them feeding. It's in the script you wrote. That reminds me. We won't be shooting here tomorrow. We'll be on the waterproof set at Warner's. We're doing the below deck flood scene first."

"That's a big change. When did that happen?"

"This morning. It's movie biz. You have to be flexible. We can't get the Warner's set next week. We have to take it tomorrow and we can't have any screwups. We have only two days to shoot, unless we want to pay an additional thirty thousand and wait until next month. Anyway, that's not the problem. It's Lucille, who plays Mary."

"I know who Lucille is. What's wrong with her?"

"She can't swim."

"What?" I asked.

"You heard me."

"So? She doesn't have a swimming scene."

"Andy told her that. But she's nervous about tomorrow. The water will be up to her chest. Andy's afraid she's going to freak. They both want you to rewrite it so that Mary doesn't have to be below deck while the others are trying to plug the holes in the ship."

"That's out of the question. The whole point of the scene is that they're eyeing one another to see who will make a break for the remaining lifeboat. How are we going to explain their faith in Mary?"

"I don't know," Henry said. "You're the writer."

"It can't be done. Lucille will just have to set aside her fears if she wants to be in this movie."

"We can't fire her," Henry said. "We fired two people yesterday."

"One. That's another thing that annoys me. Why did you stick up for Bob?"

"I didn't 'stick up' for him. He's impossible to replace at the last minute. I was simply trying to mediate the crisis. And then, in the end, you asked him to stay."

"I was afraid Roger was going to hit him again."

Henry's face darkened. "Did you see the way he hit Bob? Like he wouldn't have minded killing him?"

I waved my hand. "Roger's all right. I think he grew up in a tough part of Chicago. He actually likes Bob. I talked to him after we left your house."

"Can he swim?"

"I don't know. We didn't go swimming." I paused. "But it's an important question. He has a big swim scene. You know, now that I think about it, we didn't ask anybody if they could swim."

Henry laughed. "*You* didn't. I was only joking a second

ago. It was the first thing I asked Roger. Let's worry about this Mary/Lucille thing tomorrow. I'm sure Andy can shoot it so that Lucille doesn't feel like she's going to die." He paused. "You look tired. Preproduction jitters? Trouble sleeping?"

I rubbed my bloodshot eyes. "I was up late writing."

"A new story? What's it about?"

I had to smile. "I don't know. I have to write more. Maybe one of the characters will eventually tell me."

"I'm sure it'll sell millions."

I shrugged. "It's a different kind of story. It may not sell at all."

Just then Roger drove up in his sleek black Corvette with the top down. Dressed entirely in black, and wearing black shades, he looked like the star I hoped my movie would make him. As I walked toward his car, leaving Henry to deal with the bulldozer men, I realized I hadn't asked him about his acting background. Not that it mattered. When someone had it, they had it. And Roger definitely had it.

But what is it? *Sex? Huh, Shari?*

"Hi," I said. "How did you find this place?"

"The director told me where it was."

"Andy? Isn't he conducting rehearsals?"

"Yes."

"Aren't you supposed to be there?"

Roger laughed. "The boss is back."

I softened. "I'm sorry. I was just wondering."

"Andy told us we could take a ninety-minute break. We've been going at it since eight this morning." Roger glanced at his watch. "I thought maybe you and I could have lunch together."

"I'd love to, but I already have plans." I was supposed to pick up Peter and have lunch with him. He was coaching the future Cy Young award winner that afternoon, the blind one. But . . . Roger had such a beautiful jawline, and his body looked as if it had been programmed into a computer—to my specifications—before being stamped out. I added, "Maybe tomorrow."

"We'll be all wet tomorrow." He looked me up and down. "Lightning only strikes once."

"Is that what you are? Lightning?"

He leaned out of his car, brushing my bare arm. "No. I'm destiny. And it only knocks once. Come with me. We'll have fun. You can call your friend and tell him you were held up."

"Oh, I wasn't having lunch with anyone," I lied, and hated myself for it. "I was just busy with Henry." I stopped and giggled nervously. "Hell, why not? Where do you want to go?"

He spoke in a sinister voice. "Somewhere dark and quiet."

I continued to giggle. "I'm not drinking any wine. I'm not falling for that trick again."

He clasped my hand. "Did you fall, Shari? Is that what happened?"

I didn't know what to say. I said nothing.

~ ~ ~

Roger had expensive tastes. We went to the restaurant inside the Beverly Hills Hotel, and after we were seated, I found out that was where he was staying.

"But this place must cost five hundred a night," I said.

"My suite is actually closer to a thousand a night. Why are you so shocked? You make twenty times that a day."

"But—" I began.

"But I'm not a famous writer like you?" Roger asked.

"I wasn't going to say that."

"But you were thinking it." He shrugged. "I come from an affluent background."

I remembered my comment to Henry about Roger's background. "What does your father do?" I asked.

"He's dead."

"What did he do?"

"I never knew my father or mother."

"Are you adopted?"

"In a manner of speaking. Tell me about your father."

I thought of Jean's father. "He died when I was young."

"Where did you grow up?"

"In east L.A."

"But Jo's from Huntingdon Beach. And you said the two of you went to high school together."

I hesitated. "We did. Didn't Jo tell you we did?"

"Yes. But I don't see how it's possible." He raised a hand as I began to protest. "It doesn't matter. I have my secrets.

You have your secrets. There's nothing wrong with that."

I held his eye a heartbeat too long to deny that what he had just said was true. "I don't have many secrets," I said softly. There was something about his eyes that was so familiar. My response amused him.

"You have a few more every day, Shari."

He was referring to my being with him last night, this afternoon. His comment should have been enough to make me get up and leave. Yet I stayed. Curiosity and pride kept me in my seat.

"We're both adults," I said. "Tell me about your adopted parents?"

"They were good people." He changed the subject. "Where did you learn to write?"

"I'm self-taught."

"But you must have some inspiration?"

I had to smile. "Are you asking me where I get my ideas?"

"Why is that funny?"

"Everyone asks me that." I paused. "There's a troll in my bedroom closet. He inspires me."

"Have you ever met him?"

"He comes out occasionally."

Roger leaned over and took my hand, studying my palm, holding it close to the candle. Close enough that I felt its heat. His face was serious.

"You know, they say you can read a person's whole life

in the lines of their palm." He stroked my open hand gently with his fingertips—the sensation was delicious. He traced a line that led from beneath my small finger in a straight line below my other fingers. "This is your heart line. It predicts your love life."

"How is it?" I asked.

"It forks at the end. A fork in one of the major lines shows great power in that area of life. You have a big heart, Jean. You're compassionate and kind. But your heart line is also splintered." He pointed to a spot one-third of the way down the line. "Here, where the break is, you're about twenty-one years old."

"What does a splinter mean?"

"That your heart will be divided at that time."

"But I'm twenty-one now."

Roger nodded. "So you're in for interesting times. Let's see your intellect line. It comes from the other direction, and curves downward. You see it?"

"Yes. It's also forked."

"Yes. You're obviously intelligent. It has no breaks in it. Come what may, you will always keep your head."

I smiled nervously. "Even if my heart breaks?"

"That appears to be the case." He frowned. "This is strange."

"What?"

"Your life line. It breaks around this time in your life. In fact, there are large gaps in the line. And then, a little later, it just runs out."

"What does that mean?"

He glanced up. "It means you're going to die."

I took back my palm. "I hardly think so," I replied sharply.

He sat back and chuckled. "It's only pretend, Shari. Don't get upset."

"I'm not upset."

"You're acting upset. Anyway, the first break in your life line occurred three years ago. If there was anything to it, you would be dead already."

Three years ago. That was when I was born.

CHAPTER VIII

THAT SAME AFTERNOON I visited Private Detective John Garrett, who earlier had been Lieutenant John Garrett. Four years ago Garrett's brilliant detective work had been largely responsible for acquitting me of suicide and balcony diving. After I returned to Earth in Jean Rodrigues's body, and subsequently became rich and famous, I sent Garrett a cashiers' check for fifty thousand dollars. I made the gift anonymously. Garrett promptly quit the force and set up shop as a private eye. I had kept loose track of his career, but never gathered the courage to visit him. Until today I'd had no burning need for a private detective. Now I thought I did.

"I have my secrets. You have your secrets. There's nothing wrong with that."

Had Roger's line been innocent? Or was he trying to tell me that he knew I was a Wanderer? I would have immediately dismissed the possibility except he had gone out of his way to point out the discrepancy between Jo's story and mine. The guy was the star of my movie, I thought. I was making out with him. I had to know more about him.

The résumé on the back of his picture, or headshot, was vague. He had done some Chicago theater, taken a few acting classes. Everything he listed had been done in the past twelve months. His permanent address was a P.O. box, his home phone number—a message service. Briefly I considered trying to research his past myself, but decided I didn't have the time. Besides, I didn't know the ins and outs of detecting. Garrett it would have to be.

I could have gone to any private detective, but I chose Garrett because I wanted to see him, with human eyes. See how he was doing. Thank him again, somehow, for what he had done for me.

When I walked into his office in Century City's twin towers and saw who his secretary was, I almost fainted.

"A leg! Give me her legs! They taste so good with sausage and eggs!"

His cute dark-haired daughter, the one Peter and I had gotten off drugs—by scaring the crap out of her—sat behind the desk. She seemed healthier and more stable than I was. She glanced up as I entered.

"Hello. May I help you?"

"I cannot stop him without your help, child. If you die on drugs, he will come for you."

I took a moment to collect my wits. "Is your father here?" I asked.

The young woman appeared surprised. "How did you know Detective Garrett and I were related?"

I hesitated. "The person who referred me to your father told me."

"Oh. Who was that?"

"I can't remember his name." I nodded to her appointment book. "I called an hour ago. I was supposed to be here at three sharp. I'm sorry I'm twenty minutes late. I got caught in traffic."

I was late because I had gone back to ask Henry what he knew about Roger. Garrett would need something to start his investigation, that is, if he took the case. The office was nice, the rent high. Garrett was obviously doing well.

"Have a seat please," the daughter said. "I'll tell my father you're here. Ms—?"

"Jean Rodrigues." I couldn't meet him as Shari Cooper. That was one name he would remember, I was sure.

She stood. "I'll be just a minute."

I was left waiting ten minutes, but finally I was ushered into Garrett's office, which had a glorious view of Beverly Hills and Westwood, gold plaques on the walls, and leather furniture. The smell of success. He was talking on the phone and gestured for me to have a seat in front of his imposing desk. Settling myself, I recalled how I had described him in my book.

He was a man on his way down in life. In his midforties, he had on a frumpy green sports coat and a wrinkled white shirt with a loosely knotted purple tie caught beneath his oversize belt. He needed a good meal. His thin brown hair was going gray, and his red wizened face had seen either too much sun or too much life. He looked burned out. He was lifting a pint of whiskey to his lips when I tapped on his window.

Garrett had found a new chef and tailor. Besides having gained weight and improved his wardrobe, I believed he must have had a facelift. He looked five years younger than when I met him the night I died. He showed no signs of being an alcoholic now. Finally he set down the phone and glanced over at me.

"I'm sorry to have kept you waiting," he said. "I have a few rather intense clients. They call at all hours and want to know that everything's going to be all right."

"I imagine that it would take an intense person to come see you."

He chuckled. "Let's just say I haven't met many normal people lately. Except perhaps you. What can I do for you?"

"I need background information on a certain young man." I handed him Roger's picture and résumé. "I work for a production company and this actor has recently been hired to star in a new film. A few members of the company feel uncomfortable about comments he's made about his past. There's a lot of money riding on this film"—I shrugged—"so you can understand why we're curious about the guy."

"What is the name of the production company?" Garrett asked, studying Roger's picture.

I paused. "Cooper Productions."

"What is your position in the company?"

Damn, I thought. He'd know I was *the* Shari Cooper before the week was out. God, what if he read *Remember Me*? I had changed his name to Garrison in the book, but that would stop him for maybe two seconds. Maybe Jimmy was right, I thought. I shouldn't have published the book, not and made it so close to actual events. I thought of my mother then and wondered if she had already read the story.

I had been naive, however, to think Garrett wouldn't question me about why I wanted the information. Obviously he had to be careful to protect himself. I took too long to answer his question.

"I'm the president," I said. He would quickly learn the truth if I lied. He sat up in surprise.

"Forgive me for saying this, Ms. Rodrigues, but you look kind of young to be president of a company."

"Thank you," I said, hoping my wit could deflect his curiosity.

He smiled again. "What is the title of the film you're producing?"

"It's called *First to Die*. It's a thriller."

He frowned. "That sounds familiar. I think my daughter may have read that book."

"It's a popular title." I didn't want to get into a discussion about the author, so I continued hastily. "Our production company would be happy to pay you double your normal salary to research this guy. We are about to start shooting so you can understand our need for haste."

Garrett was blunt. "Not really. What has the guy said that makes you suspicious of him?"

"He's been vague about his past."

"So? Forgive me, Ms. Rodrigues, but if he can act and stay sober throughout the shoot, why do you care about his history?"

I spoke carefully. "We have learned from past experience that it's risky to have an actor who is, say, addicted to drugs, on the set of a film." I added, "I'm sure you can understand how volatile that would make our working relationship."

My indirect reference to his daughter's past behavior had a settling effect on Garrett, but he remained wary. "What do you want to know about the guy?"

"Anything you can find out. Where he was born. Who his family is. Does he have a police record. Where he came by his money."

"He has money? How much?"

"I don't know, but he's staying at the Beverly Hills Hotel." I removed a scrap of paper from my purse. "He drives a brand-new black Corvette. I took the liberty of writing down his license plate number." I handed the paper to Garrett. "I would like you to run a DMV check on him as well. I assume that presents no problem for you."

He studied the number. "Is this a California license plate?"

"Yes."

He sighed softly. Something about the case bothered him. "My normal fee is two hundred dollars an hour."

"Then we'll pay you four hundred dollars an hour." I took out my checkbook. "Speed is essential. If you could start researching him today, it would be appreciated. Would a ten thousand dollar retainer be satisfactory?"

"More than satisfactory. Tell me, Ms. Rodrigues, are you personally involved with this guy?"

I paused as I wrote. "Why do you ask?"

"Just curious. Are you?"

"No." I finished writing the check and handed it to him. "When do you think you'll have something for me?"

"Probably tomorrow. But it would help if you could be more specific about what you want to know about him."

"I've told you what I want."

"Maybe, but I get the idea you're searching for a particular incident in his past. Am I correct?"

I paused. "I want to know if there was a point in Roger Teller's life when everything changed for him."

"For good or bad?"

I shrugged. "Either way."

I could see Garrett wanted to ask why I phrased my request

the way I did. I was glad he didn't. How could I explain that I wanted to know if Roger was a Wanderer? With his charisma, he was definitely a candidate. And if he was a Wanderer, I wanted to know if he was aware of the fact. And what his mission was.

Garrett agreed to take the case.

I thanked him, left his office, and started back to Henry's to see how rehearsals were progressing. I had the yogi's lecture to attend that evening. Peter had made me swear I would come. Yet I wouldn't be going with Peter because Roger had insisted on going, too, and I planned to take him with me. Over lunch, after reading my palm, Roger had become unusually curious about this saint from India.

CHAPTER IX

WE ARRIVED at the lecture only minutes before it was to start. The Unity Church in Santa Monica was already full. If Peter and Jimmy hadn't saved me a seat, I would have had to stand in the back. Peter did not occupy a seat proper; his wheelchair hugged a pew near the front. Although I'd forgotten to call Peter to cancel our lunch date, I did phone to let him know I was bringing Roger. Peter hadn't minded. I could only hope Roger played it cool, and didn't try to hold my hand or anything. But *cool* was one thing Roger seemed to have no difficulty being. I wondered if he would learn of my probing into his past. Garrett had promised me that discretion was his middle name.

I introduced Roger to Peter and Jimmy, both of whom were too excited about the holy man to pay much attention to Roger. For his part, Roger was low key. He had said little on the drive over from Henry's. Peter leaned over and kissed me as I sat down. It was a brief, friendly kiss. Peter was on my left, Roger on my right. Jimmy sat next to Roger, with no Jo to hang on to—not that he would have in public anyway. Jo had wanted to come but also wanted to work on lines, she said. Her interest in the esoteric had waned as she grew older.

"Is he here yet?" I asked Peter.

"You'll know when he gets here. Everyone stands. How are rehearsals going?"

"Great. Andy and Henry think we're ready."

Peter whispered in my ear. "Is that guy your new star?" he asked.

"Yes. He's playing Daniel."

"He looks like an actor."

"Are you saying he looks handsome?" I asked.

Peter thought a moment. "Has he been in something we've seen?"

"Not that I know of. Why do you ask?"

"He looks familiar."

Interesting, I thought. I'd had the same reaction.

The yogi entered a few minutes later and, as Peter said, everyone stood up out of respect. He looked much like his picture, with his long flowing black hair and black beard. Yet his youth surprised me—he couldn't have been thirty-five. Also, he was much smaller than I'd expected, slighter. He moved with incredible grace, carrying flowers in his hands. He wore a simple white *dhoti*, a strand of beads around his neck. He entered slowly, allowing everyone a chance to greet him as he moved up the center aisle. His accent, though distinct, was not heavy. He spoke the King's English, and had obviously been educated in the language by someone from Britain. He smiled as he walked, sometimes chuckling softly. There was no doubt, he was a happy man.

Nevertheless, I found myself disappointed. He didn't exude the power of the Rishi, and I sensed his kindness but not any divine energy. I know it was ridiculous of me to want to be hit over the head, to experience instant nirvana. Perhaps I'd heard too many things about the man—my expectations were so high. As he swept by, our eyes momentarily locked and a smile broke over my own face. Yet I did not feel I was in the presence of a Master. I watched as he made his way to the sheet-draped chair at the front and sat down cross-legged. He nodded to an assistant and the lights were dimmed. Peter leaned over and spoke in my ear.

"He always starts with a few minutes of silence."

"What do we do during this few minutes?" I asked.

"Just sit with the eyes closed and relax and enjoy the good vibes."

I glanced at Roger. "We're going to meditate for a few minutes."

"I don't know how to meditate," Roger said.

"You're not the only one," I said.

As a group we closed our eyes and sat quietly. Honestly, I tried to relax and enjoy whatever was supposed to be happening, but I felt nothing, absolutely nothing, except a growing head pain. That afternoon, after seeing Garrett, I had swallowed one Tylenol-3 pill. Since this was supposed to be a holy man, I didn't want to take another and act drugged in his presence. At the same time I wondered if I would be able to make it through the night without taking something more. It seemed that lately I had a headache more often than I didn't.

The minutes passed slowly. Several times I opened my eyes to peek at the holy man, who was only twenty feet away. He sat so silently, so still, he could have been a statue. He didn't even appear to breathe. Feeling silly, I tried to see his aura, figuring it must be real bright if he was so enlightened and all. Yet the only colorful things I saw were the flowers arranged around his seat. Finally, after twenty minutes, he stirred and the lights were turned back on. As the saint opened his eyes, he smiled and played with his long beads, twirling them in front of him. He nodded to his assistant, a young man in a blue suit, who briefly introduced the yogi.

"Guruji" was traveling around the world teaching meditation and something called *kriya*. His organization was nonprofit and educational. He had centers on every continent and a large orphanage in India. That weekend—beginning the next day—Guruji would personally teach his techniques of meditation and kriya. Those who wanted to take the course could sign up after the lecture. The introduction was brief. The assistant sat down and the audience was left staring at the yogi. But for his part Guruji seemed to be reveling in an inner joke. He kept smiling, twirling his beads, and looking around.

"Now I'm going to play the role of the teacher," he said finally in a soft but clear voice. "And you're going to play the role of the students. It is like that, nothing more than a play. But it would be nice if the teacher would speak of something of interest to the students. If there are any questions on your mind, you can ask them now."

Many people's arms went up. A bombardment of questions.

"Could you speak on reincarnation?"

"Was Jesus an enlightened Master or the son of God?"

"Were you Buddha in a past life?"

"Is your form of meditation more powerful than TM?"

"Is kriya the fastest way to get enlightened?"

"If there is a God, why does he allow so much suffering?"

"Are you enlightened?"

"Are there angels?"

"How much money do you make a year?"

"Can a person gain enlightenment through sex?"

The questions went on and on. The yogi took them for half an hour, simply nodding at each one. I wondered how he could possibly keep track of them all, and how he would have time to answer half of them. Finally, however, the arms came down and he sat silently for a minute or two, smiling and staring off into space. Then he burst out laughing.

"I don't know the answers to any of these questions," he said. "What are we going to do now?"

The audience exploded with laughter; it was such a perfect response. Peter leaned over and spoke in my ear. "See what I mean?" he asked.

I nodded. "He's funny." Of course, I had wanted to hear his opinion on several of the topics. The Rishi had answered many of my questions in a straightforward manner.

"Why do you want my opinion on these things?" the yogi asked. "If I say something that agrees with your point of view, you'll be happy. You'll go home and say he is a wise man. If my opinion is the opposite of yours, you will leave here and say I'm a fool. In either case what I say doesn't affect what is. The reality is not affected by our opinions. It is what it is. For that reason I have no opinions."

An old woman stood up. "But are you enlightened?"

The yogi considered. "If I say I'm enlightened, then you will want me to prove it in some way. I will have to give a wonderful talk or else strike you with divine energy. Or I might even have to heal someone. People expect this sort of proof from someone who says he's enlightened." He paused to chuckle. "For that reason I always say, 'No, I'm not enlightened.' It's much easier that way for me."

The audience chuckled again. To my surprise, my hand went up. He nodded in my direction and I stood, feeling weak in the knees. "I would like to learn to meditate. Could you tell us a little about the technique you teach?"

His gaze lingered on me for a moment before he spoke. "Meditation is very valuable. It allows us to fathom our inner being, and gives meaning to our life. The time we spend in meditation is the most important time of all. The technique I teach is very simple, very natural, completely effortless. Correct meditation never involves effort. You see in life we do things with our body and we do things with our minds. When you want to accomplish something physical, there is always some effort. You want to climb the stairs, you have to move your legs up and down. You sweat and get out of breath. You cannot shine your car perfectly without putting a hundred percent into it. On the other hand, when it comes to mental things, if you try too hard you accomplish nothing. When it is time to sleep, if you try to nod off, you'll be up all night. You go to a movie or play and want to enjoy it because you have heard so many good things about it. But if you sit there trying to enjoy it, you get frustrated. The only way to enjoy is to let go."

"I write for a living and that is a purely mental activity," I said. "But when I write it is hard work. I have to concentrate on what I'm doing or I get nowhere."

He shook his head. "That is not so."

I forced a smile. "But it's true. It's hard work. There is effort."

"No. Thinking is an effortless process. It happens automatically. The creator designed the human brain that way. The human brain is the greatest creation of the creator. You write best when you let go, and let it flow. It is only when you settle down that you experience true inspiration. Isn't it?"

I started to disagree, but paused. It was true; I wrote best when the words flowed effortlessly. The trouble was it didn't always do that. I said as much to him and he nodded.

"That is why you will enjoy meditation. After you meditate, your writing will be inspired. What do you write? Books?"

"Yes. Scary books."

He made a scared face. "Ohhh. You must be a scary person."

I had to laugh. "It depends what time of the day it is."

He laughed with me. "Scary books are good. Contrast in life is good. If everything was the same every day, it would be no fun. You cannot have great heroes without evil villains."

I sat down. Roger raised his hand but didn't stand. The yogi nodded in his direction. "I have read that certain yogis develop amazing powers through meditation," Roger said. "They can levitate and move objects without touching them and even read people's minds. I was wondering if the meditation you teach develops these abilities?"

The yogi played with a rose. "Why do you want these things?"

"Everyone wants more personal power."

The yogi acted surprised. "Really?"

Roger spoke firmly. "Yes, which raises a concern of mine. Your followers look up to you. As you walked in, I saw many of them handing you flowers, greeting you as if you were some kind of guru. What do you have to say about that?"

The yogi was a picture of innocence. "If people want to give me flowers, I can't very well throw them back at them." He waved his hand. "It doesn't matter to me what they do. I never ask for flowers."

"You didn't answer my question."

"Which question was that?"

"Don't you think it's a mistake for people to give up their personal power? To you or any other guru?"

The yogi was serious for once. "What power do you have? You have no power. The only power is in the divine consciousness. You don't even know how to breathe, how to keep your heart pumping. If the divine stopped doing that for you, you would be dead in a moment. We do not lose strength by surrendering our life to God, to a genuine Master. We gain real strength. And then these abilities you crave—if they come, good and fine. You will know how to use them for good. But we do not meditate to gain powers. They are an obstacle to divine realization, not a boon."

"You equate God and a genuine Master," Roger persisted. "How can we know a genuine Master when we meet him?"

"You can only know him or her in your heart. There is no other way."

"I'm sure the followers of Jim Jones and David Koresh would have said the same thing," Roger said.

"Who are they?" the yogi asked.

Roger snorted softly. "Can't you *tune* into that information?"

The yogi paused. "They were cult leaders. Their followers followed them to their deaths."

"That's correct," Roger said. "I'm sure you read about them in the papers. Anyway, such people are a menace to society. They delude the weak-willed, take their money, their possessions. They take over their whole lives. How do we know you're not planning to do the same with people here tonight?"

"A genuine Master is like the sun, complete in himself. He needs nothing, asks for nothing. But for those who wish to stand and walk to the window and pull aside the curtains, he is there. He warms their path. He guides them, nothing more. He does not steal their lives from them. The opposite—he shows them how to live to their full potential."

"But shouldn't we rely upon ourselves for guidance?" Roger asked. "What do we need you for?"

The yogi was amused. "I don't know."

"Is that all you have to say?"

"It's all up to you. Just relax and enjoy."

Roger crossed his arms over his chest impatiently. He started to speak again but then thought better of it. I leaned over and whispered in his ear.

"Those were good questions," I said.

Roger shook his head. "You notice he didn't answer any of them."

"He answered them in his own way," I said uncertainly.

Someone behind us raised her arm. "Could you please tell us about the kriya you teach? What it is? How it works?"

"Kriya and meditation go together. Kriya brings spontaneous meditation. You don't have to do anything. The mind dives deep inside after kriya. We see our emotions, our thoughts, they flow in rhythms. We are happy at certain times of the day, not so happy at other times. A person says I am a morning person. I can only do my best work before lunch. Other people say they are night people. Their lives have that rhythm.

"Likewise, our emotions and thoughts are tied to the rhythm of our breath. When we are upset, our breath is rapid. We may even pant. When we're sad, our breath is heavy. We sigh. Then again, when we're happy, our breath is long and light. We feel as if we're floating. We are breathing in the same air through the same two nostrils, but the state of our mind affects it. The breath is the most intimate aspect of our lives. The first act of life is inhalation. The last act is exhalation. All of life occurs between these two acts. Yet we seldom think of our breath. Only if we choke on something—then we quickly realize how important it is.

"Breath is the bridge between the inner and outer world. If we can handle the breath, we can handle our minds, thoughts, and emotions. Using the breath, kriya brings rhythm to our lives. You hear an orchestra tuning up. One person is playing this, another that. It is just noise. But when the conductor comes and waves his baton then everyone plays together, and it's music. Kriya brings that music to our lives. It's a simple technique."

"Why does it have to be taught?" someone else asked. "Why don't we just do it spontaneously?"

The yogi smiled. "I don't know why. It would make my job easier if it happened spontaneously. I wouldn't have to travel everywhere teaching it. The next time I speak to God, I will ask Him that question."

People laughed. Jimmy stood and raised his hand. "I would like to take your course on meditation and kriya this weekend. But I'm afraid I won't be able to do it because my mind is always wandering. Just now, when we sat in silence, my mind was all over the place. What can I do?"

"This is a common experience. Normally the mind shifts among the past, the present, and the future. We feel angry about something that's happened to us, or else we regret the way things have turned out. See how much time your mind spends on yesterday, last year, when you were a child. Yet the past is the past. It is gone, finished. Why waste so much life there?

"Then there is the tendency to worry about tomorrow. When you were in school, you were anxious about what you would do when you graduated. Then, when you started your career, you worried if you would ever reach your goals. You can spend your whole life concerned about tomorrow.

"Yet you look to the future to make you happy. I'll be happy, you say, when I'm married. Then, after you get married, you think, I'll be very happy when we have children. Of course, when you have kids you can't enjoy yourself without a house. You postpone your happiness until that perfect future date, but it never arrives.

"Be in the present moment. If you live fully now, tomorrow will take care of itself. If you are happy now, the past will not torment you." The yogi paused. "Meditation and kriya will help you have this experience. Don't worry, you will do just fine. I see it."

"Thank you," Jimmy said, sitting down.

Peter raised his hand. Our little group was asking half the questions. The rest of the audience must have thought we were desperate people, or genuine seekers. I had enjoyed the yogi's last reply. It had hit me right on the head. My mind was never in the present moment. Some of what he was saying was beginning to remind me of the Rishi. Yet he still seemed so ordinary—funny and insightful, true—but lacking supernatural powers. As he had said, I was looking for proof of his God realization. I wished he would heal someone—Peter, for example. It was ironic that Peter would ask the question he did right then.

"I am paralyzed from the waist down," he said. "Is it possible that I can be healed through meditation and kriya? What I mean is—is it my karma to be crippled?"

"What do you think? Do you have some karma?"

Peter fidgeted. "I think so. I just wish I could get rid of it."

"You want to be able to walk again? Do all the things you could before?"

"Yes. I love to play baseball." Peter glanced at me. "I love many things."

"Do you love football?" the yogi asked out of left field.

Peter stuttered. "Not as much as baseball, but I enjoy watching it."

The yogi scratched his head. "I watched a football game yesterday on TV. A few minutes of it. I kept thinking: why are all these grown men fighting over this ball? What would an intelligent race from another planet think if they were watching this game? Why doesn't someone just give them each a ball so they can relax?" The yogi laughed, as did many people in the audience. He added by way of explanation, "It was the first time I saw a football game."

Peter forced a smile. "In baseball we don't actually fight over the ball."

The yogi waved his hand. "All sports are silly. That's what makes them fun. Now, I have not forgotten your question. You sit here in what you think of as a broken physical body. You imagine you are physical, and it would take something physical to fix your spine. But I tell you that is not so. Your body is pure consciousness. The whole of creation is nothing but an ocean of pure consciousness. It is that consciousness that upholds the entire creation. You can call it God or Jesus or Krishna or Buddha—it doesn't matter. It is all the same. It is that consciousness that maintains your body in the state it's in."

"Can you tell it to fix itself?" Peter asked, a note of hope in his voice.

The yogi shrugged. "Why don't you tell it yourself? Learn kriya and meditation. Dive deep inside. There is no physical injury that cannot be healed through the power of God's grace."

"What is grace?" someone asked.

The yogi played with a carnation now. "That is the same as asking what is the meaning of life. That is a great secret. If you ask someone that and they answer you, it means they do not know the answer. No one who knows the answer ever answers that question."

"That's convenient," Roger said, a sharp edge to his voice.

The yogi laughed. "I think so, too!"

Roger stood this time. "You are vague with many of your answers. It's like you don't really know anything."

The yogi nodded. "That's a beautiful state, the state of 'I don't know.' Meditation and kriya lead to that state. If knowledge doesn't—if you still feel that you do know—then that knowledge has not taken you to the goal. You see, first we think we are someone. We believe we are special, that we know everything. Then, as we progress on the path, we see that we are no one. We are nothing. We are like grass. It is good to live as if you are grass. Then, when you reach the goal, you realize that you are everyone. That is the flow of life. From someone, to no one, to everyone. Do you understand?"

"No," Roger said.

"It doesn't matter," the yogi said.

Peter had another question. "Could you talk about relationships?"

"I'm a monk. I'm the last person who should talk about relationships."

"Please? I really would like to hear your opinion on them."

"Relationships are mysterious. We doubt the positive qualities in others, seldom the negative. You will say to your partner: do you really love me? Are you sure you love me? You will ask this a dozen times and drive the person nuts. But you never ask: are you really mad at me? Are you sure you're angry? When someone is angry, you don't doubt it for a moment. Yet the reverse should be true. We should doubt the negative in life, and have faith in the positive." He paused and stared at Peter. "Assume that your partner loves you. No matter what happens. Remember this: love is not an emotion, it is your very existence." He momentarily closed his eyes, almost as if he were checking on Peter's injury. When he spoke next, it was in a soft voice. "It is this love that will heal you. Nothing ever heals except divine love. It is all there is."

More questions were asked: about reincarnation, the New Age, the return of Christ. The yogi danced around most of them, seemingly tired of talking. He was fascinating, not what I had expected at all. Obviously he had depth, but was also so childlike. It was hard to tell when he was being serious and when he was playing with the audience. Yet maybe it was as he had said at the start—it was all a play to him. At one point he asked for someone to sing a song.

"Singing is important in all spiritual traditions," he said. "When we sit here, with our minds busy with whatever, we are separate from one another. But when we sing together, we leave our small egos behind and merge in the group. That is a form of enlightenment. To feel as if everyone belongs to you, and you belong to them. That is something a Master will always teach. There is no hierarchy in the family of man. We are all equal, all children of the divine. The Master is the same as the student, the disciple, the devotee. The Master never places himself above them because if he did, he wouldn't be able to help them." The yogi glanced at Roger. "That's why we don't seek power. Those things separate us from each other. They lead to ignorance, to darkness."

"Does it matter what we sing?" someone asked.

"We can sing a devotional song in English," the yogi said. "Then we will chant a *mantra*. A mantra is a sound that has a specific effect. Certain mantras are for meditation. They are to be kept secret inside. Other mantras are for chanting out loud.

One such mantra is *Om Namah Shivaya*. It is very powerful. We don't mediate silently with it, but we can sing it. It brings harmony to the whole life. That is the effect of its six syllables on our nervous system. Some might ask: is this a Hindu mantra? Is it Buddhist? In reality it is not connected to any religion, race, or sect. It is very ancient, before there existed such divisions on Earth. *Shiva* is not the name of a particular deity. It is that state of perfect innocence we all have inside. No matter what we may have done in life. No matter how many regrets we have, how many sins we think we've committed—that state of innocence is always there for us to embrace. This mantra takes us there straight away. Then, after we chant, we will sit silently for a few minutes, and let the sound vibrate in our consciousness, in the depths of our being. We never chant to gain something selfish. We do it only to perfect ourselves and come closer to God. It is important to have this attitude of surrender. Innocence and surrender are two keys to the spiritual path."

Before he began, however, he invited people to take a brief break and stretch. Jimmy went to get a drink of water. Peter turned to me, excited.

"This chant really gets you high." Peter looked over at Roger. "You have to try it. You'll like it."

Roger was bored. "I feel like I'm at a Hare Krishna meeting." He turned to me. "Do you want to go?"

"She isn't going," Peter said. "I want her to meet the yogi after the meeting."

"Shouldn't we ask Shari what she wants?" Roger said.

I spoke hesitantly. "I would like to try the chant."

Roger stood. "I'll wait for you outside."

Peter peered up at him. "You don't have to wait if you don't want to."

Roger looked Peter up and down, then chuckled. "You're a true believer, aren't you? You'll follow any Joe or Harry who comes along. This man is interested in your money, nothing more. When he has it, that will be the last you see of him. I pity you."

Peter was unimpressed. "I see no pockets on his dhoti. I think he's just here to help people." Peter paused and gave him a cold stare. "What are you here for?"

Roger ignored him. "Remember, we have to get up early," he said to me and stepped past us, leaving. Peter was concerned.

"*We* have to get up early," he said to me. "What is this *we*?"

I shrugged. "It's nothing. We start shooting tomorrow. We both have to be there at six."

"You're not interested in this guy, are you?"

I forced a smile. "No. Don't be ridiculous. Relax. Enjoy the chant."

Yet I had been wrong. Roger had not stood up to leave. Not yet, anyway. Staring warily at the yogi, he crept toward him. The yogi was speaking softly to his assistant; he seemed unaware of Roger's approach until Roger was only a few feet from him. Then the yogi raised his eyes and smiled.

"Yes?" he said pleasantly, so that only those of us up front could hear. His microphone was turned off. Roger stopped when he saw the yogi's bright smile, and seemed on the verge of leaving. But then he drilled the holy man one last time.

"I won't be staying for the chant," he said. "The only power in a mantra is what you tell yourself there is. It's all self-hypnosis, a bunch of nonsense. I'm not into playing head games." He turned his back on the man.

"Wait," the yogi said.

Roger glanced over his shoulder. "Huh?"

"You are a fool."

Roger was instantly livid. His face flushed with blood and he drew in a shuddering breath. "How dare you call me a fool! You charlatan! Just because I don't bow at your feet!"

The yogi chuckled softly. "You see the power of one little word? I called you a fool and your whole state of mind was transformed. Not only that, your breathing and heart rate accelerated. Your blood pressure leapt off the scale. Now when a normal word such as *fool* can have such a powerful effect on you, can you imagine how much more the sacred name of God can change you?" He shook his head. "Don't be in such a hurry to dismiss this chant. Not, at least, until you have tried it."

Roger didn't listen to the advice. Obviously embarrassed, and without saying another thing, he turned and walked briskly from the church. Peter watched him go with a smug expression.

"It looks like your star will never be a star," he said. "Not in the sky, anyway."

"Don't be so hard on him," I said, thinking Roger had been a fool to try to match wits with the yogi.

A few minutes later we sang an English song, "Amazing Grace," and then settled into the chant. The yogi started us off, then the group continued on its own, as the yogi closed his eyes and appeared to meditate. The yogi had such a delightful singing voice: I wished he would continue to chant with us. It reminded me of the melodious words of the Rishi.

The power of the mantra, said out loud, was immediately evident. First I began to relax, and the pressure in my head lessened. Then, as I let myself go into the sound of the words, not minding what I was doing or where I was, I felt the endless chatter in my mind easing. It was as if I were tapping into the peace I experienced when I had entered the light after dying. The spot between my eyebrows and another spot close to my heart began to vibrate, as if touched by a powerful magnet. A stream of gladness flowed through me at those two points. I was not imagining it; I enjoyed it immensely. My consciousness was "high up," swimming free in a place devoid of restrictions. I no longer felt as if *I* chanted the mantra. I felt it chanted itself. There was a nectar in the sound, I realized, an inexhaustible well to quench my thirst.

I felt a pang of regret when we stopped.

Only for a moment, however. Then I was just gone. I

didn't fall asleep, yet the idea of Shari, of my individual personality, suddenly dropped off. I'd experienced this as well, when I entered the light after death, a taste of the soul. It was nice to know I could contact it while still in my physical body. How long I stayed in that state, I have no idea. It could have been ten minutes or two hours. The yogi's words seemed to come to me from a million light-years away. He was telling us to open our eyes slowly. Not to jump up from our seats. Drawing a nourishing breath into my body, I opened my eyes and stared at the yogi. He seemed to glow. I thought, *He must be magical.* He was twirling his beads again, smiling. Peter tugged on my arm and I glanced over.

"Did you enjoy it?" he asked.

I patted his arm. "Very much. Thank you for bringing me here."

"Do you want to meet him?"

"Yes. If he will meet me."

"He stays afterward. Anyone who wants to speak to him can."

"You want to get in line immediately," Jimmy said softly. "Everyone wants to talk to him."

I smiled at my brother. "You look stoned."

Jimmy shook his head. "This guy is better than drugs or alcohol."

Jimmy was right. The moment the yogi ended the session, the line to see him formed quickly. Fortunately, being near the

Christopher Pike

front, I was able to get a good spot. I had to wait only five minutes before I was allowed to speak to him. The people behind waited at a respectful distance. The audience was essentially private. I didn't know the proper protocol for meeting such a person. Folding my hands together, I bowed as the Japanese do, figuring Japan was in the same part of the world as India. The yogi chuckled, playing with a long-stemmed red rose.

"Ah," he said in his sweet voice. "The writer of scary stories. How are you?"

I smiled shyly. "Wonderful. I really enjoyed the chant. I want to thank you for teaching it to me."

"You're welcome. What is your name?"

"Shari Cooper. I mean, it's really Jean Rodrigues. Well, I go by Shari. That's the name I feel most comfortable with." I paused. "Do you understand?"

His eyes sparkled, and for a moment I believed he really did understand that I was a Wanderer. That I had returned from the dead to write scary stories and help save the world. Yet my stories, I now saw, were nothing compared to what this man had to offer people. For the first time I sensed what I had been looking for, the Rishi's divine love. The yogi's eyes seemed to shine as if they were windows into that pure consciousness he spoke of. He was not a man like other men. Nothing in this world could shake him, I saw. And I wanted that peace for myself. Yet it frightened me that I might have to give up too much to get it. Briefly I wondered if Roger had left the church without me.

652

"I understand," he said softly. "Will we see you tomorrow?"

"Tomorrow? Oh, that's when you start your course. I don't know. I don't think so. I'm making a movie of one of my books, and I have to be on the set early. I know it's weird to shoot on Saturday, but that's movie biz." I paused to catch my breath. "I'd like to come tomorrow. I feel I need to meditate and do your kriya."

He frowned slightly and touched his head. "How is this?"

"How is what? My head? It's all right. I get headaches sometimes, but I suppose everyone does." I paused again, thinking that it was remarkable he should know my head often hurt. "Do you think it's all right?"

He studied me thoughtfully. Then he nodded to himself. "Kriya and meditation will help this problem. Check your schedule, see if you can come."

"I'll try." I paused, feeling silly about the question I was about to put to him. "I know this is an odd thing to ask, but are there such things as chakra centers in the body? I mean, is chakra even a word?"

He nodded. "You experienced two of them when you sat in silence."

"In my forehead and heart?"

"Yes."

"Wow. I mean, that's interesting, that they're real." How did he know my experience so intimately? He *must* be enlightened,

I decided. I leaned closer, unsure what I wanted from him but knowing it was a lot. "I wanted to ask you something else. It's about myself. Who I am."

He waved away the question. "Who you are cannot be explained with words. It can only be experienced. You experienced that a few minutes ago, when you were sitting quietly."

"I understand. I've had the experience before. That's what I wanted to talk to you about. You see, I feel like I'm here on Earth for a purpose and I might be missing it. I want to do so many things, but I get so busy that I feel like I'm missing the boat, while trying so hard to catch it. Do you know what I mean?"

He nodded and tapped me lightly on the head with his rose. "You must get to know the captain better. The boat will wait for you." He glanced past me. "Where is the other?"

"Who? The guy who was sitting beside me?"

"Yes."

"He's waiting for me outside." The thought of Roger distracted me. He had left in a huff. "I'd better go."

The yogi smiled and handed me the rose. "Listen to your heart, Shari. Not to the world. The world is a place to visit, to enjoy. It is not your permanent residence. When you don't know what to do, you return to your true home."

His words touched me deeply; the way he said my name. With so much love. I felt tears well up in my eyes. "I know that. Thank you so much."

Peter and Jimmy wanted to speak to me as I returned to the pew, but I was too overwhelmed. Collecting my purse, I kissed Peter quickly on the head and said I would be home soon, I just had to drop Roger off. Outside, I found Roger sitting on a bench and smoking a cigarette. His mood was upbeat—he said he hadn't minded the wait at all. On the drive back to Henry's, where Roger had left his car, we listened to the radio and chatted about the scene we were shooting the next day. The yogi didn't come up.

Roger gave me a kiss just before he climbed out of my car. A brief kiss, it was true, but a hungry one. Enough to stimulate my appetite. Had I not still been floating in the grace of the yogi, I might have fallen right then. But that is the thing about temptation. It will always be there tomorrow, always waiting. Temptation is like the waves of the ocean gently but persistently wearing away the shoreline. Like temptation, it knows the day will eventually come when everything softens, then crumbles.

Roger laughed softly as he stepped toward his black Corvette.

He had me and he knew it.

I would not be taking the yogi's course tomorrow and I knew it.

CHAPTER X

ONCE MORE, in the middle of the night, after waking from a strange dream, I went to sit at my computer. Off to my right, in the bedroom, Peter slept peacefully. Thirty feet to my left, in the living room, Peter's blind baseball prodigy, Jacob, slept on the sofa. Not only was Jacob missing his eyes—his *real* eyes, he had glass ones—he had no home now either. Peter said he would only be staying with us for a few days; I didn't mind. He had been at the apartment when I returned from dropping Roger off. A tall, gangly, black seventeen-year-old, Jacob had struck me as a polite young man. But, boy, could he eat. Before going to bed he had cleaned out the leftover turkey in our icebox and a large bag of potato chips, plus three cans of Coke. Not to mention the chocolate cake he'd eaten. Tomorrow I planned to send him to the supermarket with Peter and a hundred dollar bill to let him buy what he wanted.

THE LAST STORY

I couldn't sleep because I felt compelled to write. I didn't know what I'd say. Only that it would come.

THE STARLIGHT CRYSTAL

Sarteen sat in her quarters and stared at the column of jewels she had built to represent the twelve chakras that each human being supposedly possessed. The precious stones glowed, shedding a soft pastel luster across the dim room. It was as if each stone resonated with a portion of her inner being. Even in her desperate situation, she felt unexpected peace as she sat with the golden rod and knew with a certainty that transcended logic that the Elders had not lied to them. That they had come to humanity in love and light, and that this invasion had been unforeseen. Something thrust upon humanity from a place so alien, so hideous, that it didn't belong in the same dimension. Many insights intuitively came to Sarteen in that moment The beings that commanded the ship that chased them were evil. They wanted to dominate humanity for perverse reasons. The Elders, and the column of jewels, emanated love. Love was what gave all beneficent creatures sustenance. The beings who pursued their vessel came in hate. They wanted to create a hate-filled planet, from which they would drink like psychic vampires. They would not destroy the Earth; not right away, at least. Not until there was nothing left to suck from it. They had to be stopped.

Yet they would not be stopped. Sarteen understood that with heartrending certainty as she meditated on the column. She must have grasped it the instant Pareen told her of the attack. It was why she had ordered her ship away from Earth. The enemy was too powerful. They could not be beaten back by physical means. Help would have to come from outside.

"Or inside," Sarteen whispered to herself. Perhaps, in the eternal scheme of things, there was a reason the enemy should come at this crucial time, when all of humanity was supposed to turn to the light. Perhaps their eyes were still drowsy with sleep, and they weren't quite ready for the transition to a higher state of consciousness. Perhaps it was not destined that they should all see the dawn. But one thing was sure—she thought the enemy would erect a quarantine around Earth. No cosmic rays would reach the planet for the foreseeable future, not unless the Elders managed to break the blockade. Yet Sarteen knew that was not their role. Humanity had to be saved by humanity. She had to get her ship out of the solar system, to safety, so that in another time, from another world, the descendants of those on board could return to Earth and guide it back home to the Elders.

Eons in the future. When the enemy least expected them.

Today, however, she had an unexpected surprise for the enemy. Pareen had located a gaseous cloud that hung between two icy comet relics like snowflakes sprayed against a black canvas. As soon as they reached the cloud, the alien ship would *almost* reach them. Sarteen had ordered Pareen to adjust their speed so that these two events coincided. Once inside the cloud, they would release a thousand nanoeggs, those tiny containers of condensed antimatter that could create such a tremendous explosion when they collided with ordinary matter. The eggs would rake the alien vessel. It should explode and leave the *Crystal* free to escape into hyperspace. The other alien ships would not be able to chase them. No instrument, no matter how elaborate, could track another vessel through hyperspace.

The communicator of Sarteen's desk beeped.

"Yes?" she said.

"It's almost time," Pareen said.

Sarteen stood. "I'm on my way."

On the viewing screen on the bridge, the images were divided. One showed the two giant balls of ice that lay before them, the elongated gas that floated between the dead comets. This far out from the sun, there was scarcely any light. The cold rocks were black as coal, the gas colorless as frosty breath in an underground cave.

The other side of the screen showed the alien vessel, long and sleek, with aerodynamic fins shaped like purple talons. The ship, though clearly spaceworthy, was also built to enter the atmosphere of worlds. Sarteen wondered if dozens of them had already dropped into the skies of Earth. The last word they had heard from their fleet was that they were surrendering. Since then there had been only eerie silence. The ruins of Malanak tumbled around the sun like a belt of meteors. Sarteen took her command seat on the bridge.

"How long till we enter the cloud?" she asked.

"Two minutes, ten seconds," Pareen said.

"is the alien vessel precisely behind us?"

"Yes. And closing quickly." He paused. "They are within disrupter range."

"If we fire, they will just raise their shields. Then our nano-eggs will be ineffective." Pareen began to protest, but Sarteen cut him off. "We know from the experience of our battered fleet that our disrupters have little effect when their shields are up."

"They could fire on us any second," Pareen warned.

"Raise our own shields." Sarteen was thoughtful. "Hail them."

"It won't help the situation."

"I'll be the judge of that. Do as I say."

Pareen opened communications with the alien vessel. Sarteen assumed they could translate Earth language. They must have been observing the Earth a long time before launching such an extensive attack. It was her intention to stall for time, nothing more.

"This is Captain Sarteen of the Earth vessel *Crystal*," she said. "We have noted your pursuit and are curious as to the nature of your mission. Please respond."

A minute passed in silence. Then there came a voice, heavy and deep, obviously straining with inhuman vocal cords to mimic Earth language. There was much hissing in the words, labored breathing. The creature who spoke sounded large and far from civil. They received only audio, no video.

"This is Captain Eworl of the Orion vessel *Adharma*. Surrender immediately and prepare for boarding, or be destroyed."

"Why do you attack us?" Sarteen asked.

"They are charging their energy beams," Pareen shouted, bent over his instruments.

"You are now subjects of the Orion Empire," Eworl responded. "We will brook no form of disobedience, no arguments. Surrender now or die."

"What are the terms of surrender?" Sarteen asked.

"Surrender must be immediate and unconditional," Eworl said.

"Surely you can give us a few minutes to prepare ourselves to comply with your demands?"

In response, a bright blue beam darted from the top of the Orion ship. The *Crystal* shook as if it had rammed one of the comets. The lights on the bridge momentarily failed. Deep in the bowels of the ship, Sarteen heard loud screeching sounds, painful wails. The emergency lights came on sober red.

"Shields?" she called out.

"They've failed!" Pareen shouted back.

"From just one shot? What are they using?"

"Their source of energy is unknown. But one thing is certain: we cannot take another hit. Do you wish us to return fire?"

"No. How long to the cloud?"

"Sixty seconds. But we'll never make it. Release the eggs now."

"No. Are they still running with shields down?"

"Yes. They have no respect for our weapons."

"We will not release the eggs until we enter the cloud. Hail the Orion ship again." The channel was reopened. "Captain Eworl, we are anxious to comply with your request. How can we best surrender?"

"Veer away from the gaseous cloud that lies directly in your course," Eworl said.

"Unfortunately, your attack has disrupted our navigational instruments. But if you can give us one minute, we should have them repaired."

The alien paused before answering. "In one minute you will be in the cloud. That is not acceptable to us."

"Their energy beams are being recharged," Pareen warned.

"Our instruments are coming back on line now," Sarteen said hastily. "We are implementing a turn." She signaled to Pareen to close the hailing frequency and spoke to him, "Fire all our retro rockets simultaneously."

"They'll cancel each other out," Pareen said. "We will still enter the cloud."

"Yes. But it will look like we're trying."

Pareen nodded. "Firing retros. Twenty-eight seconds to cloud-contact."

"Are they still preparing to fire?" Sarteen asked, hearing the roar of the retros firing.

"Yes."

"With our shields down, can we withstand the run through the cloud?"

"It's questionable," Pareen said.

"Reopen hailing frequencies." Her order was obeyed. "Captain Eworl, in an effort to comply with your instructions, we are going to use an auxiliary power source. Please stand by. Captain Sarteen out."

"What auxiliary power source is that?" Pareen asked.

Sarteen shrugged. "I will say anything at this point." She gripped the arms of her chair. "Give me a countdown on entry into the cloud."

"Ten—nine—eight—seven—"

"Prepare to release the eggs," Sarteen said.

"Six—five—They are locking their energy beams on us! We don't have time to—"

"Wait the four seconds!" Sarteen screamed back.

The seconds passed. They would have done so even if they had been destroyed. Yet the alien beams did not strike.

Sarteen was still alive and breathing when the first wisps of the cloud rocked the *Crystal*. Her eyes locked with Pareen's and she nodded.

"Releasing the nanoeggs," he said, pushing a button.

For a moment nothing changed. The eggs were too small to be seen over a distance of any kind. That was the beauty of them. They were virtually undetectable, especially inside the cloud. Their main viewing screen was now turned solely toward the Orion ship.

Without warning the Orion ship turned a brilliant white.

Everyone on the bridge yelled in delight.

"Did they explode?" Sarteen shouted out, not waiting for the glare of the bombs to subside. Pareen stood hunched over his instrument panels.

"Their ship hit several of the eggs," he said. "It did not explode, but the Orion vessel appears damaged. They have ceased accelerating."

The hull of the *Crystal* protested as they plunged deeper into the cloud. The lights flickered once more and the bridge rocked. "How are we doing?" Sarteen asked.

"Not as bad as it sounds," Pareen answered. "Well be past it in ten seconds."

His prediction proved accurate. The pressure on the hull stopped as the glare from the bombs subsided. Finally they were able to see the Orion ship. It had been seriously damaged; an entire fin had blown off and the region from which the aliens fired their mysterious energy beams was a mass of charred wreckage. As Pareen had announced, their engines had cut off. As the minutes passed it became obvious they were falling back. Sarteen breathed a sigh of relief. But they were not safe yet.

"How long until we have enough velocity for a hyper-jump?" she asked.

"At our current rate of acceleration," Pareen said, "two hours, one minute."

"Does the alien vessel have shields up?"

"No."

"What if we divert all power to our disrupters?" Sarteen asked.

"With our damage, we would be forced to cease accelerating for over an hour. I don't recommend it."

Sarteen pondered, swinging back and forth between her choices. She was tempted to finish off the Orion ship while they had the chance. Yet she was also concerned about putting as much distance between them as possible. It was not necessary to destroy the enemy. The *Crystal* only needed to escape. Logic said as much. Plus she could divert all their power to their weapons and still not destroy the Orion vessel. Standing, she paced back and forth in front of her seat, Pareen watching her.

"If we turn off our engines," he said, "we'll drift with them, at least until we build up enough power to restart our engines."

"Can we fire *one* shot of our disrupters and keep the engines going?"

"No."

"Do we have definite life signs coming from their ship?"

Pareen checked his instruments. "Yes. Many of them are still alive."

Sarteen stared at the screen. "I do not trust their captain."

"For all we know, he's dead," Pareen said.

She shook her head. "He's alive. We have hurt him, but he's eager to fight again."

"You don't know that."

"I do." She closed her eyes. "I feel him watching us."

"We need only two hours at our current rate of acceleration," Pareen counseled. "Then we will be free of the solar system."

Sarteen took a deep breath. What she did now would determine whether a portion of humanity survived as a free people or not. Her head said to escape; her heart wanted to fight. She didn't know which was wiser. Feeling the eyes of the crew on her, she slowly opened her own.

"Continue to accelerate," she said softly. "Let us pray that I am wrong, and that he is dead."

Once again I stopped writing because I wasn't sure what would happen next. Plus I was tired. Six in the morning would come too soon. Glancing at the clock, I saw that I had only another hour to sleep before the alarm went off. Why was I writing like this in the middle of the night? It was insane, with everything else I had to do. Yet I didn't begrudge the lost sleep. The story intrigued me. The more time I spent with Sarteen, the more I *knew* her and respected the tremendous burden that had been placed on her. Her last decision, however, had been a mistake. After licking his wounds, the alien captain would come after her again. And he wasn't a nice guy.

After backing up what I had written on the hard drive onto a jump drive, I turned off the computer and stumbled in the direction of my bedroom. Out of the corner of my eye, I noticed Jacob sitting up on the couch.

"Jacob," I said softly. "It's just me. Do you need to use the bathroom? I can help you to it."

"No, thank you," he said in a sleepy voice. "I don't need to go. I just heard some noise and got nervous."

I went over and sat beside him on the couch. He wore a white T-shirt and dark sweatpants. A shaft of moonlight peeped through the curtains; his glass eyes glistened in the pale glow like large hailstones.

"I'm sorry I woke you," I said. "I was writing."

"Is it daytime?" he asked.

His question saddened me. It could be pitch black and he couldn't tell. Of course, blackness was all he knew. I reached out and took his hand.

"No," I said. "It's an hour or two before dawn. You should go back to sleep."

"Do you like to write so late?" he asked.

"Not this late. This is unusual. But this story—it won't let me sleep."

"What's it about?"

I chuckled. "I don't know. It takes place in the future. Humanity is out exploring the stars when it's suddenly attacked by an alien race. I don't know how it's going to turn out."

"I'd like to read it when you're done."

"Peter can read it to you. Or maybe it will be translated into Braille. Do you read many books?"

"I listen to books on tape. I've listened to some of yours."

"Did you like them?"

Jacob flashed a smile. "Yeah. They were creepy. They gave me nightmares." He paused. "Peter's going to take me to meet this yogi tomorrow. He told me all about him. I can hardly wait. Peter says that he has the power to heal people."

I squeezed Jacob's hand. "Maybe he does have the power, I don't know. But I think the healing this man gives is on the inside. If you go to him expecting to be able to see, you will be disappointed. It's important that you understand that."

Jacob shook his head. "I wasn't thinking he could fix me. I've always been blind. I don't know what's it's like to see. I don't care that much one way or the other. As long as I can play baseball. But I hope he can heal Peter. Peter used to be able to

walk—he's used to walking." He added, "I know Peter wants
to go walking with you."

I had to bite my lip to keep from crying. Often I went
walking along the beach in the evening. But because of his
wheelchair and the sand and water, Peter was unable to accompany
me. Why couldn't I just stay on the concrete sidewalk
that ran along the beach?

"He told you that?" I whispered. Peter had never said anything
to me. Hearing the pain in my voice, Jacob was instantly
concerned.

"Did I say something wrong?" he asked.

"No. Everything you say is right. Tell me, Jacob, and tell
me the truth. How do you pitch when you can't see whom
you're pitching to? I know the catcher talks the whole time to
give you direction, but I still don't see how you do it."

Jacob considered. "I don't know. When I wind up to throw
the ball, I just know where to throw it." He added hastily, "I've
never hit anybody. I wouldn't play if I hit people."

"But how do you know?"

Jacob paused. "I never thought about it. Maybe the yogi
could tell me if I asked him. Would that be a good question to
ask him?"

I had to laugh. "I think it would be the perfect question
to ask. He may or may not be able to work miracles, as I said,
but you are a miracle, Jacob. I'm going to come see you play
the first chance I get."

Jacob beamed. "I'd like that."

"I like you," I said. "You stay here as long as you want. I mean that."

"Thank you, Shari."

"You don't have to thank me." Standing, I kissed him on the forehead. "Now go to sleep."

I went to bed and crawled under the covers. I felt as if I'd barely closed my eyes when the alarm went off.

God, my head was throbbing with pain.

I need a miracle.

CHAPTER XI

LUCILLE DID NOT LIKE WATER. No, actually, Lucille was terrified of water. The terror could be used in later scenes because we were, after all, making a scary movie. If only Lucille could have learned to save it, bottle it somehow. But we couldn't have her character Mary screaming as soon as the incoming water went above her knees. The water was supposed to go up to their necks before they abandoned their attempt to plug the holes. Andy shouted "Cut!" so many times that I thought he would walk the first day of shooting. Finally he threw in the towel—literally, at Lucille. All the actors had to dry themselves off between cuts. Fortunately they were wearing bathing suits. We just had to blow-dry their legs, bikinis, and trunks. Jo took Lucille aside to comfort her while I retreated to a corner to have a private nervous breakdown with Henry.

"Has anything like this ever happened to you before?" I complained.

"I was once filming a movie about skydiving," he began.

"Don't tell me," I interrupted. "Your star was afraid of heights?"

"No. He was suicidal. He jumped out of the plane without a parachute."

I made a face. "Did he die?"

"He didn't bounce." He paused. "What are we going to do?"

"I'm supposed to ask you that question."

Henry considered. "We could cancel the day's shoot. Call some of the others on our backup lists."

I waved my hand. "Most of them couldn't act."

"Yeah, but they could probably all swim. Mary's not a crucial role. We don't need an Academy Award-winning performance."

"All the roles are crucial. Have one bad actor in the lot and they'll all look bad. Besides, I hate to fall a whole day behind at the beginning." I stopped and glanced over at Lucille, who was sobbing into a towel. She knew we were talking about her. She would have had to be brain-dead not to know. "Maybe we could give her a stiff drink."

"We could if this was a western," Henry said. "We have to face reality. Lucille can't be in this movie. If she's nervous here, she'll be hysterical when we shoot with the sharks and out on the ocean."

Roger came over. "I know what the problem is and I know what the solution is," he said boldly.

Henry and I exchanged looks. "We're all ears," Henry said.

"Shari can play Mary," he said. He raised his hand as I started to protest. "I watched you read the other day. You're a wonderful actress, completely natural, very expressive. Also, you know every scene, every line of dialogue. If you bring in someone new, we'll all have to rehearse with her for a couple of days. You'll lose time and money."

Henry was staring at me. "He has a point."

"He's forgetting one small thing," I said. "I have never acted in front of a camera in my life. Besides, I can't be in my own movie. That's the height of egotism."

"Hollywood is all about ego," Henry said. "But I agree with Roger, I think you can play the role. The camera is not as frightening as you think. It just takes pictures."

"That millions of people see," I said.

"We hope millions will see this movie," Henry reminded me.

"Shari," Roger said, taking my hand. "Your fear of the camera will vanish quickly. In this scene the camera is hardly ever focused on Mary. She's just reacting with the others. She has two lines. Think about it—we can shoot all day if you can say those two lines."

I considered. "Will I have to wear a bikini?"

"You'll look funny if you're the only one dressed like an executive producer," Henry said in his most helpful manner.

I grumbled, yet inside my heart was racing. Me, in the movies? What a thought. Besides being absolutely terrifying, it was also terribly exciting. If I was good, I thought, maybe I'd get work in other films. Films other than my own. Anything was possible, especially for a cosmic Wanderer like myself. I burst out laughing.

"All right, I'll do it," I said.

Roger patted me on the shoulder. "Good."

"This better not be a setup to embarrass me," I told him, pinching his darling face.

Roger grinned. "I know better ways to do that."

"I bet you do," I said, catching his eye.

"Who gets to fire Lucille?" Henry asked.

I glanced at the weeping girl. "I think she's ready to quit."

An hour later we were ready to shoot again. Lucille hadn't been happy about leaving, but she was reasonable enough to see that we had no choice. Of course, we had her safely off the set before we announced I was taking her part. Bob was the only one to burst out laughing. I felt like throwing something at him.

"This is turning into a B movie," he said. "Who told you you can act? Your money?"

"Why don't you at least let me make a fool of myself before ridiculing me," I said.

Bob nodded. "But then I have your permission to ridicule you?"

Roger came up and stood at my side. "You don't have my permission," he said.

Bob gave him a dark look. "You know, I could sue you for punching me out."

Roger held his eye. "You could, but then you'd have to suffer the consequences. And I don't mean in court."

"All right," I said, stepping between them. "This is all make-believe. We don't need hard reality here. Andy, are you ready to roll? Good. *Lights. Camera. Action.* Let's do it."

So I made my acting debut and I was damn good—in one out of nine of the takes we shot. But, hey, it only takes one great slice of celluloid—taped together with sixty other great slices—to win an Oscar. And it wasn't as if I was bad in the other eight takes. In four of them someone else caused Andy to yell, "Cut!" We each took turns screwing up, except for Roger, who was the consummate pro. Andy said he would have the camera on Roger more than on anyone else. It wasn't until later, when I saw the dailies, that I realized how much the camera loved Roger. His strong jaw line, his dark eyes—his face seemed to leap off the screen. A star is born, and it was happening before our eyes.

I didn't look bad either. I enjoyed acting. It was like being a kid and playing let's pretend. I knew how to pretend to be Mary because I had created Mary. She was me—she was a part of me. And I suppose that made me her God. Yeah, stepping in front of the camera went straight to my head. Yet, even though the experience gave me a huge rush, it didn't bring the deeper contentment that writing did. Acting was emotional for me, but constructing a story out of nothing—more spiritual.

I thought of the yogi as we watched the dailies, and wondered how Peter and Jimmy were doing with the kriya and meditation. My headache had receded, somewhat, as the afternoon went on, but it never really left me. Once again, I wished the yogi was staying in Los Angeles a few days longer. Even though I wasn't taking his course, I planned to try to see him that evening. But Roger headed me off as I was leaving and asked what I was doing that evening. We were alone in the parking lot. The sun was still up but close to the horizon. The orange light on his face played up his strong features. When I explained where I was going, he didn't laugh as I thought he would.

"I know I must have sounded like a smart-ass at his lecture," he said. "And the way he pushed my buttons at the end did embarrass me. I also admit that in his own way, he is a brilliant speaker. He has something special—there's no denying it."

"I think so," I said, pleased that he was being open about the subject.

"But," he said, "let me explain where I was coming from, and see if some of what I say doesn't make sense. I've had to fight for everything I've ever gotten in life. No one's ever given me a thing. In a way, I think that's good. It's made me a strong person. When I raised my concern about giving up my personal power, I meant it. I think our world is a jungle and we have to struggle for what we can get. I'm sorry if that doesn't sound as idealistic as the blissful creation the yogi talked about, but I think it's reality. When I challenged him on that point and he maneuvered around it, it made me mad. I think you can understand why."

"I don't think he maneuvered around it," I said diplomatically. "I just think his point of view is different from yours. It doesn't mean that you're wrong and he's right."

Roger took a breath. "All right, let me put it another way. He's a monk. He says he's just here to help people and I believe him. That's fine as far as it goes. Maybe he isn't interested in money, I don't know. But because he is a monk, he lives in a different world from the rest of us. He doesn't have to go to work every day and scrape to make a living. Do you see what I'm saying?"

I wondered what had happened to Roger's affluent background.

"Sort of," I said.

"Let me be specific. The people around him obviously look up to him as a Master. Although he doesn't come right out and say he is one, he never denies it. As he travels around the world, he collects followers. God knows half the people at the lecture last night signed up for his course. I even saw that sitting outside. Now as time goes by, these people will idolize him more and more. They hang on to his every word already. But what happens when he gives the wrong advice? I'm not saying he's going to tell them to drink poisoned Kool-Aid or anything like that. Comparing him to Jim Jones or David Koresh was unfair on my part. But I'm saying he's a human being like you and me. He's not perfect."

"I suppose he could make a mistake," I muttered.

"Exactly. The trouble is the people around him think he's perfect. That's my main complaint. They stop looking to themselves for guidance and put their trust totally in him. I don't like that. I think it's dangerous."

"But he did say that a true Master will always teach a person to think for herself or himself. I don't think he wants to interfere with our personal lives in any way. I don't think it's his style."

"You're missing the point. He says one thing, which he may sincerely believe, I don't know—but something quite different is happening around him. Look at your friend Peter. If that yogi told him to jump off a cliff, he'd do it."

"But Peter can't jump," I said softly.

"I'm sorry. I didn't mean it that way. But Peter's known this guy—what? Three days? And already he stares at him like he's Jesus returned to Earth. That kind of adulation disturbs me. You're smart, Shari. In your books you write about how people behave, how they fool themselves. Surely you can see that Peter's fooling himself?"

I hesitated. "Much of what you say is reasonable. I think blind faith can be dangerous. I'm suspicious of cults and always have been. But I know from my own experience that the yogi made me feel better. Not just mentally or emotionally, but physically as well. I had a terrible headache when I went to see him and he took it away."

Roger flashed a nasty smile. "Well, I know how to get rid of headaches, too."

I giggled. "You do? How?"

He touched my shoulder. "A long back massage with warm oil to start."

I blushed. "I don't know. That sounds dangerous. You might do that and I might jump when you say jump."

He continued to stroke me. His dark eyes so big, so friendly. "A full-body massage is especially effective at removing stress. You feel so relaxed afterward, you feel you can do anything. What do you say?"

I blinked. "To what?"

"Dinner."

I shook my head. "I don't know. I'm pretty tired. I should take it easy tonight."

"But you weren't going to take it easy. You were going to go see the yogi. Remember?"

"Yeah. I guess you're right."

He moved closer, spoke softly in my ear. "Why don't you see me instead? I won't tell Peter."

I leaned against him. "I don't know. I feel funny about it."

He stroked my hair. "Fun is good. It's good fun."

"But I did want to see the yogi. He's only here for a short time."

He lightly kissed my ear. "What will you do with the yogi? He'll say wise things and you'll nod your head and go home and feel a little more spiritual. With me you won't even have to speak. You can just lie there and feel wonderful."

I giggled again. "You make it sound tempting."

He lightly kissed my cheek. "That's what I'm here for—to tempt you."

I nodded. "I believe it."

He kissed me then, on the lips, in the middle of the parking lot, with no one around. The setting sun lit his hair on fire. He kissed me long and deep—and deep was the operative word. Because I felt as if I were falling as I sank into his arms. Down a long dark tunnel, at the end of which a white light shone, or a purple light smoldered. Which it was, a path of light or one of darkness, I didn't know. And suddenly I didn't care.

I only knew that, once again, I was going to miss seeing the yogi.

CHAPTER XII

OVER THE PAST THREE YEARS, because I have been so busy, Peter and I have often communicated via voicemail. At dinner with Roger, drinking wine and eating steak, I excused myself to check on my messages. I knew Peter would leave me his evening schedule, and I wanted to plan my time with Roger around that schedule. To my surprise, Peter had left me a message saying he was going to a program with the yogi, and that he wouldn't be home until eleven o'clock. It was almost as if he were giving me permission to cheat on him.

And that was the question of the hour, wasn't it? Was I going to betray my dear friend? Was I going to let Roger seduce me, as he clearly intended? For all my internal dialogue concerning my situation, I had not decided where I wanted my relationship with Roger to lead. God knows I was feeling horny. I hadn't had sex since I'd been in my *last* body. True,

Jean had had a few good times in *this* body, but those memories only whetted my appetite for more. A million fantasies of being alone with Roger ran through my head. What would it be like to have him give me a full-body massage? It was better not even to think about it, not while standing up. But what would it be like to sleep beside Peter after I'd had sex with another guy? Somehow, I didn't think I could bear that.

I will never find another Peter.

Yet when Roger asked me where I wanted to go as we left the restaurant, I said, My place.

It was eight-thirty.

Honestly, I thought it was safer to go to the apartment than his room. If we went to the Beverly Hills Hotel, we would just end up in bed. I thought at home I wouldn't let things get out of hand.

Yet when we got there Roger asked me if I wanted a massage.

I said yes.

It was nine o'clock.

Honestly, I didn't know he would actually take off my clothes. He just pulled up my shirt to start, and then he got some baby oil, so I had to take off my shirt because I didn't want to get oil on it. His hands felt so good, moving up and down and around and around, pressing all the sore and sensitive spots. I don't remember exactly when I took off my pants, but I do remember when he started kissing me again, and how it felt like the most delicious act imaginable in all of creation. His lips, his tongue, his hands—they were what I *needed*. If this was sin, then maybe I belonged in hell. I felt so good. Soon the oil was over both of us. The hot sweaty oil.

Suddenly I didn't know what time it was.

Until I heard someone standing behind us.

I sat up with a start.

Actually, I almost leaped out of my skin.

Jacob was standing in the doorway of my bedroom in his swimming trunks, dazed and confused, his white cane in his pitching hand. In an instant I understood what had happened. Peter had dropped Jacob back at the apartment so that the young man could relax and use the pool and sauna. Jacob had said something earlier about wanting to try them out. I had not forgotten that Jacob was staying with us, but had just never thought Peter would leave the blind boy home alone. Yet Jacob was seventeen; he was used to being out on the streets. Once Peter had shown him how to get from the pool back to the apartment, Jacob was more than capable of taking care of himself. Indeed, the possibility should have crossed my mind when I reentered the apartment. The door had been unlocked, and Peter never left without throwing the dead bolt.

In either case I had been caught with my pants down and I felt as terrible as a human being could feel and still be breathing. Before Jacob appeared, I realized how loud we had both been groaning, me in particular. Yet we hadn't had sex yet, although we were as close as two people could get. Jacob turned away.

"I'm sorry," he said. "I didn't mean to intrude. I didn't know you were home—Shari, Peter."

Hastily I put a finger to my lip, signaling Roger not to speak. Grabbing a robe from beside the bed, I threw it on and chased after Jacob. I found him sitting on the couch, trembling, on the verge of tears. Obviously, even if he had the participants confused, he knew what we had been in the middle of, so there would be no point in trying to deny it. Clearly he felt terrible for having walked in on us. Sitting beside him, I put my arm around his shoulder.

"That's all right, Jacob," I said. "You didn't disturb us. Don't be upset."

He moaned, his head down. "I'm so sorry."

I forced a laugh. "No. You have no reason to be sorry. Hey, how was the pool? Pretty cool, huh?"

He looked up, or at least, raised his head. "I liked it. I've never been in a pool before."

"Really? Did you go in the sauna?"

"Yeah. Boy, it was hot in there. I couldn't stop sweating."

I giggled nervously. "That's what you're supposed to do, silly. Hey, can I get you something to drink?"

"Sure."

"A Coke? Three Cokes?"

He smiled sheepishly. "Could I have two, please?"

I jumped up. "You got it. How was the yogi today?"

"Wonderful. He gave me a flower and taught me to meditate."

I opened the refrigerator. "Did you like it?"

"Yes. I got so relaxed I almost went to sleep. But he said that was OK." He paused, frowning in the direction of the bedroom. "Is Peter mad at me?"

"No. I told you, no one's mad. Would you like your Coke in a can or a glass?"

"I like it in a can. How come Peter hasn't come out of the room?"

"He's tired." So far Roger was wisely staying put. "He's resting."

"What time is it?"

"I don't know. Around ten. Maybe a little later."

"It's that late?"

"Yes," I lied.

"I didn't think Peter would be home. He said he was going to the yogi's evening meeting. That's what he told me when he dropped me off."

"Really? I think he did go." I returned to Jacob with the Cokes, both opened. "He just got home a few minutes ago."

"If he's not asleep yet, could I speak to him? I want to tell him I'm sorry."

I giggled again. Boy, I sounded guilty. "You don't have to tell him anything. It's better to drop it. Trust me on this. He won't want to talk about it." I lowered my voice, speaking confidentially. "It would just embarrass him."

Jacob was uncertain. "OK, I won't say anything. As long as he doesn't want to kick me out."

I gave Jacob a quick squeeze. "No one's going to kick you out. I told you last night, you can stay as long as you want. Now drink your Cokes and stop worrying. Oh, maybe you should change out of your swimming trunks first. You don't want to get the couch all wet."

Jacob felt his trunks. "They're dry from the sauna."

"Yeah, but you should probably still change. Here, let me help you into the bathroom. I got your sweats here. You can change and be all ready for bed." I helped him up.

"Do I have to go to bed now? Can't I watch TV?"

Jacob enjoyed several shows, and knew many TV characters well, even though he had trouble following action scenes. "Sure," I said. "You can watch whatever you want. I just think you should get ready for bed."

"OK."

The moment I had the bathroom door closed, I gestured to Roger. He was no fool. He was already dressed and ready to go. We had driven to the apartment in our own cars. He kissed me quickly as he headed out the door.

"Do I get a rain check?" he whispered.

"We'll see."

"Did you have fun?"

"Yes! Now go! Shoo!"

Roger grinned, enjoying my discomfort. "Do you love me?"

"Do you love me?" I asked.

He snorted. "I love what you do for me."

I pushed him away. "Get out of here!"

Jacob came out of the bathroom a few minutes later. He had changed and used the bathroom and brushed his teeth. With a dread bordering on nausea, I tried to think what he would say when Peter came rolling through the front door in a couple of hours. I could only hope Jacob was sound asleep by then. But even if he was, surely he would wake when his hero came home. Hey, Peter, I thought you were asleep in the bedroom. I could just see it now. What was I going to do?

"Hey, Jacob," I said. "Are you tired?"

"A little. Do I have to go to bed?"

"No. In fact, I was just thinking we should go to Disneyland."

"Disneyland? Right now?"

"Yes. Have you ever been to Disneyland?"

"No."

"It's great."

"But you want to go now?"

"Yes. What's wrong with now?"

"I thought you wanted me to get ready for bed?"

"Yeah, but you said you're not tired. So we should go to Disneyland."

"Is it open at this time?"

"Yeah. It's only nine o'clock."

"I thought you said it was ten o'clock?"

"I was wrong. I think, in the summer, Disneyland stays open late." I patted Jacob on the back. "Come on, you'll love it."

Jacob finally smiled. "Let's go."

Of course, I wanted to keep Jacob out long enough so Peter would be asleep when we came home. By tomorrow morning, I hoped, Jacob would have forgotten all about walking in on us.

Disneyland was crowded. It was a weekend night in the summer, and a warm evening to boot. The line for Space Mountain was the longest but we went on it three times because the fun of it wasn't affected by whether you could see or not. In fact, each time I rode it, I kept my eyes clenched shut. Jacob howled; he was having the time of his life. We also went on the train ride because Jacob liked trains, and Thunder Mountain, which was another roller coaster-like ride. Jacob ate four hot dogs and two bags of popcorn and one slice of pizza. No stomach problems with this guy.

We got home at two in the morning and Peter was still up.

He glowed, I swear. I was jealous. Like the two preceding nights, he sat under the lamp in the corner reading. I had left him a note saying that I was taking Jacob to Disneyland, and that he shouldn't wait up for us. He smiled happily as we came through the door. Kriya and meditation obviously agreed with him.

"How was it?" he asked.

Jacob was still shaking with excitement. "Awesome! We went on every ride!"

I hadn't explained to Jacob that there was only one Space Mountain. I just gave it a new name each time. Leaning over to give Peter a kiss, I said, "It was a blast. How's the course going? Or do I need to ask?"

Peter nodded. "It's everything we hoped for. First we did some simple breathing exercises, then he taught us the kriya. During it you repeat certain set rhythms of breathing. Each rhythm is supposed to correspond to a different level: one to the body, one to the mind, another to the soul. The kriya integrates the different levels. I know that sounds abstract, but what it all boils down to is that after you do it, you feel incredible. You go really deep inside and when you come out it's like everything is brand-new. All your stress is gone and you feel like a little kid. You just want to play and have fun and enjoy life. It's amazing, you have to do it."

"I want to do it," I said honestly. I could have used a little less stress in my life. Especially when Jacob spoke next.

"Hey, Pete," he said. "I thought you were tired. I thought you went to bed early."

Peter was confused. "No. I went to the yogi's evening meeting. I told you I was going there when I dropped you off. Remember?"

"Yeah," Jacob said, "but when you came home you went to bed."

"Well," I broke in. "We don't know how long he's been home. It doesn't matter. Let's all go to bed. We all have to get up early tomorrow. Jacob, let me get your sweats for you. Here, I'll lead you to the bathroom. Peter, do you need anything?"

He still seemed a little puzzled. "No. I'm fine."

We were in bed ten minutes—Peter was already beginning to doze—when I spoke. There was no way I could sleep if I didn't. And I knew there would be no easy rest for me after I did, but that was the consequence of the choice I had made.

"Peter," I said softly.

"Huh?" he mumbled, his back to me.

"Roger was here this evening."

"What?"

"Roger was here this evening."

Peter rolled over and looked at me. "What are you talking about?"

I continued to stare at the ceiling, wishing I could leave my body, and soar through the roof and come once again to a place where there was no pain. I cleared my throat.

"Roger was here this evening."

"I heard you the first time. Why was he here?"

I swallowed. "I don't know."

"Shari?"

Tears formed in my eyes. "He was here with me. He was

here when Jacob walked in. He was here and we were—We were here together, in this bed."

There was a long painful silence. Peter's voice came out like a croak.

"Why?"

I sat up and bent over, feeling as if I would vomit. Burying my face in my knees, I started to shake. "I'm sorry," I mumbled.

"Shari?"

"Yes."

His voice cracked. "Did you sleep with him?"

"Peter."

"Did you sleep with him?"

I sat up and looked over. His face was a burnt-out star.

"Almost," I said.

He died then, a little. I believe we both did. Certainly I felt like a murderer. He couldn't speak, he could scarcely breathe. I wanted to touch him, to comfort him. I tried, but he shook my hand off and I quickly withdrew it, knowing how my touch must feel to him. Like the skin of a rattler pulled across his skin. I turned away and put my feet on the floor, wondering if I had the strength to stand.

"I'm sorry," I told the wall.

He didn't speak. He only wept.

"Do you want me to leave?" I asked.

He didn't answer. His tears said it all.

I stood, swaying. "I think I should leave."

I dressed and packed an overnight bag and grabbed my laptop, slipping the jump drive from my other computer into the laptop. Peter sat hugging his lifeless legs the whole time, forcing air into his lungs, awash in tears that burned both our souls. There were a million things I could have said to him. I was a writer and a genius at inventing lines of dialogue. Yet there was nothing to say now that would make things better. There comes a time, I suppose, when words fail. Love knows no reason, the yogi said. If that was true, I thought, then pain knew no answer. My pain was like a cancer, a disease I had freely chosen to share. How much I hated myself then was matched only by how little I understood myself. Above all else, I wished I had never been reborn.

I stepped to the bedroom door. On the living room couch, Jacob continued to sleep peacefully. Turning, I looked back at Peter, my dearest love.

"Goodbye," I said.

He didn't look up. "Goodbye."

I love you. More than anything in the whole creation, I love you.

"Take care of yourself, Peter," I whispered.

Then I was gone, into the night, where everything was and always would be black.

CHAPTER XIII

THE LOBBY OF THE Beverly Hills Hotel was plush. For a thousand bucks a night, it should have been. The guy at the desk took one look at me and was obviously inclined to point me in the direction of Motel 6. Without a spot of makeup and on the verge of a nervous breakdown, I was no sight for sore eyes. But when I pulled out my platinum American Express card his expression changed. The card had no limit. I didn't ask him for the room number of Roger Teller, or even if he could ring him for me. For the first time in a long time, I wasn't in the mood for sex and didn't even know why I had chosen to stay at that particular hotel.

My room was lovely. There were flowers on the coffee table and champagne on ice. The bathroom was as large as the egos of most people who probably stayed in the suite. I sampled the expensive Swiss chocolates that had been laid out for me, finding them tasteless. The champagne also tasted like vinegar. I spat it out after the first sip.

"Jesus," I whispered.

I got ready for bed. Turned out the lights. It didn't help. Sleep was not on good terms with broken hearts. It would have nothing to do with them. Thirty minutes later I was back up and turning on my laptop. If I couldn't rest, I decided, I'd work. Telling stories, lies, was the only thing I was good for.

THE STARLIGHT CRYSTAL

An hour after disabling the Orion vessel and deciding to flee—sixty minutes before Sarteen's starship would be in position to jump into hyperspace—the alien ship began to accelerate in their direction again. Pareen gave Sarteen the bad news.

"Captain," he said anxiously. "They're coming."

"Will they get to us before we jump?" she asked, sitting in her command chair on the bridge.

"It will be very close, one way or the other. But if I were to guess—Yes, they will just catch us."

Sarteen nodded to herself. She had erred. She should have fired the disrupters when she had the chance. Captain Eworl was probably laughing at her now. The extent of her mistake weighed heavily on her.

"Do we have any nanoeggs left?" she asked.

"I released our entire stock." Pareen shrugged. "I thought it was our last chance."

She gave him a reassuring smile, "I understand. I would have released them all as well. Now, what do we do? We must assume they'll catch up to us. They are damaged, and perhaps their shields aren't working. Can we defeat them in a direct fight?"

Pareen shook his head. "Doubtful. They only need to hit us once with their energy beams. I cannot believe we destroyed all their weaponry."

"By your best estimate, how close will we come to having sufficient velocity to jump into hyperspace?" she asked.

"We will have ninety-eight percent of required velocity."

"What if we implode our engines? Just as they come within firing range?"

Pareen was aghast. "That will permanently destroy our engines. When we come out of hyperspace on the other side we won't be able to slow."

"We can decelerate using our retro rockets."

"That'll take years."

"Will we be in a hurry? We have already spent a thousand years aboard this ship. What are a few more? If we implode the engines that will give us the last shove we need to jump into hyperspace."

"Are you forgetting that we already have serious structural damage? The implosion will probably destroy us."

"It is a chance we'll have to take since it is our only chance."
Sarteen stood. "I am going to my quarters. I will be back in time
for our jump."

Once more Sarteen turned to her golden column of precious
stones for guidance. Its proximity soothed her, brought her
into a state of calm clarity and intuition where she felt as if
she could almost touch the great secrets of the universe to
understand the reason for this attack. Yet in her heart she felt
she already knew the answer to the riddle. The invasion had
occurred because, as a people, they were not ready to be with
the Elders. And even the Elders had not known that. Perhaps in
their great love for humanity, they had reached out too soon to
bring their children home. Perhaps the Elders, too, were under
attack. That was a disturbing thought. Yet Sarteen somehow
doubted that that was the case. The Orions were physical, the
Elders interdimensional. The Elders could not be fenced in as
Earth could be. Sarteen had tried repeatedly to contact home,
any of the planets, without success. Sadly, she felt there was no
escape for them. Not in the foreseeable future.

"But we must escape," she said to the empty room. "We
must live."

Even before speaking to Eworl, she had sensed the hatred
of the Orions. Now that they'd had contact, there was no doubt
in her mind that the enemy planned to turn Earth into a planet
of pain. To gloat over when they grew angry or bored.

What could defeat these hideous creatures? Where was their vulnerable point? Before contact was lost with the galactic center, the Elders had explained that three feelings in the heart guided the destiny of all creatures: love, hatred, and fear. Clearly the Orions had hatred in abundance and seemed to have no use for love. But what about fear? Were they easily frightened? Could their captain be tricked—out of fear—into making a mistake? Perhaps she would get the chance to test the idea. The Elders had said where there was no love, fear always lurked close.

The communicator on her desk beeped.

"Yes?" she said.

"The Orion vessel is closing more rapidly than I thought possible."

"Will we still be able to implode the engines and get into hyperspace?"

"The farther we are from our desired velocity, the more difficult it will be. You'd better return to the bridge. Also, we have another problem, if it is a problem. The aliens have fixed a peculiar beam on us. it is not a weapon of any sort, not one that I am familiar with anyway. But it is causing minute changes in the hull of our ship."

"What kind of changes?"

"It is irradiating the hull—slightly. I'm puzzled because this level of radiation could not possibly harm us. It's more as if we are being marked."

"For what purpose?"

"I have no idea. But it makes me nervous."

Sarteen stood. "I am on my way."

On the bridge Pareen continued to analyze the energy beam from the Orion ship. Sarteen stood by his side as he worked. She had made the decision to implode the engines because it was, as she had said, their only chance. Her feeling on the matter had not changed, yet as the time of implosion approached, she grew anxious. Pareen was correct: implosion was dangerous with a sound ship, but with the deep gashes in the hull, it was doubly so. The procedure called for them to transform their engines into the equivalent of a huge bomb, which would give them an extra kick in velocity as it was spent. The trouble was that sometimes an implosion could go out of control and annihilate everything in the immediate vicinity. In her youth, centuries ago, Sarteen had witnessed a starship that had been forced to implode its engines. It had not survived.

"Are you certain their beam is not harming us?" Sarteen asked.

"It isn't. As I said, it just seems to be marking us. Perhaps they use it before firing their weapons, to get a better fix on us."

"I don't think so. They had no trouble getting a fix on us last time. I want to implode the engines now, and take our chances."

"I advise against it," Pareen said. "The closer we are to light velocity, the greater chance we'll have of surviving the jump into hyperspace."

"Another thirty minutes of acceleration will make little difference. Also, we don't know the actual range of their weapons."

"Last time they waited until they were close before they opened fire," Pareen said.

Sarteen stepped away, toward her seat. "It means nothing. Prepare the engines for implosion. Alert all decks. It will be a rough ride."

"It may be a short ride," Pareen said grimly.

A few minutes later, just as the Orion ship came into view, they were set for their big gamble. Under maximum magnification, it still looked seriously damaged. Yet Sarteen noticed another weapons port on the far side, steadily increasing its energy discharge; an angry red eye in the black well of space. Wary of another trick, Captain Eworl was preparing to attack from a distance. Let him try firing over hundreds of light-years, Sarteen thought. If the implosion worked, they'd be that far from the solar system in a matter of seconds.

"What is our destination?" Pareen asked.

"The Pleiades star cluster," Sarteen said, having made the decision earlier. There were numerous planets in that particular system capable of supporting life. Plus Pleiadian skies, filled with hundreds of blue stars floating in rivers of nebulae, were glorious. A fitting heaven to give the children of humanity. Pareen nodded at her choice, approving.

"We are ready," he said a minute later, sitting down and fastening his seat belt

"What are our chances?" Sarteen asked.

"Less than one in three."

"If we don't make it, I want it to go on the official record that you opposed this idea. That way history will say you should have been the captain."

"You are clever," Pareen said. "History will only have a chance to read the record if you're right. Let's leave our last entry blank. That way we're both wrong—or right."

Sarteen smiled. "Agreed." She sat back in her chair and fastened her belt. "Initiate implosion."

Her command was obeyed. Unlike when they were struck with the Orion energy beam, the ship did not convulse with shock waves. The *Crystal* had a dampening field around it that kept their frail human bodies from being crushed while they were under acceleration. Obviously, with the implosion of their engines, the increase in acceleration was dramatic, yet even that pressure was canceled out by the field. Nevertheless, Sarteen felt terrific *internal* motion when Pareen pushed the button. It was as if her consciousness was momentarily split open, and it was able to extend in two separate directions. Her body hummed; every cell could have suddenly begun vibrating at a high rate. She had closed her eyes and therefore could not be sure if the lights failed. Yet inside everything went black. And cold—it was an eerie sensation to feel as if she had been dropped into a galactic vortex, a whirlwind of colliding forces, that spun around and around and never reached bottom. It was like being dead; at least, what she would have imagined nonexistence to be. How long she remained in that state, she didn't know. Out of nowhere Pareen was shouting something important.

"We have made the jump! We are outside the Pleiades!"

Sarteen opened her eyes, seeing the blazing blue splendor of the cluster on the main viewing screen.

She smiled. "Thank God."

"Don't thank anybody too soon!" Pareen cried. "The Orions have made the jump, too!"

Sarteen leaped to her feet. "That's impossible. Nothing can track a ship through hyperspace"

Pareen shook his head. "Now we know why they were irradiating our hull. That radiation must have left a trail of our jump. Their technology is even more advanced than we imagined."

"How far behind us are they?" Sarteen asked.

"Two minutes."

"Can we maneuver? Fire weapons?"

"No. We're dead in space, drifting. Our engines are gone. We have to surrender."

"We will not surrender!" Sarteen shouted.

"Then we will die, this time without a fight." Pareen consulted his instruments. "They are energizing their weapons."

Sarteen thought frantically. Their weak spot must be fear;

the clarity bestowed on her by the golden column would not have misled her. Yet how could she frighten them when she had only minutes to live? Or was she asking the question backward? If fear was their blind spot, would they not assume it was humanity's weakness as well? How could she make it appear that they—her crew and herself—were helpless because of fear?

"We will go to Parting mode," she said.

Parting, as they called it, involved separating the living quarters of the ship from the control and power sections. The living quarters could slip off from the spherical *Crystal* like pieces of a sliced fruit. Lacking contact with the main engines, the sections could scarcely maneuver, and certainly could not fight. Yet, with the help of retro rockets, they would still be able to steer toward an Earth-like planet—and take fifty years to get there. It was better than going up in a ball of flame. But as Pareen's stunned expression said, what was the point of executing a Parting? The Orions would just blow the other sections out of the ether.

"Why bother?" Pareen asked. "Shouldn't we die together?"

Sarteen shook her head. "Their captain must be able to see we are helpless. If we initiate Parting, he may bring his ship in close." She nodded to Pareen. "Clear the bridge. Notify the remainder of the crew. I alone will stay to greet this Eworl."

"Wait," Pareen said.

"Do it! We don't have time for argument."

"I merely wanted to ask permission to stay with you."

Sarteen smiled as she sat back down. "Permission granted. After Parting is complete—and assuming we're still alive—I want you to go to the lab and get a nanoegg and bring it to the bridge. Attach it to the communication board. Rig it to explode on my voice command."

"But I told you—we have no nanoeggs left."

"You forget our experimental original. It is not space-worthy, and contains only typical antimatter, not the condensed version. But it will still do nicely as a self-destruct weapon."

"Why not just self-destruct now?" Pareen asked.

Sarteen leaned forward, studying the screen and the approaching alien ship. "This Captain Eworl will want to gloat over his prey before destroying it. That will be his style, I think. But he may make a mistake and come too close." She glanced over at Pareen. "Are you sure you want to stay with me?"

He didn't hesitate. "It will be my honor to die by your side."

Her plan was built on several factors. She had explained some but not all the details to Pareen. Because the *Crystal*'s weapon systems and engines were as good as dead, Eworl would see her vessel as harmless. Yet if he were human, he would not bring his ship close enough to be destroyed by a self-destruct command on her part. Nevertheless, that was her hope, and she didn't believe it a vain hope. Because Captain Eworl was *not* human. He was the product of a hateful race, a race that probably cared as little for its own members as it did for those of another race. It was possible he could not conceive of an act of total sacrifice; that she should stay behind and give up her life to save the lives of her crew. Also, as she had said to Pareen, he might want to take captives, to take her prisoner. To have her stand by his side while he wiped out the remaining sections of her ship. Yes, she thought, he would enjoy that. He would not start the killing until he had her.

But he would never have her.

Together, Pareen and Sarteen watched as the four living-quarter sections of the *Crystal* fired their retro rockets and plowed away. Each section was self-contained; her people could survive in space for centuries if need be. If it took that long to reach a life-sustaining world. Silently, she wished them good luck. Beside her, Pareen shook his head.

"If they do survive," he said. "Will their descendants remember this day?"

"It will take only one to remember," Sarteen said thoughtfully, again feeling the sensation she had experienced during the hyperjump. As If she were in two places at one time, in two minds. Shaking herself, she turned back to her seat. "Put the Orion ship on the screen. Hail their captain."

Pareen turned to obey. "He won't believe anything you have to say."

She sat down with a sigh. "He doesn't have to believe me.

He just has to want something from me. Are their weapons still energized?"

"Yes. They have us in their sights. Hailing frequencies open."

"Captain Eworl," she said pleasantly. "We await your instructions."

Once again they received only audio, no video, from their pursuers. The alien captain did not sound as if he were in a good mood. "Prepare for boarding."

Sarteen winked at Pareen. "Our docking bays are open and ready. Do you require special atmospheric conditions?"

"Negative. Disarm and prepare to be taken captive." Captain Eworl paused. "We will tolerate no further deception."

"Understood. Our surrender is total and unconditional. We await your arrival." Sarteen made a motion to Pareen to cut the signal. "The beast falls for the bait," she muttered.

"I'm surprised. I thought he would have been more careful."

Sarteen continued to stare at the approaching Orion ship. Its purple taloned fin, its glowing weapons ports—they reminded her of a nightmare of a half-seen monster she faintly remembered having had. Maybe the recurring dream was the reason she knew mankind's day of rejoicing had not yet arrived. Maybe it was something else. Something older.

"I'm not surprised," she said. "Victory is hollow without the spoils of war. For him to merely destroy us is not enough. He has to bring something back to show his comrades. A trophy to place on his shelf." She nodded to herself. "He wants me."

The Orion vessel, the *Adharma,* docked a short time afterward. At that instant Sarteen's plot could have borne fruit. She could have ignited the nanoegg implanted beneath the bridge communication board, and blown both ships to dust. Impatient, Pareen awaited the command but she shook her head. No, wait, she said. We will wait. Here, at the end, was she suddenly afraid to die? Did she honestly believe that there was a hope of escape? To these questions she had no answers. Yet she knew she needed to confront the enemy. To look into his face, his eyes, and see whether she had seen him before.

"And whether I will see him again," she whispered.

"What did you say?" Pareen asked.

"Nothing. Are their airlocks compatible with ours?"

Pareen checked his instruments. "Apparently. Several of them have already entered the lock. There are six of them. They are pressurizing the chamber." He paused. "They'll reach the bridge in two minutes."

"Have you set the nanoegg to explode on my voice command?"

"Not yet. What word would you like to use as the trigger?"

"The word *Cira.*"

"Why that word?"

Sarteen smiled sadly. "Did you know I had a daughter?"

"You never told me."

"It was many years ago. Her name is Cira. Was Cira." She added softly, "She lived on Malanak, the fifth planet."

Pareen was sympathetic. "I'm sorry."

Sarteen sighed. "At least it ended quickly for her. That's why this captain lets us live this long. He wants our end to be painful. It's pain that feeds him."

"How do you know that?" Pareen asked, working his instruments.

"You will understand when you see him."

"Surely the captain will not be a member of the boarding team."

Sarteen shrugged. "Why not? He thinks we're helpless. He can't imagine we would intentionally kill ourselves. He can't imagine an existence beyond the body. You know, that's what this is all about. The Orions don't believe we have souls." She paused. "Maybe *they* don't."

"Don't say your daughter's name again unless you want the nanoegg detonated."

"Understood. Where are they now?"

"Coming up the elevator." He pointed to the door at the rear of the bridge. "They will come through there."

Sarteen stood, faced the elevator. "How long?"

"One minute. Maybe less."

Sarteen gestured for him to stand beside her. "Pareen," she said. "This last thousand years, has it ever bothered you that I was the captain and not you? We're about to die. You can tell me the truth."

He came close. "Yes. Many times. When I disagreed with you. But at each of those times I later saw the wisdom of your decisions." He nodded toward the elevator door. "This plan was clever. We can stop them now. The others will escape."

"If I say my daughter's name."

"I believe that would be the wise thing to do."

She put an arm around him. "Trust me this last time, Pareen. I won't let you down."

"I trust you, Sarteen."

She leaned over and kissed his cheek. "They have taken the Earth, but it does not belong to them. Let's make a vow to each other. If we are ever given the chance—in whatever time, whatever place—to get the Earth back, we will give it our whole heart. We will not rest until our home is returned to us."

"Agreed." Pareen paused and stared into her eyes. "Did I ever tell you how I feel about you, Sarteen?"

She smiled sadly. "No. Did I ever tell you?"

"No." He glanced at the elevator. "And now there's no time."

She hugged him again. "There's time."

But maybe she was wrong.

At that moment the elevator door opened.

"What does Eworl look like?" I asked my computer screen. "How does Sarteen trick him? How does she get out of this mess?"

Word processors were great inventions. They allowed you to cut and paste and delete and replace. But they could not write your books for you. Certainly they could not help you with your own life. The questions I asked—I wondered if they were for Sarteen or for myself. I felt a deep kinship with her— the whole universe was tumbling down on both our heads.

Turning off the machine, I went to bed.

I slept, a little. There were no dreams.

CHAPTER XIV

THE FOLLOWING AFTERNOON, Sunday, after shooting another wet scene as Mary, Garrett agreed to meet me in his office on my lunch hour. Mary was also in the scenes that were to be shot that afternoon and evening; I had only a few minutes to spare, but I had asked him to meet me in person, rather than talk to me on the phone, because I wanted an excuse to leave the set. After coming so close to having sex with Roger the previous night, I found it difficult to act casual around him. I was ashamed and in lust at the same time. He kept smiling at me; it was unnerving.

Garrett offered me coffee, which I refused. He came straight to the point.

"You were right when you said Roger Teller was an elusive guy," he said. "I ran into problems with something as simple as the DMV check on his car."

"What kind of problems?"

"It turned up nothing."

"What does that mean?"

"His license plate is phony. Assuming you wrote down the number correctly."

"I gave you the right number. How could he have a phony license plate?"

Garrett shrugged. "It's not hard to make a fake license plate, if you're so inclined. It's just that I've never met anyone who went to the trouble."

"*Why* would he have a phony license plate?" I asked.

"To prevent someone from checking up on him, and it worked. It was a dead end for me. So I decided to check into his past acting jobs."

"They also turned out to be fake?"

"No. Each of the places he said he'd been, he really had been. The two acting classes he took, the three plays he was in were genuine. What was curious was how the people in those places talked about him."

"Go on," I said, my curiosity sparked.

"Let me tell you what his last acting teacher, a Mr. Hatcher, said. This Hatcher was on a sci-fi TV series a few years ago. He was, and is, a pretty good actor. Anyway, Hatcher runs a workshop where actors write one-act scripts alone or in pairs and then act them out with a partner in front of the class. Being a producer, I assume you're familiar with the format. By the final class, everyone in the workshop—except Roger and his partner—had done their scenes. Roger was determined to be last. He had gone out of his way to choose the most beautiful young woman in the group as his partner. Hatcher said she seemed very sensible when she joined the workshop. Yet when Roger performed his scene with her, Hatcher had doubts."

"Why?" I asked.

"In front of a class of approximately thirty people, Roger and the girl did a scene where he simulated raping her and stabbing her in the leg, before finally befriending her."

I frowned. "I don't see how that would work."

Garrett snorted. "It's not a question of whether it would work. It's disgusting!"

I nodded. "I understand that. But you don't work in Hollywood. There are rape scenes on prime time TV. That he wrote and performed such a scene is odd, but it doesn't mean he's disturbed."

Garrett stared at me. "I don't think I would fit in in Hollywood very well."

I shrugged. "On a clear day you can see the city out the window of your office. What did the other people say about him?"

"Hatcher gave me a list of people who had taken the workshop. So far, I've been unable to reach the young woman who worked with Roger on the scene. But I did talk to a guy who occasionally went out drinking with him afterward. They would go to a nearby bar and stay out late. Roger, the guy said, could really put them away."

"So? Lots of people drink."

"You asked me to check up on him. To a detective, this is significant. The guy drinks a lot. Not only that, the man I spoke to said he never saw Roger drunk."

"Yes? Am I missing something?"

Garrett scratched his head. "I don't know. I don't even know why I'm telling you this. Except the guy I spoke to— he found Roger's tolerance amazing. He said Roger could put away two bottles of wine and six beers and be perfectly sober." Garrett paused. "Have you seen him drink on the set?"

I hesitated. "Not on the set. But afterward."

Garrett consulted his notes. "Next I spoke to the director of a play Roger was in called *Summer Sleep*. Are you familiar with the story? A woman by the name of Annette Ginger wrote it at the turn of the century. She's not well known nowadays, but in her time she was considered brilliant."

"I'm afraid I've never heard of her."

"*Summer Sleep* is a murder mystery. A group of young men and women travel to a large mansion in upstate New York. There's the usual big storm to isolate them from the rest of the world, and the typical history about how people have died in the mansion under strange circumstances. Yet the mystery is unique; it goes in unexpected directions. Roger played the role of the villain, who was in reality the grandchild of one of the mansion's original victims. It will take me too long to explain the whole story but suffice it to say the role is a demanding one because it requires the actor to be the obvious suspect from the beginning, yet disarm the audience with his innocence. The character does and says one thing after another that incriminates himself. Yet the way Ms. Ginger wrote the play, if the actor can pull it off, he can stun the audience."

"Because his guilt is so obvious he couldn't possibly have committed the crime?"

"Exactly. You should read the play. You'd enjoy it."

"I'll see if I can find a copy of it." I paused. "How did Roger do in the role?"

"Excellent. The Chicago *Herald* reviewed him. It said he was someone to keep an eye on. The only trouble was the play closed after opening night."

"Why?"

"The actress who played the heroine got beat up."

I grimaced. "How bad?"

"Her jaw was broken. She was cut on her cheek. The director said the wound took twenty stitches to close. Something like that would scar, I'd think. I know the question you want to ask. Was Roger responsible for what happened to her? The police say no, although Roger was taken in for questioning. The girl herself never said it was Roger."

"Then why are you building this up to make it seem it might have been Roger?"

"Because the director thought it might have been him."

"Did he have any proof?"

"No hard proof. But I find it strange that a director who worked daily with an actor would suspect him of such a heinous crime. You see, Roger was involved with this young lady. They were living together. And the police report on the crime does state that the girl refused to cooperate with the police in apprehending the criminal."

"Why would the girl protect Roger if he had hurt her so badly? It makes no sense."

"Why would she refuse to cooperate with the authorities if she wasn't protecting someone? Sometimes you have to ask the question backward to arrive at the real question. I had a case a few years ago—when I was still with the police force—where everyone thought a seventeen-year-old girl had committed suicide by jumping off a balcony. On purely circumstantial evidence, even her friends assumed the girl had killed herself. Yet, at the time, I kept asking myself, why would she have done such a thing? She had her whole life in front of her. And until someone could prove to me that she wanted to die, I proceeded on the assumption that she had been murdered. Turned out I was right. Oh, by the way, you might have heard of the girl. Her name was Shari Cooper—the same as your pen name."

I had to remember to breathe. "You know who I am?"

"Yes," he said casually. "You're the writer."

"Have you been checking up on me as well, Mr. Garrett?"

He snorted. "Hardly. My daughter has read a couple of your books. I mentioned to her that you were the producer on a movie called *First to Die* and she got all excited. I guess it's one of her favorite books. Since you told me you were president of Cooper Productions, I put two and two together." He paused, uncertain. "You are Shari Cooper, aren't you?"

I smiled faintly. "I'm Jean Rodrigues. But I would be happy to sign a book for your daughter, if she wishes." God, I thought. It had been madness to come to this office. I continued. "It seems to me you're condemning Roger on purely circumstantial evidence. The same way this Shari Cooper's friends did."

Garrett watched me closely. Somehow, I had pushed a button in him, not a wise move. I had to remind myself how shrewd he was; how he could take the obvious, and see the hidden motive behind it. He had caught Amanda easily enough, thank God. She was another person I had to look up someday, when I was feeling reckless. I wondered if she was still locked away. I never talked to Jimmy about her. The subject pained him too much. Garrett took his time responding.

"You misunderstand me," he said. "I'm not out to condemn Roger. I'm impartial. He's your employee, not mine. You have to work with him on a daily basis. Once again, you hired me to find out these things I'm telling you. For that reason, I must in good conscience offer you my personal evaluation of what I've uncovered. Already I see a pattern here. You may not recognize it, but I do. Roger Teller is a young man who uses young women. I don't care how fanatical you are about your art. You don't write a scene about rape and stabbing and play it out in front of people unless you have serious emotional problems. And you don't beat up your girlfriend and simultaneously scare her so badly that she's afraid to talk to the police." He added, "Not unless you have serious emotional problems."

"Why do you assume he hurt her? I don't get it."

"Why do you assume he didn't?" Garrett paused. "Unless you're personally involved with him."

I stiffened. "My personal business is just that—personal. I don't pay you to pry into it. Have you anything else to tell me?"

Garrett was unmoved by my rebuff. President of a production company or not, I was still just a punk kid to him. "Nothing new. Just a reminder that two separate men—an accomplished actor and a respected director—did not like Roger Teller. They didn't trust him, and I don't think you should trust him either. Not a guy who goes to the trouble to manufacture a phony license plate."

"I will take your advice under consideration. What about Roger's family? His source of income?"

"I'm still looking into that. I have a buddy who works for the Chicago Police. He's supposed to get back to me by tomorrow. He said he had a lead on Roger Teller that might prove interesting."

"Could you elaborate?"

Garrett shook his head. "He refused to elaborate. He wanted to check it out first. That's a cop for you. But this guy's good. He won't go running all over town wasting your money."

"Am I paying him as well?"

Garrett smiled. "Indirectly. I'm sorry if I was heavy-handed a moment ago. It comes with the job. Hey, there's a question I wanted to ask you."

I forced a chuckle. "Where do I get my ideas?"

"Yeah. Does everyone ask you that?"

I stood. "Ninety-nine percent of people. The truth is, I get them in the strangest places. You have no idea how strange. May I see you tomorrow at this time?"

He stood up to walk me out. "Yes, that would be fine. My Chicago buddy should have reported in by then. Oh, if it wouldn't be too much trouble, my daughter left a copy of one of your books on her desk for you to sign. It would mean a lot to her."

I smiled again. "No problem. I'll be glad to sign it."

Garrett followed me into the reception area. Because it was Sunday, his daughter had the day off or else was at lunch. I had eaten nothing all day, but wasn't hungry. When you went to hell and back you didn't pack a lunch. Nothing worked as effectively as the pain and suffering diet. *Cry Those Calories Away.* I should write such a diet book and sell millions of copies.

Garrett's daughter had left a copy of *First to Die.* Quickly

I scribbled my best wishes and name. Garrett took the book and held it as if it was worth its weight in gold. It never ceased to amaze me how much my sloppy signature meant to people. Yet as I was leaving, he made a remark that stopped me cold.

"Actually, she was hesitant to have you sign this book," he said.

"I don't understand?"

"She didn't want to impose on you twice. She wanted you to sign the other one."

I froze. "What other one?"

"Your new one. She was going to pick up a copy today at the mall. What's it called? *Remember Me?*"

I smiled thinly. "Tell her not to bother buying it. It's my worst book." Quickly I turned away. "Have a nice afternoon, Mr. Garrett."

"You too, Shari. I mean, Jean."

His slip of the tongue had been accidental. Nothing more. But what about tomorrow?

CHAPTER XV

MY HEAD STARTED TO THROB the moment I set foot back on the set. I had no choice, I had to take two Tylenol-3. The pain medicine worked, yet I wasn't sure if the same could be said for my celluloid luster. That evening, watching the dailies, I thought I either had to rewrite Mary as a dope-smoking chick or else get a new actress to play my body double. My eyes were out of focus in every shot.

Roger, warm-blooded American boy that he was, wanted to take me to dinner and bed. But I begged off, telling him that I had a headache. He was sympathetic and didn't pressure me. I didn't tell him where I was staying.

When I reached my hotel suite, I called Peter. Hardest thing I ever had to do.

Harder than dying. I died a little when he answered and I heard the pain in his voice. "Hello?" he said.

"Peter, this is Shari. I'm so sorry."

There was a long pause. "Where are you?" he asked.

"At a hotel. By myself. How are you?"

He sighed. "Not so good."

"I'm sorry. I don't know how it happened."

I could hear him breathing. "Are you going to see him again?"

I knew he'd ask me that, of course. I tried to decide how I would respond. After the lies I'd put him through, the truth was all I could offer him now.

"I have to see him every day at the set. He's our star and we're stuck with him. At this point Henry won't let me make another change. But I don't plan to go out with him anymore. I don't want to do that. I didn't want to do it to begin with. I just did. He has some kind of hold on me—I can't explain it." I stopped. "I know that isn't exactly what you wanted to hear, but it's the best I can give you."

Peter moaned softly. "Are you sure you didn't have sex with him?"

"Yes, I'm sure. I'd remember, you know."

"Shari."

"I'm sorry," I said quickly. "That didn't come out the way I meant it. What I was trying to say is, it went too far. I crossed the line." I added, although it broke my heart to do so, "You have every right to leave me if you want."

Another long painful silence. "Do you want to leave me?"

"No. Not for anything in the world."

"Then how come you can't swear that you'll never see him again?"

I began to cry. "I don't know how come."

Peter pleaded. "Don't go to the movie set. They can make it without you. Henry's a genius. He's made dozens of movies. You're a writer—that's your gift. That's what you came back for—to tell stories. To inspire people. You don't need to be a producer or a director. Come back here to me. It can be like it was before. We've been happy, Shari. We belong together. Please?"

I sobbed. "I can't!"

He wept with me. "Why not? What's stopping you?"

"I don't deserve you!"

"Shari."

"I betrayed you! I might betray you again!"

He lowered his voice. "Is it the sex thing? Is that what you need?"

"It's more complicated than that. I feel I have to confront . . ." My voice trailed off.

"Confront what?"

I paused, feeling cold. The words had just come out of my mouth. "I don't know—the unreal maybe."

"What's the *unreal*?"

I spoke as if I were suddenly far away. On a spaceship, light-years from Earth. "Everything that isn't real." My mind felt split then as Sarteen's had when she leaped through the uncharted region of hyperspace. Indeed, I felt very close to her then. As if our mutual dilemmas were simply two sides of the same coin. Yet I did not understand what my affinity with a fictional character meant any more than I knew how to end that story. "The Starlight Crystal"—why had I called it that? In reference to the crystals in her golden column? The precious jewels that vibrated with my heroine's chakras? I remembered how my forehead and heart had vibrated in the company of the yogi.

"Shari?" Peter said, confused. Some time must have gone by.

"How's your course?" I asked. "Did you complete it today?"

"Yes. It was wonderful. It kept me from jumping off a balcony."

"Or driving head on into a truck?"

He was sad. "Yeah."

"That was a sick joke. I'm sorry."

"Mine was, too. I guess we're both sorry."

"How's the yogi?" I asked.

"Wonderful." Peter hesitated. "I told him what was happening between us."

"That's OK. I'm sure he knew anyway."

"As a matter of fact he did. He said it was inevitable."

I didn't know if I liked the sound of that. "What does that mean?"

"He said this situation was all set up by nature, and by ourselves. That we test ourselves."

I forced a chuckle. "Did he say I was failing the test?"

"I asked him—"

"And?"

"He didn't answer. He doesn't always answer. It's his way."

I spoke with feeling. "I'd love to see him again."

"He wants to see you. He asked for you to come see him."

"I thought he was leaving."

"He decided to stay longer." Peter paused. "Please come home. We can go see him together. He can help us through this difficult time."

"I don't deserve his help."

"Shari! Why do you keep saying these crazy things?"

"It's not crazy. I didn't keep my end of the bargain. I don't know what that means either, but I know it's true." I paused. Someone was knocking at my door. "Peter, I have to go now."

"What is it? We need to talk more."

"We can talk later. I'll call you."

He sounded so pitiful. "You promise?"

"I promise. I love you, Peter. You have to believe that. Whatever happens, that will never change."

He sighed. "The yogi said I had to believe that."

The knock came again. "He's a wise man. Trust him. Take care of yourself."

"I love you, Shari."

I smiled, feeling the tears well up again. "I know you do. Try to relax. Goodbye."

Yet it was a false alarm, the knock at the door. The maid simply wanted to know if I needed fresh flowers. Sure, I said. I could sit and smell them all by myself. She arranged a silver vase with two dozen red roses on the mantle above the fireplace and then discreetly departed. Because of my vow not to call Roger, I had nothing to do except finish my story and rest. Certainly I didn't feel like going out and painting the town. But when I turned on my laptop, I discovered that my muse was off helping a college student write a term paper or something. I felt about as inspired as a crashed disk. Turning off my magical machine, I tried the TV, not a favorite pastime of mine. If I wanted to watch something, I usually rented a movie. The remote control had several buttons for pay TV. The bottom one on the left let you watch X-rated features. Briefly, I wondered what Roger was doing, if he was alone.

I won't call him. I won't see him. I love Peter.

I wondered what Garrett's buddy in Chicago would discover.

The night crept by. Fifty channels on TV and I couldn't find anything to watch. I took a bath. The hotel offered an assortment of expensive oils to pour in the water. Wanting to get my thousand-bucks-a-night's worth, I dumped them all in. Came out of the tub smelling like the vase above the fireplace. I blow-dried my hair and ordered a hot fudge sundae from room service—that was a smart move. Tasted yummy, even though I was on the second day of my pain and suffering diet. I had ordered a turkey sandwich as well, but it didn't appeal to me. But I could see how people grew addicted to staying at expensive hotels. You just had to pick up the phone and dial a number and life was taken care of for you. I probably could have ordered stronger pills for my headache. The pain was coming back. Playing with my bottle of pills, I wondered how I would look and feel in the morning if I swallowed another two before I went to bed. Probably like the cheerleader after the sharks got her.

It was ironic that I should think about sharks as I turned out the light.

The call came at two in the morning. Groaning, I rolled over and turned on the light. Earlier, as a compromise, I had taken only one pill before putting my head on the pillow. Unfortunately, the *pleasant* half of the medicine had already worn off. Now I had only side effects percolating in my system. As I sat up, a vein pounded at my right temple, and I felt hung over. Picking up the phone, I hoped it was a wrong number.

"Hello?" I mumbled.

"Shari, this is Bob. I'm down at the shark set. I've got to talk to you about tomorrow's scene."

"Now? Bob, it's the middle of the night. How did you get this number?"

"Henry gave it to me. You gave it to him. This is important, Shari. We have to talk."

I yawned. "All right, I'm awake. What do you want to talk about?"

"Not on the phone. You have to come down here."

"No way. Knowing you, you'll probably shove me in the water and I'd be eaten alive."

He lowered his voice. "It's funny you should say that. Someone is planning to do exactly that tomorrow."

"What are you talking about? Who?"

"This is not something we can discuss on the phone. Be here in forty minutes. I'll be waiting by the boat. Don't be late."

"Wait a second," I began. But he had already hung up. For the life of me, I couldn't understand why Henry would have given Bob my number. I had specifically told him to keep my whereabouts secret. Of course, he knew where Roger was staying and must have figured we were having a wild old time.

I don't know why I called Roger. I had told myself a million times that I wouldn't. I guess I just needed someone to bounce Bob's crazy conversation off. Roger answered after the fifth ring. He sounded dead to the world.

"Yeah?"

"Roger, this is Shari. I'm sorry to wake you. We have a problem. It's Bob."

He groaned. "What time is it?"

"Two in the morning. I wouldn't have disturbed you if I didn't think this was important. Bob called me a minute ago and said that someone plans to push one of our crew in the water with the sharks—while we're shooting tomorrow."

Roger snorted. "The entire cast has joked about pushing someone in the water with sharks. We all grew up with *Jaws*. It's nothing. Bob's pulling your leg. Go back to sleep."

"I'd like to. But there was something in his voice—I don't think he was joking. He wants me to meet him down by the shark set. I want you to come with me."

He paused. "Are you serious about this?"

"Yes. I can come get you in a few minutes."

"In a few minutes? Where are you?"

I bit my lower lip. "I'm staying here, in your hotel."

"Shari. Why didn't you tell me that?"

"I'll explain when I see you. Get dressed. We have to see what Bob wants. Something's happening here that I don't understand."

Roger yawned. "You're not the only one."

CHAPTER XVI

ON THE WAY TO SEE BOB, sitting in the passenger seat of Roger's black Corvette, I explained to Roger that Peter and I were having difficulties but that they were unrelated to what had happened between us. Roger nodded and didn't press me for details. He was remarkably cool about the whole thing. He even confessed to feeling guilty about moving in on me while I was living with Peter. Yet, grinning, he added that he wasn't losing any sleep over it.

"I was sleeping fine until you called," he said. "You know, Bob's going to laugh when he sees how he managed to get us out of bed. In fact, I wouldn't be surprised if he's not even there."

"Whatever happens, don't get in a fight with him around the sharks."

"I know I have a temper. I'll watch it." He paused. "Tell me about the story you're working on?"

"Did I tell you that I was writing a story?"

"You write for a living. I assume you're always working on a story."

"Not always. I think a gap between stories is important. It allows what's inside to ripen. That's my take on the creative process anyway. Actually, though, I am working on a short story called 'The Starlight Crystal.' It's sci-fi—it takes place in the future."

Roger lowered the radio. "Tell me about it."

"Now? It's so late. Let me tell you another time."

"No. I want to hear it, honestly. I told you, your stories affect me deeply."

He sure knew the way to a writer's heart. Tell an author he or she is a genius and he or she will give you the world in exchange. "I probably should tell you," I said. "You're the one who inspired the story."

"Really? How?"

"A few nights ago I had a dream where I was flying around the city, visiting people I knew, putting my hands on them and entering their dreams,"

Roger watched me. "The girl in your latest book did that. When she was dead."

I had forgotten that he had read *Remember Me*. That book haunted me everywhere I turned. I spoke hastily. "That's probably why I dreamed it. Anyway, in the dream I visited you and put my hands on your head. And you were dreaming about a

great interstellar battle. Humanity versus the invading aliens."
I paused, wanting to ask a question.

"Do you remember the dream, Roger?"

But it was too peculiar a thing to say. Especially since I was
supposed to be unrelated to the Shari Cooper in my book.

"It sounds neat," Roger said. "What do the aliens look
like?"

"I don't know."

"How much of this story have you written?"

"It's almost done."

"And you don't know what the aliens look like?"

"No. I have no idea."

"Who wins in the end? Humanity or the aliens?"

"I don't know."

Roger acted exasperated. "Tell me what you *do* have."

I did as he requested, starting with Sarteen and Pareen's
journey home, to the moment when Captain Eworl was supposed to emerge from the elevator. Roger listened closely.
Indeed, I would say he was rapt with attention. When I was
finished, he remained still for a long time, thinking.

"You know you can't have Sarteen lose," he said finally. "It
will wreck the story."

"She's not about to lose. She's preparing to die so that she
can save the rest of her people."

Roger shook his head. "That's no good. You have to figure
out a way for her to survive, too."

"She can only survive by surrendering. She won't do that. It's against her nature."

"You're the writer. You can adapt her nature any way you choose. Besides, you're missing my point. You can't have a downer ending. People don't like them. It won't sell."

"Not everything I write has to sell. The story can have meaning in and of itself."

"Couldn't Sarteen fake surrender? Give in for the time being? Plan for a future revenge?"

"I don't think so. Once the Orions get their hands on you, I think you're pretty much their property. Sarteen would rather die first."

"You can't have her be a failure."

I had to smile. "Who's the writer here? Who's the actor?"

He nodded. "I wouldn't mind being in a movie made from this story. I could play Captain Eworl."

"So far he's only a voice across black space. He hasn't even been on stage."

"You said it yourself, the story isn't complete." Roger nodded. "Before it's over, I think he'll have a significant role."

The property Henry had chosen to build our "shark set" on was in the valley, actually in the foothills of the San Bernardino Mountains. The two hundred acres were a mismatch of hard orange soil and lovely pine and spruce trees. It was entirely fenced in—twenty-foot-high barriers topped with barbed wire.

Even so, for insurance reasons, we had been required by law to have a security guard on the premises at all times. Couldn't have little boys and girls who lived in the vicinity digging under the fence and going for a swim with the sharks. Such a thing wouldn't enhance my newborn production company's reputation. I had personally hired the night security guard and he was only too happy to let us on the property. Yet he said he hadn't seen Bob. Roger shook his head at the comment.

"I told you so," he said. "He's home, sleeping. A guy that fat needs his rest."

"He told me he'd meet me at the boat. We've come this far. We may as well check it out."

Because of the bumps in the path, we couldn't drive the Corvette to the boat and manmade lake, although I would have preferred driving. The set was located at the far end of the property; it was a good quarter-mile walk from the entrance, a long hike in the middle of the night without a flashlight. If Bob was on the set, he had come in via an unknown back way. Roger took my hand as we walked. It wasn't easy to pull away from him. Light from the waning moon aided us, although I did stumble several times. But each time Roger was there to catch me.

"He said this situation was all set up by nature, and by ourselves. That we test ourselves."

I wondered what the yogi had meant.

We found Bob standing in the center of the boat, which

was tied to the shore, his back to us. Moving closer, I noted the fins of the sharks as the maneaters circulated in the oval pond, vicious silver knives in the glow of the moon. Henry had rented four sharks. With the right angles and editing, he said, we could make it look like a whole school. Four was enough for my tastes. Andy's boyfriend had completed the backdrop. The fake daytime Caribbean sky, dimmed by the night, pressed in on us from three separate angles. Bob must have heard us approaching but he didn't turn until we actually stepped aboard the boat.

He had a gun in his hand.

"Bob," I said, stunned. "What the hell?"

He flashed the fiendish grin that worked so well on the screen. That made you believe that, yes, here was a young man capable of stranding kids aboard a sinking sailboat in the middle of shark-infested waters. At that moment he looked exactly as I had created Bob, before I even met him. Bob *was* Bob.

"Hello, Shari," he said. "Hello, Roger. Nice of you both to come. Please don't shout out or I'll have to shoot you."

"What do you want?" Roger asked.

Bob shook his gun a bit. "Oh, I'd think what I want is obvious. I want to rehearse."

"Huh?" I said.

Bob laughed bitterly. "You think you have such a great imagination, Ms. Bestselling Shari Cooper. You plot your stories so carefully. You sit at your computer and develop the motivation for your characters. What they were like as children. What they suffered as they went to school. Why they became criminals when they grew older. But you know nothing! Real criminals don't need motivation at all. We want to kill someone, we kill them. It's as simple as that."

Roger took a step forward. "Give me that gun, punk."

Bob raised the gun sharply, pointing it at Roger's face. "I will give you what's inside the gun before I hand it over. Understand me, Pretty Boy?"

Roger paused, chewed on that for a few seconds. "You say you want to rehearse. What scene?"

Bob nodded in admiration. "Pretty Boy is pretty smart. Yeah, the three of us are going to rehearse *First to Die*'s climactic scene. Shari's going to take the lifeboat here, and ride it to the far side of the pond, then return for you to do it. If you both make it, you both live. Easy, huh? Of course, if she makes it that far, she can always run for safety. Hide in the trees. The idea might occur to her, and she might get away from me. I'm not in the best shape. On the other hand, she might not escape. I do have a gun. There aren't many places to hide here. Besides, if she does choose to flee, I get to push you in the water, Pretty Boy. Then you get to swim to the far side of the pond. Get out on this side and I shoot you."

"You're insane," Roger swore.

"Perhaps. I'm also creative. I'm a budding director. To add drama to the scene, before you guys appeared, I dropped a handful of bloody meat in the pond. Not enough to satisfy the sharks' hunger, you understand, but enough to get them thinking about their next meal. You can see how restlessly they're circling. They know good things are coming their way."

I moved to Roger's side, feeling oddly removed from the scene, as if this couldn't be happening to me. But my disinterest was rooted in shock and gave me no comfort. Bob was deadly serious. He was my own nightmare come to life. With his small revolver, he motioned me toward the small rubber lifeboat.

"There's no point in waiting," he said.

I had to struggle to draw a breath, to speak. "There's something wrong with this lifeboat."

Bob acted surprised. "Really? Is that possible? The union boys went over it this afternoon, just to be sure it was safe. It couldn't have a hole in it. Not unless it developed one recently. But maybe you're right, and the raft does have a small hole leaking air. Maybe that's another plot twist. You're the writer, Shari, you tell me. Could it be that the longer you delay taking the lifeboat, the more air runs out of it?"

"Does the motor work?" I asked.

Bob shrugged. "Can't tell you. You might take the time to check it out. Or you might just get your ass in gear and paddle to the other side of the pond and back."

I moved toward the lifeboat. Roger grabbed my arm. "Don't," he said. "It's a setup. You'll die."

I shook him off. "I'd rather the sharks got me than him."

Roger caught my eye. "Be careful."

Bob laughed. "How romantic! Be careful! What clever dialogue! God, if you don't need a regular doctor in a few minutes, you certainly need a script doctor."

"I should never have hired you," I muttered under my breath as I leaned over and studied the lifeboat floating off the port side. Bob, at least, had gone to the trouble to put it in the water for me. The problem was, in the poor light, I was unable to judge how much air it had lost. I wouldn't know until I jumped into it. Then, if it sank, it would probably be the last thing I knew. "Jesus," I whispered.

What would it feel like to have a hand bitten off? A foot? My blood would squirt into the water in a warm red stream. The only thing that would stop it would be another, larger bite, one that ripped off an entire limb, and forced my heart to stop beating. That's all the victim of a multiple shark attack could pray for, a quick end. For the second time since I had returned to Earth as a Wanderer, I could not believe the Rishi could have allowed me to fall into such a terrible predicament.

"But can't you protect me?"

"Protect you from what? Death? There is no death. I have nothing to protect you from."

That was easy to say when you didn't have a physical body to worry about.

"Shari," Roger said behind me.

"I can do it," I said tightly. Summoning my courage, I

crouched down and planted my left arm on the sailboat deck. Spinning through a half hop, I swung my legs over and into the lifeboat. It didn't sink, but wobbled badly. The sharks sensed the movement and swam closer. Glancing up, I saw Roger creep to the edge and peer down at me. Bob stood behind him, the pistol to Roger's head.

"Since you performed that move so gracefully," Bob said, "I will give you a helpful hint. There's no gas in the motor." He gestured to the far side of the pond. "Better hurry, Shari. A sinking raft always takes longer to paddle back."

There was one paddle in the lifeboat, not two. Picking it up, I scooted to the center of the raft and began to paddle frantically. Naturally I began to swing in circles. On the deck of the sailboat set, Bob hooted.

"She's playing with the sharks! She thinks they're really dolphins!"

"Shut up," I muttered. The key to successful paddling must be not to freak out. Stabilizing the raft by paddling first on one side, then on the other, I steadily began to plow toward the far shore, increasing my speed as I gained confidence. In reality, the pond was only forty yards across, less than half the length of a football field. It took me only a minute to traverse it. Behind me, I heard Roger call out.

"Run!" he cried. "He's playing with us! It's like your book! He'll kill us anyway."

In my heart I knew Roger was right. Bob couldn't possibly

allow us to live if he planned to stay out of jail for the next forty years. Unfortunately, I couldn't leave Roger to such a gruesome death. Yet I lacked the ingenuity of the hero in my book. The raft was low on air, the sides were getting squishier. Bob intended for Roger to paddle across and back next. A second of delay could make all the difference for him. Yet, in the end, it would probably make no difference at all. Bob would keep making us take turns until one of us went under and was turned into shark food.

Master! Help me! I promise to be good.

No brilliant insight came to me. Good was not good enough.

I paddled the lifeboat back to the sailboat.

Several feet above my head, Bob saluted my nobility by clapping.

"She thought about fleeing," he said. "But in the end true love won out over fear." He turned to Roger. "Your turn, Pretty Boy. Let's see what you're made of. The conditions are the same as before. If you flee, she goes in the water."

Roger glanced at the waning moon, seemed to think for a moment, then turned and straightened in Bob's direction. "No," he said firmly.

"Roger," I gasped.

Bob chuckled. "No? You say no to the Bad Boy with the big gun?" He cocked the hammer on the gun. "Not a smart move, Pretty Boy."

"I don't believe you have the guts to shoot me in cold

blood," Roger said, staring him hard in the eye. His words were powerful—Bob actually took a step back, and for a moment seemed uncertain.

"What do you mean?" Bob asked.

Roger took a step toward him. "I mean you won't shoot me. You're too fat, too slow, too stupid to destroy me. Isn't that so?"

Bob smiled quickly. "Yeah, that's it. I'm nothing next to you. Are you going in the raft or not?"

"No. You're going in the water."

"What?"

Roger lashed out with his right foot. He could have had a black belt in karate, his blow was that swift, that accurate. Suddenly the gun was not in Bob's hand. Bob was in Roger's hands. Wearing an expression of absolute terror, Bob was dangling over the edge of the sailboat, held only by Roger's vicelike grip.

"Time to meet the Grim Reaper," Roger said coldly.

"Wait!" Bob cried. "Don't! The sharks! They—Eeehh!"

Roger threw him overboard, over me. Bob's left foot caught my right cheek before he bellyflopped into the dark pond. Before he could resurface, the fins converged. Four silver arrows aimed at one thrashing late supper. Just prior to closing my eyes and ears to the screams, Bob managed to get his head above the water. His expression was as much bewildered as terror stricken. He started to say something to me, but water rolled into his mouth and he choked. Before he could recover, he jerked down slightly, a couple of times in a row. The jerks were not because of his own wild flailing, but were being applied externally. His face was as white as the pale moonlight that shone on him from high above. Yet, from far below, a dark liquid began to spread out from his struggling form. A warm, sticky fluid that would have been bright red had it been midday, but which, this many hours after midnight, was as black as an oil gusher.

The sharks had begun to feed.

I screamed as Bob screamed.

It seemed as if they fed a long time.

CHAPTER XVII

THE NEXT TWELVE HOURS were a blur for me. Roger ran for the guard, who called for the police. Twenty minutes later, five black and white units and two ambulances braved the bumps and drove up to the set. Their flashing lights spread hideous color over Bob's remains; the pieces of flesh bobbed like torn apples at a disastrous Halloween party. On a boulder fifty feet from the pond, I sat with my eyes closed and tried to block out the universe.

A death, especially one as bizarre as Bob's, was not something the LAPD brushed over without exhaustive hours of questioning and requestioning. Roger and I were separated and taken down to the station. Obviously the authorities wanted to see if our stories matched. It was only after five hours of questioning that I wondered if I should have freely waived my right to remain silent. What I was telling them sounded like a

Shari Cooper novel! Trying to explain that what Bob had done was based on a novel of mine didn't help. The odd thing was, in the midst of it all, I never knew if I was under arrest. And here I was a mystery writer. Research had not prepared me for reality. Aliens were predictable next to people; they just wanted to conquer the Earth.

What had Bob wanted? I wondered that as the sun came up outside and my head throbbed with pain and fatigue. My questioning cops would not allow me a Tylenol-3, even though it was prescription medicine and I begged them for just one. They wanted me sharp. No drugged excuses for a defense attorney to drag up later in court. To put it simply, the men didn't believe me.

Poor Roger, I thought. He was the one who had thrown Bob in the water. I wondered how he was doing. Foolishly, I asked if I could see him. They shook their heads. Right then I would have stood a better chance of obtaining an audience with the Pope. I needed to have my confession heard. Even though, technically, I had done nothing wrong, I was plagued with guilt. The detectives must have sensed that and because of it didn't let me go or even rest. They hoped I would crack, spill my guts, sort of like the way Bob's had been spilled.

Finally I lost it. Pacing, I demanded that they at least give me a chance to place one call. I ranted about lawsuits and how they had no right to hold me and how I was a famous writer. A *New York Times* bestselling author, I yelled! That did it; that bestseller list always pushed the right buttons. They exchanged worried glances and shoved a phone in my direction. But who do you call at a time of crisis? Your family? Your lover? I felt as if I had already lost both. My producer was supposed to manage everything that happened on the set. I called Henry.

He was beautiful. He was down at the station within an hour with a high-priced lawyer who made the detectives scowl and go for doughnuts. Within the hour, I walked out of the station a free woman. The press was waiting for me, not at the back door—but at the front. Henry said the story had already hit the airways. The media even had a slogan ready. "Bob was first to die. Who will be next?" Henry promised he would get Roger out next. He drove me back to my hotel and there, after swallowing three of my pain pills, I collapsed on my bed and tried not to think, to even exist.

Yet, this time, I did dream.

If it was that, and not a vision.

I floated through outer space, the leader of a group of golden entities that needed no vessel to traverse vast distances. Up ahead, a blue-white globe shimmered in the endless river of stars, a living planet of inexpressible potential. This world was my destination. And although I was a creature of spirit and not of flesh and blood, I felt as if I might weep when I saw it again. Too long, I thought, to be isolated from Mother Earth. It didn't look so different from the last time I had seen it. Yet

I knew much had changed since then. Much had died. The quarantine was to blame.

But that was why my partners and I had returned. To break it.

To plug the two strands of humanity's DNA back into the natural twelve.

To reconnect humanity to eternity.

Yet it took almost an eternity of time to accomplish the simplest task. I entered one body, lived a productive life. Tried to help where I could, to speak truth where superstition prevailed. To offer love where hate dominated. Then I died and had to start all over. Another body, another set of parents, of genes, of characteristics that make up a human personality. Around and around I traveled the wheel of reincarnation. Yet each time, between each birth and death, I was allowed a chance to pause, to rest and gather my strength, to see that not all our efforts were in vain. Despite the continuing dominance of the enemy, humanity slowly evolved over the centuries. Discarding the illusions of fear, of separateness, of not trusting in the divine plan. Of having no faith in their own immortality. It was to increase this faith that I fought the hardest. For it constituted the enemy's greatest hold on humanity. Without the fear of death and the dogma of judgmental religions and brain-washing cults that grew up around them, the quarantine would have crumbled in the twinkling of a distant star. So again I returned to life to shout out that there was only life and no end to our being. No devil could claim our souls for all eternity unless we created the devil ourselves. Some heard me; most did not. It didn't matter. In my soul I knew that in the end, we would be triumphant.

Yet, occasionally, even I stumbled. The enemy fooled me. And those were not lives I remembered with joy. Indeed, sometimes, in my desire to make my mark on the world, I made the mistake of doing the enemy's work.

When I opened my eyes it was almost dark. Immediately I sat up and turned on the light. I had slept away the entire day. If my dream were true—and I could only recall fragments of it—then I had also slept away the last few years. Had the Rishi ever told me that I was special? I assumed he had. Since my rebirth, I had taken pride in the fact that I was a Wanderer. A bestselling writer who could save humanity with my amazing stories. Right—I couldn't even save myself. Yet the Rishi had said many things that emphasized the specialness of each of us.

"Those of negative vibration crave power and dominance. That is their trademark. You can spot them that way. They try to place themselves above others. They feel they are especially chosen by God for a great purpose. But God chooses everyone and all his purposes are great."

The yogi had said similar words.

"That is a form of enlightenment. To feel like everyone belongs to you, and you belong to them. That is something a Master will

always teach. There is no hierarchy in the family of man. We are all equal, all children of the divine. The Master is the same as the student, the disciple, the devotee. The Master never places himself above them because if he did then he wouldn't be able to help them. That's why we don't seek power. Those things separate us from each other. They lead to ignorance, to darkness."

Why hadn't I been able to see that it was the Rishi who spoke to me through the body of the yogi? That their truth was one? I had wanted proof, a miracle. Even after the yogi had given me the miracle of my own inner peace, I left him. And for what? To make out with Roger? What had my choice brought me but misery?

Reaching over, I picked up the phone and called Peter.

Jacob answered.

"Hello?"

"Jacob, this is Shari. How are you?"

He hesitated. "I'm OK, but we want you to come home. Peter misses you. I miss you."

I forced a laugh. "I'll come home, tonight. I promise. Is Peter there?"

"No. He's with the yogi."

"The yogi is still in town? I thought he was leaving."

"He is tonight. He's giving a talk at a house in Orange County now."

"Do you know where the house is? The address?"

"No."

"Did Peter happen to write down the address on a scrap of paper? Is there one lying around?"

"I can't see one."

"Oh God, I'm sorry, Jacob. That was stupid of me to say."

"There probably is a scrap of paper here that has directions on it. I know Peter was talking to the people at the house just before he left."

I paused. "Did Peter call these people for directions?"

"Yes."

"Have you made any calls since then?"

"No. I wouldn't use your phone without permission. I couldn't use this one if I wanted to. The buttons are different than the ones on other phones. I don't know what to push."

"Jacob, listen very carefully. The button on the lower right-hand side is the Redial button. Don't push it now, but when I hang up I want you to push it. It will almost certainly dial the number of the house where Peter and the yogi are. Whoever answers, tell that person it is crucial for Peter Jacobs to call me immediately at the Beverly Hills Hotel. Can you remember that?"

"Yes. I have a good memory. I will get him for you and have him call you. I know he wants to talk to you a whole bunch."

"I want to talk to him a whole bunch. Hey, when's your next game?"

"Tomorrow. Can you come?"

"You bet. I'll be there."

"Can we go to Disneyland again?"

"Yes. Tomorrow." I don't know why there were tears in my eyes. "We can do everything tomorrow, Jacob."

We exchanged goodbyes. A few minutes later the phone rang. It wasn't Peter but a woman at the house where the yogi was staying. Peter, she said, was in a private meeting with the yogi. But she would be happy to give me her address, which was what I wanted most. She told me to be sure to hurry, the yogi's plane was to leave in two hours.

"Tell him I'm coming," I cried.

"What's your name?" she asked.

"He knows my name."

CHAPTER XVIII

BUT I HAD PUT OFF seeing the yogi one time too many. When I reached the house, he had gone. Peter waited outside in front for me, in his wheelchair, a red rose resting in his lap. When he told me the news, I was devastated.

"But I need to talk to him," I cried. "Can we go to the airport?"

Peter shook his head. "He leaves from LAX, on the other side of town. He left here a while ago. By the time we got there he would probably be boarding." He handed me the rose. "He told me to give you this."

I smelled it—such a lovely fragrance. "Did he say anything else about me?"

"Yes. He said to tell you, 'The writer has many stories in her. Whenever one comes to an end, another begins.'" Peter paused, then added, "He also told me to say that you have nothing to fear, that all has been taken care of."

"What did he mean?"

"I don't know. He acted like you'd know what he meant."

I was puzzled. Every word of his meant so much. It was difficult to know where to apply his advice to my life. But perhaps it had yet to be applied. Leaning over, I gave Peter a big hug.

"I missed you, my love," I whispered in his ear. "Do you still want me back?"

He had tears in his eyes. "Yes. Will you come back?"

"Yes." I kissed him. "And I will never leave you. Never ever."

"What made up your mind?"

I straightened up, glancing up and down the street. The strangest sensation flowed through me. It was as if I were being filmed, studied, dissected. Yet no one was there. A shiver made its way through my body as I thought of Bob, what was left of him.

"Something happened last night," I said. "It was terrible. Then something beautiful happened this afternoon while I slept."

"While you were asleep?"

"Yes. I had a dream. It explained so much to me. It put me in my place, so to speak, and also reminded me of several important things the Rishi and the yogi both said. Plus it helped me remember other dreams I've been having lately, and what they mean." I shrugged. "I know I'm speaking like a crazy woman again. But what's important is that I feel clearer now. I won't be seeing Roger anymore."

Peter was grateful. "Good." He paused. "What are you looking for?"

I shrugged, although I continued to feel watched. "Nothing."

"What happened last night?"

"It's a long story. Can I tell you later? At home?"

"Yes," he said. "Do you want to go there now?"

"Yes. It's a shame we came in separate cars. We can't drive together." I kissed him again. "I don't want to leave you for a minute!"

He patted my side. "We'll live happily ever after," he promised. "Like in the movies."

I laughed. "Like in a book, silly. Books are better."

Peter followed me in his van, as was our custom. I always fought my way to the front to be the leader. To be important. That would stop now, I vowed. I would live as the yogi had said: simply, naturally, like grass.

Stopped at a light, I picked up my cell phone and checked my messages. There were several from Garrett. His tone was urgent, I dialed him immediately. He answered on the first ring.

"This is Garrett."

"This is Jean Rodrigues. I'm sorry about missing our appointment. I was tied up."

"I heard about why you were tied up. Roger Teller was with you when the young man died?"

"Yes. Bob tried to kill Roger and me."

"Really?" Garrett said sarcastically.

"You sound doubtful. I was there, I know what happened."

"You sound doubtful yourself. It doesn't matter. I have to meet with you tonight."

"You found out something about Roger?"

There was an odd note in his voice. "Yes. Among other things."

"I see," I replied, although I didn't really. "Where would you like to meet?"

"Where are you now?"

"In my car, in Newport Beach."

"That's perfect. I'm in Orange County as well. Let's meet at the entrance to the Huntingdon Beach Pier."

My old stomping ground. "Why there?"

That odd tone again. "Is there something wrong with it?"

"No. I can come. I'll be there in twenty minutes."

"I'll be waiting," Garrett said as he hung up.

I called Peter's cell phone, and after explaining that I had to meet with Garrett about Roger, I told him to go on home and take care of Jacob. I'd catch up with him soon. But Peter insisted on accompanying me. I believe he was curious to see Garrett. Together, we drove to Huntington Beach Pier, which was only two miles south of where I had died as Shari Cooper.

"*Why there?*"

Garrett had sounded like he had a lot on his mind.

He was standing at the pier entrance as we arrived. We just pulled over to the side of the road, staying on the Coast Highway. Garrett walked over to my Jag, and I rolled down the window. He nodded to the van behind me.

"Who's your friend?" he asked.

"My boyfriend." I looked around. "Do you want us to park and maybe talk in a coffee shop or something?"

"No, and I don't want to talk here. Can I just get in?"

I hesitated. "Sure. You want to go somewhere else?"

"Yes," he said. "It's not far."

"Fine. Get in."

As Garrett climbed into the passenger seat, I called Peter and told him to follow us. Everything was cool. But maybe *cool* was the wrong word. Garrett, as he glanced over at me, looked like he had just seen a ghost. Or *was* seeing a ghost. His skin was pale with a sheen of fine perspiration, yet his eyes were as sharp as ever.

"Where do you want to go?" I asked.

"Don't you know?"

Damn! "No."

He noticed my discomfort. "It's just down the road a bit."

"What is?"

"A certain condominium. You're sure you're not familiar with it?"

"I don't know what you're talking about."

"Would you have any objection to going to this condo? I've already been there this afternoon. It's unoccupied—a bunch of empty rooms. Even the carpet's gone. The manager, Rita Wilde, said I could drop by it whenever I wished." He paused. "Do you know Rita?"

"No," I lied.

He nodded to himself as he studied my reaction. "I know her from a few years back. I met her when I was investigating a death at the condo."

I shuddered. "We don't have to go there."

"But I want to. I think it's the right place to talk." He reached over and put his hand on my arm. "What do you think?"

My voice was shaky. "I told you what I think."

"Are you afraid?"

"No."

"Are you concerned that the place might be haunted?"

"No."

"Then let's go. We're blocking traffic. It's only two miles north of here."

"OK." I put my Jag in gear.

Peter must have known our destination because he fell back a bit as if he didn't want to follow. Yet he did not drive away. Garret was, of course, right. For me the condo was as haunted as a cemetery. I hadn't been back to it since the day

I reacquainted myself with Jimmy. With my badly disguised uneasiness, I wasn't fooling Garrett one bit. Clearly he had read *Remember Me*; nevertheless, I decided to let him wonder and admit to nothing. The whole way there, I forced him to give me directions.

We parked outside the condo, I believe, exactly where my friends and I had parked the night I died. Peter rolled out the van's side door in his wheelchair as we walked over to him. He wasn't happy about our meeting place.

"Why are we here?" he demanded.

"Garrett wants to talk to us here," I said. "Detective Garrett, this is my boyfriend—Lenny. Lenny, meet Garrett."

Garrett shook Peter's hand. "How did you two meet?" he asked.

"It's a long story," I muttered.

He gave me a knowing look. "I'm sure it is."

We went upstairs, took the elevator. To the fourth floor. When you fall off a fourth floor—if you're into such things, which I don't recommend—the police speak of your falling *three* stories to your death. Because you fall only three stories since you begin such a plunge from the *floor* of the fourth floor. The details don't really matter. If you land on your head on concrete—as I had—you die.

Garrett led us to what had once been the Palmone residence.

The door was unlocked. We went inside. Turned on the lights. It was dark now.

A cool ocean breeze blew in from the open balcony door. I tried but couldn't stop trembling.

I ran from the room then, through the kitchen and out onto the balcony and into the night. I remember standing by the rail, feeling the smooth wood beneath my shaking fingers. I remember seeing the flat black ocean and thinking how nice it would be if I could only exercise my magical powers and fly over to it and disappear beneath its surface for ages to come. I remember time passing.

Then things went bad.

"Are you cold?" Garrett asked.

I lowered my head. "Yes," I whispered.

"Have you been here before?" he asked.

I shook my head.

"Did you know that someone died here?"

"You just told me."

"Shari Cooper died here. Did you know her?"

"No."

"Why did you choose that name for your pen name?"

His gaze was steady and bored into me, but his will wavered. He didn't really want the truth from me. When all was said and done, the truth was terrifying. Especially when we needed to hang on to our limited ideas of selves and the universe. Truly, as the Rishi had said, modern religion's attempt to define with words the ultimate reality was the ultimate blasphemy. Garrett looked at me as if he couldn't decide to swear at me or plead with me.

"It's just a name," I said. "It means nothing."

Garrett shook his head. "I read your book."

I sighed. "Did you enjoy it?"

"How could you write that book? How could you know those things? You put me in your book!"

"I had never met you until three days ago."

"You put my daughter in your book!" He took a step toward me, roughly grabbed my shoulder.

"She went into hysterics when she read your epilogue!"

Peter started to intervene but I motioned him to stay back. I continued to hold Garrett's eyes, trying to tell him silently that these were questions better left unasked and unanswered. For his own sanity. Yet I was the one who had decided the story should be published. I was as responsible for his daughter's confusion as I was responsible for her recovery from drug addiction.

"I'm sorry I upset your daughter," I said. "I realize my book upset a lot of people. But it will help even more people. It's an important story. I had to tell it. But it's just a story. Think of it that way. For you, I believe, that would be best." I paused. "We don't need to stay here. Whatever happened here, it's in the past. We should go."

Garrett released me and turned away, his shoulders sagging. He could have aged fifteen years since I walked into his office three days ago. It was as if I had stabbed him with my revelations of how he had solved the mystery of my death, stabbed him with a blade that had created deeper mysteries. The condo was cool but he was now drenched with sweat.

"You're not going to tell me anything?" he said, his back to me.

"It's just a story," I repeated.

"But the things you described. No one could . . ." He whirled as if to pounce on me with another barrage of questions. Then the strength seemed to flow out of him. He glanced around the empty rooms, shaking his head. He spoke in a soft, weary voice. "That night, after I finished questioning the kids, I sat here and drank scotch and tried to figure out what had really happened. I drew a sketch of the condo layout. I paced through the rooms several times and drew an X where I believed the murderer—if there had been a murderer—must have stood when he or she pushed Shari Cooper to her death. Then I found an orange stain on the floor. Clay that matched the tiles on the roof. It was a fresh stain, not the sort of thing you would leave on your floor if you were about to invite people over for a birthday party. It was then I knew someone at the party had been up on the roof. It was then I knew that Shari had probably been killed."

"That soon?" I asked despite myself.

He nodded. "Yes. I knew at the beginning. But what I didn't know was—" He paused.

"What?" I asked.

"That Shari Cooper was watching me that night. That

the whole time I drank and worked to figure out who had killed her, she was pacing nearby. That she was there, trying to help me. It's an amazing thought." He rubbed his head and groaned. "If you think about it, it could drive you crazy."

"I'm sure she'd have liked to help you," I said gently.

He nodded and briefly closed his eyes. When he opened them, his expression was softer. He didn't want to interrogate me; he just wanted peace of mind. Even before he asked his last question, I knew I had to try to give him that peace. I owed him so much.

"Do you know if Shari and Peter did finally enter the light?" he asked.

I glanced at Peter and smiled at Garrett. "Yes. They made it into the light. It waits for all of us. In this world or the next."

He nodded faintly. "Thank you."

"Thank you," I said. "From both of us."

Garrett let my comment sink in, then suddenly glanced at Peter, then nodded again to himself. He was a good man, a smart man. I believe he understood much more than I said aloud. After a moment he shook himself as if emerging from a dream.

"I have to tell you about Roger Teller," he said. "He's a bad seed. Much worse than either of us imagined."

I raised my hand. "Not here. This is not a good place to talk about such things." I turned for the door. "Let's get out of here."

But before we could move the lights went out.

The darkness was absolute. I couldn't see the others.

Then the lights clicked on. Roger stood just inside the doorway.

The gun he carried looked like Bob's.

Bob, I understood at that moment, had not intended to harm us.

In that awful moment I understood many mysterious things.

"Am I a bad seed?" Roger asked Garrett. "I've never been described that way before." He motioned to all of us. "Out on the balcony."

I stood firm. "It's me you want. Let the others go."

Roger chuckled. "I can have you that much better with the others out of the way." He shook his gun again. "I'm an impatient individual."

And he didn't want to be kept waiting. We went out onto the balcony. The cool breeze continued to blow. The ocean was not a flat black lagoon as it had been the night I died, but rough—a sorcerer's dark pot of boiling brew. Three stories below I saw the lamppost, which had rushed toward me during my fatal plunge. I also saw the faint outline of my bloodstain. Rita Wilde said the mark refused to wash away completely.

"What do you want?" Garrett demanded.

Roger motioned to the railing. "Sit up there."

"You're insane," Garrett swore.

Roger raised his gun and pointed it at Garrett's face. He cocked the hammer, and put enough pressure on the trigger that a single sneeze would fire the gun, and Garrett would have a hole in his head.

"Do as I say," Roger said coldly.

Garrett sat on the railing. Peter and I waited. But what we waited for, I didn't know. God may have worked in mysterious ways, but he didn't work as well when the other guy had the gun. Yet I prayed to him all the same, and to the Rishi and the yogi.

Garrett is a wonderful man! The world needs his wonder!

Roger put the gun to Garrett's forehead. "Tell me," he said. "What kind of crop does a bad seed bring?"

Garrett was fearless. "The usual scum like you."

Roger grinned. "I don't like your answer."

Garrett snorted. "Go to hell."

Roger lost his grin. "I may go there. But not today."

Roger shoved Garrett hard in the chest. The man went over the side.

Like me, he didn't scream. Like me, he landed hard, and on his head.

His skull cracked. Blood splattered everywhere.

Such a gruesome sight—no human should have to behold it.

My eyes closed. God closed both our eyes. Garrett died instantly.

"It waits for all of us. In this world or the next."

"I know," I whispered. "The light will wait for a man such as you."

A hand roughly grabbed my arm.

"Come," Roger said. "The night's young. We have somewhere special to go."

CHAPTER XIX

HE TOOK US TO the cemetery where I was buried. I knew he would. He had a flair for the dramatic, and he was a sick person. It was getting on toward eleven o'clock. The cemetery was a large, lonely field of rolling blackness. As he goaded us toward my grave, I was surprised to see that he had already visited the spot earlier. The gravesite had been uncovered, not an easy task, what with concrete liners and other stuff grave diggers used nowadays. My tombstone lay toppled nearby. A shovel rested on top of the mound of brown dirt. Roger had probably worked up a sweat digging it all out. I remarked on the fact and he shoved his gun deeper into my spine, causing me to bump into Peter's wheelchair, which I helped wheel over the uneven ground.

"Shut up and keep moving," he said.

"Talk about bad dialogue," I said. "You were going to edit

my script? You couldn't edit the ingredients on a can of dog food."

"Your mouth is going to be the death of you."

"Then I may as well talk while I can. You've been following me."

"For longer than you know, sister."

"How did you set Bob up?"

"Easy. He wanted to play a prank on you. I showed him how. Getting into the secured area was easy; he just dug a hole and went under the fence. He was going to let us go after I returned in the lifeboat. We just took a little air out of the tubes. There was no hole. There was never any real danger from the sharks."

"For you and me," I said.

"For me," he corrected. "I almost put you in the pond last night."

"Why didn't you? Death by shark bite—you can't get much better than that."

"Just wait," he promised.

"Who are you?" I asked. "Or should I say, *what* are you?"

"I'm surprised you haven't figured that out"

"Just as many Wanderers are incarnating on Earth to help with the transition, many with negative vibrations are also returning to stop it. They will not succeed, but they can upset the plans of many men and women of good will. In particular, they dislike Wanderers and attack them when they have the chance."

"You're a Black Wanderer. You're an Orion. You're a lousy kisser."

He smacked me on the back of my head with his gun. "Shut up!"

"You're an out-of-work actor," Peter said, putting in his own two cents' worth.

Roger was bitter. "I don't need your money or your starring roles. Our kind are well financed. We have structure. We obey orders. Your friend's detective friend in Chicago will discover that the hard way tomorrow. He will pay for snooping into our business."

"How old were you when you realized what you were?" I asked curiously.

"I have always known I had a great destiny."

I stopped thirty feet short of my grave and turned around, knowing he might shoot me, but not really giving a damn. I was so pissed at him. The hatred drowned out my fear. Yet I doubted it would hold the fear at bay when the mud began to fill my lungs. That he intended to bury me alive was a given.

"Why did you come after me?" I asked. "What was I doing that was so disturbing?"

Surprisingly, he acted pleased to tell me the truth. "You know the answer to that. You were beginning to write books that broke down established concepts. We couldn't have that. Those concepts are the keys to control. Control is the secret of power. We especially couldn't allow you to publish your story of the invasion and the establishment of the quarantine. People might not consciously understand it, but it could stir ancient memories."

What he said shocked me, and I had written the story. The whole situation was madness. From the outside he was just a cute guy. Except he was pointing a gun at me.

"My story took place in the future," I protested.

Roger shook his head. "In the past. Three hundred thousand years ago."

"But in my story humanity had starships. We traveled the galaxy."

"And so your people did. Until we stopped them and put them in their place."

"Wow," I mumbled, astonished I had such a heavy muse working for me. Then my pride resurfaced. "You didn't stop all of us. I know now what Sarteen did. She exploded that egg. She wasn't afraid to sacrifice her life. I see the moral of the tale, why I wrote it. Others will as well. It is better to die free of the lies of the quarantine than to live beneath the tyranny of its illusions. Sarteen defeated your precious Captain Eworl. Not all of humanity was trapped."

Roger was haughty. "So what? The few of you who come here accomplish nothing. We find you and we kill you. Look at your supposedly great leaders. They never last long."

"Yeah, but we keep coming. We don't give up. And I think we've got you by the throat now. A new era is rolling in. Your fire-and-brimstone fear tactics don't work anymore. People don't buy the devil chasing their souls. They're coming back to what's inside. They're listening to what the yogi and others like him are teaching."

Roger snorted. "Him? He's just another ignored prophet."

"I didn't ignore him. Yeah, maybe for a short time I fell for your charm. But in my heart I was always with him, and he with me. He's with Peter and me now. Go ahead and put us in the ground. You won't see either of us beg for mercy. We know you have no mercy. We've died before and know that death doesn't exist. It's just another lie you propagate on the ignorant." I spat in his face. "I'm glad I never had sex with you. That's one thing I have to be proud of. The snake never got to me."

He slapped me in the face with his gun. A numbing pain spread through both my cheeks and a wave of dizziness swept over me. Sticky blood dripped from my nose. I believed he'd broken it. This time I had pushed him too far. Yet it was interesting what his anger revealed, and what my choice of words indicated. Ancient memories were indeed being stirred. For a moment his features blurred and elongated. I blinked and thought I saw a toothy maw, a wide snout, and knew it was a vision similar to what Sarteen had beheld when the elevator door aboard her starship had opened. In fact, for all I knew, I had been Sarteen.

And Roger, he was a lizard.

"You *will* scream before I'm through with you," he promised.

I laughed. "You sound like Bob in my book."

He threw me into the grave on top of my black coffin with its gold trim, which had faded. I landed on my back, smashing my skull on the metal. The shock brought another wave of dizziness. Red stars, the color and consistency of fireworks, danced across my field of vision. Peter, strangely silent, was forced to sit at the edge of the hole and watch it all. Roger picked up his shovel and threw a few pounds of dirt in my face as I struggled to climb out. The force of the earth caused me to stumble and fall. While I lay momentarily helpless, another two shovelfuls landed on top of me. My resolve not to cry out weakened. Edgar Allan Poe had been right. There was no worse way to go than live burial.

"Peter." I coughed, trying to roll over and push myself up, to at least die standing on my feet. But such a position was not recommended in Roger Teller's *Book of Games & Graves*. I got as far as my knees when Roger swung his shovel through a wide curving arc and caught me on the right temple with the steel blade. The pain was intense, a thing of Biblical proportions. Smashing against the wall of the hole, I felt as if my scalp had been lifted three inches and a balloon filled with red liquid beneath it had popped. I lost a pint of blood in five seconds. It spread over the top of my coffin like the melting wax of a red candle. Worse, he had hit me precisely where I was weakest, where my headaches always started. The internal damage became very much external. It was a miracle I didn't lose consciousness or topple over. Yet it was not a miracle I would have prayed for to God. Better that my nightmare should end quickly, I thought. From out of the corner of my left eye, I watched Roger toss his shovel aside and crouch beside the hole, peering down at me with a grin so idiotic that if I hadn't been bleeding so much, I swear I would have vomited in his face.

"Now," Roger said pleasantly. "If you will just open the coffin and take out what's inside, I might stop throwing dirt on top of you. What do you say?"

I wiped at my face, trying to get one last look at Peter. In either body, he was my darling. I wanted to leave this life with him on my mind. I didn't imagine Roger would let him live long after I was gone.

Yet I couldn't find him.

He wasn't in his chair.

Roger continued to grin.

"Does that sound like a deal, Shari Ann Cooper?" he asked.

Then I saw Peter. He was standing!

"No," I replied.

Peter was bending over and picking up the shovel!

Roger leaned over to hear me better. "You said no? To me?"

Peter raised the shovel over his head.

I smiled through my blood. "Yes, Roger. I'm turning you down again."

Peter brought down the shovel hard on the back of Roger's head. Peter's aim was precise, driven by a supernatural will. The monster tumbled into the grave; he fell facedown onto the coffin. The back of his head was split open. His blood poured out and mingled with my mine, creating a puddle of ooze that looked as if it had been spilled from a victim of the black plague. A cursed puddle that spread as if pumped from within, even though Roger's dark eyes lay wide open and staring at nothingness as hopeless as his long-range plans had been. He was dead.

"Thank God," I whispered.

Then I collapsed beside the enemy.

CHAPTER XX

THE ANSWER TO THE MYSTERY of Peter's healing lay in the yogi's words to him at the public lecture. *"It is this love that will heal you. Nothing ever heals except divine love. It is all that there is."* Peter later said that watching me be tortured to death was painful beyond belief. Yet it was that pain that forced him to act on a love that we, as mere mortals, have trouble believing exists, divine love. It was grace, truly, that allowed him to stand, to defeat the enemy. It was grace that allowed the change in his spinal cord to remain permanent. It is now five days after the attack and he walks fine. The karma of his past suicide has been burnt to ash.

But what about my karma? Peter took me to the hospital after the struggle at the cemetery. There I regained consciousness and allowed the doctors to sew my scalp together—forty prickling stitches. Yet I refused to stay for further tests, even though the pain in my head was unbearable. Intuitively, I understood there was nothing they could do for me.

Roger shattered the last threads of blood vessel that had kept Jean Rodrigues's brain functioning the past three years. There was not much time left. Knowing that, I went home to write this story, my last story.

It is dark in my apartment as I work. Peter and Jacob are asleep. Outside my window, I see the wide expanse of the black ocean, feel the cool salty breeze. It is a childish observation but it has always amazed me how the color of the sea changes with the color of the sky. Yet, in the same way, life also changes with the color of our emotions. Now, as I write these words, even though it is night, the world looks bright to me. At last, I am at peace.

I know how to finish "The Starlight Crystal."

At that moment the elevator door opened.

Sarteen saw Captain Eworl.

She *did* recognize him.

Just a second. Before I continue I have to jot down an old fable. Sarteen's grandmother told it to the future starship captain one night when the then five-year-old girl was about to go to bed. The story comes to me as I write, like an old memory.

There was once a dragon who lived in a wishing well. He had been there for many years, but always stayed out of sight, at the bottom in the pitch dark, where the water was cold as ice. When people visited the well, they never saw the dragon. Yet sometimes they heard him—his voice more like thoughts in their minds than whispers in their ears. Standing beside the well, people would be seized by the belief that if they wished for something, it would come true. But only if they wished hard and offered to give something in return. For that was the condition the dragon always made. He had the power to fulfill dreams, yet his price was high. Because people, not knowing that they were praying to a dragon, would sometimes say out loud, "I would give my right arm to be famous." Or, "I would give my health to live in such a wonderful house." Or, "I would give anything to find true love."

This last wish pleased the dragon the most because then he could take *everything* from that person, and give nothing in return. Because, of course, love is the one thing a dragon can never give. It is the one thing a dragon knows nothing about, and the person would die broken-hearted. Yet if the person wished for fame or a house, the dragon could easily dole that out, and then take the person's arm or health, whatever had been offered in return for the prize. The man would become well-known and then have an accident and his arm would be severed from his body. The woman would move into her new home and then have a nervous breakdown trying to take care of it. Always the dragon would get his reward, and always the person would suffer for having asked for anything.

THE LAST STORY

But one day a young but wise girl came to the well. Knowing its reputation as a wish-giving well, she asked for happiness. The request was unusual; the dragon had never received it before. True, many people asked for certain things to make them happy, but no one asked for happiness itself. Curious to know this person better, the dragon crawled out of the well and showed the girl his true form. He was surprised that she didn't back away from him in horror. Indeed, his first question to her was "Why aren't you afraid of me?"

"Why should I be?" the girl asked.

"Because I'm a dragon. Everybody is afraid of me."

The girl laughed. "Well, I'm not. You don't scare me one bit. You just look like a big, ugly lizard to me. Do you really have magical powers?"

The dragon was offended. "Yes. My powers are well known."

"Then grant me my wish. Give me happiness."

"Not so fast. If I give you this, what will you give me in return?"

"My sorrow," the girl said simply.

The dragon laughed. "What kind of bargain is that? I don't want your sorrow. If I give you happiness, then you must give me something special in return."

"What do you want from me?"

The dragon thought. "How about your heart?"

The girl considered. "All right. You give me happiness, and in return I'll give you my heart. In fact, to show you what a good sport I am, I'll give you my heart first. But if afterward you fail to give me happiness, then you must give me your head. You must allow me to cut it off with a sword."

"What do you want with my head?"

"It's none of your business. I just want it."

The dragon was amused. He believed the girl was a fool. If I take her heart, he thought, she'll be dead. I'll have what I want and I won't have to give her anything in return. The dragon believed he was making the best bargain of his long life.

"Agreed," the dragon said. "I'll cut out your heart and then I'll give you happiness. If I fail to do so, you can cut off my head."

"Fine." The girl stepped close so that the dragon could reach her. Spreading out her arms, she said, "Take my heart, you ugly lizard."

The dragon reached over and clawed open the girl's chest and pulled out her heart. Immediately the girl fell to the ground dead, and the dragon laughed long and loud.

"What a wonderful day," he said. "I have won a human heart for free."

Satisfied, the dragon took the heart and crawled back down into his well. There he sat for a long time in the dark thinking how wonderful the heart would taste for dinner. He planned to eat it just as soon as it stopped beating. He planned to have it with potatoes and maybe a bottle of wine. The dragon got all excited imagining the wonderful feast he would have.

The only trouble was that after many days, the heart still

hadn't stopped beating. Indeed, the sound of it pounding in the cold dark began to disturb the dragon. Because—as is well known—dragons have very sensitive ears. It got so the dragon couldn't even sleep, and he grew dizzy and bad-tempered. Yet never for a minute did he think of throwing the heart away. His hunger for it was too immense.

Finally, though, seven days after killing the girl, the dragon's hunger and fatigue grew so great that he could bear it no longer. Lifting the girl's heart in his scaly claws, he stuffed it in his mouth and swallowed it whole. For a moment he was satisfied; it had tasted good going down. But then he realized the heart was still beating inside him, and that scared him. Because, besides having very sensitive ears, dragons have no hearts. He didn't know what to do now that he had one. He didn't know how to get it out of him. He only knew that it was driving him crazy, the sound of it, pounding and pounding, even when he closed his eyes and pressed his claws over his ears and tried to rest.

"Oh," he moaned. "Poor me."

For another seven days the dragon wandered helplessly at the bottom of the well, banging his lizard head on the stone walls In frustration. Finally he called out for someone to help him—this monster that had never turned for help to anyone. At that moment he heard the girl's voice in his mind.

"What do you want?" she asked.

He stopped his pacing. "Who's there?"

"The girl whose heart you stole."

"It can't be. You're dead."

She ignored his remark. "You called out. What do you want?"

"Your heart—it's driving me crazy. I want you to take it away."

"You stole my heart, which contained all my sorrow and all my happiness. Yet you gave me nothing in return. Why should I help you?"

The dragon wept, another thing it had never done before. "Please. I will do anything you ask if you will just take it away."

"Are you sure? Anything?"

"Yes! Just get rid of it!"

"All right," the girl said. "But I have one condition. You must keep your end of your bargain first. You must give me your head."

The dragon was afraid. "But then I will die."

"Maybe. But you said you would give up anything for me to take it away. You are bound by your word, as you bound all the people who came to you before me."

The dragon was terrified. "But I have lived for centuries. I don't want to die."

"Then I can't help you," the girl said. "Goodbye."

"Wait!" the dragon called. "Come back! You have to help me!"

But the girl was gone. Yet her heart remained, pounding

inside the dragon's chest, and with her departure, there was no hope for him ever to rest, ever to have a moment's peace. And, because of the heart he now possessed, the dragon knew that. He realized that it was *he* who had been tricked. That the only thing that would make the girl happy would be to slay him, and that she had done so even though it had cost her her very life.

"Damn you," the dragon said.

Picking up his sword, the dragon fell on it and cut off his own head.

The dragon died. Yet the girl's heart happily lived on. . . .

Beholding the Orion commander, Sarteen remembered her grandmother's story, and finally understood what it meant, for her, at least for her own soul. She turned to Pareen and smiled.

"I love you," she said.

Pareen smiled. "I love you."

Sarteen nodded in the direction of the alien invader, who stood poised with a sharp purple weapon pointed at her chest. "Welcome, Captain Eworl. I am Sarteen, commander of the starship *Crystal*. This is my first officer, Pareen." Then, gesturing in the direction of the communication board, where the nanoegg was hidden, she added, "And there's the ghost of my daughter. Do you see her? Do you recognize her? You met her once, a few hours ago, when you destroyed her world." Sarteen took a defiant step toward the enemy. "Do you remember her? You goddamn dragon! Her name's . . . *Cira!*"

The human starship, *Crystal*, exploded, as did the alien vessel, *Adharma*.

Cool story. Both of them, all of them.

I am finished.

Except there is someone I must see. Someone I must say goodbye to. Perhaps, after I see her, I will not have a chance to make a final entry. My head pain weighs on me like ancient burdens. A last few concluding paragraphs should be no problem for me, however, even from a ghostly distance. I believe I do have a muse who helps me with my stories, an angel who watches over my life. In the same way, I have played my brother's muse before, when I dictated *Remember Me* to him. Perhaps I will play his muse one more time.

My old house, in Huntington Beach, is not entirely dark as I park out front. There is a light on in the kitchen. Someone is up late, probably unable to sleep. As I walk to the door, I wonder if this someone is sipping warm milk and thinking of me. I knock lightly, making it sound like the wind brushing against the wood. I do not wish to startle her. Yet my mother is quick to answer.

My mother bore my father scant resemblance, except that she was also attractive. She was tall and sleek, quick and loose. Her wide, thick-lipped mouth and her immaculately conceived black hair were her prizes.

Standing in her wrinkled bathrobe, she looks frail and tired, as if it has been a long time since she won a beauty prize.

"May I help you?" she asks.

"My name is Jean Rodrigues. I am the author of *Remember Me.* I am a friend of your son, Jimmy's. He told me you wanted to talk to me."

"Jim told you that?"

"Sort of. He said you had read my book."

"It's late. Why are you here?"

I shrug. "Honestly, I don't know, Mrs. Cooper."

She stares at me a long time and then steps aside. "Please come in."

We end up in the kitchen, where I came a few minutes after waking from my fatal fall. Then, four years ago, my mother and father sat around the table smoking and eating cake and talking about me as if I wasn't even there. Of course, they didn't know I was there. I was a ghost, invisible. Studying my mother across the table, I wonder if she knows now.

"Can I get you anything?" she asks.

I shake my head. "I'm fine, thank you."

She grips her glass of warm milk with both hands and stares into it as if it were a crystal ball. She has trouble looking at me. I understand. I appear completely different, but a part of her recognizes me *through* my eyes, the windows of my soul. Yet I will have to part the curtains on those windows if she is to see all the way inside. And I don't know if I want to do that.

"So," she begins. "You're the famous writer."

"Yes."

She nods. "I did read your book—*Remember Me*." Her lower lip trembles. "It was a very good book. It touched me."

"Thank you," I say.

She glances up uneasily. "How long did it take you to write?"

"Not long. It came to me all at once, like a movie playing on a screen."

The questions are hard for her. She wants the truth but, like the rest of us, she knows intuitively it is too much for her. "Did something in particular inspire the story?"

"Yes."

She swallows. "Can you tell me what it was?"

"Your daughter."

"I see." She shudders. "Did you know Shari? Is that why you adopted her name for your pen name?"

"Yes, I knew her. Better than anybody. She wanted me to write her story and I did." I hold up my hand as she starts to interrupt. "Please don't ask me where I knew her from. I can't tell you, and I'm sorry. Just know that her story is true and that she is fine. I know that above all else she would want you to know that."

Tears appear on my mother's face. "I don't understand."

I reach across the table and take her hand. "She goes on, we all go on. That's the point of the story. And wherever she is I know she would want me to tell you how much she loved you. That may not have come out as clearly as it should have in the story, but it's true. You were a great mother to her."

She sobs, shaking. "Who are you?"

"I'm a friend." I let go of her and sit back and put my hand to my head. A wave of severe pain rolls over me and I have trouble seeing. For a moment the world goes completely black and I have to strain to maintain consciousness. Forcing in a breath, I whisper, "I'm no one."

"Are you all right?" my mother asks, concerned.

I speak with effort. "I had a head injury. Sometimes it acts up and I get dizzy. Then I just have to lie down."

My mother stands and gently takes my arm. "Come, why don't you lie down in the living room."

I can barely get to my feet. "Thank you."

My mother is anxious. "Oh dear, you're as white as a ghost. Maybe you should lie down upstairs, in my daughter's old bedroom. I'll call for a doctor."

I smile faintly. "That's not necessary. I'll feel better in a few minutes. Just let me rest in her room. That's all I need." I pat her hand as she leads me toward the stairs. "Don't worry about me, really. This headache thing is nothing. It's so nice for me to be here with you."

"The world is a place to visit, to enjoy. It is not your permanent residence. When you don't know what to do, you return to your true home."

"It was nice of you to come to see me," she says with feeling.

My bed is freshly made. I sit down on the edge and my mother removes my shoes. Lying back, I feel the familiar comfort of a small child as she tucks a blanket over me. She leans over and I am surprised when she kisses me on the forehead.

"I feel like I know you," she says.

I brush her cheek with my hand, wipe away another tear that has come. How much I had prayed to do that for her in the days after I died. "You do know me," I say. "You remember me."

She doesn't fully understand but that is OK. After squeezing my hand and telling me to rest, she leaves the room, carefully closing the door behind her. In the same way I close my eyes. I know I will not open them again.

My peace is a divine gift, my joy a wonderful miracle. As I listen to my breathing slowly begin to run down, I remember how the last time I left I wished that I could have made my mark on the world, done something that would have changed the course of history. Something to be remembered by. Now I don't care about those things. I have been given the chance and done my best. No one waits on the other side to judge me. Besides, it doesn't really matter. It's all a play. God is not impressed by our acts, only by how much we love. I don't have to be important. I am grass, no one. Perhaps, in another place and time, I will learn the last of the yogi's lesson, and complete the flow of life. I will become everyone.

EPILOGUE

PETER NICHOLS AND JIMMY COOPER gathered in Jimmy's bedroom two hours after the funeral for Jean Rodrigues, bestselling author of numerous teenage thrillers and aspiring moviemaker. Jimmy sat at his desk in front of his computer, Peter on the edge of Jimmy's bed. From his back pocket, Peter withdrew a jump drive and handed it to Jimmy.

"She was almost done with it when she went to see your mother," Peter said.

Jimmy nodded, studying the drive. "She wrote this during the last week?"

"Yes."

"How could she when she was in so much pain?"

Peter shrugged. "Writing always made her feel better. It was her first love."

Jimmy sadly shook his head. "You were her first love."

Peter nodded. "We both were." He bowed his head and a single tear slid down his cheek. He had not wept at the funeral, nor had Jimmy. There seemed no point; Shari would have just laughed at them. Yet the loss was hard for both of them, very hard. Peter added, "I can't believe how much she did in such a short time."

"Yeah. She was great." Jimmy's voice fell to a whisper as he remembered the end of her most important story. "She was the best sister a guy could've had."

Peter sighed and stood. "I have to go. There are things that have to be wrapped up right away."

Jimmy also stood. "I understand. How's your back?"

"Perfect. Not even a twinge."

"That's amazing."

"It's a miracle." Peter patted him on the shoulder. "Take care of yourself."

"You, too." Jimmy hugged him. "Will you be all right?"

Peter sniffed. "Yeah. It'll take time, but I'll be fine. I have my work to do."

"Coaching?"

Peter nodded. "There's that—I won't quit helping the kids. But Shari left me a pile of money. Now I'll be able to do more. The Rishi and the yogi said to serve. I want to try to help the Hispanic community in the inner cities somehow."

"Good for you. I saw Shari's will. She left her Hispanic family a tidy sum as well. Not that I'm complaining—she left me far more than I deserved. I never knew she was so rich."

Peter was sad. "She was rich in many ways." He touched Jimmy's arm. "Let's stay in touch, OK?"

"Sure. We'll talk tomorrow."

"Good." Peter paused as he stepped toward the door, and glanced at the computer. "Are you sure you'll be able to finish her story?"

"She once dictated a whole book to me, and after she returned to Earth, we were closer than ever. I don't think there will be any problem."

Peter smiled faintly. "It will probably be another bestseller."

"I'm sure that would have made her laugh."

"Goodbye, Jimmy."

"Goodbye, Peter."

After Peter was gone, Jimmy turned on his computer and loaded the story onto his hard drive. For the next four hours he read his sister's last story, and when he came to the part where she went to see his mother, he briefly closed his eyes and prayed for guidance. He was not praying long when a tap on his shoulder made him jump. He opened his eyes and whirled around.

But, of course, the room was empty.

Jimmy smiled. "All right, I'll start writing. If I make a mistake, we can always fix it in galleys."

Rolling up his sleeves, Jimmy began to type. This time he was awake and knew he wasn't dreaming. Her funeral had been nothing more than a social obligation he had to attend. His sister was alive. He would see her again someday. They would meet in a place of light and splendor and both would remember today and yesterday and days so long ago their history could only be found in forgotten ancient myths, such as "The Starlight Crystal."

ABOUT THE AUTHOR

CHRISTOPHER PIKE is the author of more than forty teen thrillers, including the series Thirst, Final Friends, and Chain Letter.

Sink your teeth into Christopher Pike's
bestselling Thirst series.

THIRST

NO. 1

INCLUDES
THE LAST VAMPIRE
BLACK BLOOD
RED DICE

By Christopher Pike

I am a vampire, and that is the truth. But the modern meaning of the word *vampire*, the stories that have been told about creatures such as I, are not precisely true. I do not turn to ash in the sun, nor do I cringe when I see a crucifix. I wear a tiny gold cross now around my neck, but only because I like it. I cannot command a pack of wolves to attack or fly through the air. Nor can I make another of my kind simply by having him drink my blood. Wolves do like me, though, as do most predators, and I can jump so high that one might imagine I can fly. As to blood—ah, blood, the whole subject fascinates me. I do like that as well, warm and dripping, when I am thirsty. And I am often thirsty.

My name, at present, is Alisa Perne—just two words, something to last for a couple of decades. I am no more attached to them than to the sound of the wind. My hair is blond and silklike, my eyes like sapphires that have stared long at a volcanic fissure. My stature is slight by modern standards, five two in sandals, but my arms and legs are muscled, although not unattractively so. Before I speak I appear to be only eighteen years of age, but something in my voice—the coolness of my expressions, the echo of endless experience—makes people think I am much older. But even I seldom think about when I was born, long before the pyramids were erected beneath the pale moon. I was there, in that desert in those days, even though I am not originally from that part of the world.

Do I need blood to survive? Am I immortal? After all this time, I still don't know. I drink blood because I crave it. But I can eat normal food as well, and digest it. I need food as much as any other man or woman. I am a living, breathing creature. My heart beats—I can hear it now, like thunder in my ears. My hearing is very sensitive, as is my sight. I can hear a dry leaf break off a branch a mile away, and I can clearly see the craters on the moon without a telescope. Both senses have grown more acute as I get older.

My immune system is impregnable, my regenerative system miraculous, if you believe in miracles—which I don't. I can be stabbed in the arm with a knife and heal within minutes without scarring. But if I were to be stabbed in the heart, say with the currently fashionable wooden stake, then maybe I would die. It is difficult for even a vampire's flesh to heal around an implanted blade. But it is not something I have experimented with.

But who would stab me? Who would get the chance? I have the strength of five men, the reflexes of the mother of all cats. There is not a system of physical attack and defense of which I am not a master. A dozen black belts could corner me in a dark alley, and I could make a dress fit for a vampire out of the sashes that hold their fighting jackets closed. And I do love to fight, it is true, almost as much as I love to kill. Yet I kill less and less as the years go by because the need is not there, and the ramifications of murder in modern society are complex and a waste of my precious but endless time. Some loves have to be given up, others have to be forgotten. Strange as it may sound, if you think of me as a monster, but I can love most passionately. I do not think of myself as evil.

Why am I talking about all this? Who am I talking to? I send out these words, these thoughts, simply because it is time. Time for what, I do not know, and it does not matter because it is what I want and that is always reason enough for me. My wants—how few they are, and yet how deep they burn. I will not tell you, at present, who I am talking to.

The moment is pregnant with mystery, even for me. I stand outside the door of Detective Michael Riley's office. The hour is late; he is in his private office in the back, the light down low—I know this without seeing. The good Mr. Riley called me three hours ago to tell me I had to come to his office to have a little talk about some things I might find of interest. There was a note of threat in his voice, and more. I can sense emotions, although I cannot read minds. I am curious as I stand in this cramped and stale hallway. I am also annoyed, and that doesn't bode well for Mr. Riley. I knock lightly on the door to his outer office and open it before he can respond.

"Hello," I say. I do not sound dangerous—I am, after all, supposed to be a teenager. I stand beside the secretary's unhappy desk, imagining that her last few paychecks have been promised to her as "practically in the mail." Mr. Riley is at his desk, inside his office, and stands as he notices me. He has on a rumpled brown sport coat, and in a glance I see the weighty bulge of a revolver beneath his left breast. Mr. Riley thinks I am dangerous, I note, and my curiosity goes up a notch. But I'm not afraid he knows what I really am, or he would not have chosen to meet with me at all, even in broad daylight.

"Alisa Perne?" he says. His tone is uneasy.

"Yes."

He gestures from twenty feet away. "Please come in and have a seat."

I enter his office but do not take the offered chair in front of his desk, but rather, one against the right wall. I want a straight line to him if he tries to pull a gun on me. If he does try, he will die, and maybe painfully.

He looks at me, trying to size me up, and it is difficult for him because I just sit here. He, however, is a montage of many impressions. His coat is not only wrinkled but stained—greasy burgers eaten hastily. I note it all. His eyes are red rimmed, from a drug as much as fatigue. I hypothesize his poison to be speed—medicine to nourish long hours beating the pavement. After me? Surely. There is also a glint of satisfaction in his eyes, a prey finally caught. I smile privately at the thought, yet a thread of uneasiness enters me as well. The office is stuffy, slightly chilly. I have never liked the cold, although I could survive an Arctic winter night naked to the bone.

"I guess you wonder why I wanted to talk to you so urgently," he says.

I nod. My legs are uncrossed, my white slacks hanging loose. One hand rests in my lap, the other plays with my hair. Left-handed, right-handed—I am neither, and both.

"May I call you Alisa?" he asks.

"You may call me what you wish, Mr. Riley."

My voice startles him, just a little, and it is the effect I want. I could have pitched it like any modern teenager, but I have allowed my past to enter, the power of it. I want to keep Mr. Riley nervous, for nervous people say much that they later regret.

"Call me Mike," he says. "Did you have trouble finding the place?"

"No."

"Can I get you anything? Coffee? A soda?"

"No."

He glances at a folder on his desk, flips it open. He clears his throat, and again I hear his tiredness, as well as his fear. But is he afraid of me? I am not sure. Besides the gun under his coat, he has another beneath some papers at the other side of his desk. I smell the gunpowder in the bullets, the cold steel. A lot of firepower to meet a teenage girl. I hear a faint scratch of moving metal and plastic. He is taping the conversation.

"First off I should tell you who I am," he says. "As I said on the phone, I am a private detective. My business is my own—I work entirely freelance. People come to me to find loved ones, to research risky investments, to provide protection, when necessary, and to get hard-to-find background information on certain individuals."

I smile. "And to spy."

He blinks. "I do not spy, Miss Perne."

"Really." My smile broadens. I lean forward, the tops of my breasts visible at the open neck of my black silk blouse. "It is late, Mr. Riley. Tell me what you want."

He shakes his head. "You have a lot of confidence for a kid."

"And you have a lot of nerve for a down-on-his-luck private dick."

He doesn't like that. He taps the open folder on his desk. "I have been researching you for the last few months, Miss Perne, ever since you moved to Mayfair. You have an intriguing past, as well as many investments. But I'm sure you know that."

"Really."

"Before I begin, may I ask how old you are?"

"You may ask."

"How old are you?"

"It's none of your business."

He smiles. He thinks he has scored a point. He does not realize that I am already considering how he should die, although I still hope to avoid such an extreme measure. Never ask a vampire her age. We don't like that question. It's very impolite. Mr. Riley clears his throat again, and I think that maybe I will strangle him.

"Prior to moving to Mayfair," he says, "you lived in Los Angeles—in Beverly Hills in fact—at Two-Five-Six Grove Street. Your home was a four-thousand-square-foot mansion, with two swimming pools, a tennis court, a sauna, and a small observatory. The property is valued at six-point-five million. To this day you are listed as the sole owner, Miss Perne."

"It's not a crime to be rich."

"You are not just rich. You are very rich. My research indicates that you own five separate estates scattered across this country. Further research tells me that you probably own as much if not more property in Europe and the Far East. Your stock and bond assets are vast—in the hundreds of millions. But what none of my research has uncovered is how you came across this incredible wealth. There is no record of a family anywhere, and believe me, Miss Perne, I have looked far and wide."

"I believe you. Tell me, whom did you contact to gather this information?"

He enjoys that he has my interest. "My sources are of course confidential."

"Of course." I stare at him; my stare is very powerful. Sometimes, if I am not careful, and I stare too long at a flower, it shrivels and dies. Mr. Riley loses his smile and shifts uneasily. "Why are you researching me?"

"You admit that my facts are accurate?" he asks.

"Do you need my assurances?" I pause, my eyes still on him. Sweat glistens on his forehead. "Why the research?"

He blinks and turns away with effort. He dabs at the perspiration on his head. "Because you fascinate me," he says. "I think to myself, here is one of the wealthiest women in the world, and no one knows who she is. Plus she can't be more than twenty-five years old, and she has no family. It makes me wonder."

"What do you wonder, Mr. Riley?"

He ventures a swift glance at me; he really does not like to look at me, even though I am very beautiful. "Why you go to such extremes to remain invisible," he says.

"It also makes you wonder if I would pay to stay invisible," I say.

He acts surprised. "I didn't say that."

"How much do you want?"

My question stuns him, yet pleases him. He does not have to be the first to dirty his hands. What he does not realize is that blood stains deeper than dirt, and that the stains last much longer. Yes, I think again, he may not have that long to live.

"How much are you offering?" he ventures.

I shrug. "It depends."

"On what?"

"On whether you tell me who pointed you in my direction."

He is indignant. "I assure you that I needed no one to point me in your direction. I discovered your interesting qualities all by myself."

He is lying, of that I am positive. I can always tell when a person lies, almost always. Only remarkable people can fool me, and then they have to be lucky. But I do not like to be fooled—so one has to wonder at even their luck.

"Then my offer is nothing," I say.

He straightens. He believes he is ready to pounce. "Then my counteroffer, Miss Perne, is to make what I have discovered public knowledge." He pauses. "What do you think of that?"

"It will never happen."

He smiles. "You don't think so?"

I smile. "You would die before that happened."

He laughs. "You would take a contract out on my life?"

"Something to that effect."

He stops laughing, now deadly serious, now that we are talking about death. Yet I keep my smile since death amuses me. He points a finger at me.

"You can be sure that if anything happened to me the police would be at your door the same day," he says.

"You have arranged to send my records to someone else," I say. "Just in case something should happen to you?"

"Something to that effect." He is trying to be witty. He is also lying. I slide back farther into my chair. He thinks I am relaxing, but I position myself so that my legs are straight out. If I am to strike, I have decided, it will be with my right foot.

"Mr. Riley," I say. "We should not argue. You want something from me, and I want something from you. I am prepared to pay you a million dollars, to be deposited in whatever account you wish, in whatever part of the world you desire, if you will tell me who made you aware of me."

He looks me straight in the eye, tries to, and surely he feels the heat building up inside me because he flinches before he speaks. His voice comes out uneven and confused. He does not understand why I am suddenly so intimidating.

"No one is interested in you except me," he says.

I sigh. "You are armed, Mr. Riley."

"I am?"

I harden my voice. "You have a gun under your coat. You have a gun on your desk under those papers. You are taping this conversation. Now, one might think these are all standard blackmail precautions, but I don't think so. I am a young woman. I don't look dangerous. But someone has told you that I am more dangerous than I look and that I am to be treated with extreme caution. And you know that that someone is right." I pause. "Who is that someone, Mr. Riley?"

He shakes his head. He is looking at me in a new light, and he doesn't like what he sees. My eyes continue to bore into him. A splinter of fear has entered his mind.

"H-how do you know all these things?" he asks.

"You admit my facts are accurate?" I mimic him.

He shakes his head again.

Now I allow my voice to change, to deepen, to resonate with the fullness of my incredibly long life. The effect on him is pronounced; he shakes visibly, as if he is suddenly aware that he is sitting next to a monster. But I am not just any monster. I am a vampire, and in many ways, for his sake, that may be the worst monster of all.

"Someone has hired you to research me," I say. "I know that for a fact. Please don't deny it again, or you will make me angry. I really am uncontrollable when I am angry. I do things I later regret, and I would regret killing you, Mr. Riley—but not for long." I pause. "Now, for the last time, tell me who sent you after me, and I will give you a million dollars and let you walk out of here alive."

He stares at me incredulously. His eyes see one thing and his ears hear another, I know. He sees a pretty blond girl with startlingly blue eyes, and he hears the velvety voice of a succubus from hell. It is too much for him. He begins to stammer.

"Miss Perne," he begins. "You misunderstand me. I mean

you no harm. I just want to complete a simple business deal with you. No one has to . . . get hurt."

I take in a long, slow breath. I need air, but I can hold my breath for over an hour if I must. Yet now I let out the breath before speaking again, and the room cools even more. And Mr. Riley shivers.

"Answer my question," I say simply.

He coughs. "There is no one else."

"You'd better reach for your gun."

"Pardon?"

"You are going to die now. I assume you prefer to die fighting."

"Miss Perne—"

"I am five thousand years old."

He blinks. "What?"

I give him my full, uncloaked gaze, which I have used in the past—alone—to kill. "I am a vampire," I say softly. "And you have pissed me off."

He believes me. Suddenly he believes every horror story he has been told since he was a little boy. That they were all true: the dead things hungering for the warm living flesh; the bony hand coming out of the closet in the black of night; the monsters from another page of reality, the unturned page—who could look so human, so cute.

He reaches for his gun. Too slowly, much too.

I shove myself out of my chair with such force that I am

momentarily airborne. My senses switch into a hyper-accelerated mode. Over the last few thousand years, whenever I am threatened, I have developed the ability to view events in extreme slow motion. But this does not mean that I slow down; quite the opposite. Mr. Riley sees nothing but a blur flying toward him. He does not see that as I'm moving, I have cocked my leg to deliver a devastating blow.

My right foot lashes out. My heel catches him in the center of the breastbone. I hear the bones crack as he topples backward onto the floor, his weapon still holstered inside his coat. Although I moved toward him in a horizontal position, I land smoothly on my feet. He sprawls on the floor at my feet beside his overturned chair. Gasping for breath, blood pouring out of his mouth. I have crushed the walls of his heart as well as the bones of his chest, and he is going to die. But not just yet. I kneel beside him and gently put my hand on his head. Love often flows through me for my victims.

"Mike," I say gently. "You would not listen to me."

He is having trouble breathing. He drowns in his own blood—I hear it gurgling deep in his lungs—and I am tempted to put my lips to his and suck it away for him. Such a temptation, to sate my thirst. Yet I leave him alone.

"Who?" he gasps at me.

I continue to stroke his head. "I told you the truth. I am a vampire. You never stood a chance against me. It's not fair, but it is the way it is." I lean close to his mouth, whisper in his ear.

"Now tell me the truth and I will stop your pain. Who sent you after me?"

He stares at me with wide eyes. "Slim," he whispers.

"Who is Slim? A man?"

"Yes."

"Very good, Mike. How do you contact him?"

"No."

"Yes." I caress his cheek. "Where is this Slim?"

He begins to cry. The tears, the blood—they make a pitiful combination. His whole body trembles. "I don't want to die," he moans. "My boy."

"Tell me about Slim and I will take care of your boy," I say. My nature is kind, deep inside. I could have said if you don't tell me about Slim, I will find your dear boy and slowly peel off his skin. But Riley is in too much pain to hear me, and I immediately regret striking so swiftly, not slowly torturing the truth out of him. I did tell him that I was impulsive when I'm angry, and it is true.

"Help me," he pleads, choking.

"I'm sorry. I can only kill, I cannot heal, and you are too badly hurt." I sit back on my heels and glance around the office. I see on the desktop a picture of Mr. Riley posed beside a handsome boy of approximately eighteen. Removing my right hand from Mr. Riley, I reach for the picture and show it to him. "Is this your son?" I ask innocently.

Terror consumes his features. "No!" he cries.

I lean close once more. "I am not going to hurt him. I only want this Slim. Where is he?"

A spasm of pain grips Riley, a convulsion—his legs shake off the floor like two wooden sticks moved by a poltergeist. I grab him, trying to settle him down, but I am too late. His grimacing teeth tear into his lower lip, and more blood messes his face. He draws in a breath that is more a shovel of mud on his coffin. He makes a series of sick wet sounds. Then his eyes roll back in his head, and he goes limp in my arms. Studying the picture of the boy, I reach over and close Mr. Michael Riley's eyes.

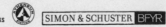